50 BEST AMERICAN SHORT STORIES

50 BEST AMERICAN SHORT STORIES

EDITED BY

Martha Foley

WINGS BOOKS

New York • Avenel, New Jersey

Copyright © 1965 by Houghton Mifflin Company.

This 1994 edition is published by Wings Books,
distributed by Random House Value Publishing, Inc.,
40 Engelhard Avenue, Avenel, New Jersey 07001,
by arrangement with Houghton Mifflin Company.

Random House
New York • Toronto • London • Sydney • Auckland

Printed and bound in the United States of America

Library of Congress Cataloging-in-Publication Data

Main entry under title:

Fifty best American short stories.
  I. Short Stories, American. 2. American fiction—
20th century.   I. Foley, Martha.
PS648.S5F535 1986   813'.01'08   85-24705
ISBN 0-517-60354-3

18 17 16 15 14 13 12 11 10

Contents

Foreword

CONTENTS

Foreword

FOUNDED IN 1915 by a young New England poet, Edward J. O'Brien, *The Best American Short Stories* for fifty years has presented annually the most distinguished short fiction appearing in the periodicals of this country. From its inception it has been recognized by authors, editors, teachers and librarians as occupying an important place in the American literary scene. But it has been the general reader who welcomed it most enthusiastically and has made its continued success possible.

When *The Best American Short Stories* was started, the American short story was on a downward path. It had become the victim of dishonest contrivances, of lifeless characters and absurd plots. The long and honorable history of the short story in this country, beginning with Irving, Poe and Hawthorne, and progressing through Melville and Crane, was threatened with an end. This was happening despite the fact that the American short story throughout the Nineteenth Century and the beginning of the Twentieth had been recognized as a unique, indigenous form influencing the literature of many other countries.

By emphasizing the excellence of the good short stories in contrast to the many meretricious ones, the anthology encouraged all that was finest in our fiction. The long list of famous authors first receiving recognition in the annual collections proves how valuable has been the function of these volumes.

Without diminution of its effect, *The Best American Short Stories* continued through the First World War, the carefree Twenties, the Great Depression, the Second World War and the Atomic Age of the present. Literary trends often changed but the main purpose of the series—to stress definite merit—remained the same. Regrettably, due either to estate or copyright complications, a few authors deserving of inclusion in this volume have had to be omitted.

Edward J. O'Brien died during the Blitz of London in 1942. The present editor took his place although she felt she could never hope to equal his achievement. During her editorship there have been many exciting literary developments and the rise of an entire new generation of splendid authors.

xi

Since 1958 she has had the help of David Burnett as an associate editor. She has also been greatly helped by Joyce Hartman, now the New York editor of Houghton Mifflin Company. In addition much is owed to many editors and writers throughout the country who have been faithful in their cooperation. Appreciation is more than deserved by the staff of Houghton Mifflin in Boston. Primarily, though, it is to the readers of America who enjoy stories of permanent literary distinction that we must all be grateful.

MARTHA FOLEY

50 BEST AMERICAN SHORT STORIES

ELSIE SINGMASTER

*It is somehow appropriate that a volume commemorating the fiftieth
anniversary of* The Best American Short Stories *should begin with a
story that commemorated the fiftieth anniversary of the end of the Civil
War. It is also ironic that today, a hundred years after the end of that
war, the reconciliation described here should still remain so timely for us.*

*Elsie Singmaster, who was born in 1879, was a well-known writer of
history and fiction in the early part of this century. She lived in Gettysburg and so was close to the scene of such stories as "The Survivors,"
in which she writes about two former enemies and their finally acknowl-
edged need for one another.*

The Survivors

A Memorial Day Story

In the year 1868, when Memorial Day was instituted, Fosterville had
thirty-five men in its parade. Fosterville was a border town; in it enthusiasm had run high, and many more men had enlisted than those required
by the draft. All the men were on the same side but Adam Foust, who,
slipping away, joined himself to the troops of his mother's Southern
State. It could not have been any great trial for Adam to fight against
most of his companions in Fosterville, for there was only one of them
with whom he did not quarrel. That one was his cousin Henry, from
whom he was inseparable, and of whose friendship for any other boys he
was intensely jealous. Henry was a frank, open-hearted lad who would
have lived on good terms with the whole world if Adam had allowed
him to.

Adam did not return to Fosterville until the morning of the first Memorial Day, of whose establishment he was unaware. He had been ill for
months, and it was only now that he had earned enough to make his way
home. He was slightly lame, and he had lost two fingers of his left hand.

He got down from the train at the station, and found himself at once in a great crowd. He knew no one, and no one seemed to know him. Without asking any questions, he started up the street. He meant to go, first of all, to the house of his cousin Henry, and then to set about making arrangements to resume his long-interrupted business, that of a saddler, which he could still follow in spite of his injury.

As he hurried along he heard the sound of band music, and realized that some sort of a procession was advancing. With the throng about him he pressed to the curb. The tune was one which he hated; the colors he hated also; the marchers, all but one, he had never liked. There was Newton Towne, with a sergeant's stripe on his blue sleeve; there was Edward Green, a captain; there was Peter Allinson, a color-bearer. At their head, taller, handsomer, dearer than ever to Adam's jealous eyes, walked Henry Foust. In an instant of forgetfulness Adam waved his hand. But Henry did not see; Adam chose to think that he saw and would not answer. The veterans passed, and Adam drew back and was lost in the crowd.

But Adam had a parade of his own. In the evening, when the music and the speeches were over and the half-dozen graves of those of Fosterville's young men who had been brought home had been heaped with flowers, and Fosterville sat on doorsteps and porches talking about the day, Adam put on a gray uniform and walked from one end of the village to the other. These were people who had known him always; the word flew from step to step. Many persons spoke to him, some laughed, and a few jeered. To no one did Adam pay any heed. Past the house of Newton Towne, past the store of Ed Green, past the wide lawn of Henry Foust, walked Adam, his hands clasped behind his back, as though to make more perpendicular than perpendicularity itself that stiff backbone. Henry Foust ran down the steps and out to the gate.

"Oh, Adam!" cried he.

Adam stopped, stock-still. He could see Peter Allinson and Newton Towne, and even Ed Green, on Henry's porch. They were all having ice-cream and cake together.

"Well, what?" said he, roughly.

"Won't you shake hands with me?"

"No," said Adam.

"Won't you come in?"

"Never."

Still Henry persisted.

"Some one might do you harm, Adam."

"Let them!" said Adam.

Then Adam walked on alone. Adam walked alone for forty years.

Not only on Memorial Day did he don his gray uniform and make the rounds of the village. When the Fosterville Grand Army Post met on Friday evenings in the post room, Adam managed to meet most of the members either going or returning. He and his gray suit became gradually so familiar to the village that no one turned his head or glanced up from book or paper to see him go by. He had from time to time a new suit, and he ordered from somewhere in the South a succession of gray, broad-brimmed military hats. The farther the war sank into the past, the straighter grew old Adam's back, the prouder his head. Sometimes, early in the forty years, the acquaintances of his childhood, especially the women, remonstrated with him.

"The war's over, Adam," they would say. "Can't you forget it?"

"Those G.A.R. fellows don't forget it," Adam would answer. "They haven't changed their principles. Why should I change mine?"

"But you might make up with Henry."

"That's nobody's business but my own."

"But when you were children you were never separated. Make up, Adam."

"When Henry needs me, I'll help him," said Adam.

"Henry will never need you. Look at all he's got!"

"Well, then, I don't need him," declared Adam, as he walked away. He went back to his saddler shop, where he sat all day stitching. He had ample time to think of Henry and the past.

"Brought up like twins!" he would say. "Sharing like brothers! Now he has a fine business and a fine house and fine children, and I have nothing. But I have my principles. I ain't never truckled to him. Some day he'll need me, you'll see!"

As Adam grew older, it became more and more certain that Henry would never need him for anything. Henry tried again and again to make friends, but Adam would have none of him. He talked more and more to himself as he sat at his work.

"Used to help him over the brook and bait his hook for him. Even built corn-cob houses for him to knock down, that much littler he was than me. Stepped out of the race when I found he wanted Annie. He might ask me for *something!*" Adam seemed often to be growing childish.

By the year 1875 fifteen of Fosterville's thirty-five veterans had died. The men who survived the war were, for the most part, not strong men, and weaknesses established in prisons and on long marches asserted themselves. Fifteen times the Fosterville Post paraded to the cemetery and read its committal service and fired its salute. For these parades Adam did not put on his gray uniform.

During the next twenty years deaths were fewer. Fosterville prospered as never before; it built factories and an electric car line. Of all its enterprises Henry Foust was at the head. He enlarged his house and bought farms and grew handsomer as he grew older. Everybody loved him; all Fosterville, except Adam, sought his company. It seemed sometimes as though Adam would almost die from loneliness and jealousy.

"Henry Foust sittin' with Ed Green!" said Adam to himself, as though he could never accustom his eyes to this phenomenon. "Henry consortin' with Newt Towne!"

The Grand Army Post also grew in importance. It paraded each year with more ceremony; it imported fine music and great speakers for Memorial Day.

Presently the sad procession to the cemetery began once more. There was a long, cold winter, with many cases of pneumonia, and three veterans succumbed; there was an intensely hot summer, and twice in one month the Post read its committal service and fired its salute. A few years more, and the Post numbered but three. Past them still on Post evenings walked Adam, head in air, hands clasped behind his back. There was Edward Green, round, fat, who puffed and panted; there was Newton Towne, who walked, in spite of palsy, as though he had won the battle of Gettysburg; there was, last of all, Henry Foust, who at seventy-five was hale and strong. Usually a tall son walked beside him, or a grandchild clung to his hand. He was almost never alone; it was as though everyone who knew him tried to have as much as possible of his company. Past him with a grave nod walked Adam. Adam was two years older than Henry; it required more and more stretching of arms behind his back to keep his shoulders straight.

In April Newton Towne was taken ill and died. Edward Green was terrified, though he considered himself, in spite of his shortness of breath, a strong man.

"Don't let anything happen to you, Henry," he would say. "Don't let anything get you, Henry. I can't march alone."

"I'll be there," Henry would reassure him. Only one look at Henry, and the most alarmed would have been comforted.

"It would kill me to march alone," said Edward Green.

As if Fosterville realized that it could not continue long to show its devotion to its veterans, it made this year special preparations for Memorial Day. The Fosterville Band practiced elaborate music, the children were drilled in marching. The children were to precede the veterans to the cemetery and were to scatter flowers over the graves. Houses were gaily decorated, flags and banners floated in the pleasant spring breeze. Early in the morning carriages and wagons began to bring in the country folk.

Adam Foust realized as well as Fosterville that the parades of veterans were drawing to their close.

"This may be the last time I can show my principles," said he, with grim setting of his lips. "I will put on my gray coat early in the morning."

Though the two veterans were to march to the cemetery, carriages were provided to bring them home. Fosterville meant to be as careful as possible of its treasures.

"I don't need any carriage to ride in, like Ed Green," said Adam proudly. "I could march out and back. Perhaps Ed Green will have to ride out as well as back."

But Edward Green neither rode nor walked. The day turned suddenly warm, the heat and excitement accelerated his already rapid breathing, and the doctor forbade his setting foot to the ground.

"But I will!" cried Edward, in whom the spirit of war still lived.

"No," said the doctor.

"Then I will ride."

"You will stay in bed," said the doctor.

So without Edward Green the parade was formed. Before the courthouse waited the band, and the long line of school children, and the burgess, and the fire company, and the distinguished stranger who was to make the address, until Henry Foust appeared, in his blue suit, with his flag on his breast and his bouquet in his hand. On each side of him walked a tall, middle-aged son, who seemed to hand him over reluctantly to the marshal, who was to escort him to his place. Smilingly he spoke to the marshal, but he was the only one who smiled or spoke. For an instant men and women broke off in the middle of their sentences, a husky something in their throats; children looked up at him with awe. Even his own grandchildren did not dare to wave or call from their places in the ranks. Then the storm of cheers broke.

Round the next corner Adam Foust waited. He was clad in his gray uniform — those who looked at him closely saw with astonishment that it was a new uniform; his brows met in a frown, his gray moustache seemed to bristle.

"How he hates them!" said one citizen of Fosterville to another. "Just look at poor Adam!"

"Used to bait his hook for him," Adam was saying. "Used to carry him pick-a-back! Used to go halves with him on everything. Now he walks with Ed Green!"

Adam pressed forward to the curb. The band was playing "Marching Through Georgia," which he hated; everybody was cheering. The volume of sound was deafening.

"Cheering Ed Green!" said Adam. "Fat! Lazy! Didn't have a wound. Dare say he hid behind a tree! Dare say — "

The band was in sight now, the back of the drum-major appeared, then all the musicians swung round the corner. After them came the little children with their flowers and their shining faces.

"Him and Ed Green next," said old Adam.

But Henry walked alone. Adam's whole body jerked in his astonishment. He heard someone say that Edward Green was sick, that the doctor had forbidden him to march, or even to ride. As he pressed nearer the curb he heard the admiring comments of the crowd.

"Isn't he magnificent!"

"See his beautiful flowers! His grandchildren always send him his flowers."

"He's our first citizen."

"He's mine!" Adam wanted to cry out. "He's mine!"

Never had Adam felt so miserable, so jealous, so heartsick. His eyes were filled with the great figure. Henry was, in truth, magnificent, not only in himself, but in what he represented. He seemed symbolic of a great era of the past, and at the same time of a new age which was advancing. Old Adam understood all his glory.

"He's mine!" said old Adam again, foolishly.

Then Adam leaned forward with startled, staring eyes. Henry had bowed and smiled in answer to the cheers. Across the street his own house was a mass of color — red, white, and blue over windows and doors, gay dresses on the porch. On each side the pavement was crowded with a shouting multitude. Surely no hero had ever had a more glorious passage through the streets of his birthplace!

But old Adam saw that Henry's face blanched, that there appeared suddenly upon it an expression of intolerable pain. For an instant Henry's step faltered and grew uncertain.

Then old Adam began to behave like a wild man. He pushed himself through the crowd, he flung himself upon the rope as though to tear it down, he called out, "Wait! wait!" Frightened women, fearful of some sinister purpose, tried to grasp and hold him. No man was immediately at hand, or Adam would have been seized and taken away. As for the feeble women — Adam shook them off and laughed at them.

"Let me go, you geese!" said he.

A mounted marshal saw him and rode down upon him; men started from under the ropes to pursue him. But Adam eluded them or outdistanced them. He strode across an open space with a surety which gave no hint of the terrible beating of his heart, until he reached the side of Henry. Him he greeted, breathlessly and with terrible eagerness.

"Henry," said he, gasping, "Henry, do you want me to walk along?"

Henry saw the alarmed crowds, he saw the marshal's hand stretched to seize Adam, he saw most clearly of all the tearful eyes under the beetling brows. Henry's voice shook, but he made himself clear.

"It's all right," said he to the marshal. "Let him be."

"I saw you were alone," said Adam. "I said, 'Henry needs me.' I know what it is to be alone. I — "

But Adam did not finish his sentence. He found a hand on his, a blue arm linked tightly in his gray arm, he felt himself moved along amid thunderous roars of sound. "Of course I need you!" said Henry. "I've needed you all along."

Then, old but young, their lives almost ended, but themselves immortal, united, to be divided no more, amid an ever-thickening sound of cheers, the two marched down the street.

THEODORE DREISER

Seldom is Theodore Dreiser, celebrated for his novels, thought of as a short story writer. The lyrical quality of this story of a man calling for his lost mate reveals a quite different writer from the one known for such ruggedly realistic novels as Sister Carrie *and* An American Tragedy. *As the story is called "The Lost Phoebe," one wonders how much the plaintive, repetitious cry of the bird called the phoebe, or pewee, may have inspired it.*

Theodore Dreiser, one of the giants of American literature, was born in Terre Haute, Indiana, in 1871. He was educated at the University of Indiana and had wide experience as a newspaperman and magazine editor. He was often called "the American Zola."

The Lost Phoebe

THEY lived together in a part of the country which was not so prosperous as it had once been, about three miles from one of those small towns that, instead of increasing in population, is steadily decreasing. The territory was not very thickly settled; perhaps a house every other mile or so, with large areas of corn- and wheat-land and fallow fields that at odd seasons had been sown to timothy and clover. Their particular house was part log and part frame, the log portion being the old original home of Henry's grandfather. The new portion, of now rain-beaten, time-worn slabs, through which the wind squeaked in the chinks at times, and which several overshadowing elms and a butternut tree made picturesque and reminiscently pathetic, but a little damp, was erected by Henry when he was twenty-one and just married.

That was forty-eight years before. The furniture inside, like the house outside, was old and mildewy and reminiscent of an earlier day. You have seen the whatnot of cherry wood, perhaps, with spiral legs and fluted top. It was there. The old-fashioned four-poster bed, with its ball-like protuberances and deep curving incisions, was there also, a sadly alienated descendant of an early Jacobean ancestor. The bureau of cherry was also high and wide and solidly built, but faded-looking, and with a musty odor. The rag carpet that underlay all these sturdy examples of enduring furniture was a weak, faded, lead-and-pink-colored affair woven by Phoebe Ann's own hands, when she was fifteen years younger than she was when she died. The creaky wooden loom on which it had been done now stood like a dusty, bony skeleton, along with a broken rocking chair, a worm-eaten clothes-press — Heaven knows how old — a lime-stained bench that had once been used to keep flowers on outside the door, and other decrepit factors of household utility, in an east room that was a lean-to against this so-called main portion. All sorts of other broken-down furniture were about this place; an antiquated clotheshorse, cracked in two of its ribs; a broken mirror in an old cherry frame, which had fallen from a nail and cracked itself three days before their youngest son, Jerry, died; an extension hat-rack, which once had had porcelain knobs on the ends of its pegs; and a sewing machine, long since outdone in its clumsy mechanism by rivals of a newer generation.

The orchard to the east of the house was full of gnarled old apple trees, worm-eaten as to trunks and branches, and fully ornamented with green and white lichens, so that it had a sad, greenish-white, silvery effect in moonlight. The low outhouses which had once housed chickens, a horse or two, a cow, and several pigs, were covered with patches of moss as to their roof, and the sides had been free of paint for so long that they were blackish gray as to color, and a little spongy. The picket fence in front, with its gate squeaky and askew, and the side fences of the stake-and-rider type were in an equally run-down condition. As a matter of fact, they had aged synchronously with the persons who lived here, old Henry Reifsneider and his wife Phoebe Ann.

They had lived here, these two, ever since their marriage, forty-eight years before, and Henry had lived here before that from his childhood up. His father and mother, well along in years when he was a boy, had invited him to bring his wife here when he had first fallen in love and decided to marry; and he had done so. His father and mother were the companions of himself and his wife for ten years after they were married, when both died; and then Henry and Phoebe were left with their five children growing lustily apace. But all sorts of things had happened since then. Of the seven children, all told, that had been born to them, three had died; one girl had gone to Kansas; one boy had gone to Sioux Falls, never even to be heard of after; another boy had gone to Washington; and the last girl lived five counties away in the same state, but was so burdened with cares of her own that she rarely gave them a thought. Time and a commonplace home-life that had never been attractive had weaned them thoroughly, so that, wherever they were, they gave little thought as to how it might be with their father and mother.

Old Henry Reifsneider and his wife Phoebe were a loving couple. You perhaps know how it is with simple natures that fasten themselves like lichens on the stones of circumstance and weather their days to a crumbling conclusion. The great world sounds widely, but it has no call for them. They have no soaring intellect. The orchard, the meadow, the cornfield, the pig-pen, and the chicken-lot measure the range of their human activities. When the wheat is headed it is reaped and threshed; when the corn is browned and frosted it is cut and shocked; when the timothy is in full head it is cut, and the haycock erected. After that comes winter, with the hauling of grain to market, the sawing and splitting of wood, the simple chores of fire-building, meal-getting, occasional repairing, and visiting. Beyond these and the changes of weather — the snows, the rains, and the fair days — there are no immediate, significant things. All the rest of life is a far-off, clamorous phantasmagoria, flickering like Northern lights in the night, and sounding as faintly as cowbells tinkling in the distance.

Old Henry and his wife Phoebe were as fond of each other as it is possible for two old people to be who have nothing else in this life to be fond of. He was a thin old man, seventy when she died, a queer, crotchety person with coarse gray-black hair and beard, quite straggly and unkempt. He looked at you out of dull, fishy, watery eyes that had deep-brown crow's feet at the sides. His clothes, like the clothes of many farmers, were aged and angular and baggy, standing out at the pockets, not fitting about the neck, protuberant and worn at elbow and knee. Phoebe Ann was thin and shapeless, a very umbrella of a woman, clad in shabby black, and with a black bonnet for her best wear. As time had passed, and they had only themselves to look after, their movements had become slower and slower, their activities fewer and fewer. The annual keep of pigs had been reduced from five to one grunting porker, and the single horse which Henry now retained was a sleepy animal, not over-nourished and not very clean. The chickens, of which formerly there was a large flock, had almost disappeared, owing to ferrets, foxes, and the lack of proper care, which produces disease. The former healthy garden was now a straggling memory of itself, and the vines and flower-beds that formerly ornamented the windows and dooryard had now become choking thickets. A will had been made which divided the small tax-eaten property equally among the remaining four, so that it was really of no interest to any of them. Yet these two lived together in peace and sympathy only that now and then old Henry would become unduly cranky, complaining almost invariably that something had been neglected or mislaid which was of no importance at all.

"Phoebe, where's my corn-knife? You ain't never minded to let my things alone no more."

"Now you hush, Henry," his wife would caution him in a cracked and squeaky voice. "If you don't, I'll leave yuh. I'll git up and walk out of here some day, and then where would y' be? Y' ain't got anybody but me to look after yuh, so yuh just behave yourself. Your corn-knife's on the mantel where it's allus been unless you've gone an' put it sommers else."

Old Henry, who knew his wife would never leave him in any circumstances, used to speculate at times as to what he would do if she were to die. That was the one leaving that he really feared. As he climbed on the chair at night to wind the old, long-pendulumed, double-weighted clock, or went finally to the front and the back door to see that they were safely shut in, it was a comfort to know that Phoebe was there, properly ensconced on her side of the bed, and that if he stirred restlessly in the night, she would be there to ask what he wanted.

"Now, Henry, do lie still! You're as restless as a chicken."

"Well, I can't sleep, Phoebe."

"Well, yuh needn't roll so, anyhow. Yuh kin let me sleep."

This usually reduced him to a state of somnolent ease. If she wanted a pail of water, it was a grumbling pleasure for him to get it; and if she did rise first to build the fires, he saw that the wood was cut and placed within easy reach. They divided this simple world nicely between them.

As the years had gone on, however, fewer and fewer people had called. They were well known for a distance of as much as ten square miles as old Mr. and Mrs. Reifsneider, honest, moderately Christian, but too old to be really interesting any longer. The writing of letters had become an almost impossible burden, too difficult to continue or even negotiate via others, although an occasional letter still did arrive from the daughter in

Pemberton County. Now and then some old friend stopped with a pie or cake or a roasted chicken or duck, or merely to see that they were well; but even these kindly-minded visits were no longer frequent.

One day in the early spring of her sixty-fourth year Mrs. Reifsneider took sick, and from a low fever passed into some indefinable ailment which, because of her age, was no longer curable. Old Henry drove to Swinnerton, the neighboring town, and procured a doctor. Some friends called, and the immediate care of her was taken off his hands. Then one chill spring night she died, and old Henry, in a fog of sorrow and uncertainty, followed her body to the nearest graveyard, an unattractive space with a few pines growing in it. Although he might have gone to the daughter in Pemberton or sent for her, it was really too much trouble and he was too weary and fixed. It was suggested to him at once by one friend and another that he could come to stay with them awhile, but he did not see fit. He was so old and so fixed in his notions and so accustomed to the exact surroundings he had known all his days, that he could not think of leaving. He wanted to remain near where they had put his Phoebe; and the fact that he would have to live alone did not trouble him in the least. The living children were notified, and the care of him offered if he would leave, but he would not.

"I kin make a shift for myself," he continually announced to old Dr. Morrow, who had attended his wife in this case. "I kin cook a little, and, besides, it don't take much more'n coffee an' bread in the mornin's to satisfy me. I'll git along now well enough. Yuh just let me be." And after many pleadings and proffers of advice, with supplies of coffee and bacon and baked bread duly offered and accepted, he was left to himself. For a while he sat idly outside his door brooding in the spring sun. He tried to revive his interest in farming, and to keep himself busy and free from thought by looking after the fields, which of late had been much neglected. It was a gloomy thing to come in of an evening, however, or in the afternoon and find no shadow of Phoebe where everything suggested her. By degrees he put a few of her things away. At night he sat beside his lamp and read in the papers that were left him occasionally or in a Bible that he had neglected for years, but he could get little solace from these things. Mostly he held his hand over his mouth and looked at the floor as he sat and thought of what had become of her, and how soon he himself would die. He made a great business of making his coffee in the morning and frying himself a little bacon at night; but his appetite was gone. The shell in which he had been housed so long seemed vacant, and its shadows were suggestive of immedicable griefs. So he lived quite dolefully for five long months, and then a change began.

It was one night, after he had looked after the front and the back door, wound the clock, blown out the light, and gone through all the selfsame motions that he had indulged in for years, that he went to bed not so much to sleep as to think. It was a moonlight night. The green lichen-covered orchard just outside and to be seen from his bed where he now lay was a silvery affair, sweetly spectral. The moon shone through the east windows, throwing the pattern of the panes on the wooden floor, and making the old furniture, to which he was accustomed, stand out dimly in the room. As usual he had been thinking of Phoebe and the years when they had been young together, and of the children who had gone, and the poor shift he was making of his present days. The house was coming to be in a very bad state indeed. The bed-clothes were in disorder and not clean, for he made a wretched shift of washing. It was a terror to him. The roof leaked, causing things (some of them) to remain damp for weeks at a time, but he was getting into that brooding state where he would accept anything rather than exert himself. He preferred to pace slowly to and fro or to sit and think.

By twelve o'clock on this particular night he was asleep, however, and by two had waked again. The moon by this time had shifted to a position on the western side of the house, and it now shone in through the windows of the living room and those of the kitchen beyond. A certain combination of furniture — a chair near a table, with his coat on it, the half-open kitchen door casting a shadow, and the position of a lamp near a paper — gave him an exact representation of Phoebe leaning over the table as he had often seen her do in life. It gave him a great start. Could it be she — or her ghost? He had scarcely ever believed in spirits; and still. . . . He looked at her fixedly in the feeble half-light, his old hair tingling oddly at the roots, and then sat up. The figure did not move. He put his thin legs out of the bed and sat looking at her, wondering if this could really be Phoebe. They had talked of ghosts often in their lifetime, of apparitions and omens; but they had never agreed that such things could be. It had never been a part of his wife's creed that she could have a spirit that could return to walk the earth. Her after-world was quite a different affair, a vague heaven, no less, from which the righteous did not trouble to return. Yet here she was now, bending over the table in her black skirt and gray shawl, her pale profile outlined against the moonlight.

"Phoebe," he called, thrilling from head to toe and putting out one bony hand, "have yuh come back?"

The figure did not stir, and he arose and walked uncertainly to the door, looking at it fixedly the while. As he drew near, however, the apparition resolved itself into its primal content — his old coat over the high-backed chair, the lamp by the paper, the half-open door.

"Well," he said to himself, his mouth open, "I thought shore I saw her." And he ran his hand strangely and vaguely through his hair, the while his nervous tension relaxed. Vanished as it had, it gave him the idea that she might return.

Another night, because of this first illusion, and because his mind was now constantly on her and he was old, he looked out of the window that was nearest his bed and commanded a hen-coop and pig-pen and a part of the wagon-shed, and there, a faint mist exuding from the damp of the ground, he thought he saw her again. It was one of those little wisps of mist, one of those faint exhalations of the earth that rise in a cool night after a warm day, and flicker like small white cypresses of fog before they disappear. In life it had been a custom of hers to cross this lot from her kitchen door to the pig-pen to throw in any scrap that was left from her cooking, and here she was again. He sat up and watched it strangely, doubtfully, because of his previous experience, but inclined, because of the nervous titillation that passed over his body, to believe that spirits really were, and that Phoebe, who would be concerned because of his lonely state, must be thinking about him, and hence returning. What other way would she have? How otherwise could she express herself? It would be within the province of her charity so to do, and like her loving interest in him. He quivered and watched it eagerly; but, a faint breath of air stirring, it wound away toward the fence and disappeared.

A third night, as he was actually dreaming, some ten days later, she came to his beside and put her hand on his head.

"Poor Henry!" she said. "It's too bad."

He roused out of his sleep, actually to see her, he thought, moving from his bedroom into the one living room, her figure a shadowy mass of black. The weak straining of his eyes caused little points of light to flicker about the outlines of her form. He arose, greatly astonished, walked the floor in the cool room, convinced that Phoebe was coming back to him. If he only thought sufficiently, if he made it perfectly clear by his feeling that he needed her greatly, she would come back, this kindly wife, and tell him what to do. She would perhaps be with him much of the time, in the night, anyhow; and that would make him less lonely, his state more endurable.

In age and with the feeble it is not such a far cry from the subtleties of illusion to actual hallucination, and in due time this transition was made for Henry. Night after night he waited, expecting her return. Once in his weird mood he thought he saw a pale light moving about the room, and another time he thought he saw her walking in the orchard after dark. It was one morning when the details of his lonely state were virtually unendurable that he woke with the thought that she was not dead. How he had arrived at this conclusion it is hard to say. His mind had gone. In its place was a fixed illusion. He and Phoebe had had a senseless quarrel. He had reproached her for not leaving his pipe where he was accustomed to find it, and she had left. It was an aberrated fulfillment of her old jesting threat that if he did not behave himself she would leave him.

"I guess I could find yuh ag'in," he had always said. But her crackling threat had always been:

"Yuh'll not find me if I ever leave yuh. I guess I kin git some place where yuh can't find me."

This morning when he arose he did not think to build the fire in the customary way or to grind his coffee and cut his bread, as was his wont, but solely to meditate as to where he should search for her and how he should induce her to come back. Recently the one horse had been dispensed with because he found it cumbersome and beyond his needs. He took down his soft crush hat after he had dressed himself, a new glint of interest and determination in his eye, and taking his black crook cane from behind the door, where he had always placed it, started out briskly to look for her among the nearest neighbors. His old shoes clumped soundly in the dust as he walked, and his gray-black locks, now grown rather long, straggled out in a dramatic fringe or halo from under his hat. His short coat stirred busily as he walked, and his hands and face were peaked and pale.

"Why, hello, Henry! Where're yuh goin' this mornin'?" inquired Farmer Dodge, who, hauling a load of wheat to market, encountered him on the public road. He had not seen the aged farmer in months, not since his wife's death, and he wondered now, seeing him looking so spry.

"Yuh ain't seen Phoebe, have yuh?" inquired the old man, looking up quizzically.

"Phoebe who?" inquired Farmer Dodge, not for the moment connecting the name with Henry's dead wife.

"Why, my wife Phoebe, o' course. Who do yuh s'pose I mean?" He stared up with a pathetic sharpness of glance from under his shaggy, gray eyebrows.

"Wall, I'll swan, Henry, yuh ain't jokin', are yuh?" said the solid Dodge, a pursy man, with a smooth, hard, red face. "It can't be your wife yuh're talkin' about. She's dead."

"Dead! Shucks!" retorted the demented Reifsneider. "She left me early this mornin', while I was sleepin'. She allus got up to build the fire, but she's gone now. We had a little spat last night, an' I guess that's the reason. But I guess I kin find her. She's gone over to Matilda Race's; that's where she's gone."

He started briskly up the road, leaving the amazed Dodge to stare in wonder after him.

"Well, I'll be switched!" he said aloud to himself. "He's clean out'n his head. That poor old feller's been livin' down there till he's gone outen his mind. I'll have to notify the authorities." And he flicked his whip with great enthusiasm. "Geddap!" he said, and was off.

Reifsneider met no one else in this poorly populated region until he reached the whitewashed fence of Matilda Race and her husband three miles away. He had passed several other houses *en route,* but these not being within the range of his illusion were not considered. His wife, who had known Matilda well, must be here. He opened the picket-gate which guarded the walk, and stamped briskly up to the door.

"Why, Mr. Reifsneider," exclaimed old Matilda herself, a stout woman, looking out of the door in an answer to his knock, "what brings yuh here this mornin'?"

"Is Phoebe here?" he demanded eagerly.

"Phoebe who? What Phoebe?" replied Mrs. Race, curious as to this sudden development of energy on his part.

"Why, my Phoebe, o' course. My wife Phoebe. Who do yuh s'pose? Ain't she here now?"

"Lawsy me!" exclaimed Mrs. Race, opening her mouth. "Yuh pore man! So you're clean out'n your mind now. Yuh come right in and sit down. I'll git you a cup o' coffee. O' course your wife ain't here; but yuh come in an' sit down. I'll find her fer yuh after a while. I know where she is."

The old farmer's eyes softened, and he entered. He was so thin and pale a specimen, pantalooned and patriarchal, that he aroused Mrs. Race's extremest sympathy as he took off his hat and laid it on his knees quite softly and mildly.

"We had a quarrel last night, an' she left me," he volunteered.

"Laws! laws!" sighed Mrs. Race, there being no one present with whom to share her astonishment as she went to her kitchen. "The pore man! Now somebody's just got to look after him. He can't be allowed to run around the country this way lookin' for his dead wife. It's turrible."

She boiled him a pot of coffee and brought in some of her new-baked bread and fresh butter. She set out some of her best jam and put a couple of eggs to boil, lying whole-heartedly the while.

"Now yuh stay right there, Uncle Henry, till Jake comes in, an' I'll send him to look for Phoebe. I think it's more'n likely she's over to Swinnerton with some o' her friends. Anyhow, we'll find out. Now yuh just drink this coffee an' eat this bread. Yuh must be tired. Yuh've had a long walk this mornin'." Her idea was to take counsel with Jake, "her man," and perhaps have him notify the authorities.

She bustled about, meditating on the uncertainties of life, while old Reifsneider thrummed on the rim of his hat with his pale fingers and later ate abstractedly of what she offered. His mind was on his wife, however, and since she was not here, or did not appear, it wandered vaguely away to a family by the name of Murray, miles away in another direction. He decided after a time that he would not wait for Jake Race to hunt his wife but would seek her for himself. He must be on, and urge her to come back.

"Well, I'll be goin'," he said, getting up and looking strangely about him. "I guess she didn't come here after all. She went over to the Murrays, I guess. I'll not wait any longer, Mis' Race. There's a lot to do over to the house today." And out he marched in the face of her protests, taking to the dusty road again in the warm spring sun, his cane striking the earth as he went.

It was two hours later that this pale figure of a man appeared in the Murrays' doorway, dusty, perspiring, eager. He had tramped all of five miles, and it was noon. An amazed husband and wife of sixty heard his strange query, and realized also that he was mad. They begged him to stay to dinner, intending to notify the authorities later and see what could be done; but though he stayed to partake of a little something, he did not stay long, and was off again to another distant farmhouse, his idea of many things to do and his need of Phoebe impelling him. So it went for that day and the next and the next, the circle of his inquiry ever widening.

The process by which a character assumes the significance of being peculiar, his antics weird, yet harmless, in such a community is often involute and pathetic. This day, as has been said, saw Reifsneider at other doors, eagerly asking his unnatural question and leaving a trail of amazement, sympathy, and pity in his wake. Although the authorities were informed — the county sheriff, no less — it was not deemed advisable to take him into custody; for when those who knew old Henry, and had for so long, reflected on the condition of the county insane asylum, a place which, because of the poverty of the district, was of staggering aberration and sickening environment, it was decided to let him remain at large; for, strange to relate, it was found on investigation that at night he returned peaceably enough to his lonesome domicile there to discover whether his wife had returned, and to brood in loneliness until the morning. Who would lock up a thin, eager, seeking old man with iron-gray hair and an attitude of kindly, innocent inquiry, particularly when he was well known for a past of only kindly servitude and reliability? Those who had known him best rather agreed that he should be allowed to roam at large. He could do no harm. There were many who were willing to help him as to food, old clothes, the odds and ends of his daily life — at least at first. His figure after a time became not so much a commonplace as an accepted curiosity, and the replies, "Why, no, Henry; I ain't see her," or "No, Henry; she ain't been here today," more customary.

For several years thereafter then he was an odd figure in the sun and rain, on dusty roads and muddy ones, encountered occasionally in strange and unexpected places, pursuing his endless search. Under-nourishment, after a time — although the neighbors and those who knew his history gladly contributed from their store — affected his body: for he walked much and ate little. The longer he roamed the public highway in this manner, the deeper became his strange hallucination; and finding it harder and harder to return from his more and more distant pilgrimages, he finally began taking a few utensils with him from his home, making a small package of them, in order that he might not be compelled to return. In an old tin coffee-pot of large size he placed a small tin cup, a knife, fork, and spoon, some salt and pepper, and to the outside of it, by a string forced through a pierced hole, he fastened a plate, which could be released, and which was his woodland table. It was no trouble for him to secure the little food that he needed, and with a strange, almost religious dignity, he had no hesitation in asking for that much. By degrees his hair became longer and longer, his once black hair became an earthen brown, and his clothes threadbare and dusty.

For all of three years he walked, and none knew how wide were his perambulations, nor how he survived the storms and cold. They could not see him, with homely rural understanding and forethought, sheltering himself in haycocks, or by the sides of cattle, whose warm bodies protected him from the cold, and whose dull understandings were not opposed to his harmless presence. Overhanging rocks and trees kept him at times from the rain, and a friendly hayloft or corn-crib was not above his humble consideration.

The involute progression of hallucination is strange. From asking at doors and being constantly rebuffed or denied, he finally came to the conclusion that although his Phoebe might not be in any of the houses at the doors of which he inquired, she might nevertheless be within the sound of his voice. And so, from patient inquiry, he began to call sad, occasional cries, that ever and anon waked the quiet landscapes and ragged hill regions, and set to echoing his thin "O-o-o Phoebe! O-o-o Phoebe!" It had a pathetic, albeit insane, ring, and many a farmer or ploughboy came to know it even from afar and say, "There goes old Reifsneider."

Another thing that puzzled him greatly after a time and after many hundreds of inquiries was when he no longer had any particular dooryard in view and no special inquiry to make, which way to go. These crossroads, which occasionally led in four or even six directions, came after a time to puzzle him. But to solve this knotty problem, which became more and more of a puzzle, there came to his aid another hallucination: Phoebe's spirit or some power of the air or wind or nature would tell him. If he stood at the center of the parting of the ways, closed his eyes, turned thrice about, and called "O-o-o Phoebe!" twice, and then threw his cane straight before him, that would surely indicate which way to go for Phoebe, or one of these mystic powers would surely govern its direction and fall! In whichever direction it went, even though, as was not infrequently the case, it took him back along the path he had already come, or across fields, he was not so far gone in his mind but that he gave himself ample time to search before he called again. Also the hallucination seemed to persist that at some time he would surely find her. There were hours when his feet were sore, and his limbs weary, when he would stop in the heat to wipe his seamed brow, or in the cold to beat his arms. Sometimes, after throwing away his cane, and finding it indicating the direction from which he had just come, he would shake his head wearily and philosophically, as if contemplating the unbelievable or an untoward fate, and then start briskly off. His strange figure came finally to be known in the farthest reaches of three or four counties. Old Reifsneider was a pathetic character. His fame was wide.

Near a little town called Watersville, in Green County, perhaps four miles from that minor center of human activity, there was a place or precipice locally known as the Red Cliff, a sheer wall of red sandstone, perhaps a hundred feet high which raised its sharp face for half a mile or more above the fruitful corn-fields and orchards that lay beneath, and which was surmounted by a thick grove of trees. The slope that slowly led up to it from the opposite side was covered by a rank growth of beech, hickory, and ash, through which threaded a number of wagon-tracks crossing at various angles. In fair weather it had become old Reifsneider's habit, so inured was he by now to the open, to make his bed in some such patch of trees as this, to fry his bacon or boil his eggs at the foot of some tree before laying himself down for the night. Occasionally, so light and inconsequential was his sleep, he would walk at night. More often, the moonlight or some sudden wind stirring in the trees or a reconnoitering animal arousing him, he would sit up and think, or pursue his quest in the moonlight or the dark, a strange, unnatural, half wild, half savage-looking but utterly harmless creature, calling at lonely road-crossings, staring at dark and shuttered houses, and wondering where, where Phoebe could really be.

That particular lull that comes in the systole-diastole of this earthly ball at two o'clock in the morning invariably aroused him, and though he might not go any farther he would sit up and contemplate the darkness or the stars, wondering. Sometimes in the strange processes of his mind he would fancy that he saw moving among the trees the figure of his lost wife, and then he would get up to follow, taking his utensils, always on a string, and his cane. If she seemed to evade him too easily he would run, or plead, or, suddenly losing track of the fancied figure, stand awed or disappointed, grieving for the moment over the almost insurmountable difficulties of his search.

It was in the seventh year of these hopeless peregrinations, in the dawn of a similar springtime to that in which his wife had died, that he came at last one night to the vicinity of this self-same patch that crowned the rise to the Red Cliff. His far-flung cane, used as a divining-rod at the last crossroads, had brought him hither. He had walked many, many miles. It was after ten o'clock at night, and he was very weary. Long wandering and little eating had left him but a shadow of his former self. It was a question now not so much of physical strength but of spiritual endurance which kept him up. He had scarcely eaten this day, and now exhausted he set himself down in the dark to rest and possibly to sleep.

Curiously on this occasion a strange suggestion of the presence of his wife surrounded him. It would not be long now, he counseled with himself, although the long months had brought him nothing, until he should see her — talk to her. He fell asleep after a time, his head on his knees. At midnight the moon began to rise, and at two in the morning, his wakeful hour, was a large silver disc shining through the trees to the east. He opened his eyes when the radiance became strong, making a silver pattern at his feet and lighting the woods with strange lustres and silvery, shadowy forms. As usual, his old notion that his wife must be near occurred to him on this occasion, and he looked about him with a speculative, anticipatory eye. What was it that moved in the distant shadows along the path by which he had entered — a pale, flickering will-o'-the-wisp that bobbed gracefully among the trees and riveted his expectant gaze? Moonlight and shadows combined to give it a strange form and a stranger reality, this fluttering of bogfire or dancing of wandering fireflies. Was it truly his lost Phoebe? By a circuitous route it passed about him, and in his fevered state he fancied that he could see the very eyes of her, not as she was when he last saw her in the black dress and shawl but now a strangely younger Phoebe, gayer, sweeter, the one whom he had known years before as a girl. Old Reifsneider got up. He had been expecting and dreaming of this hour all these years, and now as he saw the feeble light dancing lightly before him he peered at it questioningly, one thin hand in his gray hair.

Of a sudden there came to him now for the first time in many years the full charm of her girlish figure as he had known it in boyhood, the pleasing, sympathetic smile, the brown hair, the blue sash she had once worn about her waist at a picnic, her gay, graceful movements. He walked around the base of the tree, straining with his eyes, forgetting for once his cane and utensils, and following eagerly after. On she moved before him, a will-o'-the-wisp of the spring, a little flame above her head, and it seemed as though among the small saplings of ash and beech and the thick trunks of hickory and elm that she signaled with a young, a lightsome hand.

"O Phoebe! Phoebe!" he called. "Have yuh really come? Have yuh really answered me?" And hurrying faster, he fell once, scrambling lamely to his feet, only to see the light in the distance dancing illusively on. On and on he hurried until he was fairly running, brushing his ragged arms against the trees, striking his hands and face against impeding twigs. His hat was gone, his lungs were breathless, his reason quite astray, when coming to the edge of the cliff he saw her below among a silvery bed of apple trees now blooming in the spring.

"O Phoebe!" he called. "O Phoebe! Oh, no, don't leave me!" And feeling the lure of a world where love was young and Phoebe as this vision presented her, a delightful epitome of their quondam youth, he gave a gay cry of "Oh, wait, Phoebe!" and leaped.

Some farmer-boys reconnoitering this region of bounty and prospect some few days afterward, found first the tin utensils tied together under the tree where he had left them, and then later at the foot of the cliff, pale, broken, but elate, a moulded smile of peace and delight upon his lips, his body. His old hat was discovered lying under some low-growing saplings the twigs of which had held it back. No one of all the simple population knew how eagerly and joyously he had found his lost mate.

RING W. LARDNER

*On the surface "Golden Honeymoon" seems like a funny story told with
colloquial good humor. But its perceptions go far deeper. Edward J.
O'Brien, referring to another of this author's stories, said, "Mistaken by
the general public for many years as an idle entertainer, Lardner actually was a devastating portrayer of the American jungle. With a contained fury that reminds us of Swift, his portraits of his contemporaries
were deeply bitten with the acid perception of reality."*

*A native of Niles, Michigan, Ring Lardner was born in 1885 and
spent most of his life as a sports writer and editor for American newspapers. He was the author of several collections of short stories which
achieved the rare combination of both literary and popular esteem.*

The Golden Honeymoon

MOTHER says that when I start talking I never know when to stop. But
I tell her the only time I get a chance is when she ain't around, so I have
to make the most of it. I guess the fact is neither one of us would be
welcome in a Quaker meeting, but as I tell Mother, what did God give us
tongues for if He didn't want we should use them? Only she says He
didn't give them to us to say the same thing over and over again, like I
do, and repeat myself. But I say:

"Well, Mother," I say, "when people is like you and I and been
married fifty years, do you expect everything I say will be something you
ain't heard me say before? But it may be new to others, as they ain't
nobody else lived with me as long as you have."

So she says, "You can bet they ain't, as they couldn't nobody else
stand you that long."

"Well," I tell her, "you look pretty healthy."

"Maybe I do," she will say, "but I looked even healthier before I
married you."

You can't get ahead of Mother.

Yes, sir, we was married just fifty years ago the seventeenth day of last December and my daughter and son-in-law was over from Trenton to help us celebrate the Golden Wedding. My son-in-law is John H. Kramer, the real estate man. He made $12,000 one year and is pretty well thought of around Trenton; a good, steady, hard worker. The Rotarians was after him a long time to join, but he kept telling them his home was his club. But Edie finally made him join. That's my daughter.

Well, anyway, they come over to help us celebrate the Golden Wedding and it was pretty crimpy weather and the furnace don't seem to heat up no more like it used to and Mother made the remark that she hoped this winter wouldn't be as cold as the last, referring to the winter previous. So Edie said if she was us, and nothing to keep us home, she certainly wouldn't spend no more winters up here and why didn't we just shut off the water and close up the house and go down to Tampa, Florida? You know we was there four winters ago and staid five weeks, but it cost us over three hundred and fifty dollars for hotel bill alone. So Mother said we wasn't going no place to be robbed. So my son-in-law spoke up and said that Tampa wasn't the only place in the South, and besides we didn't have to stop at no high price hotel but could rent us a couple rooms and board out somewheres, and he had heard that St. Petersburg, Florida, was *the* spot and if we said the word he would write down there and make inquiries.

Well, to make a long story short, we decided to do it and Edie said it would be our Golden Honeymoon and for a present my son-in-law paid the difference between a section and a compartment so as we could have a compartment and have more privatecy. In a compartment you have an upper and lower berth just like the regular sleeper, but it is a shut in room by itself and got a wash bowl. The car we went in was all compartments and no regular berths at all. It was all compartments.

We went to Trenton the night before and staid at my daughter and son-in-law and we left Trenton the next afternoon at 3:23 P.M.

This was the twelfth day of January. Mother set facing the front of the train, as it makes her giddy to ride backwards. I set facing her, which does not affect me. We reached North Philadelphia at 4:03 P.M. and we reached West Philadelphia at 4:14, but did not go into Broad Street. We reached Baltimore at 6:30 and Washington, D.C., at 7:25. Our train laid over in Washington two hours till another train come along to pick us up and I got out and strolled up the platform and into the Union Station.

When I come back, our car had been switched on to another track, but I remembered the name of it, the La Belle, as I had once visited my aunt out in Oconomowoc, Wisconsin, where there was a lake of that name, so I had no difficulty in getting located. But Mother had nearly fretted herself sick for fear I would be left.

"Well," I said, "I would of followed you on the next train."

"You couldn't of," said Mother, and she pointed out that she had the money.

"Well," I said, "we are in Washington and I could of borrowed from the United States Treasury. I would of pretended I was an Englishman."

Mother caught the point and laughed heartily.

Our train pulled out of Washington at 9:40 P.M. and Mother and I turned in early, I taking the upper. During the night we passed through the green fields of old Virginia, though it was too dark to tell if they was green or what color. When we got up in the morning, we was at Fayette-ville, North Carolina. We had breakfast in the dining car and after breakfast I got in conversation with the man in the next compartment to ours. He was from Lebanon, New Hampshire, and a man about eighty years of age. His wife was with him and two unmarried daughters and I made the remark that I should think the four of them would be crowded in one compartment, but he said they had made the trip every vinter for fifteen years and knowed how to keep out of each other's way. He said they was bound for Tarpon Springs.

We reached Charleston, South Carolina, at 12:50 P.M. and arrived at Savannah, Georgia, at 4:20. We reached Jacksonville, Florida, at 8:45 P.M. and had an hour and a quarter to lay over there, but Mother made a fuss about me getting off the train, so we had the darkey make up our berths and retired before we left Jacksonville. I didn't sleep good as the train done a lot of hemming and hawing, and Mother never sleeps good on a train as she says she is always worrying that I will fall out. She says she would rather have the upper herself, as then she would not have to worry about me, but I tell her I can't take the risk of having it get out that I allowed my wife to sleep in an upper berth. It would make talk.

We was up in the morning in time to see our friends from New Hampshire get off at Tarpon Springs, which we reached at 6:53 A.M.

Several of our fellow passengers got off at Clearwater and some at Belleair, where the train backs right up to the door of the mammoth hotel. Belleair is the winter headquarters for the golf dudes and every-body that got off there had their bag of sticks, as many as ten and twelve in a bag. Women and all. When I was a young man we called it shinny and only needed one club to play with and about one game of it would of been a-plenty for some of these dudes, the way we played it.

The train pulled into St. Petersburg at 8:20 and when we got off the train you would think they was a riot, what with all the darkeys barking for the different hotels.

I said to Mother, I said, "It is a good thing we have got a place picked out to go to and don't have to choose a hotel, as it would be hard to choose amogst them if every one of them is the best."

She laughed.

We found a jitney and I give him the address of the room my son-in-law had got for us and soon we was there and introduced ourselves to the lady that owns the house, a young widow about forty-eight years of age. She showed us our room, which was light and airy with a comfortable bed and bureau and washstand. It was twelve dollars a week, but the location was good, only three blocks from Williams Park.

St. Pete is what folks calls the town, though they also call it the Sunshine City, as they claim they's no other place in the country where they's fewer days when Old Sol don't smile down on Mother Earth, and one of the newspapers gives away all their copies free every day when the sun don't shine. They claim to of only give them away some sixty-odd times in the last eleven years. Another nickname they have got for the town is "the Poor Man's Palm Beach," but I guess they's men that comes there that could borrow as much from the bank as some of the Willie boys over to the other Palm Beach.

During our stay we paid a visit to the Lewis Tent City, which is the headquarters for the Tin Can Tourists. But maybe you ain't heard about them. Well, they are an organization that takes their vacation trips by auto and carries everything with them. That is, they bring along their tents to sleep in and cook in and they don't patronize no hotels or cafeterias, but they have got to be bona fide auto campers or they can't belong to the organization.

They tell me they's over 200,000 members to it and they call themselves the Tin Canners on account of most of their food being put up in tin cans. One couple we seen in the Tent City was a couple from Brady, Texas, named Mr. and Mrs. Pence, which the old man is over eighty years of age and they had came in their auto all the way from home, a distance of 1641 miles. They took five weeks for the trip, Mr. Pence driving the entire distance.

The Tin Canners hails from every State in the Union and in the summer time they visit places like New England and the Great Lakes region, but in the winter the most of them comes to Florida and scatters all over the State. While we was down there, they was a national convention of them at Gainesville, Florida, and they elected a Fredonia, New York man as their president. His title is Royal Tin Can Opener of the World. They have got a song wrote up which everybody has got to learn it before they are a member:

> The tin can forever! Hurrah, boys! Hurrah!
> Up with the tin can! Down with the foe!
> We will rally round the campfire, we'll rally once again,
> Shouting, "We auto camp forever!"

That is something like it. And the members has also got to have a tin can fastened on to the front of their machine.

I asked Mother how she would like to travel around that way and she said, "Fine, but not with an old rattle brain like you driving."

"Well," I said, "I am eight years younger than this Mr. Pence who drove here from Texas."

"Yes," she said, "but he is old enough to not be skittish."

You can't get ahead of Mother.

Well, one of the first things we done in St. Petersburg was to go to the Chamber of Commerce and register our names and where we was from as they's great rivalry amongst the different States in regards to the number of their citizens visiting in town and of course our little State don't stand much of a show, but still every little bit helps, as the fella says. All and all, the man told us, they was 11,000 names registered, Ohio leading with some 1500-odd and New York State next with 1200. Then come Michigan, Pennsylvania and so on down, with one man each from Cuba and Nevada.

The first night we was there, they was a meeting of the New York-New Jersey Society at the Congregational Church and a man from Ogdensburg, New York State, made the talk. His subject was Rainbow Chasing. He is a Rotarian and a very convicting speaker, though I forget his name.

Our first business, of course, was to find a place to eat and after trying several places we run on to a cafeteria on Central Avenue that suited us up and down. We eat pretty near all our meals there and it averaged about two dollars per day for the two of us, but the food was well cooked and everything nice and clean. A man don't mind paying the price if things is clean and well cooked.

On the third day of February, which is Mother's birthday, we spread ourselves and eat supper at the Poinsettia Hotel and they charged us seventy-five cents for a sirloin steak that wasn't hardly big enough for one.

I said to Mother, "Well," I said, "I guess it's a good thing every day ain't your birthday or we would be in the poorhouse."

"No," says Mother, "because if every day was my birthday, I would be old enough by this time to of been in my grave long ago."

You can't get ahead of Mother.

In the hotel they had a cardroom where they was several men and ladies playing five hundred and this new fangled whist bridge. We also seen a place where they was dancing, so I asked Mother would she like to trip the light fantastic too and she said no, she was too old to squirm like you have got to do nowdays. We watched some of the young folks at it awhile till Mother got disgusted and said we would have to see a good movie to take the taste out of our mouth. Mother is a great movie heroyne and we go twice a week here at home.

But I want to tell you about the Park. The second day we was there we visited the Park, which is a good deal like the one in Tampa, only bigger, and they's more fun goes on here every day than you could shake a stick at. In the middle they's a big bandstand and chairs for the folks to set and listen to the concerts, which they give you music for all tastes, from Dixie up to classical pieces like "Hearts and Flowers."

Then all around they's places marked off for different sports and games —chess and checkers and dominoes for folks that enjoys those kind of games, and roque and horseshoes for the nimbler ones. I used to pitch a pretty fair shoe myself, but ain't done much of it in the last twenty years.

Well, anyway, we bought a membership ticket in the club which costs one dollar for the season, and they tell me that up to a couple years ago it was fifty cents, but they had to raise it to keep out the riffraff.

Well, Mother and I put in a great day watching the pitchers and she wanted I should get in the game, but I told her I was all out of practice and would make a fool of myself, though I seen several men pitching who I guess I could take their measure without no practice. However, they was some good pitchers, too, and one boy from Akron, Ohio, who could certainly throw a pretty shoe. They told me it looked like he would win the championship of the United States in the February tournament. We come away a few days before they held that and I never did hear if he win. I forget his name, but he was a clean cut young fella and he has got a brother in Cleveland that's a Rotarian.

Well, we just stood around and watched the different games for two or three days and finally I set down in a checker game with a man named Weaver from Danville, Illinois. He was a pretty fair checker player, but he wasn't no match for me, and I hope that don't sound like bragging. But I always could hold my own on a checkerboard and the folks around here will tell you the same thing. I played with this Weaver pretty near all morning for two or three mornings and he beat me one game and the only other time it looked like he had a chance, the noon whistle blowed and we had to quit and go to dinner.

While I was playing checkers, Mother would set and listen to the band, as she loves music, classical or no matter what kind, but anyway she was setting there one day and between selections the woman next to her opened up a conversation. She was a woman about Mother's own age, seventy or seventy-one, and finally she asked Mother's name and Mother told her her name and where she was from and Mother asked her the same question, and who do you think the woman was?

Well, sir, it was the wife of Frank M. Hartsell, the man who was engaged to Mother till I stepped in and cut him out, fifty-two years ago!

Yes, sir!

You can imagine Mother's surprise! And Mrs. Hartsell was surprised, too, when Mother told her she had once been friends with her husband, though Mother didn't say how close friends they had been, or that Mother and I was the cause of Hartsell going out West. But that's what we was. Hartsell left his town a month after the engagement was broke off and ain't never been back since. He had went out to Michigan and become a veterinary, and that is where he had settled down, in Hillsdale, Michigan, and finally married his wife.

Well, Mother screwed up her courage to ask if Frank was still living and Mrs. Hartsell took her over to where they was pitching horseshoes and there was old Frank, waiting his turn. And he knowed Mother as soon as he seen her, though it was over fifty years. He said he knowed her by her eyes.

"Why, it's Lucy Frost!" he says, and he throwed down his shoes and quit the game.

Then they come over and hunted me up and I will confess I wouldn't of knowed him. Him and I is the same age to the month, but he seems to show it more, some way. He is balder for one thing. And his beard is all white, where mine has still got a streak of brown in it. The very first thing I said to him, I said, "Well, Frank, that beard of yours makes me feel like I was back north. It looks like a regular blizzard."

"Well," he said, "I guess yourn would be just as white if you had it dry cleaned."

But Mother wouldn't stand that.

"Is that so!" she said to Frank. "Well, Charley ain't had no tobacco in his mouth for over ten years!"

And I ain't!

Well, I excused myself from the checker game and it was pretty close to noon, so we decided to all have dinner together and they was nothing for it only we must try their cafeteria on Third Avenue. It was a little more expensive than ours and not near as good, I thought. I and Mother had about the same dinner we had been having every day and our bill was $1.10. Frank's check was $1.20 for he and his wife. The same meal wouldn't of cost them more than a dollar at our place.

After dinner we made them come up to our house and we all set in the parlor, which the young woman had give us the use of to entertain company. We begun talking over old times and Mother said she was ascared Mrs. Hartsell would find it tiresome listening to we three talk over old times, but as it turned out they wasn't much chance for nobody else to talk with Mrs. Hartsell in the company. I have heard lots of women that could go it, but Hartsell's wife takes the cake of all the women I ever seen. She told us the family history of everybody in the State of Michigan and bragged for a half hour about her son, who she said is in the drug business in Grand Rapids, and a Rotarian.

When I and Hartsell could get a word in edgeways we joked one another back and forth and I chafed him about being a horse doctor.

"Well, Frank," I said, "you look pretty prosperous, so I suppose they's been plenty of glanders around Hillsdale."

"Well," he said, "I've managed to make more than a fair living. But I've worked pretty hard."

"Yes," I said, "and I suppose you get called out all hours of the night to attend births and so on."

Mother made me shut up.

Well, I thought they wouldn't never go home and I and Mother was in misery trying to keep awake, as the both of us generally always takes a

nap after dinner. Finally they went, after we had made an engagement to
meet them in the Park the next morning, and Mrs. Hartsell also invited
us to come to their place the next night and play five hundred. But she
had forgot that they was a meeting of the Michigan Society that evening,
so it was not till two evenings later that we had our first card game.

Hartsell and his wife lived in a house on Third Avenue North and had
a private setting room besides their bedroom. Mrs. Hartsell couldn't quit
talking about their private setting room like it was something wonderful.
We played cards with them, with Mother and Hartsell partners against
his wife and I. Mrs. Hartsell is a miserable card player and we certainly
got the worst of it.

After the game she brought out a dish of oranges and we had to
pretend it was just what we wanted, though oranges down there is like a
young man's whiskers; you enjoy them at first, but they get to be a pesky
nuisance.

We played cards again the next night at our place with the same
partners and I and Mrs. Hartsell was beat again. Mother and Hartsell
was full of compliments for each other on what a good team they made,
but the both of them knowed well enough where the secret of their
success laid. I guess all and all we must of played ten different evenings
and they was only one night when Mrs. Hartsell and I come out ahead.
And that one night wasn't no fault of hern.

When we had been down there about two weeks, we spent one evening
as their guest in the Congregational Church, at a social give by the
Michigan Society. A talk was made by a man named Bitting of Detroit,
Michigan, on How I was Cured of Story Telling. He is a big man in the
Rotarians and give a witty talk.

A woman named Mrs. Oxford rendered some selections which Mrs.
Hartsell said was grand opera music, but whatever they was my daughter
Edie could of give her cards and spades and not made such a hullaballoo
about it neither.

Then they was a ventriloquist from Grand Rapids and a young woman
about forty-five years of age that mimicked different kinds of birds. I
whispered to Mother that they all sounded like a chicken, but she nudged
me to shut up.

After the show we stopped in a drug store and I set up the refresh-
ments and it was pretty close to ten o'clock before we finally turned in.
Mother and I would of preferred tending the movies, but Mother said we
mustn't offend Mrs. Hartsell, though I asked her had we came to Florida

to enjoy ourselves or to just not offend an old chatterbox from Michigan.

I felt sorry for Hartsell one morning. The women folks both had an engagement down to the chiropodist's and I run across Hartsell in the Park and he foolishly offered to play me checkers.

It was him that suggested it, not me, and I guess he repented himself before we had played one game. But he was too stubborn to give up and set there while I beat him game after game and the worst part of it was that a crowd of folks had got in the habit of watching me play and there they all was, looking on, and finally they seen what a fool Frank was making of himself, and they began to chafe him and pass remarks. Like one of them said, "Who ever told you you was a checker player!"

And, "You might maybe be good for tiddle-de-winks, but not checkers!"

I almost felt like letting him beat me a couple games. But the crowd would of knowed it was a put up job.

Well, the women folks joined us in the Park and I wasn't going to mention our little game, but Hartsell told about it himself and admitted he wasn't no match for me.

"Well," said Mrs. Hartsell, "checkers ain't much of a game anyway, is it?" She said, "It's more of a children's game, ain't it? At least, I know my boy's children used to play it a good deal."

"Yes, ma'am," I said. "It's a children's game the way your husband plays it, too."

Mother wanted to smooth things over, so she said, "Maybe they's other games where Frank can beat you."

"Yes," said Mrs. Hartsell, "and I bet he could beat you pitching horseshoes."

"Well," I said, "I would give him a chance to try, only I ain't pitched a shoe in over sixteen years."

"Well," said Hartsell, "I ain't played checkers in twenty years."

"You ain't never played it," I said.

"Anyway," says Frank, "Lucy and I is your master at five hundred."

Well, I could of told him him why that was, but had decency enough to hold my tongue.

It had got so now that he wanted to play cards every night and when I or Mother wanted to go to a movie, why one of us would have to pretend we had a headache and then trust to goodness that they wouldn't see us sneak into the theater. I don't mind playing cards when my partner keeps their mind on the game, but you take a woman like Hartsell's wife and how can they play cards when they have got to stop every couple seconds and brag about their son in Grand Rapids?

Well, the New York-New Jersey Society announced that they was going to give a social evening too and I said to Mother, I said, "Well, that is one evening when we will have an excuse not to play five hundred."

"Yes," she said, "but we will have to ask Frank and his wife to go to the social with us as they asked us to go to the Michigan social."

"Well," I said, "I had rather stay home than drag that chatterbox everywheres we go."

So Mother said, "You are getting too cranky. Maybe she does talk a little too much but she is good hearted. And Frank is always good company."

So I said, "I suppose if he is such good company you wished you had of married him."

Mother laughed and said I sounded like I was jealous. Jealous of a cow doctor!

Anyway we had to drag them along to the social and I will say that we give them a much better entertainment than they had given us.

Judge Lane of Paterson made a fine talk on business conditions and a Mrs. Newell of Westfield imitated birds, only you could really tell what they was the way she done it. Two young women from Red Bank sung a choral selection and we clapped them back and they gave us "Home to Our Mountains" and Mother and Mrs. Hartsell both had tears in their eyes. And Hartsell, too.

Well, some way or another the chairman got wind that I was there and asked me to make a talk and I wasn't even going to get up, but Mother made me, so I got up and said, "Ladies and gentlemen," I said. "I didn't expect to be called on for a speech on an occasion like this or no other occasion as I do not set myself up as a speech maker, so will have to do the best I can, which I often say is the best anybody can do."

Then I told them the story about Pat and the motorcycle, using the brogue, and it seemed to tickle them and I told them one or two other stories, but altogether I wasn't on my feet more than twenty or twenty-five minutes and you ought to of heard the clapping and hollering when I set down. Even Mrs. Hartsell admitted that I am quite a speechifier and said if I ever went to Grand Rapids, Michigan, her son would make me talk to the Rotarians.

When it was over, Hartsell wanted we should go to their place and play cards, but his wife reminded him that it was after 9:30 P.M., rather a late hour to start a card game, but he had went crazy on the subject of cards, probably because he didn't have to play partners with his wife. Anyway, we got rid of them and went home to bed.

It was the next morning, when we met over to the Park, that Mrs. Hartsell made the remark that she wasn't getting no exercise so I suggested that why didn't she take part in the roque game.

She said she had not played a game of roque in twenty years, but if Mother would play she would play. Well, at first Mother wouldn't hear of it, but finally consented, more to please Mrs. Hartsell than anything else.

Well, they had a game with a Mrs. Ryan from Eagle, Nebraska, and a young Mrs. Morse from Rutland, Vermont, who Mother had met down to the chiropodist's. Well, Mother couldn't hit a flea and they all laughed at her and I couldn't help from laughing at her myself and finally she quit and said her back was too lame to stoop over. So they got another lady and kept on playing and soon Mrs. Hartsell was the one everybody was laughing at, as she had a long shot to hit the black ball, and as she made the effort her teeth fell out on to the court. I never seen a woman so flustered in my life. And I never heard so much laughing, only Mrs. Hartsell didn't join in and she was madder than a hornet and wouldn't play no more, so the game broke up.

Mrs. Hartsell went home without speaking to nobody, but Hartsell staid around and finally he said to me, he said, "Well, I played you checkers the other day and you beat me bad and now what do you say if you and me play a game of horseshoes?"

I told him I hadn't pitched a shoe in sixteen years, but Mother said, "Go ahead and play. You used to be good at it and maybe it will come back to you."

Well, to make a long story short, I give in. I oughtn't to of never tried it, as I hadn't pitched a shoe in sixteen years, and I only done it to humor Hartsell.

Before we started, Mother patted me on the back and told me to do my best, so we started in and I seen right off that I was in for it, as I hadn't pitched a shoe in sixteen years and didn't have my distance. And besides, the plating had wore off the shoes so that they was points right where they stuck into my thumb and I hadn't throwed more than two or three times when my thumb was raw and it pretty near killed me to hang on to the shoe, let alone pitch it.

Well, Hartsell throws the awkwardest shoe I ever seen pitched and to see him pitch you wouldn't think he would ever come nowheres near, but he is also the luckiest pitcher I ever seen and he made some pitches where the shoe lit five and six feet short and then schoonered up and was a ringer. They's no use trying to beat that kind of luck.

They was a pretty fair size crowd watching us and four or five other ladies besides Mother, and it seems like, when Hartsell pitches, he has got to chew and it kept the ladies on the anxious seat as he don't seem to care which way he is facing when he leaves go.

You would think a man as old as him would of learnt more manners.

Well, to make a long story short, I was just beginning to get my distance when I had to give up on account of my thumb, which I showed it to Hartsell and he seen I couldn't go on, as it was raw and bleeding. Even if I could of stood it to go on myself, Mother wouldn't of allowed it after she seen my thumb. So anyway I quit and Hartsell said the score was nineteen to six, but I don't know what it was. Or don't care, neither.

Well, Mother and I went home and I said I hoped we was through with the Hartsells as I was sick and tired of them, but it seemed like she had promised we would go over to their house that evening for another game of their everlasting cards.

Well, my thumb was giving me considerable pain and I felt kind of out of sorts and I guess maybe I forgot myself, but anyway, when we was about through playing Hartsell made the remark that he wouldn't never lose a game of cards if he could always have Mother for a partner.

So I said, "Well, you had a chance fifty years ago to always have her for a partner, but you wasn't man enough to keep her."

I was sorry the minute I had said it and Hartsell didn't know what to say and for once his wife couldn't say nothing. Mother tried to smooth things over by making the remark that I must of had something stronger than tea or I wouldn't talk so silly. But Mrs. Hartsell had froze up like an iceberg and hardly said good night to us and I bet her and Frank put in a pleasant hour after we was gone.

As we was leaving, Mother said to him, "Never mind Charley's nonsense, Frank. He is just mad because you beat him all hollow pitching horseshoes and playing cards."

She said that to make up for my slip, but at the same time she certainly riled me. I tried to keep ahold of myself, but as soon as we was out of the house she had to open up the subject and begun to scold me for the break I had made.

Well, I wasn't in no mood to be scolded. So I said, "I guess he is such a wonderful pitcher and card player that you wished you had married him."

"Well," she said, "at least he ain't a baby to give up pitching because his thumb has got a few scratches."

"And how about you," I said, "making a fool of yourself on the roque court and then pretending your back is lame and you can't play no more!"

"Yes," she said, "but when you hurt your thumb I didn't laugh at you, and why did you laugh at me when I sprained my back?"

"Who could help from laughing!" I said.

"Well," she said, "Frank Hartsell didn't laugh."

"Well," I said, "why didn't you marry him?"

"Well," said Mother, "I almost wished I had!"

"And I wished so, too!" I said.

"I'll remember that!" said Mother, and that's the last word she said to me for two days.

We seen the Hartsells the next day in the Park and I was willing to apologize, but they just nodded to us. And a couple days later we heard they had left for Orlando, where they have got relatives.

I wished they had went there in the first place.

Mother and I made it up setting on a bench.

"Listen, Charley," she said. "This is our Golden Honeymoon and we don't want the whole thing spoilt with a silly old quarrel."

"Well," I said, "did you mean that about wishing you had married Hartsell?"

"Of course not," she said, "that is, if you didn't mean that you wished I had, too."

So I said, "I was just tired and all wrought up. I thank God you chose me instead of him as they's no other woman in the world who I could of lived with all these years."

"How about Mrs. Hartsell?" says Mother.

"Good gracious!" I said. "Imagine being married to a woman that plays five hundred like she does and drops her teeth on the roque court!"

"Well," said Mother, "it wouldn't be no worse than being married to a man that expectorates towards ladies and is such a fool in a checker game."

So I put my arm around her shoulder and she stroked my hand and I guess we got kind of spooney.

They was two days left of our stay in St. Petersburg and the next to the last day Mother introduced me to a Mrs. Kendall from Kingston, Rhode Island, who she had met at the chiropodist's.

Mrs. Kendall made us acquainted with her husband, who is in the grocery business. They have got two sons and five grandchildren and one great-grandchild. One of their sons lives in Providence and is way up in the Elks as well as a Rotarian.

We found them very congenial people and we played cards with them the last two nights we was there. They was both experts and I only wished we had met them sooner instead of running into the Hartsells. But the Kendalls will be there again next winter and we will see more of them, that is, if we decide to make the trip again.

We left the Sunshine City on the eleventh day of February, at 11 A.M. This give us a day trip through Florida and we seen all the country we had passed through at night on the way down.

We reached Jacksonville at 7 P.M. and pulled out of there at 8:10 P.M. We reached Fayetteville, North Carolina, at nine o'clock the following morning, and reached Washington, D.C., at 6:30 P.M., laying over there half an hour.

We reached Trenton at 11:01 P.M. and had wired ahead to my daughter and son-in-law and they met us at the train and we went to their house and they put us up for the night. John would of made us stay up all night, telling about our trip, but Edie said we must be tired and made us go to bed. That's my daughter.

The next day we took our train for home and arrived safe and sound, having been gone just one month and a day.

Here comes Mother, so I guess I better shut up.

SHERWOOD ANDERSON

One of the most difficult ways of telling a story, although it appears the most simple, is to write it in the first person. "I'm a Fool" is a masterpiece of the genre as well as a masterpiece in itself. What could have been comedy comes through as heartbreak. It is doubtful that anyone who has read this story has ever forgotten it.

Sherwood Anderson was the first of our great modern short story writers. He was born in Camden, Ohio, in 1876. His collection, Winesburg, Ohio, *published in 1919, was a turning point in the life of the American short story. It anticipated Ernest Hemingway by several years and also greatly influenced William Faulkner who, unlike Hemingway, never ceased to pay tribute to Anderson.*

I'm a Fool

IT WAS a hard jolt for me, one of the most bitterest I ever had to face. And it all came about through my own foolishness too. Even yet, sometimes, when I think of it, I want to cry or swear or kick myself. Perhaps, even now, after all this time, there will be a kind of satisfaction in making myself look cheap by telling of it.

It began at three o'clock one October afternoon as I sat in the grandstand at the fall trotting and pacing meet at Sandusky, Ohio.

To tell the truth, I felt a little foolish that I should be sitting in the grandstand at all. During the summer before I had left my home town with Harry Whitehead and, with a nigger named Burt, had taken a job as swipe with one of the two horses Harry was campaigning through the fall race meets that year. Mother cried and my sister Mildred, who wanted to get a job as a schoolteacher in our town that fall, stormed and scolded about the house all during the week I left. They both thought it something disgraceful that one of our family should take a place as a swipe with race horses. I've an idea Mildred thought my taking the place would stand in the way of her getting the job she'd been working so long for.

But after all I had to work and there was no other work to be got. A big lumbering fellow of nineteen couldn't just hang around the house and I had got too big to mow people's lawns and sell newspapers. Little chaps who could get next to people's sympathies by their sizes were always getting jobs away from me. There was one fellow who kept saying to everyone who wanted a lawn mowed or a cistern cleaned, that he was saving his money to work his way through college, and I used to lay awake nights thinking up ways to injure him without being found out. I kept thinking of wagons running over him and bricks falling on his head as he walked along the street. But never mind him.

I got the place with Harry and I liked Burt fine. We got along splendid together. He was a big nigger with a lazy sprawling body and soft kind eyes, and when it came to a fight he could hit like Jack Johnson. He had Bucephalus, a big black pacing stallion that could do 2.09 or 2.10 if he had to, and I had a little gelding named Doctor Fritz that never lost a race all fall when Harry wanted him to win.

We set out from home late in July in a boxcar with the two horses and after that, until late November, we kept moving along to the race meets and the fairs. It was a peachy time for me, I'll say that. Sometimes, now, I think that boys who are raised regular in houses, and never have a fine nigger like Burt for best friend, and go to high schools and college, and never steal anything or get drunk a little, or learn to swear from fellows who know how, or come walking up in front of a grandstand in their shirt sleeves and with dirty horsey pants on when the races are going on and the grandstand is full of people all dressed up — What's the use talking about it? Such fellows don't have nothing at all. They've never had no opportunity.

But I did. Burt taught me how to rub down a horse and put the bandages on after a race and steam a horse out and a lot of valuable things for any man to know. He could wrap a bandage on a horse's leg so smooth that if it had been the same color you would think it was his skin, and I guess he'd have been a big driver too and got to the top like Murphy and Walter Cox and the others if he hadn't been black.

Gee whizz, it was fun. You got to a county seat town maybe, say, on a Saturday or Sunday, and the fair began the next Tuesday and lasted until Friday afternoon. Doctor Fritz would be, say, in the 2.25 trot on Tuesday afternoon and on Thursday afternoon Bucephalus would knock 'em cold in the "free-for-all" pace. It left you a lot of time to hang around and listen to horse talk, and see Burt knock some yap cold that got too gay, and you'd find out about horses and men and pick up a lot of stuff you could use all the rest of your life if you had some sense and salted down what you heard and felt and saw.

And then at the end of the week when the race meet was over, and Harry had run home to tend up to his livery stable business, you and Burt hitched the two horses to carts and drove slow and steady across country to the place for the next meeting so as to not overheat the horses, etc., etc., you know.

Gee whizz, gosh amighty, the nice hickorynut and beechnut and oaks and other kinds of trees along the roads, all brown and red, and the good smells, and Burt singing a song that was called "Deep River," and the country girls at the windows of houses and everything. You can stick your colleges up your nose for all me. I guess I know where I got my education.

Why, one of those little burgs of towns you come to on the way, say now, on a Saturday afternoon, and Burt says, "Let's lay up here." And you did.

And you took the horses to a livery stable and fed them and you got your good clothes out of a box and put them on.

And the town was full of farmers gaping, because they could see you were race horse people, and the kids maybe never see a nigger before and was afraid and run away when the two of us walked down their main street.

And that was before prohibition and all that foolishness, and so you went into a saloon, the two of you, and all the yaps come and stood around, and there was always someone pretended he was horsey and knew things and spoke up and began asking questions, and all you did was to lie and lie all you could about what horses you had, and I said I owned them, and then some fellow said, "Will you have a drink of whiskey?" and Burt knocked his eye out the way he could say, offhand like, "Oh, well, all right, I'm agreeable to a little nip. I'll split a quart with you." Gee whizz.

But that isn't what I want to tell my story about. We got home late in November and I promised mother I'd quit the race horses for good. There's a lot of things you've got to promise a mother because she don't know any better.

And so, there not being any work in our town any more than when I left there to go to the races, I went off to Sandusky and got a pretty good place taking care of the horses for a man who owned a teaming and delivery and storage business there. It was a pretty good place with good eats and a day off each week and sleeping on a cot in the big barn, and mostly just shoveling in hay and oats to a lot of big good-natured skates of horses that couldn't have trotted a race with a toad. I wasn't dissatisfied and I could send money home.

And then, as I started to tell you, the fall races come to Sandusky and I got the day off and I went. I left the job at noon and had on my good clothes and my new brown derby hat I'd just bought the Saturday before, and a stand-up collar.

First of all I went downtown and walked about with the dudes. I've always thought to myself, Put up a good front, and so I did it. I had forty dollars in my pocket and so I went into the West House, a big hotel, and walked up to the cigar stand. "Give me three twenty-five cent cigars," I said. There was a lot of horse men and strangers and dressed-up people from other towns standing around in the lobby and in the bar, and I·mingled amongst them. In the bar there was a fellow with a cane and a Windsor tie on, that it make me sick to look at him. I like a man to be a man and dress up, but not to go put on that kind of airs. So I pushed him aside, kind of rough, and had me a drink of whiskey. And then he looked at me as though he thought maybe he'd get gay, but he changed his mind and didn't say anything. And then I had another drink of whiskey, just to show him something, and went out and had a hack out to the races all to myself, and when I got there I bought myself the best seat I could get up in the grandstand, but didn't go in for any of these boxes. That's putting on too many airs.

And so there I was, sitting up in the grandstand as gay as you please and looking down on the swipes coming out with their horses and with their dirty horsey pants on and the horse blankets swung over their shoulders same as I had been doing all the year before. I liked one thing about the same as the other, sitting up there and feeling grand and being down there and looking up at the yaps and feeling grander and more important too. One thing's about as good as another if you take it just right. I've often said that.

Well, right in front of me, in the grandstand that day, there was a fellow with a couple of girls and they was about my age. The young fellow was a nice guy all right. He was the kind maybe that goes to college and then comes to be a lawyer or maybe a newspaper editor or something like that, but he wasn't stuck on himself. There are some of that kind are all right and he was one of the ones.

He had his sister with him and another girl and the sister looked around over his shoulder, accidental at first, not intending to start anything — she wasn't that kind — and her eyes and mine happened to meet.

You know how it is. Gee, she was a peach. She had on a soft dress, kind of a blue stuff and it looked carelessly made, but was well sewed and made and everything. I knew that much. I blushed when she looked right at me and so did she. She was the nicest girl I've ever seen in my life. She wasn't stuck on herself and she could talk proper grammar without being like a schoolteacher or something like that. What I mean is, she was O.K. I think maybe her father was well-to-do, but not rich to make her chesty because she was his daughter, as some are. Maybe he owned a drugstore or a dry-goods store in their home town, or something like that. She never told me and I never asked.

My own people are all O.K. too, when you come to that. My grandfather was Welsh and over in the old country, in Wales he was — but never mind that.

The first heat of the first race come off and the young fellow setting there with the two girls left them and went down to make a bet. I knew what he was up to, but he didn't talk big and noisy and let everyone around know he was a sport, as some do. He wasn't that kind. Well, he come back and I heard him tell the two girls what horse he'd bet on, and when the heat was trotted they all half got to their feet and acted in the excited, sweaty way people do when they've got money down on a race, and the horse they bet on is up there pretty close at the end, and they think maybe he'll come on with a rush, but he never does because he hasn't got the old juice in him, come right down to it.

And then, pretty soon, the horses came out for the 2.18 pace and there was a horse in it I knew. He was a horse Bob French had in his string, but Bob didn't own him. He was a horse owned by a Mr. Mathers down at Marietta, Ohio.

This Mr. Mathers had a lot of money and owned some coal mines or something, and he had a swell place out in the country, and he was stuck on race horses, but was a Presbyterian or something, and I think more than likely his wife was one, too, maybe a stiffer one than himself. So he never raced his horses hisself, and the story round the Ohio race tracks was that when one of his horses got ready to go to the races he turned him over to Bob French and pretended to his wife he was sold.

So Bob had the horses and he did pretty much as he pleased and you can't blame Bob, at least, I never did. Sometimes he was out to win and sometimes he wasn't. I never cared much about that when I was swiping a horse. What I did want to know was that my horse had the speed and could go out in front if you wanted him to.

And, as I'm telling you, there was Bob in this race with one of Mr. Mathers' horses, was named "About Ben Ahem" or something like that, and was fast as a streak. He was a gelding and had a mark of 2.21, but could step in .08 or .09.

Because when Burt and I were out, as I've told you, the year before, there was a nigger Burt knew, worked for Mr. Mathers, and we went out there one day when we didn't have no race on at the Marietta Fair and our boss Harry was gone home.

And so everyone was gone to the fair but just this one nigger, and he took us all through Mr. Mathers' swell house and he and Burt tapped a bottle of wine Mr. Mathers had hid in his bedroom, back in a closet, without his wife knowing, and he showed us this Ahem horse. Burt was always stuck on being a driver, but didn't have much chance to get to the top, being a nigger, and he and the other nigger gulped the whole bottle of wine and Burt got a little lit up.

So the nigger let Burt take this About Ben Ahem and step him a mile in a track Mr. Mathers had all to himself, right there on the farm. And Mr. Mathers had one child, a daughter, kinda sick and not very good looking, and she came home and we had to hustle and get About Ben Ahem stuck back in the barn.

I'm only telling you to get everything straight. At Sandusky, that afternoon I was at the fair, this young fellow with the two girls was fussed, being with the girls and losing his bet. You know how a fellow is that way. One of them was his girl and the other his sister. I had figured that out.

Gee whizz, I says to myself, I'm going to give him the dope.

He was mightily nice when I touched him on the shoulder. He and the girls were nice to me right from the start and clear to the end. I'm not blaming them.

And so he leaned back and I gave him the dope on About Ben Ahem. "Don't bet a cent on this first heat because he'll go like an oxen hitched to a plough, but when the first heat is over go right down and lay on your pile." That's what I told him.

Well, I never saw a fellow treat anyone sweller. There was a fat man sitting beside the little girl that had looked at me twice by this time, and I at her, and both blushing, and what did he do but have the nerve to turn and ask the fat man to get up and change places with me so I could set with his crowd.

Gee whizz, amighty. There I was. What a chump I was to go and get gay up there in the West House bar, and just because that dude was standing there with a cane and that kind of a necktie on, to go and get all balled up and drink that whiskey, just to show off.

Of course she would know, me setting right beside her and letting her smell of my breath. I could have kicked myself right down out of that grandstand and all around that race track and made a faster record than most of the skates of horses they had there that year.

Because that girl wasn't any mutt of a girl. What wouldn't I have give right then for a stick of chewing gum to chew, or a lozenger, or some licorice, or most anything. I was glad I had those twenty-five-cent cigars in my pocket, and right away I give that fellow one and lit one myself. Then that fat man got up and we changed places and there I was plunked right down beside her.

They introduced themselves, and the fellow's best girl he had with him was named Miss Elinor Woodbury, and her father was a manufacturer of barrels from a place called Tiffin, Ohio. And the fellow himself was named Wilbur Wessen and his sister was Miss Lucy Wessen.

I suppose it was their having such swell names got me off my trolley. A fellow, just because he has been a swipe with a race horse, and works taking care of horses for a man in the teaming, delivery and storage business, isn't any better or worse than anyone else. I've often thought that, and said it, too.

But you know how a fellow is. There's something in that kind of nice clothes, and the kind of nice eyes she had, and the way she had looked at me, awhile before, over her brother's shoulder, and me looking back at her, and both of us blushing.

I couldn't show her up for a boob, could I?

I made a fool of myself, that's what I did. I said my name was Walter Mathers from Marietta, Ohio, and then I told all three of them the smashingest lie you ever heard. What I said was that my father owned the horse About Ben Ahem, and that he had let him out to this Bob

French for racing purposes, because our family was proud and had never gone into racing that way, in our own name, I mean. Then I had got started and they were all leaning over and listening, and Miss Lucy Wessen's eyes were shining, and I went the whole hog.

I told about our place down at Marietta, and about the big stables and the grand brick house we had on a hill, up above the Ohio River, but I knew enough not to do it in no bragging way. What I did was to start things and then let them draw the rest out of me. I acted just as reluctant to tell as I could. Our family hasn't got any barrel factory, and, since I've known us, we've always been pretty poor, but not asking anything of anyone at that, and my grandfather, over in Wales — but never mind that.

We set there talking like we had known each other for years and years, and I went and told them that my father had been expecting maybe this Bob French wasn't on the square, and had sent me up to Sandusky on the sly to find out what I could.

And I bluffed it through I had found out all about the 2.18 pace in which About Ben Ahem was to start.

I said he would lose the first heat by pacing like a lame cow and then he would come back and skin 'em alive after that. And to back up what I said I took thirty dollars out of my pocket and handed it to Mr. Wilbur Wessen and asked him would he mind, after the first heat, to go down and place it on About Ben Ahem for whatever odds he could get. What I said was that I didn't want Bob French to see me and none of the swipes.

Sure enough the first heat come off and About Ben Ahem went off his stride, up the back stretch, and looked like a wooden horse or a sick one, and come in to be last. Then this Wilbur Wessen went down to the betting place under the grandstand and there I was with the two girls, and when that Miss Woodbury was looking the other way once, Lucy Wessen kinda, with her shoulder you know, kinda touched me. Not just tucking down, I don't mean. You know how a woman can do. They get close, but not getting gay either. You know what they do. Gee whizz.

And then they give me a jolt. What they had done when I didn't know, was to get together, and they had decided Wilbur Wessen would bet fifty dollars, and the two girls had gone and put in ten dollars each of their own money, too. I was sick then, but I was sicker later.

About the gelding, About Ben Ahem, and their winning their money, I wasn't worried a lot about that. It come out O.K. Ahem stepped the next three heats like a bushel of spoiled eggs going to market before they could be found out, and Wilbur Wessen had got nine to two for the money. There was something else eating at me.

Because Wilbur come back after he had bet the money, and after that he spent most of his time talking to that Miss Woodbury, and Lucy Wessen and I was left alone together like on a desert island. Gee, if I'd only been on the square or if there had been any way of getting myself on the square. There ain't any Walter Mathers, like I said to her and them, and there hasn't ever been one, but if there was, I bet I'd go to Marietta, Ohio, and shoot him tomorrow.

There I was, big boob that I am. Pretty soon the race was over, and Wilbur had gone down and collected our money, and we had a hack downtown, and he stood us a swell dinner at the West House, and a bottle of champagne beside.

And I was with that girl and she wasn't saying much, and I wasn't saying much either. One thing I know. She wasn't stuck on me because of the lie about my father being rich and all that. There's a way you know. . . . Craps amighty. There's a kind of girl you see just once in your life, and if you don't get busy and make hay then you're gone for good and all and might as well go jump off a bridge. They give you a look from inside of them somewhere, and it ain't no vamping, and what it means is — you want that girl to be your wife, and you want nice things around her like flowers and swell clothes, and you want her to have the kids you're going to have, and you want good music played and no ragtime. Gee whizz.

There's a place over near Sandusky, across a kind of bay, and it's called Cedar Point. And when we had had that dinner we went over to it in a launch, all by ourselves. Wilbur and Miss Lucy and that Miss Woodbury had to catch a ten o'clock train back to Tiffin, Ohio, because when you're out with girls like that you can't get careless and miss any trains and stay out all night like you can with some kinds of Janes.

And Wilbur blowed himself to the launch and it cost him fifteen cold plunks, but I wouldn't ever have knew if I hadn't listened. He wasn't no tin horn kind of a sport.

Over at the Cedar Point place we didn't stay around where there was a gang of common kind of cattle at all.

There was big dance halls and dining places for yaps, and there was a beach you could walk along and get where it was dark, and we went there.

She didn't talk hardly at all and neither did I, and I was thinking how glad I was my mother was all right, and always made us kids learn to eat with a fork at table and not swill soup and not be noisy and rough like a gang you see around a race track that way.

Then Wilbur and his girl went away up the beach and Lucy and I set down in a dark place where there was some roots of old trees the water had washed up, and after that, the time, till we had to go back in the launch and they had to catch their trains, wasn't nothing at all. It went like winking your eye.

Here's how it was. The place we were setting in was dark, like I said, and there was the roots from that old stump sticking up like arms, and there was a watery smell, and the night was like — as if you could put your hand out and feel it — so warm and soft and dark and sweet like a orange.

I most cried and I most swore and I most jumped up and danced, I was so mad and happy and sad.

When Wilbur come back from being alone with his girl, and she saw him coming, Lucy she says, "We got to go to the train now," and she was most crying, too, but she never knew nothing I knew, and she couldn't be so all busted up. And then, before Wilbur and Miss Woodbury got up to where she was, she put her face up and kissed me quick and put her head up against me and she was all quivering and — Gee whizz.

Sometimes I hope I have cancer and die. I guess you know what I mean. We went in the launch across the bay to the train like that, and it was dark too. She whispered and said it was like she and I could get out of the boat and walk on the water, and it sounded foolish, but I knew what she meant.

And then quick, we were right at the depot, and there was a big gang of yaps, the kind that goes to the fairs, and crowded and milling around like cattle, and how could I tell her? "It won't be long because you'll write and I'll write to you." That's all she said.

I got a chance like a hay barn afire. A swell chance I got.

And maybe she would write me, down at Marietta that way, and the letter would come back, and stamped on the front of it by the U.S.A. "There ain't any such guy," or something like that, whatever they stamp on a letter that way.

And me trying to pass myself off for a bigbug and a swell — to her, as decent a little body as God ever made. Craps amighty. A swell chance I got.

And then the train come in and she got on, and Wilbur Wessen come and shook hands with me and that Miss Woodbury was nice and bowed to me and I at her and the train went and I busted out and cried like a kid.

Gee, I could have run after that train and made Dan Patch look like a freight train after a wreck, but socks amighty, what was the use? Did you ever see such a fool?

I'll bet you what — if I had an arm broke right now or a train had run over my foot — I wouldn't go to no doctor at all. I'd go set down and let her hurt and hurt — that's what I'd do.

I'll bet you what — if I hadn't a drunk that booze I'd never been such a boob as to go tell such a lie — that couldn't never be made straight to a lady like her.

I wish I had that fellow right here that had on a Windsor tie and carried a cane. I'd smash him for fair. Gosh darn his eyes. He's a big fool — that's what he is.

And if I'm not another you just go find me one and I'll quit working and be a bum and give him my job. I don't care nothing for working and earning money and saving it for no such boob as myself.

ERNEST HEMINGWAY

The 1923 volume of The Best American Short Stories, *in which "My Old Man" was first published, is a collector's item for two reasons. It contains the only story in the entire series which did not first appear in a magazine. More important, the publication of this story led Hemingway to decide to keep on writing at a time when his stories had not only been rejected but all the manuscripts and their carbons had been stolen. As he tells in* A Moveable Feast, *Hemingway was planning to give up fiction writing when he first met Edward J. O'Brien, to whom he told his tale of woe. He had only two manuscripts left, one of which was "My Old Man." O'Brien read it and printed it. Moreover, he dedicated that year's volume to Hemingway. What happened after is literary history too well known to be repeated here.*

Ernest Hemingway was born in Oak Park, Illinois, in 1898. He was educated in private schools and joined the Italian army during the First World War. Later he was to work with the Loyalists in Spain and to cover the Second World War as a correspondent. He was both novelist and short story writer. His finest short stories are to be found in the volumes In Our Time, Men Without Women, Winner Take Nothing *and* To Have and Have Not.

My Old Man

I GUESS looking at it, now, my old man was cut out for a fat guy, one of those regular little roly-poly fat guys you see around, but he sure never got that way, except a little toward the last, and then it wasn't his fault, he was riding over the jumps only and he could afford to carry plenty of weight then. I remember the way he'd pull on a rubber shirt over a couple of jerseys and a big sweat shirt over that, and get me to run with him in the forenoon in the hot sun. He'd have, maybe, taken a trial trip with one of Razzo's skins early in the morning after just getting in from Torino at four o'clock in the morning and beating it out to the stables in a cab and then with the dew all over everything and the sun just starting to get going, I'd help him pull off his boots and he'd get into a pair of sneakers and all these sweaters and we'd start out.

"Come on, kid," he'd say, stepping up and down on his toes in front of the jock's dressing room, "let's get moving."

Then we'd start off jogging around the infield once, maybe, with him ahead, running nice, and then turn out the gate and along one of those roads with all the trees along both sides of them that run out from San Siro. I'd go ahead of him when we hit the road and I could run pretty stout and I'd look around and he'd be jogging easy just behind me and after a little while I'd look around again and he'd begun to sweat. Sweating heavy and he'd just be dogging it along with his eyes on my back, but when he'd catch me looking at him he'd grin and say, "Sweating plenty?" When my old man grinned, nobody could help but grin too. We'd keep right on running out toward the mountains and then my old man would yell, "Hey, Joe!" and I'd look back and he'd be sitting under a tree with a towel he'd had around his waist wrapped around his neck.

I'd come back and sit down beside him and he'd pull a rope out of his pocket and start skipping rope out in the sun with the sweat pouring off his face and him skipping rope out in the white dust with the rope going cloppetty, cloppetty, clop, clop, clop, and the sun hotter, and him working harder up and down a patch of the road. Say, it was a treat to see my old man skip rope, too. He could whirr it fast or lop it slow and fancy. Say, you ought to have seen wops look at us sometimes, when they'd come by, going into town walking along with big white steers hauling the cart. They sure looked as though they thought the old man was nuts. He'd start the rope whirring till they'd stop dead still and watch him, then give the steers a cluck and a poke with the goad and get going again.

When I'd sit watching him working out in the hot sun I sure felt fond of him. He sure was fun and he done his work so hard and he'd finish up with a regular whirring that'd drive the sweat out of his face like water and then sling the rope at the tree and come over and sit down with me and lean back against the tree with the towel and a sweater wrapped around his neck.

"Sure is hell keeping it down, Joe," he'd say and lean back and shut his eyes and breathe long and deep, "it ain't like when you're a kid." Then he'd get up before he started to cool and we'd jog along back to the stables. That's the way it was keeping down to weight. He was worried all the time. Most jocks can just about ride off all they want to. A jock loses about a kilo every time he rides, but my old man was sort of dried out and he couldn't keep down his kilos without all that running.

I remember once at San Siro, Regoli, a little wop, that was riding for Buzoni, came out across the paddock going to the bar for something cool; and flicking his boots with his whip, after he'd just weighed in and my old man had just weighed in too, and came out with the saddle under his arm looking red-faced and tired and too big for his silks and he stood there looking at young Regoli standing up to the outdoors bar, cool and kid-looking, and I says, "What's the matter, Dad?" 'cause I thought maybe Regoli had bumped him or something and he just looked at Regoli and said, "Oh, to hell with it," and went on to the dressing room.

Well, it would have been all right, maybe, if we'd stayed in Milan and ridden at Milan and Torino, 'cause if there ever were any easy courses, it's those two. "Pianola, Joe," my old man said when he dismounted in the winning stall after what the wops thought was a hell of a steeplechase. I asked him once. "This course rides itself. It's the pace you're going at, that makes riding the jumps dangerous, Joe. We ain't going any pace here, and they ain't any really bad jumps either. But it's the pace always — not the jumps that makes the trouble."

San Siro was the swellest course I'd ever seen but the old man said it was a dog's life. Going back and forth between Mirafiore and San Siro and riding just about every day in the week with a train ride every other night.

I was nuts about the horses, too. There's something about it, when they come out and go up the track to the post. Sort of dancy and tight looking with the jock keeping a tight hold on them and maybe easing off a little and letting them run a little going up. Then once they were at the barrier it got me worse than anything. Especially at San Siro with that big green infield and the mountains way off and the fat wop starter with his big whip and the jocks fiddling them around and then the barrier snapping up and that bell going off and them all getting off in a bunch and then commencing to string out. You know the way a bunch of skins get off. If you're up in the stand with a pair of glasses all you see is them plunging off and then that bell goes off and it seems like it rings for a thousand years and then they come sweeping round the turn. There wasn't ever anything like it for me.

But my old man said one day, in the dressing room, when he was getting into his street clothes, "None of these things are horses, Joe. They'd kill that bunch of skates for their hides and hoofs up at Paris." That was the day he'd won the Premio Commercio with Lantorna shooting her out of the field the last hundred meters like pulling a cork out of a bottle.

It was right after the Premio Commercio that we pulled out and left Italy. My old man and Holbrook and a fat wop in a straw hat that kept wiping his face with a handkerchief were having an argument at a table in the Galleria. They were all talking French and the two of them were after my old man about something. Finally he didn't say anything any more but just sat there and looked at Holbrook, and the two of them kept after him, first one talking and then the other, and the fat wop always butting in on Holbrook.

"You go out and buy me a *Sportsman,* will you, Joe?" my old man said, and handed me a couple of soldi without looking away from Holbrook.

So I went out of the Galleria and walked over to in front of the Scala and bought a paper, and came back and stood a little way away because I didn't want to butt in and my old man was sitting back in his chair looking down at his coffee and fooling with a spoon and Holbrook and the big wop were standing and the big wop was wiping his face and shaking his head. And I came up and my old man acted just as though the two of them weren't standing there and said, "Want an ice, Joe?" Holbrook looked down at my old man and said slow and careful, "You son of a b——," and he and the fat wop went out through the tables.

My old man sat there and sort of smiled at me, but his face was white and he looked sick as hell and I was scared and felt sick inside because I knew something had happened and I didn't see how anybody could call my old man a son of a b——, and get away with it. My old man opened up the *Sportsman* and studied the handicaps for a while and then he said, "You got to take a lot of things in this world, Joe." And three days later we left Milan for good on the Turin train for Paris, after an auction sale out in front of Turner's stables of everything we couldn't get into a trunk and a suitcase.

We got into Paris early in the morning in a long, dirty station the old man told me was the Gare de Lyon. Paris was an awful big town after Milan. Seems like in Milan everybody is going somewhere and all the trams run somewhere and there ain't any sort of a mixup, but Paris is all balled up and they never do straighten it out. I got to like it, though, part of it, anyway, and say it's got the best race courses in the world. Seems as though that were the thing that keeps it all going and about the only thing you can figure on is that every day the buses will be going out to whatever track they're running at, going right out through everything to the track. I never really got to know Paris well, because I just came in about once or twice a week with the old man from Maisons and he always sat at the Café de la Paix on the Opéra side with the rest of the gang from Maisons and I guess that's one of the busiest parts of the town. But, say, it is funny that a big town like Paris wouldn't have a Galleria, isn't it?

Well, we went out to live at Maisons-Lafitte, where just about everybody lives except the gang at Chantilly, with a Mrs. Meyers that runs a boardinghouse. Maisons is about the swellest place to live I've ever seen in all my life. The town ain't so much, but there's a lake and a swell forest that we used to go off bumming in all day, a couple of us kids, and my old man made me a slingshot and we got a lot of things with it but the best one was a magpie. Young Dick Atkinson shot a rabbit with it one day and we put it under a tree and were all sitting around and Dick had some cigarettes and all of a sudden the rabbit jumped up and beat it into the brush and we chased it but we couldn't find it. Gee, we had fun at Maisons. Mrs. Meyers used to give me lunch in the morning and I'd be gone all day. I learned to talk French quick. It's an easy language.

As soon as we got to Maisons, my old man wrote to Milan for his license and he was pretty worried till it came. He used to sit around the Café de Paris in Maisons with the gang, there were lots of guys he'd known when he rode up at Paris, before the war, lived at Maisons, and there's a lot of time to sit around because the work around a racing stable, for the jocks, that is, is all cleaned up by nine o'clock in the morning. They take the first batch of skins out to gallop them at five-thirty in the morning and they work the second lot at eight o'clock. That means getting up early all right and going to bed early, too. If a jock's riding for somebody too, he can't go boozing around because the trainer always has an eye on him if he's a kid and if he ain't a kid he's always got an eye on himself. So mostly if a jock ain't working he sits around the Café de Paris with the gang and they can all sit around about two or three hours in front of some drink like vermouth and seltz and they talk and tell stories and shoot pool and it's sort of like a club or the Galleria in Milan. Only it ain't really like the Galleria because there everybody is going by all the time and there's everybody around at the tables.

Well, my old man got his license all right. They sent it through to him without a word and he rode a couple of times. Amiens, up country and that sort of thing, but he didn't seem to get any engagement. Everybody liked him and whenever I'd come in to the Café in the forenoon I'd find somebody drinking with him because my old man wasn't tight like most of these jockeys that have got the first dollar they made riding at the World's Fair in St. Louis in nineteen ought four. That's what my old man would say when he'd kid George Burns. But it seemed like everybody steered clear of giving my old man any mounts.

We went out to wherever they were running every day with the car from Maisons and that was the most fun of all. I was glad when the horses came back from Deauville and the summer. Even though it meant no more bumming in the woods, 'cause then we'd ride to Enghien or Tremblay or St. Cloud and watch them from the trainers' and jockeys' stand. I sure learned about racing from going out with that gang and the fun of it was going every day.

I remember once out at St. Cloud. It was a big two hundred thousand franc race with seven entries and Kzar a big favorite. I went around to the paddock to see the horses with my old man and you never saw such horses. This Kzar is a great big yellow horse that looks like just nothing but run. I never saw such a horse. He was being led around the paddocks with his head down and when he went by me I felt all hollow inside he was so beautiful. There never was such a wonderful, lean, running built horse. And he went around the paddock putting his feet just so and quiet and careful and moving easy like he knew just what he had to do and not jerking and standing up on his legs and getting wild eyed like you see these selling platers with a shot of dope in them. The crowd was so thick I couldn't see him again except just his legs going by and some yellow and my old man started out through the crowd and I followed him over to the jocks' dressing room back in the trees and there was a big crowd around there, too, but the man at the door in a derby nodded to my old man and we got in and everybody was sitting around and getting dressed and pulling shirts over their heads and pulling boots on and it all smelled hot and sweaty and linimenty and outside was the crowd looking in.

The old man went over and sat down beside George Gardner that was getting into his pants and said, "What the dope, George?" just in an ordinary tone of voice 'cause there ain't any use him feeling around because George either can tell him or he can't tell him.

"He won't win," George says very low, leaning over and buttoning the bottoms of his pants.

"Who will?" my old man says, leaning over close so nobody can hear.

"Kircubbin," George says, "and if he does, save me a couple of tickets."

My old man says something in a regular voice to George and George says, "Don't ever bet on anything, I tell you," kidding like, and we beat it out and through all the crowd that was looking in over to the 100 franc mutuel machine. But I knew something big was up because George is Kzar's jockey. On the way he gets one of the yellow odds-sheets with the starting prices on and Kzar is only paying 5 for 10, Cefisidote is next at 3 to 1 and fifth down the list this Kircubbin at 8 to 1. My old man bets five thousand on Kircubbin to win and puts on a thousand to place and we went around back of the grandstand to go up the stairs and get a place to watch the race.

We were jammed in tight and first a man in a long coat with a gray tall hat and a whip folded up in his hand came out and then one after another the horses, with the jocks up and a stable boy holding the bridle on each side and walking along, followed the old guy. That big yellow horse Kzar came first. He didn't look so big when you first looked at him until you saw the length of his legs and the whole way he's built and the way he moves. Gosh, I never saw such a horse. George Gardner was riding him and they moved along slow, back of the old guy in the gray tall hat that walked along like he was the ring master in a circus. Back of Kzar, moving along smooth and yellow in the sun, was a good looking black with a nice head with Tommy Archibald riding him; and after the black was a string of five more horses all moving along slow in a procession past the grandstand and the pesage. My old man said the black was Kircubbin and I took a good look at him and he was a nice looking horse, all right, but nothing like Kzar.

Everybody cheered Kzar when he went by and he sure was one swell-looking horse. The procession of them went around on the other side past the pelouse and then back to the near end of the course and the circus master had the stable boys turn them loose one after another so they could gallop by the stands on their way up to the post and let everybody have a good look at them. They weren't at the post hardly any time at all when the gong started and you could see them way off across the infield all in a bunch starting on the first swing like a lot of little toy horses. I was watching them through the glasses and Kzar was running well back, with one of the bays making the pace. They swept down and around and came pounding past and Kzar was way back when they passed us and this Kircubbin horse in front and going smooth. Gee, it's awful when they go by you and then you have to watch them go farther

away and get smaller and smaller and then all bunched up on the turns
and then come around towards into the stretch and you feel like swearing
and goddamming worse and worse. Finally they made the last turn and
came into the straightaway with this Kircubbin horse way out in front.
Everybody was looking funny and saying "Kzar" in a sort of a sick way
and them pounding nearer down the stretch, and then something came
out of the pack right into my glasses like a horse-headed yellow streak
and everybody began to yell "Kzar" as though they were crazy. Kzar
came on faster than I'd ever seen anything in my life and pulled up on
Kircubbin that was going fast as any black horse could go with the jock
flogging hell out of him with the gad and they were right dead neck and
neck for a second but Kzar seemed going about twice as fast with those
great jumps and that head out — but it was while they were neck and
neck that they passed the winning post and when the numbers went up
in the slots the first one was 2 and that meant Kircubbin had won.

I felt all trembly and funny inside, and then we were all jammed in
with the people going downstairs to stand in front of the board where
they'd post what Kircubbin paid. Honest, watching the race I'd forgot
how much my old man had bet on Kircubbin. I'd wanted Kzar to win so
damned bad. But now it was all over it was swell to know we had the
winner.

"Wasn't it a swell race, Dad?" I said to him.

He looked at me sort of funny with his derby on the back of his head.
"George Gardner's a swell jockey, all right," he said. "It sure took a great
jock to keep that Kzar horse from winning."

Of course I knew it was funny all the time. But my old man saying
that right out like that sure took the kick all out of it for me and I didn't
get the real kick back again ever, even when they posted the numbers up
on the board and the bell rang to pay off and we saw that Kircubbin paid
67.50 for 10. All round people were saying, "Poor Kzar! Poor Kzar!"
And I thought, I wish I were a jockey and could have rode him instead
of that son of a b——. And that was funny, thinking of George Gardner
as a son of a b——because I'd always liked him and besides he'd given us
the winner, but I guess that's what he is, all right.

My old man had a big lot of money after that race and he took to
coming into Paris oftener. If they raced at Tremblay he'd have them drop
him in town on their way back to Maisons, and he and I'd sit out in front
of the Café de la Parix and watch the people go by. It's funny sitting

there. There's streams of people going by and all sorts of guys come up and want to sell you things, and I loved to sit there with my old man. That was when we'd have the most fun. Guys would come by selling funny rabbits that jumped if you squeezed a bulb and they'd come up to us and my old man would kid with them. He could talk French just like English and all those kind of guys knew him 'cause you can always tell a jockey — and then we always sat at the same table and they got used to seeing us there. There were guys selling matrimonial papers and girls selling rubber eggs that when you squeezed them a rooster came out of them and one old wormy-looking guy that went by with postcards of Paris, showing them to everybody, and, of course, nobody ever bought any, and then he would come back and show the under side of the pack and they would all be smutty postcards and lots of people would dig down and buy them.

Gee, I remember the funny people that used to go by. Girls around suppertime looking for somebody to take them out to eat and they'd speak to my old man and he'd make some joke at them in French and they'd pat me on the head and go on. Once there was an American woman sitting with her kid daughter at the next table to us and they were both eating ices and I kept looking at the girl and she was awfully good-looking and I smiled at her and she smiled at me but that was all that ever came of it because I looked for her mother and her every day and I made up ways that I was going to speak to her and I wondered if I got to know her if her mother would let me take her out to Auteuil or Tremblay but I never saw either of them again. Anyway, I guess it wouldn't have been any good, anyway, because looking back on it I remember the way I thought out would be best to speak to her was to say, "Pardon me, but perhaps I can give you a winner at Enghien today?" and, after all, maybe she would have thought I was a tout instead of really trying to give her a winner.

We'd sit at the Café de la Paix, my old man and me, and we had a big drag with the waiter because my old man drank whisky and it cost five francs, and that meant a good tip when the saucers were counted up. My old man was drinking more than I'd ever seen him, but he wasn't riding at all now and besides he said that whisky kept his weight down. But I noticed he was putting it on, all right, just the same. He'd busted away from his old gang out at Maisons and seemed to like just sitting around on the boulevard with me. But he was dropping money every day at the track. He'd feel sort of doleful after the last race, if he'd lost on the day until we'd get to our table and he'd have his first whisky and then he'd be fine.

He'd be reading the *Paris-Sport* and he'd look over at me and say, "Where's your girl, Joe?" to kid me on account I had told him about the girl that day at the next table. And I'd get red, but I liked being kidded about her. It gave me a good feeling. "Keep your eye peeled for her, Joe," he'd say, "she'll be back."

He'd ask me questions about things and some of the things I'd say he'd laugh. And then he'd get started talking about things. About riding down in Egypt, or at St. Moritz on the ice before my mother died, and about during the war when they had regular races down in the south of France without any purses, or betting or crowd or anything just to keep the breed up. Regular races with the jocks riding hell out of the horses. Gee, I could listen to my old man talk by the hour, especially when he'd had a couple or so of drinks. He'd tell me about when he was a boy in Kentucky and going coon hunting, and the old days in the States before everything went on the bum there. And he'd say, "Joe, when we've got a decent stake, you're going back there to the States and go to school."

"What've I got to go back there to go to school for when everything's on the bum there?" I'd ask him.

"That's different," he'd say and get the waiter over and pay the pile of saucers and we'd get a taxi to the Gare St. Lazare and get on the train out to Maisons.

One day at Auteuil, after a selling steeplechase, my old man bought in the winner for 30,000 francs. He had to bid a little to get him but the stable let the horse go finally and my old man had his permit and his colors in a week. Gee, I felt proud when my old man was an owner. He fixed it up for stable space with Charles Drake and cut out coming in to Paris, and started his running and sweating out again, and him and I were the whole stable gang. Our horse's name was Gilford, he was Irish bred and a nice, sweet jumper. My old man figured that training him and riding him, himself, he was a good investment. I was proud of everything and I thought Gilford was as good a horse as Kzar. He was a good, solid jumper, a bay, with plenty of speed on the flat, if you asked him for it, and he was a nice looking horse, too.

Gee, I was fond of him. The first time he started with my old man up, he finished third in a 2500 meter hurdle race and when my old man got off him, all sweating and happy in the place stall, and went in to weigh, I felt as proud of him as though it was the first race he'd ever placed in.

You see, when a guy ain't been riding for a long time, you can't make yourself really believe that he has ever rode. The whole thing was different now, 'cause down in Milan, even big races never seemed to make any difference to my old man, if he won he wasn't ever excited or anything, and now it was so I couldn't hardly sleep the night before a race and I knew my old man was excited, too, even if he didn't show it. Riding for yourself makes an awful difference.

Second time Gilford and my old man started was a rainy Sunday at Auteuil, in the Prix du Marat, a 4500 meter steeplechase. As soon as he'd gone out I beat it up in the stand with the new glasses my old man had bought for me to watch them. They started way over at the far end of the course and there was some trouble at the barrier. Something with goggle blinders on was making a great fuss and rearing around and busted the barrier once, but I could see my old man in our black jacket, with a white cross and a black cap, sitting up on Gilford, and patting him with his hand. Then they were off in a jump and out of sight behind the trees and the gong going for dear life and the pari-mutuel wickets rattling down. Gosh, I was so excited, I was afraid to look at them, but I fixed the glasses on the place where they would come out back of the trees and then out they came with the old black jacket going third and they all sailing over the jump like birds. Then they went out of sight again and then they came pounding out and down the hill and all going nice and sweet and easy and taking the fence smooth in a bunch, and moving away from us all solid. Looked as though you could walk across on their backs they were all so bunched and going so smooth. Then they bellied over the big double Bullfinch and something came down. I couldn't see who it was, but in a minute the horse was up and galloping free and the field, all bunched still, sweeping around the long left turn into the straightaway. They jumped the stone wall and came jammed down the stretch toward the big water jump right in front of the stands. I saw them coming and hollered at my old man as he went by, and he was leading by about a length and riding way out, and light as a monkey, and they were racing for the water jump. They took off over the big hedge of the water jump in a pack and then there was a crash, and two horses pulled sideways out of it, and kept on going and three others were piled up. I couldn't see my old man anywhere. One horse kneed himself up and the jock had hold of the bridle and mounted and went slamming on after the place money. The other horse was up and away by himself, jerking his head and galloping with the bridle rein hanging and the jock staggered over to one side of the track against the fence. Then Gilford rolled over to one side off my old man and got up and started to run on three legs with his off hoof dangling and there was my old man laying there on the grass flat out with his face up and blood all over the side of his head. I ran down the stand and bumped into a jam of people and got to the rail and a cop grabbed me and held me and two big stretcher bearers were going out after my old man and around on the other side of the course I saw three horses, strung way out, coming out of the trees and taking the jump.

My old man was dead when they brought him in and while a doctor was listening to his heart with a thing plugged in his ears, I heard a shot up the track that meant they'd killed Gilford. I lay down beside my old man, when they carried the stretcher into the hospital room, and hung on to the stretcher and cried and cried, and he looked so white and gone and so awfully dead, and I couldn't help feeling that if my old man was dead maybe they didn't need to have shot Gilford. His hoof might have got well. I don't know. I loved my old man so much.

Then a couple of guys came in and one of them patted me on the back and then went over and looked at my old man and then pulled a sheet off the cot and spread it over him; and the other was telephoning in French for them to send the ambulance to take him out to Maisons. And I couldn't stop crying, crying and choking, sort of, and George Gardner came in and sat down beside me on the floor and put his arm around me and says, "Come on, Joe, old boy. Get up and we'll go out and wait for the ambulance."

George and I went out to the gate and I was trying to stop bawling and George wiped off my face with his handkerchief and we were standing back a little ways while the crowd was going out of the gate and a couple of guys stopped near us while we were waiting for the crowd to get through the gate and one of them was counting a bunch of mutuel tickets and he said, "Well, Butler got his, all right."

The other guy said, "I don't give a good goddam if he did, the crook. He had it coming to him on the stuff he's pulled."

"I'll say he had," said the other guy, and tore the bunch of tickets in two.

And George Gardner looked at me to see if I'd heard and I had all right and he said, "Don't you listen to what those bums said, Joe. Your old man was one swell guy."

But I don't know. Seems like when they get started they don't leave a guy nothing.

DOROTHY PARKER

"A Telephone Call" could have been a long love story. Instead, in a few pages, the author lets us know the people, what has happened, what is happening and "the inevitable end," to borrow Max Beerbohm's description of how a story should finish. The intense emotion of this monologue would be almost unbearable were it not for the writer's empathic skill.

When Dorothy Parker's name is mentioned, most people think of the wit for which she is famous. In her short stories, however, she shows great compassion and social awareness. She was born in West End, New Jersey, in 1893.

A Telephone Call

PLEASE, God, let him telephone me now. Dear God, let him call me now. I won't ask anything else of You, truly I won't. It isn't very much to ask. It would be so little to You, God, such a little, little thing. Only let him telephone now. Please, God. Please, please, please.

If I didn't think about it, maybe the telephone might ring. Sometimes it does that. If I could think of something else. If I could think of something else. Maybe if I counted five hundred by fives, it might ring by that time. I'll count slowly. I won't cheat. And if it rings when I get to three hundred, I won't stop; I won't answer it until I get to five hundred. Five, ten, fifteen, twenty, twenty-five, thirty, thirty-five, forty, forty-five, fifty. . . . Oh, please ring. Please.

This is the last time I'll look at the clock. I will not look at it again. It's ten minutes past seven. He said he would telephone at five o'clock. "I'll call you at five, darling." I think that's where he said "darling." I'm almost sure he said it there. I know he called me "darling" twice, and the other time was when he said good-bye. "Good-bye, darling." He was busy, and he can't say much in the office, but he called me "darling" twice. He couldn't have minded my calling him up. I know you shouldn't keep telephoning them — I know they don't like that. When you do that, they know you are thinking about them and wanting them, and that makes them hate you. But I hadn't talked to him in three days — not in three days. And all I did was ask him how he was; it was just the way anybody might have called him up. He couldn't have minded that. He couldn't have thought I was bothering him. "No, of course you're not," he said. And he said he'd telephone me. He didn't have to say that. I didn't ask him to, truly I didn't. I'm sure I didn't. I don't think he would say he'd telephone me, and then just never do it. Please don't let him do that, God. Please don't.

"I'll call you at five, darling." "Good-bye, darling." He was busy, and he was in a hurry, and there were people around him, but he called me "darling" twice. That's mine, that's mine. I have that, even if I never see him again. Oh, but that's so little. That isn't enough. Nothing's enough, if I never see him again. Please let me see him again, God. Please, I want him so much. I want him so much. I'll be good, God. I will try to be better, I will, if You will let me see him again. If You will let him telephone me. Oh, let him telephone me now.

Ah, don't let my prayer seem too little to You, God. You sit up there, so white and old, with all the angels about You and the stars slipping by. And I come to You with a prayer about a telephone call. Ah, don't laugh, God. You see, You don't know how it feels. You're so safe, there on Your throne, with the blue swirling under You. Nothing can touch You; no one can twist Your heart in his hands. This is suffering, God, this is bad, bad suffering. Won't you help me? For Your Son's sake, help me. You said You would do whatever was asked of You in His name. Oh, God, in the name of Thine only beloved Son, Jesus Christ, our Lord, let him telephone me now.

I must stop this. I mustn't be this way. Look. Suppose a young man says he'll call a girl up, and then something happens, and he doesn't. That isn't so terrible, is it? Why, it's going on all over the world, right this minute. Oh, what do I care what's going on all over the world? Why can't that telephone ring? Why can't it, why can't it? Couldn't you ring? Ah, please, couldn't you? You damned, ugly, shiny thing. It would hurt you to ring, wouldn't it? Oh, that would hurt you. Damn you, I'll pull your filthy roots out of the wall, I'll smash your smug black face in little bits. Damn you to hell.

No, no, no. I must stop. I must think about something else. This is what I'll do. I'll put the clock in the other room. Then I can't look at it. If I do have to look at it, then I'll have to walk into the bedroom, and that will be something to do. Maybe, before I look at it again, he will call me. I'll be so sweet to him, if he calls me. If he says he can't see me tonight, I'll say, "Why, that's all right, dear. Why, of course it's all right." I'll be the way I was when I first met him. Then maybe he'll like me again. I was always sweet, at first. Oh, it's so easy to be sweet to people before you love them.

I think he must still like me a little. He couldn't have called me "darling" twice today, if he didn't still like me a little. It isn't all gone, if he still likes me a little; even if it's only a little, little bit. You see, God, if You would just let him telephone me, I wouldn't have to ask You anything more. I would be sweet to him, I would be gay, I would be just the way I used to be, and then he would love me again. And then I would never have to ask You for anything more. Don't You see, God? So won't You please let him telephone me? Won't You please, please, please?

Are You punishing me, God, because I've been bad? Are You angry with me because I did that? Oh, but, God, there are so many bad people —You could not be hard only to me. And it wasn't very bad; it couldn't have been bad. We didn't hurt anybody, God. Things are only bad when they hurt people. We didn't hurt one single soul; You know that. You know it wasn't bad, don't You, God? So won't You let him telephone me now?

If he doesn't telephone me, I'll know God is angry with me. I'll count five hundred by fives, and if he hasn't called me then, I will know God isn't going to help me, ever again. That will be the sign. Five, ten, fifteen, twenty, twenty-five, thirty, thirty-five, forty, forty-five, fifty, fifty-five. . . . It was bad. I knew it was bad. All right, God, send me to hell. You think You're frightening me with Your hell, don't You? You think Your hell is worse than mine.

I mustn't. I mustn't do this. Suppose he's a little late calling me up — that's nothing to get hysterical about. Maybe he isn't going to call — maybe he's coming straight up here without telephoning. He'll be cross if he sees I have been crying. They don't like you to cry. He doesn't cry. I wish to God I could make him cry. I wish I could make him cry and tread the floor and feel his heart heavy and big and festering in him. I wish I could hurt him like hell.

He doesn't wish that about me. I don't think he even knows how he makes me feel. I wish he could know, without my telling him. They don't like you to tell them they've made you cry. They don't like you to tell them you're unhappy because of them. If you do, they think you're possessive and exacting. And then they hate you. They hate you whenever you say anything you really think. You always have to keep playing little games. Oh, I thought we didn't have to; I thought this was so big I could say whatever I meant. I guess you can't, ever. I guess there isn't ever anything big enough for that. Oh, if he would just telephone, I wouldn't tell him I had been sad about him. They hate sad people. I would be so sweet and so gay, he couldn't help but like me. If he would only telephone. If he would only telephone.

Maybe that's what he is doing. Maybe he is coming up here without calling me up. Maybe he's on his way now. Something might have happened to him. No, nothing could ever happen to him. I can't picture anything happening to him. I never picture him run over. I never see him lying still and long and dead. I wish he were dead. That's a terrible wish. That's a lovely wish. If he were dead, he would be mine. If he were dead, I would never think of now and the last few weeks. I would remember only the lovely times. It would be all beautiful. I wish he were dead. I wish he were dead, dead, dead.

This is silly. It's silly to go wishing people were dead just because they don't call you up the very minute they said they would. Maybe the clock's fast; I don't know whether it's right. Maybe he's hardly late at all. Anything could have made him a little late. Maybe he had to stay at his office. Maybe he went home, to call me up from there, and somebody came in. He doesn't like to telephone me in front of people. Maybe he's worried, just a little, little bit, about keeping me waiting. He might even hope that I would call him up. I could do that. I could telephone him.

I mustn't. I mustn't, I mustn't. Oh, God, please don't let me telephone him. Please keep me from doing that. I know, God, just as well as You do, that if he were worried about me, he'd telephone no matter where he was or how many people there were around him. Please make me know that, God. I don't ask You to make it easy for me — You can't do that, for all that You could make a world. Only let me know it, God. Don't let me go on hoping. Don't let me say comforting things to myself. Please don't let me hope, dear God. Please don't.

I won't telephone him. I'll never telephone him again as long as I live. He'll rot in hell, before I'll call him up. You don't have to give me strength, God; I have it myself. If he wanted me, he could get me. He knows where I am. He knows I'm waiting here. He's so sure of me, so sure. I wonder why they hate you, as soon as they are sure of you. I should think it would be so sweet to be sure.

It would be so easy to telephone him. Then I'd know. Maybe it wouldn't be a foolish thing to do. Maybe he wouldn't mind. Maybe he'd like it. Maybe he has been trying to get me. Sometimes people try and try to get you on the telephone, and they say the number doesn't answer. I'm not just saying that to help myself; that really happens. You know that really happens, God. Oh, God, keep me away from that telephone. Keep me away. Let me still have just a little bit of pride. I think I'm going to need it, God. I think it will be all I'll have.

Oh, what does pride matter, when I can't stand it if I don't talk to him? Pride like that is such a silly, shabby little thing. The real pride, the big pride, is in having no pride. I'm not saying that just because I want to call him. I am not. That's true, I know that's true. I will be big. I will be beyond little prides.

Please, God, keep me from telephoning him. Please, God.

I don't see what pride has to do with it. This is such a little thing, for me to be bringing in pride, for me to be making such a fuss about. I may have misunderstood him. Maybe he said for me to call him up, at five. "Call me at five, darling." He could have said that, perfectly well. It's so possible that I didn't hear him right. "Call me at five, darling." I'm almost sure that's what he said. God, don't let me talk this way to myself. Make me know, please make me know.

I'll think about something else. I'll just sit quietly. If I could sit still. If I could sit still. Maybe I could read. Oh, all the books are about people who love each other, truly and sweetly. What do they want to write about that for? Don't they know it isn't true? Don't they know it's a lie, it's a God damned lie? What do they have to tell about that for, when they know how it hurts? Damn them, damn them, damn them.

I won't. I'll be quiet. This is nothing to get excited about. Look. Suppose he were someone I didn't know very well. Suppose he were another girl. Then I'd just telephone and say, "Well, for goodness' sake, what happened to you?" That's what I'd do, and I'd never even think about it. Why can't I be casual and natural, just because I love him? I can be. Honestly, I can be. I'll call him up, and be so easy and pleasant. You see if I won't, God. Oh, don't let me call him. Don't, don't, don't.

God, aren't You really going to let him call me? Are You sure, God?

Couldn't You please relent? Couldn't You? I don't even ask You to let him telephone me now, God; only let him do it in a little while. I'll count five hundred by fives. I'll do it so slowly and so fairly. If he hasn't telephoned then, I'll call him. I will. Oh, please, dear God, dear kind God, my blessed Father in Heaven, let him call before then. Please, God. Please.

Five, ten, fifteen, twenty, twenty-five, thirty, thirty-five. . . .

WILLA CATHER

Despite the references to Prohibition and a post-revolutionary Russia, which would seem to place "Double Birthday" in the nineteen-twenties, it really seems to be a story of people living in that idyllic age which preceded the First World War. And so is its way of telling in the rounded, warm, almost cozy descriptions of the characters and their manners.

Willa Cather was born in Winchester, Virginia, in 1876. She was educated at the University of Nebraska. In her early life she was engaged in newspaper work and as a magazine editor. She became one of the country's most distinguished authors. Primarily a novelist, she wrote few short stories. With the exception of "Double Birthday," the best of these are printed in Youth and the Bright Medusa *and* Obscure Destinies.

Double Birthday

EVEN in American cities, which seem so much alike, where people seem all to be living the same lives, striving for the same things, thinking the same thoughts, there are still individuals a little out of tune with the times — there are still survivals of a past more loosely woven, there are disconcerting beginnings of a future yet unforeseen.

Coming out of the gray stone Court House in Pittsburgh on a dark November afternoon, Judge Hammersley encountered one of these men whom one does not readily place, whom one is, indeed, a little embarrassed to meet, because they have not got on as they should. The Judge saw him mounting the steps outside, leaning against the wind, holding his soft felt hat on with his hand, his head thrust forward — hurrying with a light, quick step, and so intent upon his own purposes that the Judge could have gone out by a side door and avoided the meeting. But that was against his principles.

"Good day, Albert," he muttered, seeming to feel, himself, all the embarrassment of the encounter, for the other snatched off his hat with a smile of very evident pleasure, and something like pride. His gesture

bared an attractive head — small, well-set, definite and smooth — one of
those heads that look as if they had been turned out of some hard, rich
wood by a workman deft with the lathe. His smooth-shaven face was
dark — a warm coffee color — and his hazel eyes were warm and lively.
He was not young, but his features had a kind of quicksilver mobility.
His manner toward the stiff, frowning Judge was respectful and admiring — not in the least self-conscious.

The Judge inquired after his health and that of his uncle.

"Uncle Albert is splendidly preserved for his age. Frail, and can't stand
any strain, but perfectly all right if he keeps to his routine. He's going to
have a birthday soon. He will be eighty on the first day of December, and
I shall be fifty-five on the same day. I was named after him because I was
born on his twenty-fifth birthday."

"Umph." The judge glanced from left to right as if this announcement
were in bad taste, but he put a good face on it and said with a kind of
testy heartiness, "That will be an — occasion. I'd like to remember it in
some way. Is there anything your uncle would like, any — recognition?"
He stammered and coughed.

Young Albert Engelhardt, as he was called, laughed apologetically, but
with confidence. "I think there is, Judge Hammersley. Indeed, I'd
thought of coming to you to ask a favor. I am going to have a little
supper for him, and you know he likes good wine. In these dirty bootleg-
ging times, it's hard to get."

"Certainly, certainly." The Judge spoke up quickly, and for the first
time looked Albert squarely in the eye. "Don't give him any of that
bootleg stuff. I can find something in my cellar. Come out tomorrow
night after eight, with a gripsack of some sort. Very glad to help you out,
Albert. Glad the old fellow holds up so well. Thank'ee, Albert," as
Engelhardt swung the heavy door open and held it for him to pass.

Judge Hammersley's car was waiting for him, and on the ride home to
Squirrel Hill he thought with vexation about the Engelhardts. He really
was a sympathetic man, and though so stern of manner, he had deep
affections; was fiercely loyal to old friends, old families, and old ideals.
He didn't think highly of what is called success in the world today, but
such as it was he wanted his friends to have it, and was vexed with them
when they missed it. He was vexed with Albert for unblushingly, almost
proudly, declaring that he was fifty-five years old, when he had nothing
whatever to show for it. He was the last of the Engelhardt boys, and they
had none of them had anything to show. They all died much worse off in

the world than they began. They began with a flourishing glass factory
up the river, a comfortable fortune, a fine old house on the park in
Allegheny, a good standing in the community; and it was all gone,
melted away.

Old August Engelhardt was a thrifty, energetic man, though pig-
headed — Judge Hammersley's friend and one of his first clients. August's five sons had sold the factory and wasted the money in fantastic
individual enterprises, lost the big house, and now they were all dead
except Albert. They ought all to be alive, with estates and factories and
families. To be sure, they had that queer German streak in them; but so
had old August, and it hadn't prevented his amounting to something.
Their bringing-up was wrong; August had too free a hand, he was too
proud of his five handsome boys, and too conceited. Too much tennis,
Rhine wine punch, music, and silliness. They were always running over
to New York, like this Albert. Somebody, when asked what in the world
young Albert had ever done with his inheritance, had laughingly replied
that he had spent it on the Pennsylvania Railroad.

Judge Hammersley didn't see how Albert could hold his head up. He
had some small job in the County Clerk's office, was dependent upon it,
had nothing else but the poor little house on the South Side where he
lived with his old uncle. The county took care of him for the sake of his
father, who had been a gallant officer in the Civil War, and afterwards a
public-spirited citizen and a generous employer of labor. But, as Judge
Hammersley had bitterly remarked to Judge Merriman when Albert's
name happened to come up: "If it weren't for his father's old friends
seeing that he got something, that fellow wouldn't be able to make a
living." Next to a charge of dishonesty, this was the worst that could be
said of any man.

Judge Hammersley's house out on Squirrel Hill sat under a grove of
very old oak trees. He lived alone, with his daughter, Margaret Parmenter, who was a widow. She had a great many engagements, but she
usually managed to dine at home with her father, and that was about as
much society as he cared for. His house was comfortable in an old-fashioned way, well appointed — especially the library, the room in which he
lived when he was not in bed or at the Court House. Tonight, when he
came down to dinner, Mrs. Parmenter was already at the table, dressed
for an evening party. She was tall, handsome, with a fine, easy carriage,
and her face was both hard and sympathetic, like her father's. She had
not, however, his stiffness of manner, that contraction of the muscles

which was his unconscious protest at any irregularity in the machinery of life. She accepted blunders and accidents smoothly if not indifferently.

As the old colored man pulled back the Judge's chair for him, he glanced at his daughter from under his eyebrows.

"I saw that son of old Gus Engelhardt's this afternoon," he said in an angry, challenging tone.

As a young girl his daughter had used to take up the challenge and hotly defend the person who had displeased or disappointed her father. But as she grew older she was conscious of that same feeling in herself when people fell short of what she expected; and she understood now that when her father spoke as if he were savagely attacking someone, it merely meant that he was disappointed or sorry for them; he never spoke thus of persons for whom he had no feeling. So she said calmly, "Oh, did you really? I haven't seen him for years, not since the war. How was he looking? Shabby?"

"Not so shabby as he ought to. That fellow's likely to be in want one of these days."

"I'm afraid so," Mrs. Parmenter sighed. "But I believe he would be rather plucky about it."

The Judge shrugged. "He's coming out here tomorrow night, on some business for his uncle."

"Then I'll have a chance to see for myself. He must look much older. I can't imagine his ever looking really old and settled, though."

"See that you don't ask him to stay. I don't want the fellow hanging around. He'll transact his business and get it over. He had the face to admit to me that he'll be fifty-five years old on the first of December. He's giving some sort of birthday party for old Albert, a-hem." The Judge coughed formally, but was unable to check a smile; his lips sarcastic, but his eyes full of sly humor.

"Can he be as old as that? Yes, I suppose so. When we were both at Mrs. Sterrett's in Rome, I was fifteen, and he must have been about thirty."

Her father coughed. "He'd better have been in Homestead!"

Mrs. Parmenter looked up; that was rather commonplace, for her father. "Oh, I don't know. Albert would never have been much use in Homestead, and he was very useful to Mrs. Sterrett in Rome."

"What did she want the fellow hanging round for? All the men of her family amounted to something."

"To too much! There must be some butterflies if one is going to give house parties, and the Sterretts and Dents were all heavyweights. He was in Rome a long while; three years, I think. He had a gorgeous time. Anyway, he learned to speak Italian very well, and that helps him out now, doesn't it? You still send for him at the Court House when you need an interpreter?"

"That's not often. He picks up a few dollars. Nice business for his father's son."

After dinner the Judge retired to his library, where the gas-fire was lit, and his book at hand, with a paper-knife inserted to mark the place where he had left off reading last night at exactly ten-thirty. On his way he went to the front door, opened it, turned on the porch light, and looked at the thermometer, making an entry in a little notebook. In a few moments his daughter, in an evening cloak, stopped at the library door to wish him good night and went down the hall. He listened for the closing of the front door; it was a reassuring sound to him. He liked the feeling of an orderly house, empty for himself and his books all evening. He was deeply read in divinity, philosophy, and in the early history of North America.

II

While Judge Hammersley was settling down to his book, Albert Engelhardt was sitting at home in a garnet velvet smoking-jacket, at an upright piano, playing Schumann's *Kreisleriana* for his old uncle. They lived, certainly, in a queer part of the city, on one of the dingy streets that run uphill off noisy Carson Street, in a little two-story brick house, a working man's house, that Albert's father had taken over long ago in satisfaction of a bad debt. When his father had acquired this building, it was a mere nothing — the Engelhardts were then living in their big, many-gabled, so-German house on the Park, in Allegheny; and they owned many other buildings, besides the glass factory up the river. After the father's death, when the sons converted houses and lands into cash, this forgotten little house on the South Side had somehow never been sold or mortgaged. A day came when Albert, the last surviving son, found this piece of property the only thing he owned in the world beside his personal effects. His uncle, having had a crushing disappointment, wanted at that time to retire from the practice of medicine, so Albert settled in the South Side house and took his uncle with him.

He had not gone there in any mood of despair. His impoverishment had come about gradually, and before he took possession of these quarters he had been living in a boarding house; the change seemed going up instead of going down in the world. He was delighted to have a home again, to unpack his own furniture and his books and pictures — the most valuable in the world to him, because they were full of his own history and that of his family, were like part of his own personality. All the years and the youth which had slipped away from him still clung to these things.

At his piano, under his Degas drawing in black and red — three ballet girls at the bar — or seated at his beautiful inlaid writing table, he was still the elegant young man who sat there long ago. His rugs were fine ones, his collection of books was large and very personal. It was full of works which, though so recent, were already immensely far away and diminished. The glad, rebellious excitement they had once caused in the world he could recapture only in memory. Their power to seduce and stimulate the young, the living, was utterly gone. There was a complete file of the *Yellow Book,* for instance; who could extract sweet poison from these volumes now? A portfolio of the drawings of Aubrey Beardsley — decadent, had they been called? A slender, padded volume — the complete works of a great new poet, Ernest Dowson. Oscar Wilde, whose wickedness was now so outdone that he looked like the poor old hat of some Victorian belle, wired and feathered and garlanded and faded.

Albert and his uncle occupied only the upper floor of their house. The ground floor was let to an old German glass engraver who had once been a workman in August Engelhardt's factory. His wife was a good cook, and every night sent their dinner up hot on the dumb waiter. The house opened directly upon the street and to reach Albert's apartment one went down a narrow paved alley at the side of the building and mounted an outside flight of wooden stairs at the back. They had only four rooms — two bedrooms, a snug sitting-room in which they dined, and a small kitchen where Albert got breakfast every morning. After he had gone to work, Mrs. Rudder came up from downstairs to wash the dishes and do the cleaning, and to cheer up old Doctor Engelhardt.

At dinner this evening Albert had told his uncle about meeting Judge Hammersley, and of his particular inquiries after his health. The old man was very proud and received this intelligence as his due, but could not conceal a certain gratification.

"The daughter, she still lives with him? A damned fine-looking woman!" he muttered between his teeth. Uncle Albert, a bachelor, had been a professed connoisseur of ladies in his day.

Immediately after dinner, unless he were going somewhere, Albert always played for his uncle for an hour. He played extremely well. Doctor Albert sat by the fire smoking his cigar. While he listened, the look of wisdom and professional authority faded, and many changes went over his face, as if he were playing a little drama to himself; moods of scorn and contempt, of rakish vanity, sentimental melancholy . . . and something remote and lonely. The Doctor had always flattered himself that he resembled a satyr, because the tops of his ears were slightly pointed; and he used to hint to his nephews that his large pendulous nose was the index of an excessively amorous disposition. His mouth was full of long, yellowish teeth, all crowded irregularly, which he snapped and ground together when he uttered denunciations of modern art or the Eighteenth Amendment. He wore his moustache short and twisted up at the corners. His thick gray hair was cut close and upright, in the bristling French fashion. His hands were small and fastidious, high-knuckled, quite elegant in shape.

Across the Doctor's throat ran a long, jagged scar. He used to mutter to his young nephews that it had been justly inflicted by an outraged husband — a pistol shot in the dark. But his brother August always said that he had been cut by glass, when, wandering about in the garden one night after drinking too much punch, he had fallen into the cold-frames.

After playing Schumann for some time, Albert, without stopping, went into Stravinsky.

Doctor Engelhardt by the gas-fire stirred uneasily, turned his important head towards his nephew, and snapped his teeth. "Br-r-r, that stuff! Poverty of imagination, poverty of musical invention; *fin-de-siècle!*"

Albert laughed. "I thought you were asleep. Why will you use that phrase? It shows your vintage. Like this any better?" He began the second act of *Pelléas et Mélisande.*

The Doctor nodded. "Yes, that is better, though I'm not fooled by it." He wrinkled his nose as if he were smelling out something, and squinted with superior discernment. "To this *canaille* that is all very new; but to me it goes back to Bach."

"Yes, if you like."

Albert, like Judge Hammersley, was jealous of his solitude — liked a few hours with his books. It was time for Uncle Doctor to be turning in.

He ended the music by playing half a dozen old German songs which the old fellow always wanted but never asked for. The Doctor's chin sank into his shirt front. His face took on a look of deep, resigned sadness; his features, losing their conscious importance, seemed to shrink a good deal. His nephew knew that this was the mood in which he would most patiently turn to rest and darkness. Doctor Engelhardt had had a heavy loss late in life. Indeed, he had suffered the same loss twice.

As Albert left the piano, the Doctor rose and walked a little stiffly across the room. At the door of his chamber he paused, brought his hand up in a kind of military salute and gravely bowed, so low that one saw only the square upstanding gray brush on the top of his head and the long pear-shaped nose. After this he closed the door behind him. Albert sat down to his book. Very soon he heard the bath water running. Having taken his bath, the Doctor would get into bed immediately to avoid catching cold. Luckily, he usually slept well. Perhaps he dreamed of that unfortunate young singer whom he sometimes called, to his nephew and himself, "the lost Lenore."

III

Long years ago, when the Engelhardt boys were still living in the old house in Allegheny with their mother, after their father's death, Doctor Engelhardt was practicing medicine, and had an office on the Park, five minutes' walk from his sister-in-law. He usually lunched with the family, after his morning office hours were over. They always had a good cook, and the Allegheny market was one of the best in the world. Mrs. Engelhardt went to market every morning of her life; such vegetables and poultry, such cheeses and sausages and smoked and pickled fish as one could buy there! Soon after she had made her rounds, boys in white aprons would come running across the Park with her purchases. Everyone knew the Engelhardt house, built of many-colored bricks, with gables and turrets and, on the west a large stained-glass window representing a scene on the Grand Canal in Venice, the Church of Santa Maria della Salute in the background, in the foreground a gondola with a slender gondolier. People said August and Mrs. Engelhardt should be solidly seated in the prow to make the picture complete.

Doctor Engelhardt's especial interest was the throat, preferably the singing throat. He had studied every scrap of manuscript that Manuel Garcia had left behind him, every reported conversation with him. He had doctored many singers, and imagined he had saved many voices. Pittsburgh air is not good for the throat, and traveling artists often had need of medical assistance. Conductors of orchestras and singing societies recommended Doctor Engelhardt because he was very lax about collecting fees from professionals, especially if they sent him a photograph floridly inscribed. He had been a medical student in New York while Patti was still singing; his biography fell into chapters of great voices as a turfman's falls into chapters of fast horses. This passion for the voice had given him the feeling of distinction, of being unique in his profession, which had made him all his life a well-satisfied and happy man, and had left him a poor one.

One morning when the Doctor was taking his customary walk about the Park before office hours, he stopped in front of the Allegheny High School building because he heard singing — a chorus of young voices. It was June, and the chapel windows were open. The Doctor listened for a few moments, then tilted his head on one side and laid his forefinger on his pear-shaped nose with an anxious, inquiring squint. Among the voices he certainly heard one Voice. The final bang of the piano was followed by laughter and buzzing. A boy ran down the steps. The Doctor stopped him and learned that this was a rehearsal for Class Day exercises. Just then the piano began again, and in a moment he heard the same voice alone:

Still wie die Nacht, tief wie das Meer.

No, he was not mistaken; a full, rich, soprano voice, so easy, so sure; a golden warmth, even in the high notes. Before the second verse was over he went softly into the building, into the chapel, and for the first time laid eyes on Marguerite Thiesinger. He saw a sturdy, blooming German girl standing beside the piano; good-natured one knew at a glance, glowing with health. She looked like a big peony just burst into bloom and full of sunshine — sunshine in her auburn hair, in her rather small hazel eyes. When she finished the song, she began waltzing on the platform with one of the boys.

Doctor Albert waited by the door, and accosted her as she came out carrying her coat and schoolbooks. He introduced himself and asked her if she would go over to Mrs. Engelhardt's for lunch and sing for him.

Oh, yes! she knew one of the Engelhardt boys, and she'd always wanted to see that beautiful window from the inside.

She went over at noon and sang for them before lunch, and the family took stock of her. She spoke a very ordinary German, and her English was still worse; her people were very ordinary. Her flat, slangy speech was somehow not vulgar because it was so naive — she knew no other way. The boys were delighted with her because she was jolly and interested in everything. She told them about the glorious good times she had going to dances in suburban Turner halls, and to picnics in the damp, smoke-smeared woods up the Allegheny. The boys roared with laughter at the unpromising places she mentioned. But she had the warm bubble in her blood that makes everything fair; even being a junior in the Allegheny High School was "glorious," she told them!

She came to lunch with them again and again, because she liked the boys, and she thought the house magnificent. The Doctor observed her narrowly all the while. Clearly she had no ambition, no purpose; she sang to be agreeable. She was not very intelligent, but she had a kind of personal warmth that, to his way of thinking, was much better than brains. He took her over to his office and poked and pounded her. When he had finished his examination, he stood before the foolish, happy young thing and inclined his head in his peculiar fashion.

"Miss Thiesinger, I have the honor to announce to you that you are on the threshold of a brilliant, possibly a great career."

She laughed her fresh, ringing laugh. "Aren't you nice, though, to take so much trouble about me!"

The Doctor lifted a forefinger. "But for that you must turn your back on this childishness, these sniveling sapheads you play marbles with. You must uproot this triviality." He made a gesture as if he were wringing a chicken's neck, and Marguerite was thankful she was able to keep back a giggle.

Doctor Engelhardt wanted her to go to New York with him at once, and begin her studies. He was quite ready to finance her. He had made up his mind to stake everything upon this voice.

But not at all. She thought it was lovely of him, but she was very fond of her classmates, and she wanted to graduate with her class next year. Moreover, she had just been given a choir position in one of the biggest churches in Pittsburgh, though she was still a schoolgirl; she was going to have money and pretty clothes for the first time in her life and wouldn't miss it all for anything.

All through the next school year Doctor Albert went regularly to the church where she sang, watched and cherished her, expostulated and lectured, trying to awaken fierce ambition in his big peony flower. She was very much interested in other things just then, but she was patient with him; accepted his devotion with good nature, respected his wisdom, and bore with his "stagey" manners as she called them. She graduated in June, and immediately after commencement, when she was not quite nineteen, she eloped with an insurance agent and went to Chicago to live. She wrote Doctor Albert: "I do appreciate all your kindness to me, but I guess I will let my voice rest for the present."

He took it hard. He burned her photographs and the foolish little scrawls she had written to thank him for presents. His life would have been dull and empty if he hadn't had so many reproaches to heap upon her in his solitude. How often and how bitterly he arraigned her for the betrayal of so beautiful a gift. Where did she keep it hidden now, that jewel, in the sordid life she had chosen?

Three years after her elopement, suddenly, without warning, Marguerite Thiesinger walked into his office on Arch Street one morning and told him she had come back to study! Her husband's "affairs were involved"; he was now quite willing that she should make as much as possible of her voice — and out of it.

"My voice is better than it was," she said, looking at him out of her rather small eyes — greenish-yellow, with a glint of gold in them. He believed her. He suddenly realized how uncommonly truthful she had always been. Rather stupid, unimaginative, but carried joyously along on a flood of warm vitality, and truthful to a degree he had hardly known in any woman or in any man. And now she was a woman.

He took her over to his sister-in-law's. Albert, who chanced to be at home, was sent to the piano. She was not mistaken. The Doctor kept averting his head to conceal his delight, to conceal, once or twice, a tear — the moisture that excitement and pleasure brought to his eyes. The voice, after all, he told himself, is a physical thing. She had been growing and ripening like fruit in the sun, and the voice with the body. Doctor Engelhardt stepped softly out of the music-room into the conservatory and addressed a potted palm, his lips curling back from his teeth: "So we get that out of you, *Monsieur le commis-voyageur,* and now we throw you away like a squeezed lemon."

When he returned to his singer, she addressed him very earnestly from under her spring hat covered with lilacs: "Before my marriage, Doctor Engelhardt, you offered to take me to New York to a teacher, and lend me money to start on. If you still feel like doing it, I'm sure I could repay

you before very long. I'll follow your instructions. What was it you used
to tell me I must have — application and ambition?"

He glared at her: "Take note, Gretchen, that I change the prescription.
There is something vulgar about ambition. Now we will play for higher
stakes; for *ambition* read *aspiration!*" His index finger shot upward.

In New York he had no trouble in awakening the interest of his
friends and acquaintances. Within a week he had got his protégée to a
very fine artist, just then retiring from the Opera, a woman who had
been a pupil of Pauline Garcia Viardot. In short, Doctor Engelhardt had
realized the dream of a lifetime; he had discovered a glorious voice,
backed by a rich vitality. Within a year Marguerite had one of the best
church positions in New York; she insisted upon repaying her benefac-
tor before she went abroad to complete her studies. Doctor Engelhardt
went often to New York to counsel and advise, to gloat over his treasure.
He often shivered as he crossed the Jersey ferry, he was afraid of Fate. He
would tell over her assets on his fingers to reassure himself. You might
have seen a small, self-important man of about fifty, standing by the rail
of the ferry boat, his head impressively inclined as if he were addressing
an amphitheater full of students, gravely counting upon his fingers.

But Fate struck, and from the quarter least under suspicion —
through that blooming, rounded, generously molded young body, from
that abundant, glowing health which the Doctor proudly called peasant
vigor. Marguerite's success had brought to his office many mothers of
singing daughters. He was not insensible to the compliment, but he
usually dismissed them by dusting his fingers delicately in the air and
growling: "Yes, she can sing a little, she has a voice; *aber kleine, kleine!*"
He exulted in the opulence of his cabbage rose. To his nephews he used
to match her possibilities with the singers of that period. Emma Eames
he called *die Puritan,* Geraldine Farrar *la voix blanche,* another was *trop
raffinée.*

Marguerite had been in New York two years, her path one of uninter-
rupted progress, when she wrote the Doctor about a swelling of some
sort; the surgeons wanted to operate. Doctor Albert took the next train
for New York. An operation revealed that things were very bad indeed;
a malignant growth, so far advanced that the knife could not check it.
Her mother and grandmother had died of the same disease.

Poor Marguerite lived a year in a hospital for incurables. Every weekend when Doctor Albert went over to see her he found great changes —
it was rapid and terrible. That winter and spring he lived like a man lost

in a dark morass, the Slave in the Dismal Swamp. He suffered more than his Gretchen, for she was singularly calm and hopeful to the very end, never doubting that she would get well.

The last time he saw her she had given up. But she was noble and sweet in mood, and so piteously apologetic for disappointing him — like a child who has broken something precious and is sorry. She was wasted, indeed, until she was scarcely larger than a child, her beautiful hair cut short, her hands like shadows, but still a stain of color in her cheeks.

"I'm so sorry I didn't do as you wanted instead of running off with Phil," she said. "I see now how little he cared about me — and you've just done everything. If I had my twenty-six years to live over, I'd live them very differently."

Doctor Albert dropped her hand and walked to the window, the tears running down his face. *"Pourquoi, pourquoi?"* he muttered, staring blindly at that brutal square of glass. When he could control himself and come back to the chair at her bedside, she put her poor little sheared head out on his knee and lay smiling and breathing softly.

"I expect you don't believe in the hereafter," she murmured. "Scientific people hardly ever do. But if there is one, I'll not forget you. I'll love to remember you."

When the nurse came to give her her hypodermic, Doctor Albert went out into Central Park and wandered about without knowing where or why, until he smelled something which suddenly stopped his breath, and he sat down under a flowering linden tree. He dropped his face in his hands and cried like a woman. Youth, art, love, dreams, true-heartedness — why must they go out of the summer world into darkness? *Warum, warum?* He thought he had already suffered all that man could, but never had it come down on him like this. He sat on that bench like a drunken man or like a dying man, muttering Heine's words: "God is a grimmer humorist than I. Nobody but God could have perpetrated anything so cruel." She was ashamed, he remembered it afresh and struck his bony head with his clenched fist — ashamed at having been used like this; she was apologetic for the power, whatever it was, that had tricked her. "Yes, by God, she apologized for God!"

The tortured man looked up through the linden branches at the blue arch that never answers. As he looked, his face relaxed, his breathing grew regular. His eyes were caught by puffy white clouds like the cherub-heads in Raphael's pictures, and something within him seemed to rise and travel with those clouds. The moment had come when he could bear no more. . . . When he went back to the hospital that evening, he learned that she had died very quietly between eleven and twelve, the hour when he was sitting on the bench in the park.

Uncle Doctor now sometimes spoke to Albert out of a long silence: "Anyway, I died for her; that was given to me. She never knew a death-struggle — she went to sleep. That struggle took place in my body. Her dissolution occurred within me."

IV

Old Doctor Engelhardt walked abroad very little now. Sometimes on a fine Sunday his nephew would put him aboard a street car that climbs the hills beyond Mount Oliver and take him to visit an old German graveyard and a monastery. Every afternoon, in good weather, he walked along the pavement which ran past the front door, as far as the first corner, where he bought his paper and cigarettes. If Elsa, the pretty little granddaughter of his housekeeper, ran out to join him and see him over the crossings, he would go a little farther. In the morning, while Mrs. Rudder did the sweeping and dusting, the Doctor took the air on an upstairs back porch, overhanging the court.

The court was bricked, and had an old-fashioned cistern and hydrant, and three ailanthus trees — the last growing things left to the Engel-hardts, whose flowering shrubs and greenhouses had once been so well known in Allegheny. In these trees, which he called *les Chinoises,* the Doctor took a great interest. The clothes line ran about their trunks in a triangle, and on Monday he looked down upon the washing. He was too nearsighted to be distressed by the sooty flakes descending from neighbor-ing chimneys upon the white sheets. He enjoyed the dull green leaves of his *Chinoises* in summer, scarcely moving on breathless, sticky nights, when the moon came up red over roofs and smoke-stacks. In autumn he watched the yellow fronds drop down upon the brick pavement like great ferns. Now, when his birthday was approaching, the trees were bare; and he thought he liked them best so, especially when all the knotty, curly twigs were outlined by a scurf of snow.

As he sat there, wrapped up in rugs, a stiff felt hat on his head — he would never hear to a cap — and woolen gloves on his hands, Elsa, the granddaughter, would bring her cross-stitch and chatter to him. Of late she had been sewing on her trousseau, and that amused the Doctor highly — though it meant she would soon go to live in Lower Allegheny, and he would lose her. Her young man, Carl Abberbock, had now a half-interest in a butcher stall in the Allegheny market, and was in a hurry to marry.

When Mrs. Rudder had quite finished her work and made the place neat, she would come and lift the rug from his knees and say, "Time to go in, Herr Doctor."

MORLEY CALLAGHAN

"The Faithful Wife" is typical of that period of understatement when characters were presented in a situation without resolution and without comment. It permits most of the story to develop in the reader's own mind. Such a way of narration can have a force all its own, as is proven here.

Morley Callaghan was born in Toronto, Ontario, in 1903. He was educated at the University of Toronto. He has studied law and done newspaper work. He is one of the foremost Canadian authors. Edmund Wilson has paid tribute to him as a great writer too little known in the United States.

The Faithful Wife

UNTIL a week before Christmas George worked in the station restaurant at the lunch counter. The last week was extraordinarily cold, then the sun shone strongly for a few days, though it was always cold again in the evenings. There were three other men working at the counter. For years they must have had a poor reputation. Women, unless they were careless and easy-going, never started a conversation with them when having a light lunch at noontime. The girls at the station always avoided the red-capped porters and the countermen.

George, who was working there till he got enough money to go back home for a week and then start late in the year at college, was a young fellow with fine hair retreating far back on his forehead and rather bad upper teeth, but he was very polite and generous. Steve, the plump Italian, with the waxed black mustaches, who had charge of the restaurant, was very fond of George.

Many people passed the restaurant window on the way to the platform and the trains. The four men, watching them frequently, got to know some of them. Girls, brightly dressed and highly powdered, loitered in front of the open door, smiling at George, who saw them so often he knew their first names. At noontime, other girls, with a few minutes to spare before going back to work, used to walk up and down the tiled tunnel to the waiting-room, loafing the time away, but they never even glanced in at the countermen. It was cold outside, the streets were slippery, and it was warm in the station, that was all. George got to know most of these girls too, and talked about them with the other fellows.

George watched carefully one girl every day at noon hour. The other men had also noticed her, and two or three times she came in for a cup of coffee, but she was so gentle, and aloofly pleasant, and so unobtrusively beyond them, they were afraid to try and amuse her with easy cheerful talk. George wished earnestly that she had never seen him there in the restaurant behind the counter, even though he knew she had never noticed him at all. Her cheeks were usually rosy from the cold wind outside. When she went out the door to walk up and down for a few minutes, an agreeable expression on her face, she never once looked back at the restaurant. George, following her with his eye while pouring coffee slowly, did not expect her to look back. She was about twenty-eight, pretty, rather shy, and dressed plainly and poorly in a thin blue-cloth coat without any fur on it. Most girls managed to have a piece of fur of some kind on their coats.

With little to do in the middle of the afternoon, George used to think of her because of seeing her every day and looking at her face in profile when she passed the window. Then, on the day she had on the light-fawn felt hat, she smiled politely at him, when having a cup of coffee, and as long as possible, he remained opposite her, cleaning the counter with a damp cloth.

The last night he worked at the station he went out at about half past eight in the evening, for he had an hour to himself, and then worked on till ten o'clock. In the morning he was going home, so he walked out of the station and down the side street to the docks, and was having only pleasant thoughts, passing the warehouses, looking out over the dark cold lake and liking the tang of the wind on his face. Christmas was only a week away. The snow was falling lazily and melting slowly when it hit the sidewalk. He was glad he was through with the job at the restaurant.

An hour later, back at the restaurant, Steve said, "A dame just phoned you, George, and left her number."

"Do you know who she was?"

"No, you got too many girls, George. Don't you know the number?"

"I never saw it before."

He called the number and did not recognize the voice that answered him. A woman was asking him pleasantly enough if he remembered her. He said he did not. She said she had had a cup of coffee that afternoon at noontime, and added that she had worn a blue coat and a tan-colored felt hat, and even though she had not spoken to him, she thought he would remember her.

"Good Lord," he said.

She wanted to know if he would come and see her at half past ten that evening. Timidly he said he would, and hardly heard her giving the address. Steve and the other boys started to kid him brightly, but he was too astonished, wondering how she had found out his name, to bother with them. The boys, saying good-bye to him later, winked and elbowed him in the ribs, urging him to celebrate on his last night in the city. Steve, who was very fond of him, shook his head sadly and pulled the ends of his mustaches down into his lips.

The address the girl had given him was only eight blocks away, so he walked, holding his hands clenched tightly in his pockets, for he was cold from nervousness. He was watching the automobile headlights shining on slippery spots on the sidewalk. The house, opposite a public-school ground on a side street, was a large old rooming house. A light was in a window on the second story over the door. Ringing the bell he didn't really expect anyone to answer, and was surprised when the girl herself opened the door.

"Good evening," he said shyly.

"Oh, come upstairs," she said, smiling and practical.

In the front room he took off his overcoat and hat and sat down slowly, noticing, out of the corner of his eye, that she was even slimmer, and had nice fair hair and lovely eyes. But she was moving very nervously. He had intended to ask at once how she found out his name, but forgot about it as soon as she sat down opposite him on a camp bed and smiled shyly. She had on a red woollen sweater, fitting her tightly at the waist. Twice he shook his head, unable to get used to having her there opposite him, nervous and expectant. The trouble was she had always seemed so aloof.

"You're not very friendly," she said awkwardly.

"Oh, yes, I am. Indeed I am."

"Why don't you come over here and sit beside me?"

Slowly he sat down beside her on the camp bed, smiling stupidly. He was even slow to see that she was waiting for him to put his arms around her. Ashamed of himself, he finally kissed her eagerly and she held on to him tightly. Her heart was thumping underneath the red woollen sweater. She just kept on holding him, almost savagely, closing her eyes slowly and breathing deeply every time he kissed her. She was so delighted and satisfied to hold him in her arms that she did not bother talking at all. Finally he became very eager and she got up suddenly, walking up and down the room, looking occasionally at the cheap alarm clock on a bureau. The room was clean but poorly furnished.

"What's the matter?" he said irritably.

"My girl friend, the one I room with, will be home in twenty minutes."

"Come here anyway."

"Please sit down, please do," she said.

Slowly she sat down beside him. When he kissed her she did not object, but her lips were dry, her shoulders were trembling, and she kept on watching the clock. Though she was holding his wrist so tightly her nails dug into the skin, he knew she would be glad when he had to go. He kissed her again and she drew her left hand slowly over her lips.

"You really must be out of here before Irene comes home," she said.

"But I've only kissed and hugged you and you're wonderful." He noticed the red ring mark on her finger. "Are you sure you're not waiting for your husband to come home?" he said a bit irritably.

Frowning, looking away vaguely, she said, "Why do you have to say that?"

"There's a ring mark on your finger."

"I can't help it," she said, and began to cry quietly. "Yes, oh, yes, I'm waiting for my husband to come home. He'll be here at Christmas."

"It's too bad. Can't we do something about it?"

"I tell you I love my husband. I do, I really do, and I'm faithful to him too."

"Maybe I'd better go," he said uncomfortably, feeling ridiculous.

"Eh, what's that? My husband, he's at a sanitarium. He got his spine hurt in the war, then he got tuberculosis. He's pretty bad. They've got to carry him around. We want to love each other every time we meet, but we can't."

"That's tough, poor kid, and I suppose you've got to pay for him."

"Yes."

"Do you have many fellows?"

"No. I don't want to have any."

"Do they come here to see you?"

"No. No, I don't know what got into me. I liked you, and felt a little crazy."

"I'll slide along then. What's your first name?"

"Lola. You'd better go now."

"Couldn't I see you again?" he said suddenly.

"No, you're going away tomorrow," she said, smiling confidently.

"So you've got it all figured out. Supposing I don't go?"

"Please, you must."

Her arms were trembling when she held his overcoat. She wanted him to go before Irene came home. "You didn't give me much time," he said flatly.

"No. Irene comes in at this time. You're a lovely boy. Kiss me."

"You had that figured out too."

"Just kiss and hold me once more, George." She held on to him as if she did not expect to be embraced again for a long time, and he said, "I think I'll stay in the city a while longer."

"It's too bad, but you've got to go. We can't see each other again."

In the poorly lighted hall she looked lovely. Her cheeks were flushed, and though still eager, she was quite satisfied with the whole affair. Everything had gone perfectly for her.

As he went out the door and down the walk to the street he remembered that he hadn't asked how she had found out his name. Snow was falling lightly and there were hardly any footprints on the sidewalk. All he could think of was that he ought to go back to the restaurant and ask Steve for his job again. Steve was fond of him. But he knew he could not spoil it for her. "She had it all figured out," he muttered, turning up his coat collar.

WILLIAM MARCH

The reader can receive the catharsis of Greek tragedy from "The Little Wife" even though the main character is a "little man" and not that loftily placed personage asserted by orthodox critics to be the only correct tragic hero. The stricken husband unable to face reality is one of the most touching characters ever to appear in an American short story.

William March was a dual personality. Under his real name of William Campbell, he was the executive of a successful steamship line in his native city, Mobile, Alabama. Under the name of William March, he wrote several novels and three collections of short stories, the best known being Company K, *and the highly successful Broadway play,* The Bad Seed.

The Little Wife

JOE HINCKLEY selected a seat on the shady side of the train and carefully stowed away his traveling bag and his heavy, black catalogue case. It was unusually hot for early June. Outside the heat waves shimmered and danced above the hot slag roadbed and the muddy river that ran by the station was low between its red banks. "If it's as hot as this in June, it sure will be awful in August," he thought. He looked at his watch: 2:28 — the train was five minutes late in getting out. If he had known the 2:23 was going to be late he might have had time to pack his sample trunk and get it to the station, but he couldn't have anticipated that, of course. He had had so little time after getting that telegram from Mrs. Thompkins: barely time to pack his bag and check out of the hotel. Joe loosened his belt and swabbed his neck with a limp handkerchief. "It don't matter so much about the trunk," he thought; "one of the boys at the hotel can express it to me, or I can pick it up on my way back."

Joe noticed that one end of his catalogue case protruded slightly. With his foot he shoved it farther under the seat. It was a battered, black case, made strongly to withstand constant traveling, and re-enforced at its corners with heavy copper cleats. One of the handles had been broken and mended with newer leather. On the front of the case there had once been stamped in gilt the firm name of Boykin & Rosen, Wholesale Hardware, Chattanooga, Tenn., but time had long since worn away the gold lettering.

The telegram had upset Joe: it had come so suddenly, so unexpectedly. He felt vaguely that somebody was playing a joke on him. He felt confused and helpless. It was difficult to believe that Bessie was so desperately sick. He sat for a time staring at his fingernails. Suddenly he remembered an appointment at four o'clock with the buyer for Snowdoun and Sims and he rose quickly from his seat with some dim idea of telephoning or sending a message to explain his absence. Then he realized that the train was already in motion. "I'll write him a letter when I get to Mobile," said Joe to himself; "he'll understand all right when I explain the circumstances. He won't blame me for breaking that date when I tell him about my wife being so sick." He sat down heavily in his seat and again looked at his hands.

Ahead of him two young girls were leaning out of the window and waving to their friends. Their eyes were shining and their cheeks were flushed and they were laughing with excitement at the prospect of going away.

Across the aisle sat a gaunt farm-woman. Her red-veined eyes protruded. Her neck was swollen with a goiter. In her arms she held a bouquet of red crêpe-myrtle which was already wilting in the heat. Beside her she had placed her straw suitcase and several bulky, paper-wrapped parcels. She gazed steadily out of the window as if afraid that someone would catch her eye and try to talk to her.

It was very hot in the coach. The small electric fan at the end of the car droned and wheezed sleepily but succeeded only in stirring up the hot air.

Joe took from his pocket the telegram that he had received from his mother-in-law and read it again: "J. G. Hinckley, American Hotel, Montgomery, Ala. Come home at once. Doctor says Bessie not expected live through day. Will wire again if necessary. It was a boy. Mother."

Joe's hands clenched suddenly and then relaxed. It had all happened so suddenly; he couldn't quite get it through his head, even yet. He had taken a buyer to lunch that day and they had laughed and talked and told each other stories. Then at two o'clock he had gone back to the hotel to freshen up and the clerk had reached in his box and taken out the key to his room and the telegram. The telegram had been waiting for him for two hours the clerk said. Joe read it through twice and then looked at the address to make sure that the message was really for him. He hadn't understood. Bessie was getting along so nicely — she had had no trouble at all — and the baby wasn't expected for a month. He had arranged his itinerary so that he would be with her when the baby was born. They had gone over all that and had arranged everything. And now everything was upset. He thought: "I was out talking and laughing with that buyer and the telegram was waiting here all the time." That thought hurt him. He stood repeating stupily, "I was out laughing and telling smutty stories and that telegram was here all the time."

Joe leaned his head against the red plush of the seat. He felt numb and very tired. At first the signature "Mother" had puzzled him. He couldn't understand what his mother would be doing in Mobile with Bessie; then he realized that it was Bessie's mother who had sent the telegram. He had never thought of Bessie's mother by any name except Mrs. Thompkins.

When he had married Bessie her mother had come to live with them as a matter of course. He was rather glad of that arrangement; he was really fond of the old lady in an impersonal sort of way. Then, too, it was pleasant for Bessie to have someone with her while he was on the road. His work made it impossible for him to get home oftener than every other weekend, and many times it was difficult for him to get home that often, but he had always managed to make it, one way or another. He couldn't disappoint Bessie, no matter what happened. Their year of married life had been the happiest that he had ever known. And Bessie had been happy too. Suddenly he had a clear picture of her lying on their bed, her face white with suffering, and a quick panic gripped his heart. To reassure himself he whispered, "Those doctors don't know everything. She'll be all right. Mrs. Thompkins was just excited and frightened. Everything's going to be all right!"

Ahead of him a white-haired old gentleman opened his bag and took out a traveling cap. He had some difficulty in fastening the catch while holding his straw hat in his hand, but his wife, sitting with him, took the bag and fastened it at once. Then she took his hat and held it on her lap. The wife was reading a magazine. She did not look up from the magazine when she fastened the bag.

Down the aisle came the Negro porter. He had a telegram in his hand

When he reached the center of the coach he stopped and called out: "Telegram for Mr. J. G. Hinckley!" Joe let him call the name three times before he claimed the message. The porter explained that the telegram had been delivered to the train by a messenger from the American Hotel just as the train was getting under way. Joe gave the porter twenty-five cents for a tip and went back to his seat.

The country woman looked up for an instant and then turned her eyes away. The young girls giggled and whispered and looked boldly at Joe, and the old gentleman, after settling his cap firmly on his head, took a cigar from his case and went to the smoking-room.

Joe's throat felt tight and he noticed that his hands were shaking. He wanted to put his head on the window-sill but he was afraid that people would think him sick and try to talk to him. He placed the unopened telegram on the seat beside him and stared at it for a long time. At last he re-read the first telegram very slowly. "It must be from Mrs. Thompkins, all right," he thought, "she said she'd wire again if —" Then he thought: "It may not be from Mrs. Thompkins at all; it may be from somebody else; it may be from Boykin & Rosen about that cancellation in Meridian. That's who it's from: it's from the House, it's not from Mrs. Thompkins at all!" He looked up quickly and saw that the two young girls had turned around and were watching him, making laughing remarks to each other behind their hands.

He arose from his seat feeling weak and slightly nauseated, the unopened telegram in his hand. He passed through several coaches until he reached the end of the train and went out on the rear vestibule. He had a sudden wish to jump from the end of the train and run off into the woods, but a brakeman was there tinkering with a red lantern and Joe realized that such an act would look very strange. When the brakeman looked up and saw Joe's face he put down his lantern and asked, "Are you feeling all right, mister?" Joe said, "Yes, I'm feeling all right but it's a little hot, though." Finally the brakeman finished his job and left and Joe was very glad of that. He wanted to be alone. He didn't want anybody around him.

The rails clicked rhythmically and the wilted country-side flew past. A little Negro girl . . . in a patched pink dress . . . ran down to the track . . . and waved her hand. A lame old country man . . . ploughing in his stumpy field . . . pulled up his mangy mule . . . to stare at the passing train. The rails clattered and clicked and the train flew over the hot slag roadbed. "There's no need of going so fast," thought Joe, "we've got all the time in the world." He felt sick. In the polished metal of the car he caught a distorted glimpse of his face. It was white and terrified. He thought: "No wonder that brakeman asked me how I was feeling." Then he thought: "Do I look so bad that people can tell it?" That worried him. He didn't want people to notice him or to talk to him. There was nothing that anybody could say, after all.

He kept turning the telegram over in his hand thinking: "I've got to open it now; I've got to open it and read it." Finally he said aloud, "It's not true! I don't believe it!" He repeated these words a number of times and then he said; "It's from the House about that cancellation in Meridian — it isn't from Mrs. Thompkins at all." He tore the unopened telegram into tiny bits and threw the pieces from the end of the train. A wind fluttered and shimmered the yellow fragments before they settled down lightly on the hard, hot roadbed. He thought: "They look like a cloud of yellow butterflies dancing and settling that way." Immediately he felt better. He drew back his shoulders and sucked in lungfuls of the country air. "Everything's all right," he said. "I'm going home to see the little wife and everything's all right." He laughed happily. He felt like a man who has just escaped some terrible calamity. When he could no longer see the scraps of paper on the track he went back to his seat humming a tune. He felt very gay and immensely relieved.

Joe reached his seat just as the conductor came through the train. He nodded pleasantly as he gave up his ticket.

"Don't let anybody talk you out of a free ride," he said.

"No chance of that, Cap!" said the conductor.

Joe laughed with ringing heartiness and the conductor looked at him in surprise. Then he laughed a little himself. "You sure are in a good humor, considering how hot it is," he said.

"And why shouldn't I be in a good humor?" asked Joe. "I'm going home to see the little wife." Then he whispered, as if it were a great secret, "It's a boy!"

"That's fine, that's simply fine!" said the conductor. He put his papers and his tickets on the seat and shook Joe's hand. Joe blushed and laughed again. As the conductor moved off he nudged Joe's ribs and said, "Give my regards to the madam."

"I sure will," said Joe happily.

Joe was sorry that the conductor couldn't stay longer. He felt an imperative need of talking to someone. He felt that he must talk about Bessie to someone. He looked around the car to see if he knew anybody on the train. The two young girls smiled at him. Joe understood perfectly; they were just two nice kids going on a trip. Either one, alone, would never think of smiling at a strange man but being together changed things all the way around. That made it an exciting adventure, something to be laughed over and discussed later with their friends. Joe decided that he would go over and talk to them. He walked over casually and seated himself.

"Well, where are you young ladies going?" he asked.

"Don't you think that you have a great deal of nerve?" asked the black-eyed girl.

"Sure I have. I wouldn't be the best hardware salesman on the road if I didn't have a lot of nerve," said Joe pleasantly.

Both of the girls laughed at that and Joe knew that everything was all right. He decided that the blue-eyed girl was the prettier of the two but the black-eyed girl had more snap.

"We're getting off at Flomaton," said the blue-eyed girl.

"We've been in school in Montgomery," said the black-eyed girl.

"We're going home for the summer vacation."

"And we want the cock-eyed world to know we're glad of it!"

Joe looked at them gravely. "Don't make a mistake, young ladies; get all the education you can. You'll regret it later on if you don't."

Both the girls started laughing. They put their arms around each other and laughed until tears came into their eyes. Joe laughed too although he wondered what the joke was. After a while the girls stopped laughing, but a sudden giggle from the blue-eyed girl set them off again, worse than before.

"This is awfully silly!" said the black-eyed girl.

"Please don't think us rude," gasped the blue-eyed girl.

"What's the joke?" asked Joe, who was really laughing as much as either of the girls.

"You sounded so — so — " explained the blue-eyed girl.

"So damned *fatherly!*" finished the black-eyed girl.

They went off into another whirlwind of mirth, laughing and hugging each other. The old lady across the aisle put down her magazine and started laughing too, but the woman with the goiter held her bouquet of crêpe-myrtle rigidly and stared out of the window.

Joe waited until the girls had exhausted themselves. Finally they wiped their eyes and opened their vanity cases to look at themselves in their mirrors and to repowder their faces. He said, "Well, I guess I ought to sound fatherly: I just got a telegram saying that I was a parent for the first time."

That interested the young girls and they crowded him with questions: they wanted to know all about it. Joe felt very happy. As he started to talk he noticed that the old lady had been listening and that she had moved over in her seat in order to hear better. Joe felt friendly toward everybody: "Won't you come over and join us?" he asked.

"Yes, indeed," said the old lady and Joe moved over and made a place for her.

"Now tell us all about it!" demanded the blue-eyed girl.

"You must be very happy," said the old lady.

"I sure am happy," said Joe. Then he added, "There's not a whole lot to tell except that I got a telegram from Mrs. Thompkins— Mrs. Thompkins is my mother-in-law — saying that Bessie had given birth to a fine boy and that both of them were doing just fine: the doctor said that he'd never seen anybody do so well before, but of course my wife wanted me to be with her and so I just dropped everything and here I am. You see Bessie and I have only been married for a year. We've been very happy. The only bad thing is that I don't get home very often, but it wouldn't do to have everything perfect in the world, would it? She sure is the finest little wife a man ever had. She don't complain at all about my being away so much, but some day we hope to have things different."

"There isn't anything nicer than a baby," said the blue-eyed girl.

"What are you going to name him?" asked the old lady.

"Well, Bessie wants to name him for me, but I can't see much sense in that. My first name's Joe and I think that's a little common, don't you? But I'll leave the naming part up to Bessie. She can name him anything she wants to. She sure has been a fine little wife to me."

Joe started talking rapidly. He told in detail of the first time he had met Bessie. It had been in the home of Jack Barnes, one of the boys he had met on the road, and he had been invited over for dinner and a little stud poker later. Mrs. Barnes didn't play poker so Bessie, who lived across the street, had been invited over to keep Mrs. Barnes company while the men played. He had liked Bessie at once and the boys had kidded him about not keeping his mind on the game. He had never told anybody this before, but when the boys started kidding him he made up his mind not to look at Bessie again as he didn't want her to think that he was fresh, but he couldn't stop looking at her and every time he caught her eye she would smile in a sweet, friendly sort of way. Finally everybody noticed it and they started joking Bessie too, but she hadn't minded at all. He had lost $14.50 that night, but he had met Bessie. You couldn't call Bessie exactly beautiful but she was sweet and nice. Bessie was the sort of girl that any man would want to marry.

He told of their courtship. He quoted whole paragraphs from letters that she had written to prove a particular point which he had brought up. Bessie hadn't liked him especially, not right at first, at any rate; of course she had liked him as a friend from the first but not in any serious way. There were one or two other fellows hanging around, too. Bessie had a great deal of attention; she could have gone out every night with a different man if she had wanted to. Being on the road all the time had been pretty much of a disadvantage. He didn't have an opportunity to see her often. Or maybe that was an advantage — anyway he wrote her every day. Then, finally, they had become engaged. She hadn't even let him kiss her until then. He knew from the first that she would make a wonderful little wife but he was still puzzled why a girl as superior as Bessie would want to marry *him*.

He talked on and on, rapidly — feverishly. He told how he had once determined not to get married at all, but that was before he had met Bessie. She had changed all that. Two hours passed before he knew it. His audience was getting bored, but Joe didn't realize it.

Finally the old gentleman with the cap came back from the smoking-room and his wife, glad of a chance to get away, made her excuses and went over to sit with him. Joe smiled and nodded, but paused only a moment in his story. He was in the midst of a long description of Mrs. Thompkins. Mrs. Thompkins wasn't at all like the comic supplement mother-in-law. Quite the contrary. He didn't see how he and Bessie would get along without her. To show you the sort of woman she really was, she always took his side in any dispute — not that he and Bessie ever quarreled! Oh, no! But occasionally they had little friendly discussions like all other married couples and Mrs. Thompkins always took his side of the argument. That was unusual, wasn't it? Joe talked and talked and talked, totally unconscious of the passing of time.

Finally the train reached Flomaton and the porter came to help the girls off with their bags. They were very glad to get away. They were getting a little nervous. There was something about Joe that they couldn't understand. At first they had thought him just jolly and high spirited, but after a time they came to the conclusion that he must be a little drunk, or, possibly, slightly demented. For the past hour they had been nudging each other significantly.

Joe helped them off the train and on to the station platform. Just as the train pulled out the black-eyed girl waved her hand and said, "Give my love to Bessie and the son and heir," and the blue-eyed girl said, "Be sure and kiss the baby for me."

"I sure will," said Joe.

After the train had passed the girls looked at each other for a moment. Then they started laughing. Finally the black-eyed girl said, "Well, Bessie certainly has him roped and tied." The blue-eyed girl said, "Did you ever see anything like that in your life before?"

Joe came into the coach again. "Just a couple of nice kids," he thought to himself. He looked at his watch. It was 5:25. He was surprised. The time had passed very quickly. "It won't be long now before I'm in Mobile," he thought.

He went back to his seat, but he was restless. He decided that he would have a cigarette. He found three men in the smoker. One of them was an old man with a tuft of gray whiskers. His face was yellow and sunken and blue veins stood out on his hands. He was chewing tobacco gravely and spitting into the brass cuspidor. The second man was large and flabby. When he laughed his eyes disappeared entirely and his fat belly shook. His fingernails were swollen and his underlip hung down in a petulant droop. The third man was dark and nervous looking. He had on his little finger a ring with a diamond much too large.

They were telling jokes and laughing when Joe came in. Joe wanted to talk to them about Bessie, but he couldn't bring her name up in such an atmosphere. Suddenly he thought: "I was laughing and telling smutty stories with that buyer in Montgomery and the telegram was there all the time." His face contracted with pain. He crushed the thought from his mind. Quickly he threw away his cigarette and went back to his seat.

A bright-skinned waiter came through the train announcing the first call for dinner. At first Joe thought that he would have his dinner on the train as that would break the monotony of the trip and help pass the time, but immediately he remembered that Mrs. Thompkins would have dinner for him at home — a specially prepared dinner with all of the things that he liked. "I'll wait until I get home," thought Joe. "I wouldn't disappoint Mrs. Thompkins and the little wife for the world after they went to all that trouble for me."

Again he felt that curious, compulsive need of talking about Bessie to someone. He had a feeling that as long as he talked about her she would remain safe. He saw the old lady and her husband in their seat eating a lunch which they had brought and he decided to go over and talk with them. "Can I come over and talk to you folks?" asked Joe.

"Certainly, sir," said the old gentleman with the cap. Then, in order to make conversation he said, "My wife has been telling me that you are going home to see your new son."

"That's right," said Joe, "that's right." He started talking rapidly, hardly pausing for breath. The old lady looked at her husband reproachfully. "Now see what you started!" her glance seemed to say.

Joe talked of his wedding. It had been very quiet. Bessie was the sort of a girl who didn't go in for a lot of show. There had been present only a few members of the family and one or two close friends. George Orcutt who traveled a line of rugs out of New York had been his best man. Bessie was afraid that someone would try to play a joke on them: something like tying tin cans to the automobile that was to take them to the station or marking their baggage with chalk. But everything had gone off smoothly. The Barneses had been at the wedding, of course: he had met Bessie in their home and they were such close neighbors that they couldn't overlook them, but almost nobody else outside the family was there.

Then he told of the honeymoon they had spent in New Orleans; all the places they had visited there and just what Bessie had thought and said about each one. He talked on and on and on. He told of the first weeks of their married life and how happy they were. He told what a splendid cook Bessie was and what an excellent housekeeper, how much she had loved the home he had bought for her and her delight when she knew that she was going to have a baby.

The old gentleman was staring at Joe in a puzzled manner. He was wondering if he hadn't better call the conductor as it was his private opinion that Joe had a shot of cocaine in him. The old lady had folded her hands like a martyr. She continued to look at her husband with an "I-told-you-so!" expression.

Joe had lost all idea of time. He talked on and on, rapidly, excitedly. He had got as far as Bessie's plans for the child's education when the porter touched him on the arm and told him that they were pulling into the station at Mobile. He came to himself with a start and looked at his watch: 7:35! He didn't believe it possible that two hours had passed so quickly.

"It sure has been a pleasure talking to you folks," said Joe.

"Oh, that's all right," said the man with the cap.

Joe gave the porter a tip and stepped off the train jauntily. As he turned to pick up his bag he saw that the woman with the goiter was staring at him. He walked over to the window that framed her gaunt face. "Good-bye, lady; I hope you have a nice trip." The woman answered, "The doctors said it wasn't no use operating on me. I waited too long." "Well that's fine! — That sure is fine!" said Joe. He laughed gaily and waved his hand. He picked up his bag and his catalogue case and followed the people through the gate. The woman with the goiter stared at him until he was out of sight.

On the other side of the iron fence Joe saw Mrs. Thompkins. She was dressed in black and she wore a black veil. Joe went over to her briskly and Mrs. Thompkins put her arms around him and kissed him twice. "Poor Joe!" she said. Then she looked at his smiling, excited face with amazement. Joe noticed that her eyes were red and swollen.

"Didn't you get my telegram?" she asked. Joe wrinkled his brow in an effort to remember. Finally he said, "Oh, sure. I got it at the hotel."

"Did you get my second telegram?" insisted Mrs. Thompkins.

She looked steadily into Joe's eyes. A feeling of terror swept over him. He knew that he could no longer lie to himself. He could no longer keep Bessie alive by talking about her. His face was suddenly twisted with pain and his jaw trembled like a child's. He leaned against the iron fence for support and Mrs. Thompkins held his hand and said, "You can't give in. You got to be a man. You can't give in like that, Joe!"

Finally he said, "I didn't read your telegram. I didn't want to know that she was dead. I wanted to keep her alive a little longer." He sat down on an empty baggage truck and hid his face in his hands. He sat there for a long time while Mrs. Thompkins stood guard over him, her black veil trailing across his shoulder.

"Joe!" she said patiently. . . . "Joe! . . ."

A man in a dirty uniform came up. "I'm sorry, Mister, but you'll have to move. We got to use that truck." Joe picked up his catalogue case and his bag and followed Mrs. Thompkins out of the station.

F. SCOTT FITZGERALD

The Lost Generation discovers how really lost it was — that could be one way of summing up "Babylon Revisited," but it would not do this powerful story justice. The impact of the story is too great for any simple summation. Its historical significance is the ending of the Flaming Twenties and the beginning of the Great Depression. All fiction has a springboard of reality; those who know the author's tragic life know how true this story is.

F. Scott Fitzgerald was born in St. Paul, Minnesota, in 1896. He was educated at Princeton University, and served in the American Army during the First World War. He published several novels, notably The Great Gatsby *and* Tender Is the Night, *and four collections of short stories. His life, and that of his wife Zelda, is now a legend.*

Babylon Revisited

"And where's Mr. Campbell?" Charlie asked.

"Gone to Switzerland. Mr. Campbell's a pretty sick man, Mr. Wales."

"I'm sorry to hear that. And George Hardt?" Charlie inquired.

"Back in America, gone to work."

"And where is the Snow Bird?"

"He was in here last week. Anyway, his friend, Mr. Schaeffer, is in Paris."

Two familiar names from the long list of a year and a half ago. Charlie scribbled an address in his notebook and tore out the page.

"If you see Mr. Schaeffer, give him this," he said. "It's my brother-in-law's address. I haven't settled on a hotel yet."

He was not really disappointed to find Paris was so empty. But the stillness in the Ritz bar was strange and portentous. It was not an American bar any more — he felt polite in it, and not as if he owned it. It had gone back into France. He felt the stillness from the moment he got out of the taxi and saw the doorman, usually in a frenzy of activity at this hour, gossiping with a *chasseur* by the servants' entrance.

Passing through the corridor, he heard only a single, bored voice in the once-clamorous women's room. When he turned into the bar he traveled the twenty feet of green carpet with his eyes fixed straight ahead by old habit; and then, with his foot firmly on the rail, he turned and surveyed the room, encountering only a single pair of eyes that fluttered up from a newspaper in the corner. Charlie asked for the head barman, Paul, who in the latter days of the bull market had come to work in his own custom-built car — disembarking, however, with due nicety at the nearest corner. But Paul was at his country house today and Alix giving him information.

"No, no more," Charlie said, "I'm going slow these days."

Alix congratulated him: "You were going pretty strong a couple of years ago."

"I'll stick to it all right," Charlie assured him. "I've stuck to it for over a year and a half now."

"How do you find conditions in America?"

"I haven't been to America for months. I'm in business in Prague, representing a couple of concerns there. They don't know about me down there."

Alix smiled.

"Remember the night of George Hardt's bachelor dinner here?" said Charlie. "By the way, what's become of Claude Fessenden?"

Alix lowered his voice confidentially: "He's in Paris, but he doesn't come here any more. Paul doesn't allow it. He ran up a bill of thirty thousand francs, charging all his drinks and his lunches, and usually his dinner, for more than a year. And when Paul finally told him he had to pay, he gave him a bad check."

Alix shook his head sadly.

"I don't understand it, such a dandy fellow. Now he's all bloated up —— " He made a plump apple of his hands.

Charlie watched a group of strident queens installing themselves in a corner.

"Nothing affects them," he thought. "Stocks rise and fall, people loaf or work, but they go on forever." The place oppressed him. He called for the dice and shook with Alix for the drink.

"Here for long, Mr. Wales?"

"I'm here for four or five days to see my little girl."

"Oh-h! You have a little girl?"

Outside, the fire-red, gas-blue, ghost-green signs shone smokily through the tranquil rain. It was late afternoon and the streets were in movement; the *bistros* gleamed. At the corner of the Boulevard des Capucines he took a taxi. The Place de la Concorde moved by in pink majesty; they crossed the logical Seine, and Charlie felt the sudden provincial quality of the Left Bank.

Charlie directed his taxi to the Avenue de l'Opera, which was out of his way. But he wanted to see the blue hour spread over the magnificent façade, and imagine that the cab horns, playing endlessly the first few bars of *Le Plus que Lent,* were the trumpets of the Second Empire. They were closing the iron grill in front of Brentano's Bookstore, and people were already at dinner behind the trim little bourgeois hedge of Duval's. He had never eaten at a really cheap restaurant in Paris. Five-course dinner, four francs fifty, eighteen cents, wine included. For some odd reason he wished that he had.

As they rolled on to the Left Bank and he felt its sudden provincialism, he thought, "I spoiled this city for myself. I didn't realize it, but the days came along one after another, and then two years were gone, and everything was gone, and I was gone."

He was thirty-five, and good to look at. The Irish mobility of his face was sobered by a deep wrinkle between his eyes. As he rang his brother-in-law's bell in the Rue Palatine, the wrinkle deepened till it pulled down his brows; he felt a cramping sensation in his belly. From behind the maid who opened the door darted a lovely little girl of nine who shrieked "Daddy"! and flew up, struggling like a fish, into his arms. She pulled his head around by one ear and set her cheek against his.

"My old pie," he said.

"Oh, daddy, daddy, daddy, daddy, dads, dads, dads!"

She drew him into the salon, where the family waited, a boy and girl his daughter's age, his sister-in-law and her husband. He greeted Marion with his voice pitched carefully to avoid either feigned enthusiasm or dislike, but her response was more frankly tepid, though she minimized her expression of unalterable distrust by directing her regard toward his child. The two men clasped hands in a friendly way and Lincoln Peters rested his for a moment on Charlie's shoulder.

The room was warm and comfortably American. The three children moved intimately about, playing through the yellow oblongs that led to other rooms; the cheer of six o'clock spoke in the eager smacks of the fire and the sounds of French activity in the kitchen. But Charlie did not relax; his heart sat up rigidly in his body and he drew confidence from his daughter, who from time to time came close to him, holding in her arms the doll he had brought.

"Really extremely well," he declared in answer to Lincoln's question. "There's a lot of business there that isn't moving at all, but we're doing even better than ever. In fact, damn well. I'm bringing my sister over from America next month to keep house for me. My income last year was bigger than it was when I had money. You see, the Czechs ——"

His boasting was for a specific purpose; but after a moment, seeing a faint restiveness in Lincoln's eye, he changed the subject: "Those are fine children of yours, well brought up, good manners."

"We think Honoria's a great little girl too."

Marion Peters came back from the kitchen. She was a tall woman with worried eyes, who had once possessed a fresh American loveliness. Charlie had never been sensitive to it and was always surprised when people spoke of how pretty she had been. From the first there had been an instinctive antipathy between them.

"Well, how do you find Honoria?" she asked.

"Wonderful. I was astonished how much she's grown in ten months. All the children are looking well."

"We haven't had a doctor for a year. How do you like being back in Paris?"

"It seems very funny to see so few Americans around."

"I'm delighted," Marion said vehemently. "Now at least you can go into a store without their assuming you're a millionaire. We've suffered like everybody, but on the whole it's a good deal pleasanter."

"But it was nice while it lasted," Charlie said. "We were a sort of royalty, almost infallible, with a sort of magic around us. In the bar this afternoon" — he stumbled, seeing his mistake — "there wasn't a man I knew."

She looked at him keenly. "I should think you'd have had enough of bars."

"I only stayed a minute. I take one drink every afternoon, and no more."

"Don't you want a cocktail before dinner?" Lincoln asked.

"I take only one drink every afternoon, and I've had that."

"I hope you keep to it," said Marion.

Her dislike was evident in the coldness with which she spoke, but

Charlie only smiled; he had larger plans. Her very aggressiveness gave
him an advantage, and he knew enough to wait. He wanted them to
initiate the discussion of what they knew had brought him to Paris.

At dinner he couldn't decide whether Honoria was most like him or
her mother. Fortunate if she didn't combine the traits of both that had
brought them to disaster. A great wave of protectiveness went over him.
He thought he knew what to do for her. He believed in character; he
wanted to jump back a whole generation and trust in character again as
the eternally valuable element. Everything wore out.

He left soon after dinner, but not to go home. He was curious to see
Paris by night with clearer and more judicious eyes than those of other
days. He bought a *strapontin* for the Casino and watched Josephine
Baker go through her chocolate araabesques.

After an hour he left and strolled toward Montmartre, up the Rue
Pigalle into the Place Blanche. The rain had stopped and there were a
few people in evening clothes disembarking from taxis in front of cab-
arets, and *cocottes* prowling singly or in pairs, and many Negroes. He
passed a lighted door from which issued music, and stopped with the
sense of familiarity; it was Bricktop's, where he had parted with so many
hours and so much money. A few doors farther on he found another
ancient rendezvous and incautiously put his head inside. Immediately an
eager orchestra burst into sound, a pair of professional dancers leaped to
their feet and a maître d'hôtel swooped toward him, crying, "Crowd just
arriving, sir!" But he withdrew quickly.

"You have to be damn drunk," he thought.

Zelli's was closed, the bleak and sinister cheap hotels surrounding it
were dark; up in the Rue Blanche there was more light and a local,
colloquial French crowd. The Poet's Cave had disappeared, but the two
great mouths of the Café of Heaven and the Café of Hell still yawned —
even devoured, as he watched, the meagre contents of a tourist bus — a
German, a Japanese, and an American couple who glanced at him with
frightened eyes.

So much for the effort and ingenuity of Montmartre. All the catering
to vice and waste was on an utterly childish scale, and he suddenly
realized the meaning of the word "dissipate" — to dissipate into thin air;
to make nothing out of something. In the little hours of the night every
move from place to place was an enormous human jump, an increase of
paying for the privilege of slower and slower motion.

He remembered thousand-franc notes given to an orchestra for playing a single number, hundred-franc notes tossed to a doorman for calling a cab.

But it hadn't been given for nothing.

It had been given, even the most wildly squandered sum, as an offering to destiny that he might not remember the things most worth remembering, the things that now he would always remember — his child taken from his control, his wife escaped to a grave in Vermont.

In the glare of a *brasserie* a woman spoke to him. He bought her some eggs and coffee, and then, eluding her encouraging stare, gave her a twenty-franc note and took a taxi to his hotel.

II

He woke upon a fine fall day — football weather. The depression of yesterday was gone and he liked the people on the streets. At noon he sat opposite Honoria at Le Grand Vatel, the only restaurant he could think of not reminiscent of champagne dinners and long luncheons that began at two and ended in a blurred and vague twilight.

"Now, how about vegetables? Oughtn't you to have some vegetables?"

"Well, yes."

"Here's *épinards* and *chou-fleur* and carrots and *haricots*."

"I'd like *chou-fleur*."

"Wouldn't you like to have two vegetables?"

"I usually only have one at lunch."

The waiter was pretending to be inordinately fond of children. *"Qu'elle est mignonne la petite? Elle parle exactement comme une française."*

"How about dessert? Shall we wait and see?"

The waiter disappeared. Honoria looked at her father expectantly.

"What are we going to do?"

"First, we're going to that toy store in the Rue Saint-Honoré and buy you anything you like. And then we're going to the vaudeville at the Empire."

She hesitated. "I like it about the vaudeville, but not the toy store."

"Why not?"

"Well, you brought me this doll." She had it with her. "And I've got lots of things. And we're not rich any more, are we?"

"We never were. But today you are to have anything you want."

"All right," she agreed resignedly.

When there had been her mother and a French nurse he had been inclined to be strict; now he extended himself, reached out for a new tolerance; he must be both parents to her and not shut any of her out of communication.

"I want to get to know you," he said gravely. "First let me introduce myself. My name is Charles J. Wales, of Prague."

"Oh, daddy!" her voice cracked with laughter.

"And who are you, please?" he persisted, and she accepted a rôle immediately: "Honoria Wales, Rue Palatine, Paris."

"Married or single?"

"No, not married. Single."

He indicated the doll. "But I see you have a child, madame."

Unwilling to disinherit it, she took it to her heart and thought quickly: "Yes, I've been married, but I'm not married now. My husband is dead."

He went on quickly, "And the child's name?"

"Simone. That's after my best friend at school."

"I'm very pleased that you're doing so well at school."

"I'm third this month," she boasted. "Elsie" — that was her cousin — "is only about eighteenth, and Richard is about at the bottom."

"You like Richard and Elsie, don't you?"

"Oh, yes. I like Richard quite well and I like her all right."

Cautiously and casually he asked, "And Aunt Marion and Uncle Lincoln — which do you like best?"

"Oh, Uncle Lincoln, I guess."

He was increasingly aware of her presence. As they came in, a murmur of ". . . adorable" followed them, and now the people at the next table bent all their silences upon her, staring as if she were something no more conscious than a flower.

"Why don't I live with you?" she asked suddenly. "Because mamma's dead?"

"You must stay here and learn more French. It would have been hard for daddy to take care of you so well."

"I don't really need much taking care of any more. I do everything for myself."

Going out of the restaurant, a man and a woman unexpectedly hailed him!

"Well, the old Wales!"

"Hello there, Lorraine . . . Dunc."

Sudden ghosts out of the past: Duncan Schaeffer, a friend from college. Lorraine Quarrles, a lovely, pale blonde of thirty; one of a crowd who had helped them make months into days in the lavish times of three years ago.

"My husband couldn't come this year," she said, in answer to his question. "We're poor as hell. So he gave me two hundred a month and told me I could do my worst on that. . . . This your little girl?"

"What about coming back and sitting down?" Duncan asked.

"Can't do it." He was glad for an excuse. As always he felt Lorraine's passionate, provocative attraction, but his own rhythm was different now.

"Well, how about dinner?" she asked.

"I'm not free. Give me your address and let me call you."

"Charlie, I believe you're sober," she said judicially. "I honestly believe he's sober, Dunc. Pinch him and see if he's sober."

Charlie indicated Honoria with his head. They both laughed.

"What's your address?" said Duncan skeptically.

He hesitated, unwilling to give the name of his hotel.

"I'm not settled yet. I'd better call you. We're going to see the vaudeville at the Empire."

"There! That's what I want to do," Lorraine said. "I want to see some clowns and acrobats and jugglers. That's just what we'll do, Dunc."

"We've got to do an errand first," said Charlie. "Perhaps we'll see you there."

"All right, you snob. . . . Good-bye, beautiful little girl."

"Good-bye."

Honoria bobbed politely.

Somehow, an unwelcome encounter. They liked him because he was functioning, because he was serious; they wanted to see him, because he was stronger than they were now, because they wanted to draw a certain sustenance from his strength.

At the Empire, Honoria proudly refused to sit upon her father's folded coat. She was already an individual with a code of her own, and Charlie was more and more absorbed by the desire of putting a little of himself into her before she crystallized utterly. It was hopeless to try to know her in so short a time.

Between the acts they came upon Duncan and Lorraine in the lobby where the band was playing.

"Have a drink?"

"All right, but not up at the bar. We'll take a table."

"The perfect father."

Listening abstractedly to Lorraine, Charlie watched Honoria's eyes leave their table, and he followed them wistfully about the room, wondering what they saw. He met her glance and she smiled.

"I liked that lemonade," she said.

What had she said? What had he expected? Going home in a taxi afterward, he pulled her over until her head rested against his chest.

"Darling, do you ever think about your mother?"

"Yes, sometimes," she answered vaguely.

"I don't want you to forget her. Have you got a picture of her?"

"Yes, I think so. Anyhow, Aunt Marion has. Why don't you want me to forget her?"

"She loved you very much."

"I loved her too."

They were silent for a moment.

"Daddy, I want to come and live with you," she said suddenly.

His heart leaped; he had wanted it to come like this.

"Aren't you perfectly happy?"

"Yes, but I love you better than anybody. And you love me better than anybody, don't you, now that mummy's dead?"

"Of course I do. But you won't always like me best, honey. You'll grow up and meet somebody your own age and go marry him and forget you ever had a daddy."

"Yes, that's true," she agreed tranquilly.

He didn't go in. He was coming back at nine o'clock and he wanted to keep himself fresh and new for the thing he must say then.

"When you're safe inside, just show yourself in that window."

"All right. Good-bye, dads, dads, dads, dads."

He waited in the dark street until she appeared, all warm and glowing, in the window above and kissed her fingers out into the night.

III

They were waiting. Marion sat behind the coffee service in a dignified black dinner dress that just faintly suggested mourning. Lincoln was walking up and down with the animation of one who had already been talking. They were as anxious as he was to get into the question. He opened it almost immediately: "I suppose you know what I want to see you about — why I really came to Paris."

Marion played with the black stars on her necklace and frowned.

"I'm awfully anxious to have a home," he continued. "And I'm awfully anxious to have Honoria in it. I appreciate your taking in Honoria for her mother's sake, but things have changed now" — he hesitated and then continued more forcibly — "changed radically with me, and I want to ask you to reconsider the matter. It would be silly for me to deny that about three years ago I was acting badly —— "

Marion looked up at him with hard eyes.

" —— but all that's over. As I told you, I haven't had more than a drink a day for over a year, and I take that drink deliberately, so that the idea of alcohol won't get too big in my imagination. You see the idea?"

"No," said Marion succinctly.

"It's a sort of stunt I set myself. It keeps the matter in proportion."

"I get you," said Lincoln. "You don't want to admit it's got any attraction for you."

"Something like that. Sometimes I forget and don't take it. But I try to take it. Anyhow, I couldn't afford to drink in my position. The people I represent are more than satisfied with what I've done, and I'm bringing my sister over from Burlington to keep house for me, and I want awfully to have Honoria too. You know that even when her mother and I weren't getting along well we never let anything that happened touch Honoria. I know she's fond of me and I know I'm able to take care of her and — well, there you are. How do you feel about it?"

He knew that now he would have to take a beating. It would last an hour or two hours, and it would be difficult, but if he modulated his inevitable resentment to the chastened attitude of the reformed sinner, he might win his point in the end.

Keep your temper, he told himself. You don't want to be justified. You want Honoria.

Lincoln spoke first: "We've been talking it over ever since we got your letter last month. We're happy to have Honoria here. She's a dear little thing, and we're glad to be able to help her, but of course that isn't the question —— "

Marion interrupted suddenly. "How long are you going to stay sober, Charlie?" she asked.

"Permanently, I hope."

"How can anybody count on that?"

"You know I never did drink heavily until I gave up business and came over here with nothing to do. Then Helen and I began to run around with —— "

"Please leave Helen out of it. I can't bear to hear you talk about her like that."

He stared at her grimly; he had never been certain how fond of each other the sisters were in life.

"My drinking only lasted about a year and a half — from the time we came over until I — collapsed."

"It was time enough."

"It was time enough," he agreed.

"My duty is entirely to Helen," she said. "I try to think what she would have wanted me to do. Frankly, from the night you did that terrible thing you haven't really existed for me. I can't help that. She was my sister."

"Yes."

"When she was dying she asked me to look out for Honoria. If you hadn't been in a sanitarium then, it might have helped matters."

He had no answer.

"I'll never in my life be able to forget the morning when Helen knocked at my door, soaked to the skin and shivering, and said you'd locked her out."

Charlie gripped the sides of the chair. This was more difficult than he expected; he wanted to launch out into a long expostulation and explanation, but he only said, "The night I locked her out —— " and she interrupted, "I don't feel up to going over that again."

After a moment's silence Lincoln said, "We're getting off the subject. You want Marion to set aside her legal guardianship and give you Honoria. I think the main point for her is whether she has confidence in you or not."

"I don't blame Marion," Charlie said slowly, "but I think she can have entire confidence in me. I had a good record up to three years ago. Of course, it's within human possibilities I might go wrong any time. But if we wait much longer I'll lose Honoria's childhood and my chance for a home." He shook his head, "I'll simply lose her, don't you see?"

"Yes, I see," said Lincoln.

"Why didn't you think of all this before?" Marion asked.

"I suppose I did, from time to time, but Helen and I were getting along badly. When I consented to the guardianship, I was flat on my back in a sanitarium and the market had cleaned me out. I knew I'd acted badly, and I thought if it would bring any peace to Helen, I'd agree to anything. But now it's different. I'm functioning, I'm behaving damn well, so far as——"

"Please don't swear at me," Marion said.

He looked at her, startled. With each remark the force of her dislike became more and more apparent. She had built up all her fear of life into one wall and faced it toward him. This trivial reproof was possibly the result of some trouble with the cook several hours before. Charlie became increasingly alarmed at leaving Honoria in this atmosphere of hostility against himself; sooner or later it would come out, in a word here, a shake of the head there, and some of that distrust would be irrevocably implanted in Honoria. But he pulled his temper down out of his face and shut it up inside him; he had won a point, for Lincoln realized the absurdity of Marion's remark and asked her lightly since when she had objected to the word "damn."

"Another thing," Charlie said, "I'm able to give her certain advantages now. I'm going to take a French governess to Prague with me. I've got a lease on a new apartment——"

He stopped, realizing that he was blundering. They couldn't be expected to accept with equanimity the fact that his income was again twice as large as their own.

"I suppose you can give her more luxuries than we can," said Marion. "When you were throwing away money we were living along watching every ten francs. . . . I suppose you'll start doing it again."

"Oh, no," he said. "I've learned. I worked hard for ten years, you know — until I got lucky in the market, like so many people. Terribly lucky. It didn't seem any use working any more, so I quit. It won't happen again."

There was a long silence. All of them felt their nerves straining, and for the first time in a year Charlie wanted a drink. He was sure now that Lincoln Peters wanted him to have his child.

Marion shuddered suddenly; part of her saw that Charlie's feet were planted on the earth now, and her own maternal feeling recognized the naturalness of his desire; but she had lived for a long time with a prejudice — a prejudice founded on a curious disbelief in her sister's happiness, and which, in the shock of one terrible night, had turned to hatred for him. It had all happened at a point in her life where the discouragement of ill health and adverse circumstances made it necessary for her to believe in tangible villainy and a tangible villain.

"I can't help what I think!" she cried out suddenly. "How much you were responsible for Helen's death, I don't know. It's something you'll have to square with your own conscience."

An electric current of agony surged through him; for a moment he was almost on his feet, an unuttered sound echoing in his throat. He hung on to himself for a moment, another moment.

"Hold on there," said Lincoln uncomfortably. "I never thought you were responsible for that."

"Helen died of heart trouble," Charlie said dully.

"Yes, heart trouble." Marion spoke as if the phrase had another mean-ing for her.

Then, in the flatness that followed her outburst, she saw him plainly and she knew he had somehow arrived at control over the situation. Glancing at her husband, she found no help from him, and as abruptly as if it were a matter of no importance, she threw up the sponge.

"Do what you like!" she cried, springing up from her chair. "She's your child. I'm not the person to stand in your way. I think if it were my child I'd rather see her —— " She managed to check herself. "You two decide it. I can't stand this. I'm sick. I'm going to bed."

She hurried from the room; after a moment Lincoln said, "This has been a hard day for her. You know how strongly she feels —— " His voice was almost apologetic: "When a woman gets an idea in her head."

"Of course."

"It's going to be all right. I think she sees now that you — can provide for the child, and so we can't very well stand in your way or Honoria's way."

"Thank you, Lincoln."

"I'd better go along and see how she is."

"I'm going."

He was still trembling when he reached the street, but a walk down the Rue Bonaparte to the quais set him up, and as he crossed the Seine, fresh and new by the quai lamps, he felt exultant. But back in his room he couldn't sleep. The image of Helen haunted him. Helen whom he had loved so until they had senselessly begun to abuse each other's love, tear it into shreds. On that terrible February night that Marion remembered so vividly, a slow quarrel had gone on for hours. There was a scene at the Florida, and then he attempted to take her home, and then she kissed young Webb at a table; after that there was what she had hysterically said. When he arrived home alone he turned the key in the lock in wild anger. How could he know she would arrive an hour later alone, that there would be a snowstorm in which she wandered about in slippers, too confused to find a taxi? Then the aftermath, her escaping pneumonia by a miracle, and all the attendant horror. They were "reconciled," but that was the beginning of the end, and Marion, who had seen with her own eyes and who imagined it to be one of many scenes from her sister's martyrdom, never forgot.

Going over it again brought Helen nearer, and in the white, soft light that steals upon half sleep near morning he found himself talking to her again. She said that he was perfectly right about Honoria and that she wanted Honoria to be with him. She said she was glad he was being good and doing better. She said a lot of other things — very friendly things — but she was in a swing in a white dress, and swinging faster and faster all the time, so that at the end he could not hear clearly all that she said.

IV

He woke up feeling happy. The door of the world was open again. He made plans, vistas, futures for Honoria and himself, but suddenly he grew sad, remembering all the plans he and Helen had made. She had not planned to die. The present was the thing — work to do and someone to love. But not to love too much, for he knew the injury that a father can do to a daughter or a mother to a son by attaching them too closely: afterward, out in the world, the child would seek in the marriage partner the same blind tenderness and, failing probably to find it, turn against love and life.

It was another bright, crisp day. He called Lincoln Peters at the bank where he worked and asked if he could count on taking Honoria when he left for Prague. Lincoln agreed that there was no reason for delay. One thing — the legal guardianship. Marion wanted to retain that a while longer. She was upset by the whole matter, and it would oil things if she felt that the situation was still in her control for another year. Charlie agreed, wanting only the tangible, visible child.

Then the question of a governess. Charlie sat in a gloomy agency and talked to a cross Bernaise and to a buxom Breton peasant, neither of whom he could have endured. There were others whom he would see tomorrow.

He lunched with Lincoln Peters at Griffons, trying to keep down his exultation.

"There's nothing quite like your own child," Lincoln said. "But you understand how Marion feels too."

"She's forgotten how hard I worked for seven years there," Charlie said. "She just remembers one night."

"There's another thing." Lincoln hesitated. "While you and Helen were tearing around Europe throwing money away, we were just getting along. I didn't touch any of the prosperity because I never got ahead enough to carry anything but my insurance. I think Marion felt there was some kind of injustice in it — you not even working toward the end, and getting richer and richer."

"It went just as quick as it came," said Charlie.

"Yes, a lot of it stayed in the hands of *chasseurs* and saxophone players and maîtres d'hôtel — well, the big party's over now. I just said that to explain Marion's feeling about those crazy years. If you drop in about six o'clock tonight before Marion's too tired, we'll settle the details on the spot."

Back at his hotel, Charlie found a *pneumatique* that had been redirected from the Ritz bar where Charlie had left his address for the purpose of finding a certain man.

DEAR CHARLIE: You were so strange when we saw you the other day that I wondered if I did something to offend you. If so, I'm not conscious of it. In fact, I have thought about you too much for the last year, and it's always been in the back of my mind that I might see you if I came over here. We *did* have such good times that crazy spring, like the night you and I stole the butcher's tricycle, and the time we tried to call on the president and you had the old derby rim and the wire cane. Everybody seems so old lately, but I don't feel old a bit. Couldn't we get together some time today for old time's sake? I've got a vile hangover for the moment, but will be feeling better this afternoon and will look for you about five in the sweet-shop at the Ritz.

> Always devotedly,
> LORRAINE

His first feeling was one of awe that he had actually, in his mature years, stolen a tricycle and pedaled Lorraine all over the Étoile between the small hours and dawn. In retrospect it was a nightmare. Locking out Helen didn't fit in with any other act of his life, but the tricycle incident did — it was one of many. How many weeks or months of dissipation to arrive at that condition of utter irresponsibility?

He tried to picture how Lorraine had appeared to him then — very attractive; Helen was unhappy about it, though she said nothing. Yesterday, in the restaurant, Lorraine had seemed trite, blurred, worn away. He emphatically did not want to see her, and he was glad Alix had not given away his hotel address. It was a relief to think, instead, of Honoria, to think of Sundays spent with her and of saying good morning to her and of knowing she was there in his house at night, drawing her breath in the darkness.

At five he took a taxi and bought presents for all the Peters — a piquant cloth doll, a box of Roman soldiers, flowers for Marion, big linen handkerchiefs for Lincoln.

He saw, when he arrived in the apartment, that Marion had accepted the inevitable. She greeted him now as though he were a recalcitrant member of the family, rather than a menacing outsider. Honoria had been told she was going; Charlie was glad to see that her tact made her conceal her excessive happiness. Only on his lap did she whisper her delight and the question "When?" before she slipped away with the other children.

He and Marion were alone for a minute in the room, and on an impulse he spoke out boldly: "Family quarrels are bitter things. They don't go according to any rules. They're not like aches or wounds; they're more like splits in the skin that won't heal because there's not enough material. I wish you and I could be on better terms."

"Some things are hard to forget," she answered. "It's a question of confidence." There was no answer to this and presently she asked, "When do you propose to take her?"

"As soon as I can get a governess. I hoped the day after tomorrow."

"That's impossible. I've got to get her things in shape. Not before Saturday."

He yielded. Coming back into the room, Lincoln offered him a drink.

"I'll take my daily whisky," he said.

It was warm here, it was a home, people together by a fire. The children felt very safe and important; the mother and father were serious, watchful. They had things to do for the children more important than his visit here. A spoonful of medicine was, after all, more important than the strained relations between Marion and himself. They were not dull people, but they were very much in the grip of life and circumstances. He wondered if he couldn't do something to get Lincoln out of his rut at the bank.

A long peal at the door-bell; the *bonne de toute faire* passed through and went down the corridor. The door opened upon another long ring, and then voices, and the three in the salon looked up expectantly; Richard moved to bring the corridor within his range of vision, and Marion rose. Then the maid came back along the corridor, closely followed by the voices, which developed under the light into Duncan Schaeffer and Lorraine Quarrles.

They were gay, they were hilarious, they were roaring with laughter. For a moment Charlie was astounded; unable to understand how they ferreted out the Peters' address.

"Ah-h-h!" Duncan wagged his finger roguishly at Charlie. "Ah-h-h!"

They both slid down another cascade of laughter. Anxious and at a loss, Charlie shook hands with them quickly and presented them to Lincoln and Marion. Marion nodded, scarcely speaking. She had drawn back a step toward the fire; her little girl stood beside her, and Marion put an arm about her shoulder.

With growing annoyance at the intrusion, Charlie waited for them to explain themselves. After some concentration Duncan said, "We came to invite you out to dinner. Lorraine and I insist that all this shishi, cagy business 'bout your address got to stop."

Charlie came closer to them, as if to force them backward down the corridor.

"Sorry, but I can't. Tell me where you'll be and I'll phone you in half an hour."

This made no impression. Lorraine sat down suddenly on the side of a chair, and focusing her eyes on Richard, cried, "Oh, what a nice little boy! Come here, little boy." Richard glanced at his mother, but did not move. With a perceptible shrug of her shoulders, Lorraine turned back to Charlie, "Come and dine. Sure your cousins won' mine. See you so sel'om. Or solemn."

"I can't," said Charlie sharply. "You two have dinner and I'll phone you."

Her voice became suddenly unpleasant. "All right, we'll go. But I remember once when you hammered on my door at four A.M. I was enough of a good sport to give you a drink. Come on, Dunc."

Still in slow motion, with blurred, angry faces, with uncertain feet, they retired along the corridor.

"Good night," Charlie said.

"Good night!" responded Lorraine emphatically.

When he went back into the salon Marion had not moved, only now her son was standing in the circle of her other arm. Lincoln was still swinging Honoria back and forth like a pendulum from side to side.

"What an outrage!" Charlie broke out. "What an absolute outrage!"

Neither of them answered. Charlie dropped into an armchair, picked up his drink, set it down again and said, "People I haven't seen for two years having the colossal nerve —— "

He broke off. Marion had made the sound "Oh!" in one swift, furious breath, turned her body from him with a jerk and left the room.

Lincoln set down Honoria carefully.

"You children go in and start your soup," he said, and when they obeyed, he said to Charlie, "Marion's not well and she can't stand shocks. That kind of people make her really physically sick."

"I didn't tell them to come here. They wormed your name out of somebody. They deliberately —— "

"Well, it's too bad. It doesn't help matters. Excuse me a minute."

Left alone, Charlie sat tense in his chair. In the next room he could hear the children eating, talking in monosyllables, already oblivious to the scene between their elders. He heard a murmur of conversation from a farther room and then the ticking bell of a telephone receiver picked up, and in a panic he moved to the other side of the room and out of earshot.

In a minute Lincoln came back. "Look here, Charlie. I think we'd better call off dinner for tonight. Marion's in bad shape."

"Is she angry with me?"

"Sort of," he said, almost roughly. "She's not strong and —— "

"You mean she's changed her mind about Honoria?"

"She's pretty bitter right now. I don't know. You phone me at the bank tomorrow."

"I wish you'd explain to her I never dreamed these people would come here. I'm just as sore as you are."

"I couldn't explain anything to her now."

Charlie got up. He took his coat and hat and started down the corridor. Then he opened the door of the dining room and said in a strange voice, "Good night, children."

Honoria rose and ran around the table to hug him.

"Good night, sweetheart," he said vaguely, and then trying to make his voice more tender, trying to conciliate something, "Good night, dear children."

V

Charlie went directly to the Ritz bar with the furious idea of finding Lorraine and Duncan, but they were not there, and he realized that in any case there was nothing he could do. He had not touched his drink at the Peters', and now he ordered a whisky and soda. Paul came over to say hello.

"It's a great change," he said sadly. "We do about half the business we did. So many fellows I hear about back in the States lost everything, maybe not in the first crash, but then in the second. Your friend George Hardt lost every cent, I hear. Are you back in the States?"

"No, I'm in business in Prague."

"I heard that you lost a lot in the crash."

"I did," and he added grimly, "but I lost everything I wanted in the boom."

"Selling short."

"Something like that."

Again the memory of those days swept over him like a nightmare — the people they had met traveling; then people who couldn't add a row of figures or speak a coherent sentence. The little man Helen had consented to dance with at the ship's party, who had insulted her ten feet from the table; the women and girls carried screaming with drink or drugs out of public places ——

—— The men who locked their wives out in the snow, because the snow of 'twenty-nine wasn't real snow. If you didn't want it to be snow, you just paid some money.

He went to the phone and called the Peters' apartment; Lincoln answered.

"I called up because this thing is on my mind. Has Marion said anything definite?"

"Marion's sick," Lincoln answered shortly. "I know this thing isn't altogether your fault, but I can't have her go to pieces about it. I'm afraid we'll have to let it slide for six months; I can't take the chance of working her up to this state again."

"I see."

"I'm sorry, Charlie."

He went back to his table. His whisky glass was empty, but he shook his head when Alix looked at it questioningly. There wasn't much he could do now except send Honoria some things; he would send her a lot of things tomorrow. He thought rather angrily that this was just money —he had given so many people money. . . .

"No, no more," he said to another waiter. "What do I owe you?"

He would come back some day; they couldn't make him pay forever. But he wanted his child, and nothing was much good now, beside that fact. He wasn't young any more, with a lot of nice thoughts and dreams to have by himself. He was absolutely sure Helen wouldn't have wanted him to be so alone.

WILBUR DANIEL STEELE

*That a short story can be a poem is revealed in "How Beautiful with
Shoes." Mad as the ravings of the lunatic are, they open "magic casements" for a girl who has seen little of loveliness in her life and sees
even less in the life that is awaiting her.*

*In 1886 Wilbur Daniel Steele was born in Greensboro, North Caro-
lina. He is a graduate of the University of Denver and has studied art
in Paris, New York and Boston. He is an author whose work should
be much better known today. Unlike many famous writers who appeared
in the earlier volumes of* The Best American Short Stories, *the high
quality of his work has not fluctuated.*

How Beautiful with Shoes

BY THE TIME the milking was finished, the sow, which had farrowed the
past week, was making such a row that the girl spilled a pint of warm
milk down the trough lead to quiet the animal before taking the pail to
the well house. Then in the quiet she heard a sound of hoofs on the
bridge, where the road crossed the creek a hundred yards below the
house, and she set the pail down on the ground beside her bare, barn-
soiled feet. She picked it up again. She set it down. It was as if she
calculated its weight.

That was what she was doing, as a matter of fact, setting off against its
pull toward the well house the pull of that wagon team in the road, with
little more of personal will or wish in the matter than has a wooden
weathervane between two currents in the wind. And as with the vane, so
with the wooden girl — the added behest of a whiplash cracking in the
distance was enough; leaving the pail at the barn door, she set off in a
deliberate, docile beeline through the cowyard, over the fence, and down
in a diagonal across the farm's one tilled field toward the willow brake

that walled the road at the dip. And once under way, though her mother came to the kitchen door and called in her high, flat voice, "Amarantha, where you goin', Amarantha?" the girl went on apparently unmoved, as though she had been as deaf as the woman in the doorway; indeed, if there was emotion in her it was the purely sensuous one of feeling the clods of the furrows breaking softly between her toes. It was springtime in the mountains.

"Amarantha, why don't you answer me, Amarantha?"

For moments after the girl had disappeared beyond the willows the widow continued to call, unaware through long habit of how absurd it sounded, the name which that strange man her husband had put upon their daughter in one of his moods. Mrs. Doggett had been deaf so long she did not realize that nobody else ever thought of it for the broad-fleshed, slow-minded girl, but called her Mary, or even more simply, Mare.

Ruby Herter had stopped his team this side of the bridge, the mules' heads turned into the lane to his father's farm beyond the road. A big-barreled, heavy-limbed fellow with a square, sallow, not unhandsome face, he took out youth in ponderous gestures of masterfulness; it was like him to have cracked his whip above his animals' ears the moment before he pulled them to a halt. When he saw the girl getting over the fence under the willows he tongued the wad of tobacco out of his mouth into his palm, threw it away beyond the road, and drew a sleeve of his jumper across his lips.

"Don't run yourself out o' breath, Mare; I got all night."

"I was comin'." It sounded sullen only because it was matter of fact.

"Well, keep a-comin' and give us a smack." Hunched on the wagon seat, he remained motionless for some time after she had arrived at the hub, and when he stirred it was but to cut a fresh bit of tobacco, as if already he had forgotten why he threw the old one away. Having satisfied his humor, he unbent, climbed down, kissed her passive mouth, and hugged her up to him, roughly and loosely, his hands careless of contours. It was not out of the way; they were used to handling animals both of them; and it was spring. A slow warmth pervaded the girl, formless, nameless, almost impersonal.

Her betrothed pulled her head back by the braid of her yellow hair. He studied her face, his brows gathered and his chin out.

"Listen, Mare, you wouldn't leave nobody else hug and kiss you, dang you!"

She shook her head, without vehemence or anxiety.

"Who's that?" She harkened up the road. "Pull your team out," she added, as a Ford came in sight around the bend above the house, driven at speed. "Geddap!" she said to the mules herself.

But the car came to a halt near them, and one of the five men crowded in it called, "Come on, Ruby, climb in. They's a loony loose out o' Dayville Asylum, and they got him trailed over somewheres on Split Ridge, and Judge North phoned up to Slosson's store for ever'body come help circle him — come on, hop the runnin'-board!"

Ruby hesitated, an eye on his team.

"Scared, Ruby?" The driver raced his engine. "They say this boy's a killer."

"Mare, take the team in and tell Pa." The car was already moving when Ruby jumped it. A moment after it had sounded on the bridge it was out of sight.

"Amarantha, Amarantha, why don't you come, Amarantha?"

Returning from her errand, fifteen minutes later, Mare heard the plaint lifted in the twilight. The sun had dipped behind the back ridge, though the sky was still bright with day, the dusk began to smoke up out of the plowed field like a ground fog. The girl had returned through it, got the milk, and started toward the well house before the widow saw her.

"Daughter, seems to me you might!" she expostulated without change of key. "Here's some young man friend o' yourn stopped to say howdy, and I been rackin' my lungs out after you. . . . Put that milk in the cool and come!"

Some young man friend? But there was no good to be got from puzzling. Mare poured the milk in the pan in the dark of the low house over the well, and as she came out, stooping, she saw a figure waiting for her, black in silhouette against the yellowing sky.

"Who are you?" she asked, a native timidity making her sound sulky.

"'Amarantha!'" the fellow mused. "That's poetry." And she knew then that she did not know him.

She walked past, her arms straight down and her eyes front. Strangers always affected her with a kind of muscular terror simply by being strangers. So she gained the kitchen steps, aware by his tread that he followed. There, taking courage at the sight of her mother in the doorway, she turned on him, her eyes down at the level of his knees.

"Who are you and what d' y' want?"

He still mused. "Amarantha! Amarantha in Carolina! That makes me happy!"

Mare hazarded one upward look. She saw that he had red hair, brown eyes, and hollows under his cheekbones, and though the green sweater he wore on top of a gray overall was plainly not meant for him, sizes too large as far as girth went, yet he was built so long of limb that his wrists came inches out of the sleeves and made his big hands look even bigger.

Mrs. Doggett complained. "Why don't you introduce us, daughter?"

The girl opened her mouth and closed it again. Her mother, unaware that no sound had come out of it, smiled and nodded, evidently taking to the tall, homely fellow and tickled by the way he could not seem to get his eyes off her daughter. But the daughter saw none of it, all her attention centered upon the stranger's hands.

Restless, hard-fleshed, and chap-bitten, they were like a countryman's hands; but the fingers were longer than the ordinary, and slightly spatulate at their ends, and these ends were slowly and continuously at play among themselves.

The girl could not have explained how it came to her to be frightened and at the same time to be calm, for she was inept with words. It was simply that in an animal way she knew animals, knew them in health and ailing, and when they were ailing she knew by instinct, as her father had known, how to move so as not to fret them.

Her mother had gone in to light up; from beside the lampshelf she called back, "If he's aimin' to stay to supper you should've told me, Amarantha, though I guess there's plenty of the side-meat to go 'round, if you'll bring me in a few more turnips and potatoes, though it is late."

At the words the man's cheeks moved in and out. "I'm very hungry," he said.

Mare nodded deliberately. Deliberately, as if her mother could hear her, she said over her shoulder, "I'll go get the potatoes and turnips, Ma." While she spoke she was moving, slowly, softly, at first, toward the right of the yard, where the fence gave over into the field. Unluckily her mother spied her through the window.

"Amarantha, where *are* you goin'?"

"I'm goin' to get the potatoes and turnips." She neither raised her voice nor glanced back, but lengthened her stride. He won't hurt her, she said to herself. He won't hurt her; it's me, not her, she kept repeating, while she got over the fence and down into the shadow that lay more than ever like a fog on the field.

The desire to believe that it actually did hide her, the temptation to break from her rapid but orderly walk grew till she could no longer fight it. She saw the road willows only a dash ahead of her. She ran, her feet floundering among the furrows.

She neither heard nor saw him, but when she realized he was with her she knew he had been with her all the while. She stopped, and he stopped, and so they stood, with the dark open of the field all around. Glancing sidewise presently, she saw he was no longer looking at her with those strangely importunate brown eyes of his, but had raised them to the crest of the wooded ridge behind her.

By and by, "What does it make you think of?" he asked. And when she made no move to see, "Turn around and look!" he said, and though it was low and almost tender in its tone, she knew enough to turn.

A ray of the sunset hidden in the west struck through the tops of the topmost trees, far and small up there, a thin, bright hem.

"What does it make you think of, Amarantha? . . . Answer!"

"Fire," she made herself say.

"Or blood."

"Or blood, yeh. That's right, or blood." She had heard a Ford going up the road beyond the willows, and her attention was not on what she said.

The man soliloquized. "Fire and blood, both; spare one or the other, and where is beauty, the way the world is? It's an awful thing to have to carry, but Christ had it. Christ came with a sword. I love beauty, Amarantha. . . . I say, I love beauty!"

"Yeh, that's right, I hear." What she heard was the car stopping at the house.

"Not prettiness. Prettiness'll have to go with ugliness, because it's only ugliness trigged up. But beauty!" Now again he was looking at her. "Do you know how beautiful you are, Amarantha, Amarantha sweet and fair?" Of a sudden, reaching behind her, he began to unravel the meshes of her hair braid, the long, flat-tipped fingers at once impatient and infinitely gentle. "Braid no more that shining hair!"

Flat-faced Mare Doggett tried to see around those glowing eyes so near to hers, but wise in her instinct, did not try too hard. "Yeh," she temporized. "I mean, no, I mean."

"Amarantha, I've come a long, long way for you. Will you come away with me now?"

"Yeh — that is — in a minute I will, mister — yeh . . ."

"Because you want to, Amarantha? Because you love me as I love you? Answer!"

"Yeh — sure — uh . . . *Ruby!*"

The man tried to run, but there were six against him, coming up out of the dark that lay in the plowed ground. Mare stood where she was while they knocked him down and got a rope around him; after that she walked back toward the house with Ruby and Older Haskins, her father's cousin.

Ruby wiped his brow and felt of his muscles. "Gees, you're lucky we come, Mare. We're no more'n past the town, when they come hollerin' he'd broke over this way."

When they came to the fence the girl sat on the rail for a moment and rebraided her hair before she went into the house, where they were making her mother smell ammonia.

Lots of cars were coming. Judge North was coming, somebody said. When Mare heard this she went into her bedroom off the kitchen and got her shoes and put them on. They were brand-new two-dollar shoes with cloth tops, and she had only begun to break them in last Sunday; she wished afterwards she had put her stockings on too, for they would have eased the seams. Or else that she had put on the old button pair, even though the soles were worn through.

Judge North arrived. He thought first of taking the loony straight through to Dayville that night, but then decided to keep him in the lockup at the courthouse till morning and make the drive by day. Older Haskins stayed in, gentling Mrs. Doggett, while Ruby went out to help get the man into the Judge's sedan. Now that she had them on, Mare didn't like to take the shoes off till Older went; it might make him feel small, she thought.

Older Haskins had a lot of facts about the loony.

"His name's Humble Jewett," he told them. "They belong back in Breed County, all them Jewetts, and I don't reckon there's none of 'em that's not a mite unbalanced. He went to college though, worked his way, and he taught somethin' 'rother in some academy-school a spell, till he went off his head all of a sudden and took after folks with an axe. I remember it in the paper at the time. They give out one while how the Principal wasn't goin' to live, and there was others — there was a girl he tried to strangle. That was four-five year back."

Ruby came in guffawing. "Know the only thing they can get 'im to

say, Mare? Only God thing he'll say is 'Amarantha, she's goin' with me.'
. . . Mare!"

"Yeh, I know."

The cover of the kettle the girl was handling slid off the stove with a
clatter. A sudden sick wave passed over her. She went out to the back,
out into the air. It was not till now she knew how frightened she had
been.

Ruby went home, but Older Haskins stayed to supper with them, and
helped Mare do the dishes afterward; it was nearly nine when he left.
The mother was already in bed, and Mare was about to sit down to get
those shoes off her wretched feet at last, when she heard the cow carrying
on up at the barn, lowing and kicking, and next minute the sow was in it
with a horning note. It might be a fox passing by to get at the henhouse,
or a weasel. Mare forgot her feet, took a broom handle they used in
boiling clothes, opened the back door, and stepped out. Blinking the
lamplight from her eyes, she peered up toward the outbuildings, and saw
the gable end of the barn standing like a red arrow in the dark, and the
top of a butternut tree beyond it drawn in skeleton traceries, and just
then a cock crowed.

She went to the right corner of the house and saw where the light
came from, ruddy above the woods down the valley. Returning into the
house, she bent close to her mother's ear and shouted, "Somethin's a-fire
down to the town, looks like," then went out again and up to the barn.
"Soh! Soh!" she called in to the animals. She climbed up and stood on
the top rail of the cow-pen fence, only to find she could not locate the
flame even there.

Ten rods behind the buildings a mass of rock mounted higher than
their ridgepoles, a chopped off buttress of the back ridge, covered with
oak scrub and wild grapes and blackberries, whose thorny ropes the girl
beat away from her skirt with the broom handle as she scrambled up in
the wine-colored dark. Once at the top, and the brush held aside, she
could see the tongue-tip of the conflagration half a mile away at the
town. And she knew by the bearing of the two church steeples that it
was the building where the lockup was that was burning.

There is a horror in knowing animals trapped in a fire, no matter what
the animals.

"Oh, my God!" Mare said.

A car went down the road. Then there was a horse galloping. That
would be Older Haskins probably. People were out at Ruby's father's

farm; she could hear their voices raised. There must have been another car up from the other way, for lights wheeled and shouts were exchanged in the neighborhood of the bridge. Next thing she knew, Ruby was at the house below, looking for her probably.

He was telling her mother, Mrs. Doggett was not used to him, so he had to shout even louder than Mare had to.

"What y' reckon he done, the hellion! he broke the door and killed Lew Fyke and set the courthouse afire! . . . Where's Mare?"

Her mother would not know. Mare called. "Here, up the rock here."

She had better go down. Ruby would likely break his bones if he tried to climb the rock in the dark, not knowing the way. But the sight of the fire fascinated her simple spirit, the fearful element, more fearful than ever now, with the news. "Yes, I'm comin'," she called sulkily, hearing feet in the brush. "You wait; I'm comin'."

When she turned and saw it was Humble Jewett, right behind her among the branches, she opened her mouth to screech. She was not quick enough. Before a sound came out he got one hand over her face and the other around her body.

Mare had always thought she was strong, and the loony looked gangling, yet she was so easy for him that he need not hurt her. He made no haste and little noise as he carried her deeper into the undergrowth. Where the hill began to mount it was harder though. Presently he set her on her feet. He let the hand that had been over her mouth slip down to her throat, where the broad-tipped fingers wound, tender as yearning, weightless as caress.

"I was afraid you'd scream before you knew who 'twas, Amarantha. But I didn't want to hurt your lips, dear heart, your lovely, quiet lips."

It was so dark under the trees she could hardly see him, but she felt his breath on her mouth, near to. But then, instead of kissing her, he said, "No! No!" took from her throat for an instant the hand that had held her mouth, kissed its palm, and put it back softly against her skin.

"Now, my love, let's go before they come."

She stood stock-still. Her mother's voice was to be heard in the distance, strident and meaningless. More cars were on the road. Nearer, around the rock, there were sounds of tramping and thrashing. Ruby fussed and cursed. He shouted, "Mare, dang you, where are you, Mare?" his voice harsh with uneasy anger. Now, if she aimed to do anything, was the time to do it. But there was neither breath nor power in her windpipe. It was as if those yearning fingers had paralyzed the muscles.

"Come!" The arm he put around her shivered against her shoulder blades. It was anger. "I hate killing. It's a dirty, ugly thing. It makes me sick." He gagged, judging by the sound. But then he ground his teeth. "Come away, my love!"

She found herself moving. Once when she broke a branch underfoot with an instinctive awkwardness he chided her. "Quiet, my heart, else they'll hear!" She made herself heavy. He thought she grew tired and bore more of her weight till he was breathing hard.

Men came up the hill. There must have been a dozen spread out, by the angle of their voices as they kept touch. Always Humble Jewett kept caressing Mare's throat with one hand; all she could do was hang back.

"You're tired and you're frightened," he said at last. "Get down here."

There were twigs in the dark, the overhang of a thicket of some sort. He thrust her in under this, and lay beside her on the bed of groundpine. The hand that was not in love with her throat reached across her; she felt the weight of its forearm on her shoulder and its fingers among the strands of her hair, eagerly, but tenderly, busy. Not once did he stop speaking, no louder than breathing, his lips to her ear.

"*Amarantha sweet and fair — Ah, braid no more that shining hair . . .*"

Mare had never heard of Lovelace, the poet; she thought the loony was just going on, hardly listened, got little sense. But the cadence of it added to the lethargy of all her flesh.

"*Like a dew of golden thread — Most excellently ravelled . . .*"

Voices loudened; feet came tramping; a pair went past not two rods away.

"*. . . Do not then wind up the light — In ribbands, and o'ercloud in night . . .*"

The search went on up the woods, men shouting to one another and beating the brush.

"*. . . But shake your head and scatter day.* I've never loved, Amarantha. They've tried me with prettiness, but prettiness is too cheap, yes, it's too cheap."

Mare was cold, and the coldness made her lazy. All she knew was that he talked on.

"But dogwood blowing in the spring isn't cheap. The earth of a field isn't cheap. Lots of times I've lain down and kissed the earth of a field, Amarantha. That's beauty, and a kiss for beauty." His breath moved up her cheek. He trembled violently. "No, no, not yet!" He got to his knees and pulled her by an arm. "We can go now."

They went back down the slope, but at an angle, so that when they came to the level they passed two hundred yards to the north of the house, and crossed the road there. More and more her walking was like sleepwalking, the feet numb in their shoes. Even where he had to let go of her, crossing the creek on stones, she stepped where he stepped with an obtuse docility. The voices of the searchers on the back ridge were small in distance when they began to climb the fence of Coward Hill, on the opposite side of the valley.

There is an old farm on top of Coward Hill, big hayfields as flat as tables. It had been half-past nine when Mare stood on the rock above the barn; it was toward midnight when Humble Jewett put aside the last branches of the woods and let her out on the height, and a half a moon had risen. And a wind blew there, tossing the withered tops of last year's grasses, and mists ran with the wind, and ragged shadows with the mists, and mares'-tails of clear moonlight among the shadows, so that now the boles of birches on the forest's edge beyond the fences were but opal blurs and now cut alabaster. It struck so cold against the girl's cold flesh, this wind, that another wind of shivers blew through her, and she put her hands over her face and eyes. But the madman stood with his eyes open and his mouth open, drinking the moonlight and the wet wind.

His voice, when he spoke at last, was thick in his throat.

"Get down on your knees." He got down on his and pulled her after. "And pray!"

Once in England a poet sang four lines. Four hundred years have forgotten his name, but they have remembered his lines. The daft man knelt upright, his face raised to the wild scud, his long wrists hanging to the dead grass. He began simply:

> O western wind, when wilt thou blow
> That the small rain down can rain?

The Adam's apple was big in his bent throat. As simply he finished.

> Christ, that my love were in my arms
> And I in my bed again!

Mare got up and ran. She ran without aim or feeling in the power of the wind. She told herself again that the mists would hide her from him, as she had done at dusk. And again, seeing that he ran at her shoulder, she knew he had been there all the while, making a race of it, flailing the air with his long arms for joy of play in the cloud of spring, throwing his knees high, leaping the moon-blue waves of the brown grass, shaking his bright hair; and her own hair was a weight behind her, lying level on the wind. Once a shape went bounding ahead of them for instants; she did not realize it was a fox till it was gone.

She never thought of stopping; she never thought of anything, except once, Oh, my God, I wish I had my shoes off! And what would have been the good in stopping or in turning another way, when it was only play? The man's ecstasy magnified his strength. When a snake fence came at them he took the top rail in flight, like a college hurdler, and seeing the girl hesitate and half turn as if to flee, he would have releaped it without touching a hand. But then she got a loom of buildings, climbed over quickly, before he should jump, and ran along the lane that ran with the fence.

Mare had never been up there, but she knew that the farm and the house belonged to a man named Wyker, a kind of cousin of Ruby Herter's, a violent, bearded old fellow who lived by himself. She could not believe her luck. When she had run half the distance and Jewett had not grabbed her, doubt grabbed her instead. "Oh, my God, go careful!" she told herself. "Go slow!" she implored herself, and stopped running, to walk.

Here was a misgiving the deeper in that it touched her special knowledge. She had never known an animal so far gone that its instincts failed it; a starving rat will scent the trap sooner than a fed one. Yet, after one glance at the house they approached, Jewett paid it no further attention, but walked with his eyes to the right, where the cloud had blown away, and wooded ridges, like black waves rimed with silver, ran down away toward the Valley of Virginia.

"I've never lived!" In his single cry there were two things, beatitude and pain.

Between the bigness of the falling world and his eyes the flag of her hair blew. He reached out and let it whip between his fingers. Mare was afraid it would break the spell then, and he would stop looking away and look at the house again. So she did something incredible; she spoke.

"It's a pretty — I mean — a beautiful view down that-a-way."

"God Almighty beautiful, to take your breath away. I knew I'd never loved, Beloved — " He caught a foot under the long end of one of the boards that covered the well and went down heavily on his hands and knees. It seemed to make no difference. "But I never knew I'd never lived," he finished in the same tone of strong rapture, quadruped in the grass, while Mare ran for the door and grabbed the latch.

When the latch would not give, she lost what little sense she had. She pounded with her fists. She cried with all her might: "Oh — hey — in there — hey — in there!" Then Jewett came and took her gently between his hands and drew her away, and then, though she was free, she stood in something like an awful embarrassment while he tried shouting.

'Hey! Friend! whoever you are, wake up and let my love and me come in!"

"No!" wailed the girl.

He grew peremptory. "Hey, wake up!" He tried the latch. He passed to full fury in a wink's time; he cursed, he kicked, he beat the door till Mare thought he would break his hands. Withdrawing, he ran at it with his shoulder; it burst at the latch, went slamming in, and left a black emptiness. His anger dissolved in a big laugh. Turning in time to catch her by a wrist, he cried joyously, "Come, my Sweet One!"

"No! No! Please — aw — listen. There ain't nobody there. He ain't to home. It wouldn't be right to go in anybody's house if they wasn't to home, you know that."

His laugh was blither than ever. He caught her high in his arms.

"I'd do the same by his love and him if 'twas my house, I would." At the threshold he paused and thought. "That is, if she was the true love of his heart forever."

The room was the parlor. Moonlight slanted in at the door, and another shaft came through a window and fell across a sofa, its covering dilapidated, showing its wadding in places. The air was sour, but both of them were farm-bred.

"Don't, Amarantha!" His words were pleading in her ear. "Don't be so frightened."

He set her down on the sofa. As his hands let go of her they were shaking.

"But look, I'm frightened too." He knelt on the floor before her, reached out his hands, withdrew them. "See, I'm afraid to touch you."

He mused, his eyes rounded. "Of all the ugly things there are, fear is the ugliest. And yet, see, it can be the very beautifulest. That's a strange queer thing."

The wind blew in and out of the room, bringing the thin, little bitter sweetness of new April at night. The moonlight that came across Mare's shoulders fell full upon his face, but hers it left dark, ringed by the aureole of her disordered hair.

"Why do you wear a halo, Love?" He thought about it. "Because you're an angel, is that why?" The swift, untempered logic of the mad led him to dismay. His hands came flying to hers, to make sure they were of earth; and he touched her breast, her shoulders, and her hair. Peace returned to his eyes as his fingers twined among the strands.

"*Thy hair is as a flock of goats that appear from Gilead . . .*" He spoke like a man dreaming. "*Thy temples are like a piece of pomegranate within thy locks.*"

Mare never knew that he could not see her for the moonlight.

"Do you remember, Love?"

She dared not shake her head under his hand. "Yeh, I reckon," she temporized.

"You remember how I sat at your feet, long ago, like this, and made up a song? And all the poets in all the world have never made one to touch it, have they, Love?"

"Ugh-ugh — never."

"*How beautiful are thy feet with shoes . . .* Remember?"

"Oh, my God, what's he sayin' now?" she wailed to herself.

"*How beautiful are thy feet with shoes, O prince's daughter! the joints of thy thighs are like jewels, the work of the hands of a cunning workman.*

Thy navel is like a round goblet, which wanteth not liquor; thy belly is like an heap of wheat set about with lilies.

Thy two breasts are like two young roes that are twins."

Mare had not been to church since she was a little girl, when her mother's black dress wore out. "No, no!" she wailed under her breath. "You're awful to say such awful things." She might have shouted it; nothing could have shaken the man now, rapt in the immortal, passionate periods of Solomon's Song.

"*. . . now also thy breasts shall be as clusters of the vine, and the smell of thy nose like apples.*"

Hotness touched Mare's face for the first time. "Aw, no, don't talk so!"

"*And the roof of thy mouth like the best wine for my beloved . . . causing the lips of them that are asleep to speak.*"

He had ended. His expression changed. Ecstasy gave place to anger, love to hate. And Mare felt the change in the weight of the fingers in her hair.

"What do you mean, I mustn't say it like that?" But it was not to her his fury spoke, for he answered himself straightway. "Like poetry, Mr. Jewett; I won't have blasphemy around my school."

"Poetry. My God! If that isn't poetry — if that isn't music —" . . . "It's Bible, Jewett. What you're paid to teach here is *literature*."

"Doctor Ryeworth, you're the blasphemer and you're an ignorant man." . . . "And you're principal. And I won't have you going around reading sacred allegory like earthly love."

"Ryeworth, you're an old man, a dull man, a dirty man, and you'd be better dead."

Jewett's hands had slid down from Mare's head. "Then I went to put my fingers around his throat, so. But my stomach turned, and I didn't do it. I went to my room. I laughed all the way to my room. I sat in my room at my table and laughed. I laughed all afternoon and long after dark came. And then, about ten, somebody came and stood beside me in my room."

" 'Wherefore dost thou laugh, son?'

"Then I knew who He was, He was Christ.

" 'I was laughing about that dirty, ignorant, crazy old fool, Lord.'

" 'Wherefore dost thou laugh?'

"I didn't laugh any more. He didn't say any more. I kneeled down, bowed my head.

" 'Thy will be done! Where is he, Lord?'

" 'Over at the girls' dormitory, waiting for Blossom Sinckley.'

"Brassy Blossom, dirty Blossom . . ."

It had come so suddenly it was nearly too late. Mare tore at his hands with hers, tried with all her strength to pull her neck away.

"Filthy Blossom! and him an old filthy man, Blossom! and you'll find him in Hell when you reach there, Blossom. . . ."

It was more the nearness of his face than the hurt of his hands that gave her power of fright to choke out three words.

"I — ain't — Blossom!"

Light ran in crooked veins. Through the veins she saw his face bewildered. His hands loosened. One fell down and hung; the other he lifted and put over his eyes, took it away again and looked at her.

"Amarantha!" His remorse was fearful to see. "What have I done!" His hands returned to hover over the hurts, ravening with pity, grief and tenderness. Tears fell down his cheeks. And with that, dammed desire broke its dam.

"Amarantha, my love, my dove, my beautiful love — "

"And I ain't Amarantha neither, I'm Mary! Mary, that's my name!"

She had no notion what she had done. He was like a crystal crucible that a chemist watches, changing hue in a wink with one adeptly added drop; but hers was not the chemist's eye. All she knew was that she felt light and free of him; all she could see of his face as he stood away above the moonlight were the whites of his eyes.

"Mary!" he muttered. A slight paroxysm shook his frame. So in the transparent crucible desire changed its hue. He retreated farther, stood in the dark by some tall piece of furniture. And still she could see the whites of his eyes.

"Mary! Mary Adorable!" A wonder was in him. "Mother of God."

Mare held her breath. She eyed the door, but it was too far. And already he came back to go on his knees before her, his shoulders so bowed and his face so lifted that it must have cracked his neck, she thought; all she could see on the face was pain.

"Mary Mother, I'm sick to my death. I'm so tired."

She had seen a dog like that, one she had loosed from a trap after it had been there three days, its caught leg half gnawed free. Something about the eyes.

"Mary Mother, take me in your arms . . ."

Once again her muscles tightened. But he made no move.

". . . and give me sleep."

No, they were worse than the dog's eyes.

"Sleep, sleep! why won't they let me sleep? Haven't I done it all yet, Mother? Haven't I washed them yet of all their sins? I've drunk the cup that was given me; is there another? They've mocked me and reviled me, broken my brow with thorns and my hands with nails, and I've forgiven them, for they knew not what they did. Can't I go to sleep now, Mother?"

Mare could not have said why, but now she was more frightened than she had ever been. Her hands lay heavy on her knees, side by side, and she could not take them away when he bowed his head and rested his face upon them.

After a moment he said one thing more. "Take me down gently when you take me from the Tree."

Gradually the weight of his body came against her shins, and he slept.

The moon streak that entered by the eastern window crept north across the floor, thinner and thinner; the one that fell through the southern doorway traveled east and grew fat. For a while Mare's feet pained her terribly and her legs too. She dared not move them, though, and by and by they did not hurt so much.

A dozen times, moving her head slowly on her neck, she canvassed the shadows of the room for a weapon. Each time her eyes came back to a heavy earthenware pitcher on a stand some feet to the left of the sofa. It would have had flowers in it when Wyker's wife was alive; probably it had not been moved from its dust ring since she died. It would be a long grab, perhaps too long; still, it might be done if she had her hands.

To get her hands from under the sleeper's head was the task she set herself. She pulled first one, then the other, infinitesimally. She waited. Again she tugged a very, very little. The order of his breathing was not disturbed. But at the third trial he stirred.

"Gently! gently!" His own muttering waked him more. With some drowsy instinct of possession he threw one hand across her wrists, pinning them together between thumb and fingers. She kept dead quiet, shut her eyes, lengthened her breathing, as if she too slept.

There came a time when what was pretense grew a peril; strange as it was, she had to fight to keep her eyes open. She never knew whether or not she really napped. But something changed in the air, and she was wide awake again. The moonlight was fading on the doorsill, and the light that runs before dawn waxed in the window behind her head.

And then she heard a voice in the distance, lifted in maundering song. It was old man Wyker coming home after a night, and it was plain he had had some whiskey.

Now a new terror laid hold of Mare.

"Shut up, you fool you!" she wanted to shout. "Come quiet, quiet!"

She might have chanced it now to throw the sleeper away from her and scramble and run, had his powers of strength and quickness not taken her simple imagination utterly in thrall.

Happily the singing stopped. What had occurred was that the farmer had espied the open door and, even befuddled as he was, wanted to know more about it quietly. He was so quiet that Mare had begun to fear he had gone away. He had the squirrel-hunter's foot, and the first she knew of him was when she looked and saw his head in the doorway, his hard, soiled, whiskery face half upside-down with craning.

He had been to the town. Between drinks he had wandered in and out of the night's excitement; had even gone a short distance with one search party himself. Now he took in the situation in the room. He used his forefinger. First he held it to his lips. Next he pointed it with a jabbing motion at the sleeper. Then he tapped his own forehead and described wheels. Lastly, with his whole hand, he made pushing gestures, for Mare to wait. Then he vanished as silently as he had appeared.

The minutes dragged. The light in the east strengthened and turned rosy. Once she thought she heard a board creaking in another part of the house, and looked down sharply to see if the loony stirred. All she could see of his face was a temple with freckles on it and the sharp ridge of a cheekbone, but even from so little she knew how deeply and peacefully he slept. The door darkened. Wyker was there again. In one hand he carried something heavy; with the other he beckoned.

"Come jumpin'!" he said out loud.

Mare went jumping, but her cramped legs threw her down halfway to the sill; the rest of the distance she rolled and crawled. Just as she tumbled through the door it seemed as if the world had come to an end above her; two barrels of a shotgun discharged into a room make a noise. Afterwards all she could hear in there was something twisting and bumping on the floor boards. She got up and ran.

Mare's mother had gone to pieces; neighbor women put her to bed when Mare came home. They wanted to put Mare to bed, but she would not let them. She sat on the edge of her bed in her lean-to bedroom off the kitchen, just as she was, her hair down all over her shoulders and her shoes on, and stared away from them, at a place in the wallpaper.

"Yeh, I'll go myself. Lea' me be!"

The women exchanged quick glances, thinned their lips, and left her be. "God knows," was all they would answer to the questionings of those that had not gone in, "but she's gettin' herself to bed."

When the doctor came through he found her sitting just as she had been, still dressed, her hair down on her shoulders and her shoes on.

"What d' y' want?" she muttered and stared at the place in the wall-paper.

How could Doc Paradise say, when he did not know himself?

"I didn't know if you might be — might be feeling very smart, Mary."

"I'm all right. Lea' me be."

It was a heavy responsibility. Doc shouldered it. "No, it's all right," he said to the men in the road. Ruby Herter stood a little apart, chewing sullenly and looking another way. Doc raised his voice to make certain it carried. "Nope, nothing."

Ruby's ears got red, and he clamped his jaws. He knew he ought to go in and see Mare, but he was not going to do it while everybody hung around waiting to see if he would. A mule tied near him reached out and mouthed his sleeve in idle innocence; he wheeled and banged a fist against the side of the animal's head.

"Well, what d' y' aim to do 'bout it?" he challenged its owner.

He looked at the sun then. It was ten in the morning. "Hell, I got work!" he flared, and set off down the road for home. Doc looked at Judge North, and the Judge started after Ruby. But Ruby shook his head angrily. "Lea' me be!" He went on, and the Judge came back.

It got to be eleven and then noon. People began to say, "Like enough she'd be as thankful if the whole neighborhood wasn't camped here." But none went away.

As a matter of fact they were no bother to the girl. She never saw them. The only move she made was to bend her ankles over and rest her feet on the edge; her shoes hurt terribly and her feet knew it, though she did not. She sat all the while staring at that one figure in the wallpaper, and she never saw the figure.

Strange as the night had been, this day was stranger. Fright and physical pain are perishable things once they are gone. But while pain merely dulls and telescopes in memory and remains diluted pain, terror looked back upon has nothing of terror left. A gambling chance taken, at no matter what odds, and won was a sure thing since the world's beginning; perils come through safely were never perilous. But what fright does do in retrospect is this — it heightens each sensuous recollection, like a hard, clear lacquer laid on wood, bringing out the color and grain of it vividly.

Last night Mare had lain stupid with fear on groundpine beneath a bush, loud footfalls and light whispers confused in her ear. Only now, in her room, did she smell the groundpine.

Only now did the conscious part of her brain begin to make words of the whispering.

Amarantha, she remembered, *Amarantha sweet and fair.* That was as far as she could go for the moment, except that the rhyme with "fair" was "hair." But then a puzzle, held in abeyance, brought other words. She wondered what "ravel Ed" could mean. *Most excellently ravell-ed.* It was left to her mother to bring the end.

They gave up trying to keep her mother out at last. The poor woman's prostration took the form of fussiness.

"Good gracious, daughter, you look a sight. Them new shoes, half ruined; ain't your feet *dead*? And look at your hair, all tangled like a wild one!"

She got a comb.

"Be quiet, daughter; what's ailin' you. Don't shake your head!"

"But shake your head and scatter day."

"What you say, Amarantha?" Mrs. Doggett held an ear down.

"Go 'way! Lea' me be!"

Her mother was hurt and left. And Mare ran, as she stared at the wallpaper.

Christ, that my love were in my arms . . .

Mare ran. She ran through a wind white with moonlight and wet with "the small rain." And the wind she ran through, it ran through her, and made her shiver as she ran. And the man beside her leaped high over the waves of the dead grasses and gathered the wind in his arms, and her hair was heavy and his was tossing, and a little fox ran before them across the top of the world. And the world spread down around in waves of black and silver, more immense than she had ever known the world could be, and more beautiful.

God Almighty beautiful, to take your breath away!

Mare wondered, and she was not used to wondering. "Is it only crazy folks ever run like that and talk that way?"

She no longer ran; she walked; for her breath was gone. And there was some other reason, some other reason. Oh, yes, it was because her feet were hurting her. So, at last, and roundabout, her shoes had made contact with her brain.

Bending over the side of the bed, she loosened one of them mechanically. She pulled it half off. But then she looked down at it sharply, and she pulled it on again.

How beautiful . . .

Color overspread her face in a slow wave.

How beautiful are thy feet with shoes . . .

"Is it only crazy folks ever say such things?"

O prince's daughter!

"Or call you that?"

By and by there was a knock at the door. It opened, and Ruby Herter came in.

"Hello, Mare old girl!" His face was red. He scowled and kicked at the floor. "I'd 'a' been over sooner, except we got a mule down sick." He looked at his dumb betrothed. "Come on, cheer up, forget it! He won't scare you no more, not that boy, not. what's left o' him. What you lookin' at, sourface? Ain't you glad to see me?"

Mare quit looking at the wallpaper and looked at the floor.

"Yeh," she said.

"That's more like it, babe." He came and sat beside her, reached down behind her and gave her a spank. "Come on, give us a kiss, babe!" He wiped his mouth on his jumper sleeve, a good farmer's sleeve, spotted with milking. He put his hands on her; he was used to handling animals. "Hey, you, warm up a little; reckon I'm goin' to do all the lovin'?"

"Ruby, lea' me be!"

"What!"

She was up, twisting. He was up, purple.

"What's ailin' of you, Mare? What you bawlin' about?"

"Nothin' — only go 'way!"

She pushed him to the door and through it with all her strength, and closed it in his face, and stood with her weight against it, crying, "Go 'way! Go 'way! Lea' me be!"

WILLIAM SAROYAN

Pure mint Saroyan is probably the most adequate way to describe "Resurrection of a Life." It is one of the author's earliest short stories. When he was first published, Edward J. O'Brien said of his writing, "It is a free fantasia in which he pours forth his feelings and his thoughts about himself and America with extraordinary brilliance and perceptive power . . . He has invented a new form for the short story."

Of Armenian ancestry, William Saroyan was born in the San Joaquin Valley, California, in 1908. He is the author of novels, many collections of short stories, of which The Daring Young Man on the Flying Trapeze *is the best known, and plays.*

Resurrection of a Life

EVERYTHING begins with inhale and exhale, and never ends, moment after moment, yourself inhaling, and exhaling, seeing, hearing, smelling, touching, tasting, moving, sleeping, waking, day after day and year after year, until it is now, this moment, the moment of *your* being, the last moment, which is saddest and most glorious. It is because we remember, and I remember having lived among dead moments, now deathless because of my remembrance, among people now dead, having been a part of the flux which is now only a remembrance, of myself and this earth, a street I was crossing and the people I saw walking in the opposite direction, automobiles going away from me. Saxons, Dorts, Maxwells, and the streetcars and trains, the horses and wagons, and myself, a small boy, crossing a street, alive somehow, going somewhere.

First he sold newspapers. It was because he wanted to do something, standing in the city, shouting about what was happening in the world. He used to shout so loud, and he used to need to shout so much, that he would forget he was supposed to be selling papers; he would get the idea that he was only supposed to shout, to make people understand what was going on. He used to go through the city like an alley cat, prowling all over the place, into saloons, upstairs into whore houses, into gambling joints, to see: their faces, the faces of those who were alive with him on the earth, and the expressions of their faces, and their forms, the faces of old whores, and the way they talked, and the smell of all the ugly places, and the drabness of all the old and rotting buildings, all of it, of his time and his life, a part of him. He prowled through the city, seeing and smelling, talking, shouting about the big news, inhaling and exhaling, blood moving to the rhythm of the sea, coming and going, to the shore of self and back again to selflessness, inhale and newness, exhale and new death, and the boy in the city, walking through it like an alley cat, shouting headlines.

The city was ugly, but his being there was splendid and not an ugliness. His hands would be black with the filth of the city and his face would be black with it, but it was splendid to be alive and walking, of the events of the earth, from day to day, new headlines every day, new things happening.

In the summer it would be very hot and his body would thirst for the sweet fluids of melons, and he would long for the shade of thick leaves and the coolness of a quiet stream, but always he would be in the city, shouting. It was his place and he was the guy, and he wanted the city to be the way it was, if that was the way. He would figure it out somehow. He used to stare at rich people sitting at tables in hightone restaurants eating dishes of ice cream, electric fans making breezes for them, and he used to watch them ignoring the city, not going out to it and being of it, and it used to make him mad. Pigs, he used to say, having everything you want, having everything. What do you know of this place? What do you know of me, seeing this place with a clean eye, any of you? And he used to go, in the summer, to the Crystal Bar, and there he would study the fat man who slept in a chair all summer, a mountain of somebody, a man with a face and substance that lived, who slept all day every summer day, dreaming what? This fat man, three hundred pounds? What did he dream, sitting in the saloon, in the corner, not playing poker or pinochle like the other men, only sleeping and sometimes brushing the flies from his fat face? What was there for him to dream, anyway, with a body like that, and what was there hidden beneath the fat of that body, what grace or gracelessness? He used to go into the saloon and spit on the floor as the men did and watch the fat man sleeping, trying to figure it out. Him alive, too? he used to ask. That great big sleeping thing alive? Like myself?

In the winter he wouldn't see the fat man. It would be only in the summer. The fat man was like the hot sun, very near everything, of everything, sleeping, flies on his big nose. In the winter it would be cold and there would be much rain. The rain would fall over him and his clothes would be wet, but he would never get out of the rain, and he would go on prowling around in the city, looking for whatever it was that was there and that nobody else was trying to see, and he would go in and out of all the ugly places to see how it was with the faces of the people when it rained, how the rain changed the expressions of their faces. His body would be wet with the rain, but he would go from one place to another, shouting headlines, telling the city about the things that were going on in the world.

I was this boy and he is dead now, but he will be prowling through the city when my body no longer makes a shadow upon the pavement, and if it is not this boy it will be another, myself again, another boy alive on earth, seeking the essential truth of the scene, seeking the static and precise beneath that which is in motion and which is imprecise.

The theatre stood in the city like another universe, and he entered its darkness, seeking there in the falsity of pictures of man in motion the truth of his own city, and of himself, and the truth of all living. He saw their eyes: *While London Sleeps*. He saw the thin emaciated hand of theft twitching toward crime: *Jean Valjean*. And he saw the lecherous eyes of lust violating virginity. In the darkness the false universe unfolded itself before him and he saw the phantoms of man going and coming, making quiet horrifying shadows: *The Cabinet of Doctor Caligari*. He saw the endless sea, smashing against rocks, birds flying, the great prairie and herds of horses, New York and greater mobs of men, monstrous trains, rolling ships, men marching to war, and a line of infantry charging another line of infantry: *The Birth of a Nation*. And sitting in the secrecy of the theatre he entered the houses of the rich, saw them, the male and the female, the high ceilings, the huge marble pillars, the fancy furniture, great bathrooms, tables loaded with food, rich people laughing and eating and drinking, and then secrecy again and a male seeking a female, and himself watching carefully to understand, one pursuing and the other fleeing, and he felt the lust of man mounting in him, desire for the loveliest of them, the universal lady of the firm white shoulders and the thick round thighs, desire for her, he himself, ten years old, in the darkness.

He is dead and deathless, staring at the magnification of the kiss, straining at the mad embrace of male and female, walking alone from the theatre, insane with the passion to live. And at school their shallowness was too much. Don't try to teach me, he said. Teach the idiots. Don't try to tell me anything. I am getting it direct, straight from the pit, the ugliness with the loveliness. Two times two is many millions all over the earth, lonely and shivering, groaning one at a time, trying to figure it out. Don't try to teach me. I'll figure it out for myself.

Daniel Boone? he said. Don't tell me. I knew him. Walking through Kentucky. He killed a bear. Lincoln? A big fellow walking alone, looking at things as if he pitied them, a face like the face of man. The whole countryside full of dead men, men he loved, and he himself alive. Don't ask me to memorize his speech. I know all about it, the way he stood, the way the words came from his being.

He used to get up before daybreak and walk to the San Joaquin Baking Company. It was good, the smell of freshly baked bread, and it was good to see the machine wrapping the loaves in wax paper. *Chicken bread,* he used to say, and the important man in the fine suit of clothes used to smile at him. The important man used to say. What kind of chickens you got at your house, kid? And the man would smile nicely so that there would be no insult, and he would never have to tell the man that he himself and his brother and sisters were eating the chicken bread. He would just stand by the bin, not saying anything, not asking for the best loaves, and the important man would understand, and he would pick out the best of the loaves and drop them into the sack the boy held open. If the man happened to drop a bad loaf into the sack the boy would say nothing, and a moment later the man would pick out the bad loaf and throw it back into the bin. Those chickens, he would say, they might not like that loaf. And the boy would say nothing. He would just smile. It was good bread, not too stale and sometimes very fresh, sometimes still warm, only it was bread that had fallen from the wrapping machine and couldn't be sold to rich people. It was made of the same dough, in the same ovens, only after the loaves fell they were called chicken bread and a whole sackful cost only a quarter. The important man never insulted. Maybe he himself had known hunger once; maybe as a boy he had known how it felt to be hungry for bread. He was very funny, always asking about the chickens. He knew there were no chickens, and he always picked out the best loaves.

Bread to eat, so that he could move through the city and shout. Bread to make him solid, to nourish his anger, to fill his substance with vigor that shouted at the earth. Bread to carry him to death and back again to life, inhaling, exhaling, keeping the flame within him alive. Chicken bread, he used to say, not feeling ashamed. We eat it. Sure, sure. It isn't good enough for the rich. There are many at our house. We eat every bit of it, all the crumbs. We do not mind a little dirt on the crust. We put all of it inside. A sack of chicken bread. We know we're poor. When the wind comes up our house shakes, but we don't tremble. We can eat the bread that isn't good enough for the rich. Throw in the loaves. It is too good for chickens. It is our life. Sure we eat it. We're not ashamed. We're living on the money we earn selling newspapers. The roof of our house leaks and we catch the water in pans, but we are all there, all of us alive, and the floor of our house sags when we walk over it, and it is full of crickets and spiders and mice, but we are in the house, living there. We eat this bread that isn't quite good enough for the rich, this bread that you call chicken bread.

Walking, this boy vanished, and now it is myself, another, no longer the boy, and the moment is now this moment, of my remembrance. The fig tree he loved: of all graceful things it was the most graceful, and in the winter it stood leafless, dancing, sculptural whiteness dancing. In the spring the new leaves appeared on the fig tree and the hard green figs. The sun came closer and closer and the heat grew, and he climbed the tree, eating the soft fat figs, the flowering of the lovely white woman, his lips kissing.

But always he returned to the city, back again to the place of man, the street, the structure, the door and window, the hall, the roof and floor, back again to the corners of dark secrecy, where they were dribbling out their lives, back again to the movement of mobs, to beds and chairs and stoves, away from the tree, away from the meadow and the brook. The tree was of the other earth, the older and lovelier earth, solid and quiet and of godly grace, of earth and water and of sky and of the time that was before, ancient places, quietly in the sun, Rome and Athens, Cairo, the white fig tree dancing. He talked to the tree, his mouth clenched, pulling himself over its smooth limbs, to be of you, he said, to be of your time, to be there, in the old world, and to be here as well, to eat your fruit, to feel your strength, to move with you as you dance, myself, alone in the world, with you only, my tree, that in myself which is of thee.

Dead, dead, the tree and the boy, yet everlastingly alive, the white tree moving slowly in dance, and the boy talking to it in unspoken, unspeakable language; you, loveliness of the earth, the street waits for me, the moment of my time calls me back, and there he was suddenly, running through the streets, shouting that ten thousand Huns had been destroyed. Huns? he asked. What do you mean, Huns? They are men, aren't they? Call me, then, a Hun. Call me a name, if they are to have a name dying. And he saw the people of the city smiling and talking with pleasure about the good news. He himself appreciated the goodness of the news because it helped him sell his papers, but after the shouting was over and he was himself again, he used to think of ten thousand men smashed from life to violent death, one man at a time, each man himself as he, the boy, was himself, bleeding, praying, screaming, weeping, remembering life as dying men remember it, wanting it, gasping for breath, to go on inhaling and exhaling, living and dying, but always living somehow, stunned, horrified, ten thousand faces suddenly amazed at the monstrousness of the war, the beastliness of man, who could be so godly.

There were no words with which to articulate his rage. All that he could do was shout, but even now I cannot see the war as the historians see it. Succeeding moments have carried the germ of myself to this face and form, the one of this moment, now, my being in this small room, alone, as always, remembering the boy, resurrecting him, and I cannot see the war as the historians see it. Those clever fellows study all the facts and they see the war as a large thing, one of the biggest events in the legend of man, something general, involving multitudes. I see it as a large thing too, only I break it into small units of one man at a time, and I see it as a large and monstrous thing for each man involved. I see the war as death in one form or another for men dressed as soldiers, and all the men who survived the war, including myself, I see as men who died with their brothers, dressed as soldiers.

There is no such thing as a soldier. I see death as a private event, the destruction of the universe in the brain and in the senses of one man, and I cannot see any man's death as a contributing factor in the success or failure of a military campaign. The boy had to shout what had happened. Whatever happened, he had to shout it, making the city know. *Ten thousand Huns killed, ten thousand,* one at a time, one, two, three, four, inestimably many, ten thousand, alive, and then dead, killed, shot, mangled, ten thousand Huns, ten thousand men. I blame the historians for the distortion. I remember the coming of the gas mask to the face of man, the proper grimace of the horror of the nightmare we were performing, artfully expressing the monstrousness of the inward face of man. To the boy who is dead the war was the international epilepsy which brought about the systematic destruction of one man at a time until millions of men were destroyed.

There he is suddenly in the street, running, and it is 1917, shouting the most recent crime of man, extra, extra, ten thousand Huns killed, himself alive, inhaling, exhaling, *ten thousand, ten thousand,* all the ugly buildings solid, all the streets solid, the city unmoved by the crime, *ten thousand,* windows opening, doors opening, and the people of the city smiling about it, good, ten thousand of them killed, good. *Johnny, get your gun, get your gun, Johnny get your gun: we'll be over, we're coming over, and we won't come back till it's over, over there,* and another trainload of boys in uniforms, going to the war. And the fat man, sleeping in a corner of the Crystal Bar, what of him? Sleeping there, somehow alive in spite of the lewd death in him, but never budging. Pig, he said, ten thousand Huns killed, ten thousand men with solid bodies mangled to death. Does it mean nothing to you? Does it not disturb your fat dream? Boys with loves, men with wives and children. What have you, sleeping? They are all dead, all of them dead. Do you think you are alive? Do you dream you are alive? The fly on your nose is more alive than you.

Sunday would come, *O day of, rest and gladness, O day of joy and light, O balm of care and sadness, Most beautiful, most bright,* and he would put on his best shirt and his best trousers, and he would try to comb his hair down, to be neat and clean, meeting God, and he would go to the small church and sit in the shadow of religion: in the beginning, the boy David felling the giant Goliath, beautiful Rebecca, mad Saul, Daniel among lions, Jesus talking quietly to the men, and in the boat shouting at them because they feared, angry at them because they had fear, calm yourselves, boys, calm yourselves, let the storm rage, let the boat sink, do you fear going to God? Ah, that was lovely, that love of death was lovely, Jesus loving it: calm yourselves, boys, God damn you, calm yourselves, why are you afraid? *Still, still with thee, when purple morning breaketh, abide, abide, with me, fast falls the eventide,* ah, lovely. He sat in the basement of the church, among his fellows, singing at the top of his voice. I do not believe, he said. I cannot believe. There cannot be a God. But it is lovely, lovely, these songs we sing, *Saviour, breathe an evening blessing, sun of my soul, begin, my tongue, some heavenly theme, begin, my tongue, begin, begin.* Lovely, lovely, but I cannot believe. The poor and the rich, those who deserve life and those who deserve death, and the ugliness everywhere. Where is God? Big ships sinking at sea, submarines, men in the water, cannon booming, machine guns, men dying, ten thousand, where? But our singing, *Joy to the world, the Lord is come. Let earth receive her King. Silent night, holy night. What grace, O Lord, my dear redeemer. Ride on, ride on, in majesty. Angels, roll the rock away; death, yield up thy mighty prey.*

No, he could not believe. He had seen for himself. It was there, in the city, all the godlessness, the eyes of the whores, the men at cards, the sleeping fat man, and the mad headlines, it was all there, unbelief, ungodliness, everywhere, all the world forgetting. How could he believe? But the music, so good and clean, so much of the best in man: *lift up, lift up your voices now. Lo, he comes with clouds descending once for favored sinners slain. Arise, my soul, arise, shake off thy guilty fears, O for a thousand tongues to sing. Like a river glorious, holy Bible, book divine, precious treasure, thou art mine.* And spat, right on the floor of the Crystal Bar. And into Madam Juliet's Rooms, over the Rex Drug Store, the men buttoning their clothes, ten thousand Huns killed, madam. *Break thou the bread of life, dear Lord, to me, as thou didst break the loaves, beside the sea.* And spat, on the floor, hearing the fat man snoring. Another ship sunk. The Marne. Ypres. Russia. Poland. Spat. *Art thou weary, art thou languid, art thou sore distressed?* Zeppelin over Paris. The fat man sleeping. *Haste, traveler, haste, the night comes on.* Spat. *The storm is gathering in the west.* Cannon. Hutt! two three, four! Hutt! two three, four, how many men marching, how many? Onward, onward, unChristian soldiers. *I was a wandering sheep.* Spat. *I did not love my home.* Your deal, Jim. Spat. *Take me, O my father, take me.* Spat. *This holy bread, this holy wine. My God, is any hour so sweet?* Submarine plunging. Spat. *Take my life and let it be consecrated, Lord, to thee.* Spat.

He sat in the basement of the little church, deep in the shadow of faith, and of no faith: I cannot believe: where is the God of whom they speak, where? *Your harps, ye trembling saints, down from the willows take.* Where? Cannon. *Lead, oh lead, lead kindly light, amid the encircling gloom.* Spat. *Jesus, Saviour, pilot me.* Airplane: spat: smash. *Guide me, O thou great Jehovah. Bread of heaven, feed me till I want no more.* The universal lady of the dark theatre: thy lips, beloved, thy shoulders and thighs, thy sea-surging blood. The tree, black figs in sunlight. Spat. *Rock of ages, cleft for me, let me hide myself in thee.* Spat. *Let the water and the blood, from thy riven side which flowed, be of sin the double cure.* Lady, your arm, your arm: spat. The mountain of flesh sleeping through the summer. Ten thousand Huns killed.

Sunday would come, turning him from the outward world to the inward, to the secrecy of the past, endless as the future, back to Jesus, to God; *when the weary, seeking rest, to thy goodness flee;* back to the earliest quiet: *He leadeth me, O blessed thought.* But he did not believe. He could not believe. Jesus was a remarkable fellow: you couldn't figure him out. He had a pious love of death. An heroic fellow. And as for God. Well, he could not believe.

But the songs he loved and he sang them with all his might: *hold thou my hand, O blessed nothingness, I walk with thee. Awake, my soul, stretch every nerve, and press with vigor on. Work, for the night is coming, work, for the day is done.* Spat. Right on the floor of the Crystal Bar. It is Sunday again: O blessed nothingness, we worship thee. Spat. And suddenly the sleeping fat man sneezes. Hallelujah. Amen. Spat. Sleep on, beloved, sleep, and take thy rest. *Lay down thy head upon thy Saviour's breast.* We love thee well, but Jesus loves thee best. Jesus loves thee. For the Bible tells you so. Amen. The fat man sneezes. He could not believe and he could not disbelieve. Sense? There was none. But glory? There was an abundance of it. Everywhere. Madly everywhere. Those crazy birds vomiting song. Those vast trees, solid and quiet. And clouds. And sun. And night. And day. *It is not death to die,* he sang: *to leave this weary road, to be at home with God.* God? The same. Nothingness. Nowhere. Everywhere. The crazy glory, everywhere: Madam Juliet's Rooms, all modern conveniences, including beds. Spat. *I know not, O I know not, what joys await us there.* Where? Heaven? No. Madam Juliet's. In the church, the house of God, the boy singing, remembering the city's lust.

Boom: Sunday morning: and the war still booming: after the singing he would go to the newspaper office and get his Special Sunday Extras and run through the city with them, his hair combed for God, and he would shout the news: amen, *I gave my life for Jesus.* Oh, yeah? Ten thousand Huns killed, and I am the guy, inhaling, exhaling, running through the town, I, myself, seeing, hearing, touching, shouting, smelling, singing, wanting, I, the guy, the latest of the whole lot, alive by the grace of God: ten thousand, two times ten million, by the grace of God dead, by His grace smashed, amen, extra, extra: five cents a copy, extra, ten thousand killed.

I was this boy who is now lost and buried in the succeeding forms of myself, and I am now of this last moment, of this small room, and the night hush, time going, time coming, breathing, this last moment, inhale, exhale, the boy dead and alive. All that I have learned is that we breathe, and remember, and we see the boy moving through a city that has become lost, among people who have become dead, alive among dead moments, crossing a street, the scene thus, or standing by the bread bin in the bakery, a sack of chicken bread please so that we can live and shout about it, and it begins nowhere and it ends nowhere, and all that I know is that we are somehow alive, all of us in the light, making shadows, the sun overhead, space all around us, inhaling, exhaling, the face and form of man everywhere, pleasure and pain, sanity and madness, war and no war, and peace and no peace, the earth solid and unaware of us, unaware of our cities, our dreams, the earth everlastingly itself, and the sea sullen with movement like my breathing, waves coming and going, and all that I know is that I am alive and glad to be, glad to be of this ugliness and this glory, somehow glad that I can remember the boy climbing the fig tree, unpraying but religious with joy, somehow of the earth, of the time of earth, somehow everlastingly of life, nothingness, blessed or unblessed, somehow deathless, insanely glad to be here, and so it is true, there is no death, somehow there is no death, and can never be.

THOMAS WOLFE

To Thomas Wolfe's southern ear, the Brooklyn dialect sounded exotic, and he tended to overemphasize its intricacies in this famous story, "Only the Dead Know Brooklyn." The story, nevertheless, is deserving of its fame for Wolfe's depiction of the characters of the obtuse narrator and the despairing man with a map.

Like that of Fitzgerald, the life of Thomas Wolfe is another sad and familiar saga in American literature. He was born in Asheville, North Carolina, in 1900 and died in 1939. He taught at New York University and is most known for his novels Look Homeward, Angel, Of Time and the River, *and* You Can't Go Home Again.

Only the Dead Know Brooklyn

DERE's no guy livin' dat knows Brooklyn t'roo an' t'roo, because it'd take a guy a lifetime just to find his way aroun' duh f —— town.

So like I say, I'm waitin' for my train t' come when I sees dis big guy standin' deh — dis is duh foist I eveh see of him. Well, he's lookin' wild, y'know, an' I can see dat he's had plenty, but still he's holdin' it; he talks good an' is walkin' straight enough. So den, dis big guy steps up to a little guy dat's standin' deh, an' says, "How d'yuh get t' Eighteent' Avenoo an' Sixty-sevent' Street?" he says.

"Jesus! Yuh got me, chief," duh little guy says to him. "I ain't been heah long myself. Where is duh place?" he says. "Out in duh Flatbush section somewhere?"

"Nah," duh big guy says. "It's out in Bensonhoist. But I was neveh deh befoeh. How d'yuh get deh?"

"Jesus," duh little guy says, scratchin' his head, y'know — yuh could see duh little guy didn't know his way about — "yuh got me, chief. I neveh hoid of it. Do any of youse guys know where it is?" he says to me.

"Sure," I says. "It's out in Bensonhoist. Yuh take duh Fourt' Avenoo express, get off at Fifty-nint' Street, change to a Sea Beach local deh, get off at Eighteent' Avenoo an' Sixty-toid, an' den walk down foeh blocks. Dat's all yuh got to do," I says.

"G'wan!" some wise guy dat I neveh seen befoeh pipes up. "Whatcha talkin' about?" he says — oh, he was wise, y'know. "Duh guy is crazy! I tell yuh what yuh do," he says to duh big guy. "Yuh change to duh West End line at Toity-sixt'," he tells him. "Get off at Noo Utrecht an' Sixteent' Avenoo," he says. "Walk two blocks oveh, foeh blocks up," he says, "an' you'll be right deh." Oh, a *wise* guy, y'know.

"Oh, yeah?" I says. "Who told *you* so much?" He got me sore because he was so wise about it. "How long you been livin' heah?" I says.

"All my life," he says. "I was bawn in Williamsboig," he says. "An' I can tell you t'ings about dis town you neveh hoid of," he says.

"Yeah?" I says.

"Yeah," he says.

"Well, den, you can tell me t'ings about dis town dat nobody else has eveh hoid of, either. Maybe you make it all up yoehself at night," I says, "befoeh you go to sleep — like cuttin' out papeh dolls, or somp'n."

"Oh, yeah?" he says. "You're pretty wise, ain't yuh?"

"Oh, I don't know," I says. "Duh boids ain't usin' my head for Lincoln's statue yet," I says. "But I'm wise enough to know a phony when I see one."

"Yeah?" he says. "A wise guy, huh? Well, you're so wise dat someone's goin' t'bust yuh one right on duh snoot some day," he says. "Dat's how wise *you* are."

Well, my train was comin', or I'da smacked him den and dere, but when I seen duh train was comin', all I said was, "All right, mugg! I'm sorry I can't stay to take keh of you, but I'll be seein' yuh sometime, I hope, out in duh cemetery." So den I says to duh big guy, who'd been standin' deh all duh time, "You come wit me," I says. So when we gets onto duh train I says to him, "Where yuh goin' out in Bensonhoist?" I says. "What numbeh are yuh lookin' for?" I says. *You* know — I t'ought if he told me duh address I might be able to help him out.

"Oh," he says. "I'm not lookin' for no one. I don't know no one out deh."

"Then whatcha goin' out deh for?" I says.

"Oh," duh guy says, "I'm just goin' out to see duh place," he says. "I like duh sound of duh name — Bensonhoist, y'know — so I t'ought I'd go out an' have a look at it."

"Whatcha tryin t'hand me?" I says. "Whatcha tryin t'do — kid me?"
You know, I t'ought duh guy was bein' wise wit me.

"No," he says, "I'm tellin' yuh duh troot. I like to go out an' take a
look at places wit nice names like dat. I like to go out an' look at all
kinds of places," he says.

"How'd yuh know deh was such a place," I says, "if yuh neveh been
deh befoeh?"

"Oh," he says, "I got a map."

"A *map?*" I says.

"Sure," he says, "I got a map dat tells me about all dese places. I take it
wit me every time I come out heah," he says.

And Jesus! Wit dat, he pulls it out of his pocket, an' so help me, but
he's *got* it — he's tellin' duh troot — a big map of duh whole f —— place
with all duh different pahts mahked out. You know — Canarsie an' East
Noo Yawk an' Flatbush, Bensonhoist, Sout' Brooklyn, duh Heights, Bay
Ridge, Greenpernt — duh whole goddam layout, he's got it right deh **on**
duh map.

"You been to any of dose places?" I says.

"Sure," he says, "I been to most of 'em. I was down in Red Hook just
last night," he says.

"Jesus! Red Hook!" I says. "Whatcha do down deh?"

"Oh," he says, "nuttin' much. I just walked aroun'. I went into a
coupla places an' had a drink," he says, "but most of the time I just
walked aroun'."

"Just walked aroun'?" I says.

"Sure," he says, "just lookin' at t'ings, y'know."

"Where'd yuh go?" I asts him.

"Oh," he says, "I don't know duh name of duh place, but I could find
it on my map," he says. "One time I was walkin' across some big fields
where deh ain't no houses," he says, "but I could see ships oveh deh all
lighted up. Dey was loadin'. So I walks across duh fields," he says, "to
where duh ships are."

"Sure," I says, "I know where you was. You was down to duh Erie
Basin."

"Yeah," he says, "I gues dat was it. Dey had some of dose big elevators
an' cranes an' dey was loadin' ships, an' I could see some ships in drydock
all lighted up, so I walks across duh fields to where dey are," he says.

"Den what did yuh do?" I says.

"Oh," he says, "nuttin' much. I came on back across duh fields after a while an' went into a coupla places an' had a drink."

"Didn't nuttin' happen while yuh was in dere?" I says.

"No," he says. "Nuttin' much. A coupla guys was drunk in one of duh places an' started a fight, but dey bounced 'em out," he says, "an' den one of duh guys stahted to come back again, but duh bartender gets his baseball bat out from under duh counteh, so duh guy goes on."

"Jesus!" I said. "Red Hook!"

"Sure," he says. "Dat's where it was, all right."

"Well, you keep outa deh," I says. "You stay away from deh."

"Why?" he says. "What's wrong wit it?"

"Oh," I says, "It's a good place to stay away from, dat's all. It's a good place to keep out of."

"Why?" he says. "Why is it?"

Jesus! Whatcha gonna do wit a guy as dumb as dat? I saw it wasn't no use to try to tell him nuttin', he wouldn't know what I was talkin' about, so I just says to him, "Oh, nuttin'. Yuh might get lost down deh, dat's all."

"Lost?" he says. "No, I wouldn't get lost. I got a map," he says.

A map! Red Hook! Jesus.

So den duh guy begins to ast me all kinds of nutty questions: how big was Brooklyn an' could I find my way aroun' in it, an' how long would it take a guy to know duh place.

"Listen!" I says. "You get dat idea outa yoeh head right now," I says. "You ain't neveh gonna get to know Brooklyn," I says. "Not in a hunderd yeahs. I been livin' heah all my life," I says, "an' I don't even know all deh is to know about it, so how do you expect to know duh town," I says, "when you don't even live heah?"

"Yes," he says, "but I got a map to help me find my way about."

"Map or no map," I says, "yuh ain't gonna get to know Brooklyn wit no map," I says.

"Can you swim?" he says, just like dat. Jesus! By dat time, y'know, I begun to see dat duh guy was some kind of nut. He'd had plenty to drink, of course, but he had dat crazy look in his eye I didn't like. "Can you swim?" he says.

"Sure," I says. "Can't you?"

"No," he says. "Not more'n a stroke or two. I neveh loined good."

"Well, it's easy," I says. "All yuh need is a little confidence. Duh way I loined, me older bruddeh pitched me off duh dock one day when I was eight yeahs old, cloes an' all. 'You'll swim,' he says. 'You'll swim all right — or drown.' An' believe me, I *swam!* When yuh know yuh got to, you'll do it. Duh only t'ing yuh need is confidence. An' once you've loined," I says, "you've got nuttin' else to worry about. You'll neveh forget it. It's somp'n dat stays wit yuh as long as yuh live."

"Can yuh swim good?" he says.

"Like a fish," I tells him. "I'm a regulah fish in duh wateh," I says. "I loined to swim right off duh docks wit all duh oddeh kids," I says.

"What would you do if yuh saw a man drownin'?" duh guy says.

"Do? Why, I'd jump in an' pull him out," I says. "Dat's what I'd do."

"Did yuh eveh see a man drown?" he says.

"Sure," I says. "I see two guys — bot' times at Coney Island. Dey got out too far, an' neider one could swim. Dey drowned befoeh anyone could get to 'em."

"What becomes of people after dey've drowned out heah?" he says.

"Drowned out where?" I says.

"Out heah in Brooklyn."

"I don't know whatcha mean," I says. "Neveh hoid of no one drownin' heah in Brooklyn, unless you mean a swimmin' pool. Yuh can't drown in Brooklyn," I says. "Yuh gotta drown somewhere else — in duh ocean, where dere's wateh."

"Drownin'," duh guy says, lookin' at his map. "Drownin'." Jesus! I could see by den he was some kind of nut, he had dat crazy expression in his eyes when he looked at you, an' I didn't know what he might do. So we was comin' to a station, an' it wasn't my stop, but I got off anyway, an' waited for duh next train.

"Well, so long, chief," I says. "Take it easy, now."

"Drownin'," duh guy says, lookin' at his map. "Drownin'."

Jesus! I've t'ought about dat guy a t'ousand times since den an' wondered what eveh happened to 'm goin' out to look at Bensonhoist because he liked duh name! Walkin' aroun' t'roo Red Hook by himself at night an' lookin' at his map! How many people did I see get drowned out heah in Brooklyn! How long would it take a guy wit a good map to know all deh was to know about Brooklyn!

Jesus! What a nut *he* was! I wondeh what eveh happened to 'im, anyway! I wondeh if someone knocked him on duh head, or if he's still wanderin' aroun' in duh subway in duh middle of duh night wit his little map! Duh poor guy! Say, I've got to laugh, at dat, when I t'ink about him! Maybe he's found out by now dat he'll neveh live long enough to know duh whole of Brooklyn. It'd take a guy a lifetime to know Brooklyn t'roo an' t'roo. An' even den, yuh wouldn't know it all.

TESS SLESINGER

Superb stream-of-consciousness writing is found in "A Life in the Day of a Writer." It is also an illuminating text on how a writer approaches his task, for it shows that writing is organic and grows as it is written.
    A beautiful, vibrant girl, Tess Slesinger was born in New York City in 1905 and died young. In her brief life she wrote a fine novel, The Unpossessed, *and short stories collected in a volume,* Time: the Present. *If she had lived, she probably would be known today as one of our major authors.*

A Life in the Day of a Writer

O SHINING stupor, O glowing idiocy, O crowded vacuum, O privileged pregnancy, he prayed, morosely pounding X's on his typewriter, I am a writer if I never write another line, I am alive if I never step out of this room again; Christ, oh, Christ, the problem is not to stretch a feeling, it is to reduce a feeling, *all* feeling, all thought, all ecstasy, tangled and tumbled in the empty crowded head of a writer, to one clear sentence, one clear form, and still preserve the hugeness, the hurtfulness, the enormity, the unbearable all-at-once-ness, of being alive and knowing it too . . .

He had been at it for three hours, an elbow planted on either side of his deaf-mute typewriter, staring like a passionate moron round the walls that framed his life — for a whole night had passed, he had nothing or everything to say, and he awoke each morning in terror of his typewriter until he had roused it and used it and mastered it, he was always afraid it might be dead forever — when the *telephone* screamed like an angry siren across his nerves. It was like being startled out of sleep; like being caught making faces at yourself in the mirror — by an editor or a book-critic; like being called to account again by your wife. His hand on the telephone, a million short miles in time and space from his writing-desk, he discovered that he was shaking. He had spoken to no one all the morning since Louise — shouting that she could put up with being the wife of a non-best-seller, or even the wife of a chronic drunk with a fetich for carrying away coat-hangers for souvenirs, but not, by God, the duenna of a conceited, adolescent flirt — had slammed the door and gone off cursing to her office. Voices are a proof of life, he explained gently to the angry telephone, and I have not for three hours heard my own; supposing I have lost it? Courage, my self! he said, as he stupidly lifted the receiver and started when nothing jumped out at him. All at once he heard his own voice, unnaturally loud, a little hoarse. *I wish to report a fire,* he wanted to say, but he said instead, roaring it: *Hello.* The answering *Hello, sunshine,* came from an immeasurable distance, from America, perhaps, or the twentieth century — a rescue party! but he had grown, in three long hours, so used to his solitary island! And though he was a writer and said to be gifted with a fine imagination, it was beyond his uttermost power to imagine that this voice addressing him was really a voice, that since it was a voice it must belong to a person, especially to the person identifying herself as Louise.

Ho, Louise! he said, going through with it for the purpose of establishing his sanity, at least in her ears if not actually in his own: he spoke courteously as though her voice were a voice, as though it did belong to her, as though she really were his wife; *now, darling, don't go on with —* But then he discovered that she was not going on with anything but being a wife, a voice, an instrument of irrelevant torture. *How goes the work,* she said kindly. What in hell did she think he was, a half-witted baby playing with paper-dolls? *Oh, fine, just fine,* he answered deprecatingly. (I'm a writer if I never write another line, he said fiercely to his typewriter, which burst out laughing.) *Well, look,* she was saying, *Freddie called up* (who in hell was Freddie?), and then her voice went on, making explanations, and it seemed that he was to put away his paper-dolls and meet her at five at Freddie's, because Freddie was giving a cocktail party. *Cocktail party,* he said obediently; *wife; five.* Cocktail party, eh — and a dim bell sounded in his brain, for he remembered cocktail parties from some other world, the world of yesterday; a cocktail party meant reprieve from typewriters, rescue from desert islands; and it might also mean Betsey — he cocked a debonair eye at his typewriter to see if it was jealous — Betsey, who, along with half a dozen coat-hangers, had been the cause of this morning's quarrel! *Yes, your wife for a change,* came the off-stage tinkle over the telephone again; *and you might try taking her home for a change too, instead of someone else's—* and *by the way, my treasure, don't bring those coat-hangers with you, Freddie has plenty of his own.—Right you are, my pet,* he said, feeling smart and cheap and ordinary again, *right you are, my lamb-pie, my song of songs, ace of spades, queen of hearts, capital of Wisconsin, darling of the Vienna press—* But she had got off somewhere about Wisconsin.

He looked, a little self-conscious, about his now twice-empty room; aha, my prison, my lonely four-walled island, someone has seen the smoke from my fire at last, someone has spied the waving of my shirt-tails; at five o'clock today, he said, thumbing his nose at his typewriter, the rescue plane will swoop down to pick me up, see, and for all you know, my black-faced Underwood, my noiseless, portable, publisher's stooge, my conscience, my slave, my master, my mistress—for all you know it may lead to that elegant creature Betsey, whom my rather plump Louise considers a bit too much on the thin side . . . ah, but my good wife is a bit short-sighted there, she doesn't look on the *other* side, the bright side, the sunny side, the side that boasts the little, hidden ripples that it takes imagination, courage, to express; the little hiding ripples that the male eye can't stop looking for . . .

He seated himself again before his typewriter, like an embarrassed schoolboy.

Black anger descended upon him. It was easy enough for her, for Louise, to put out a hand to her telephone where it sat waiting on her office desk, and ring him up and order him to report at a cocktail party—Louise, who sat in a room all day surrounded matter-of-factly by people and their voices and her own voice. But for him it was gravely another matter. Her ring summoned him out of his own world—what if he hadn't written a line all morning except a complicated series of coat-hanger designs in the shape of X's? —and because he couldn't really make the crossing, it left him feeling a little ashamed, a little found-out, caught with his pants down, so to speak—and a little terrified, too, to be reminded again that he was not "like other people." He was still shaking. She had no right, damn it, no damn right, to disturb him with that sharp malicious ringing, to present him with the bugbear, the insult, the indignity, of a cocktail party—she, who was proud enough of him in public (Bertram Kyle, author of *Fifty Thousand Lives,* that rather brilliant book), although at home she was inclined to regard him, as his family had when he refused to study banking, as something of a sissy.

Still, when you have accepted an invitation to a party for the afternoon, you have that to think about, to hold over your typewriter's head, you can think of how you will lock it up at half-past four and shave and shower and go out with a collar and a tie around your neck to show people that you can look, talk, drink, like any of them, like the worst of them. But a party! Christ, the faces, the crowds of white faces (like the white keys of the typewriter I had before you, my fine Underwood), and worst of all, the voices. . . . The party became abnormally enlarged in his mind, as though it would take every ounce of ingenious conniving — not to speak of courage! — to get to it at all; and as he fell face downward on his typewriter, he gave more thought to the party than even the party's host was likely to do, Freddie, whoever the devil "Freddie" was . . .

O degrading torture, lying on the smug reproachful keys with nothing to convey to them. He remembered how he had once been afraid of every women he met until he kissed her, beat her, held her captive in his arms; but this typewriter was a thing to master every day, it was a virgin every morning. If I were Thomas Wolfe, he thought, I should start right off: O country of my birth and land I have left behind me, what can I, a youth with insatiable appetite, do to express what there is in me of everlasting hunger, loneliness, nakedness, a hunger that feeds upon hunger and a loneliness that grows in proportion to the hours I lend to strangers . . . If I were Saroyan I should not hesitate either: But I am young, young and hungry (thank God), and why must I listen to the rules the old men make or the rich ones, this is not a story, it is a life, a simple setting down in words of what I see of men upon this earth. No, no, I am not Saroyan (thank God), I am not Thomas Wolfe either, and I am also not Louise's boss (ah, *there's* a man!). And I cannot write an essay; I am a natural liar, I prefer a jumbled order to chronology, and poetry to logic; I don't like facts, I like to imagine their implications. O to get back, get back, to the pre-telephone stupor, the happy mingled pregnancy, the clear confusion of myself only with myself . . .

And so Bertram Kyle opened up his notebooks. He felt again that the story he had outlined so clearly there, of the "lousy guy" whom everyone thought was lousy including himself, but who was so only because of a simple happening in his childhood, might be a fine story; but it was one he could not do today. Nor could he do the story (which had occurred to him on a train to Washington) of the old lady, prospective grandmother, who went mad thinking it was her own child to be born. Nor could he do the story — partly because he did not know it yet — which would begin: "He lived alone with a wife who had died and two children who had left him." Perhaps, he thought bitterly, he could never do those stories, for in the eagerness of begetting them he had told them to Louise; too often when he told her a story it was finished then, it was dead, like killing his lust by confiding an infidelity.

And so, desperately, he turned to those thoughtful little flaps in the backs of his notebooks, into which he poured the findings in his pockets each night; out came old menus, the torn-off backs of matchbooks, hotel stationery that he had begged of waiters, ticket-stubs, a time-table, a theatre program, and odd unrecognizable scraps of paper he had picked up anywhere. The writing on these was born of drinking sometimes; of loneliness in the midst of laughing people; of a need to assert himself, perhaps, a desire to remind himself — that he was a writer; but more than anything, he thought, for the sheer love of grasping a pencil and scratching with it on a scrap of paper. "If I were a blind man I should carry a typewriter before me on a tray suspended from my neck by two blue ribbons; I think I *am* blind" — he had written that on a tablecloth once, and Louise was very bored.

"It is always later than you think, said the sundial finding itself in the shade" — from the back of an old match-box, and undoubtedly the relic of an evening on which he had strained to be smart. A night-club menu: "Dear Saroyan: But take a day off from your writing, *mon vieux,* or your writing will get to be a habit . . ." Another menu — and he remembered the evening well, he could still recall the look of tolerance growing into anger on Louise's face as he wrote and wrote and went on writing: "Nostalgia, a nostalgia for all the other nostalgic nights on which nothing would suffice . . . a thing of boredom, of content, of restlessness, *velleities,* in which the sweetness of another person is irrelevant and intolerable, and indifference or even cruelty hurt in the same way . . . linking up with gray days in childhood when among bewilderingly many things to do one wanted to do none of them, and gray evenings with Louise when everything of the adult gamut of things to do would be the same thing . . ." (At that point Louise had reached down to her anger and said, "All right, sunshine, we come to a place I loathe because you like to see naked women and then, when they come on, you don't even watch them; I wouldn't complain if you were Harold Bell Wright or something . . .") "In order to make friends," he discovered from another match-box, "one need not talk seriously, any more than one needs to make love in French" — and that, he recalled tenderly, was plagiarized from a letter he had written to a very young girl, Betsey's predecessor in his fringe flirtations. "A man's underlying motives are made up of his thwarted, or unrealized, ambitions," "The war between men and women consists of left-overs from their unsatisfactory mating." "But the blinking of the eye" — this on a concert program — "must go on; perhaps one catches the half-face of the player and sees, despite the frenzied waving of his head, a thing smaller than his playing, but perhaps the important, the vital thing: like the heart-beat, at once greater and smaller than the thing it accompanies . . ." "We are not so honest as the best of our writing, for to be wholly honest is to be brave, braver than any of us dares to be with another human being, especially with a woman." *"At bottom one is really grave."*

He was pulled up short by that last sentence, which was the only one of the lot that made sense. "At bottom one is really grave."

Suddenly he raised his head and stared wildly round the room. He was terrified, he was elated. Here was his whole life, in these four walls. This year he had a large room with a very high ceiling; he works better in a big room, Louise told people who came in. Last year he had worked in a very small room with a low ceiling; he works better, Louise used to tell people, in a small place. He worked better at night, he worked better in the daytime, he worked better in the country, better in the city, in the winter, in the summer . . . But he was frightened. Here he was all alone with his life until five o'clock in the afternoon. Other people (Louise) went out in the morning, left their life behind them somewhere, or else filed it away in offices and desks; he imagined that Louise only remembered her life and took it up again in the late afternoon when she said good night to her boss and started off for home — or a cocktail party. But he had to live with his life, and work with it; he couldn't leave it alone and it couldn't leave him alone, not for a minute — except when he was drunk, and that, he said, smugly surveying the scattered coat-hangers, relic of last night's debauch, that is why a writer drinks so much. Hell, he thought, proud, I'm living a life, my own whole life, right here in this room each day; I can still feel the pain I felt last night when I was living part of it and Louise said . . . and I can still feel the joy I felt last week when Betsey said . . . and I can feel the numbness and the excitement of too many Scotch-and-sodas, of too perfect dancing, of too many smooth-faced, slick-haired women; I can remember saying *Listen — listen* to anyone who would or would not, and the truth of it is I had nothing to say anyway because I had too much to say . . . Hell, he thought, my coat-hangers lie on the floor where I flung them at three this morning when Louise persuaded me that it was better not to sleep in my clothes again, I have not hung up my black suit, I have not emptied yesterday's waste-basket nor last week's ashtrays (nor my head of its thirty years' fine accumulation) . . . everything in my room and in my head is testimony to the one important fact, that I am alive, alive as hell, and all I have to do is wait till the whole reeling sum of things adds itself up or boils itself down, to a story . . .

There seemed now to be hunger in his belly, and it was a fact that he had not eaten since breakfast and then only of Louise's anger. But the turmoil in his insides was not, he felt, pure hunger. It came from sitting plunged in symbols of his life, it came because he did not merely have to live with his life each day, but he had to give birth to it over again every morning. Of course, he thought with a fierce joy, I am hungry. I am ravenously hungry, and I have no appetite, I am parched but I am not thirsty, I am dead tired and wide awake and passionately, violently alive.

But he lifted his elbows now from his typewriter, he looked straight before him, and he could feel between his eyes a curious knot, not pain exactly, but tension, as though all of him were focused on the forefront of his brain, as though his head were a packed box wanting to burst. It was for this moment that, thirty years before, he had been born; for this moment that he had tossed peanuts to an elephant when he was a child; that he had by a miracle escaped pneumonia, dropping from an airplane, death by drowning, concussion from football accidents; that he had fallen desperately and permanently in love with a woman in a yellow hat whose car had been held up by traffic, and whom he never saw again; that he had paused at sight of the blue in Chartres Cathedral and wept, and a moment later slapped angrily at a mosquito; that he had met and married Louise, met and coveted Kitty Braithwaite, Margery, Connie, Sylvia, Elinor, Betsey; for this moment that he had been born and lived, for this moment that he was being born again.

His fingers grew light. The room was changing. Everything in it was integrating; pieces of his life came together like the odd-shaped bits of a puzzle-map, forming a pattern as one assembles fruits and flowers for a still-life. Listen, there is a name. Bettina Gregory. Bettina is a thin girl, wiry, her curves so slight as to be ripples, so hidden that the male eye cannot stop searching for them; she drinks too much; she is nicer when she is sober, a little shy, but less approachable. Bettina Gregory. She is the kind of girl who almost cares about changing the social order, almost cares about people, almost is *at bottom really grave*. She is the kind of girl who would be at a cocktail party when someone named Fr — named Gerry — would call up and say he couldn't come because he was prosecuting a taxi-driver who had robbed him of four dollars. She is the kind of girl who would then toss off another drink and think it funny to take old Carl along up to the night-court to watch old Gerry prosecute a taxi-man. She is the kind of girl who will somehow collect coat-hangers (I give you my coat-hangers, Betsey-Bettina, Bertram Kyle almost shouted in his joy) and who will then go lilting and looping into the night-court armed to the teeth with coat-hangers and defense mechanisms, who will mock at the whores that have been rounded up, leer at the taxi-driver, ogle the red-faced detective, mimic the rather sheepish Gerry — all the time mocking, leering, ogling, mimicking — nothing but herself. Frankly we are just three people, she explains to the detective, with an arm about Gerry and Carl, who love each other veddy veddy much. She must pretend to be drunker than she is, bcause she is bitterly and deeply ashamed; she must wave with her coat-hangers and put on a show because she knows it is a rotten show and she cannot stop it. It is not merely the liquor she has drunk; it is the wrong books she has read, the Noel Coward plays she has gone to, the fact that there is a drought in the Middle West, that there was a war when she was a child, that there will be another when she has a child, that she and Carl have something between them but it is not enough, that she is sorry for the taxi-driver and ashamed of being sorry, that *at bottom she is almost grave*. In the end, Bertram Kyle said to anybody or nobody, in the end I think . . .

But there was no reason any more to think. His fingers were clicking, clicking, somehow it developed that Gerry had muddled things because he was drunk so that the taxi-man must go to jail pending special sessions, and then Bettina and Gerry and Carl take the detective out to a bar someplace; explaining frankly to waiters that they are just four people who love each other veddy veddy much . . . and, perhaps because they all hate themselves so veddy veddy much, Carl and Gerry let Bettina carry them all off in her car for a three-day spree which means that Gerry misses the subpoena and the taxi-driver spends a week in jail, earning himself a fine prison record because he stole four dollars to which Carl and Gerry and Bettina think him wholly and earnestly entitled, and perhaps in the end they give the four dollars to the Communist Party, or perhaps they just buy another round of drinks, or perhaps they throw it in the river, or perhaps they frankly throw themselves . . .

And is this all, Bertram Kyle, all that will come out today of your living a life by yourself, of your having been born thirty years ago and tossed peanuts to elephants, wept at the Chartres window, slapped at mosquitoes, survived the hells and heavens of adolescence to be born again, today — is this all, this one short story which leaves out so much of life? But neither can a painter crowd all the world's rivers and mountains and railroad tracks onto one canvas, yet if his picture is any good at all it is good because he has seen those rivers and mountains and puts down all that he knows and all that he has felt about them, even if his painting is of a bowl of flowers and a curtain . . . And here, thought that thin layer of consciousness which went on as an undercurrent to his fingers' steady tapping, here is my lust for Betsey, my repentance for Louise, my endless gratitude to the woman who wore a yellow hat, my defeatism, my optimism, the fact that I was born when I was, all of my last night's living and much that has gone before . . .

The room grew clouded with the late afternoon and the cigarettes that he forgot to smoke. His fingers went faster, they ached like the limbs of a tired lover and they wove with delicacy and precision because the story had grown so real to him that it was physical. He knew that his shoulders were hunched, that his feet were cramped, that if he turned his desk about he would have a better light — but all the time he was tearing out sheet after sheet and with an odd accuracy that was not his own at any other time, inserting the next ones with rapidity and ease, he typed almost perfectly, he made few mistakes in spelling, punctuation, or the choice of words, and he swung into a rhythm that was at once uniquely his and yet quite new to him.

Now each idea as he pounded it out on his flying machine gave birth to three others, and he had to lean over and make little notes with a pencil on little pieces of paper that later on he would figure out and add together and stick in all the gaping stretches of his story. He rediscovered the miracle of something on page twelve tying up with something on page seven which he had not understood when he wrote it, the miracle of watching a shapeless thing come out and in the very act of coming take its own inevitable shape. He could feel his story growing out of the front of his head, under his moving fingers, beneath his searching eye . . . his heart was beating as fast as the keys of his typewriter, he wished that his typewriter were also an easel, a violin, a sculptor's tools, a boat he could sail, a plane he could fly, a woman he could love, he wished it were something he could not only bend over in his passion but lift in his exultation, he wished it could sing for him and paint for him and breathe for him.

And all at once his head swims, he is in a fog, sitting is no longer endurable to him, and he must get up, blind, not looking at his words, and walk about the room, the big room, the small room, whether it is night or day or summer or winter, he must get up and walk it off . . . *Listen, non-writers, I am not boasting when I tell you that writing is not a sublimation of living, but living is a pretty feeble substitute for art. Listen, non-writers, this is passion. I am trembling, I am weak, I am strong, pardon me a moment while I go and make love to the world, it may be indecent, it may be mad — but as I stalk about the room now I am not a man and I am not a woman, I am Bettina Gregory and Gerry and the taxi-driver and all the whores and cops and stooges in the night-court, I am every one of the keys of my typewriter, I am the clean white pages and the word-sprawled used ones, I am the sunlight on my own walls — rip off your dress, life, tear off your clothes, world, let me come closer; for listen: I am a sated, tired, happy writer, and I have to make love to the world.*

Sometimes it was night when this happened and then he must go to bed because even a writer needs sleep, but at those times he went to bed and then lay there stark and wide awake with plots weaving like tunes in his head and characters leaping like mad chess-men, and words, words and their miraculous combinations, floating about on the ceiling above him and burying themselves in the pillow beneath him till he thought that he would never sleep and knew that he was mad . . . till Louise sometimes cried out that she could not sleep beside him, knowing him to be lying there only on sufferance, twitching with his limbs like a mad-man in the dark . . .

Louise! For it was not night, it was late afternoon, with the dark of coming night stealing in to remind him, to remind him that if he were ever again to make the break from his life's world back to sanity, back to normalcy and Louise, he must make it now, while he remembered to; he must leave this room, stale with his much-lived life, his weary typewriter, he must shake off his ecstasy and his bewilderment, his passion, his love, his hate, his glorious rebirth and his sated daily death — and go to meet Louise; go to a cocktail party . . .

He was shocked and terrified when he met his own face in the mirror because it was not a face, it was a pair of haggard, gleaming eyes, and because like Rip Van Winkle he seemed to have grown heavy with age and yet light with a terrible youth. He managed somehow to get by without letting the elevator man know that he was crazy, that he was afraid of him because he was a face and a voice, because he seemed to be looking at him queerly. On the street Bettina appeared and walked beside him, waving her drunken coat-hangers and announcing, "Frankly there is nothing like a coat-hanger," while Gerry leaned across him rather bitterly to say, "If I hear you say frankly again, Bettina, frankly I shall kill you." But they walked along, all of them, very gay and friendly, despite the taxi-driver's slight hostility, and then at the corner they were joined by Carl with the detective's arm about him, and Carl was saying to anybody and nobody that they passed — "Frankly we are veddy veddy mad." And they came at last to Freddie's house, and there Bertram Kyle stood for a moment, deserted by Bettina and Carl and Gerry — even the detective was gone — hiding behind a collar and a tie and frankly panic-stricken. The door opens, he enters mechanically — good God, is it a massacre, a revolution, is it the night-court, a nightmare? . . .

But he pushed in very bravely and began to reel toward all his friends. "Hello, I'm cockeyed!" he roared at random. "Hell, I've been floating for forty days, where's a coat-hanger, Freddie, frankly, if there's anything I'm nuts about it's coat-hangers, and frankly have you seen my friends, some people I asked along, Bettina Gregory, Gerry, and a detective?" He saw Louise, ominous and tolerant, placing her hands in disgust on her soft hips at sight of him. Frankly, he shouted at her, frankly, Louise, I am just three or four people who love you veddy veddy much, and where's a drink, my pearl, my pet, my bird, my cage, my night-court, my nightmare — for frankly I need a little drink to sober down . . .

LOVELL THOMPSON

Often called as powerful as the writing of Joseph Conrad, "The Iron City" attracted wide attention when it was published. The conflict between two lonely men at sea over a girl only one of the men has ever seen has the surge of the ocean itself in its narration.

Lovell Thompson was born in Nahant, Massachusetts, in 1902. He was educated at Harvard University and has worked in the Boston publishing house of Houghton Mifflin Company most of his life.

The Iron City

THERE is a rawness in the city of Liverpool that permeates the flesh and grips the vitals of a man who, like Gideon Grimes, is not vigorous. The city, as it stood in his mind, appeared coated with cold, cohesive dust. When he thought of the city he felt sticky particles rasping upon his fingertips and saw heavy dust-hardened raindrops, and fog stiffened by the filth of Liverpool. The odor of Liverpool was to him that of stale grease; even after he had crossed the Mersey Bar a taste of Liverpool clung in the back of his throat. Was it the queer name of the city that stamped this impression on him, or was it that it was the place where he had met Shank?

Gideon Grimes hated the city — and yet it was this city, phlegmatic and depraved, that beyond all others lay closest to the varied and beautiful ocean. The graceful ships of a hundred nations rested here close to the stinking rawboned docks. In the harbor the water was smooth, sluggish, and crusted with a gelatinous scum. Yet here, in spite of ugliness and crudity, the thousand-fingered hand of the ocean gently soothed the land. The mighty rhythm of the ocean's breath is sensitively felt in Liverpool. The scum upon the surface of the water assiduously charts upon the piles of the docks the record of each breath. Twice a year the ocean heaves a few vast equinoctial signs, the tide rises high and in Liverpool the highest tide is more permanently recorded than the rest, by the scum mark on the piles, by the bits of débris shoved far up to a damp and rotting security beneath the bellies of the docks. Here on the harbor's edge human scum is also deposited and left till the next high tide reaches up for it once more. Thus the hand of the ocean reached for the man Shank, on the same September night that Gideon Grimes also embarked for America.

Under the shelter of the dock a few electric light bulbs shone listlessly. They were on the ends of long rods which stretched down out of darkness. They lit up the sordid dirt and scraps of paper upon the dock floor. Gideon Grimes tightened his muscles to try to stop shivering. The anguished clatter of a winch banged at the back of his head. He was weak. He was depressed. He gazed down the dockway into the murk as if in search of a reason.

And out of the murk came the man Shank whose name he did not then know. He, too, bore a duffle bag upon his shoulder. He leaned forward with it and thus was able to support it partly on his back and partly also upon his elbow, cocked up for the purpose with a hand upon his hip. His other arm, the left, with the fingers of the hand hooked into the fastening of the sea bag upon his right shoulder, concealed his face. So Grimes observed the rest of him. He was shabby, neither dirty nor clean, neither tidy nor unkempt — he was utterly ordinary and he bent beneath his load like a tallow taper before a hot blaze.

When he had come quite close to the gangplank before which Grimes stood, he threw down his duffle bag. He was small, about the size of Gideon, and astonishingly thin, and his pinched face except for his eyes was no more unusual than the rest of him. His eyes looked as if their owner's line of vision traveled about twenty feet and then turned a right angle. The man looked as if he were trying to see around a corner; looked as if he did see around one; looked as if he saw nowhere else. He looked at Gideon Grimes, seeming to have to look away to get him in his line of vision, and he spoke.

"Say, Brother, ain't there extra quarters on these ships, fellars like you going back — extra bunks I mean? Think I could stow away with you fellars — no one would notice? Won't show up for boat drill. Slip ashore in Boston. What do you think, eh?"

"I guess so," said Gideon.

"I'll stick close to you," said Shank, and close he remained.

They labored into the black belly of the ship.

On a ship of this type what is often called the first deck is beneath the actual outside deck of the ship. By outside deck is meant what the ordinary man considers the deck of a ship — the outermost uppermost side which roofs in the hold and upon which the officers' quarters, funnels, and what not appears to be a superstructure. Beneath this outside deck then is the first deck — a subterranean deck, as it were, and on it, forward in the bow, are quarters for the crew, rooms lined with bunks.

They walked this deck, Shank and Grimes, between rows of iron supports. The deck was dark and for the most part empty.

On this freighter, as on other ships of the same line, there were the extra quarters which Shank had asked about. These had been put in after the building of the ship, to accommodate extra hands required for the shipping of certain cargoes — a deckload of livestock, for instance. Thereafter these quarters were used as a sort of unofficial sub-steerage, where men whom the line desired to transport across the ocean were quartered.

The *Iron City* had a cabin for four next these quarters. It was designed for those who were in charge of the men who worked on the cargo. Grimes made for this cabin, in the hope that the other free passengers might be sufficiently few for him to occupy it alone. Shank, however, followed him into the room, so Grimes directed him to throw his bag into a lower bunk and to crawl into an upper himself. Gideon did the same and the cabin was occupied. Other men following looked in but were directed to the larger bunk-room further along.

Shank's scheme of stowing away was extraordinarily feasible. The captain of a freighter pays no attention to this idle element of his crew. There are say ten men in the extra quarters — most of them probably have been employed in bringing livestock from America to England; no one ever sees them all together. The face of the stowaway becomes familiar. No one realizes that he is an extra. The officers are searching for a name on their lists which has no corresponding face, not for a face which has no name.

With blankets given out later by the purser, and with a dry straw mattress beneath him, Gideon felt warm and slept. As he dropped off, he noticed that a rod of light from one of the bulbs on the dock came through a doorway and through a port and at last rested upon the recumbent figure of Shank — this leech who clung to him — it lit Shank's face, his strange eyes now closed and his mouth now gently ajar.

During the next day, the *Iron City* steamed through choppy water along the coast of Ireland. Hour after hour the high green coast passed by — the long miles marked by bulging headlands. Each, when first seen, appeared to come no nearer; ship and headland moved together, carried on the same subaqueous belt. But when attention was turned from the progress of the boat the headlands leapt up upon it and stopped again when the eye was turned upon them as if they played a game.

As the day dwindled, the long, blinking beam of Fastnet Light rose in the west. The beam of this revolving star, like a gigantic compass describing an arc, traversed every few seconds a three-hundred-mile circle and yet found time in its passing to pierce the eyeball of Grimes, who looked at it, with a fierce, curious stare.

Summoned by this wonder, and still smelling of stale daylight sleep, up the forward hatchway, rose the fate-sent Shank to ask, "What light is that?"

"Fastnet," said Grimes.

Shank looked while the night wind, sharp upon the forecastlehead, hewed his heavy frowsy hair into a sculptured grace. Then he turned away to walk a stretch down the deck and return. Thus he came at intervals, bringing his pale face to meet the swinging light, then turned again to vanish as if into another world. And each time he came Gideon asked a question and Shank replied, gradually drawing the picture of a life.

With an artificial tension produced by his periodic walks down the deck, from which he would return still more stirred by the contemplation of his past, Shank held his listener, there on the deck of the *Iron City*. A constantly freshening wind gave to the man's talk an ominous crescendo and the scene was unified by one powerful trait of the man which emerged slowly from his story.

This was a genius for taking care of himself in perilous situations — a genius for always attaching himself to the person who was best fitted to look after him — a genius which had thus far never forsaken him.

In Egypt during the war he had found a six-foot-five Australian. He had followed this man as a jackal does a lion; he had watched with furtive curiosity the unending process of satisfying the lion's appetites, and he had picked up the mouthfuls which were thrown aside as too small to fill the throat of his patron.

Into Arab villages where voluminous Arab women with tattooed faces beckoned, Shank followed Australia; he wet his feet where the big man wallowed; drank a glass where his companion drank a gallon; used the Australian's size and boldness to aid him in gleaning a small harvest of dissipation which Shank alone would never have had the courage or impressiveness to find, and in the end he would take Australia home.

"Women listen," said Shank, "when six-foot-five speaks to them."

On the bow of the battleship that the English were to beach as part of their desperate plan to land at Gallipoli, stood the big Australian. After the vessel had gently forced its keel into the smooth sand, he was one of the first over the gangplank toward shore, and one of the many to be killed on that gangplank — his superhuman appetites quenched by human death. Perhaps the last tremor of departing life woke the big man to consciousness once more, told him that, in his loneliness, many feet were stepping over him; then left him only time to curse the day that man was born to die. Perhaps, however, he never knew that Shank was not to take him home from this night of adventure as from the others.

Shank saw, and the bile of his belly was sour in his throat. Turkish lights and Turkish guns were trained upon the landing point. Shank knew that the other end of that plank did not lie on the beach but in unending unconscious.

Then he saw a few men running to the unnoticed and slightly more seaward side of the bow, from there they dropped into the water and swam ashore. This was the thin road out that fate always sent to Shank. He hurled himself over the side and fell feet first into the bloody water with a thick splash like a June-bug in a mug of beer. But he was soon gathering his feet under him in the shallow water, safely landed beyond the feline stare of the searchlights.

Fastnet Light was barely discernible now and as the *Iron City* left the sheltering coast of Ireland, the wind grew stronger. The ship took the waves on her quarter. She wallowed deeply while each wave rolled upward along her side toward the scuppers amidships. Then as the lifting power of the wave passed forward beneath the center of the boat, the stern fell back and the bow rose dripping and stars and shreds of cloud appeared beneath the ship's rail. The last step in the cycle was a shuffling, falling movement as the ship fell backward and crabwise down the long back of the wave, while the wave cantered easily forward into the darkness like some unwieldy prehistoric animal wearing a small white nightcap of phosphorescent foam. The light upon the mast indicated upon the sky, as if with an extended little finger, an ellipse; and drew it neatly to a close as each wave passed. Shank's talk ceased; he felt sick and went below.

Often during the next thirty-six hours Grimes watched Shank stick his head out of the porthole above his bunk. He looked at these moments like a mouse with its head in a trap, hind quarters protruding, passionately limp. He was very sick.

The fourth morning, however, was sunny with a light steadying headwind, and Shank with a two days' beard upon his face peered over the edge of his bunk with the light of life in his eye. After breakfast Shank followed Gideon up to the wheelhouse where it was sheltered — where the sun was tropical and where they lay half naked upon the deck. Here, stimulated by his sudden freedom from nausea and by his heavy drinking of tea, and hypnotized by the droning of the ship's propeller beneath them — Shank grew confidential.

"I've got a girl," said Shank. "And I've got money."

He reached for his coat, stiffly, as one from death revivified, and pulled out of it a worn imitation-leather wallet. From the wallet he drew a photograph and holding it in his wan yellow palm, he studied it for a long time. Grimes leaned over the man's shoulder to look at the picture and noticed that he smelt like an old man, and that the high sun made the hairs on his chest cast long shadows on his belly.

Gideon was looking down at the picture of a woman — Shank's "girl." Momentarily the bright day and all it showed to his eyes became a frame to the picture. The tarry pleasant smell of a bit of marlin he was twisting in his hands perfumed the moment.

There was a long silence, for the face before Grimes was beautiful. The face of that woman had the seductive patience of a fair-weather sea. It was a smooth-skinned face, deeply shadowed beneath the eyes, which were lighter than the surrounding skin. The hair was heavy, like the flow of oil, and was drawn back from the round cheeks to leave the pale ears showing. The woman wore a round-necked dress with a collar that lay smooth upon it and a sort of coif above her smooth crown. The points of her shoulders were thrown forward slightly so that there was an area above a full, deep bosom which was slightly concave.

"There's the girl," said Shank, and added abruptly, "She's a trained nurse."

"Now," said Shank, "I'll tell ye how I got the money." So he began, blinking at the wide ocean with his eyes that made only the knight's move.

The new regiment to which, after Gallipoli and toward the end of the war, Shank was shifted was in a camp, close behind the lines in France. In this regiment there was a man who owned a roulette wheel. Daily this man spread out the marked cloth that was the board and amid an attendant circle he spun the wheel and was the banker — but Shank was the croupier.

And Shank was glad to be croupier, for he felt that he won, himself, and yet at no risk; the banker in turn permitted Shank's offices good-humoredly at first, and then as his game grew larger depended on them. The banker was Sergeant Cooper — a man with a squat frame and a huge U-shaped smile and a nose that plunged down between the upright arms of the U. His smile parted his lips from one corner of his mouth to the other; it looked like a horseshoe turned upright for luck.

One night a soldier came hurrying to the grinning sergeant's group to say that the regiment was ordered forward.

On the following night Shank got himself settled comfortably in a front-line trench. After settling himself he took a walk down the trench to pay a call and to ask a question. He called on a second lieutenant whom he had known before and who had been given a command which included Sergeant Cooper. His question was, "How's Sergeant Cooper?" "Oh, he's fine," replied the lieutenant, and Shank retired.

Regularly once a day for four days Shank made this inquiry, and at last on the fourth day the answer he sought was given him.

"I sent Cooper out this morning with a couple of men, to look around, and he didn't come back. They all got separated and Cooper's two men don't know what became of him." Shank thanked the lieutenant and returned to his place.

He shed no tears for the good sergeant whose wheel had given so much pleasure to so many and so much profit to its owner and who somewhere in No Man's Land had encountered a run on the bank.

"I got back then quick to my post," Shank went on, and he waited at his post until full darkness, then crawled over the parapet and began, on hands and knees, a search for Sergeant Cooper.

Now and then a star shell went up and caught the thin little man turning over a corpse with his hand for a better look at the face. Instantly he would crouch and be like the dead man himself, using the light, however, for a glance at the dead face, looking eagerly for that horseshoe smile.

Shank told Grimes that it was safer to be in No Man's Land than in a trench, if you knew the shell holes, for there was less shelling there and less sniping.

Sometimes Shank could tell by the smell of a body that it was not that of Sergeant Cooper, for Cooper had not been dead long. Sometimes Shank must have turned over one that still retained life enough to roll a comprehending eye; but he never said this. Perhaps he crept quickly away when this happened, disliking the suspicious glance of these men whose problem was suddenly so far removed from his and who were already cooling in the final chill. He would then have had to come back when such a man had died to make sure that none of them was Cooper. He continued with perseverance his squirming inspection of that dark rat-ridden graveyard for the unburied, returning in the gray of morning.

Thus the man worked to rob the dead. And when Gideon said this Shank turned upon him and said, dropping his 'H' as he seldom did: "Well, 'oo are the dead?"

"It was the third night," said Shank, "I found him, and in the pocket of his tunic the money, mostly coins."

Shank took the grinning sergeant's identification disk, his money, and his wrist watch and warily returned to the home trench. He was not one to believe fortune a friend because fortune had done him a favor. . . .

Shank's voice had stopped and the regular beat of the propeller upon the water now became noticeable. It rose, this sound, to take the place of Shank's voice, to fill in the interval as water runs into a depression, leveling it off. The small waves ran out from the wake, upon the surface of the ocean, as upon a hard surface; and the sound of them came regularly as upon a beach. The long, straight wake appeared to have been once a flowing substance, long since congealed, though retaining still the pattern of its boiling. It lay now behind the ship like a fault in the surface of a vast blue earth. Shank pulled a layer of skin-like red paint off the deck and made no further move to speak. The slow strong pulse of calm weather beat everywhere about them.

While Grimes fidgeted, Shank slept, and between the blue concentric spheres of sky and ocean, three white birds appeared, painted when they flew high a yellowed amber by the late afternoon light and reflecting the blue light from the ocean on their bellies when they flew low. The birds looked like tubby cigars with a stiff unjointed wing, shaped like a razor blade attached to each side of the center of the cigar. With wings as unmoving as if transfixed by the taxidermist's wire, these birds apparently freed from the laws of gravity rose and fell in the air. Going nowhere, seeking no food, they were only superficially appropriate, the touch of a landlubber's brush upon the afternoon marine.

The birds passed on ahead of the ship, outdistancing it as did the sun and the lazy waves. One bird before it disappeared, swept toward the boat and passed over it, casting thus a momentary shadow, like a mask, across Shank's eyes. With the passing of the shadow and the resuming of the glare of the sun upon his face, Shank opened his eyes and looked at once at Gideon. He started, feeling guilty at having been caught thus staring at Shank while he slept.

"I've been thinking the face of that girl was familiar, Shank. Just let me have another glance at the photo, will you?" Gideon repeated these words to himself trying to find the casual emphasis.

When at last he spoke the question aloud, Shank said, "What girl?"

"I mean the photo of the trained nurse you showed me."

"You don't know her," said Shank, as if to close the conversation.

But Grimes persisted, "Let me see it at any rate."

"What the Jesus for?" mumbled Shank; but he unfolded his coat and reached into the inner pocket. Then at last he placed that beautiful victim in Gideon's hand.

Gideon looked but did not dare to gaze too long. Passing the photo back he said, "What's her name?"

"She's Mary Slade," said Shank.

Before Grimes slept that night he dared to ask Shank another question. "Shank," he said, "where is she now, your friend Mary Slade?"

And at this Shank rose out of his bunk, and Grimes saw his head silhouetted against the portal which showed, a round gray hole in the surrounding darkness. "Say," said Shank, "you're struck on that picture, ain't you?"

Grimes saw as he examined the silhouette from the shelter of his dark bunk that Shank was right; Gideon was struck on Mary Slade.

At last the silhouette vanished and Grimes saw the round port unbroken once more; the straw of Shank's mattress hissed dryly with the movement of his body and Shank's voice said: "She's in Blackwell. A town in the east of England." No more was said that night.

What had taken seed on the fourth day, on the fifth grew rankly, so that the position of Shank as tyrant keeper of the well was a thing established by night. This was natural since Shank and Grimes were day and night together, and had no occupation to keep them from continual consciousness of one another's thoughts; and since there could come no other woman's face to divert these two from the voluptuous contemplation of the face of Mary Slade.

Furthermore it was necessary for Shank not to displease Grimes too much, for at disembarkation comes another time when the stowaway must have a man to assist him. Someone must carry his duffle ashore, leaving him in hiding aboard until nightfall, when he can walk off unquestioned by the authorities on shore. Once ashore, he can look up his accomplice, get his baggage, and depart about his business. For this task Grimes was the ideal man. And the desire of Grimes's fingers to know exactly the temperature of the gray opalescent fine-textured skin on Mary Slade's throat was Shank's assurance.

On the sixth day of the voyage the *Iron City* passed in the late afternoon a ship headed back to England. The smokestack of this vessel was a rich weathered pink that shone out even at a great distance. The smoke from the vessel's funnel rose gently upward — for the wind was on her quarter — and then lay in a huge flimsy cloud above the ship. Thoughtful and brooding, as if with a distracted eye upon the ship, the cloud appeared like a mother who patiently slows her pace for the child that bustles by her hand. Other shreds of cloud, fatigued by their defeat at the hands of the sunny day, struggled down the sky and made a white background for the dark brooding smoke.

On one of the *Iron City*'s tarpaulin-covered hatches a stoker sat; his face was pasty, his eyes were darkened about the lashes by coal dust imperfectly removed. He looked like a great actor wearied and resting after the playing of a tragic rôle. He crooned upon a harmonica softly to the receding day, and noiselessly dusk gathered in the zenith.

And Gideon, too, sat there on the hatch and watched the ship go slowly back to England. Shank sat beside him.

"That ship," said Shank, "will be steaming up the Mersey in a week, and if ye were aboard her ye'd be in Blackwell the same day."

"I'll go back there, as soon as I get to America," said Grimes. It was a threat, but Shank laughed. He laughed first silently with his lower jaw agape, like the swinging jaw of a steam shovel; then he laughed through his nose, noisily and with his mouth wide open and his stinking breath pouring out between his rotten teeth. Then he banged the tragic actor on the back and asked him did he hear that. The harmonica sputtered, uttered a discord, and then resumed exactly where it left off . . . "save the king."

Then in the full early night, while Shank beside him dreamed not of the deadly thrust he made at him, Grimes swore to himself to visit Blackwell as soon as he could get back to England. Shank in silence enjoyed Grimes's despondent air. He did not know that Gideon's oath made him like a man pushed from a cliff-top; as yet unharmed, he fell through space.

Shank felt a need to play upon Grimes's admiration for Mary and thus to assure himself of Gideon's protection. Every time that Grimes was permitted to see the picture of Mary, and this was really often though never without preliminary resistance, Shank accompanied the revelation of the beautiful face with a new tale of the woman's extraordinary humbleness. These relations, coming with the sight of the picture as they did, filled Grimes with envy and passion. This made Shank exaggerate. Nonetheless, the succession of anecdotes as the days passed built a picture detailed and essentially truthful.

Mary's strength drew her to Shank's weakness. The more she battled for him and against him, the more she had at stake and the further she was from leaving him. She was like a mother persisting in her love for a vicious child.

During the war the poor women of Blackwell had been organized to do a share in the war work. They knitted and rolled bandages; and Mary, whose hands were quick, soon began to be noticed. A hospital was started in the neighborhood, and Mary's capabilities soon drew her out of her natural sphere and into another. Mary became a trained nurse.

As a nurse Mary was distinguished by her calm strength. She tended her patients placidly, disregarding their complaints, her mind fixed only on the signs of their recovery.

The war ended. Mary Slade returned to Blackwell; and when Shank returned also, all her natural affection and all her newly acquired gift for watching over the unreasonable flowed out upon him. In this nerve-racking atmosphere of endless patience Shank soon grew restless again.

There was still one other chapter in the six-day epic of Shank's leechdom. It was apparently almost a final scene in that part of Shank's life which preceded his brief acquaintance with Grimes. The effect of its

telling upon Gideon's mind was subtle and final. It grew into his mind
during the next day of the voyage like roots into soft earth, laying a fine
fatal tendril on every particle. For it showed to Grimes how the fear of
dying hung over Shank, excluding consideration for the world. It made
Grimes feel strong — he seemed to hold a weapon built and weighted to
his hand. . . .

During the summer following the peace Shank was finally mustered
out of France and crossed the Channel on his way to Blackwell. He
found among the troops that accompanied him another man who was
also going to Blackwell. With this man Shank made friends. They had
drunk many drinks together by the time Blackwell was reached, and
Shank had shown his friend the picture of Mary. Meanwhile Shank had
thought of a joke with which to celebrate his homecoming.

"Go to her house and tell her I'm dead," said Shank.

Shank's friend, a handsome man, impressed by Mary's beauty and
feeling that the embrace of a handsome man is often a quick road away
from grief for the death of a runt, consented — already feeling the soft
skin of Mary on his lips.

The handsome man went to the house where Mary lived and spoke his
piece, and Mary wept at the news and screamed under his kisses and he
fled.

Such was Shank's joke — and Shank waited at a nearby saloon to hear
the outcome. His friend, of course, never bothered to report, and Shank
after waiting and drinking set out for Mary's house himself. The woman
who came to the door in answer to Shank's ring said that Mary had left
the house. Shank knew Blackwell and knew where she would have gone.
Shank was pretty drunk but he kept walking. Just outside of the town
the road crossed a brook, and at its crossing there was a break in the
hedge that bordered the road and a footway ran through it along the side
of the brook. The path ended where the brook crossed another road a
mile further along its course. Here Shank and Mary had walked in the
early days of Shank's courting.

Unsteadily then Shank walked down this path in search of his beautiful Mary. He found her remembering in torture the kisses of the handsome man, and wondering in yet greater pain if the terrible story he had
told her was true.

Shank's snuffling laugh announced to Mary his return from death, for
the sight of Mary's grief was funny to him. Shaken with laughter he half

fell, half willingly sat down in the coarse strong-growing grass at the brook's edge. Mary seeing him ran to him, crouched beside him pressing her wet face upon his in joy. Shank laughed on, and between drunken giggles explained his joke. Mary was not a woman to spank a long-lost child because he had run away. She was glad of Shank's return and went on kissing him. Under her kisses his gloating suddenly turned from mirth to heat.

The soft upper edge of Mary's breast might just have showed at the pointed neck of her dress — so Grimes thought where its smooth arch sprang from her chest. It might have looked in the half light of the long twilight a gray cream color — soft and giving way elusively under the touch as if the skin actually floated upon a smooth rich liquid.

Shank's breath smelling of stale beer warmed Mary's neck; perhaps she saw in his face more human emotion than she had seen for many years. Thus the picture was before Grimes's eyes when Shank paused to grab the shoulder of the intent listener, startling him so that he shivered. "Wot 'appened then? 'ere's wot 'appened — a goddam rabbit, his guts a-swim with fear, scrambled clean over the two of us" — as intent upon its separate terror as Shank upon the soft throat of Mary. But here something had laid hold of Mary. Suddenly the smell of decaying vegetation in the brook bed, the reasonless cancerous profusion of growth all about her, smothered for a moment the intentness of her love of Shank. She stopped him in mid-caress.

While he paused, the rabbit, still near, began to scream; the enemy that had invisibly pursued had now caught up. The rabbit gave forth a series of cries each less strong, a significant diminuendo, without emotion, a purely mechanical announcement that that which was alive understood that it was losing in agony all the world of created things. The mad desire to go on living, the great condition of all life, was in the presence of Mary and Shank undergoing the final chastening which it was born to meet, the ultimate agony which dwarfs all joy. Shank felt Mary's body stiffen and relax as if the outcry were her own, and Shank's hand, like a scaled lizard, withdrew cringing from that dim and oddly cool chamber between Mary's breasts where it had crept.

Between that time and the time of his seeking out the *Iron City,* Shank did not again make love to Mary Slade. Death had waggled a finger at him. He was impressed by his bad luck. Perhaps he had hoped the *Iron City* would wall it out, but it had walled it in. Grimes, too, feared it and felt himself shaken by a strange anticipatory tremble, like a bride before her lover, but the embrace that now encircled him was sinister and invisible.

"Does Mary know why you have gone or where?" asked Grimes.

"I'll write," said Shank, "when I'm well ready."

There were two things only which served to make one day different from the next aboard the *Iron City*. The weather and the photograph of Mary Slade. The rotation of stew and hash was as monotonous and as inevitable as the turn of the ship's propeller. The rotation of distant officers upon the bridge was the same. One had a beard, one had a mustache, one was clean-shaven. These faces appeared against the sky in a succession as imperturbable as the alternation of sun and moon against the same sky, and the faces seemed, if anything, more distant. Sun and moon and officers and hash all moved like figures on an elaborate clock to the rhythmic, melodious, distant sound of the ship's bells.

But the weather and the photograph were full of change. They maintained an interrelationship of mood, an irrelevant coquettishness. They smiled, then sneered; they played tricks with time, they spun the moon in its orbit at will; they rang the ship's bells and toyed with the succession of beards and mustaches. Gideon was bound by their spell day and night. He was alone with the *Iron City* surrounded by hallucinations; he sailed in an empty sea.

By the eighth day Mary was flesh and blood for Grimes and he had set up about her picture all those fetishes of love that men set up about the moods of real women.

It was a cruel tyranny. He tried to think of a way by which he might break it. In the first place he might steal the photograph. When Shank discovered its absence, he would become infuriated — for he would thus lose a hostage for his security, and the implement with which, in this dull interval, he tortured Grimes. He would realize just where his picture had gone and Grimes would not dare sleep in a room with a man thus enraged who was moreover in possession of a bag of murderous tackler's tools — mechanic's hammers nicely weighted, punches, and the like. If he dared not sleep with Shank after the theft, so Grimes reasoned, he should have to get rid of him, and this he might do by hastily informing the ship's officers of the presence of a stowaway aboard the ship. This scheme would leave Grimes quit of Shank and in possession of the photograph.

In the darkness of the eighth night — stimulated by the wheezing of the unconscious Shank — Grimes plotted on. A stowaway is put in the brig and he goes back with the ship to his native port. Shank would go back to England and very likely, after a short jail term, back to Mary. Grimes, without money, having to work his passage back, could hardly get there before Shank. It would not do to expose Shank.

Here the sleeping Shank paused in his wheezing to moisten his lips, and for Gideon from this thought there arose another anxiety. Suppose Shank were to lose the photograph? He would be quite as sure that Grimes had taken it, as if he really had, and Grimes would be in the same danger of violence.

On the ninth day of the voyage a new piece of information was thrust at Gideon. The finger of God appeared and pointed to it.

Early in the ninth night Shank and Grimes stood on the fo'c'slehead. The wind was behind the ship so that it was comfortable to be in the bow. Two figures moved silently on the bridge. A third man was tinkering with the searchlight on the bridge; it went on and off at rare intervals; a lantern was near him to light his work.

There were only two topics of conversation between Grimes and Shank now. There was the problem of getting Shank ashore, and there was Mary Slade.

"Mary's a fine big woman," said Shank. He drew out his wallet. "If the searchlight comes on again ye might have a look." Grimes tried in the half darkness to prepare his eyes to take advantage of every moment of light by filling them in advance with the image of the photograph so that no time should be wasted in recognition of details already sufficiently impressed on his mental eye. Thus his eye was fixed upon Shank's hands that held his wallet and the photograph. Many moments passed but the light was not turned on. After a while it went on and shone out over the water, throwing only a reflected grayness upon the photograph.

Shank and Grimes waited, but at last Shank grew tired and began to put it back in its place. As he was doing this and while Gideon's eyes still stared at his hands, a rod of light leapt into the air. It did not progress from the searchlight and illuminate Shank's hands. It was dropped into place whole; one end rested in the socket of the searchlight on the bridge, the other rested on the wallet in Shank's hands and slipped a tributary beam into every crevice and pocket in it. The finger of light pointed into the long pocket at the back of the wallet. There, deep in the bowels of the greasy wallet, ephemeral, perishable, Grimes perceived two notes of the Bank of England. The bar of light vanished, not sucked in like a lizard's tongue, but lifted out of place whole and instantaneously, and put down somewhere else out of sight. Grimes had not fixed his anxious gaze upon Mary's face, but what had he seen?

In the darkness that follows blinding light and that slowly returns again to the normal gray like blood returning to a frightened face, Grimes saw that Shank's eyes were fixed upon his and that they asked him that same question.

Grimes had not envisaged the winnings of Sergeant Cooper in the form of two bank notes in Shank's pocket. He had supposed the money hidden or in a bank. Now it appeared to be within reach of his hand. That money, could he procure it, would see him back to England at once.

After an interval Shank went below but Grimes remained where he was. Smoke, black and angry, was pushed out of the funnel and blown forward above him, darkening the night. The many sounds of the traveling ship made in his ear a monotonous whisper, a woven harlequin pattern of sound unheard. An ocean of jet a-sparkle with gray highlights stood before his eyes unseen. Eyes and ears turned inwards and fixed themselves upon one thought. When Grimes took the photograph from Shank, he must also take the money.

He saw himself upon the bridge telling the two men about the stowaway. He saw an officer asking him why he had not reported this sooner; he heard Shank's voice saying that he had only done it now because he had taken Shank's money; Grimes saw himself locked with Shank below decks. While Shank had a voice, a memory, while Shank was on the ship, Grimes would not be safe.

Then, upon that instant, Shank must have no voice, no memory; he must leave the ship.

From every angle both in space and in time, Gideon saw a long line of circumstances converging with a fitness born of fatality upon the deed of murder. No one knew that Shank was aboard the *Iron City*. A day or so before the vessel's arrival in harbor it was necessary that Shank disappear so that when the final roundup came he would be well hidden, waiting for evening to enable him to slip off the ship unseen. When Shank was no longer on the ship, Grimes would only have to say to his companions, who knew Shank was a stowaway, that Shank had begun his term of hiding. Grimes then would walk off the vessel when it made port with Shank's duffle as already arranged, and who was to know that Shank, who had been last seen in Blackwell, had met death upon the Grand Banks of Newfoundland?

The heavy bag of tools, the mechanic's hammer, now seemed to Gideon as providential as the revelation of the money and the chance of having come to know the photograph.

With this thought of violence tightening its unfamiliar grip upon him, Gideon waited upon the bow beneath the heavy train of smoke that went into the west. Its mass concealed him, its hot breath warmed him. He wanted to go beneath it, toward the shore. He felt that the smoke would guide him, and conceal him from the stars. He saw himself upon a bicycle outdistancing the ship, riding upon the sea with Shank already done to death in stealth.

He climbed down the iron stairway to the castle deck. At the foot of it was the doorway to that four-bunk cabin which Shank and he had so successfully held against their companions. The round brass ring that was a doorknob stared at him as soon as he had stepped off the last step; he laid hand upon it; he stepped over the high sill and closed the door behind him. Into the deeper blackness of the cabin the grayer light of the open night flowed from the portal over Shank's bunk and lit with a faint austere light the head that Gideon hoped to crush, forty-eight hours hence; the eyes, their uneven flicker of deceit now vanished, moved idly beneath their lids. The faithful, forward motion of the ship gave peace. Shank's face wore the composed yet faintly drawn expression of a death mask. Below the gray calm-sharpened face Gideon saw, as his eyes became accustomed to yet deeper shades of night, protruding from the bunk beneath Shank's, the handle of his mechanic's hammer.

Grimes undressed silently so as not to wake Shank. He climbed into his bunk. He did not sleep. Hour upon hour his muscles twitched with the effort of wielding that hammer. He caught it with both hands and swung it above his head, but found he had swung it too freely and the metal girder above Shank's bunk rang where the blow fell. He realized that he could not strike as he would drive a spike with a sledge. He struck again, with a more circumspect swing; the blow fell strong upon the face of Shank, but the high side of the bunk was struck by the handle of his weapon at the same time that its head struck the sleeping face, the force of the blow was broken, it was not fatal, it did not even stun. Gideon wiped the slate clean again, and the next time he stood upon the lower bunk giving himself thus height from which to strike. His stroke this time was very cramped but the hammer was heavy, it shattered the skull like cardboard. It caught inside the hole it had made and could not easily be withdrawn. Gideon did not have the remotest idea how much force a skull would resist nor did he know how it would resist. Was it like a hen's egg, he wondered, or like a turtle's egg? A last time he rehearsed the blow, and this time he used the flat of the hammer and was successful. Would there be blood, he wondered? Was it a sure way to kill a man?

The ship traveled methodically on. It carried Shank and Gideon; and it carried all about Gideon a thousand other Shanks all variously mutilated and resisting his hammer. The room was crowded with their forms, they overlapped. There was one form with many heads; not one was whole. Gideon suffered the tortures of one who repents a crime. Yet he had not as yet committed any crime and certainly did not regret it. In the light of morning he resolved against the business and then slept.

Grimes opened his eyes, puffed with short hours of stuffy sleep. He knew at once that his life had become an unpleasant business. He looked forward to the day with dread and to all days. He sought in his mind for the reason and found at once the feeling of the murder of Shank, hastily following down the thoughts of the passed day, to overtake the present, he found his mind too slow for his anxiety. He rose out of his bed and hastily and fearfully looked into Shank's bunk. Shank lay there asleep. Grimes was at once overjoyed and disappointed: the situation was unchanged. He had nothing to fear today that he did not have to fear yesterday; he had no new hope today. Then in the same moment he remembered the outcome of the night's deliberations — he had decided not to kill Shank. He was free.

From the breakfast of sluggish gruel, stiffened bread, dusty butter, brightened only by the sunny light of marmalade, the untouchables on the tenth day arose and went on deck. The sun drew them up as it drew the light mists that lay here and there upon the ocean, like clouds dozing.

Grimes chose the forward end of the ship. He paced back and forth on the windward side of the deck and slowly he felt purged of the night. For this tenth day was lively. In its light all things moved lightly, briskly — waves, clouds, sun, and ship. The officer on the bridge moved quickly. He minced as if he walked a treadmill which supplied the power for the sprightly motion of the world around him. There in the ship's bow, Shank found Grimes, and crept away again frightened by his fierce silence.

Grimes stood staring at the flat sea as it came toward the ship. The boat was stationary, only the sea moved. Someone behind drew the huge flat sheet of water toward the vessel. The sheet was torn asunder in its exact center by the bow of the stationary boat. The material parted with a faint hiss. The dark scar of those parted edges showed behind the ship as far as the eye could see. Grimes watched the roll come toward him from the west. The lunch hour came and passed, he did not go below. The sea grew flatter. The cloth ran from the bolt smoothly and still more smoothly. The sun leapt with one exuberant bound into the zenith and through the bright morning. There it stood as still as if Grimes were a Joshua, and while it stood there and while the sea grew calm it waned, it paled. It was like a last ember in the grate at which you warm your hands. It died in mid-leap, and before the day had reached maturity it had dwindled into a premature and waxen twilight.

Then at last as the day fainted and night stood close — Grimes perceived the end of the bolt on which the smooth ocean was wound, the loom from which it came. For all about there now appeared wisps of mist, string-like shreds of vapor rising from the taut silken surface. And while Grimes watched, the ship was swallowed in the machinery of the loom. It plunged into a wall of fog.

Grimes now found himself in a new, cramped world, a world hardly bigger than the ship itself, and far from other worlds. Heralding this accomplished passage out of the world that Grimes knew, came an enormous sound. It filled the fog-bound sphere in which the ship was cased. This sound flowed alike between the particles of air and the particles of Gideon's body. It was as loud in his stomach as in the air above his head. It drew his knees toward his chin in a convulsion of fear. Upon the bridge the officer with a mustache had drawn down the wire that ran up the fog horn upon the funnel. Summoned by that trumpet of doom, Gideon went to his cabin scarce knowing whether he was judge or judged and fearing to be either.

He was too late for supper. He could only crawl shivering between his blankets; and his belly made savage with hunger paced within him like a caged cat, and at two-minute intervals throughout the night his whole body was dissolved in sound.

At every blast throughout the unrelenting night, Gideon's eyes leapt open. Morning came again, the eleventh morning, and as the sun rose higher the fog withdrew, not altogether but to a good distance — a besieging army which takes counsel after an unexpected rebuff. The fog horn ceased its braying — the wind had not risen since it had dropped twenty hours before. There was no sound of waves rebounding from iron flanks, no grunting of strained bolts; the ship moved stealthily. Relieved from the tension produced by the blasts of the horn which seemed to demand an accounting of him, Gideon fell asleep.

The morning passed. After lunch, feeling more cheerful, Grimes returned on deck with Shank. The sun was losing its strength, the boat still skated upon a stricken sea. Then the sun vanished altogether and the world, bounded by fog, shrank. With this new contraction of the cage surrounding Grimes and Shank, announcing their approach to a fog-bound Newfoundland, announcing the beginning of the end of the voyage, the separation of Grimes from Shank and consequently the separation of Grimes from the picture of Mary, came a scream from the fog horn, and Grimes jumped the more because this time he saw the sound was coming, but could not tune his ears to its loudness. He winced before it as if it were a cry for help that called him into danger. In two minutes the scream came again and yet again, the fog came closer and the afternoon crept on, two minutes at a time.

A half hour later there came out of the fog another sign of the approaching end of the voyage. Four gulls signifying anew the nearness of land appeared in the ship's wake. Two of the birds cackled malevolently, one wailed melodiously and pityingly, and one made a sound that was like the voice of a woman. This voice, low, smooth and rich, was raised in speech, but before it had time to articulate it halted as if embarrassed by emotion. Unmoved, however, by threat or tears the ship slid slowly forward and the afternoon drew to a close.

After supper with the world about the *Iron City* even more constricted by darkness that arrived to reinforce the fog, Grimes went to the wheelhouse. Here also came Shank. They leaned upon the ship's rail together. The voices of the gulls spoke to them of the end of the strange voyage watched over by the beauty of Mary Slade. "Shank," said Grimes, finally, "let's have a look at Mary before it's too dark."

Shank reached into his inner pocket and brought out his wallet. He held it in his hand. Grimes waited and under the pressure of Shank's delay he added another plea. "Give me the picture," he said. "You'll never give happiness more easily."

"I can give it easier to Mary," said Shank, but he drew from the wallet the picture — he was about to do as Grimes asked.

Holding the small white square between his hands, his elbows on the rail, and hands above the wake of the ship, his deliberations produced the effect of a pause. During this pause, while Grimes was putting forth a hand to receive from Shank the photograph, Shank let slip the picture of

Mary just before Gideon's fingers could close upon it. While the face of
Mary was still visible to Gideon, the falling photograph was far beyond
his reach, as irrevocably removed as are the living from the dead. Mary
was gone.

With her went Grimes's tolerance of Shank. He began to get angry.
Shank laughed at the accident. He, in that moment, reached the peak of
his power over Grimes. Had some breath of wind played the final trick
that Shank dared not play, yet now he could laugh and appear as if he
had permitted the accident.

Grimes was helpless. "God damn you, Shank," he said. "You bastard."
He sought for some supreme blasphemy, there was none; only the daily
oaths came to his tongue.

Shank savored the impotent insults, they rolled down his scraggy
throat as easily as they shot up from Grimes's. Grimes rattled the loose
ship's rail in his hand. He stamped his foot. Then suddenly a great
feeling of freedom rolled over him; there was now no reason to preserve
the forms of friendship with Shank. He had tolerated Shank's nauseous
personality in order that he might be permitted to look at the picture of
Mary. What reason was there for Grimes to control his dislike now? And
Shank's laughs were echoed by Grimes's own. Shank stopped in surprise.
Grimes, watching, grew cold and deliberate.

"You think you've got Mary, Shank," he said. "Why do you think I've
asked questions about her? Why do I know her address and where she
works: because I'm going back to Blackwell and get her. I'm going to
have her now, not you. What's more, you're going to be damn polite the
rest of this voyage or I'll tell an officer you're a stowaway and you'll be
starved below decks, handcuffed so you can't brush off the rats. Damn
you, Shank."

Shank might have tried to hit Gideon then; but Grimes turned and left
him.

The fog horn split the silence. Its two-minute interval had just brack-
eted the scene. It hurried Gideon on his way.

The fog about the ship shut out sound and sight and air and held in
the demon who yelled in the cabin. Grimes slept; awoke and perceived
that not yet had Shank come to bed. Why in hell was he up so late? Was
he out behind the wheelhouse, terrified by threats and wondering how he
could escape exposure?

One more night and the *Iron City* would raise Highland Light; the
fog horn bellowed, there might be fishing schooners near.

What was Shank thinking? Gideon asked himself. Then he saw. "Where's my Buddy, did ye ask?" Shank would say to the fo'c'sle cook; " 'e's going to hide out this last day. Let me get his landing card. The officers don't know one of us for another. I'll get ashore, then he'll have his passport, says he can manage all right." It wasn't a very good idea, but who would think about it, and where would Gideon be? Gideon asked in the dark cabin and Gideon answered. He would be overboard with the hammer thrown after, gone the way he had thought of sending Shank. Shank would have his papers, passport and all. It was simple; that was what Shank was thinking. He, who had crawled about in the cold blood of dead men, would not fumble the doing. He simply waited for Gideon to go to sleep. "I must not sleep," thought Gideon.

He turned on the light to help him stay awake. He lay and blinked at the dull light. Now the blaring fog horn became a lullaby. When it blew, its loudness suspended the action of Gideon's senses and held his eyes closed. They flew open again as soon as the sound ceased to tell him if Shank had come into the room. There was a perceptible time between the moment at which Gideon's eyes flew open and the succeeding temporary allaying of his fears. During this moment he could visualize the form of Shank; head and shoulders leaning over his bunk, hammer poised flat side toward his head. Feverishly Gideon's brain would hasten to compare this anticipated image with what his eyes actually saw. When he found that they did not coincide, his terror was allayed for two minutes more, but when his eyes closed again the hammer rose as before and his scalp crawled upon his skull, awaiting the shock. He rubbed the place.

Then he dozed and dreamed.

He dreamed that he opened his eyes, that he hastened to compare as always the two images, the one that he feared with the one that he actually beheld, and that he found to his utter terror that they exactly coincided. This time with certainty and in spite of the fact that his eyes were surely open he still beheld the thin wrist, the bony hand with fingers whitened by the strength of the grip upon the handle of the heavy hammer. He tried to grab the wrist, to shout. He writhed in his bunk in a death agony and then he overcame the force that held shut his eyes. The deafening horn which held him asleep suddenly ceased, his eyelids flew up; and waking he beheld neither the familiar sight of the iron girder above his bunk or the anticipated grim face and upraised hammer. He beheld nothing. The room was dark. The light had been turned out.

Was Shank there above him? He did not know. He rose up. He could see only the round port, dimly gray. He got out of his bunk and he reached into the bunk below Shank's to see if the hammer were there. He felt the handle; why had he not thought to possess himself of it before? Next, he stood upon the edge of the lower bunk and looked into Shank's bunk to see if he were there. He was there, and in the faint light from the port his eyes showed dark in the lighter tone of his face. They were open. He must be seeing Gideon leaning over him with the hammer in his hand. He would kill Gideon. Gideon must strike while sleep still stifled his mind, if not his sight. Gideon brought down the hammer flat side foremost, swinging short from his elbow to avoid the girder: Shank tried to shout; sleep still held him for one split instant more. The flat side of the hammer struck the head. It was not like a hen's egg; it was not like a turtle's egg; it was like an apple inside a sock.

The fog horn blew again. It was two minutes since Gideon had got out of his bunk.

Gideon shuddered and — rolled in his blankets. Shank too shuddered, as if the idea of death were repugnant to him. Gideon did not dare to touch Shank's heart to see if he were dead; instead he put his heavy blanket over Shank's head so that if he should not be dead and should groan the sound would be muffled. Then Gideon dressed, and went to the galley.

This part was simple and Gideon was quick, for he had thought it out before. In the galley was a sackful of potato peelings and the galley was empty. Gideon took the sack to his cabin quickly lest Shank should be alive. Shank had not moved. He emptied the sack on the floor of the cabin.

Then he climbed laboriously into the top bunk and straddling the warm form of Shank which, for all he knew, might still be alive, he shudderingly pulled the blanket from Shank's head and all in one motion hurled it to the floor among the potato peelings. The head was still and Gideon saw that it was queerly shaped. He pulled the bag hastily over it, then down to the waist of the limp little man.

In the end, after lifting the whole unwieldy burden to the floor, he was able to shake the whole of the man, Shank, in an inverted squat down into the bag. He tried not to jounce the crushed head too hard upon the floor in doing this. Once he waited for the blare of the fog horn to conceal the sound of his operation. When the little man was in the bag, Gideon shoved his tool kit in after him, tying it to one ankle. He got the burden onto his shoulder by resting it on an upper bunk, paused, adjusting the weight, and it seemed to him that the pulse of the ship's engine went slower. The world became still more quiet; between the blasts of the fog horn there was no sound in the world but the expiring distant beat of the ship's engine.

Gideon opened the door of the cabin and peered out as well as he could with that awkward hundred-odd pounds upon his shoulder. He saw no one, once out of his room he was all right or almost. He might have been working late for the cook and now be carrying the week's collection of potato peels to the door in the ship's side to throw it out. He staggered out upon the darkened underdeck.

The concrete floor was slippery with dampness of the fog. Bent as Shank had been bent that first day in Liverpool when he came down the dock with his duffle bag, Gideon walked uncertainly aft. Before he had taken two steps the dying rhythm of the ship's engine ceased altogether. Silence fell upon the world. Gideon, too, felt forced to stop, his bundle settled upon his shoulder as if making itself comfortable. Now creeping up behind Gideon came that deadly brazen shout. The bridge again! Gideon started aft in the dead ship with a dead burden nestling to him and there came to him now a faint answering bellow, as if spectators were assembling for the burial of Shank at sea.

Gideon came to the door in the side of the ship. The whole unrippling ocean waited to hear the sound of Shank's plunge. He lowered the bag to the deck and waited for the salute from the bridge which would conceal the sound of the splash. In the sluggish sea the ship was losing way. Across the water came the answering bleat. He knew that the call of the *Iron City* would follow soon. He got ready. "Get set," it said to him and GO cried the signal from the bridge.

Forward and outward fell the bag. Gideon leaned over and grasped the two lower corners and whipped back his body. That shriveled parasite, Grimes's strange companion, Shank, fell free of the bag, unsheltered by any shroud, into the ocean which quivered now beneath the *Iron City*'s brazen blast. As Shank struck the water it seemed to Gideon to fall away beneath, forming momentarily a smooth bowl-like cradle for the huddled form, a cradle festooned about its edges with a pale fire of phosphorescence. Then the water grew calm above the spot where Shank had fallen. He sank slowly, dragged down by the feet to which Gideon had tied the kit of tools. The face looked up and Gideon could see it; for phosphorescent bubbles issued from the nose and mouth and escaped from the hair and drew in livid light the outline of a bodiless, eyeless face.

While Gideon looked down thus and Shank looked up there came, winding like a garter snake through tall grass, a gigantic serpent of light, a curious fish which left behind it a trail of phosphorescence and was drawn by this sudden commotion in the sea. For one final instant the upturned face seemed like the head of this serpentine body, like the fabulous serpent of the garden of Eden human-headed; then all was lost in a knot of fiery coils which fell shining into a hell of velvet in the shadow of the ship.

Gideon straightened his aching back and turned about. Little Shank was gone like big Australia, a cockroach in a mug of beer.

In the end it was light. Grimes got himself on deck. He rose, still stupid with the shock of murder, out of the darkness and stench of the ship, out of the cabin where the smell of Shank's living body still hung, into the opalescent misty morning. The fog had retreated somewhat and the fog horn no longer blew. He went to the rail and looked upon the sea. No wind stirred it; yet everywhere there was life. As far as he could see, spread out at geometrically even intervals like fleur-de-lis on a wall-paper, there were small black and white birds. They could not rise off the water because the day was still. They rested each in its appointed place upon the endless pewter plane and waited for the wind. As the ship moved upon this strange sea, the birds became frightened by its approach and flapped their short strong wings vainly. Around each bird then ripples arose widening evenly, slowly, until the graceful circles became tangent to one another. The *Iron City* lay upon a sheet of ancient silver chased with an inscrutable design.

PIETRO DI DONATO

The accident befalling Geremio, the foreman, and his fellow Italian laborers could have happened anywhere, anytime. "Christ in Concrete," however, grows straight out of the Depression years with desperate men struggling to keep their families and themselves alive no matter what the danger. Much of the so-called "proletarian writing" of the thirties was done by authors with not enough perspective. This is one of the few examples from that period to achieve permanent distinction.

Pietro di Donato was born in West Hoboken, New Jersey, in 1911. When his father was killed on the job, he left school at thirteen to support his widowed mother and seven brothers and sisters. He is the author of a book, also called Christ in Concrete.

Christ in Concrete

MARCH whistled stinging snow against the brick walls and up the gaunt girders. Geremio, the foreman, swung his arms about, and gaffed the men on.

Old Nick, the "Lean," stood up from over a dust-flying brick pile, and tapped the side of his nose.

"Master Geremio, the devil himself could not break his tail any harder than we here."

Burly Vincenzo of the walrus moustache, and known as the "Snout-nose," let fall the chute door of the concrete hopper and sang over in the Lean's direction: "Mari-Annina's belly and the burning night will make of me once more a milk-mouthed stripling lad . . ."

The Lean loaded his wheelbarrow and spat furiously. "Sons of two-legged dogs . . . despised of even the devil himself! Work! Sure! For America beautiful will eat you and spit your bones into the earth's hole! Work!" And with that his wiry frame pitched the barrow violently over the rough floor.

Snoutnose waved his head to and fro and with mock pathos wailed, "Sing on, oh guitar of mine . . ."

Short, cherry-faced Joe Chiappa, the scaffoldman, paused with hatchet in hand and tenpenny spike sticking out from small dice-like teeth to tell the Lean as he went by, in a voice that all could hear, "Ah, father of countless chicks, the old age is a carrion!"

Geremio chuckled and called to him: "Hey, little Joe, who are you to talk? You and big-titted Cola can't even hatch an egg, whereas the Lean has just to turn the doorknob of his bedroom and old Philomena becomes a balloon!"

Coarse throats tickled and mouths opened wide in laughter.

Mike, the "Barrel-mouth," pretended he was talking to himself and yelled out in his best English . . . he was always speaking English while the rest carried on in their native Italian: "I don't know myself, but somebodys whose gotta bigga buncha keeds and he alla times talka from somebodys elsa!"

Geremio knew it was meant for him and he laughed. "On the tomb of Saint Pimplelegs, this little boy my wife is giving me next week shall be the last! Eight hungry little Christians to feed is enough for any man."

Joe Chiappa nodded to the rest. "Sure, Master Geremio had a telephone call from the next bambino. Yes, it told him it had a little bell there instead of a rosebush . . . It even told him its name!"

"Laugh, laugh all of you," returned Geremio, "but I tell you that all my kids must be boys so that they someday will be big American builders. And then I'll help them to put the gold away in the basements for safe keeping!"

A great din of riveting shattered the talk among the fast-moving men. Geremio added a handful of "Honest" tobacco to his corncob, puffed strongly, and cupped his hands around the bowl for a bit of warmth. The chill day caused him to shiver, and he thought to himself, "Yes, the day is cold, cold . . . but who am I to complain when the good Christ himself was crucified?

"Pushing the job is all right (when has it been otherwise in my life?) but this job frightens me. I feel the building wants to tell me something; just as one Christian to another. I don't like this. Mr. Murdin tells me, 'Push it up!' That's all he knows. I keep telling him that the underpinning should be doubled and the old material removed from the floors, but he keeps the inspector drunk and . . . 'Hey, Ashes-ass! Get away from under that pilaster! Don't pull the old work. Push it away from you or you'll have a nice present for Easter if the wall falls on you!' . . . Well, with the help of God I'll see this job through. It's not my first, nor the . . . 'Hey, Patsy number two! Put more cement in that concrete; we're putting up a building, not an Easter cake!'"

Patsy hurled his shovel to the floor and gesticulated madly. "The padrone Murdin-sa tells me, 'Too much, too much! Lil' bit is plenty!' And you tell me I'm stingy! The rotten building can fall after I leave!"

Six floors below, the contractor called: "Hey Geremio! Is your gang of dagos dead?"

Geremio cautioned to the men: "On your toes, boys. If he writes out slips, someone won't have big eels on the Easter table."

The Lean cursed that "the padrone could take the job and shove it . . . !"

Curly-headed Sandino, the roguish, pigeon-toed scaffoldman, spat a clod of tobacco-juice and hummed to his own music.

"Yes, certainly yes to your face, master padrone . . . and behind, this to you and all your kind!"

The day, like all days, came to an end. Calloused and bruised bodies sighed, and numb legs shuffled towards shabby railroad flats. . . .

"Ah, *bella casa mia*. Where my little freshets of blood, and my good woman await me. Home where my broken back will not ache so. Home where midst the monkey chatter of my *piccolinos* I will float off to blessed slumber with my feet on the chair and the head on the wife's soft full breast."

These great child-hearted ones leave each other without words or ceremony, and as they ride and walk home, a great pride swells the breast. . . .

"Blessings to Thee, oh Jesus. I have fought winds and cold. Hand to hand I have locked dumb stones in place and the great building rises. I have earned a bit of bread for me and mine."

The mad day's brutal conflict is forgiven, and strained limbs prostrate themselves so that swollen veins can send the yearning blood coursing and pulsating deliciously as though the body mountained leaping streams.

The job alone remained behind . . . and yet, they too, having left the bigger part of their lives with it. The cold ghastly beast, the Job, stood stark, the eerie March wind wrapping it in sharp shadows of falling dusk.

That night was a crowning point in the life of Geremio. He bought a house! Twenty years he had helped to mould the New World. And now he was to have a house of his own! What mattered that it was no more than a wooden shack? It was his own!

He had proudly signed his name and helped Annunziata to make her **X** on the wonderful contract that proved them owners. And she was happy to think that her next child, soon to come, would be born under their own rooftree. She heard the church chimes, and cried to the children: "Children, to bed! It is near midnight. And remember, shut-mouth to the *paesanos!* Or they will send the evil eye to our new home even before we put foot."

The children scampered off to the icy yellow bedroom where three slept in one bed and three in the other. Coltishly and friskily they kicked about under the covers; their black iron-cotton stockings not removed . . . what! and freeze the peanut-little toes?

Said Annunziata, "The children are so happy, Geremio; let them be, for even I would a Tarantella dance." And with that she turned blushing. He wanted to take her on her word. She patted his hands, kissed them, and whispered, "Our children will dance for us . . . in the American style some day."

Geremio cleared his throat and wanted to sing. "Yes, with joy I could sing in a richer feeling than the great Caruso." He babbled little old country couplets and circled the room until the tenant below tapped the ceiling.

Annunziata whispered: "Geremio, to bed and rest. Tomorrow is a day for great things . . . and the day on which our Lord died for us."

The children were now hard asleep. Heads under the cover, over . . . moist noses whistling, and little damp legs entwined.

In bed Geremio and Annunziata clung closely to each other. They mumbled figures and dates until fatigue stilled their thoughts. And with chubby Johnnie clutching fast his bottle and warmed between them . . . life breathed heavily, and dreams entertained in far, far worlds, the nation-builder's brood.

But Geremio and Annunziata remained for a while staring into darkness, silently.

"Geremio?"

"Yes?"

"This job you are now working. . . ."

"So?"

"You used always to tell me about what happened on the jobs . . . who was jealous, and who praised. . . ."

"You should know by now that all work is the same. . . ."

"Geremio. The month you have been on this job, you have not spoken a word about the work . . . And I have felt that I am walking in a dream. Is the work dangerous? Why don't you answer . . . ?"

Job loomed up damp, shivery gray. Its giant members waiting.

Builders quietly donned their coarse robes, and waited.

Geremio's whistle rolled back into his pocket and the symphony of struggle began.

Trowel rang through brick and slashed mortar rivets were machine-gunned fast with angry grind Patsy number one check Patsy number two check the Lean three check Vincenzo four steel bellowed back at hammer donkey engines coughed purple Ashes-ass Pietro fifteen chisel point intoned stone thin steel whirred and wailed through wood liquid stone flowed with dull rasp through iron veins and hoist screamed through space Carmine the Fat twenty-four and Giacomo Sangini check . . . The multitudinous voices of a civilization rose from the surroundings and welded with the efforts of the Job.

To the intent ear, Nation was voicing her growing pains, but, hands that create are attached to warm hearts and not to calculating minds. The Lean as he fought his burden on looked forward to only one goal, the end. The barrow he pushed, he did not love. The stones that brutalized his palms, he did not love. The great God Job, he did not love. He felt a searing bitterness and a fathomless consternation at the queer consciousness that inflicted the ever mounting weight of structure that he HAD TO! HAD TO! raise above his shoulders! When, when and where would the last stone be? Never . . . did he bear his toil with the rhythm of song! Never . . . did his gasping heart knead the heavy mortar with lilting melody! A voice within him spoke in wordless language.

The language of worn oppression and the despair of realizing that his life had been left on brick piles. And always, there had been hunger and her bastard, the fear of hunger.

Murdin bore down upon Geremio from behind and shouted:

"Goddamnit, Geremio, if you're givin' the men two hours off today with pay, why the hell are they draggin' their tails? And why don't you turn that skinny old Nick loose, and put a young wop in his place?"

"Now, listen-a to me, Mister Murdin — "

"Don't give me that! And bear in mind that there are plenty of good barefoot men in the streets who'll jump for a day's pay!"

"Padrone — padrone, the underpinning gotta be make safe and — "

"Lissenyawopbastard! If you don't like it, you know what you can do!"
And with that he swung swaggering away.

The men had heard, and those who hadn't knew instinctively.

The new home, the coming baby, and his whole background, kept the fire from Geremio's mouth and bowed his head. "Annunziata speaks of scouring the ashcans for the children's bread in case I didn't want to work on a job where . . . But am I not a man, to feed my own with these hands? Ah, but day will end and no boss in the world can then rob me of the joy of my home!"

Murdin paused for a moment before descending the ladder.

Geremio caught his meaning and jumped to, nervously directing the rush of work . . . No longer Geremio, but a machine-like entity.

The men were transformed into single, silent, beasts. Snoutnose steamed through ragged moustache whip-lashing sand into mixer Ashes-ass dragged under four by twelve beam Lean clawed wall knots jumping in jaws masonry crumbled dust billowed thundered choked. . . .

At noon, Geremio drank his wine from an old-fashioned magnesia bottle and munched a great pepper sandwich . . . no meat on Good Friday. Said one, "Are some of us to be laid off? Easter is upon us and communion dresses are needed and . . ."

That, while Geremio was dreaming of the new house and the joys he could almost taste. Said he: "Worry not. You should know Geremio." It then all came out. He regaled them with his wonderful joy of the new house. He praised his wife and children one by one. They listened respectfully and returned him well wishes and blessings. He went on and on. . . . "Paul made a radio — all by himself, mind you! One can hear Barney Google and many American songs! How proud he."

The ascent to labor was made, and as they trod the ladder, heads turned and eyes communed with the mute flames of the brazier whose warmth they were leaving, not with willing heart, and in that fleeting moment, the breast wanted so, so much to speak of hungers that never reached the tongue.

About an hour later, Geremio called over to Pietro: "Pietro, see if Mister Murdin is in the shanty and tell him I must see him! I will convince him that the work must not go on like this . . . just for the sake of a little more profit!"

Pietro came up soon. "The padrone is not coming up. He was drinking from a large bottle of whisky and cursed in American words that if you did not carry out his orders — "

Geremio turned away disconcerted, stared dumbly at the structure and mechanically listed in his mind's eye the various violations of construction safety. An uneasy sensation hollowed him. The Lean brought down an old piece of wall and the structure palsied. Geremio's heart broke loose and out-thumped the floor's vibrations, a rapid wave of heat swept him and left a chill touch in its wake. He looked about to the men, a bit frightened. They seemed usual, life-size, and moved about with the methodical deftness that made the moment then appear no different than the task of toil had ever been.

Snoutnose's voice boomed into him. "Master Geremio, the concrete is rea — dy!"

"Oh, yes, yes, Vincenz." And he walked gingerly towards the chute, but, not without leaving behind some part of his strength, sending out his soul to wrestle with the limbs of Job, who threatened in stiff silence. He talked and joked with Snoutnose. Nothing said anything, nor seemed wrong. Yet a vague uneasiness was to him as certain as the foggy murk that floated about Job's stone and steel.

"Shall I let the concrete down now, Master Geremio?"

"Well, let me see — no, hold it a minute. Hey, Sandino! tighten the chute cables!"

Snoutnose straightened, looked about, and instinctively rubbed the sore small of his spine. "Ah," sighed he, "all the men feel as I — yes, I can tell. They are tired but happy that today is Good Friday and we quit at three o'clock . . ." And he swelled in human ecstasy at the anticipation of food, drink, and the hairy flesh-tingling warmth of wife, and then, extravagant rest. In truth, they all felt as Snoutnose, although perhaps with variations on the theme.

It was the Lean only who had lived, and felt otherwise. His soul, accompanied with time, had shredded itself in the physical war to keep the physical alive. Perhaps he no longer had a soul, and the corpse continued from momentum. May he not be the Slave, working on from the birth of Man — He of whom it was said, "It was not for Him to reason"? And probably He who, never asking, taking, nor vaunting, created God and the creatable? Nevertheless, there existed in the Lean a sense of oppression suffered, so vast that the seas of time could never wash it away.

Geremio gazed about and was conscious of seeming to understand many things. He marveled at the strange feeling which permitted him to sense the familiarity of life. And yet — all appeared unreal, a dream pungent and nostalgic. Life, dream, reality, unreality, spiraling ever about each other. "Ha," he chuckled, "how and from where do these thoughts come?"

Snoutnose had his hand on the hopper latch and was awaiting the word from Geremio. "Did you say something, Master Geremio?"

"Why, yes, Vincenz, I was thinking — funny! A — yes, what is the time — yes, that is what I was thinking."

"My American can of tomatoes says ten minutes from two o'clock. It won't be long now, Master Geremio."

Geremio smiled. "No, about an hour . . . and then, home."

"Oh, but first we stop at Mulberry Street, to buy their biggest eels, and the other finger-licking stuffs."

Geremio was looking far off, and for a moment happiness came to his heart without words, a warm hand stealing over. Snoutnose's words sang to him pleasantly, and he nodded.

"And Master Geremio, we ought really to buy the seafruits with the shells — you know, for the much needed steam they put into the — "

He flushed despite himself and continued. "It is true, I know it — especially the juicy clams . . . uhmn, my mouth waters like a pump."

Geremio drew on his unlit pipe and smiled acquiescence. The men around him were moving to their tasks silently, feeling of their fatigue, but absorbed in contemplations the very same as Snoutnose's. The noise of labor seemed not to be noise, and as Geremio looked about, life settled over him a gray concert — gray forms, atmosphere, and gray notes . . . Yet his off-tone world felt so near, and familiar.

"Five minutes from two," swished through Snoutnose's moustache.

Geremio automatically took out his watch, rewound, and set it. Sandino had done with the cables. The tone and movement of the scene seemed to Geremio strange, differently strange, and yet, a dream familiar from a timeless date. His hand went up in motion to Vincenzo. The molten stone gurgled low, and then with heightening rasp. His eyes followed the stone-cementy pudding, and to his ears there was no other sound than its flow. From over the roofs somewhere, the tinny voice of *Barney Google* whined its way, hooked into his consciousness and kept itself a revolving record beneath his skull-plate.

"Ah, yes, Barney Google, my son's wonderful radio machine . . . wonderful Paul." His train of thought quickly took in his family, home and hopes. And with hope came fear. Something within asked, "Is it not possible to breathe God's air without fear dominating with the pall of unemployment? And the terror of production for Boss, Boss and Job? To rebel is to lose all of the very little. To be obedient is to choke. Oh, dear Lord, guide my path."

Just then, the floor lurched and swayed under his feet. The slipping of the underpinning below rumbled up through the undetermined floors.

Was he faint or dizzy? Was it part of the dreamy afternoon? He put his hands in front of him and stepped back, and looked up wildly. "No! No!"

The men poised stricken. Their throats wanted to cry out and scream but didn't dare. For a moment they were a petrified and straining pageant. Then the bottom of their world gave way. The building shuddered violently, her supports burst with the crackling slap of wooden gunfire. The floor vomited upward. Geremio clutched at the air and shrieked agonizingly. "Brothers, what have we done? Ahhh-h, children of ours!" With the speed of light, balance went sickeningly awry and frozen men went flying explosively. Job tore down upon them madly. Walls, floors, beams became whirling, solid, splintering waves crashing with detonations that ground man and material in bonds of death.

The strongly shaped body that slept with Annunziata nights and was perfect in all the limitless physical quantities, thudded as a worthless sack amongst the giant debris that crushed fragile flesh and bone with centrifugal intensity.

Darkness blotted out his terror and the resistless form twisted, catapulted insanely in its directionless flight, and shot down neatly and deliberately between the empty wooden forms of a foundation wall pilaster in upright position, his blue swollen face pressed against the form and his arms outstretched, caught securely through the meat by the thin round bars of reinforcing steel.

The huge concrete hopper that was sustained by an independent structure of thick timber, wavered a breath or so, its heavy concrete rolling uneasily until a great sixteen-inch wall caught it squarely with all the terrific verdict of its dead weight and impelled it downward through joists, beams and masonry, until it stopped short, arrested by two girders, an arm's length above Geremio's head; the gray concrete gushing from the hopper mouth, and sealing up the mute figure.

Giacomo had been thrown clear of the building and dropped six floors to the street gutter, where he lay writhing.

The Lean had evinced no emotion. When the walls descended, he did not move. He lowered his head. One minute later he was hanging in mid-air, his chin on his chest, his eyes tearing loose from their sockets, a green foam bubbling from his mouth and his body spasming, suspended by the shreds left of his mashed arms pinned between a wall and a girder.

A two-by-four hooked little Joe Chiappa up under the back of his jumper and swung him around in a circle to meet a careening I-beam. In the flash that he lifted his frozen cherubic face, its shearing edge sliced through the top of his skull.

When Snoutnose cried beseechingly, "Saint Michael!" blackness enveloped him. He came to in a world of horror. A steady stream, warm, thick, and sickening as hot wine bathed his face and clogged his nose, mouth, and eyes. The nauseous syrup that pumped over his face, clotted his moustache red and drained into his mouth. He gulped for air, and swallowed the rich liquid scarlet. As he breathed, the pain shocked him to oppressive semi-consciousness. The air was wormingly alive with cries, screams, moans and dust, and his crushed chest seared him with a thousand fires. He couldn't see, nor breathe enough to cry. His right hand moved to his face and wiped at the gelatinizing substance, but it kept coming on, and a heartbreaking moan wavered about him, not far. He wiped his eyes in subconscious despair. Where was he? What kind of a dream was he having? Perhaps he wouldn't wake up in time for work, and then what? But how queer; his stomach beating him, his chest on fire, he sees nothing but dull red, only one hand moving about, and a moaning in his face!

The sound and clamor of the rescue squads called to him from far off.

Ah, yes, he's dreaming in bed, and far out in the streets, engines are going to a fire. Oh poor devils! Suppose his house were on fire? With the children scattered about in the rooms he could not remember! He must do his utmost to break out of this dream! He's swimming under water, not able to raise his head and get to the air. He must get back to consciousness to save his children!

He swam frantically with his one right hand, and then felt a face beneath its touch. A face! It's Angelina alongside of him! Thank God, he's awake! He tapped her face. It moved. It felt cold, bristly, and wet. "It moves so. What is this?" His fingers slithered about grisly sharp bones and in a gluey, stringy, hollow mass, yielding as wet macaroni. Gray light brought sight, and hysteria punctured his heart. A girder lay across his chest his right hand clutched a grotesque human mask, and suspended almost on top of him was the twitching, faceless body of Joe Chiappa. Vincenzo fainted with an inarticulate sigh. His fingers loosed and the bodyless-headless face dropped and fitted to the side of his face while the drippings above came slower and slower.

The rescue men cleaved grimly with pick and axe.

Geremio came to with a start . . . far from their efforts. His brain told him instantly what had happened and where he was. He shouted wildly. "Save me! Save me! I'm being buried alive!"

He paused exhausted. His genitals convulsed. The cold steel rod upon which they were impaled froze his spine. He shouted louder and louder. "Save me! I am hurt badly! I can be saved, I can — save me before it's too late!" But the cries went no farther than his own ears. The icy wet concrete reached his chin. His heart was appalled. "In a few seconds I shall be entombed. If I can only breathe, they will reach me. Surely they will!" His face was quickly covered, its flesh yielding to the solid, sharp-cut stones. "Air! Air!" screamed his lungs as he was completely sealed. Savagely, he bit into the wooden form pressing upon his mouth. An eighth of an inch of its surface splintered off. Oh, if he could only hold out long enough to bite even the smallest hole through to air! He must! There can be no other way! He is responsible for his family! He cannot leave them like this! He didn't want to die! This could not be the answer to life! He had bitten halfway through when his teeth snapped off to the gums in the uneven conflict. The pressure of the concrete was such, and its effectiveness so thorough, that the wooden splinters, stumps of teeth, and blood never left the choking mouth.

Why couldn't he go any farther?

Air! Quick! He dug his lower jaw into the little hollowed space and gnashed in choking agonized fury. "Why doesn't it go through? Mother of Christ, why doesn't it give? Can there be a notch, or two-by-four stud behind it? Sweet Jesu! No! No! Make it give. . . . Air! Air!"

He pushed the bone-bare jaw maniacally; it splintered, cracked, and a jagged fleshless edge cut through the form, opening a small hole to air. With a desperate burst the lung-prisoned air blew an opening through the shredded mouth and whistled back greedily a gasp of fresh air. He tried to breathe, but it was impossible. The heavy concrete was settling immutably, and its rich cement-laden grout ran into his pierced face. His lungs would not expand, and were crushing in tighter and tighter under the settling concrete.

"Mother mine — mother of Jesu-Annunziata — children of mine — dear, dear, for mercy, Jesu-Giuseppe e 'Maria," his blue-foamed tongue called. It then distorted in a shuddering coil and mad blood vomited forth. Chills and fire played through him and his tortured tongue stuttered, "Mercy, blessed Father — salvation, most kind Father — Saviour — Saviour of His children help me — adored Saviour — I kiss your feet eternally — you are my Lord — there is but one God — you are my God of infinite mercy — Hail Mary divine Virgin — our Father who art in heaven hallowed by thy — name — our Father — my Father," and the agony excruciated with never-ending mount, "our Father — Jesu, Jesu, soon Jesu, hurry dear Jesu Jesu! Je-sssu . . . !" His mangled voice trebled hideously, and hung in jerky whimperings.

The unfeeling concrete was drying fast, and shrinking into monolithic density. The pressure temporarily de-sensitized sensation; leaving him petrified, numb, and substanceless. Only the brain remained miraculously alive.

"Can this be death? It is all too strangely clear. I see nothing nor feel nothing, my body and senses are no more, my mind speaks as it never did before. Am I or am I not Geremio? But I am Geremio! Can I be in the other world? I never was in any other world except the one I knew of; that of toil, hardship, prayer . . . of my wife who awaits with child for me, of my children and the first home I was to own. Where do I begin in this world? Where do I leave off? Why? I recall only a baffled life of cruelty from every direction. And hope was always as painful as fear, the fear of displeasing, displeasing the people and ideas whom I could never understand; laws, policemen, priests, bosses, and a rag with colors waving on a stick. I never did anything to these things. But what have I done with my life? Yes, my life! No one else's! Mine — mine — MINE — Geremio! It is clear. I was born hungry, and have always been hungry for freedom — life! I married and ran away to America so as not to kill and be killed in Tripoli for things they call 'God and Country.' I've never known the freedom I wanted in my heart. There was always an arm upraised to hit at me. What have I done to them? I did not want to make them toil for me. I did not raise my arm to them. In my life I could never breathe, and now without air, my mind breathes clearly for me. Wait! There has been a terrible mistake! A cruel crime! The world is not right! Murderers! Thieves! You have hurt me and my kind, and have taken my life from me! I have long felt it — yes, yes, yes, they have cheated me with flags, signs and fear . . . I say you can't take my life! I want to live! My life! To tell the cheated to rise and fight! Vincenz! Chiappa! Nick! Men! Do you hear me? We must follow the desires within us for the world has been taken from us; we, who made the world! Life!"

Feeling returned to the destroyed form.

"Ahhh-h, I am not dead yet. I knew it — you have not done with me. Torture away! I cannot believe you, God and Country, no longer!" His body was fast breaking under the concrete's closing wrack. Blood vessels burst like mashed flower stems. He screamed. "Show yourself now, Jesu! Now is the time! Save me! Why don't you come! Are you there! I cannot stand it — ohhh, why do you let it happen — it is bestial — where are you! Hurry, hurry, hurry! You do not come! You make me suffer, and what have I done! Come, come — come now — now save me, save me now! Now, now, now! If you are God, save me!"

The stricken blood surged through a weltering maze of useless pipes and exploded forth from his squelched eyes and formless nose, ears and mouth, seeking life in the indifferent stone.

"Aie — aie, aie — devils and Saints — beasts! Where are you — quick, quick, it is death and I am cheated — cheat — ed! Do you hear, you whoring bastards who own the world? Ohhh-ohhh aie-aie — haha-haha!" His bones cracked mutely and his sanity went sailing distorted in the limbo of the subconscious.

With the throbbing tones of an organ in the hollow background, the fighting brain disintegrated and the memories of a baffled lifetime sought outlet.

He moaned the simple songs of barefoot childhood, scenes flashed desperately on and off in disassociated reflex, and words and parts of words came pitifully high and low from his inaudible lips, the hysterical mind sang cringingly and breathlessly, "Jesu my Lord my God my all Jesu my Lord my God my all Jesu my Lord my God my all Jesu my Lord my God my all," and on as the whirling tempo screamed now far, now near, and came in soul-sickening waves as the concrete slowly contracted and squeezed his skull out of shape.

JOHN STEINBECK

Readers who always seek for symbols in stories can have almost too easy a time with this story, "The Chrysanthemums." In spite of such "deep readers," stories are not about symbols but about people. The chrysanthemums here, like all flowers, are sex organs, of course. The woman, whose physical strength is described in such passionate detail, knows this meaning and when she reaches out almost to touch the old mending man it is because she feels its presence so deeply.

John Steinbeck, a recipient of the Nobel Award in Literature, was born in Salinas, California, in 1902 and was educated at Stanford University. He is the author of many noted novels and short stories.

The Chrysanthemums

THE high gray-flannel fog of winter closed off the Salinas Valley from the sky and from all the rest of the world. On every side it sat like a lid on the mountains and made of the great valley a closed pot. On the broad, level land floor the gang ploughs bit deep and left the black earth shining like metal where the shares had cut. On the foothill ranches across the Salinas River, the yellow stubble fields seemed to be bathed in pale cold sunshine, but there was no sunshine in the valley now in December. The thick willow scrub along the river flamed with sharp and positive yellow leaves.

It was a time of quiet and of waiting. The air was cold and tender. A light wind blew up from the southwest so that the farmers were mildly hopeful of a good rain before long; but fog and rain do not go together. Across the river, on Henry Allen's foothill ranch there was little work to be done, for the hay was cut and stored and the orchards were ploughed up to receive the rain deeply when it should come. The cattle on the higher slopes were becoming shaggy and rough-coated.

Elisa Allen, working in her flower garden, looked down across the yard and saw Henry, her husband, talking to two men in business suits. The three of them stood by the tractor shed, each man with one foot on the side of the little Fordson. They smoked cigarettes and studied the machine as they talked.

Elisa watched them for a moment and then went back to her work. She was thirty-five. Her face was lean and strong and her eyes were as clear as water. Her figure looked blocked and heavy in her gardening costume, a man's black hat pulled low down over her eyes, clod-hopper shoes, a figured print dress almost completely covered by a big corduroy apron with four big pockets to hold the snips, the trowel and scratcher, the seeds and the knife she worked with. She wore heavy leather gloves to protect her hands while she worked.

She was cutting down the old year's chrysanthemum stalks with a pair of short and powerful scissors. She looked down toward the men by the tractor shed now and then. Her face was eager and mature and handsome; even her work with the scissors was over-eager, over-powerful. The chrysanthemum stems seemed too small and easy for her energy.

She brushed a cloud of hair out of her eyes with the back of her glove, and left a smudge of earth on her cheek in doing it. Behind her stood the neat white farm house with red geraniums close-banked around it as high as the windows. It was a hard-swept-looking little house, with hard-polished windows, and a clean mud-mat on the front steps.

Elisa cast another glance toward the tractor shed. The strangers were getting into their Ford coupé. She took off a glove and put her strong fingers down into the forest of new green chrysanthemum sprouts that were growing around the old roots. She spread the leaves and looked down among the close-growing stems. No aphids were there, no sow bugs or snails or cutworms. Her terrier fingers destroyed such pests before they could get started.

Elisa started at the sound of her husband's voice. He had come near quietly, and he leaned over the wire fence that protected her flower garden from cattle and dogs and chickens.

"At it again," he said. "You've got a strong new crop coming."

Elisa straightened her back and pulled on the gardening glove again. "Yes. They'll be strong this coming year." In her tone and on her face there was a little smugness.

"You've got a gift with things," Henry observed. "Some of those yellow chrysanthemums you had this year were ten inches across. I wish you'd work out in the orchard and raise some apples that big."

Her eyes sharpened. "Maybe I could do it, too. I've a gift with things, all right. My mother had it. She could stick anything in the ground and make it grow. She said it was having planters' hands that knew how to do it."

"Well, it sure works with flowers," he said.

"Henry, who were those men you were talking to?"

"Why, sure, that's what I came to tell you. They were from the Western Meat Company. I sold those thirty head of three-year-old steers. Got nearly my own price, too."

"Good," she said. "Good for you."

"And I thought," he continued, "I thought how it's Saturday afternoon, and we might go into Salinas for dinner at a restaurant, and then to a picture show — to celebrate, you see."

"Good," she repeated. "Oh, yes. That will be good."

Henry put on his joking tone. "There's fights tonight. How'd you like to go to the fights?"

"Oh, no," she said breathlessly. "No, I wouldn't like fights."

"Just fooling, Elisa. We'll go to a movie. Let's see. It's two now. I'm going to take Scotty and bring down those steers from the hill. It'll take us maybe two hours. We'll go in town about five and have dinner at the Cominos Hotel. Like that?"

"Of course I'll like it. It's good to eat away from home."

"All right, then. I'll go get up a couple of horses."

She said: "I'll have plenty of time to transplant some of these sets, I guess."

She heard her husband calling Scotty down by the barn. And a little later she saw the two men ride up the pale yellow hillside in search of the steers.

There was a little square sandy bed kept for rooting the chrysanthemums. With her trowel she turned the soil over and over, and smoothed it and patted it firm. Then she dug ten parallel trenches to receive the sets. Back at the chrysanthemum bed she pulled out the little crisp shoots, trimmed off the leaves of each one with her scissors and laid it on a small orderly pile.

A squeak of wheels and plod of hoofs came from the road. Elisa looked up. The country road ran along the dense bank of willows and cottonwoods that bordered the river, and up this road came a curious vehicle, curiously drawn. It was an old spring-wagon, with a round canvas top on it like the cover of a prairie schooner. It was drawn by an old bay horse and a little gray-and-white burro. A big stubble-bearded man sat between the cover flaps and drove the crawling team. Underneath the wagon, between the hind wheels, a lean and rangy mongrel dog walked sedately. Words were painted on the canvas, in clumsy, crooked letters. "Pots, pans, knives, sisors, lawn mores, Fixed." Two rows of articles, and the triumphantly definitive "Fixed" below. The black paint had run down in little sharp points beneath each letter.

Elisa, squatting on the ground, watched to see the crazy, loose-jointed wagon pass by. But it didn't pass. It turned into the farm road in front of her house, crooked old wheels skirling and squeaking. The rangy dog darted from between the wheels and ran ahead. Instantly the two ranch shepherds flew out at him. Then all three stopped, and with stiff and quivering tails, with taut straight legs, with ambassadorial dignity, they slowly circled, sniffing daintily. The caravan pulled up to Elisa's wire fence and stopped. Now the newcomer dog, feeling out-numbered, lowered his tail and retired under the wagon with raised hackles and bared teeth.

The man on the wagon seat called out: "That's a bad dog in a fight when he gets started."

Elisa laughed. "I see he is. How soon does he generally get started?"

The man caught up her laughter and echoed it heartily. "Sometimes not for weeks and weeks," he said. He climbed stiffly down, over the wheel. The horse and the donkey drooped like unwatered flowers.

Elisa saw that he was a very big man. Although his hair and beard were graying, he did not look old. His worn black suit was wrinkled and spotted with grease. The laughter had disappeared from his face and eyes the moment his laughing voice ceased. His eyes were dark, and they were full of the brooding that gets in the eyes of teamsters and of sailors. The calloused hands he rested on the wire fence were cracked, and every crack was a black line. He took off his battered hat.

"I'm off my general road, ma'am," he said. "Does this dirt road cut over across the river to the Los Angeles highway?"

Elisa stood up and shoved the thick scissors in her apron pocket. "Well, yes, it does, but it winds around and then fords the river. I don't think your team could pull through the sand."

He replied with some asperity: "It might surprise you what them beasts can pull through."

"When they get started?" she asked.

He smiled for a second. "Yes. When they get started."

"Well," said Elisa, "I think you'll save time if you go back to the Salinas road and pick up the highway there."

He drew a big finger down the chicken wire and made it sing. "I ain't in any hurry, ma'am. I go from Seattle to San Diego and back every year. Takes all my time. About six months each way. I aim to follow nice weather."

Elisa took off her gloves and stuffed them in the apron pocket with the scissors. She touched the under edge of her man's hat, searching for fugitive hairs. "That sounds like a nice kind of a way to live," she said.

He leaned confidentially over the fence. "Maybe you noticed the writing on my wagon. I mend pots and sharpen knives and scissors. You got any of them things to do?"

"Oh, no," she said quickly. "Nothing like that." Her eyes hardened with resistance.

"Scissors is the worst thing," he explained. "Most people just ruin scissors trying to sharpen 'em, but I know how. I got a special tool. It's a little bobbit kind of thing, and patented. But it sure does the trick."

"No. My scissors are all sharp."

"All right, then. Take a pot," he continued earnestly, "a bent pot, or a pot with a hole. I can make it like new so you don't have to buy no new ones. That's a saving for you."

"No," she said shortly. "I tell you I have nothing like that for you to do."

His face fell to an exaggerated sadness. His voice took on a whining undertone. "I ain't had a thing to do today. Maybe I won't have no supper tonight. You see I'm off my regular road. I know folks on the highway clear from Seattle to San Diego. They save their things for me to sharpen up because they know I do it so good and save them money."

"I'm sorry," Elisa said irritably. "I haven't anything for you to do."

His eyes left her face and fell to searching the ground. They roamed about until they came to the chrysanthemum bed where she had been working. "What's them plants, ma'am?"

The irritation and resistance melted from Elisa's face. "Oh, those are chrysanthemums, giant whites and yellows. I raise them every year, bigger then anybody around here."

"Kind of a long-stemmed flower? Looks like a quick puff of colored smoke?" he asked.

"That's it. What a nice way to describe them."

"They smell kind of nasty till you get used to them," he said.

"It's a good bitter smell," she retorted, "not nasty at all."

He changed his tone quickly. "I like the smell myself."

"I had ten-inch blooms this year," she said.

The man leaned farther over the fence. "Look. I know a lady down the road a piece, has got the nicest garden you ever seen. Got nearly every kind of flower but no chrysanthemums. Last time I was mending a copper-bottom washtub for her (that's a hard job but I do it good), she said to me: 'If you ever run acrost some nice chrysantheums I wish you'd try to get me a few seeds.' That's what she told me."

Elisa's eyes grew alert and eager. "She couldn't have known much about chrysanthemums. You *can* raise them from seed, but it's much easier to root the little sprouts you see there."

"Oh," he said. "I s'pose I can't take none to her, then."

"Why yes you can," Elisa cried. "I can put some in damp sand, and you can carry them right along with you. They'll take root in the pot if you keep them damp. And then she can transplant them."

"She'd sure like to have some, ma'am. You say they're nice ones?"

"Beautiful," she said. "Oh, beautiful." Her eyes shone. She tore off the battered hat and shook out her dark pretty hair. "I'll put them in a flower pot, and you can take them right with you. Come into the yard."

While the man came through the picket gate Elisa ran excitedly along the geranium-bordered path to the back of the house. And she returned carrying a big red flower pot. The gloves were forgotten now. She kneeled on the ground by the starting bed and dug up the sandy soil with her fingers and scooped it into the bright new flower pot. Then she picked up the little pile of shoots she had prepared. With her strong fingers she pressed them into the sand and tamped around them with her knuckles. The man stood over her. "I'll tell you what to do," she said. "You remember so you can tell the lady."

"Yes, I'll try to remember."

"Well, look. These will take root in about a month. Then she must set them out, about a foot apart in good rich earth like this, see?" She lifted a handful of dark soil for him to look at. "They'll grow fast and tall. Now remember this: In July tell her to cut them down, about eight inches from the ground."

"Before they bloom?" he asked.

"Yes, before they bloom," Her face was tight with eagerness. "They'll grow right up again. About the last of September the buds will start."

She stopped and seemed perplexed. "It's the budding that takes the most care," she said hesitantly. "I don't know how to tell you." She looked deep into his eyes, searchingly. Her mouth opened a little, and she seemed to be listening. "I'll try to tell you," she said. "Did you ever hear of planting hands?"

"Can't say I have, ma'am."

"Well, I can only tell you what it feels like. It's when you're picking off the buds you don't want. Everything goes right down into your finger-tips. You watch your fingers work. They do it themselves. You can feel how it is. They pick and pick the buds. They never make a mistake. They're with the plant. Do you see? Your fingers and the plant. You can feel that, right up your arm. They know. They never make a mistake. You can feel it. When you're like that you can't do anything wrong. Do you see that? Can you understand that?"

She was kneeling on the ground looking up at him. Her breast swelled passionately.

The man's eyes narrowed. He looked away self-consciously. "Maybe I know," he said. "Sometimes in the night in the wagon there — "

Elisa's voice grew husky. She broke in on him: "I've never lived as you do, but I know what you mean. When the night is dark — why, the stars are sharp-pointed, and there's quiet. Why, you rise up and up! Every pointed star gets driven into your body. It's like that. Hot and sharp and — lovely."

Kneeling there, her hand went out toward his legs in the greasy black trousers. Her hesitant fingers almost touched the cloth. Then her hand dropped to the ground. She crouched low like a fawning dog.

He said: "It's nice, just like you say. Only when you don't have no dinner, it ain't."

She stood up then, very straight, and her face was ashamed. She held the flower pot out to him and placed it gently in his arms. "Here. Put it in your wagon, on the seat, where you can watch it. Maybe I can find something for you to do."

At the back of the house she dug in the can pile and found two old and battered aluminum saucepans. She carried them back and gave them to him. "Here, maybe you can fix these."

His manner changed. He became professional. "Good as new I can fix them." At the back of his wagon he set a little anvil, and out of an oily tool-box dug a small machine hammer. Elisa came through the gate to watch him while he pounded out the dents in the kettles. His mouth grew sure and knowing. At a difficult part of the work he sucked his under-lip.

"You sleep right in the wagon?" Elisa asked.

"Right in the wagon, ma'am. Rain or shine I'm dry as a cow in there."

"It must be nice," she said. "It must be very nice. I wish women could do such things."

"It ain't the right kind of a life for a woman."

Her upper lip raised a little, showing her teeth. "How do you know? How can you tell?" she said.

"I don't know, ma'am," he protested. "Of course I don't know. Now here's your kettles, done. You don't have to buy no new ones."

"How much?"

"Oh, fifty cents'll do. I keep my prices down and my work good. That's why I have all them satisfied customers up and down the highway."

Elisa brought him a fifty-cent piece from the house and dropped it in his hand. "You might be surprised to have a rival sometime. I can sharpen scissors, too. And I can beat the dents out of little pots. I could show you what a woman might do."

He put his hammer back in the oily box and shoved the little anvil out of sight. "It would be a lonely life for a woman, ma'am, and a scarey life, too, with animals creeping under the wagon all night." He climbed over the single-tree, steadying himself with a hand on the burro's white rump. He settled himself in the seat, picked up the lines. "Thank you kindly, ma'am," he said. "I'll do like you told me; I'll go back and catch the Salinas road."

"Mind," she called, "if you're long in getting there, keep the sand damp."

"Sand, ma'am? . . . Sand? Oh, sure. You mean around the chrysantheums. Sure I will." He clucked his tongue. The beasts leaned luxuriously into their collars. The mongrel dog took his place between the back wheels. The wagon turned and crawled out the entrance road and back the way it had come, along the river.

Elisa stood in front of her wire fence watching the slow progress of the caravan. Her shoulders were straight, her head thrown back, her eyes half-closed, so that the scene came vaguely into them. Her lips moved silently, forming the words "Good-bye—good-bye." Then she whispered: "That's a bright direction. There's a glowing there." The sound of her whisper startled her. She shook herself free and looked about to see whether anyone had been listening. Only the dogs had heard. They lifted their heads toward her from their sleeping in the dust, and then stretched out their chins and settled asleep again. Elisa turned and ran hurriedly into the house.

In the kitchen she reached behind the stove and felt the water tank. It was full of hot water from the noonday cooking. In the bathroom she tore off her soiled clothes and flung them into the corner. And then she scrubbed herself with a little block of pumice, legs and thighs, loins and chest and arms, until her skin was scratched and red. When she had dried herself she stood in front of a mirror in her bedroom and looked at her body. She tightened her stomach and threw out her chest. She turned and looked over her shoulder at her back.

After a while she began to dress, slowly. She put on her newest under-clothing and her nicest stockings and the dress which was the symbol of her prettiness. She worked carefully on her hair, pencilled her eyebrows and rouged her lips.

Before she was finished she heard the little thunder of hoofs and the shouts of Henry and his helper as they drove the red steers into the corral. She heard the gate bang shut and set herself for Henry's arrival.

His step sounded on the porch. He entered the house calling: "Elisa, where are you?"

"In my room, dressing. I'm not ready. There's hot water for your bath. Hurry up. It's getting late."

When she heard him splashing in the tub, Elisa laid his dark suit on the bed, and shirt and socks and tie beside it. She stood his polished shoes on the floor beside the bed. Then she went to the porch and sat primly and stiffly down. She looked toward the river road where the willow-line was still yellow with frosted leaves so that under the high gray fog they seemed a thin band of sunshine. This was the only color in the gray afternoon. She sat unmoving for a long time. Her eyes blinked rarely.

Henry came banging out of the door, shoving his tie inside his vest as he came. Elisa stiffened and her face grew tight. Henry stopped short and looked at her. "Why — why, Elisa. You look so nice!"

"Nice? You think I look nice? What do you mean by 'nice'?"

Henry blundered on. "I don't know. I mean you look different, strong and happy."

"I am strong? Yes, strong. What do you mean 'strong'?"

He looked bewildered. "You're playing some kind of a game," he said helplessly. "It's a kind of a play. You look strong enough to break a calf over your knee, happy enough to eat it like a watermelon."

For a second she lost her rigidity. "Henry! Don't talk like that. You didn't know what you said." She grew complete again. "I'm strong," she boasted. "I never knew before how strong."

Henry looked down toward the tractor shed, and when he brought his eyes back to her, they were his own again. "I'll get out the car. You can put on your coat while I'm starting."

Elisa went into the house. She heard him drive to the gate and idle down his motor, and then she took a long time to put on her hat. She pulled it here and pressed it there. When Henry turned the motor off she slipped into her coat and went out.

The little roadster bounced along on the dirt road by the river, raising the birds and driving the rabbits into the brush. Two cranes flapped heavily over the willow-line and dropped into the river-bed.

Far ahead on the road Elisa saw a dark speck. She knew.

She tried not to look as they passed it, but her eyes would not obey. She whispered to herself sadly: "He might have thrown them off the road. That wouldn't have been much trouble, not very much. But he kept the pot," she explained. "He had to keep the pot. That's why he couldn't get them off the road."

The roadster turned a bend and she saw the caravan ahead. She swung full around toward her husband so she could not see the little covered wagon and the mis-matched team as the car passed them.

In a moment it was over. The thing was done. She did not look back.

She said loudly, to be heard above the motor: "It will be good, tonight, a good dinner."

"Now you're changed again," Henry complained. He took one hand from the wheel and patted her knee. "I ought to take you in to dinner oftener. It would be good for both of us. We get so heavy out on the ranch."

"Henry," she asked, "could we have wine at dinner?"

"Sure we could. Say! That will be fine."

She was silent for a while; then she said: "Henry, at those prize-fights, do the men hurt each other very much?"

"Sometimes a little, not often. Why?"

"Well, I've read how they break noses, and blood runs down their chests. I've read how the fighting gloves get heavy and soggy with blood."

He looked around at her. "What's the matter, Elisa? I didn't know you read things like that." He brought the car to a stop, then turned to the right over the Salinas River bridge.

"Do any women ever go to the fights?" she asked.

"Oh, sure, some. What's the matter, Elisa? Do you want to go? I don't think you'd like it, but I'll take you if you really want to go."

She relaxed limply in the seat. "Oh, no. No. I don't want to go. I'm sure I don't." Her face was turned away from him. "It will be enough if we can have wine. It will be plenty." She turned up her coat collar so he could not see that she was crying weakly — like an old woman.

RICHARD WRIGHT

"Bright and Morning Star," the first published story by Richard Wright, marked the emergence of Negro authors as major contributors to American literature. The cruelty laid bare in it would seem incredible if we did not have too many recent examples. It is especially notable for the nobly moving character of the dark-skinned mother.

Richard Wright was born in 1908 in Natchez, Mississippi. During the Depression he won first prize in the WPA Writers' Contest for his collection of stories, Uncle Tom's Children. *His book,* Black Boy, *attracted international attention. Until his death in 1960, he lived in Paris.*

Bright and Morning Star

SHE stood with her black face some six inches from the moist window-pane and wondered when on earth would it ever stop raining. It might keep up like this all week, she thought. She heard rain droning upon the roof, and high up in the wet sky her eyes followed the silent rush of a bright shaft of yellow that swung from the airplane beacon in far-off Memphis. Momently she could see it cutting through the rainy dark; it would hover a second like a gleaming sword above her head, then vanish. She sighed, troubling, Johnny-Boys been trampin in this slop all day wid no decent shoes on his feet. . . . Through the window she could see the rich black earth sprawling outside in the night. There was more rain than the clay could soak up; pools stood everywhere. She yawned and mumbled, "Rains good n bad. It kin make seed bus up thu the groun, er it kin bog things down lika watah-soaked coffin." Her hands were folded loosely over her stomach and the hot air of the kitchen traced a filmy veil of sweat on her forehead. From the cookstove came the soft singing of burning wood and now and then a throaty bubble rose from a pot of simmering greens.

"Shucks, Johnny-Boy coulda let somebody else do all tha runnin in the rain. Theres others bettah fixed fer it than he is. But, naw! Johnny-Boy ain the one t trust nobody t do nothin. Hes gotta do it *all* hissef. . . ."

She glanced at a pile of damp clothes in a zinc tub. Waal, Ah bettah git to work. She turned, lifted a smoothing iron with a thick pad of cloth, touched a spit-wet finger to it with a quick, jerking motion: *smiiitz!* Yeah; its hot! Stooping, she took a blue work-shirt from the tub and shook it out. With a deft twist of her shoulder she caught the iron in her right hand; the fingers of her left hand took a piece of wax from a tin box and a frying sizzle came as she smeared the bottom. She was thinking of nothing now; her hands followed a life-long ritual of toil. Spreading a sleeve, she ran the hot iron to and fro until the wet cloth became stiff. She was deep in the midst of her work when a song rose out of the far off days of her childhood and broke through half-parted lips:

> *Hes the Lily of the Valley, the Bright n Mawnin Star*
> *Hes the Fairest of Ten Thousan t mah soul . . .*

A gust of wind dashed rain against the window. Johnny-Boy oughta c mon home n eat his suppah. Aw Lawd! Itd be fine ef Sug could eat wid us tonight! Itd be like ol times! Mabbe aftah all it wont be long fo he'll be back. Tha lettah Ah got from im las week said *Don give up hope.* . . . Yeah; we gotta live in hope. Then both of her sons, Sug and Johnny-Boy, would be back with her.

With an involuntary nervous gesture, she stopped and stood still, listening. But the only sound was the lulling fall of rain. Shucks, ain no usa me ackin this way, she thought. Ever time they gits ready to hol them meetings Ah gits jumpity. Ah been a lil scared ever since Sug went t jail. She heard the clock ticking and looked. Johnny-Boys a *hour* late! He sho mus be havin a time doin all tha trampin, trampin thu the mud. . . . But her fear was a quiet one; it was more like an intense brooding than a fear; it was a sort of hugging of hated facts so closely that she could feel their grain, like letting cold water run over her hand from a faucet on a winter morning.

She ironed again, faster now, as if the more she engaged her body in work the less she would think. But how could she forget Johnny-Boy out there on those wet fields rounding up white and black Communists for a meeting tomorrow? And that was just what Sug had been doing when the sheriff had caught him, beat him, and tried to make him tell who and where his comrades were. Po Sug! They sho musta beat tha boy something awful! But, thank Gawd, he didnt talk! He ain no weaklin' Sug ain! Hes been lion-hearted all his life long.

That had happened a year ago. And now each time those meetings came around the old terror surged back. While shoving the iron a cluster of toiling days returned; days of washing and ironing to feed Johnny-Boy and Sug so they could do party work; days of carrying a hundred pounds of white folks' clothes upon her head across fields sometimes wet and sometimes dry. But in those days a hundred pounds was nothing to carry carefully balanced upon her head while stepping by instinct over the corn and cotton rows. The only time it had seemed heavy was when she had heard of Sug's arrest. She had been coming home one morning with a bundle upon her head, her hands swinging idly by her sides, walking slowly with her eyes in front of her, when Bob, Johnny-Boy's pal, had called from across the fields and had come and told her that the sheriff had got Sug. That morning the bundle had become heavier than she could ever remember.

And with each passing week now, though she spoke of it to no one, things were becoming heavier. The tubs of water and the smoothing iron and the bundle of clothes were becoming harder to lift, her with her back aching so, and her work was taking longer, all because Sug was gone and she didn't know just when Johnny-Boy would be taken too. To ease the ache of anxiety that was swelling her heart, she hummed, then sang softly:

> He walks wid me, He talks wid me
> He tells me Ahm His own. . . .

Guiltily, she stopped and smiled. Looks like Ah jus cant seem t fergit them ol songs, no mattah how hard Ah tries. . . . She had learned them when she was a little girl living and working on a farm. Every Monday morning from the corn and cotton fields the slow strains had floated from her mother's lips, lonely and haunting; and later, as the years had filled with gall, she had learned their deep meaning. Long hours of scrubbing floors for a few cents a day had taught her who Jesus was, what a great boon it was to cling to Him, to be like Him and suffer without a mumbling word. She had poured the yearning of her life into the songs, feeling buoyed with a faith beyond this world. The figure of the Man nailed in agony to the Cross, His burial in a cold grave, His transfigured Resurrection, His being breath and clay, God and Man — all had focused her feelings upon an imagery which had swept her life into a wondrous vision.

But as she had grown older, a cold white mountain, the white folks and their laws, had swum into her vision and shattered her songs and their spell of peace. To her that white mountain was temptation, something to lure her from her Lord, a part of the world God had made in order that she might endure it and come through all the stronger, just as Christ had risen with greater glory from the tomb. The days crowded with trouble had enhanced her faith and she had grown to love hardship with a bitter pride; she had obeyed the laws of the white folks with a soft smile of secret knowing.

After her mother had been snatched up to heaven in a chariot of fire, the years had brought her a rough workingman and two black babies, Sug and Johnny-Boy, all three of whom she had wrapped in the charm and magic of her vision. Then she was tested by no less than God; her man died, a trial which she bore with the strength shed by the grace of her vision; finally even the memory of her man faded into the vision itself, leaving her with two black boys growing tall, slowly into manhood.

Then one day grief had come to her heart when Johnny-Boy and Sug had walked forth demanding their lives. She had sought to fill their eyes with her vision, but they would have none of it. And she had wept when they began to boast of the strength shed by a new and terrible vision.

But she had loved them, even as she loved them now; bleeding, her heart had followed them. She could have done no less, being an old woman in a strange world. And day by day her sons had ripped from her startled eyes her old vision; and image by image had given her a new one, different, but great and strong enough to fling her into the light of another grace. The wrongs and sufferings of black men had taken the place of Him nailed to the Cross; the meager beginnings of the party had become another Resurrection; and the hate of those who would destroy her new faith had quickened in her a hunger to feel how deeply her strength went.

"Lawd, Johnny-Boy," she would sometimes say, "Ah jus wan them white folks t try t make me tell *who* is *in* the party n who *ain!* Ah jus wan em t try, n Ahll show em something they never thought a black woman could have!"

But sometimes like tonight, while lost in the forgetfulness of work, the past and the present would become mixed in her; while toiling under a strange star for a new freedom the old songs would slip from her lips with their beguiling sweetness.

The iron was getting cold. She put more wood into the fire, stood again at the winow and watched the yellow blade of light cut through the wet darkness. Johnny-Boy ain here yit. . . . Then, before she was aware of it, she was still, listening for sounds. Under the drone of rain she heard the slosh of feet in mud. Tha ain Johnny-Boy. She knew his long, heavy footsteps in a million. She heard feet come on the porch. Some woman. . . . She heard bare knuckles knock three times, then once. Thas some of them comrades! She unbarred the door, cracked it a few inches, and flinched from the cold rush of damp wind.

"Whos tha?"

"Its me!"

"Who?"

"Me, Reva!"

She flung the door open.

"Lawd, chile, c mon in!"

She stepped to one side and a thin, blonde-haired white girl ran through the door; as she slid the bolt she heard the girl gasping and shaking her wet clothes. Somethings wrong! Reva wouldna walked a mile t mah house in all this slop fer nothin! Tha gals stuck onto Johnny-Boy; Ah wondah ef anything happened t im?

"Git on inter the kitchen, Reva, where its warm."

"Lawd, Ah sho is wet!"

"How yuh reckon yuhd be, in all tha rain?"

"Johnny-Boy ain here *yit?*" asked Reva.

"Naw! N ain no usa yuh worryin bout im. Jus yuh git them shoes off! Yuh wanna ketch yo deatha col?" She stood looking absently. Yeah; its something bout the party er Johnny-Boy thas gone wrong. Lawd, Ah wondah ef her pa knows how she feels bout Johnny-Boy? "Honey, yuh hadnt oughta come out in sloppy weather like this."

"Ah had t come, An Sue."

She led Reva to the kitchen.

"Git them shoes off an git close t the stove so yuhll git dry!"

"An Sue, Ah got something to tell yuh . . ."

The words made her hold her breath. Ah bet its something bout Johnny-Boy!

"Whut, honey?"

"The sheriff wuz by our house tonight. He come see pa."

"Yeah?"

"He done got word from somewheres bout tha meetin tomorrow."

"Is it Johnny-Boy, Reva?"

"Aw, naw, An Sue! Ah ain hearda word bout im. Ain yuh seen im tonight?"

"He ain come home t eat yit."

"Where kin he be?"

"Lawd knows, chile."

"Somebodys gotta tell them comrades tha meetings off," said Reva. "The sheriffs got men watchin our house. Ah had t slip out t git here widout em followin me."

"Reva?"

"Hunh?"

"Ahma ol woman n Ah wans yuh t tell me the truth."

"Whut, An Sue?"

"Yuh ain tryin t fool me, is yuh?"

"*Fool* yuh?"

"Bout Johnny-Boy?"

"Lawd, naw, An Sue!"

"Ef theres anything wrong jus tell me, chile. Ah kin stan it."

She stood by the ironing board, her hands as usual folded loosely over her stomach, watching Reva pull off her waterclogged shoes. She was feeling that Johnny-Boy was already lost to her; she was feeling the pain that would come when she knew it for certain; and she was feeling that she would have to be brave and bear it. She was like a person caught in a swift current of water and knew where the water was sweeping her and did not want to go on but had to go on to the end.

"It ain nothin bout Johnny-Boy, An Sue," said Reva. "But we gotta do somethin er we'll all git inter trouble."

"How the sheriff know bout tha meetin?"

"Thas whut pa wans t know."

"Somebody done turned Judas."

"Sho looks like it."

"Ah bet it wuz some of them new ones," she said.

"Its hard t tell," said Reva.

"Lissen, Reva, yuh oughta stay here n git dry, but yuh bettah git back n tell yo pa Johnny-Boy ain here n Ah don know when hes gonna show up. *Some*bodys gotta tell them comrades t stay erway from yo pas house."

She stood with her back to the window, looking at Reva's wide, blue eyes. Po critter! Gotta go back thu all tha slop! Though she felt sorry for Reva, not once did she think that it would not have to be done. Being a woman, Reva was not suspect; she would have to go. It was just as natural for Reva to go back through the cold rain as it was for her to iron night and day or for Sug to be in jail. Right now, Johnny-Boy was out there on those dark fields trying to get home. Lawd, don let em git im tonight! In spite of herself her feelings became torn. She loved her son and, loving him, she loved what he was trying to do. Johnny-Boy was happiest when he was working for the party, and her love for him was for his happiness. She frowned, trying hard to fit something together in her feelings: for her to try to stop Johnny-Boy was to admit that all the toil of years meant nothing; and to let him go meant that sometime or other he would be caught, like Sug. In facing it this way she felt a little stunned, as though she had come suddenly upon a blank wall in the dark. But outside in the rain were people, white and black, whom she had known all her life. Those people depended upon Johnny-Boy, loved him and looked to him as a man and leader. Yeah; hes gotta keep on; he cant stop now. . . . She looked at Reva; she was crying and pulling her shoes back on with reluctant fingers.

"Whut yuh carryin on tha way fer, chile?"

"Yuh done los Sug, now yuh sendin Johnny-Boy . . ."

"Ah got t, honey."

She was glad she could say that. Reva believed in black folks and not for anything in the world would she falter before her. In Reva's trust and acceptance of her she had found her first feelings of humanity; Reva's love was her refuge from shame and degradation. If in the early days of her life the white mountain had driven her back from the earth, then in her last days Reva's love was drawing her toward it, like the beacon that swung through the night outside. She heard Reva sobbing.

"Hush, honey!"

"Mah brothers in jail too! Ma cries ever day . . ."

"Ah know, honey."

She helped Reva with her coat; her fingers felt the scant flesh of the girl's shoulders. She don git ernuff t eat, she thought. She slipped her arms around Reva's waist and held her close for a moment.

"Now, yuh stop tha cryin."

"A-a-ah c-c-cant hep it. . . ."

"Everythingll be awright; Johnny-Boyll be back."

"Yuh think so?"

"Sho, chile. Cos he will."

Neither of them spoke again until they stood in the doorway. Outside they could hear water washing through the ruts of the street.

"Be sho n send Johnny-Boy t tell the folks t stay erway from pas house," said Reva.

"Ahll tell im. Don yuh worry."

"Good-bye!"

"Good-bye!"

Leaning against the door jamb, she shook her head slowly and watched Reva vanish through the falling rain.

II

She was back at her board, ironing, when she heard feet sucking in the mud of the back yard; feet she knew from long years of listening were Johnny-Boy's. But tonight with all the rain and fear his coming was like a leaving, was almost more than she could bear. Tears welled to her eyes and she blinked them away. She felt that he was coming so that she could give him up; to see him now was to say good-bye. But it was a good-bye she knew she could never say; they were not that way toward each other. All day long they could sit in the same room and not speak; she was his mother and he was her son; most of the time a nod or a grunt would carry all the meaning that she wanted to say to him, or he to her.

She did not even turn her head when she heard him come stomping into the kitchen. She heard him pull up a chair, sit, sigh, and draw off his muddy shoes; they fell to the floor with heavy thuds. Soon the kitchen was full of the scent of his drying socks and his burning pipe. Tha boys hongry! She paused and looked at him over her shoulder; he was puffing at his pipe with his head tilted back and his feet propped up on the edge of the stove; his eyelids drooped and his wet clothes steamed from the heat of the fire. Lawd, tha boy gits mo like his pa ever day he lives, she mused, her lips breaking in a faint smile. Hols tha pipe in his mouth jus like his pa usta hol his. Wondah how they woulda got erlong ef his pa hada lived? They oughta liked each other, they so mucha like. She wished there could have been other children besides Sug, so Johnny-Boy would not have to be so much alone. A man needs a woman by his side. . . . She thought of Reva; she liked Reva; the brightest glow her heart had ever known was when she had learned that Reva loved Johnny-Boy. But beyond Reva were cold white faces. Ef theys caught it means *death*. . . . She jerked around when she heard Johnny-Boy's pipe clatter to the floor. She saw him pick it up, smile sheepishly at her, and wag his head.

"Gawd, Ahm sleepy," he mumbled.

She got a pillow from her room and gave it to him.

"Here," she said.

"Hunh," he said, putting the pillow between his head and the back of the chair.

They were silent again. Yes, she would have to tell him to go back out into the cold rain and slop; maybe to get caught; maybe for the last time; she didn't know. But she would let him eat and get dry before telling him that the sheriff knew of the meeting to be held at Lem's tomorrow. And she would make him take a big dose of soda before he went out; soda always helped to stave off a cold. She looked at the clock. It was eleven. Theres time yit. Spreading a newspaper on the apron of the stove, she placed a heaping plate of greens upon it, a knife, a fork, a cup of coffee, a slab of cornbread, and a dish of peach cobbler.

"Yo suppahs ready," she said.

"Yeah," he said.

He did not move. She ironed again. Presently, she heard him eating. Wen she could no longer hear his knife tinkling against the edge of the plate, she knew he was through. It was almost twelve now. She would let him rest a little while longer before she told him. Till one er'clock, mabbe. Hes so tired. . . . She finished her ironing, put away the board, and stacked the clothes in her dresser drawer. She poured herself a cup of coffee, drew up a chair, sat, and drank.

"Yuh almos dry," she said, not looking around.

"Yeah," he said, turning sharply to her.

The tone of voice in which she had spoken let him know that more was coming. She drained her cup and waited a moment longer.

"Reva wuz here."

"Yeah?"

"She lef bout a hour ergo."

"Whut she say?"

"She said ol man Lem hada visit from the sheriff today."

"Bout the meetin?"

"Yeah."

She saw him stare at the coals glowing red through the crevices of the stove and run his fingers nervously through his hair. She knew he was wondering how the sheriff had found out. In the silence he would ask a wordless question and in the silence she would answer wordlessly. Johnny-Boys too trustin, she thought. Hes tryin t make the party big n hes takin in folks fastern he kin git t know em. You cant trust ever white man yuh meet. . . .

"Yuh know, Johnny-Boy, yuh been takin in a lotta them white folks lately . . ."

"Aw, ma!"

"But, Johnny-Boy . . ."

"Please, don talk t me bout tha now, ma."

"Yuh ain t ol t lissen n learn, son," she said.

"Ah know whut yuh gonna say, ma. N yuh wrong. Yuh cant judge folks jus by how yuh feel bout em n by how long yuh done knowed em. Ef we start tha we wouldnt have *no*body in the party. When folks pledge they word t be with us, then we gotta take em in. Wes too weak t be choosy."

He rose abruptly, rammed his hands into his pockets, and stood facing the window; she looked at his back in a long silence. She knew his faith; it was deep. He had always said that black men could not fight the rich bosses alone; a man could not fight with every hand against him. But he believes so hard hes blind, she thought. At odd times they had had these arguments before; always she would be pitting her feelings against the hard necessity of his thinking, and always she would lose. She shook her head. Po Johnny-Boy; he don know . . .

"But ain nona our folks tol, Johnny-Boy," she said.

"How yuh know?" he asked. His voice came low and with a tinge of anger. He still faced the window and now and then the yellow blade of light flicked across the sharp outline of his black face.

"Cause Ah know em," she said.

"*Any*body mighta tol," he said.

"It wuznt nona *our* folks," she said again.

She saw his hand sweep in a swift arc of disgust.

"*Our* folks! Ma, who in Gawds name is *our* folks?"

"The folks we wuz born n raised wid, son. The folks we *know!*"

"We cant make the party grow tha way, ma."

"It mighta been Booker," she said.

"Yuh don know."

". . . er Blattbert . . ."

"Fer Chrissakes!"

". . . er any of the fo-five others whut joined las week."

"Ma, yuh jus don wan me t go out tonight," he said.

"Yo ol ma wans yuh t be careful, son."

"Ma, when yuh start doubtin folks in the party, then there ain no end."

"Son, Ah knows ever black man n woman in this parta the county," she said, standing too. "Ah watched em grow up; Ah even heped birth n nurse some of em; Ah knows em *all* from way back. There ain none of em tha *coulda* tol! The folks Ah know jus don open they dos n ast death t walk in! Son, it wuz some of them white folks! Yuh jus mark mah word!"

"Why is it gotta be *white* folks?" he asked. "Ef they tol, then theys jus Judases, thas all."

"Son, look at whuts befo yuh."

He shook his head and sighed.

"Ma, Ah done tol yuh a hundred times Ah cant see white an Ah cant see black," he said. "Ah sees rich men an Ah sees po men."

She picked up his dirty dishes and piled them in a pan. Out of the corners of her eyes she saw him sit and pull on his wet shoes. Hes goin! When she put the last dish away he was standing fully dressed, warming his hands over the stove. Just a few mo minutes now n he'll be gone, like Sug, mabbe. Her throat swelled. This black mans fight takes *ever*thing! Looks like Gawd puts us in this worl jus t beat us down!

"Keep this, ma," he said.

She saw a crumpled wad of money in his outstretched fingers.

"Naw; yuh keep it. Yuh might need it."

"It ain mine, ma. It berlongs t the party."

"But, Johnny-Boy, yuh might hafta go erway!"

"Ah kin make out."

"Don fergit yousef too much, son."

"Ef Ah don come back theyll need it."

He was looking at her face and she was looking at the money.

"Yuh keep tha," she said slowly. "Ahll give em the money."

"From where?"

"Ah got some."

"Where yuh git it from?"

She sighed.

"Ah been savin a dollah a week fer Sug ever since hes been in jail."

"Lawd, ma!"

She saw the look of puzzled love and wonder in his eyes. Clumsily, he put the money back into his pocket.

"Ahm gone," he said.

"Here; drink this glass of soda watah."

She watched him drink, then put the glass away.

"Waal," he said.

"Take the stuff outta yo pockets!"

She lifted the lid of the stove and he dumped all the papers from his pocket into the hole. She followed him to the door and made him turn round.

"Lawd, yuh tryin to maka revolution n yuh cant even keep yo coat buttoned." Her nimble fingers fastened his collar high around his throat. "There!"

He pulled the brim of his hat low over his eyes. She opened the door and with the suddenness of the cold gust of wind that struck her face, he was gone. She watched the black fields and the rain take him, her eyes burning. When the last faint footstep could no longer be heard, she closed the door, went to her bed, lay down, and pulled the cover over her while fully dressed. Her feelings coursed with the rhythm of the rain: Hes gone! Lawd, Ah *know* hes gone! Her blood felt cold.

III

She was floating in a gray void somewhere between sleeping and dreaming and then suddenly she was wide awake, hearing and feeling in the same instant the thunder of the door crashing in and a cold wind filling the room. It was pitch black and she stared, resting on her elbows, her mouth open, not breathing, her ears full of the sound of tramping feet and booming voices. She knew at once: They lookin fer im! Then, filled with her will, she was on her feet, rigid, waiting, listening.

"The lamps burnin!"

"Yuh see her?"

"Naw!"

"Look in the kitchen!"

"Gee, this place smells like niggers!"

"Say, somebodys here er been here!"

"Yeah; theres fire in the stove!"

"Mabbe hes been here n gone?"

"Boy, look at these jars of jam!"

"Niggers make good jam!"

"Git some bread!"

"Heres some cornbread!"

"Say, lemme git some!"

"Take it easy! Theres plenty here!"

"Ahma take some of this stuff home!"

"Look, heres a pota greens!"

"N some hot cawffee!"

"Say, yuh guys! C mon! Cut it out! We didnt come here fer a feas!"

She walked slowly down the hall. They lookin fer im, but they ain got im yit! She stopped in the doorway, her gnarled, black hands as always folded over her stomach, but tight now, so tightly the veins bulged. The kitchen was crowded with white men in glistening raincoats. Though the lamp burned, their flashlights still glowed in red fists. Across her floor she saw the muddy tracks of their boots.

"Yuh white folks git outta mah house!"

There was quick silence; every face turned toward her. She saw a sudden movement, but did not know what it meant until something hot and wet slammed her squarely in the face. She gasped, but did not move. Calmly, she wiped the warm, greasy liquor of greens from her eyes with her left hand. One of the white men had thrown a handful of greens out of the pot at her.

"How they taste, ol bitch?"

"Ah ast yuh t git outta mah house!"

She saw the sheriff detach himself from the crowd and walk toward her.

"Now Anty . . ."

"White man, don yuh *Anty* me!"

"Yuh ain got the right sperit!"

"Sperit hell! Yuh git these men outta mah house!"

"Yuh ack like yuh don like it!"

"Naw, Ah don like it, n yuh knows dam waal Ah don!"

"What yuh gonna do about it?"

"Ahm tellin yuh t git outta mah house!"

"Gittin sassy?"

"Ef tellin yuh t git outta mah house is sass, then Ahm sassy!"

Her words came in a tense whisper; but beyond, back of them, she was watching, thinking, and judging the men.

"Listen, Anty," the sheriff's voice came soft and low. "Ahm here t hep yuh. How come yuh wanna ack this way?"

"Yuh ain never heped you *own* sef since yuh been born," she flared. "How kin the likes of yuh hep me?"

One of the white men came forward and stood directly in front of her.

"Lissen, nigger woman, yuh talkin t *white* men!"

"Ah don care who Ahm talkin t!"

"Yuhll wish some day yuh did!"

"Not t the likes of yuh!"

"Yuh need somebody t teach yuh how t be a good nigger!"

"*Yuh* cant teach it t me!"

"Yuh gonna change yo tune."

"Not longs mah bloods warm!"

"Don git smart now!"

"Yuh git outta mah house!"

"Spose we don go?" the sheriff asked.

They were crowded around her. She had not moved since she had taken her place in the doorway. She was thinking only of Johnny-Boy as she stood there giving and taking words; and she knew that they, too, were thinking of Johnny-Boy. She knew they wanted him, and her heart was daring them to take him from her.

"Spose we don go?" the sheriff asked again.

"Twenty of yuh runnin over one ol woman! Now, ain yuh white men glad yuh so brave?"

The sheriff grabbed her arm.

"C mon, now! Yuh done did ernuff sass fer one night. Wheres tha nigger son of yos?"

"Don yuh wished yuh knowed?"

"Yuh wanna git slapped?"

"Ah ain never seen one of yo kind tha wuznt too low fer . . ."

The sheriff slapped her straight across her face with his open palm. She fell back against a wall and sank to her knees.

"Is tha whut white men do t nigger women?"

She rose slowly and stood again, not even touching the place that ached from his blow, her hands folded over her stomach.

"Ah ain never seen one of yo kind tha wuznt too low fer . . ."

He slapped her again; she reeled backward several feet and fell on her side.

"Is tha whut we too low t do?"

She stood before him again, dry-eyed, as though she had not been struck. Her lips were numb and her chin was wet with blood.

"Aw, let her go! Its the nigger we wan!" said one.

"Wheres that nigger son of yos?" the sheriff asked.

"Find im," she said.

"By Gawd, ef we hafta find im we'll kill im!"

"He wont be the only nigger yuh ever killed," she said.

She was consumed with a bitter pride. There was nothing on this earth, she felt then, that they could not do to her but that she could take. She stood on a narrow plot of ground from which she would die before she was pushed. And then it was, while standing there feeling warm blood seeping down her throat, that she gave up Johnny-Boy, gave him up to the white folks. She gave him up because they had come tramping into her heart demanding him, thinking they could get him by beating her, thinking they could scare her into making her tell where he was. She gave him up because she wanted them to know that they could not get what they wanted by bluffing and killing.

"Wheres this meetin gonna be?" the sheriff asked.

"Don yuh wish yuh knowed?"

"Ain there gonna be a meetin?"

"How come yuh astin me?"

"There *is* gonna be a meetin," said the sheriff.

"Is it?"

"Ah gotta great mind t choke it outta yuh!"

"Yuh so smart," she said.

"We ain playin wid yuh!"

"Did Ah say yuh wuz?"

"Tha nigger son of yos is erroun here somewheres an we aim t find im," said the sheriff. "Ef yuh tell us where he is n ef he talks, mabbe he'll git off easy. But ef we hafta find im, we'll kill im! Ef we hafta find im, then yuh git a sheet t put over im in the mawnin, see? Git yuh a sheet, cause hes gonna be dead!"

"He wont be the only nigger yuh ever killed," she said again.

The sheriff walked past her. The others followed. Yuh didn't git whut yuh wanted! she thought exultingly. N yuh ain gonna *never* git it! Hotly something ached in her to make them feel the intensity of her pride and freedom; her heart groped to turn the bitter hours of her life into words of a kind that would make them feel that she had taken all they had done to her in her stride and could still take more. Her faith surged so strongly in her she was all but blinded. She walked behind them to the door, knotting and twisting her fingers. She saw them step to the muddy ground. Each whirl of the yellow beacon revealed glimpses of slanting rain. Her lips moved, then she shouted, "Yuh didn't git whut yuh wanted! N yuh ain gonna nevah git it!"

The sheriff stopped and turned; his voice came low and hard.

"Now, by Gawd, thas ernuff outta yuh!"

"Ah know when Ah done said ernuff!"

"Aw, naw, yuh don!" he said. "Yuh don know when yuh done said ernuff, but Ahma teach yuh ternight!"

He was up the steps and across the porch with one bound. She backed into the hall, her eyes full on his face.

"Tell me when yuh gonna stop talkin!" he said, swinging his fist.

The blow caught her high on the cheek; her eyes went blank; she fell flat on her face. She felt the hard heel of his wet shoes coming into her temple and stomach.

"Lemme hear yuh talk some mo!"

She wanted to, but could not; pain numbed and choked her. She lay still and somewhere out of the gray void of unconsciousness she heard someone say: *Aw fer chrissakes leave her erlone its the nigger we wan . . . .*

IV

She never knew how long she had lain huddled in the dark hallway. Her first returning feeling was of a nameless fear crowding the inside of her, then a deep pain spreading from her temple downward over her body. Her ears were filled with the drone of rain and she shuddered from the cold wind blowing through the door. She opened her eyes and at first saw nothing. As if she were imagining it, she knew she was half-lying and half-sitting in a corner against a wall. With difficulty she twisted her neck, and what she saw made her hold her breath — a vast white blur was suspended directly above her. For a moment she could not tell if her fear was from the blur or if the blur was from her fear. Gradually the blur resolved itself into a huge white face that slowly filled her vision. She was stone still, conscious really of the effort to breathe, feeling somehow that she existed only by the mercy of that white face. She had seen it before; its fear had gripped her many times; it had for her the fear of all the white faces she had ever seen in her life. *Sue* . . . As from a great distance, she heard her name being called. She was regaining consciousness now, but the fear was coming with her. She looked into the face of a white man, wanting to scream out for him to go; yet accepting his presence because she felt she had to. Though some remote part of her mind was active, her limbs were powerless. It was as if an invisible knife had split her in two, leaving one half of her lying there helpless, while the other half shrank in dread from a forgotten but familiar enemy. *Sue its me Sue its me* . . . Then all at once the voice came clearly.

"Sue, its me! Its Booker!"

And she heard an answering voice speaking inside of her, Yeah, its Booker . . . The one whut jus joined . . . She roused herself, struggling for full consciousness; and as she did so she transferred to the person of Booker the nameless fear she felt. It seemed that Booker towered above her as a challenge to her right to exist upon the earth.

"Yuh awright?"

She did not answer; she started violently to her feet and fell.

"Sue, yuh hurt!"

"Yeah," she breathed.

"Where they hit yuh?"

"Its mah head," she whispered.

She was speaking even though she did not want to; the fear that had hold of her compelled her.

"They beat yuh?"

"Yeah."

"Them bastards! Them Gawddam bastards!"

She heard him saying it over and over; then she felt herself being lifted.

"Naw!" she gasped.

"Ahma take yuh t the kitchen!"

"Put me down!"

"But yuh cant stay here like this!"

She shrank in his arms and pushed her hands against his body; when she was in the kitchen she freed herself, sank into a chair, and held tightly to its back. She looked wonderingly at Booker; there was nothing about him that should frighten her so; but even that did not ease her tension. She saw him go to the water bucket, wet his handkerchief, wring it, and offer it to her. Distrustfully, she stared at the damp cloth.

"Here; put this on yo fohead . . ."

"Naw!"

"C mon; itll make yuh feel bettah!"

She hesitated in confusion; what right had she to be afraid when someone was acting as kindly as this toward her? Reluctantly, she leaned forward and pressed the damp cloth to her head. It helped. With each passing minute she was catching hold of herself, yet wondering why she felt as she did.

"Whut happened?"

"Ah don know."

"Yuh feel bettah?"

"Yeah."

"Who all wuz here?"

"Ah don know," she said again.

"Yo head still hurt?"

"Yeah."

"Gee, Ahm sorry."

"Ahm awright," she sighed and buried her face in her hands.

She felt him touch her shoulder.

"Sue, Ah got some bad news fer yuh . . ."

She knew; she stiffened and grew cold. It had happened; she stared dry-eyed with compressed lips.

"Its mah Johnny-Boy," she said.

"Yeah; Ahm awful sorry t hafta tell yuh this way. But Ah thought yuh oughta know . . ."

Her tension eased and a vacant place opened up inside of her. A voice whispered, Jesus, hep me!

"W-w-where is he?"

"They got im out t Foley's Woods tryin t make im tell who the others is."

"He ain gonna tell," she said. "They just as waal kill im, cause he ain gonna nevah tell."

"Ah hope he don," said Booker. "But he didnt hava chance t tell the others. They grabbed im just as he got t the woods."

Then all the horror of it flashed upon her; she saw flung out over the rainy countryside an array of shacks where white and black comrades were sleeping; in the morning they would be rising and going to Lem's; then they would be caught. And that meant terror, prison, and death. The comrades would have to be told; she would have to tell them; she could not entrust Johnny-Boy's work to another, and especially not to

Booker as long as she felt toward him as she did. Gripping the bottom of the chair with both hands, she tried to rise; the room blurred and she swayed. She found herself resting in Booker's arms.

"Lemme go!"

"Sue, yuh too weak t walk!"

"Ah gotta tell em!" she said.

"Set down, Sue! Yuh hurt; yuh sick!"

When seated she looked at him helplessly.

"Sue, lissen! Johnny-Boys caught. Ahm here. Yuh tell me who they is n Ahll tell em."

She stared at the floor and did not answer. Yes; she was too weak to go. There was no way for her to tramp all those miles through the rain tonight. But should she tell Booker? If only she had somebody like Reva to talk to. She did not want to decide alone; she must make no mistake about this. She felt Booker's fingers pressing on her arm and it was as though the white mountain was pushing her to the edge of a sheer height; she again exclaimed inwardly, Jesus, hep me! Booker's white face was at her side, waiting. Would she be doing right to tell him? Suppose she did not tell and then the comrades were caught? She could not ever forgive herself for doing a thing like that. But maybe she was wrong; maybe her fear was what Johnny-Boy had always called "jus foolishness." She remembered his saying, Ma we cant make the party ef we start doubtin everybody. . . .

"Tell me who they is, Sue, n Ahll tell em. Ah just joined n Ah don know who they is."

"Ah don know who they is," she said.

"Yuh *gotta* tell me who they is, Sue!"

"Ah tol yuh Ah don know!"

"Yuh *do* know! C mon! Set up n talk!"

"Naw!"

"Yuh wan em all t git *killed?*"

She shook her head and swallowed. Lawd, Ah don blieve in this man!

"Lissen, Ahll call the names n yuh tell me which ones is in the party n which ones ain, see?"

"Naw!"

"Please, Sue!"

"Ah don know," she said.

"Sue, yuh ain doin right by em. Johnny-Boy wouldnt wan yuh t be this way. Hes out there holdin up his end. Les hol up ours. . . ."

"Lawd, Ah don know. . . ."

"Is yuh scareda me cause Ahm *white?* Johnny-Boy ain like tha. Don let all the work we done go fer nothin."

She gave up and bowed her head in her hands.

"Is it Johnson? Tell me, Sue?"

"Yeah," she whispered in horror; a mounting horror of feeling herself being undone.

"Is it Green?"

"Yeah."

"Murphy?"

"Lawd, Ah don know!"

"Yuh gotta tell me, Sue!"

"Mistah Booker, please leave me erlone. . . ."

"Is it Murphy?"

She answered yes to the names of Johnny-Boy's comrades; she answered until he asked her no more. Then she thought, How he know the sheriffs men is watchin Lems house? She stood up and held on to her chair, feeling something sure and firm within her.

"How yuh know bout Lem?"

"Why . . . How Ah know?"

"Whut yuh doin here this tima night? How yuh know the sheriff got Johnny-Boy?"

"Sue, don yuh blieve in me?"

She did not, but she could not answer. She stared at him until her lips hung open; she was searching deep within herself for certainty.

"You meet Reva?" she asked.

"Reva?"

"Yeah; Lems gal?"

"Oh, yeah. Sho, Ah met Reva."

"She tell yuh?"

She asked the question more of herself than of him; she longed to believe.

"Yeah," he said softly. "Ah reckon Ah oughta be goin t tell em now."

"Who?" she asked. "Tell *who?*"

The muscles of her body were stiff as she waited for his answer; she felt as though life depended upon it.

"The comrades," he said.

"Yeah," she sighed.

She did not know when he left; she was not looking or listening. She just suddenly saw the room empty, and from her the thing that had made her fearful was gone.

V

For a space of time that seemed to her as long as she had been upon the earth, she sat huddled over the cold stove. One minute she would say to herself, They both gone now; Johnny-Boy n Sug . . . Mabbe Ahll never see em ergin. Then a surge of guilt would blot out her longing. "Lawd, Ah shouldna tol!" she mumbled. "But no man kin be so low-down as t do a thing like tha . . ." Several times she had an impulse to try to tell the comrades herself; she was feeling a little better now. But what good would that do? She had told Booker the names. He just couldn't be a Judas t po folks like us . . . He *couldnt!*

"An Sue!"

Thas Reva! Her heart leaped with an anxious gladness. She rose without answering and limped down the dark hallway. Through the open door, against the background of rain, she saw Reva's face lit now and then to whiteness by the whirling beams of the beacon. She was about to call, but a thought checked her. Jesus, hep me! Ah gotta tell her bout Johnny-Boy . . . Lawd, Ah cant!

"An Sue, yuh there?"

"C mon in, chile!"

She caught Reva and held her close for a moment without speaking.

"Lawd, Ahm sho glad yuh here," she said at last.

"Ah thought something had happened t yuh," said Reva, pulling away. "Ah saw the do open . . . Pa tol me to come back n stay wid yuh tonight . . ." Reva paused and stared. "W-w-whuts the mattah?"

She was so full of having Reva with her that she did not understand what the question meant.

"Hunh?"

"Yo neck . . ."

"Aw, it ain nothin, chile. C mon in the kitchen."

"But theres blood on yo neck!"

"The sheriff wuz here . . ."

"Them fools! Whut they wanna bother yuh fer? Ah could kill em! So hep me Gawd, Ah could!"

"It ain nothin," she said.

She was wondering how to tell Reva about Johnny-Boy and Booker. Ahll wait a lil while longer, she thought. Now that Reva was here, her fear did not seem as awful as before.

"C mon, lemme fix yo head, An Sue. Yuh hurt."

They went to the kitchen. She sat silent while Reva dressed her scalp. She was feeling better now; in just a little while she would tell Reva. She felt the girl's finger pressing gently upon her head.

"Tha hurt?"

"A lil, chile."

"Yuh po thing."

"It ain nothin."

"Did Johnny-Boy come?"

She hesitated.

"Yeah."

"He done gone t tell the others?"

Reva's voice sounded so clear and confident that it mocked her. Lawd, Ah cant tell this chile . . .

"Yuh tol im, didnt yuh, An Sue?"

"Y-y-yeah . . ."

"Gee! Thas good! Ah tol pa he didn't hafta worry if Johnny-Boy got the news. Mabbe thingsll come out awright."

"Ah hope . . ."

She could not go on; she had gone as far as she could; for the first time that night she began to cry.

"Hush, An Sue! Yuh awways been brave. It'll be awright!"

"Ain nothin awright, chile. The worls just too much fer us, Ah reckon."

"Ef yuh cry that way it'll make me cry."

She forced herself to stop. Naw; Ah cant carry on this way in fronta Reva. . . . Right now she had a deep need for Reva to believe in her. She watched the girl get pine-knots from behind the stove, rekindle the fire, and put on the coffee pot.

"Yuh wan some cawffee?" Reva asked.

"Naw, honey."

"Aw, c mon, An Sue."

"Jusa lil, honey."

"Thas the way t be. Oh, say, Ah fergot," said Reva, measuring out spoonfuls of coffee. "Pa tol me t tell yuh t watch out fer tha Booker man. Hes a stool."

She showed not one sign of outward movement or expression, but as the words fell from Reva's lips she went limp inside.

"Pa tol me soon as Ah got back home. He got word from town . . ."

She stopped listening. She felt as though she had been slapped to the extreme outer edge of life, into a cold darkness. She knew now what she had felt when she had looked up out of her fog of pain and had seen Booker. It was the image of all the white folks, and the fear that went with them, that she had seen and felt during her lifetime. And again, for the second time that night, something she had felt had come true. All she could say to herself was, Ah didn't like im! Gawd knows, Ah didn't! Ah tol Johnny-Boy it wuz some of them white folks . . .

"Here; drink yo cawffee . . ."

She took the cup; her fingers trembled, and the steaming liquid spilt onto her dress and leg.

"Ahm sorry, An Sue!"

Her leg was scalded, but the pain did not bother her.

"Its awright," she said.

"Wait; lemme put something on tha burn!"

"It don hurt."

"Yuh worried bout something."

"Naw, honey."

"Lemme fix yuh so mo cawffee."

"Ah don wan nothin now, Reva."

"Waal, buck up. Don be tha way . . ."

They were silent. She heard Reva drinking. No; she would not tell Reva; Reva was all she had left. But she had to do something, some way, somehow. She was undone too much as it was; and to tell Reva about Booker or Johnny-Boy was more than she was equal to; it would be too coldly shameful. She wanted to be alone and fight this thing out with herself.

"Go t bed, honey. Yuh tired."

"Naw; Ahm awright, An Sue."

She heard the bottom of Reva's empty cup clank against the top of the stove. Ah *got* t make her go t bed! Yes; Booker would tell the names of the comrades to the sheriff. If she could only stop him some way! That was the answer, the point, the star that grew bright in the morning of new hope. Soon, maybe half an hour from now, Booker would reach Foley's Woods. Hes boun t go the long way, cause he don know no short cut, she thought. Ah could wade the creek n beat im there. . . . But what would she do after that?

"Reva, honey, go t bed. Ahm awright. Yuh need res."

"Ah ain sleepy, An Sue."

"Ah knows whuts bes fer yuh, chile. Yuh tired n wet."

"Ah wanna stay up wid yuh."

She forced a smile and said:

"Ah don think they gonna hurt Johnny-Boy . . ."

"Fer *real,* An Sue?"

"Sho, honey."

"But Ah wanna wait up wid yuh."

"Thas mah job, honey. Thas whut a mas fer, t wait up fer her chullun."

"Good night, An Sue."

"Good night, honey."

She watched Reva pull up and leave the kitchen; presently she heard the shucks in the mattress whispering, and she knew that Reva had gone to bed. She was alone. Through the cracks of the stove she saw the fire dying to gray ashes; the room was growing cold again. The yellow beacon continued to flit past the window and the rain still drummed. Yes; she was alone; she had done this awful thing alone; she must find some way out, alone. Like touching a festering sore, she put her finger upon that moment when she had shouted her defiance to the sheriff, when she had shouted to feel her strength. She had lost Sug to save others; she had let Johnny-Boy go to save others; and then in a moment of weakness that came from too much strength she had lost all. If she had not shouted to the sheriff, she would have been strong enough to have resisted Booker; she would have been able to tell the comrades herself. Something tightened in her as she remembered and understood the fit of fear she had felt on coming to herself in the dark hallway. A part of her life she thought she had done away with forever had had hold of her then. She had thought the soft, warm past was over; she had thought that it did not mean much when now she sang: "Hes the Lily of the Valley, the Bright n Mawnin Star." . . . The days when she had sung that song were the days when she had not hoped for anything on this earth, the days when the cold mountain had driven her into the arms of Jesus. She had thought that Sug and Johnny-Boy had taught her to forget Him, to fix her hope upon the fight of black men for freedom.

Through the gradual years she had believed and worked with them, had felt strength shed from the grace of their terrible vision. That grace had been upon her when she had let the sheriff slap her down; it had been upon her when she had risen time and again from the floor and faced him. But she had trapped herself with her own hunger; to water the long dry thirst of her faith her pride had made a bargain which her flesh could not keep. Her having told the names of Johnny-Boy's comrades was but an incident in a deeper horror. She stood up and looked at the floor while call and counter-call, loyalty and counter-loyalty struggled in her soul. Mired she was between two abandoned worlds, living, dying without the strength of the grace that either gave. The clearer she felt it the fuller did something well up from the depths of her for release; the more urgent did she feel the need to fling into her black sky another star, another hope, one more terrible vision to give her the strength to live and act. Softly and restlessly she walked about the kitchen, feeling herself naked against night, the rain, the world; and shamed whenever the thought of Reva's love crossed her mind. She lifted her empty hands and looked at her writhing fingers. Lawd, whut kin Ah do now? She could still wade the creek and get to Foley's Woods before Booker. And then what? How could she manage to see Johnny-Boy or Booker? Again she heard the sheriff's threatening voice: Git yuh a sheet, cause hes gonna be dead! The sheet! Thas it, the sheet! Her whole being leaped with will; the long years of her life bent toward a moment of focus, a point. Ah kin go wid mah sheet! Ahll be doin whut he said! Lawd Gawd in Heaven, Ahma go lika nigger woman wid mah windin sheet t git mah dead son! But then what? She stood straight and smiled grimly; she had in her heart the whole meaning of her life; her entire personality was poised on the brink of a total act. Ah know! Ah know! She thought of Johnny-Boy's gun in the dresser drawer. Ahll hide the gun in the sheet n go aftah Johnny-Boys body. . . . She tiptoed to her room, eased out the dresser drawer, and got a sheet. Reva was sleeping; the darkness was filled with her quiet breathing. She groped in the drawer and found the gun. She wound the gun in the sheet and held them both under her apron. Then she stole to the bedside and watched Reva. Lawd, hep her! But mabbe shes bettah off. This had t happen sometimes . . . She n Johnny-Boy couldna been together in this here South . . . N Ah couldnt tell her bout Booker. Itll come out awright n she wont nevah know. Reva's trust would never be shaken. She caught her breath as the shucks in the mattress rustled dryly; then all was quiet and she breathed easily again. She tiptoed to the door, down the hall, and stood on the porch. Above her the yellow beacon whirled through the rain. She went over muddy ground, mounted a slope, stopped and looked back at her house. The lamp glowed in her window, and the yellow beacon that swung every few seconds seemed to feed it with light. She turned and started across the fields, holding the gun and sheet tightly, thinking, Po Reva . . . Po critter . . . Shes fas ersleep . . .

VI

For the most part she walked with her eyes half shut, her lips tightly compressed, leaning her body against the wind and the slanting rain, feeling the pistol in the sheet sagging cold and heavy in her fingers. Already she was getting wet; it seemed that her feet found every puddle of water that stood between the corn rows.

She came to the edge of the creek and paused, wondering at what point was it low. Taking the sheet from under her apron, she wrapped the gun in it so that her finger could be upon the trigger. Ahll cross here, she thought. At first she did not feel the water; her feet were already wet. But the water grew cold as it came up to her knees; she gasped when it reached her waist. Lawd, this creeks high! When she had passed the middle, she knew that she was out of danger. She came out of the water, climbed a grassy hill, walked on, turned a bend and saw the lights of autos gleaming ahead. Yeah; theys still there! She hurried with her head down. Wondah did Ah beat im here? Lawd, Ah hope so! A vivid image of Booker's white face hovered a moment before her eyes and a driving will surged up in her so hard and strong that it vanished. She was among the autos now. From nearby came the hoarse voices of the men.

"Hey, yuh!"

She stopped, nervously clutching the sheet. Two white men with shotguns came toward her.

"Whut in hell yuh doin out here?"

She did not answer.

"Didnt yuh hear somebody speak t yuh?"

"Ahm comin aftah mah son," she said humbly.

"Yo *son?*"

"Yessuh."

"Whut yo son doin out here?"

"The sheriffs got im."

"Holy Scott! Jim, its the niggers ma!"

"Whut yuh got there?" asked one.

"A sheet."

"A *sheet?*"

"Yessuh."

"Fer whut?"

"The sheriff tol me t bring a sheet t git his body."

"Waal, waal . . ."

"Now, ain tha something?"

The white men looked at each other.

"These niggers sho love one ernother," said one.

"N tha ain no lie," said the other.

"Take me t the sheriff," she begged.

"Yuh ain givin us *orders,* is yuh?"

"Nawsuh."

"We'll take yuh when wes good n ready."

"Yessuh."

"So yuh wan his body?"

"Yessuh."

"Waal, he ain dead yit."

"They gonna kill im," she said.

"Ef he talks they wont."

"He ain gonna talk," she said.

"How yuh know?"

"Cause he ain."

"We got ways of makin niggers talk."

"Yuh ain got no way fer im."

"Yuh thinka lot of tha black Red, don yuh?"

"He's mah son."

"Why don yuh teach im some sense?"

"Hes mah son," she said again.

"Lissen, old nigger woman, yuh stan there wid yo hair white. Yuh got bettah sense than t blieve tha niggers kin make a revolution . . ."

"A black republic," said the other one, laughing.

"Take me t the sheriff," she begged.

"Yuh his ma," said one. "Yuh kin make im talk n tell whos in this thing wid im."

"He ain gonna talk," she said.

"Don yuh wan im t live?"

She did not answer.

"C mon, les take her t Bradley."

They grabbed her arms and she clutched hard at the sheet and gun; they led her toward the crowd in the woods. Her feelings were simple; Booker would not tell; she was there with the gun to see to that. The louder became the voices of the men the deeper became her feeling of wanting to right the mistake she had made; of wanting to fight her way back to solid ground. She would stall for time until Booker showed up. Oh, ef theyll only lemme git close t Johnny-Boy! As they led her near the crowd she saw white faces turning and looking at her and heard a rising clamor of voices.

"Whos tha?"

"A nigger woman!"

"Whut she doin out here?"

"This is his ma!" called one of the men.

"Whut she wans?"

"She brought a sheet t cover his body!"

"He ain dead yit!"

"They tryin t make im talk!"

"But he will be dead soon ef he don open up!"

"Say, look! The niggers ma brought a sheet t cover up his body!"

"Now, ain tha sweet?"

"Mabbe she wans hol a prayer meetin!"

"Did she git a preacher?"

"Say, go git Bradley!"

"O.K.!"

The crowd grew quiet. They looked at her curiously; she felt their cold eyes trying to detect some weakness in her. Humbly, she stood with the sheet covering the gun. She had already accepted all that they could do to her.

The sheriff came.

"So yuh brought yo sheet, hunh?"

"Yessuh," she whispered.

"Looks like them slaps we gave yuh learned yuh some sense, didn't they?"

She did not answer.

"Yuh don need tha sheet. Yo son ain dead yit," he said, reaching.

She backed away, her eyes wide.

"Naw!"

"Now, lissen, Anty!" he said. "There ain no use in yuh ackin a fool! Go in there n tell tha nigger son of yos t tell us whos in this wid im, see? Ah promise we wont kill im ef he talks. We'll let im git outta town."

"There ain nothin Ah kin tell im," she said.

"Yuh wan us t kill im?"

She did not answer. She saw someone lean toward the sheriff and whisper.

"Bring her erlong," the sheriff said.

They lead her to a muddy clearing. The rain streamed down through the ghostly glare of the flashlights. As the men formed a semicircle she saw Johnny-Boy lying in a trough of mud. He was tied with rope; he lay hunched, one side of his face resting in a pool of black water. His eyes were staring questioningly at her.

"Speak t im," said the sheriff.

If she could only tell him why she was there! But that was impossible; she was close to what she wanted and she stared straight before her with compressed lips.

"Say, nigger!" called the sheriff, kicking Johnny-Boy. "Here's yo ma!"

Johnny-Boy did not move or speak. The sheriff faced her again.

"Lissen, Anty," he said. "Yuh got mo say wid im than anybody. Tell im t talk n hava chance. Whut he wanna pertect the other niggers n white folks fer?"

She slid her finger about the trigger of the gun and looked stonily at the mud.

"Go t him," said the sheriff.

She did not move. Her heart was crying out to answer the amazed question in Johnny-Boy's eyes. But there was no way now.

"Waal, yuhre astin fer it. By Gawd, we gotta way to *make* yuh talk t im," he said, turning away. "Say, Tim, git one of them logs n turn tha nigger upsidedown n put his legs on it!"

A murmur of assent ran through the crowd. She bit her lips; she knew what that meant.

"Yuh wan yo nigger son crippled?" she heard the sheriff ask.

She did not answer. She saw them roll the log up; they lifted Johnny-Boy and laid him on his face and stomach, then they pulled his legs over the log. His knee-caps rested on the sheer top of the log's back, the toes of his shoes pointing groundward. So absorbed was she in watching that she felt that it was she that was being lifted and made ready for torture.

"Git a crowbar!" said the sheriff.

A tall, lank man got a crowbar from a nearby auto and stood over the log. His jaws worked slowly on a wad of tobacco.

"Now, its up t yuh, Anty," the sheriff said. "Tell the man what t do!"

She looked into the rain. The sheriff turned.

"Mabbe she think wes playin. Ef she don say nothin, then break em at the knee-caps!"

"O.K., Sheriff!"

She stood waiting for Booker. Her legs felt weak; she wondered if she would be able to wait much longer. Over and over she said to herself, Ef he came now Ahd kill em both!

"She ain sayin nothin, Sheriff!"

"Waal, Gawddammit, let im have it!"

The crowbar came down and Johnny-Boy's body lunged in the mud and water. There was a scream. She swayed, holding tight to the gun and sheet.

"Hol im! Git the other leg!"

The crowbar fell again. There was another scream.

"Yuh break em?" asked the sheriff.

The tall man lifted Johnny-Boy's legs and let them drop limply again, dropping rearward from the knee-caps. Johnny-Boy's body lay still. His head had rolled to one side and she could not see his face.

"Jus lika broke sparrow wing," said the man, laughing softly.

Then Johnny-Boy's face turned to her; he screamed.

"Go way, ma! Go way!"

It was the first time she had heard his voice since she had come out to the woods; she all but lost control of herself. She started violently forward, but the sheriff's arm checked her.

"Aw, naw! Yuh had yo chance!" He turned to Johnny-Boy. "She kin go ef yuh talk."

"Mistah, he ain gonna talk," she said.

"Go way, ma!" said Johnny-Boy.

"Shoot im! Don make im suffah so," she begged.

"He'll either talk or he'll never hear yuh ergin," the sheriff said. "Theres other things we kin do t im."

She said nothing.

"Whut yuh come here fer, ma?" Johnny-Boy sobbed.

"Ahm gonna split his eardrums," the sheriff said. "Ef yuh got anything t say t im yuh bettah say it *now!*"

She closed her eyes. She heard the sheriff's feet sucking in mud. Ah could save im! She opened her eyes; there were shouts of eagerness from the crowd as it pushed in closer.

"Bus em, Sheriff!"

"Fix im so he cant hear!"

"He knows how t do it, too!"

"He busted a Jew boy tha way once!"

She saw the sheriff stoop over Johnny-Boy, place his flat palm over one ear and strike his fist against it with all his might. He placed his palm over the other ear and struck again. Johnny-Boy moaned, his head rolling from side to side, his eyes showing white amazement in a world without sound.

"Yuh wouldn't talk t im when yuh had the chance," said the sheriff. "Try n talk now."

She felt warm tears on her cheeks. She longed to shoot Johnny-Boy and let him go. But if she did that they would take the gun from her, and Booker would tell who the others were. Lawd, hep me! The men were talking loudly now, as though the main business was over. It seemed ages that she stood there watching Johnny-Boy roll and whimper in his world of silence.

"Say, Sheriff, heres somebody lookin fer yuh!"

"Who is it?"

"Ah don know!"

"Bring em in!"

She stiffened and looked around wildly, holding the gun tight. Is tha Booker? Then she held still, feeling that her excitement might betray her. Mabbe Ah kin shoot em both! Mabbe Ah kin shoot twice! The sheriff stood in front of her, waiting. The crowd parted and she saw Booker hurrying forward.

"Ah know em all, Sheriff!" he called.

He came full into the muddy clearing where Johnny-Boy lay.

"Yuh mean yuh got the names?"

"Sho! The ol nigger . . ."

She saw his lips hang open and silent when he saw her. She stepped forward and raised the sheet.

"Whut . . ."

She fired, once; then, without pausing, she turned, hearing them yell. She aimed at Johnny-Boy, but they had their arms around her, bearing her to the ground, clawing at the sheet in her hand. She glimpsed Booker lying sprawled in the mud, on his face, his hands stretched out before him; then a cluster of yelling men blotted him out. She lay without struggling, looking upward through the rain at the white faces above her. And she was suddenly at peace; they were not a white mountain now; they were not pushing her any longer to the edge of life. Its awright . . .

"She shot Booker!"

"She hada gun in the sheet!"

"She shot im right thu the head!"

"Whut she shoot im fer?"

"Kill the bitch!"

"Ah *thought* something wuz wrong bout her!"

"Ah wuz fer givin it t her from the firs!"

"Thas whut yuh git fer treatin a nigger nice!"

"Say, Bookers dead!"

She stopped looking into the white faces, stopped listening. She waited, giving up her life before they took it from her; she had done what she wanted. Ef only Johnny-Boy . . . She looked at him; he lay looking at her with tired eyes. Ef she could only tell im!

"Whut yuh kill im fer, hunh?"

It was the sheriff's voice; she did not answer.

"Mabbe she wuz shootin at yuh, Sheriff?"

"Whut yuh kill im fer?"

She felt the sheriff's foot come into her side; she closed her eyes.

"Yuh black bitch!"

"Let her have it!"

"Yuh reckon she foun out bout Booker?"

"She mighta."

"Jesus Christ, whut yuh dummies *waitin* on!"

"Yeah; kill her!"

"Kill em *both!*"

"Let her know her nigger sons dead firs!"

She turned her head toward Johnny-Boy; he lay looking puzzled in a world beyond the reach of voices. At least he cant hear, she thought.

"C mon, let im have it!"

She listened to hear what Johnny-Boy could not. They came, two of them, one right behind the other; so close together that they sounded like one shot. She did not look at Johnny-Boy now; she looked at the white faces of the men, hard and wet in the glare of the flashlights.

"Yuh hear tha; nigger woman?"

"Did tha surprise im? Hes in hell now wonderin whut hit im!"

"C mon! Give it t her, Sheriff!"

"Lemme shoot her, Sheriff! It wuz mah pal she shot!"

"Awright, Pete! Thas fair ernuff!"

She gave up as much of her life as she could before they took it from her. But the sound of the shot and the streak of fire that tore its way through her chest forced her to live again, intensely. She had not moved, save for the slight jarring impact of the bullet. She felt the heat of her own blood warming her cold, wet back. She yearned suddenly to talk. "Yuh didn't git whut yuh wanted! N yuh ain gonna nevah git it! Yuh didn't kill me; Ah come here by mahsef . . ." She felt rain falling into her wide-open, dimming eyes and heard faint voices. Her lips moved soundlessly. *Yuh didnt git yuh didnt yuh didnt . . .* Focused and pointed she was, buried in the depths of her star, swallowed in its peace and strength; and not feeling her flesh growing cold, cold as the rain that fell from the invisible sky upon the doomed living and the dead that never dies.

WILLIAM FAULKNER

Set in Yoknapatawpha County — which is so real a place to Faulkner
readers it might actually be marked on a map of the United States —
"Hand Upon the Waters" reads almost like a detective story. But the
power of the writing is such that, while the solving of Lonnie Grinnup's
death is enthralling, the characterizations, the atmosphere, and the style
far surpass what is ordinarily thought of as a "whodunit."

William Faulkner, a towering figure in American letters, was born
in New Albany, Mississippi, in 1897, and died in Oxford, Mississippi, in
1962. He published many distinguished novels and short story collections.
When he received the Nobel Award he spoke the memorable words, "I
decline to accept the end of man . . . I believe that man will not merely
endure: he will prevail. He is immortal, not because he alone among
creatures has an inexhaustible voice but because he has a soul, a spirit
capable of compassion and sacrifice and endurance. The poet's, the
writer's, duty is to write about these things."

Hand upon the Waters

I

THE two men followed the path where it ran between the river and the
dense wall of cypress and cane and gum and brier. One of them carried a
gunnysack which had been washed and looked as if it had been ironed
too. The other was a youth, less than twenty, by his face. The river was
low, at mid-July level.

"He ought to been catching fish in this water," the youth said.

"If he happened to feel like fishing," the one with the sack said. "Him
and Joe run that line when Lonnie feels like it, not when the fish are
biting."

"They'll be on the line, anyway," the youth said. "I don't reckon Lonnie cares who takes them off for him."

Presently the ground rose to a cleared point almost like a headland. Upon it sat a conical hut with a pointed roof, built partly of mildewed canvas and odd-shaped boards and partly of oil tins hammered out flat. A rusted stovepipe projected crazily above it, there was a meager woodpile and an axe, and a bunch of cane poles leaned against it. Then they saw, on the earth before the open door, a dozen or so short lengths of cord just cut from a spool near-by, and a rusted can half full of heavy fishhooks, some of which had already been bent onto the cords. But there was nobody there.

"The boat's gone," the man with the sack said. "So he ain't gone to the store." Then he discovered that the youth had gone on, and he drew in his breath and was just about to shout when suddenly a man rushed out of the undergrowth and stopped, facing him and making an urgent whimpering sound — a man not large, but with tremendous arms and shoulders; an adult, yet with something childlike about him, about the way he moved, barefoot, in battered overalls and with the urgent eyes of the deaf and dumb.

"Hi, Joe," the man with the sack said, raising his voice as people will with those who they know cannot understand them. "Where's Lonnie?" He held up the sack. "Got some fish?"

But the other only stared at him, making that rapid whimpering. Then he turned and scuttled on up the path where the youth had disappeared, who, at that moment, shouted: "Just look at this line!"

The older one followed. The youth was leaning eagerly out over the water beside a tree from which a light cotton rope slanted tautly downward into the water. The deaf-and-dumb man stood just behind him, still whimpering and lifting his feet rapidly in turn, though before the older man reached him he turned and scuttled back past him, toward the hut. At this stage of the river the line should have been clear of the water, stretching from bank to bank, between the two trees, with only the hooks on the dependent cords submerged. But now it slanted into the water from either end, with a heavy downstream sag, and even the older man could feel movement on it.

"It's big as a man!" the youth cried.

"Yonder's his boat," the older man said. The youth saw it, too — across the stream and below them, floated into a willow clump inside a point. "Cross and get it, and we'll see how big this fish is."

The youth stepped out of his shoes and overalls and removed his shirt and waded out and began to swim, holding straight across to let the current carry him down to the skiff, and got the skiff and paddled back, standing erect in it and staring eagerly upstream toward the heavy sag of the line, near the center of which the water, from time to time, roiled heavily with submerged movement. He brought the skiff in below the older man, who, at that moment, discovered the deaf-and-dumb man just behind him again, still making the rapid and urgent sound and trying to enter the skiff.

"Get back!" the older man said, pushing the other back with his arm. "Get back, Joe!"

"Hurry up!" the youth said, staring eagerly toward the submerged line, where, as he watched, something rolled sluggishly to the surface, then sank again. "There's something on there, or there ain't a hog in Georgia. It's big as a man too!"

The older one stepped into the skiff. He still held the rope, and he drew the skiff, hand over hand, along the line itself.

Suddenly, from the bank of the river behind them, the deaf-and-dumb man began to make an actual sound. It was quite loud.

II

"Inquest?" Stevens said.

"Lonnie Grinnup." The coroner was an old country doctor. "Two fellows found him drowned on his own trotline this morning."

"No!" Stevens said. "Poor damned feeb. I'll come out." As county attorney he had no business there, even if it had not been an accident. He knew it. He was going to look at the dead man's face for a sentimental reason. What was now Yoknapatawpha County had been founded, not by one pioneer, but by three simultaneous ones. They came together on horseback, through the Cumberland Gap from the Carolinas, when Jefferson was still a Chickasaw Agency post, and bought land in the Indian patent and established families and flourished and vanished, so that now, a hundred years afterward, there was in all the county they helped to found but one representative of the three names.

This was Stevens, because the last of the Holston family had died before the end of the last century, and the Louis Grenier, whose dead face Stevens was driving eight miles in the heat of a July afternoon to look at, had never even known he was Louis Grenier. He could not even spell the

Lonnie Grinnup he called himself — an orphan, too, like Stevens, a man
a little under medium size and somewhere in his middle thirties, whom
the whole county knew — the face which was almost delicate when you
looked at it again, equable, constant, always cheerful, with an invariable
fuzz of soft golden beard which had never known a razor, and light-
colored peaceful eyes — "touched," they said, but whatever it was, had
touched him lightly, taking not very much away that need be missed —
living, year in and year out, in the hovel he had built himself of an old
tent and a few mismatched boards and flattened oil tins, with the deaf-
and-dumb orphan he had taken into his hut ten years ago and clothed
and fed and raised, and who had not even grown mentally as far as he
himself had.

Actually his hut and trotline and fish trap were in almost the exact
center of the thousand and more acres his ancestors had once owned. But
he never knew it.

Stevens believed he would not have cared, would have declined to
accept the idea that any one man could or should own that much of the
earth which belongs to all, to every man for his use and pleasure — in his
own case, that thirty or forty square feet where his hut sat and the span
of river across which his trotline stretched, where anyone was welcome at
any time, whether he was there or not, to use his gear and eat his food as
long as there was food.

And at times he would wedge his door shut against prowling animals
and with his deaf-and-dumb companion he would appear without warning or invitation at houses or cabins ten and fifteen miles away, where he
would remain for weeks, pleasant, equable, demanding nothing and without servility, sleeping wherever it was convenient for his hosts to have
him sleep — in the hay of lofts, or in beds in family or company rooms,
while the deaf-and-dumb youth lay on the porch or the ground just
outside, where he could hear him who was brother and father both,
breathing. It was one sound out of all the voiceless earth. He was infalli-
bly aware of it.

It was early afternoon. The distances were blue with heat. Then, across
the long flat where the highway began to parallel the river bottom,
Stevens saw the store. By ordinary it would have been deserted, but now
he could already see clotted about it the topless and battered cars, the
saddled horses and mules and the wagons, the riders and drivers of which
he knew by name. Better still, they knew him, voting for him year after
year and calling him by his given name even though they did not quite

understand him, just as they did not understand the Harvard Phi Beta Kappa key on his watch chain. He drew in beside the coroner's car.

Apparently it was not to be in the store, but in the grist mill beside it, before the open door of which the clean Saturday overalls and shirts and the bared heads and the sunburned necks striped with the white razor lines of Saturday neck shaves were densest and quietest. They made way for him to enter. There was a table and three chairs where the coroner and two witnesses sat.

Stevens noticed a man of about forty holding a clean gunnysack, folded and refolded until it resembled a book, and a youth whose face wore an expression of weary yet indomitable amazement. The body lay under a quilt on the low platform to which the silent mill was bolted. He crossed to it and raised the corner of the quilt and looked at the face and lowered the quilt and turned, already on his way back to town, and then he did not go back to town. He moved over among the men who stood along the wall, their hats in their hands, and listened to the two witnesses — it was the youth telling it in his amazed, spent, incredulous voice — finish describing the finding of the body. He watched the coroner sign the certificate and return the pen to his pocket, and he knew he was not going back to town.

"I reckon that's all," the coroner said. He glanced toward the door. "All right, Ike," he said. "You can take him now."

Stevens moved aside with the others and watched the four men cross toward the quilt. "You going to take him, Ike?" he said.

The eldest of the four glanced back at him for a moment. "Yes. He had his burying money with Mitchell at the store."

"You, and Pose, and Matthew, and Jim Blake," Stevens said.

This time the other glanced back at him almost with surprise, almost impatiently.

"We can make up the difference," he said.

"I'll help," Stevens said.

"I thank you," the other said. "We got enough."

Then the coroner was among them, speaking testily: "All right, boys. Give them room."

With the others, Stevens moved out into the air, the afternoon again. There was a wagon backed up to the door now which had not been there before. Its tail gate was open, the bed was filled with straw, and with the others Stevens stood bareheaded and watched the four men emerge from the shed, carrying the quilt-wrapped bundle, and approach the wagon.

Three or four others moved forward to help, and Stevens moved, too, and touched the youth's shoulder, seeing again that expression of spent and incredulous wild amazement.

"You went and got the boat before you knew anything was wrong," he said.

"That's right," the youth said. He spoke quietly enough at first. "I swum over and got the boat and rowed back. I knowed something was on the line. I could see it swagged — "

"You mean you swam the boat back," Stevens said.

" — down into the — Sir?"

"You swam the boat back. You swam over and got it and swam it back."

"No, sir! I rowed the boat back. I rowed it straight back across! I never suspected nothing! I could see them fish — "

"What with?" Stevens said. The youth glared at him. "What did you row it back with?"

"With the oar! I picked up the oar and rowed it right back, and all the time I could see them flopping around in the water. They didn't want to let go! They held on to him even after we hauled him up, still eating him! Fish were! I knowed turtles would, but these were fish! Eating him! Of course it was fish we thought was there. It was! I won't never eat another one! Never!"

It had not seemed long, yet the afternoon had gone somewhere, taking some of the heat with it. Again in his car, his hand on the switch, Stevens sat looking at the wagon, now about to depart. And it's not right, he thought. It don't add. Something more that I missed, didn't see. Or something that hasn't happened yet.

The wagon was now moving, crossing the dusty banquette toward the highroad, with two men on the seat and the other two on saddled mules beside it. Stevens's hand turned the switch; the car was already in gear. It passed the wagon, already going fast.

A mile down the road he turned into a dirt lane, back toward the hills. It began to rise, the sun intermittent now, for in places among the ridges sunset had already come. Presently the road forked. In the V of the fork stood a church, white-painted and steepleless, beside an unfenced straggle of cheap marble headstones and other graves outlined only by rows of inverted glass jars and crockery and broken brick.

He did not hesitate. He drove up beside the church and turned and stopped the car facing the fork and the road over which he had just come where it curved away and vanished. Because of the curve, he could hear the wagon for some time before he saw it, then he heard the truck. It was coming down out of the hills behind him, fast, sweeping into sight, already slowing — a cab, a shallow bed with a tarpaulin spread over it.

It drew out of the road at the fork and stopped; then he could hear the wagon again, and then he saw it and the two riders come around the curve in the dusk, and there was a man standing in the road beside the truck now, and Stevens recognized him: Tyler Ballenbaugh — a farmer, married and with a family and a reputation for self-sufficiency and violence, who had been born in the county and went out West and returned, bringing with him, like an effluvium, rumors of sums he had won gambling, who had married and bought land and no longer gambled at cards, but on certain years would mortgage his own crop and buy or sell cotton futures with the money — standing in the road beside the wagon, tall in the dusk, talking to the men in the wagon without raising his voice or making any gesture. Then there was another man beside him, in a white shirt, whom Stevens did not recognize or look at again.

His hand dropped to the switch; again the car was in motion with the sound of the engine. He turned the headlights on and dropped rapidly down out of the churchyard and into the road and up behind the wagon as the man in the white shirt leaped onto the running board, shouting at him, and Stevens recognized him too: a younger brother of Ballenbaugh's, who had gone to Memphis years ago, where it was understood he had been a hired armed guard during a textile strike, but who, for the last two or three years, had been at his brother's, hiding, it was said, not from the police, but from some of his Memphis friends or later business associates. From time to time his name made one in reported brawls and fights at country dances and picnics. He was subdued and thrown into jail once by two officers in Jefferson, where, on Saturdays, drunk, he would brag about his past exploits or curse his present luck and the older brother who made him work about the farm.

"Who in hell you spying on?" he shouted.

"Boyd," the other Ballenbaugh said. He did not even raise his voice. "Get back in the truck." He had not moved — a big somber-faced man who stared at Stevens out of pale, cold, absolutely expressionless eyes. "Howdy, Gavin," he said.

"Howdy, Tyler," Stevens said. "You going to take Lonnie?"

"Does anybody here object?"

"I don't," Stevens said, getting out of the car. "I'll help you swap him."

Then he got back into the car. The wagon moved on. The truck backed and turned, already gaining speed; the two faces fled past — the one which Stevens saw now was not truculent, but frightened; the other, in which there was nothing at all save the still, cold, pale eyes. The cracked tail lamp vanished over the hill. That was an Okatoba County license number, he thought.

Lonnie Grinnup was buried the next afternoon, from Tyler Ballenbaugh's house.

Stevens was not there. "Joe wasn't there, either, I suppose," he said. "Lonnie's dummy."

"No. He wasn't there, either. The folks that went in to Lonnie's camp on Sunday morning to look at that trotline said that he was still there, hunting for Lonnie. But he wasn't at the burying. When he finds Lonnie this time, he can lie down by him, but he won't hear him breathing."

"No," Stevens said.

III

He was in Mottstown, the seat of Okatoba County, on that afternoon. And although it was Sunday, and although he would not know until he found it just what he was looking for, he found it before dark — the agent for the company which, eleven years ago, had issued to Lonnie Grinnup a five-thousand-dollar policy, with double indemnity for accidental death, on his life, with Tyler Ballenbaugh as beneficiary.

It was quite correct. The examining doctor had never seen Lonnie Grinnup before, but he had known Tyler Ballenbaugh for years, and Lonnie had made his mark on the application and Ballenbaugh had paid the first premium and kept them up ever since.

There had been no particular secrecy about it other than transacting the business in another town, and Stevens realized that even that was not unduly strange.

Okatoba County was just across the river, three miles from where Ballenbaugh lived, and Stevens knew of more men than Ballenbaugh who owned land in one county and bought their cars and trucks and banked their money in another, obeying the country-bred man's inherent, possibly atavistic, faint distrust, perhaps, not of men in white collars, but of paving and electricity.

"Then I'm not to notify the company yet?" the agent asked.

"No. I want you to accept the claim when he comes in to file it, explain to him it will take a week or so to settle it, wait three days and send him word to come in to your office to see you at nine o'clock or ten o'clock the next morning; don't tell him why, what for. Then telephone me at Jefferson when you know he has got the message."

Early the next morning, about daybreak, the heat wave broke. He lay in bed watching and listening to the crash and glare of lightning and the rain's loud fury, thinking of the drumming of it and the fierce channeling of clay-colored water across Lonnie Grinnup's raw and kinless grave in the barren hill beside the steepleless church, and of the sound it would make, above the turmoil of the rising river, on the tin-and-canvas hut where the deaf-and-dumb youth probably still waited for him to come home, knowing that something had happened, but not how, not why. Not how, Stevens thought. They fooled him someway. They didn't even bother to tie him up. They just fooled him.

On Wednesday night he received a telephone message from the Motts town agent that Tyler Ballenbaugh had filed his claim.

"All right," Stevens said. "Send him the message Monday, to come in Tuesday. And let me know when you know he has got it." He put the phone down. I am playing stud poker with a man who has proved himself a gambler, which I have not, he thought. But at least I have forced him to draw a card. And he knows who is in the pot with him.

So when the second message came, on the following Monday afternoon, he knew only what he himself was going to do. He had thought once of asking the sheriff for a deputy, or of taking some friend with him. But even a friend would not believe that what I have is a hole card, he told himself, even though I do: that one man, even an amateur at murder, might be satisfied that he had cleaned up after himself. But when there are two of them, neither one is going to be satisfied that the other has left no ravelings.

So he went alone. He owned a pistol. He looked at it and put it back into its drawer. At least nobody is going to shoot me with that, he told himself. He left town just after dusk.

This time he passed the store, dark at the roadside. When he reached the lane into which he had turned nine days ago, this time he turned to the right and drove on for a quarter of a mile and turned into a littered yard, his headlights full upon a dark cabin. He did not turn them off. He walked full in the yellow beam, toward the cabin, shouting: "Nate! Nate!"

After a moment a Negro voice answered, though no light showed.

"I'm going in to Mr. Lonnie Grinnup's camp. If I'm not back by daylight, you better go up to the store and tell them."

There was no answer. Then a woman's voice said: "You come on away from that door!" The man's voice murmured something.

"I can't help it!" the woman cried. "You come away and let them white folks alone!"

So there are others besides me, Stevens thought, thinking how quite often, almost always, there is in Negroes an instinct, not for evil, but to recognize evil at once when it exists. He went back to the car and snapped off the lights and took his flashlight from the seat.

He found the truck. In the close-held beam of the light he read again the license number which he had watched nine days ago flee over the hill. He snapped off the light and put it into his pocket.

Twenty minutes later he realized he need not have worried about the light. He was in the path, between the black wall of jungle and the river, he saw the faint glow inside the canvas wall of the hut and he could already hear the two voices — the one cold, level, and steady, the other harsh and high. He stumbled over the woodpile and then over something else and found the door and flung it back and entered the devastation of the dead man's house — the shuck mattresses dragged out of the wooden bunks, the overturned stove and scattered cooking vessels — where Tyler Ballenbaugh stood facing him with a pistol and the younger one stood half-crouched above an overturned box.

"Stand back, Gavin," Ballenbaugh said.

"Stand back yourself, Tyler," Stevens said. "You're too late."

The younger one stood up. Stevens saw recognition come into his face. "Well, by — " he said.

"Is it all up, Gavin?" Ballenbaugh said. "Don't lie to me."

"I reckon it is," Stevens said. "Put your pistol down."

"Who else is with you?"

"Enough," Stevens said. "Put your pistol down, Tyler."

"Hell," the younger one said. He began to move; Stevens saw his eyes go swiftly from him to the door behind him. "He's lying. There ain't anybody with him. He's just spying around like he was the other day, putting his nose into business he's going to wish he had kept it out of. Because this time it's going to get bit off."

He was moving toward Stevens, stooping a little, his arms held slightly away from his sides.

"Boyd!" Tyler said. The other continued to approach Stevens, not

smiling, but with a queer light, a glitter, in his face. "Boyd!" Tyler said.
Then he moved, too, with astonishing speed, and overtook the younger
and with one sweep of his arm hurled him back into the bunk. They
faced each other — the one cold, still, expressionless, the pistol held before
him aimed at nothing, the other half-crouched, snarling.

"What the hell you going to do? Let him take us back to town like
two damn sheep?"

"That's for me to decide," Tyler said. He looked at Stevens. "I never
intended this, Gavin. I insured his life, kept the premiums paid — yes.
But it was good business: if he had outlived me, I wouldn't have had any
use for the money, and if I had outlived him, I would have collected on
my judgment. There was no secret about it. It was done in open daylight.
Anybody could have found out about it. Maybe he told about it. I never
told him not to. And who's to say against it anyway? I always fed him
when he came to my house, he always stayed as long as he wanted to,
come when he wanted to. But I never intended this."

Suddenly the younger one began to laugh, half-crouched against the
bunk where the other had flung him. "So that's the tune," he said.
"That's the way it's going." Then it was not laughter any more, though
the transition was so slight or perhaps so swift as to be imperceptible.
He was standing now, leaning forward a little, facing his brother. "I
never insured him for five thousand dollars! I wasn't going to get — "

"Hush," Tyler said.

" — five thousand dollars when they found him dead on that —"

Tyler walked steadily to the other and slapped him in two motions,
palm and back, of the same hand, the pistol still held before him in the
other.

"I said, hush, Boyd," he said. He looked at Stevens again. "I never
intended this. I don't want that money now, even if they were going to
pay it, because this is not the way I aimed for it to be. Not the way I bet.
What are you going to do?"

"Do you need to ask that? I want an indictment for murder."

"And then prove it!" the younger one snarled. "Try and prove it! I
never insured his life for — "

"Hush," Tyler said. He spoke almost gently, looking at Stevens with
the pale eyes in which there was absolutely nothing. "You can't do that.
It's a good name. Has been. Maybe nobody's done much for it yet, but
nobody's hurt it bad yet, up to now. I have owed no man, I have taken
nothing that was not mine. You mustn't do that, Gavin."

"I mustn't do anything else, Tyler."

The other looked at him. Stevens heard him draw a long breath and expel it. But his face did not change at all. "You want your eye for an eye and tooth for a tooth."

"Justice wants it. Maybe Lonnie Grinnup wants it. Wouldn't you?"

For a moment longer the other looked at him. Then Ballenbaugh turned and made a quiet gesture at his brother and another toward Stevens, quiet and peremptory.

Then they were out of the hut, standing in the light from the door; a breeze came up from somewhere and rustled in the leaves overhead and died away, ceased.

At first Stevens did not know what Ballenbaugh was about. He watched in mounting surprise as Ballenbaugh turned to face his brother, his hand extended, speaking in a voice which was actually harsh now: "This is the end of the row. I was afraid from that night when you came home and told me. I should have raised you better, but I didn't. Here. Stand up and finish it."

"Look out, Tyler!" Stevens said. "Don't do that!"

"Keep out of this, Gavin. If it's meat for meat you want, you will get it." He still faced his brother, he did not even glance at Stevens. "Here," he said. "Take it and stand up."

Then it was too late. Stevens saw the younger one spring back. He saw Tyler take a step forward and he seemed to hear in the other's voice the surprise, the disbelief, then the realization of the mistake. "Drop the pistol, Boyd," he said. "Drop it."

"So you want it back, do you?" the younger said. "I come to you that night and told you you were worth five thousand dollars as soon as somebody happened to look on that trotline, and asked you to give me ten dollars, and you turned me down. Ten dollars, and you wouldn't. Sure you can have it. Take it." It flashed, low against his side; the orange fire lanced downward again as the other fell. ·

Now it's my turn, Stevens thought. They faced each other; he heard again that brief wind come from somewhere and shake the leaves overhead and fall still.

"Run while you can, Boyd," he said. "You've done enough. Run, now."

"Sure I'll run. You do all your worrying about me now, because in a minute you won't have any worries. I'll run all right, after I've said a word to smart guys that come sticking their noses where they'll wish to hell they hadn't —"

Now he's going to shoot, Stevens thought, and he sprang. For an instant he had the illusion of watching himself springing, reflected somehow by the faint light from the river, that luminousness which water gives back to the dark, in the air above Boyd Ballenbaugh's head. Then he knew it was not himself he saw, it had not been wind he heard, as the creature, the shape which had no tongue and needed none, which had been waiting nine days now for Lonnie Grinnup to come home, dropped toward the murderer's back with its hands already extended and its body curved and rigid with silent and deadly purpose.

He was in the tree, Stevens thought. The pistol glared. He saw the flash, but he heard no sound.

IV

He was sitting on the veranda with his neat surgeon's bandage after supper when the sheriff of the county came up the walk — a big man, too, pleasant, affable, with eyes even paler and colder and more expressionless than Tyler Ballenbaugh's.

"It won't take but a minute," he said, "or I wouldn't have bothered you."

"How bothered me?" Stevens said.

The sheriff lowered one thigh to the veranda rail. "Head feel all right?"

"Feels all right," Stevens said.

"That's good. I reckon you heard where we found Boyd."

Stevens looked back at him just as blankly. "I may have," he said pleasantly. "Haven't remembered much today but a headache."

"You told us where to look. You were conscious when I got there. You were trying to give Tyler water. You told us to look on that trotline."

"Did I? Well, well, what won't a man say, drunk or out of his head? Sometimes he's right too."

"You were. We looked on the line, and there was Boyd hung on one of the hooks, dead, just like Lonnie Grinnup was. And Tyler Ballenbaugh with a broken leg and another bullet in his shoulder, and you with a crease in your skull you could hide a cigar in. How did he get on that trotline, Gavin?"

"I don't know," Stevens said.

"All right. I'm not sheriff now. How did Boyd get on that trotline?"

"I don't know."

The sheriff looked at him; they looked at each other. "Is that what you answer any friend that asks?"

"Yes. Because I was shot, you see. I don't know."

The sheriff took a cigar from his pocket and looked at it for a time. "Joe — that deaf-and-dumb boy Lonnie raised — seems to have gone away at last. He was still around there last Sunday, but nobody has seen him since. He could have stayed. Nobody would have bothered him."

"Maybe he missed Lonnie too much to stay," Stevens said.

"Maybe he missed Lonnie." The sheriff rose. He bit the end from the cigar and lit it. "Did that bullet cause you to forget this too? Just what made you suspect something was wrong? What was it the rest of us seem to have missed?"

"It was that paddle," Stevens said.

"Paddle?"

"Didn't you ever run a trotline, a trotline right at your camp? You don't paddle, you pull the boat hand over hand along the line itself from one hook to the next. Lonnie never did use his paddle; he even kept the skiff tied to the same tree his trotline was fastened to, and the paddle stayed in his house. If you had ever been there, you would have seen it. But the paddle was in the skiff when that boy found it."

ROBERT M. COATES

"The Net" tells of a commonplace man in a not uncommon situation, cuckolded by his wife. The very simplicity of the man is used by Coates to draw the reader inescapably into the poor fellow's "net of night."
    Robert M. Coates, *the author of innumerable stories and former art critic for* The New Yorker, *was born in New Haven in 1897.*

The Net

WALTER had just turned the corner of Charles Street into Seventh when he saw her. She was standing a little way up the block talking to a fellow in a black overcoat and a black felt hat, and just the way they were standing — the fellow leaning back against the wall of the building there and she crowded close against him, looking up at him — was enough to let Walter know the kind of talk they were having. Almost without thinking, he stopped and stepped back a pace down Charles, out of sight around the corner.

This was the way things went, then; this was what she had left him for. He had known it, but this was the first time he had ever had sight of it, and it sent a queer feeling through him, as if more air than he could breathe had been forced into him. He was a tall man, with a pale, solemn, heavy-jawed face and a slow, slightly awkward manner of movement. He placed himself against the railing of an areaway and stood there, looking down Seventh Avenue, waiting. He knew she would have to come around the corner when she started home, and whether she was alone or the fellow was still with her, he would have a right to speak to her then. Till then he would wait. He had time.

It was growing late and the evening had been cold; there were few people walking. Down by Christopher Street there was a cluster of bright signs and illuminated buildings, but up where he was the houses were mostly dark, and the only sound was the rough, shuffling whir of the tires on pavement as the cars went flying by. Then the traffic lights changed and the cars stopped, at Charles, at Tenth, at Christopher; at Charles, a black truck crawled out across the avenue and went slowly on down the street past Walter, toward Hudson.

That was all the cross traffic there was, but for a few seconds longer the avenue was still. Then the lights went green and the headlights moved forward, sifting past each other as the cars took up their varying speeds. A moment later, Walter heard the tap of her heels on the sidewalk, coming around the corner, and she passed him.

"Hello, Ann," he said softly.

She hadn't noticed him till then; he could tell that from the way her head snapped around and the look that came over her face. Then she turned her head away. She kept on walking. "Hello, Walter," she said wearily.

He was walking along beside her. "Where you been, Ann?" he asked. "I was at your people's house and they said you'd went to the movies."

"I did."

"Yeah. The movies."

She glanced up at him, and he could see her face pinching up in the way it did when she got angry. But she didn't say anything; she just turned her face forward again, tucked her chin down in the fur collar of her coat, and walked on. He kept pace with her. "I saw you talking to that fellow back there, Ann," he went on in his slow, insistent voice. "I saw you."

"Well," she said. "So you saw me. Can't a girl meet a friend on the street?"

"Yeah. But the movies."

He knew she didn't like to be prodded like that about things, even when she was telling the truth, and he half expected her to burst out with something then and there. He could feel his chest tightening already, in that mixture of fear and excitement and stubbornness that always came over him when they got into an argument. But she just kept on walking. After a few steps she turned to him again. "You was up to the folks'?" she asked, her voice very innocent and offhand. "Who'd you see? Was Ma there?"

"Yes, your mother was there," he said. "As you doubtless know. I know what you're thinking, Ann, but I didn't think it would give you pleasure. She didn't give me no nice reception. But that don't bother me, either; that I expected. I'm not blind, and I know who it was that turned you against me and broke up our marriage. But there's an old saying, Ann, that marriages are made in heaven, and I believe it, and I believe she will get her punishment, too, for what she's done — turning a man's wife against her lawful husband. If not now, then she'll surely get it in the hereafter. But it's not her I'm worried about; I leave her to her own devices. It's you, Ann. Listen," he said. "What you don't get is, I'd take you back tomorrow. Like that. I don't care who you been with, what you done — even that fellow back there, Ann, whoever he is. I don't ask. But a fellow you got to meet on street corners, can't even show to your folks — but even him, Ann; I'd forget everything. Just so long as you'd tell me, come clean about things. But this lying and hiding. Listen, Ann — " He had thought a good deal about this meeting and had planned for it, and this was one of the things he had figured on saying, so he found himself talking faster and faster. But just then a crazy thing happened.

They were passing a series of old-fashioned houses with high-stooped entrances, and the steps running down from them made the sidewalk narrow. And there was a couple, a man and a girl, walking up the street toward them; in his excitement, Walter didn't notice them until he was upon them, and then there wasn't room for them all to pass. The man bumped him, and Walter stumbled, trying to sidestep them, but all the time his eyes were on Ann. She had walked on, never varying her pace, as if she had nothing to do with him at all, and at the sight of her tan-stockinged legs flicking briskly away beneath her black coat a kind of panic took hold of him. "I'm your husband, Ann!" he yelled suddenly. He could see both the man's and the girl's faces turned toward him, but for the moment he didn't care. He shoved past them and ran after Ann, grabbing at her arm. "I'm your husband," he repeated, his voice still loud. "Don't that mean anything to you? For better or for worse." Then he saw that she was laughing, and he let go of her arm.

It was only a little way farther on to her family's apartment house. When they reached it, she ran up the three or four steps to the entrance. Walter followed her, letting the street door swing shut behind him. They were alone in the dim vestibule. She bent her head for a moment, fumbling in her bag for the key, then she glanced up. "Well, Walter," she said. She wasn't laughing now, but she might just as well have been; he could tell from the look on her face that she was only waiting to get on upstairs to start in again. "Well, it's been a enjoyable little walk."

He could feel the air crowding into his lungs again, so hard that it made his whole chest feel hot inside. "Maybe it ain't finished yet," he said.

"Well, it is for me. I'm going up."

"I'm coming up, too."

"No, you won't."

"Why won't I?" Without his meaning it to, he could hear his voice getting louder. "What you got to conceal up there?"

"Oh, Walter! It ain't that and you know it. But you know what'll happen. You and Ma." He hadn't realized that he had moved closer to her, but he must have, for suddenly she stepped back a pace and stared up at him. "Walter," she said. "You been drinking?"

"I have not been drinking," he said, and he let his voice go louder still when he said it. Let her scare a little, he was thinking; at least she wasn't laughing at him any more. She was paying attention to him now. "Well, then," she said, and she began talking faster. "Listen, Walter. This kind of chasing around ain't getting us anywhere, you hiding around corners and laying for me and all that. Why don't we get together some other way, sometime? I could come up to your place sometime, even. You still got the apartment, haven't you? We could talk."

"You come up there," he said, "and maybe you wouldn't never leave it again." He hadn't meant to put it like that; what he'd meant was that if she came up, it would have to be because she wanted to stay there and be with him again, but the way it came out it sounded threatening, even to him, and she must have thought so too, for she stared at him blankly a moment. Then, suddenly, she made a kind of dive out of the corner where he had crowded her. "Then go home, then! Get out of here!" he heard her cry, and she began pushing with both hands against his chest. He grabbed her wrists and she screamed. When she screamed, his hands went directly to her throat.

He had only intended to stop her screaming, but as soon as he touched her a strange kind of strength flowed into his hands, a strength that came from somewhere inside him and that once released could not be recalled, so that he couldn't have let go if he'd tried. For a while she struggled, jerking her body this way and that and pulling at his arms with her hands. It didn't bother him. He had shoved her back against the wall, so hard that her head bumped against it and her hat tipped over sidewise.

He just stiffened his legs and stood there, his hands locked hard in the
flesh of her throat; he was surprised at how strongly he stood there,
meeting and conquering every move she made. "Laugh now," he said
once, not loud, but almost gently.

Her knee worked up somehow between them until it was pressing
against his thigh, but there was no strength in it; the strength was all in
him, and soon the knee slipped harmlessly down again. Then her body
lashed back and forth once or twice, fast and violently, and stopped, and
her eyelids, which had been tight shut, opened so that he could see
through her lashes the blue of her eyes, glittering in the dim light overhead. A kind of shudder ran through her. It was some time after that
before he realized that she wasn't struggling any more.

It was the strain on his arms that told him of the change. Her body
was just so much weight now, almost more than he could hold, and he
let her slide slowly down along the wall until she was sitting on the floor,
her back propped against the corner of the vestibule. Well, I did it, he
thought, I did it; and for a moment he stood looking down at her uncertainly, not knowing what he ought to do next. One leg was crooked
awkwardly sidewise, he noticed, so that the skirt was pulled up above the
stocking top, and he bent down and pulled the hem over the knee. Then
he turned and went out the door.

At the top of the steps he stopped and looked up and down the street.
At first glance it seemed there was no one in sight at all, not a soul; then
he noticed a couple of people standing in front of a house farther down
the block — a man and a girl, he thought, though he couldn't be sure;
about all he could see was their faces, and these were no more than pale
spots in the shadows where they were standing. Farther still, down almost to Hudson, he sighted two others, two men, dark against the light
from a shop window on the corner. And now there was a girl clipping
quickly along on the opposite sidewalk; it was amazing how silently they
all moved, and how easy it was not to notice them in the darkness. He
stood where he was for a while, watching them, trying to determine if
there was any sign of a concerted scheme in their actions. He had a
feeling that they were only moving as they did in order to set a trap for
him; at a signal they might all turn and begin running to surround him.

But none of them paid any attention to him. The couple down the
block just stood there, the two men walked onward, the girl hurried
around the corner and disappeared. Walter went down the steps and

turned up toward Seventh Avenue. Well, I did it, he thought again, and as before, the thought carried no emotion with it except relief. It had to be done, it was coming to her; that was the way his thoughts ran, and what little guilt he had was submerged in a kind of careless irresponsibility, the feeling that a drunken man has when he knows he has done something wrong, admits it, and doesn't care. The emotion was so close to that of drunkenness that even Walter recognized it. I could say I was drunk, he thought, his mind momentarily occupied with stratagems. But as soon as the idea came to him, he rejected it. I've got better reasons than that, he decided; her laughing at me, cheating on me, chasing at every corner. As he neared Fourth Street, another man, a new one, sprang up suddenly before him, a short, heavy-set fellow stepping out of the shadows and striding directly toward him.

The man passed without giving him a second glance, but after the man had gone by, Walter stopped and stepped back against a house wall, watching his progress down the street; suppose he was headed for *her* house, he was thinking, and the fear became so strong that he almost set out in pursuit of the stranger. I could ask him for a match, get him talking, lead him on past the door, he thought. As he hesitated, the man went by; he went three or four doors farther before he turned in.

Walter walked on. He didn't hurry, and when he reached the end of the block he even stopped for a moment, glancing, as if idly, up and down before crossing the street. The night was a net, he realized, with its streets and its people walking this way and that along them; what he had to do was to find his way out without disturbing anything or anyone. The thing that worried him most now was his breathing; he discovered that it had been bothering him for some time. He would find himself breathing fast and hard, so hard that it hurt his chest, and then he would take a deep breath, so long and so deep that when he let it out he could feel the flesh of his body shrinking away from his clothes, leaving the skin damp and prickly and cool. Then the hard, quick breathing would begin again.

Like a man that's been running, he thought. That was one thing he mustn't do; without even thinking about it, he knew he mustn't run. Or talk. For a while he had had the notion of going up to his brother-in-law's place. It was just a notion, or really it was more like a picture that had come into his mind; somehow, he didn't want to go home, and suddenly he had seen himself sitting with Frank and Ethel in their warm apartment, and then he had thought how pleasant it would be, it would rest him; they'd send out for some beer even, maybe. But he saw now that it wouldn't do. He'd get to talking, and there was no way of knowing how they'd take it. At the thought, the picture in his mind changed in a way that made him go cold all over; from seeing their faces smiling at him, friendly and companionable, he had seen them go white and staring, and hard with horror as they looked at him.

It was an awful thing he had done, all right, and the funny part was that he hadn't meant to. "God sakes!" he said. For the moment he was arguing with Frank and Ethel, and he found himself talking out loud. "If I'd meant to do it, wouldn't I have planned the thing different? Me here with no more than a couple of bucks in my pocket." If it had been Friday, even, when his pay came through at the shop; then he'd have had a matter of thirty-five dollars in his hand, enough to start out with, anyway. But maybe Frank would lend him some money; he'd done as much for him on occasion.

"I swear, Frank, it's the first time I ever even laid hands on her. I never meant to harm a hair of her head." He had stopped talking out loud, but he was still arguing to himself when he remembered that Frank was Ann's brother; he had had an idea all along that his mind was running too fast for him, sort of, so that he was overlooking things. And maybe important things. This proved it. If Frank was Ann's brother, that left him out, of course; he was the last man to turn to now. It was late, too. His mind had been racing ahead, full of confidence, but now it was swarming with doubts and uncertainties: how could he expect to burst in on them now, at this hour, asking for money, without them asking questions? And even if he did get some money, where would he go? It would mean quitting his job, leaving everyone he knew, everything. "Me, a man that's near forty," he thought.

It was just that Frank was the only one in the family that had ever had a decent word for him.

And the thing was, he hadn't meant to do it. All the time back there in the vestibule it had seemed like all the dozens of times in the past when he and Ann would have arguments; and she'd slump down in a chair or a sofa, so mad that she couldn't keep from crying but still trying to hide it; and he'd shout something, slam the door, and go out. And then, like as not, she'd get up, slam the door too, and go off to see one of her girl friends or something. But not now. Now she would lie where she was, in the dim hallway, until someone came in from the street or down from the apartments above, and stumbled over her.

It would happen any minute now, if it hadn't happened already, and at the thought a vast sorrow rose up slowly inside him and filled him — sorrow for himself and for Ann, but mostly for himself. "What I've got myself in for," he kept thinking. A whole group of people, men and women all talking and laughing, were coming down the steps of a house ahead of him, and he slowed his pace so as not to get tangled up with them on the sidewalk. But they just stood there, and finally he had to brush past them. As he did so, he shoved one of the men and gave the whole group such a fierce look that they must have noticed it; he was sure he saw their faces change.

"I could tell you something that would stop your giggling," he thought, and this time, when he thought of the terror he could bring to their faces, he felt an odd sort of satisfaction; it would serve them right, he thought. When he had gone a few paces farther on, he looked back. They were all trailing off down the street, and on an impulse he stopped and leaned against an areaway railing, watching them. It would happen any minute now, he thought.

How long he stood there he didn't know, but it couldn't have been long, and the thing that made him conscious of time again was a thin knife sound like a scream or a siren; then a car's headlights turned into the street from away down at Hudson. He watched them, and it was some seconds before he realized what was the matter with them: the car was heading up the wrong way, against traffic.

Only a police car would do that, he thought, and as if in confirmation he saw it swing in toward the curb and stop, just about where the entrance to Ann's house would be. Well, then, the police were coming, he thought; that was right, it was proper, and if the old woman — he realized that one of the things he had been worrying about was Ann's mother; he'd known she'd be mixed up in the scene down there some way. But if the police were there and she started her ranting and scream-ing — well, they'd know how to stop her. Slowly, he pushed himself away from the railing.

He'd go on up to Frank's, he thought, but it was only when he started walking on up the street, toward Seventh, that he realized how tired he was. So maybe, after all, he'd go home. "It's too much," he thought. "It's too much to expect of a man." He was still arguing about this question of packing up and leaving town for good. But he was almost too tired, and too lonely, to bother about it. Unexpectedly, as he walked, a picture came into his mind of the couple he had bumped into when Ann and he were walking home. Down this very block, it had been, and he could see them again, their faces turning in surprise as he shoved past them shouting; somehow, the recollection only added to his feeling of lonely helplessness.

If he could only talk to them, he thought, he could explain everything; they were the only people in the world, perhaps, who would understand. But they had gone, and the thought vanished too, almost as soon as it had come to him. He walked on up to Seventh and then turned north, toward the subway. Maybe he'd go up to Frank and Ethel's after all; if there had been a reason against going there, he had forgotten it, and anyway it wasn't worth bothering about now. Most of all, now, he felt tired.

KAY BOYLE

At the outset, the reader might think the American actress is to be the main character in "Nothing Ever Breaks Except the Heart." If so, he is going to be surprised. It is the airplane pilot, already suffering battle fatigue, who recalls the nearly worldwide nervous breakdown at the beginning of World War II.

Kay Boyle was born in St. Paul, Minnesota, in 1903. She has spent much of her life abroad. She is the author of many distinguished novels and volumes of short stories.

Nothing Ever Breaks
Except the Heart

PERHAPS you have been there, and you know the Avenida and the way the trees grow the length of it — palm trees and the foreign varieties of hawthorn and maple. Perhaps you've drunk iced coffee under a colored umbrella there, with your back turned to the traffic's noise and the sight of the horses and your face turned to the strips of green, fresh-watered grass. The trees make the long avenues of shade that flow like a dark stream through the city, and on the edges of them stagger the horses, knee-deep in burning, if imaginary, sands. Perhaps you've walked up the avenue through the leafy jungle-dark toward where the American flag hangs, heavy with summer, on its white pole in this foreign city's air. Either children or tropical mirages of them must have run barefoot and scrofulous after you, asking for something as cool as money, and if you were there this summer, you must have seen Miss Del Monte eating ice cream at one of the tin tables under the trees.

Miss Del Monte used to buy all the American picture magazines there were, and she would sit there looking at them, so as not to think of the horses, with the carts they drew breaking their back and crippling their limbs beneath them, nor of the lather frothing under the harness that bound them irrevocably to man. Something was always doing it to her, taking the heart out of her breast and tearing it apart, and now she had come to the end. The first day she arrived she told this to Mr. Mc-Closkey. She said, "You can have the horses and the children with pellagra. I'll take the mint juleps," and Mr. McCloskey stopped looking at the German and the Polish and the Czech and the Russian refugees for a moment and decided, without much interest in it, that she was probably the prettiest woman he had ever seen.

Perhaps you even know Mr. McCloskey — the set of his shoulders in his American businessman's suit, and the rather jaded look in his eyes, and the thick hair just beginning to go gray. He had a roll-top desk to himself, but he never sat down at it, because for eight hours a day he stood behind the elegant glass-topped counter in the airways office and told the roomful of foreigners, and Americans even, that they wouldn't be able to board a plane and go where they wanted to go for at least another month or two. Miss Del Monte went into the office in June, the first day she got to the city, and spun the propeller of the miniature plane with one finger as she waited there. She had left her stockings at the hotel because of the heat, and her arms and legs and her head were bare and cool enough looking; her nails were long and immaculately done, and her mouth was far too brilliant. Once you'd seen her, you watched for her everywhere you went: at the Tivoli Bar before dinner, or at the Casino, or dancing at the Palace or the Atlantico. But she was never anywhere like that. She was always in the airways office, talking to Mr. McCloskey or waiting to talk to Mr. McCloskey, smoking one cigarette after another and putting fresh lip rouge on from time to time.

"I'd like to get over by Saturday," Miss Del Monte had said to him the first day, and when she said it all the refugees sitting on the benches along the wall stopped breathing for a moment and looked at something that wasn't bitterness and hopelessness at last.

"Look," said Mr. McCloskey, making a gesture. "Everyone in this country's trying to get over." His eyes were haggard and his face was a little gaunt from the heat and the amount of talking he had to do. There were three telephone calls waiting for him on three different desks and fifteen people at the counter where Miss Del Monte stood. "It's either the language that's driving them out, or else it's because they don't kill their bulls in the *corsos* here," he said.

"They broke my heart every Sunday afternoon in Spain," said Miss Del Monte. "They dragged it out with the horses, and now I'm not having any more." She took another cigarette and she said, "On account my show's opening up, I'd like to get over by Saturday."

"Saturday!" a little man in a pongee suit behind her cried out, and for a moment Miss Del Monte thought he had been stabbed. "I've been three monce waiting here — three monce!" he said, and he held up that number of fingers. He didn't speak English very well, but he had diamonds on his hand.

That was the first day, and the second day, in the morning, they were standing three-deep around the counter, so Miss Del Monte gave it up after an hour and came back in the afternoon. When she got opposite Mr. McCloskey at last, she lit a cigarette and looked at him carefully and evenly. He must have been just over thirty, in spite of the gray in his hair, and his shoulders would probably have looked too broad for any chair he sat in.

"I'm not prepared for summer," she said. "Monday's the latest I can wait. I haven't a single sharkskin to put on."

"Do you know Mr. Sumner Welles?" said Mr. McCloskey, and for the first time Miss Del Monte saw the madness in his eyes. "Have you influential friends in Washington?" he asked, and Miss Del Monte shook her head. "Then perhaps I can help you out," he said, and he walked rather handsomely to his desk, passing Mr. Concachina at the counter on his way.

Mr. Concachina was native, and his head was bald, and his mind was going. "I'm just now speaking four different languages at the same time to five different parties, Mr. McCloskey," he said, and there was sweat on his forehead. "I tell you, I can't do it much longer. I'm at the breaking point."

"You've been saying that for a year and a half," said Mr. McCloskey. He was looking among the other papers for the typewritten list of names. "But nothing ever breaks, nothing," he said, and he repeated it vaguely. "Nothing ever breaks," and he held the list in one hand while he said "Hello there" into one of the three telephones. When he came back to the counter, he looked at Miss Del Monte. "We have a very nice opening for the seventeenth of November," he said.

This went on for a week or more, and then, one Monday morning, Miss Del Monte felt she was getting somewhere at last. She was on her fourth cigarette, and she had combed back her hair and put fresh lipstick on her mouth, and she looked more beautiful than ever.

"Just a minute," said Mr. McCloskey, studying the list. "How old are you? How much do you weigh?"

"A hundred and fifteen," said Miss Del Monte quickly. "I'm twenty-four, but I feel a lot older."

Mr. McCloskey pondered for a moment, and then he said, "Did you ever think of trying a boat, Miss Del Monte?"

"A boat? Do you mean a boat?" she said.

"Yes," said Mr. McCloskey. He looked at her and moved his hand in a swaying motion. "You'd be surprised. You might like a boat."

Mr. Concachina, a little way down the counter, had a telephone receiver in one hand and a fountain pen in the other, and he was writing something down. But still he had time enough to look up at Miss Del Monte. "You know about Pola Negri?" he said, and then he spoke the other language into the mouthpiece. "Well, Pola Negri got fed up," he said, after a moment. "She went out of here in a huff this morning. She's going to take a boat."

"I'd just as soon go out of here in a huff as in what I have on," said Miss Del Monte evenly. "I'm sure it would be cooler."

"It ought to be awfully cool on shipboard," Mr. McCloskey said.

It was never Mr. McCloskey's intention to start going out in the evening with Miss Del Monte, but by the second week he had got so accustomed to seeing her around that it seemed the natural thing to find her on the Avenida one evening after dinner and walk back and forth with her beneath the trees. She carried a guidebook in one hand, with a cablegram marking a page in it, and she said she'd just had a double whiskey-and-soda.

"It breaks my heart to talk shop," she said, "but my show's opening on the first of September."

"It can't if you're not there," said Mr. McColskey. Behind them, in the fountains, illuminated water lilies with iron stems and china petals floated monstrously through the night, and the bookstalls, each one shaped like a book, and the leather tooled across the back, were open.

"If I stay much longer, I'll be right in time for the summer season," said Miss Del Monte. "It says so in the guidebook on page twenty-three. It says there are always balls and processions, varinos exhibitions, gymkhanas, and firelarks. However they want to spell it, I'd give up the varinos exhibitions any day if I could see a gymkhana or a firelark."

"You probably will without a bit of trouble if you have another double whiskey," said Mr. McCloskey, but Miss Del Monte said she'd rather hear a *fado* sung.

Mr. McCloskey had never been to a *fado* café before, but Miss Del Monte seemed quite familiar with the back street where one was. The lights were still on when they walked in and took a table, and all the men in their pongee suits and their white silk shoes turned to watch Miss Del Monte go past. The only other women there were the female *fado* singers, with their Spanish-looking shawls on their shoulders, sitting there rather grimly at separate tables, some with their fathers keeping an eye on them and some with their entrepreneurs, either sitting silent or writing out *fados* while they waited for their turn to come. In a minute the lights went out, and two guitar players mounted a little platform and sat down on the chairs that were placed on opposite sides of it and tuned their instruments up. No one looked very pleased about it, not even when the fado singer himself ran quickly up the steps in his patent-leather shoes and stood in the spotlight between the two guitarists on the platform's boards. He was a short, evil-looking man in a black suit, and his hair was wavy and very well greased, and he kept his hands in his trousers pockets all the time.

"If he takes his hands out of his pockets, he isn't a *fado* singer," said Miss Del Monte, and although the man hadn't yet started to sing, someone behind her hissed.

Presently the singer announced the title of the *fado* and added that this was the first time it had been sung in public, for it was about a stabbing that had occurred near the fish market that day. But when he opened his mouth he might just as well have been telling them all what he thought of them, one minute facing half of the room with his neck going red, and then one minute berating the other half with the veins in his forehead beginning to swell. He said the same words over and over to them, so that there could be no mistake, breaking the rhythm savagely and throwing it in their faces while the throbbing of the guitars wove steadily and systematically upward and, finding no foothold, wove steadily and carefully down again.

When he was done, the lights sprang up all over, and the applause scattered about him, and Miss Del Monte lit another cigarette.

"Did you find this in the guidebook?" Mr. McCloskey asked. He removed the crockery jug from its pail of ice and poured the green wine out.

"Don't be absurd," said Miss Del Monte. "This is neither a bewildering panorama nor a rendezvous of the élite, nor is it an imposing terrace overlooking the sea."

"It might be a gymkhana," said Mr. McCloskey, and he took another drink of wine.

The second night they went out together, again to one of the back-street cafés, Miss Del Monte explained to him further about the *fado.* She said the better ones were either patriotic or heroic, and these had been handed down from generation to generation. The ones they sat writing out quickly at the tables were only the personal ones she told him.

"You simply have to sense which kind it is," she said.

This time it was a girl who sang first, standing up on the platform between the two seated guitarists, with the fringe of the black Spanish shawl hanging just below her knees. Her throat was bare and broad, and her face was primitive under the *maquillage,* and it was only the feet that had nothing to do with the rest. She wore pink stockings, and her feet were as small as mice and twisted like mice in the traps of the open-toed, cork-soled shoes she had on. She began her statement of fact with her teeth showing white in her mouth, and her voice was husky. She said it beautifully, repeating it first to one side of the room and then to the other, with her hands clasped on her stomach, holding the shawl.

"This is a personal one," said Miss Del Monte in a whisper to Mr. Mc-Closkey.

"I'd be interested to know," said Mr. McCloskey rather wearily, "if she makes any mention of Mr. Sumner Welles."

"It's something she read in the paper," said Miss Del Monte. "It's about a girl whose fiancé kills her sister because she takes the bracelets he'd given the other one and wears them to go out dancing with another man. He couldn't stand it."

Mr. McCloskey filled their glasses up again. "Miss Del Monte," he said, "I don't know how your public's getting on without you."

It may have been later in the summer, perhaps it was in July, that Mr. McCloskey took her across on the ferry to have dinner on the other shore. They were probably sitting on the open part of the ferry's deck when Mr. McCloskey said, "She's over there." He didn't look toward the city's delicately starred hills but off into the darkness. "The only thing in life I care about is over there," he said, and as he spoke the strung lights of the battleship and the cutter went running past.

He said it again, after they had left the ferry and left the taxi and were walking down through the grass to the river's edge. The moon had risen now, and everything was as brilliantly lit as if by daylight, and although no explanation had been asked for or given as to why they had come here, and why they went down through the night-drenched grass to where the bright stream of water lay, still it seemed, and singularly without question, the one thing left for them to do.

"She's out there, tethered on the water," Mr. McCloskey said. "The plane," he said, a little impatiently, because Miss Del Monte didn't seem to be able to understand English any more. "She's out there. You can see her just to the left of the jetty." They stood on a footpath at the water's edge, where a half-dozen dories, white-flanked and rocking empty on the tide, were chained up to the shore. "We can row out to her," he said, and Miss Del Monte stepped into the boat that he held steady with his foot and sat down on the cross seat, doing it slowly and without wonder, like one hypnotized.

Mr. McCloskey followed her in and fitted the oars in their grooves and then pushed off from shore. The water was smooth, and the light and the dark moved clearly in broken pieces on it, first light and then dark around them as the oars dipped softly in the night. Every now and then he turned partway in his seat and let the oars feather while he looked ahead at the suave, enormous body of the plane.

"I love her," he said. "I love her," and Miss Del Monte couldn't think of the right thing to say. As they drew nearer he pulled hard and in silence on one oar so as to bring them up against the wing.

"Have you ever piloted one?" Mis Del Monte asked, and Mr. Mc-Closkey didn't say anything for a little while. They were riding close to the plane and he had pulled the oars in, and until the water began drying on them, the splays of them looked as bright as glass.

"That's what's the matter with me," he said after a moment. "I used to be one. I used to fly them across." He did not move from his seat, but he raised one hand and ran it along the hard, sweet, sloping, metallic breast. "I didn't have what it takes," he said, and his voice was bitter to hear. "Or, rather, I gave away what it takes. I had it. I had it." The dory gyrated slowly and without direction near the marvelously still body of the plane. "One or two whiskeys too much every now and then, and jitters," he said. "Single whiskeys when I was tired and double ones to get me out of whatever trouble I happened to be in. Jitters," he said. "So now I'm just good enough to stand up all day behind a counter and tell them what day the company's going to let them fly."

When Miss Del Monte got to the airways office the next morning, there was one Frenchwoman talking faster and better than the others, leaning across to Mr. McCloskey, with her hand in the black fish-net glove closed sharply on his arm. She was telling him, in French, that she knew Mr. Sumner Welles and that she'd been to school with Eve Curie, and Mr. Mc-Closkey stood there looking at her with a rather faded, hopeless look around his eyes.

IRWIN SHAW

*The quest of a man for the woman he loves has been described in
stories since ancient times. But the characters of the man and the woman
in "Search Through the Streets of the City" are so typically modern
American and so freshly described that the quest is as new as if it never
had been written about before.*

From the time of his first play, Bury the Dead, *in 1937, Irwin Shaw
has been one of our most renowned and productive writers. He was
born in New York City and is the author of six volumes of short stories,
six novels, a travel volume and many motion picture scripts.*

Search Through
the Streets of the City

WHEN HE FINALLY saw her he nearly failed to recognize her. He walked
behind her for a half-block, vaguely noticing that the woman in front of
him had long legs and was wearing a loose, college-girlish linen coat and
a plain brown felt hat. Suddenly something about the way she walked
made him remember — the almost affected rigidity of her back and
straightness of throat and head, with all the movement of walking flowing up to the hips and stopping there, like Negro women in the South
and Mexican and Spanish women carrying baskets on their heads.

For a moment he watched her walk along Twelfth Street, on the sunny
side of the street, in front of the little tired gardens behind which lay the
quiet, pleasantly run-down old houses. Then he caught up with her and
touched her arm.

"Low heels," he said. "I never thought I'd live to see the day."

She looked around in surprise, then smiled widely and took his arm.
"Hello, Paul," she said. "I've gone in for health."

"Whenever I think of you," he said, "I think of the highest heels in
New York City."

"The old days," Harriet said. They walked slowly down the sunny street toward Sixth Avenue. "I was a frivolous creature."

"You still walk the same way. As though you ought to have a basket of laundry on your head."

"I practiced walking like that for six months. You'd be surprised how much attention I get walking into a room that way."

"I wouldn't be surprised," Paul said, looking at her. She had black hair and pale, clear skin and a long, full body, and her eyes were deep gray and always brilliant, even after she'd been drinking for three days in a row.

Harriet began to walk a little faster. "I'm going to Wanamaker's," she said. "There's a couple of things I have to buy. Where you going?"

"Wanamaker's," Paul said. "I've been dying to go to Wanamaker's for three years."

They walked in silence for a few moments, Harriet's arm in his.

"Casual," Paul said. "I bet to the naked eye we look casual as hell. How do you feel?"

Harriet took her arm away. "Casual."

"Oh. Then that's how I feel, too." Paul whistled a few bars of the "1812 Overture." He stopped and looked critically at her, and she stopped too and turned toward him, a slight, puzzled smile on her face. "What makes you dress that way?" he asked. "You look like Monday morning in Northampton."

"I just threw on whatever was nearest," Harriet said. "I'm just going to be out about an hour."

"You used to look like a nice big box of candy in your clothes." Paul took her arm and they started off again. "Viennese bonbons. Every indentation carefully exploited in silk and satin. Even if you were just going down to the corner for a pint of gin, you'd look like something that ought to be eaten for dessert. This is no improvement."

"A girl has different periods in clothes," Harriet said. "Like Picasso. And if I'd known I was going to meet you, I'd've dressed differently."

Paul patted her arm. "That's better." He eyed her obliquely as they walked — the familiar long face, the well-known wide mouth with always a little too much lipstick on it, the little teeth that made her face, when she smiled, look suddenly like a little girl's in Sunday school.

"You're getting skinny, Paul," Harriet said.

Paul nodded. "I'm as lean as a herring. I've been leading a fevered and ascetic life. What sort of life have you been leading?"

"I got married." Harriet paused a moment. "Did you hear I got married?"

"I heard," Paul said. "The last time we crossed Sixth Avenue together the 'L' was still up. I feel a nostalgic twinge for the Sixth Avenue 'L.'" They hurried as the light changed. "On the night of January 9, 1940," Paul said, holding her elbow until they had crossed the street, "you were not home."

"Possible," Harriet said. "I'm a big girl now. I go out at night."

"I happened to pass your house and I noticed that the light wasn't on." They turned down toward Ninth Street. "I remembered how hot you kept that apartment — like the dahlia greenhouse in the Botanical Garden."

"I have thin blood," Harriet said gravely. "Long years of inbreeding in Massachusetts."

"The nicest thing about you," Paul said, "was you never went to sleep."

"Every lady to her own virtue," Harriet said. "Some women're beautiful, some're smart. Me, I never went to sleep. The secret of my great popularity —"

Paul grinned. "Shut up."

Harriet smiled back at him and they chuckled together. "You know what I mean," he said. "Any time I called you up — two, three in the morning — you'd come right over, lively and bright-eyed, all the rouge and mascara in the right places —"

"In my youth," said Harriet, "I had great powers of resistance."

"In the morning we'd eat breakfast at Beethoven. The Masterwork Hour, WNYC. Beethoven, by special permission of His Honor the Mayor, from nine to ten." Paul closed his eyes for a moment. "The Little Flower, Mayor for Lovers."

Paul opened his eyes and looked at the half-strange, half-familiar woman walking lightly at his side. He remembered lying close to her, dreamily watching the few lights of the towers of the nighttime city framed by the big window of his bedroom against the black sky, and one night when she moved sleepily against him and rubbed the back of his neck where the hair was sticking up in sharp little bristles because he had had his hair cut that afternoon. Harriet had rubbed them the wrong way, smiling dreamily, without opening her eyes. "What a delicious thing a man is," she'd murmured. And she'd sighed, then chuckled a little and fallen asleep, her hand still on the clipped back of his neck. Paul smiled, remembering.

"You still laughing at my clothes?" Harriet asked.

"I remembered something I heard someplace," Paul said. " 'What a delicious thing a man is.' "

Harriet looked at him coldly. "Who said that?"

Paul squinted suspiciously at her. "Oswald Spengler."

"Uh huh," Harriet said soberly. "It's a famous quotation."

"It's a well-turned phrase," said Paul.

"That's what I think, too." Harriet nodded and walked a little faster.

They passed the run-down bar where they'd sat afternoons all one winter, drinking Martinis and talking and talking and laughing so loud the people at the other tables would turn and smile. Paul waited for Harriet to say something about the place, but she didn't even seem to notice it. "There's Eddie's Bar," Paul said.

"Uh huh." Harriet nodded.

"He's going to start making his Martinis with sherry when all the French vermouth runs out," Paul said.

"It sounds horrible." Harriet made a face.

"Is that all you have to say?" Paul said loudly, remembering the times he'd looked in to see if she was there.

"What do you want me to say?" Harriet looked honestly puzzled, but Paul had never known when she was lying to him or telling the truth anyway, and he hadn't improved in these two years, he discovered.

"I don't want you to say anything," he said. "I'll take you in and buy you a drink."

"No, thanks. I've really got to get to Wanamaker's and back home in a hurry. Give me a rain check."

"Yeah," Paul said sourly.

They turned into Ninth Street toward Fifth Avenue.

"I knew I'd meet you someplace, finally," Paul said. "I was curious to see what would happen."

Harriet didn't say anything. She was looking absently at the buildings across the street.

"Don't you ever talk any more?" Paul asked.

"What *did* happen?"

"Every once in a while," he began, "I meet some girl I used to know — "

"I bet the country's full of them," Harriet said.

"The country's full of everybody's ex-girls."

Harriet nodded. "I never thought of it that way, but you're right."

"Most of the time I think, Isn't she a nice, decent person? Isn't it wonderful I'm no longer attached to her? The first girl I ever had," Paul said, "is a policewoman now. She subdued a gangster singlehanded in Coney Island last summer. Her mother won't let her go out of the house in her uniform. She's ashamed for the neighbors."

"Naturally," Harriet said.

"Another girl I used to know changed her name and danced in the Russian Ballet. I went to see her dance the other night. She has legs like a Fordham tackle. I used to think she was beautiful. I used to think you were beautiful, too."

"We were a handsome couple," Harriet said. "Except you always needed a shave. That electric razor — "

"I've given it up."

They were passing his old house now and he looked at the doorway and remembered all the times he and Harriet had gone in and come out, the rainy days and the early snowy mornings with the milkman's horse silent on the white street behind them. They stopped and looked at the old red house with the shabby shutters and the window on the fourth floor they had both looked out of time and time again to see what the weather was. Paul remembered the first time, on a winter's night, he and Harriet had gone through that door together.

"I was so damn polite," Paul said softly.

Harriet smiled. "You kept dropping the key and saying 'Lord, Lord' under your breath while you were looking for it."

"I was nervous. I wanted to make sure you knew exactly how matters stood. No illusions. Good friends, everybody understanding everybody else, another girl coming in from Detroit in six weeks — no claims on me, no claims on you . . ." Paul looked at the window on the fourth floor and smiled. "What a god-damn fool!"

"It's a nice, quiet street," Harriet said, looking up at the window on the fourth floor, too. She shook her head, took Paul's arm again. "I've got to get to Wanamaker's."

They started off.

"What're you buying at Wanamaker's?" Paul asked.

Harriet hesitated for a moment. "Nothing much. I'm looking at some baby clothes. I'm going to have a baby." They crowded over to one side to let a little woman with four dachshunds pass them in a busy tangle.

"Isn't it funny — me with a baby?" Harriet smiled. "I lie around all day and try to imagine what it's going to be like. In between, I sleep and drink beer to nourish us. I've never had such a good time in all my life."

"Well," said Paul, "at least it'll keep your husband out of the Army."

"Maybe. He's a raging patriot."

"Good. When he's at Fort Dix I'll meet you in Washington Square Park when you take the baby out for an airing in its perambulator. I'll put on a policeman's uniform to make it proper. I'm not such a raging patriot."

"They'll get you anyway, won't they?"

"Sure. I'll send you my picture in a lieutenant's suit. From Bulgaria. I have a premonition I'm going to be called on to defend a strategic point in Bulgaria."

"How do you feel about it?" For the first time, Harriet looked squarely and searchingly at him.

Paul shrugged. "It's going to happen. It's all damned silly, but it isn't as silly now as it was ten years ago."

Suddenly Harriet laughed.

"What's so funny?" Paul demanded.

"My asking you how you felt about something. I never used to have a chance. You'd let me know how you felt about everything. Roosevelt, James Joyce, Jesus Christ, Gypsy Rose Lee, Matisse, Yoga, liquor, sex, and architecture — "

"I was full of opinions in those days." Paul smiled. "Lust and conversation. The firm foundations of civilized relations between the sexes."

He turned and looked back at the window on the fourth floor. "That was a nice apartment," he said softly. "Lust and conversation — "

"Come on, Paul," Harriet said. "Wanamaker's isn't going to stay open all night."

"You were the only girl I ever knew I could sleep in the same bed with," Paul said.

"That's a hell of a thing to say to a girl." Harriet laughed. "Is that your notion of a compliment?"

Paul shrugged. "It's an irrelevant fact. Or a relevant fact. Is it polite to talk to a married lady this way?"

"No."

Paul walked along with her. "What do you think of when you look at me?" he asked.

"Nothing much," Harriet said.

"What're you lying about?"

"Nothing much," Harriet said.

"Don't you ever think, what in the name of God did I ever see in him?"

"No." Harriet began to walk faster.

"Should I tell you what I think of when I look at you?"

"No."

"I've been looking for you for two years," Paul said.

"My name's been in the telephone book." Harriet hurried even more, wrapping her coat tightly around her.

"I didn't realize I was looking for you until I saw you."

"Please, Paul —"

"I would walk along the street and I'd pass a bar we'd been in together and I'd go in and sit there even though I didn't want a drink, not knowing why I was sitting there. Now I know. I was waiting for you to come in. I didn't pass your house by accident."

"Look, Paul," Harriet pleaded. "It was a long time ago and it was fine and it ended —"

"I was wrong," Paul said. "Do you like hearing that? I was wrong. You know, I never did get married after all."

"I know," Harriet said. "Please shut up."

"I walk along Fifth Avenue and every time I pass Saint Patrick's I half look up to see if you're passing, because I met you that day right after you'd had a tooth pulled. And it was cold and you were walking along with the tears streaming from your eyes and your eyes red and that was the only time I ever met you by accident any place."

Harriet smiled. "That certainly sounds like a beautiful memory."

"Two years," Paul said. "I've gone out with a lot of girls in the last two years." He shrugged. "They've bored me and I've bored them. I keep looking at every woman who passes to see if it's you. All the girls I go out with bawl the hell out of me for it. I've been walking around, following girls with dark hair to see if it'll turn out to be you, and girls with a fur jacket like that old one you had, and girls that walk in that silly, beautiful way you walk. I've been searching the streets of the city for you for two years and this is the first time I've admitted it even to myself. That little Spanish joint we went the first time. Every time I pass it I remember everything — how many drinks we had and what the band played and what we said and the fat Cuban who kept winking at you from the bar and the very delicate way we landed up in my apartment . . ."

They were both walking swiftly now, Harriet holding her hands stiffly down at her sides.

"There is a particular, wonderful way you are joined together — "

"Paul, stop it!" Harriet's voice was flat but loud.

"Two years. In two years the edge should be dulled off things like that. Instead . . ." How can you make a mistake as big as that? Paul thought. How can you deliberately be as wrong as that? And no remedy. So long as you live, no remedy. He looked harshly at Harriet. Her face was set, as though she weren't listening to him and was intent only on getting across the street as quickly as possible. "How about you?" he asked. "Don't you remember?"

"I don't remember anything," she said. And then, suddenly, the tears sprang up in her eyes and streamed down the tight, distorted cheeks. "I don't remember a god-damn thing!" She wept. "I'm not going to Wanamaker's. I'm going home! Good-bye." She ran over to a cab that was parked at the corner and opened the door and sprang in. The cab spurted past Paul and he had a glimpse of Harriet sitting stiffly upright, the tears bitter and unheeded in her eyes.

He watched the cab go down Fifth Avenue until it turned. Then he turned the other way and started walking, thinking, I must move away from this neighborhood, I've lived here long enough.

NANCY HALE

If a short story should be an emotional adventure in reading, "Who Lived and Died Believing" is precisely that. One woman whose heart has broken, one woman whose heart is breaking are brought dramatically together here at a turning point in both their lives.

Nancy Hale is from a New England family illustrious in American life and letters. She is a descendant of Nathan Hale, the patriot, and the granddaughter of Edward Everett Hale who wrote The Man Without a Country. *Among her great-aunts were Harriet Beecher Stowe, author of* Uncle Tom's Cabin, *and Lucretia Hale, author of* The Peterkin Papers. *Miss Hale herself was born in Boston in 1908 and has been widely praised for both her fiction and nonfiction.*

Who Lived and Died Believing

It was a strange, hot summer. The days throbbed and the nights were exhausted and melancholy. In August the temperature rose over ninety and hung there; the heat shimmered over the buildings and the streets of the town. Every afternoon at two Elizabeth Percy came down the steps of the house that was made into apartments for nurses. She walked along the burning pavements, around the corner, past the newsstand where the magazines hung fluttering on lines of wire, to Massey's Drugstore.

Her hair was very dark and as smooth as dark brown satin; it was combed back from her calm forehead and fell curving under at the back behind her ears. She wore plain uniforms with small round collars close about her neck, and she was all white and fresh and slender and strong.

From the heat outside she would walk into the dim coolness of the drugstore that smelled of soda and candy. There was a faint sweat upon the marble of the soda fountain; Mr. Massey and the other clerks stood about in their light tan linen coats, and they smiled at her without speaking. Dave was behind the prescription counter wrapping up a small package; first the white paper and then slowly the thin bright red string.

He lifted his head as she walked down the center of the store to where the tables were, and his eyes met Elizabeth's. She sat down at the small black table and one of the boys from the fountain came and took her order of Coca-Cola. Several electric fans whirred remotely, high on the ceiling. The door opened again at the front, and three interns from the hospital came in. They leaned together on the marble counter in their whites. Their faces were young and pale with heat.

Dave came around the corner of the counter, and sat down beside Elizabeth. Mr. Massey walked slowly up toward the front of the store; he smiled absently at them; he always smiled at them as they sat together between two and three.

They never talked much. Elizabeth sucked the drink slowly through a straw, and lifted the glass and let bits of crushed ice drop into her mouth; they melted on her tongue. She loved to look at Dave. He was very thin and tall and he had straight yellow hair that fell forward in a lock on his forehead. His eyes were restless. He would glance at her suddenly and smile.

"How you doing over there?"

"She's just the same."

"Long case."

"Unh-hunh. Going to be longer."

"Tough you have to nurse one of those cases. Beckwith have any idea how long it'll be?"

One afternoon Elizabeth said, "Grainger told me yesterday he said he was going to use shock. Maybe."

"Insulin?"

"No, I don't think so."

Dave raised his eyebrows and shook his head. The damp yellow lock trembled against his forehead. He had finished the second year of medical school and was working at Massey's during the summer months.

"Oh-oh. That won't be so good."

"Grainger'll have it, in the mornings."

"No, no fun," he said.

"I'm so sorry for Mrs. Myles."

Dave shrugged his shoulders.

"Don't get tough," she said. "You're not a doctor yet. Beckwith's sorry for her, too. It's not the usual thing. She's gone through plenty."

"Sure," he said.

"Oh, real doctors have pity, you know; it's just you little boys."

She smiled at him, and he smiled back after a minute. He looked restless and impatient. He reached one hand under the table and put it on her knee, and looked into her long, calm, dark blue eyes.

"Meet you at eleven?" he said. Elizabeth nodded. He took his hand away.

"She wants to see you again."

"Oh, God."

"It doesn't hurt you any. Just go up there to her room for a minute and say good night. She gets so much out of it."

He gave a sort of groan, and shifted in his chair.

"She's got those damned eyes. I don't *mean* anything, I don't like her looking like that."

"It's just because we're going together," Elizabeth said. "It's the only thing outside herself, you see, like the only thing that's outside and ahead, and she likes to think about our going together."

"Oh, God."

"She asks me about you every day. Lots of times. I don't know whether she forgets she's asked before or whether . . . Come on, do it again once. It doesn't hurt you."

"All right. All right. Eleven."

"Eleven."

She got up and walked to the counter and laid the check down with a nickel. She went out into the heat, crossed the street, and walked up the wide steps of the hospital entrance.

In Copperthwaite Two the corridor was dim and hot. Elizabeth stopped at the desk and turned over the leaves of the order book. Doctor Beckwith had ordered the shock treatment for the morning; no breakfast. Elizabeth drew in her breath. Miss Grainger came out of the door of 53 and down the hall, without her cap.

"Hi," Elizabeth said.

"Hi."

"See you've got it ordered for tomorrow."

"Yeah, man."

"Does she know about it?"

"I'm not sure. He came up and went over her this morning, heart and all, before we went out. Told her, but not exactly; said they were going to give her a treatment and there'd be acute physical discomfort. I love Doctor Beckwith. Discomfort. I don't look forward to it, I tell you.

Seems like there's some things you don't get used to, and I don't like shock."

"What have you all done?"

"About the same. Walked. This walking miles in this weather does me in. I'm going home and go to sleep."

Elizabeth flipped back the pages of the order book.

"What is this stuff, anyhow? We didn't have it, then."

"Oh . . . camphor derivative? . . . something. Reckon I'll know plenty in the morning. How's Dave?"

"Fine," Elizabeth said. They parted and went along the long corridor in opposite directions. Elizabeth pushed open the heavy door of 53.

Mrs. Myles sat beside the open window and in the vicious heat observed passing back and forth outside (along the pavement?) back and forth from hell the doughy and grimacing faces of the damned. And a little part of the rotted grapes that rolled about within her brain watched the faces with an abstracted care; each of the faces was forever familiar, a face seen before (where?), seen before and seen again, and where, where, had been the face before? In her brain the fruit gave out a stench that she could taste in her mouth, and with it came the horror; no, no, those faces she had never seen before; it only seemed that she had; and the seeming was wrong and she could not send it away, the seeming stayed, shaking its tattered locks and grinning; yes, these faces had been seen before. The faces passed, and none of them was his. Watch, watch, observe with shrinking but insistent care each hideous face that comes nearer and nearer with death in its eyes and the unbelievable humanity, the bigness, in the coming-nearer mouths, until each face passed and was not his, was never his.

Her heart that was no longer her friend beat frantically one two three four five six seven eight eighty is a normal pulse for a woman seventy for a man but this was — hundred and forty . . . MAD.

The heavy-strained tension split with the scream of silk. The door opened and Miss Percy came in. So cool so calm so bright. With calm brow, with dark hair, and eyes like dark blue water. Cool as the little leaves that tremble in the tree. What thou among the leaves hast never known. This she has never known, with her calm eyes. Oh reach to me, thou among the leaves, reach down to me in hell with your cool hands, reach down to me.

She sees it all clean. The same world, clean. It is just me. I must remember that, it is just me; the world is cool and calm and bright. Not this. It is just me. Not mad, he said, just an exaggeration of your understandable state of tension, just an exaggeration of a normal point of view, just an exaggeration but not mad.

"Poor old Mr. Duggan next door's making quite a lot of noise," Miss Percy said, smiling. She stood before the mirror of the yellow-oak bureau and took her cap from the bureau post and pinned it to the back of her dark head. "I hope it doesn't bother you too much. Anyway, we'll go right out."

"Poor Mr. Duggan," Mrs. Myles said. "Is he getting any better at all?"

"I think they're going to give him some treatments that will make him all well."

The nurse glanced quickly at the patient.

She didn't mean to say that. She doesn't know if I know it, too. They are coming.

"You'd better wear your wide hat," Miss Percy said. "The sun's real hot this afternoon."

Obediently she put the hat upon her head and tied the ribbons that held it on under her chin.

"Put a little lipstick on," the nurse said. "It's so becoming to you to have a little color in your lips. Don't you remember what Doctor Beckwith said when he met us outside the steps yesterday, how pretty you looked? You've put on a pound and a half in two weeks. It won't be long before we have you weighing what you ought to. Before you know it you're going to be right strong."

Now to smile. Now widen the corners of the mouth and look straight into Miss Percy's eyes and hold it for a moment. But no! This is no smile. This is the terrible and tragic shape of a comic mask. Thus grimace the damned, who burn in the fires, and looking upward to the cool hand that is stretched in kindness and impotence to meet their torment, try one last time and achieve the horrible stretch, the grin, of the comic mask.

They walked down the hot dim corridor and turned to the right.

"Can't we please go down in the elevator?" Mrs. Myles said.

Miss Percy's face looked troubled.

"I know," she said. "Only he wants you to walk through the hospital."

"All right."

So once again. Endure, endure. Endure to the end.

First they walked through the children's ward. Once it had not been bad; the universal slime had not had time to foul this too; she had seen them as children, delicate and pale and sweet. But then the tide of the slime had mounted here too, and ever since it had been this way. Student nurses, nurses, interns passed them. "Afternoon, Mrs. Myles." They all know me. Can they see it in my face? . . . In the little beds the children lay or sat, with their sick faces. Sickness was everywhere. This is the great house of sickness. The children's faces were greenish with the heat. Which among them is mine? He is dead. He is not dead; which among them is mine, not well and laughing, but sick, which among them is my sick, corrupted child, infected from me all its tiny beginnings with the worm of sick sick sick? I am sick and all of mine is sick.

And she smelled the sharp recurrent fear. Fear, that clawed at the ruin of her mind; fear that rattled in her chest about the flabby palpitating boundaries of her heart. This fear is wicked, she thought: I am not afraid *for* the children, I am afraid *of* them. I am afraid of everything. I am full of poison of wickedness and fear; cold poison.

"He wants you to face things," Miss Percy said as they passed through and beyond the men's ward. "You know. Not get so you think you couldn't do something, special."

"I know."

In the beds the men lay, with sickness floating in the pools of their eyes. They passed on through the women's ward. A woman looked up. One side of her face was swollen out to huge proportions, and covered with bandages through which leaked sticky, yellow stuff. There was the long ominous smell of sweet ether and they passed suddenly across the hall of the hospital and their feet sounded sharp and loud on the stone flagging, and they went out into the loud sad heat. They descended the steps and started to walk down the road away from the town.

Suddenly from behind in the sunshine blared a loudspeaker, carried on a truck painted silver, with huge letters advertising an air-cooled movie house downtown. Slowly, slowly, the truck crept along the hot street. The enormous screaming music shook the atmosphere:

> *Fall in love, fall in love, says my heart* . . .
> Fall in love, *FALL IN LOVE* . . .

It swung slowly around a corner, out of sight. From far away in the afternoon the idiot voice still screamed:

"Fall in love, fall in love, says my heart . . ."

They walked steadily on, the nurse with a secret little smile; the woman, with a stiff and empty face.

The hours passed in gross and threatening procession. And with the hours the woman felt the always coming on, the rising walls, of the enclosing fear, like sound-proof glass, shutting her away; the terrible pawlike hand fumbling with the cork to stopper her finally into this bottle of aloneness.

She sat beside the window in the decline of the afternoon, and her hand was too sick with fear to stretch out to the shade and pull it down aginst the sun. She did not dare to move her hand. And soon the sun had bobbled behind the dreadful mountains of the west.

The nurse spoke to her several times and at last in her closing bottle she heard the voice from far away and turned, and it was supper being put before her on a tray. In the bowls of all the spoons were faces, that grinned at her and twisted their mouths into screams.

She ate, and then she was sick and the good food left her body in protest and she sat again by the window where the evening light now ran in around the edges of the shade like liquid poison, wet and lying on the floor and on the furniture of the room. The nurse put a table before her and laid out cards for a game upon its surface.

She looked down and saw the ferret faces of the kings and queens, the knaves; pinched and animal-like faces that whispered until the whispering was like a whistling in the room; and she turned her face away, but there was only the faraway flapping shade with the night running in around the edges, and she looked again at her hands but they were vast and swollen and she turned away and closed her eyes but within her was nothing but fear.

"How do you feel?" the nurse said in the evening room.

"How do you feel?" the nurse said.

"How do you feel?" the nurse said.

"HOW DO YOU FEEL?" the nurse said.

The nurse said, "Mrs. Myles, is there anything the matter?"

"It's as if," she said, "all the human things had been taken out of me and it left holes, like a cheese with great empty holes. And the holes have to be filled with something and they are all filled up with fear. So that where I had all sorts of things now I haven't got anything but fear in all the holes."

But that wasn't it at all, not only that; there was the bottle, how to tell someone of the bottle, glass, and sound-proof, where the stopper was being pushed tight home with her inside; not like a moth, no, not so clean, not like the souls in bottles, *animula, vagula, blandula.* No, like a festering purple lump of tissue.

Hell is not heat or cold, it is banishment to the ultimate ego. And in a few hours I shall be stoppered forever, she thought. I will not be able to speak, I will not be able to hear. I will be *mad.*

She asked for a pencil and paper. She wrote, and her handwriting was not her own; it was strange and inchoate like the sawings of the line of a fever chart. She looked at it with desperation. Will I scream? Will I groan? Will I grimace and mouth meaningless words? What will I do, with all of them watching me, crawling loathsomely inside the bottle, the face plastered on the purple stinking tissue like the fearful little faces in the spoons; while they watch, with their cool, well eyes, dressed all in white.

She tried to explain about the bottle on the paper with her failing handwriting, and then she folded it and wrote the doctor's name outside.

"Put it somewhere," she said urgently. "I want you to give it to Doctor Beckwith tomorrow if . . . if I . . ."

If I can no longer communicate what I feel, if I am mad.

"You're going to be fine," the nurse said. "You're going to be fine. Nothing's going to happen to you. Don't be afraid."

She thinks I mean die. No. Only the bottle. Or die?

Or die? For they are coming in the morning with something in their hands. For they are coming in the morning, footsteps measured, slow, down the corridor to me, bearing . . . the cross? . . . in their arms. No. No. You can still endure a little, do not think of Christ, that's the beginning. When the stopper is jammed at last deep into the neck of the bottle, then it will all be thoughts of Christ. Just with the last resisting inch, I can avoid the thought of Christ. . . .

But Christ. So cool, so calm, so bright. O Jesus thou art standing outside the fast-closed door. Jesus with his mild face, his mournful eyes, the bright brown beard, the suffering. Oh, no!

The minutes, the hours passed in ever-gathering procession. Miss Percy ran water and opened the high, narrow bed and helped the woman into it.

"Dave is coming to say good night to you," she said above the bed.

"Dave is coming to say GOOD NIGHT TO YOU," she said.

Oh . . . Dave is coming to say good night to me. . . . Dave? I don't know what is that word: Dave. Something; once; better; but not now. Only the bones of ego smelling of fear and dirt.

"Mrs. Myles."

"Mrs. Myles."

"Mrs. Myles."

"MRS. MYLES!"

She turned her head and in the doorway, unreal, remote, beyond hell, they stood, the nurse, white and slender, and the young man — he was Dave. They stood there, down a tiny vista beckoning, the last reminder. For they were love. It still endured, somewhere, upon the fading world. It was a flickering candle point upon the dark; flickering in the waves that even now, like the great winds of hell, blew the candle flame, tiny, tiny.

The woman on the bed strained toward what she saw. Upon these bones of ego hangs one last shred of flesh, and as long as it hesitates there, gnawed by the mouths of cockroaches, so long that shred of flesh shall reach, shall strain toward what it sees, toward love. The shred is hanging by a nerve, and the candle point flickers and grows far, far away at the end of the cone-shaped darkness.

"Good night, Mrs. Myles."

"Good night," she said. "Are you going out somewhere together?"

"Unh-hunh," Miss Percy said. "Reckon we'll go for a drive in the country to find a breeze."

"Yes," the woman said. "I hope it'll be cool, in the country. I hope you have a lovely time. I hope you're happy."

She turned her head away from the door and closed her eyes, struggling to maintain that point of light somewhere in the darkness that was growing. As long as I can see it the bones will not be wholly bare, and the world not gone. I hope they will be happy. They love each other. Here I lie: in my sepulcher, and the stopper hovers, and the smell of brimstone everywhere. But while the candle flickers I will remember. When it gutters and goes out, I will go out, and the shred of flesh shall drop at last and the paw that reeks shall push the stopper down. . . .

"Well, if you need anything, you know you just have to ring and Miss Perley will get it for you, dear. Good night," the nurse said.

But that, the woman did not hear.

After eleven the hospital was quiet and the lights along the corridors were turned out, so that only the light over the desks of the nurses in charge shone. The wards were dark and still; along some corridor could be heard occasionally the rattling trundle of a stretcher being pushed in a hurry, the stifled coming and going of a night emergency.

Elizabeth Percy went out through the hospital to the main entrance with Dave. A yawning nurse behind a desk raised her eyes and said "Hi!"; a doctor came hurriedly along the passage, wriggling his arms into a hospital coat as he went; his head was down and as Elizabeth passed he glanced upward from under his brows, nodded, and said, "Miss Percy. . . ." They came out onto the open stone flagging of the entrance hall where lights burned behind the admittance desk, and went down into the melting, melancholy night.

Elizabeth put her hand through Dave's arm and squeezed it; he glanced down at her and smiled.

"How you, babe?" he said.

"A little whipped. . . . That case is so hard, you can't do anything for her much and she's going through something awful."

"Forget it," he said. "You're off now. Climb in. Reckon it'll hold together a little longer."

She got into the old Chevrolet parked by the curb in the darkness.

They drove through the subsiding lights of the town, past the movie theatres with their electric signs turned off, now; the few people in light clothes dawdling before the doors of ice-cream parlors; there was the faint occasional hoot of a motor horn, the slam of a front door. As they passed into the outskirts of the town, the smell of the honeysuckle met them, drifting in from the country, and from far away the small sweet sawing of the crickets in the fields. They crossed a bridge and drove out along the country road, like a tunnel of darkness covered over with the branches of the trees. Their headlights made a white passage down the center of the tunnel. The smell of honeysuckle grew stronger, filling the whole night air, and sometimes they would pass a spot where the honeysuckle smell grew suddenly sharper, sweeter, bursting like fresh fountains into scent.

"My, this is nice," Elizabeth said. Her head was leaned back against the back of the seat.

He pressed her knee with his right hand and drew it toward his.

"Heat like we've been having can't last much longer," he said. "Registered over a hundred outside the store this afternoon. Got to crack sometime. May Leeds says her father and all the farmers are praying for rain."

"How's May?" Elizabeth asked in her low, quiet voice.

"Oh . . . I just took her to a movie while I was waiting around for you. She just dropped in while I was finishing up. . . . I've got to do something with the evenings, haven't I?"

"Of course, darling."

"It was a lousy movie."

She said nothing.

Far out along the road Dave stopped the car off to one side, under the boughs of the trees, and switched out the lights so that nothing could be seen; only the wide dark; the smell of the honeysuckle quivered through the darkness, and in the field beside them a whippoorwill called. Dave lit a cigarette and put his arm around Elizabeth.

"God, it's good to get out of that hellhole," he said.

After a moment Elizabeth spoke.

"I can't get Mrs. Myles out of my head," she said. "She just doesn't get any relief at all."

"Oh, skip the hospital when you're out of it."

"I know. Only I keep thinking that's what love can do to you."

"Inability to adjust."

"Yes, I know. But I guess it isn't so easy to adjust when you're too much in love, and then everything sort of came on her. I can't help picking things up. She was just mad about him and apparently he never cared much about her and she knew it, and that must be just . . . awful. And then when she got pregnant he went off with this other woman, and when she had her baby it died right away. Placenta previa. It would take quite a lot of adjusting.

"Well . . . Skip it. You can't go stewing about patients' problems. Leave that to Beckwith. How about kissing me?"

"You'd think she'd be through with love, wouldn't you? But she sort of hangs on to the idea of it. Like about . . . us."

"Yeah. Listen, I'm sorry, but I can't go up there any more and represent something for your patient. It just makes me feel too God-damn gummy."

"You don't have to. You never had to, only she seemed to get so much out of seeing you and it's awful seeing her every day, so lost. Anyway, she's getting shock in the morning."

"She is?"

"Yes. I hope it'll do the trick."

"How about skipping the hospital, baby? You're supposed to be a nurse, not an angel of mercy. Quit brooding about work out of hours. Kiss me."

She put both arms around him and kissed his mouth. His arms came around her and she felt the restlessness, the impatience in his body, and the eagerness, the searching.

"Oh, darling," she said. "I guess I'm pretty much in love with you."

"I don't mind you one bit myself," he murmured.

She started to speak, checked herself, and then spoke.

"Dave, darling, you wouldn't hurt me, would you?"

"Mmh-mmh."

"You could hurt me so easily. I'm so wide open to you."

"That's just the way I like you," he said, and he put his mouth down on hers, and his hands passed down her arms. Now they were close together, closer and closer in the satin darkness, and in the field the bird called at intervals and the smell of the honeysuckle came down in waves of shuddering sweetness. Over the country where they were the night sky seemed to brood, hanging soft and thick and vast over the land. Far away a train passed in the darkness and across the fields Elizabeth heard its whistle cry three times, three times — ah, ah, aaaah.

When they drove back into town it was very late and the air had a false coolness; there was a little breeze that would go away with the dawn. Elizabeth leaned silent against the seatback. Dave sat up straight and drove, and talked about the coming year of work.

"We get Parsons in surgery and will that be something. You remember Jim Jencks from down Eliza County, he was a real nice guy, I used to see a whole lot of him; he just had one run-in with Parsons after another, and that's one reason, I guess, he isn't going to be able to come back this year. Hope I don't get fixed up wrong with the old bastard "

"What's Jim Jencks doing now?" Elizabeth said.

"He just went on home. The damn fool, he got married. That finished him. Reckon he'll be raising pigs the rest of his life."

"I didn't know he got married."

"Yeah. Lehman, Lemmon . . . ? Married a nurse, anyway. Never had good sense."

Elizabeth made a small noise with her lips.

"Oh! . . . Beg you pardon! Only *you* know, the business of guys marrying nurses, the way they do. . . . You know just as well as I do."

"Yes."

He left her in the dark and empty street before the apartment house where she lived. In the silence of the town the car sounded noisily as he drove away. Elizabeth looked after the car for a moment and then she walked slowly up the brick steps to the house full of nurses asleep.

The woman in Room 53 was awake, passing from unconscious to conscious horror, as soon as the phlegm-gray dawn had filled the corners of the room. There was the relentless metronome beat of doom rapping everywhere. It could not be slowed, nor stopped, nor avoided, but beat faster minute by minute until at last the beat would fuse, would *be,* the footsteps coming down the corridor outside, bearing the thing that would be borne. The woman turned her head in an old and useless reflex against horror and stared out of the window into the gray light.

On the bank opposite the hospital window there were a number of little things, moving about and pecking, and she knew that they were birds; but they were not birds, they were frightful lumps of mud, mud-birds, that jerked about the dirt. She turned her eyes away from them in loathing, but there was nowhere else to look. She closed her eyes upon the horror of outside, to meet the inside horror.

The chorus sang the evil hymns. O Jesus, thou art standing outside the fast-closed door. O Jesus, thou . . . the bright brown beard, the promise that is stained and filthied with corruption, and where is there to fly to lose this wickedness? Abide with me; fast falls the eventide. The awful sweetish dripping of the notes in chorus; that seems to be a promise, that asks for comfort.

The panic grew and the metronome beat, a little faster; the tentacles within reached out in frenzy and there was nothing there to grasp, only abide with me; fast falls the eventide; the dim valley of sin, echoing in the shadows. Though I walk through the valley of the shadow of death, I shall fear no evil; for thou are with me; thy rod and thy staff. . . . Were those what they would bear? The rod and the staff? Though I walk through the valley of the shadow of death. . . . I shall fear this evil, spreading like phlegm along the valley, everywhere, and all is evil, abiding with me. . . .

Oh, no! she cried inside herself with one last straining, no! But where was there to look? And in the ultimate necessity there flickered far off the pale point of the candle flame.

And then the footsteps down the corridor. And then the footsteps, am I dreaming them? The door opened and the priests and the acolytes came in — no, the doctor and the resident and the interns and the nurse — no, the white-robed priests of this obscene observance, this sacrifice, and I am the sacrifice that lies quite still upon the altar, and they bear the weapon in their hands: the huge, brutal, long syringe lying upon a bed of gauze, and I am Christ to meet their sacrifice, to give my life. Six people in the room, and the sacrifice.

"Good morning, gentlemen," the woman said.

The nurse, by the head of the bed, laid her hand upon the patient's hand. The three interns stood grouped at the foot of the bed. The doctor stood on the right of the bed and looked down into the patient's face. The resident stood halfway down the left side of the bed, and in his hands he held the syringe.

She looked up into the doctor's face and upon it lay his eyes, flat, like gray, wet, cold oysters laid upon a plate.

"Listen," the woman said hurriedly. "Tell me quick. Does it matter what thoughts I am thinking? I mean will this fasten them permanently this way? Because my thoughts are so bad, and I can't seem to think any good thoughts. . . ."

"It doesn't matter, kiddy," said the doctor. The eyes like oysters swam at her, and spun a little round and round. He laid his fingers on her wrist. The resident took her left arm and felt with his fingers along the veins on the inside of her elbow. She closed her eyes Now let me think one good thought, that my brain may be embalmed in this sacrifice with a good thought held in it like a fly in amber. Oh, stay with me, flame, the point before the eyes, the one last point. . . .

A wave from the outside of sick; of liquid; of shuddering horror ran up her veins.

"Thrombosed," the resident said. "We'll have to try another."

"Steady, kiddy," the doctor said.

Oh, flame, abide with me in the moment of dissolution. . . .

Then crashingly a thousand carmine circles spun in her brain and there were crashes and mad carmine and the dark.

"Look at that," the leftmost intern said as the figure on the bed sat straight up, clenched in convulsion.

"Patient down on G Ward fractured three vertebrae in one of those," the resident said, watching.

"You'll have your good days and your bad days." The nurse's voice came to her. "You'll have your good days and your bad days, Mrs. Myles."

She was eating lunch off a tray and it was lettuce that she was putting in her mouth. It was thin and crisp and very cold. The world around her was hot and the sun beat through the window beside her. Everything was fatigue, and pain in her back, but the lettuce on her tongue was cool, and the nurse's voice; her name was Miss Percy and she was always there, in the revolving mist, speaking to her out of the wilderness, cool and clear.

"You'll have your good days and your bad days, Mrs. Myles."

She was walking through the jungle of the world, and she was lost. She did not know where she was. It was an utterly strange, green jungle. Only the nurse, Miss Percy, was there beside her, and so she continued to walk through this land.

They came to a brook that ran through a shady hollow and they sat down on a large stone by the margin of the brook and the nurse took off the woman's shoes, and she put her tired feet in the brook. The water was warm and fresh and ran softly past her feet. Beside the brook stood tall green trees that she had never seen before. She kept her feet in the soft running water and listened to the rustling in the leaves of the strange trees.

"How did I get here?" she asked. "Where have I been?"

The nurse's voice came with the sound of the brook, cool and clear.

"You're taking a walk in the country. You're staying at the hospital for a while."

"I don't remember . . ."

"You'll have amnesia for a little bit. It's all right."

It's all right . . .

Miss Percy stopped the doctor in the corridor.

"Doctor Beckwith, may I speak to you for a minute?"

The doctor stopped on one foot in his hurrying walk. The two horns of the stethoscope stuck up from the pocket of his white coat.

"My patient is getting hardly any sleep, doctor. I wondered if you could order something."

"Can't give sedatives, you know, with the treatments. Has a counteractive effect."

"She just seems so terribly tired."

"Well, she didn't even feel tired before. . . . I'll order insulin tonight, Miss Percy. See whether that'll put her to sleep."

"Thank you, doctor."

"You don't look as if you'd got much sleep yourself," the doctor said.

"Oh . . . it's just this heat."

"Got to break soon."

"Yes."

They were in a bowling alley, that was what it was, although she did not know where the bowling alley was or how she had got there. But the nurse was sitting on one of the wooden theatre seats behind her. She herself was standing, facing the alley with a bowl in her hand.

She continued with the action that somehow she had begun. She neither felt the bowl with her hand nor felt the floor under her feet when she moved forward. It was like moving through air. She willed herself to make the gestures that somewhere inside she knew should be made now, and her body carried out the commands, but without sensation, without seeming to touch anything at all.

It just shows what you can do by will power, she thought, surprised. I can do anything I will myself to do, even though I am moving in air.

She let go the bowl and watched down the long straight alley where the bowl rolled, and heard the rumble of the falling pins.

She watched as the three black bowls came rolling up the wooden trolley to the side, and came to a stop. She picked up one of them and although she had picked it up she felt nothing against her palm.

It's almost fun, she thought, seeing what you can do by will power.

It was night, and suddenly she could not bear to lie in bed any longer. Since the nurse had stuck the needle in her arm the strangest energy and slow hope had begun in her.

In the dim spaces of this room the nurse was moving about. She was taking off her cap.

"I want to get up," the woman said. "Can I get up? I want to talk."

The nurse turned and smiled.

"All right," she said. She pulled forward the big chair that was by the window, and helped the woman into it. The nurse sat down on a small straight chair and smiled at the woman.

"But were you going away . . ." the woman said, puzzled. Something stirred in her head, faintly remembered.

"No," the nurse said. "I haven't anywhere special to go. I'd be glad to stay a little later, Mrs. Myles."

"You don't know," she said, "what hope can feel like. It's like running water. I mean freedom. Oh, you don't know what it's like! To be able to see freedom. Even just a little bit."

"You're going to have all the freedom in the world."

"I keep thinking of the loveliest things — long straight roads and driving along them fast in an open car. You don't know what hope can feel like. It's like the wind beginning to blow. Am I really going to be free?"

Suddenly the words of something whose origin she could not remember came into her head and she began to repeat them aloud: "That this nation, under God, shall have a new birth in freedom, and that government of the people, by the people, for the people, shall not perish from the earth."

Shall not perish . . .

"That's what I mean," she said. "That's the way it feels. I can't remember but it wasn't that way before, it wasn't by the people, for the people, I mean as if I were the people, as if I were a nation. A woman like a nation."

"Yes," the nurse said. "I know. Instead of under a dictator, you mean. It's awful to live under a dictator and not belong to yourself any more, isn't it?"

"Yes," she said impatiently, pushing that part away from her, for now there was hope, forming like a five-petaled flower, like a star. Sitting forward on the edge of the chair in her excitement, she repeated the words again, whatever they were: "This nation, under God, shall have a new birth in freedom — and that government of the people . . ."

And after some time the nurse went away and came back with a tall glass that was filled with sugared water, flavored deliciously with lemon, and the woman drank it.

And on some mornings the doctor and the resident and three interns came into her room, and the resident carried the large syringe. He was always the one who inserted the needle into her vein. It was a thing that came suddenly on some mornings and it had to be faced, once more; endure, she thought, endure to the end. And always at the last she summoned to her the vision, with her eyes closed, of the candle flame, that companioned her through the darkness, through the bad days, through it all. It did not leave her, it remained to fortify her in the last extremity, when they came and the needle went into her arm and in her head spun the carmine circles and the world crashed, and then the dark. . . .

"Don't think she'll have to have another," the doctor said, as they watched the figure in convulsion on the bed. "This stuff certainly is magic in some cases."

On an afternoon in the yellow sunshine, suddenly she was sitting under an apple tree in the yard beside the hospital, and the nurse, Miss Percy, was sitting on the grass beside her. Mrs. Myles turned her head slowly and smiled. The heat had gone; it was a cool and lovely afternoon; the leaves rustled in the tree above her and from its branches came the smell of apples.

On the grass farther away some interns were playing baseball. Their voices shouted to one another, and the ball could be heard smacking their cupped palms. A breeze trickled along the air. The shadows were beginning to lengthen from the wall of the hospital, and in that light the interns, in their white clothes, ran and shouted. From a grass bank on the other side of the road from the hospital a bird called, suddenly, sweetly.

"Hello," Mrs. Myles said.

"Hello, dear. You're feeling much better, aren't you?"

"Yes," she said. Things were swimming back into her memory, the buildings here were taking their places in the world. And everything was very calm, very peaceful; there was no hurry. It doesn't matter.

She looked at the nurse, who had been there all the time. In the darkness and the long confusion, in that strange land where she had been, the nurse had been with her all the time. She studied the dark, smooth hair, the oval face, and the long, dark blue, quiet eyes.

"How is Dave?" Mrs. Myles said.

"You're remembering, aren't you?" the nurse said, without looking at the patient. "I think he's fine. I haven't seen him for a while."

"But . . ."

That did not fit. She stayed silent for a little time, while the remembrances slowly rearranged themselves within her head.

"But, you're in love with him," she said slowly. "It was you both. You are in love with each other."

"Well . . . You see, we aren't going together any more."

Something was wrong. Wait while the sifting memory slowly settled.

Her own life was dead, somehow she had learned that, someone had taught her that in the strange, twilight land. She knew that she had been reborn and that this was a new life. She could never have the things of her own old life, for they had gone and they were dead. But one thing only . . . a candle burning down a vista, some constant star that had companioned her through the dark valleys of the land she had left. . . . She remembered two figures standing in a doorway.

"You're not?"

"No," the nurse said. She looked tired. They stared at each other and then a new and curious thing happened, a wave swept upward and from her eyes the woman felt tears falling. It was not despair. It was only deepest sadness. The last thing had gone out of the old life. Now the past was wiped black and she was all alone and beginning a new life, reborn alone. The purest, quietest sadness swept her and she could not halt the tears that fell and fell.

"You musn't mind at all, dear," the nurse said. But their eyes kept meeting: the nurse's quiet and dry, the woman's full of tears.

The baseball game had broken up and a young intern came strolling by the apple tree, and looked down at the two who sat upon the grass. His face Mrs. Myles knew. It had looked at her on many mornings.

"Afternoon, Mrs. Myles, Miss Percy," the intern said, and then stopped in embarrassment at the tears on the woman's face.

"Well . . ." he said. "Seems fine to have a good cry, doesn't it?"

"Yes," she said, crying quietly, for all that was dead, now, forever, and could never be brought back. And it was fading fast. Fade far away, dissolve, and quite forget what thou among the leaves hast never known. It was all over; it was finished; the fight with death and sin, the wandering in the strange lost land. It was all gone, and love was gone too, and the candle flame had silently gone out. Above their heads where they sat upon the grass the little leaves in the apple tree whispered. It was all gone, and from now on the world was new, a page unwritten.

PAUL HORGAN

*In "The Peach Stone" four points of view by four people have been
combined into a satisfying unity. Sad though the story is, it does, for
three people at least, have a happy ending which required great skill
to make so convincing.*

*Born in Buffalo, New York, in 1903, Paul Horgan has been acclaimed
for his short stories, novels and histories. He is the author of ten novels,
the first of which won the Harper Novel Award, and many volumes
of short stories. As a historian, he is best known for* Great River: The
Rio Grande in North American History, *for which he won both the
Pulitzer and Bancroft Prizes.*

The Peach Stone

As THEY all knew, the drive would take them about four hours, all the
way to Weed, where *she* came from. They knew the way from traveling it
so often, first in the old car, and now in the new one; new to them, that
is, for they'd bought it second hand, last year, when they were down in
Roswell to celebrate their tenth wedding anniversary. They still thought
of themselves as a young couple, and *he* certainly did crazy things now
and then, and always laughed her out of it when she was cross at the
money going where it did, instead of where it ought to go. But there was
so much droll orneriness in him when he did things like that that she
couldn't stay mad, hadn't the heart, and the harder up they got, the more
she loved him, and the little ranch he'd taken her to in the rolling plains
just below the mountains.

This was a day in spring, rather hot, and the mountain was that
melting blue that reminded you of something you could touch, like a
china bowl. Over the sandy brown of the earth there was coming a green
shadow. The air struck cool and deep in their breasts. *He* came from
Texas, as a boy, and had lived here in New Mexico ever since. The word

Copyright, 1942, by Paul Horgan. First published in *The Yale Review*, 1942.

home always gave *her* a picture of unpainted, mouse-brown wooden houses in a little cluster by the rocky edge of the last mountain-step — the town of Weed, where Jodey Powers met and married her ten years ago.

They were heading back that way today.

Jodey was driving, squinting at the light. It never seemed so bright as now, before noon, as they went up the valley. He had a rangy look at the wheel of the light blue Chevvie — a bony man, but still fuzzed over with some look of a cub about him, perhaps the way he moved his limbs, a slight appealing clumsiness, that drew on thoughtless strength. On a rough road, he flopped and swayed at the wheel as if he were on a bony horse that galloped a little sidewise. His skin was red-brown from the sun. He had pale blue eyes, edged with dark lashes. *She* used to say he "turned them on" her, as if they were lights. He was wearing his suit, brown-striped, and a fresh blue shirt, too big at the neck. But he looked well dressed. But he would have looked that way naked, too, for he communicated his physical essence through any covering. It was what spoke out from him to anyone who encountered him. Until Cleotha married him, it had given him a time, all right, he used to reflect.

Next to him in the front seat of the sedan was Buddy, their nine-year-old boy, who turned his head to stare at them both, his father and mother.

She was in back.

On the seat beside her was a wooden box, sandpapered, but not painted. Over it lay a baby's coverlet of pale yellow flannel with cross-stitched flowers down the middle in a band of bright colors. The mother didn't touch the box except when the car lurched or the tires danced over corrugated places in the gravel highway. Then she steadied it, and kept it from creeping on the seat cushions. In the box was coffined the body of their dead child, a two-year-old girl. They were on their way to Weed to bury it there.

In the other corner of the back seat sat Miss Latcher, the teacher. They rode in silence, and Miss Latcher breathed deeply of the spring day, as they all did, and she kept summoning to her aid the fruits of her learning. She felt this was a time to be intelligent, and not to give way to feelings.

The child was burned to death yesterday, playing behind the adobe chickenhouse at the edge of the arroyo out back, where the fence always caught the tumbleweeds. Yesterday, in a twist of wind, a few sparks from the kitchen chimney fell in the dry tumbleweeds and set them ablaze. Jodey had always meant to clear the weeds out: never seemed to get to it: told Cleotha he'd get to it next Saturday morning, before going down to Roswell: but Saturdays went by, and the wind and the sand drove the weeds into a barrier at the fence, and they would look at it every day without noticing, so habitual had the sight become. And so for many a spring morning, the little girl had played out there, behind the gray stucco house, whose adobe bricks showed through in one or two places.

The car had something loose; they believed it was the left rear fender: it chattered and wrangled over the gravel road.

Last night Cleotha stopped her weeping.

Today something happened; it came over her as they started out of the ranch lane, which curved up toward the highway. She looked as if she were trying to see something beyond the edge of Jodey's head and past the windshield.

Of course, she had sight in her eyes; she could not refuse to look at the world. As the car drove up the valley that morning, she saw in two ways —one, as she remembered the familiar sights of this region where she lived; the other, as if for the first time she were really seeing, and not simply looking. Her heart began to beat faster as they drove. It seemed to knock at her breast as if to come forth and hurry ahead of her along the sunlighted lanes of the life after today. She remembered thinking that her head might be a little giddy, what with the sorrow in her eyes so bright and slowly shining. But it didn't matter what did it. Ready never to look at anyone or anything again, she kept still; and through the window, which had a meandering crack in it like a river on a map, all that she looked upon seemed dear to her. . . .

Jodey could only drive. He watched the road as if he expected it to rise up and smite them all over into the canyon, where the trees twinkled and flashed with bright drops of light on their new varnished leaves. Jodey watched the road and said to himself that if it thought it could turn him over or make him scrape the rocks along the near side of the hill they were going around, if it thought for one minute that he was not master of this car, this road, this journey, why, it was just crazy. The wheels spraying the gravel across the surface of the road traveled on outward from his legs; his muscles were tight and felt tired as if he were running instead of riding. He tried to *think,* but he could not; that is, nothing came about that he would speak to her of, and he believed that she sat there, leaning forward, waiting for him to say something to her.

But this he could not do, and he speeded up a little, and his jaw made hard knots where he bit on his own rage; and he saw a lump of something coming in the road, and it aroused a positive passion in him. He aimed directly for it, and charged it fast, and hit it. The car shuddered and skidded, jolting them. Miss Latcher took a sharp breath inward, and put out her hand to touch someone, but did not reach anyone. Jodey looked for a second into the rear-view mirror above him, expecting something; but his wife was looking out of the window beside her, and if he could believe his eyes, she was smiling, holding her mouth with her fingers pinched up in a little claw.

The blood came up from under his shirt, he turned dark, and a sting came across his eyes.

He couldn't explain why he had done a thing like that to her, as if it were she he was enraged with, instead of himself.

He wanted to stop the car and get out and go around to the back door on the other side, and open it, and take her hands, bring her out to stand before him in the road, and hang his arms around her until she would be locked upon him. This made a picture that he indulged like a dream, while the car ran on, and he made no change, but drove as before. . . .

The little boy, Buddy, regarded their faces, again, and again, as if to see in their eyes what had happened to them.

He felt the separateness of the three.

He was frightened by their appearance of indifference to each other. His father had a hot and drowsy look, as if he had just come out of bed. There was something in his father's face which made it impossible for Buddy to say anything. He turned around and looked at his mother, but she was gazing out the window, and did not see him; and until she should see him, he had no way of speaking to her, if not with his words, then with his eyes, but if she should happen to look at him, why, he would wait to see what she looked *like,* and if she *did,* why, then he would smile at her, because he loved her, but he would have to know first if she was still his mother, and if everything was all right, and things weren't blown to smithereens — *bla-a-ash! wh-o-o-m!* — the way the dynamite did when the highway came past their ranch house, and the men worked out there for months, and whole hillsides came down at a time. All summer long, that was, always something to see. The world, the family, he, between his father and mother, was safe.

He silently begged her to face toward him. There was no security until she should do so.

"Mumma?"

But he said it to himself, and she did not hear him this time, and it seemed intelligent to him to turn around, make a game of it (the way things often were worked out), and face the front, watch the road, delay as long as he possibly could bear to, and *then* turn around again, and *this* time, why, she would probably be looking at him all the time, and it would *be:* it would simply *be*.

So he obediently watched the road, the white gravel ribbon passing under their wheels as steadily as time.

He was a sturdy little boy, and there was a silver nap of child's dust on his face, over his plum-red cheeks. He smelled something like a raw potato that has just been pared. The sun crowned him with a ring of light on his dark hair. . . .

What Cleotha was afraid to do was break the spell by saying anything or looking at any of them. This was *vision,* it was all she could think; never had anything looked so in all her life; everything made her heart lift, when she had believed this morning, after the night, that it would never lift again. There wasn't anything to compare her grief to. She couldn't think of anything to answer the death of her tiny child with. In her first hours of hardly believing what had happened, she had felt her own flesh and tried to imagine how it would have been if she could have borne the fire instead of the child. But all she got out of that was a longing avowal to herself of how gladly she would have borne it. Jodey had lain beside her, and she clung to his hand until she heard how he breathed off to sleep. Then she had let him go, and had wept at what seemed faithless in him. She had wanted his mind beside her then. It seemed to her that the last degree of her grief was the compassion she had had to bestow upon him while he slept.

But she had found this resource within her, and from that time on, her weeping had stopped.

It was like a wedding of pride and duty within her. There was nothing she could not find within herself, if she had to, now, she believed.

And so this morning, getting on toward noon, as they rode up the valley, climbing all the way, until they would find the road to turn off on, which would take them higher and higher before they dropped down toward Weed on the other side, she welcomed the sights of that dusty trip. Even if she had spoken her vision aloud, it would not have made sense to the others.

Look at that orchard of peach trees, she thought. I never saw such color as this year; the trees are like lamps, with the light coming from within. It must be the sunlight shining from the other side, and, of course, the petals are very thin, like the loveliest silk; so any light that shines upon them will pierce right through them and glow on this side. But they are so bright! When I was a girl at home, up to Weed, I remember we had an orchard of peach trees, but the blossoms were always a deeper pink than down here in the valley.

My! I used to catch them up by the handful, and I believed when I was a girl that if I crushed them and tied them in a handkerchief and carried the handkerchief in my bosom, I would come to smell like peach blossoms and have the same high pink in my face, and the girls I knew said that if I took a peach *stone* and held it *long enough* in my hand, it would *sprout;* and I dreamed of this one time, though, of course, I knew it was nonsense; but that was how children thought and talked in those days — we all used to pretend that *nothing* was impossible, if you simply did it hard enough and long enough.

But nobody wanted to hold a peach stone in their hand until it *sprouted,* to find out, and we used to laugh about it, but I think we believed it. I think I believed it.

It seemed to me, in between my *sensible* thoughts, a thing that any woman could probably do. It seemed to me like a parable in the Bible. I could preach you a sermon about it this day.

I believe I see a tree down there in that next orchard which is dead; it has old black sprigs, and it looks twisted by rheumatism. There is one little shoot of leaves up on the top branch, and that is all. No, it is not dead, it is aged, it can no longer put forth blossoms in a swarm like pink butterflies; but there is that one little swarm of green leaves — it is just about the prettiest thing I've seen all day, and I thank God for it, for if there's anything I love, it is to see something growing. . . .

Miss Latcher had on her cloth gloves now, which she had taken from her blue cloth bag a little while back. The little winds that tracked through the moving car sought her out and chilled her nose, and the tips of her ears, and her long fingers, about which she had several times gone to visit various doctors. They had always told her not to worry, if her fingers seemed cold, and her hands moist. It was just a nervous condition, nothing to take very seriously; a good hand lotion might help the sensation, and in any case, some kind of digital exercise was a good thing — did she perhaps play the piano. It always seemed to her that doctors never *paid any attention* to her.

Her first name was Arleen, and she always considered this a very pretty name, prettier than Cleotha; and she believed that there was such a thing as an *Arleen look,* and if you wanted to know what it was, simply look at her. She had a long face, and pale hair; her skin was white, and her eyes were light blue. She was wonderfully clean, and used no cosmetics. She was a girl from "around here," but she had gone away to college, to study for her career, and what she had known as a child was displaced by what she had heard in classrooms. And she had to admit it: people *here* and *away* were not much alike. The men were different. She couldn't imagine marrying a rancher and "sacrificing" everything she had learned in college.

This poor little thing in the other corner of the car, for instance: she seemed dazed by what had happened to her — all she could do evidently was sit and stare out the window. And that man in front, simply driving, without a word. What did they have? What was their life like? They hardly had good clothes to drive to Roswell in, when they had to go to the doctor, or on some social errand.

But I must not think uncharitably, she reflected, and sat in an attitude of sustained sympathy, with her face composed in Arleenish interest and tact. The assumption of a proper aspect of grief and feeling produced the most curious effect within her, and by her attitude of concern she was suddenly reminded of the thing that always made her feel like weeping, though of course, she never did, but when she stopped and *thought* —

Like that painting at college, in the long hallway leading from the Physical Education lecture hall to the stairway down to the girls' gym: an enormous picture depicting the Agony of the Christian Martyrs, in ancient Rome. There were some days when she simply couldn't look at it; and there were others when she would pause and see those maidens with their tearful faces raised in calm prowess, and in them, she would find herself — they were all Arleens; and after she would leave the picture she would proceed in her imagination to the arena, and there she would know with exquisite sorrow and pain the ordeals of two thousand years ago, instead of those of her own lifetime. She thought of the picture now, and traded its remote sorrows for those of today until she had sincerely forgotten the mother and the father and the little brother of the dead child with whom she was riding up the spring-turning valley, where noon was warming the dust that arose from the graveled highway. It was white dust, and it settled over them in an enriching film, ever so finely. . . .

Jodey Powers had a fantastic scheme that he used to think about for taking and baling tumbleweed and make a salable fuel out of it. First, you'd compress it — probably down at the cotton compress in Roswell — where a loose bale was wheeled in under the great power-drop, and when the nigger at the handle gave her a yank, down came the weight, and packed the bale into a little thing, and then they let the steam exhaust go, and the press sighed once or twice, and just seemed to *lie* there, while the men ran wires through the gratings of the press and tied them tight. Then up came the weight, and out came the bale.

If he did that to enough bales of tumbleweed, he believed he'd get rich. Burn? It burned like a house afire. It had oil in it, somehow, and the thing to do was to get it in shape for use as a fuel. Imagine all the tumbleweed that blew around the State of New Mexico in the fall, and sometimes all winter. In the winter, the weeds were black and brittle. They cracked when they blew against fence posts, and if one lodged there, then another one caught at its thorny lace; and next time it blew, and the sand came trailing, and the tumbleweeds rolled, they'd pile up at the same fence and build out, locked together against the wires. The wind drew through them, and the sand dropped around them. Soon there was a solid-looking but airy bank of tumbleweeds built right to the top of the fence, in a long windward slope; and the next time the wind blew, and the weeds came, they would roll up the little hill of brittle twigs and leap off the other side of the fence, for all the world like horses taking a jump, and go galloping ahead of the wind across the next pasture on the plains, a black and witchy procession.

If there was an arroyo, they gathered there. They backed up in the miniature canyons of dirt-walled watercourses, which were dry except when it rained hard up in the hills. Out behind the house, the arroyo had filled up with tumbleweeds; and in November, when it blew so hard and so cold, but without bringing any snow, some of the tumbleweeds had climbed out and scattered, and a few had tangled at the back fence, looking like rusted barbed wire. Then there came a few more; all winter the bank grew. Many times he'd planned to get out back there and clear them away, just e-e-ease them off away from the fence posts, so's not to catch the wood up, and then set a match to the whole thing, and in five minutes, have it all cleared off. If he did like one thing, it was a neat place.

How Cleotha laughed at him sometimes when he said that, because she knew that as likely as not he would forget to clear the weeds away. And if he'd said it once he'd said it a thousand times, that he was going to gather up that pile of scrap iron from the front yard, and haul to to Roswell, and sell it — old car parts, and the fenders off a truck that had turned over up on the highway, which he'd salvaged with the aid of the driver.

But the rusting iron was still there, and he had actually come to have a feeling of fondness for it. If someone were to appear one night and silently make off with it, he'd be aroused the next day, and demand to know who had robbed him: for it was dear junk, just through lying around and belonging to him. What was his was part of him, even that heap of fenders that rubbed off on your clothes with a rusty powder, like a caterpillar fur.

But even by thinking hard about all such matters, treading upon the fringe of what had happened yesterday, he was unable to make it all seem long ago, and a matter of custom and even of indifference. There was no getting away from it — if anybody was to blame for the terrible moments of yesterday afternoon, when the wind scattered a few sparks from the chimney of the kitchen stove, why he was.

Jodey Powers never claimed to himself or anybody else that he was any *better* man than another. But everything he knew and hoped for, every reassurance his body had had from other people, and the children he had begotten, had been knowledge to him he was *as good* a man as any.

And of this knowledge he was now bereft.

If he had been alone in his barrenness, he could have solaced himself with heroic stupidities. He could have produced out of himself abominations, with the amplitude of biblical despair. But he wasn't alone; there they sat; there was Buddy beside him, and Clee in back, even the teacher, Arleen — even to her he owed some return of courage.

All he could do was drive the damned car, and keep *thinking* about it.

He wished he could think of something to say, or else that Clee would.

But they continued in silence, and he believed that it was one of his making. . . .

The reverie of Arleen Latcher made her almost ill, from the sad, sweet experiences she had entered into with those people so long ago. How

wonderful it was to have such a rich life, just looking up things! — And
the most wonderful thing of all was that even if they were beautiful, and
wore semitransparent garments that fell to the ground in graceful folds,
the maidens were all pure. It made her eyes swim to think how innocent
they went to their death. Could anything be more beautiful, and reassuring, than this? Far, far better. Far better those hungry lions, than the
touch of lustful men. Her breath left her for a moment, and she closed
her eyes, and what threatened her with real feeling — the presence of the
Powers family in the faded blue sedan climbing through the valley sunlight toward the turn-off that led to the mountain road — was gone.
Life's breath on her cheek was not so close. Oh, others had suffered. She
could suffer.

"All that pass by clap their hands at thee: they hiss and wag their
heads at the daughter of Jerusalem — "

This image made her wince, as if she herself had been hissed and
wagged at. Everything she knew made it possible for her to see herself as
a proud and threatened virgin of Bible times, which were more real to
her than many of the years she had lived through. Yet must not Jerusalem have sat in country like this with its sandy hills, the frosty stars that
were so bright at night, the simple Mexicans riding their burros as if to
the Holy Gates? We often do not see our very selves, she would reflect,
gazing ardently at the unreal creature which the name Arleen brought to
life in her mind.

On her cheeks there had appeared two islands of color, as if she had a
fever. What she strove to save by her anguished retreats into the memories of the last days of the Roman Empire was surely crumbling away
from her. She said to herself that she must not give way to it, and that
she was just wrought up; the fact that she really *didn't* feel anything —
in fact, it was a pity that she *couldn't* take that little Mrs. Powers in her
arms, and comfort her, just *let* her go ahead and cry, and see if it
wouldn't probably help some. But Miss Latcher was aware that she felt
nothing that related to the Powers family and their trouble.

Anxiously she searched her heart again, and wooed back the sacrifice of
the tribe of heavenly Arleens marching so certainly toward the lions. But
they did not answer her call to mind, and she folded her cloth-gloved
hands and pressed them together, and begged of herself that she might
think of some way to comfort Mrs. Powers; for if she could do that, it
might fill her own empty heart until it became a cup that would run
over. . . .

Cleotha knew Buddy wanted her to see him; but though her heart turned toward him, as it always must, no matter what he asked of her, she was this time afraid to do it because if she ever lost the serenity of her sight now she might never recover it this day; and the heaviest trouble was still before her.

So she contented herself with Buddy's look as it reached her from the side of her eye. She glimpsed his head and neck, like a young cat's, the wide bones behind the ears, and the smooth but visible cords of his nape, a sight of him that always made her want to laugh because it was so pathetic. When she caressed him she often fondled those strenuous hollows behind his ears. Heaven only knew, she would think, what went on within the shell of that topknot! She would pray between her words and feelings that those unseen thoughts in the boy's head were ones that would never trouble him. She was often amazed at things in him which she recognized as being like herself; and at those of Buddy's qualities which came from some alien source, she suffered pangs of doubt and fear. He was so young to be a stranger to her!

The car went around the curve that hugged the rocky fall of a hill; and on the other side of it, a green quilt of alfalfa lay sparkling darkly in the light. Beyond that, to the right of the road, the land leveled out, and on a sort of platform of swept earth stood a two-room hut of adobe. It had a few stones cemented against the near corner, to give it strength. Clee had seen it a hundred times — the place where that old man Melendez lived, and where his wife had died a few years ago. He was said to be simple-minded and claimed he was a hundred years old. In the past, riding by here, she had more or less delicately made a point of looking the other way. It often distressed her to think of such a helpless old man, too feeble to do anything but crawl out when the sun was bright and the wall was warm, and sit there, with his milky gaze resting on the hills he had known since he was born, and had never left. Somebody came to feed him once a day, and see if he was clean enough to keep his health. As long as she could remember, there'd been some kind of dog at the house. The old man had sons and grandsons and great-grandsons — you might say a whole orchard of them, sprung from this one tree that was dying, but that still held a handful of green days in its ancient veins.

Before the car had quite gone by, she had seen him. The sun was bright, and the wall must have been warm, warm enough to give his shoulders and back a reflection of the heat which was all he could feel. He sat there on his weathered board bench, his hands on his branch of apple tree that was smooth and shiny from use as a cane. His house door was open, and a deep tunnel of shade lay within the sagged box of the opening. Cleotha leaned forward to see him, as if to look at him were one of her duties today. She saw his jaw moving up and down, not chewing, but just opening and closing. In the wind and flash of the car going by, she could not hear him; but from his closed eyes, and his moving mouth, and the way his head was raised, she wouldn't have been surprised if she had heard him singing. He was singing some thread of song, and it made her smile to imagine what kind of noise it made, a wisp of voice.

She was perplexed by a feeling of joyful fullness in her breast, at the sight of the very same old witless sire from whom in the past she had turned away her eyes out of delicacy and disgust.

The last thing she saw as they went by was his dog, who came around the corner of the house with a caracole. He was a mongrel puppy, partly hound — a comedian by nature. He came prancing outrageously up to the old man's knees, and invited his response, which he did not get. But as if his master were as great a wag as he, he hurled himself backward, pretending to throw himself recklessly into pieces. Everything on him flopped and was flung by his idiotic energy. It was easy to imagine, watching the puppy-fool, that the sunlight had entered him as it had entered the old man. Cleotha was reached by the hilarity of the hound, and when he tripped over himself and plowed the ground with his flapping jowls, she wanted to laugh out loud.

But they were past the place, and she winked back the merriment in her eyes, and she knew that it was something she could never have told the others about. What it stood for, in her, they would come to know in other ways, as she loved them. . . .

Jodey was glad of one thing. He had telephoned from Hondo last night, and everything was to be ready at Weed. They would drive right up the hill to the family burial ground. They wouldn't have to wait for anything. He was glad, too, that the wind wasn't blowing. It always made his heart sink when the wind rose on the plains and began to change the sky with the color of dust.

Yesterday: it was all he could see, however hard he was *thinking* about everything else.

He'd been on his horse, coming back down the pasture that rose up behind the house across the arroyo, nothing particular in mind — except to make a joke with himself about how far along the peaches would get before the frost killed them all, *snap,* in a single night, like that — when he saw the column of smoke rising from the tumbleweeds by the fence. Now who could've lighted them, he reflected, following the black smoke up on its billows into the sky. There was just enough wind idling across the long front of the hill to bend the smoke and trail it away at an angle, toward the blue.

The hillside, the fire, the wind, the column of smoke.

Oh my God! And the next minute he was tearing down the hill as fast as his horse could take him, and the fire — he could see the flames now — the fire was like a bank of yellow rags blowing violently and torn in the air, rag after rag tearing up from the ground. Cleotha was there, and in a moment, so was he, but they were too late. The baby was unconscious. They took her up and hurried to the house, the back way where the screen door was standing open with its spring trailing on the ground. When they got inside where it seemed so dark and cool, they held the child between them, fearing to lay her down. They called for Buddy, but he was still at school up the road, and would not be home until the orange school bus stopped by their mailbox out front at the highway after four o'clock. The fire poured in cracking tumult through the weeds. In ten minutes they were only little airy lifts of ash off the ground. Everything was black. There were three fence posts still afire; the wires were hot. The child was dead. They let her down on their large bed.

He could remember every word Clee had said to him. They were not many, and they shamed him, in his heart, because he couldn't say a thing. He comforted her, and held her while she wept. But if he had spoken then, or now, riding in the car, all he could have talked about was the image of the blowing rags of yellow fire, and blue, blue, plaster blue behind the above, sky and mountains. But he believed that she knew why he seemed so short with her. He hoped earnestly that she knew. He might just be wrong. She might be blaming him, and keeping so still because it was more proper, now, to *be* still than full of reproaches.

But of the future, he was entirely uncertain; and he drove, and came to the turn-off, and they started winding in back among the sandhills that lifted them toward the rocky slopes of the mountains. Up and up they went; the air was so clear and thin that they felt transported, and across the valleys that dropped between the grand shoulders of the pine-haired slopes, the air looked as if it were blue breath from the trees. . . .

Cleotha was blinded by a dazzling light in the distance, ahead of them, on the road.

It was a ball of diamond-brilliant light.

It danced, and shook, and quivered above the road far, far ahead. It seemed to be traveling between the pine trees on either side of the road, and somewhat above the road, and it was like nothing she had ever seen before. It was the most magic and exquisite thing she had ever seen, and wildly, even hopefully as a child is hopeful when there is a chance and a need for something miraculous to happen, she tried to explain it to herself. It could be a star in the daytime, shaking and quivering and traveling ahead of them, as if to lead them. It was their guide. It was shaped like a small cloud, but it was made of shine, and dazzle, and quiver. She held her breath for fear it should vanish, but it did not, and she wondered if the others in the car were smitten with the glory of it as she was.

It was brighter than the sun, whiter; it challenged the daytime, and obscured everything near it by its blaze of flashing and dancing light.

It was almost as if she had approached perfect innocence through her misery, and were enabled to receive portents that might not be visible to anyone else. She closed her eyes for a moment.

But the road curved, and everything traveling on it took the curve too, and the trembling pool of diamond-light ahead lost its liquid splendor, and turned into the tin signs on the back of a huge oil truck which was toiling over the mountain, trailing its links of chain behind.

When Clee looked again, the star above the road was gone. The road and the angle of the sun to the mountaintop and the two cars climbing upward had lost their harmony to produce the miracle. She saw the red oil truck, and simply saw it, and said to herself that the sun might have reflected off the big tin signs on the back of it. But she didn't believe it, for she was not thinking, but rather dreaming; fearful of awakening. . . .

The high climb up this drive always made Miss Latcher's ears pop, and she had discovered once that to swallow often prevented the disagreeable sensation. So she swallowed. Nothing happened to her ears. But she continued to swallow, and feel her ears with her cloth-covered fingers, but what really troubled her now would not be downed, and it came into her mouth as a taste; she felt giddy — that was the altitude, of course — when they got down the other side, she would be all right.

What it was was perfectly clear to her, for that was part of having an education and a trained mind — the processes of thought often went right on once you started them going.

Below the facts of this small family, in the worst trouble it had ever known, lay the fact of envy in Arleen's breast.

It made her head swim to realize this. But she envied them their entanglement with one another, and the dues they paid each other in the humility of the duty they were performing on this ride, to the family burial ground at Weed. Here she sat riding with them, to come along and be of help to them, and she was no help. She was unable to swallow the lump of desire that rose in her throat, for life's uses, even such bitter ones as that of the Powers family today. It had been filling her gradually, all the way over on the trip, this feeling of jealousy and degradation.

Now it choked her and she knew she had tried too hard to put from her the thing that threatened her, which was the touch of life through anybody else. She said to herself that she must keep control of herself.

But Buddy turned around again, just then, slowly, as if he were a young male cat who just happened to be turning around to see what he could see, and he looked at his mother with his large eyes, so like his father's: pale petal-blue, with drops of light like the centers of cats' eyes, and dark lashes. He had a solemn look, when he saw his mother's face, and he prayed her silently to acknowledge him. If she didn't, why, he was still alone. He would never again feel safe about running off to the highway to watch the scrapers work, or the huge Diesel oil tankers go by, or the cars with strange license plates — of which he had already counted thirty-two different kinds, his collection, as he called it. So if she didn't see him, why, what might he find when he came back home at times like those, when he went off for a little while just to play?

They were climbing down the other side of the ridge now. In a few minutes they would be riding into Weed. The sights as they approached were like images of awakening to Cleotha. Her heart began to hurt when she saw them. She recognized the tall iron smokestack of the sawmill. It showed above the trees down on the slope ahead of them. There was a stone house which had been abandoned even when she was a girl at home here, and its windows and doors standing open always seemed to her to depict a face with an expression of dismay. The car dropped farther down — they were making that last long curve of the road to the left — and now the town stood visible, with the sunlight resting on so many of the unpainted houses and turning their weathered gray to a dark silver. Surely they must be ready for them, these houses: all had been talked over by now. They could all mention that they knew Cleotha as a little girl.

She lifted her head.

There were claims upon her.

Buddy was looking at her soberly, trying to predict to himself how she would *be*. He was ready to echo with his own small face whatever her face would show him.

Miss Latcher was watching the two of them. Her heart was racing in her breast.

The car slowed up. Now Cleotha could not look out the windows at the wandering earthen street, and the places alongside it. They would have to drive right through town, to the hillside on the other side.

"Mumma?" asked the boy softly.

Cleotha winked both her eyes at him, and smiled, and leaned toward him a trifle.

And then he blushed, his eyes swam with happiness, and he smiled back at her, and his face poured forth such radiance that Miss Latcher took one look at him, and with a choke, burst into tears.

She wept into her hands, her gloves were moistened, her square shoulders rose to her ears, and she was overwhelmed by what the mother had been able to do for the boy. She shook her head and made long gasping sobs. Her sense of betrayal was not lessened by the awareness that she was weeping for herself.

Cleotha leaned across to her, and took her hand, and murmured to her. She comforted her, gently.

"Hush, honey, you'll be all right. Don't you cry, now. Don't you think about us. We're almost there, and it'll soon be over. God knows you were mighty sweet to come along and be with us. Hush, now, Arleen, you'll have Buddy crying too."

But the boy was simply watching the teacher, in whom the person he knew so well every day in school had broken up, leaving an unfamiliar likeness. It was like seeing a reflection in a pond, and then throwing a stone in. The reflection disappeared in ripples of something else.

Arleen could not stop.

The sound of her 'ooping made Jodey furious. He looked into the rear-view mirror and saw his wife patting her and comforting her. Cleotha looked so white and strained that he was frightened, and he said out, without turning around: "Arleen, you cut that out, you shut up, now. I won't have you wearin' down Clee, God damn it, you quit it!"

But this rage, which arose from a sense of justice, made Arleen feel guiltier than ever; and she laid her head against the car window, and her sobs drummed her brow bitterly on the glass.

"Hush," whispered Cleotha, but she could do no more, for they were arriving at the hillside, and the car was coming to a stop. They must awaken from this journey, and come out onto the ground, and begin to toil their way up the yellow hill, where the people were waiting. Over the ground grew yellow grass that was turning to green. It was like velvet, showing dark or light, according to the breeze and the golden afternoon sunlight. It was a generous hill, curving easily and gradually as it rose. Beyond it was only the sky, for the mountains faced it from behind the road. It was called Schoolhouse Hill, and at one time, the whole thing had belonged to Cleotha's father; and before there was any schoolhouse crowning its noble swell of earth, the departed members of his family had been buried halfway up the gentle climb.

Jodey helped her out of the car, and he tried to talk to her with his holding fingers. He felt her trembling, and she shook her head at him. Then she began to walk up there, slowly. He leaned into the car and took the covered box in his arms, and followed her. Miss Latcher was out of the car on her side, hiding from them, her back turned, while she used her handkerchief and positively clenched herself back into control of her thoughts and sobs. When she saw that they weren't waiting for her, she hurried, and in humility, reached for Buddy's hand to hold it for him as they walked. He let her have it, and he marched, watching his father, whose hair was blowing in the wind and sunshine. From behind, Jodey looked like just a kid. . . .

And now for Cleotha her visions on the journey appeared to have some value, and for a little while longer, when she needed it most, the sense of being in blind communion with life was granted her, at the little graveside where all those kind friends were gathered on the slow slope up of the hill on the summit of which was the schoolhouse of her girlhood.

It was afternoon, and they were all kneeling toward the upward rise, and Judge Crittenden was reading the prayer book.

Everything left them but a sense of their worship, in the present.

And a boy, a late scholar, is coming down the hill from the school, the sunlight edging him; and his wonder at what the people kneeling there are doing is, to Cleotha, the most memorable thing she is to look upon today; for she has resumed the life of her infant daughter, whom they are burying, and on whose behalf, something rejoices in life anyway, as if to ask the mother whether love itself is not ever-living. And she watches the boy come discreetly down the hill, trying to keep away from them, but large-eyed with a hunger *to know* which claims all acts of life, for him, and for those who will be with him later; and his respectful curiosity about those kneeling mourners, the edge of sunlight along him as he walks away from the sun and down the hill, is of all those things she saw and rejoiced in, the most beautiful; and at that, her breast is full, with the heaviness of a baby at it, and not for grief alone, but for praise.

"I believe, I believe!" her heart cries out in her, as if she were holding the peach stone of her eager girlhood in her woman's hand.

She puts her face into her hands, and weeps, and they all move closer to her. Familiar as it is, the spirit has had a new discovery. . . .

Jodey then felt that she had returned to them all; and he stopped seeing, and just remembered, what happened yesterday; and his love for his wife was confirmed as something he would never be able to measure for himself or prove to her in words.

JESSE STUART

The vagaries of publishing have a wonderful example in the lyrical "Dawn of Remembered Spring." The author sent it to thirty-six magazines, all of which, including those for men, rejected it on the grounds that the snakes in it would repel women readers. This story accidentally became caught in the clip of another manuscript being sent to Harper's Bazaar. *The editors rejected the story the author hoped they would like and enthusiastically accepted the snake story. When asked for permission to reprint it in* The Best American Short Stories, *Mr. Stuart wrote, "What goes on up there anyhow? Men's magazines, afraid of women readers, turn it down, a magazine edited by women for women takes it and then a lady anthologist comes along and wants to reprint it!"*

Jesse Stuart is a native of Kentucky, where he was born in 1907, and lives in Greenup. He first made his mark with a collection of poems, Man With a Bull Tongue Plow. *He has written novels and many short stories in addition to being a school superintendent and a farmer.*

Dawn of Remembered Spring

"BE CAREFUL, Shan," Mom said. "I'm afraid if you wade that creek that a water moccasin will bite you."

"All right, Mom."

"You know what happened to Roy Deer last Sunday!"

"Yes, Mom!"

"He's nigh at the point of death," she said. "I'm going over there now to see him. His leg's swelled hard as a rock and it's turned black as black-oak bark. They're not looking for Roy to live until midnight tonight."

"All water moccasins ought to be killed, hadn't they, Mom?"

"Yes, they're pizen things, but you can't kill them," Mom said. "They're in all of these creeks around here. There's so many of them we can't kill 'em all."

Mom stood at the foot-log that crossed the creek in front of our house. Her white apron was starched stiff; I heard it rustle when Mom put her

hand in the little pocket in the right upper corner to get tobacco crumbs
for her pipe. Mom wore her slat bonnet that shaded her sun-tanned face
— a bonnet with strings that came under her chin and tied in a bowknot.

"I feel uneasy," Mom said as she filled her long-stemmed clay-stone
pipe with bright-burley crumbs, tamped them down with her index
finger, and struck a match on the rough bark of an apple tree that grew
on the creek bank by the foot-log.

"Don't feel uneasy about me," I said.

"But I do," Mom said. "Your Pa out groundhog huntin' and I'll be
away at Deers' — nobody at home but you, and so many pizen snakes
around this house."

Mom blew a cloud of blue smoke from her pipe. She walked across the
foot-log — her long clean dress sweeping the weed stubble where Pa had
mown the weeds along the path with a scythe so we could leave the
house without getting our legs wet by the dew-covered weeds.

When Mom walked out of sight around the turn of the pasture hill and
the trail of smoke that she left behind her had disappeared into the light
blue April air, I crossed the garden fence at the wild-plum thicket.

Everybody gone, I thought. I am left alone. I'll do as I please. A water
moccasin bit Roy Deer but a water moccasin will never bite me. I'll get
me a club from this wild-plum thicket and I'll wade up the creek killing
water moccasins.

There was a dead wild-plum sprout standing among the thicket of
living sprouts. It was about the size of a tobacco stick. I stepped out of
my path into the wild-plum thicket. Barefooted, I walked among the
wild-plum thorns. I uprooted the dead wild-plum sprout. There was a
bulge on it where roots had once been — now the roots had rotted in the
earth. It was like a maul with this big bulge on the end of it. It would be
good to hit water moccasins with.

The mules played in the pasture. It was Sunday — their day of rest.
And the mules knew it. This was Sunday and it was my day of rest. It
was my one day of freedom, too, when Mom and Pa were gone and I was
left alone. I would like to be a man now, I thought, I'd love to plow the
mules, run a farm, and kill snakes. A water moccasin bit Roy Deer but
one would never bite me.

The bright sunlight of April played over the green Kentucky hills.
Sunlight fell onto the creek of blue water that twisted like a crawling
snake around the high bluffs and between the high rocks. In many places
dwarf willows, horse-weeds, iron weeds, and wild grapevines shut away

the sunlight and the creek waters stood in quiet cool puddles. These little puddles under the shade of weeds, vines, and willows were the places where the water moccasins lived.

I rolled my overall legs above my knees so I wouldn't wet them and Mom wouldn't know I'd been wading the creek. I started wading up the creek toward the head of the hollow. I carried my wild-plum club across my shoulder with both hands gripped tightly around the small end of it. I was ready to maul the first water moccasin I saw.

"One of you old water moccasins bit Roy Deer," I said bravely, clinching my grip tighter around my club, "but you won't bite me."

As I waded the cool creek waters, my bare feet touched gravel on the creek bottom. When I touched a wet water-soaked stick on the bottom of the creek bed, I'd think it was a snake and I'd jump. I'd wade into banks of quicksand. I'd sink into the sand above my knees. It was hard to pull my legs out of this quicksand and when I pulled them out they'd be covered with thin quicky mud that the next puddle of water would wash away.

"A water moccasin," I said to myself. I was scared to look at him. He was wrapped around a willow that was bent over the creek. He was sleeping in the sun. I slipped toward him quietly — step by step — with my club drawn over my shoulder. Soon as I got close enough to reach him, I came over my shoulder with the club. I hit the water moccasin a powerful blow that mashed its head flat against the willow. It fell dead into the water. I picked it up by the tail and threw it up on the bank.

"One gone," I said to myself.

The water was warm around my feet and legs. The sharp-edged gravels hurt the bottoms of my feet but the soft sand soothed them. Butterflies swarmed over my head and around me — alighting on the wild pink phlox that grew in clusters along the creek bank. Wild honey bees, bumble bees, and butterflies worked on the elder blossoms, the shoe-make blossoms and the beet-red finger-long blossoms of the ironweed and the whitish pink covered smart-weed blossoms. Birds sang among the willows and flew up and down the creek with four-winged snake-feeders in their bills.

This is what I like to do, I thought. I love to kill snakes. I'm not afraid of snakes. I laughed to think how afraid of snakes Mom was — how she struck a potato-digger tine through a big rusty-golden copperhead's skin just enough to pin him to the earth and hold him so he couldn't get under our floor. He fought the potato-digger handle until Pa came home from work and killed him. Where he'd thrown poison over the ground it killed the weeds and weeds didn't grow on this spot again for four years.

Once when Mom was making my bed upstairs, she heard a noise of something running behind the paper that was pasted over the cracks between the logs — the paper split and a house snake six feet long fell onto the floor with a mouse in his mouth. Mom killed him with a bed slat. She called me once to bring her a goose-neck hoe upstairs quickly. I ran upstairs and killed two cow snakes restin' on the wall plate. And Pa killed twenty-eight copperheads out of a two-acre oat field in the hollow above the house one spring season.

"Snakes — snakes," Mom used to say, "are goin' to run us out'n this Hollow."

"It's because these woods ain't been burnt out in years," Pa'd always answer. "Back when I's a boy the old people burnt the woods out every spring to kill the snakes. Got so anymore there ain't enough good timber for a board tree and people have had to quit burning up the good timber. Snakes are about to take the woods again."

I thought about the snakes Pa had killed in the cornfield and the tobacco patch and how nearly copperheads had come to biting me and how I'd always seen the snake in time to cut his head off with a hoe or get out of his way. I thought of the times I had heard a rattlesnake's warning and how I'd run when I hadn't seen the snake. As I thought these thoughts, plop a big water moccasin fell from the creek bank into a puddle of water.

"I'll get you," I said. "You can't fool me! You can't stand muddy water."

I stirred the water until it was muddy with my wild-plum club. I waited for the water moccasin to stick his head above the water. Where wild ferns dipped down from the bank's edge and touched the water, I saw the snake's head rise slowly above the water — watchin' me with his lidless eyes. I swung sidewise with my club like batting at a ball. I couldn't swing over my shoulder, for there were willow limbs above my head.

I surely got him, I thought. I waited to see. Soon, something like milk spread over the water. "I got 'im." I raked in the water with my club and lifted from the bottom of the creek bed a water moccasin long as my club. It was longer than I was tall. I threw him up on the bank and moved slowly up the creek — looking on every drift, stump, log, and sunny spot. I looked for a snake's head along the edges of the creek bank where ferns dipped over and touched the water.

I waded up the creek all day killing water moccasins. If one were asleep on the bank, I slipped upon him quietly as a cat. I mauled him with the big end of my wild-plum club. I killed him in his sleep. He never knew what struck him. If a brush caught the end of my club and caused me to miss and let the snake get into a puddle of water, I muddied the water and waited for him to stick his head above the water. When he stuck his head above the water, I got him. Not one water moccasin got away from me. It was four o'clock when I stepped from the creek onto the bank. I'd killed fifty-three water moccasins.

Water moccasins are not half as dangerous as turtles, I thought. A water moccasin can't bite you under the water for he gets his mouth full of water. A turtle can bite you under water and when one bites you he won't let loose until it thunders, unless you cut his head off. I'd been afraid of turtles all day because I didn't have a knife in my pocket to cut one's head off if it grabbed my foot and held it.

When I left the creek, I was afraid of the snakes I'd killed. I didn't throw my club away. I gripped the club until my hands hurt. I looked below my path, above my path, and in front of me. When I saw a stick on the ground, I thought it was a snake. I eased up to it quietly as a cat trying to catch a bird. I was ready to hit it with my club.

What will Mom think when I tell her I've killed fifty-three water moccasins? I thought. A water moccasin bit Roy Deer but one's not going to bite me. I paid the snakes back for biting him. It was good enough for them. Roy wasn't bothering the water moccasin that bit him. He was just crossing the creek at the foot-log and it jumped from the grass and bit him.

Shadows lengthened from the tall trees. The Hollow was deep and the creek flowed softly in the cool recesses of evening shadows. There was one patch of sunlight. It was upon the steep broomsedge-covered bluff above the path.

"Snakes," I cried, "snakes a-fightin' and they're not water moccasins! They're copperheads!"

They were wrapped around each other. Their lidless eyes looked into each other's eyes. Their hard lips touched each other's lips. They did not move. They did not pay any attention to me. They looked at one another.

I'll kill 'em, I thought, if they don't kill one another in this fight.

I stood in the path with my club ready. I had heard snakes fought each other but I'd never seen them fight.

"What're you lookin' at, Shan?" Uncle Alf Skinner asked. He walked up the path with a cane in his hand.

"Snakes a-fightin'."

"Snakes a-fightin'?"

"Yes."

"I never saw it in my life."

"I'll kill 'em both if they don't finish the fight," I said. "I'll club 'em to death."

"Snakes a-fightin', Shan," he shouted, "you are too young to know! It's snakes in love! Snakes in love! Don't kill 'em — just keep your eye on 'em until I bring Martha over here! She's never seen snakes in love!"

Uncle Alf ran around the turn of the hill. He brought Aunt Martha back with him. She was carrying a basket of greens on her arm and the case knife that she'd been cutting greens with in her hand.

"See 'em, Martha," Uncle Alf said. "Look up there in that broomsedge!"

"I'll declare," she said. "I've lived all my life and I never saw this. I've wondered about snakes!"

She stood with a smile on her wrinkled lips. Uncle Alf stood with a wide smile on his deep-lined face. I looked at them and wondered why they looked at these copperheads and smiled. Uncle Alf looked at Aunt Martha. They smiled at each other.

"Shan! Shan!" I heard Mom calling.

"I'm here," I shouted.

"Where've you been?" she asked as she turned around the bend of the hill with a switch in her hand.

"Be quiet, Sall," Uncle Alf said. "Come here and look for yourself!"

"What is it?" Mom asked.

"Snakes in love," Uncle Alf said.

Mom was mad. "Shan, I feel like limbing you," she said. "I've hunted everyplace for you! Where've you been?"

"Killin' snakes," I answered.

"Roy Deer is dead," she said. "That's how dangerous it is to fool with snakes."

"I paid the snakes back for him," I said. "I've killed fifty-three water moccasins!"

"Look, Sall!"

"Yes, Alf, I see," Mom said.

Mom threw her switch on the ground. Her eyes were wide apart. The frowns left her face.

"It's the first time I ever saw snakes in love," Aunt Martha said to Mom.

"It's the first time I ever saw anything like this," Mom said. "Shan, you go tell your Pa to come and look at this."

I was glad to do anything for Mom. I was afraid of her switch. When I brought Pa back to the sunny bank where the copperheads were loving, Art and Sadie Baker were there and Tom and Ethel Riggs — and there were a lot of strangers there. They were looking at the copperheads wrapped around each other with their eyes looking into each other's eyes and their hard lips touching each other's lips.

"You hurry to the house, Shan," Pa said, "and cut your stove wood for tonight."

"I'd like to kill these copperheads," I said.

"Why?" Pa asked.

"Fightin'," I said.

Uncle Alf and Aunt Martha laughed as I walked down the path carrying my club. It was something — I didn't know what — all the crowd watching the snakes were smiling. Their faces were made over new. The snakes had done something to them. Their wrinkled faces were as bright as the spring sunlight on the bluff; their eyes were shiny as the creek was in the noonday sunlight. And they laughed and talked to one another. I heard their laughter grow fainter as I walked down the path toward the house. Their laughter was louder than the wild honey bees I had heard swarming over the shoe-make, alderberry, and wild phlox blossoms along the creek.

JAMES THURBER

*Thurber's war between the sexes is epitomized in "The Catbird Seat."
You will not weep when you read it. But you might have if you had
read the letter Thurber sent when giving permission to use it . . . "My
sight is almost gone now. To write this story I had to do it in large
letters on four hundred sheets of yellow manila paper."*

*James Thurber was born in Columbus, Ohio, in 1894. He attended
Ohio State University but did not graduate because he could not master
botany and military drill. He must have had a sense of humor even
then. When he died, America lost the writer who had given readers the
greatest joy since Mark Twain.*

The Catbird Seat

MR. MARTIN bought the pack of Camels on Monday night in the most
crowded cigar store on Broadway. It was theatre time and seven or eight
men were buying cigarettes. The clerk didn't even glance at Mr. Martin,
who put the pack in his overcoat pocket and went out. If any of the staff
at F & S had seen him buy the cigarettes, they would have been astonished, for it was generally known that Mr. Martin did not smoke, and
never had. No one saw him.

It was just a week to the day since Mr. Martin had decided to rub out
Mrs. Ulgine Barrows. The term "rub out" pleased him because it suggested nothing more than the correction of an error — in this case an
error of Mr. Fitweiler. Mr. Martin had spent each night of the past week
working out his plan and examining it. As he walked home now he went
over it again. For the hundredth time he resented the element of impreci-
sion, the margin of guesswork that entered into the business. The project
as he had worked it out was casual and bold, the risks were considerable.
Something might go wrong anywhere along the line. And therein lay the
cunning of his scheme. No one would ever see in it the cautious, painstak-
ing hand of Erwin Martin, head of the filing department at F & S, of

whom Mr. Fitweiler had once said, "Man is fallible but Martin isn't." No one would see his hand; that is, unless it were caught in the act.

Sitting in his apartment, drinking a glass of milk, Mr. Martin reviewed his case against Mrs. Ulgine Barrows, as he had every night for seven nights. He began at the beginning. Her quacking voice and braying laugh had first profaned the halls of F & S on March 7, 1941 (Mr. Martin had a head for dates). Old Roberts, the personnel chief, had introduced her as the newly appointed special adviser to the president of the firm, Mr. Fitweiler. The woman had appalled Mr. Martin instantly, but he hadn't shown it. He had given her his dry hand, a look of studious concentration, and a faint smile. "Well," she had said, looking at the papers on his desk, "are you lifting the oxcart out of the ditch?" As Mr. Martin recalled that moment, over his milk, he squirmed slightly. He must keep his mind on her crimes as a special adviser, not on her peccadillos as a personality. This he found difficult to do, in spite of entering an objection and sustaining it. The faults of the woman as a woman kept chattering on in his mind like an unruly witness. She had, for almost two years now, baited him. In the halls, in the elevator, even in his own office, into which she romped now and then like a circus horse, she was constantly shouting these silly questions at him. "Are you lifting the oxcart out of the ditch? Are you tearing up the pea patch? Are you hollering down the rain barrel? Are you scraping the bottom of the pickle barrel? Are you sitting in the catbird seat?"

It was Joey Hart, one of Mr. Martin's two assistants, who had explained what the gibberish meant. "She must be a Dodger fan," he had said. "Red Barber announces the Dodger games over the radio and he uses those expressions — picked 'em up down South." Joey had gone on to explain one or two. "Tearing up the pea patch" meant going on a rampage; "sitting in the catbird seat" meant sitting pretty, like a batter with three balls and no strikes on him. Mr. Martin dismissed all this with an effort. It had been annoying, it had driven him near to distraction, but he was too solid a man to be moved to murder by anything so childish. It was fortunate, he reflected as he passed on to the important charges against Mrs. Barrows, that he had stood up under it so well. He had maintained always an outward appearance of polite tolerance. "Why, I even believe you like the woman," Miss Paird, his other assistant, had once said to him. He had simply smiled.

A gavel rapped in Mr. Martin's mind and the case proper was resumed. Mrs. Ulgine Barrows stood charged with willful, blatant, and persistent attempts to destroy the efficiency and system of F & S. It was competent, material, and relevant to review her advent and rise to power. Mr. Martin had got the story from Miss Paird, who seemed always able to find things out. According to her, Mrs. Barrows had met Mr. Fitweiler at a party, where she had rescued him from the embraces of a powerfully built drunken man who had mistaken the president of F & S for a famous Middle Western football coach. She had led him to a sofa and somehow worked upon him a monstrous magic. The aging gentleman had jumped to the conclusion there and then that this was a woman of singular attainments, equipped to bring out the best in him and in the firm. A week later he had introduced her into F & S as his special adviser. On that day confusion got its foot in the door. After Miss Tyson, Mr. Brundage, and Mr. Bartlett had been fired and Mr. Munson had taken his hat and stalked out, mailing in his resignation later, old Roberts had been emboldened to speak to Mr. Fitweiler. He mentioned that Mr. Munson's department had been "a little disrupted" and hadn't they perhaps better resume the old system there? Mr. Fitweiler had said certainly not. He had the greatest faith in Mrs. Barrows' ideas. "They require a little seasoning, a little seasoning, is all," he had added. Mr. Roberts had given it up. Mr. Martin reviewed in detail all the changes wrought by Mrs. Barrows. She had begun chipping at the cornices of the firm's edifice and now she was swinging at the foundation stones with a pickaxe.

Mr. Martin came now, in his summing up, to the afternoon of Monday, November 2, 1942 — just one week ago. On that day, at 3 P.M., Mrs. Barrows had bounced into his office. "Boo!" she had yelled. "Are you scraping the bottom of the pickle barrel?" Mr. Martin had looked at her from under his green eyeshade, saying nothing. She had begun to wander about the office, taking it in with her great popping eyes. "Do you really need *all* these filing cabinets?" she demanded suddenly. Mr. Martin's heart had jumped. "Each of these files," he had said, keeping his voice even, "plays an indispensable part in the system of F & S." She had brayed at him, "Well, don't tear up the pea patch!" and gone to the door. From there she had bawled, "But you sure have got a lot of fine scrap in here!" Mr. Martin could no longer doubt that the finger was on his beloved department. Her pickaxe was on the upswing, poised for the first blow. It had not come yet; he had received no blue memo from the enchanted Mr. Fitweiler bearing nonsensical instructions deriving from the obscene woman. But there was no doubt in Mr. Martin's mind that one would be forthcoming. He must act quickly. Already a precious week had gone by.

Mr. Martin stood up in his living room, still holding his milk glass. Gentlemen of the jury, he said to himself, I demand the death penalty for this horrible person.

The next day Mr. Martin followed his routine, as usual. He polished his glasses more often and once sharpened an already sharp pencil, but not even Miss Paird noticed. Only once did he catch sight of his victim; she swept past him in the hall with a patronizing "Hi!" At five-thirty he walked home, as usual, and had a glass of milk, as usual. He had never drunk anything stronger in his life — unless you could count ginger ale. The late Sam Schlosser, the S of F & S, had praised Mr. Martin at a staff meeting several years before for his temperate habits. "Our most efficient worker neither drinks nor smokes," he had said. "The results speak for themselves." Mr. Fitweiler had sat by, nodding approval.

Mr. Martin was still thinking about that red-letter day as he walked over to the Schrafft's on Fifth Avenue near Forty-Sixth Street. He got there, as he always did, at eight o'clock. He finished his dinner and the financial page of the *Sun* at a quarter to nine, as he always did. It was his custom after dinner to take a walk. This time he walked down Fifth Avenue at a casual pace. His gloved hands felt moist and warm, his forehead cold. He transferred the Camels from his overcoat to a jacket pocket. He wondered, as he did so, if they did not represent an unnecessary note of strain. Mrs. Barrows smoked only Luckies. It was his idea to puff a few puffs on a Camel (after the rubbing-out), stub it out in the ashtray holding her lipstick-stained Luckies, and thus drag a small red herring across the trail. Perhaps it was not a good idea. It would take time. He might even choke, too loudly.

Mr. Martin had never seen the house on West Twelfth Street where Mrs. Barrows lived, but he had a clear enough picture of it. Fortunately, she had bragged to everybody about her ducky first-floor apartment in the perfectly darling three-story red-brick. There could be no doorman or other attendants; just the tenants of the second and third floors. As he walked along, Mr. Martin realized that he would get there before nine-thirty. He had considered walking north on Fifth Avenue from Schrafft's to a point from which it would take him until ten o'clock to reach the house. At that hour people were less likely to be coming in or going out. But the procedure would have an awkward loop in the straight thread of his casualness, and he had abandoned it. It was impossible to figure when people would be entering or leaving the house, anyway. There was a great risk at any hour. If he ran into anybody, he would simply have to place the rubbing-out of Ulgine Barrows in the inactive file forever. The same thing would hold true if there were someone in her apartment. In that case he would just say that he had been passing by, recognized her charming house, and thought to drop in.

It was eighteen minutes after nine when Mr. Martin turned into Twelfth Street. A man passed him, and a man and a woman, talking. There was no one within fifty paces when he came to the house, halfway down the block. He was up the steps and in the small vestibule in no time, pressing the bell under the card that said "Mrs. Ulgine Barrows." When the clicking in the lock started, he jumped forward against the door. He got inside fast, closing the door behind him. A bulb in a lantern hung from the hall ceiling on a chain seemed to give a monstrously bright light. There was nobody on the stair, which went up ahead of him along the left wall. A door opened down the hall in the wall on the right. He went toward it swiftly, on tiptoe.

"Well, for God's sake, look who's here!" bawled Mrs. Barrows, and her braying laugh rang out like the report of a shotgun. He rushed past her like a football tackle, bumping her. "Hey, quit shoving!" she said, closing the door behind them. They were in her living room, which seemed to Mr. Martin to be lighted by a hundred lamps. "What's after you?" she said. "You're as jumpy as a goat." He found he was unable to speak. His heart was wheezing in his throat. "I — yes," he finally brought out. She was jabbering and laughing as she started to help him off with his coat. "No, no," he said. "I'll put it here." He took it off and put it on a chair near the door. "Your hat and gloves, too," she said. "You're in a lady's house." He put his hat on top of the coat. Mrs. Barrows seemed larger than he had thought. He kept his gloves on. "I was passing by," he said. "I recognized — is there anyone here?" She laughed louder than ever. "No," she said, "we're all alone. You're as white as a sheet, you funny man. Whatever *has* come over you? I'll mix you a toddy." She started toward a door across the room. "Scotch-and-soda be all right? But say, you don't drink, do you?" She turned and gave him her amused look. Mr. Martin pulled himself together. "Scotch-and-soda will be all right," he heard himself say. He could hear her laughing in the kitchen.

Mr. Martin looked quickly around the living room for the weapon. He had counted on finding one there. There were andirons and a poker and something in a corner that looked like an Indian club. None of them would do. It couldn't be that way. He began to pace around. He came to a desk. On it lay a metal paper knife with an ornate handle. Would it be sharp enough? He reached for it and knocked over a small brass jar. Stamps spilled out of it and it fell to the floor with a clatter. "Hey," Mrs. Barrows yelled from the kitchen, "are you tearing up the pea patch?" Mr. Martin gave a strange laugh. Picking up the knife, he tried its point against his left wrist. It was blunt. It wouldn't do.

When Mrs. Barrows reappeared, carrying two highballs, Mr. Martin, standing there with his gloves on, became acutely conscious of the fantasy he had wrought. Cigarettes in his pocket, a drink prepared for him —it was all too grossly improbable. It was more than that; it was impossible. Somewhere in the back of his mind a vague idea stirred, sprouted. "For heaven's sake, take off those gloves," said Mrs. Barrows. "I always wear them in the house," said Mr. Martin. The idea began to bloom, strange and wonderful. She put the glasses on a coffee table in front of a sofa and sat on the sofa. "Come over here, you odd little man," she said. Mr. Martin went over and sat beside her. It was difficult getting a cigarette out of the pack of Camels, but he managed it. She held a match for him, laughing. "Well," she said, handing him his drink, "this is perfectly marvelous. You with a drink and a cigarette."

Mr. Martin puffed, not too awkwardly, and took a gulp of the highball. "I drink and smoke all the time," he said. He clinked his glass against hers. "Here's nuts to that old windbag, Fitweiler," he said, and gulped again. The stuff tasted awful, but he made no grimace. "Really, Mr. Martin," she said, her voice and posture changing, "you are insulting our employer." Mrs. Barrows was now all special adviser to the president. "I am preparing a bomb," said Mr. Martin, "which will blow the old goat higher than hell." He had only had a little of the drink, which was not strong. It couldn't be that. "Do you take dope or something?" Mrs. Barrows asked coldly. "Heroin," said Mr. Martin. "I'll be coked to the gills when I bump that old buzzard off." "Mr. Martin!" she shouted, getting to her feet. "That will be all of that. You must go at once." Mr. Martin took another swallow of his drink. He tapped his cigarette out in the ashtray and put the pack of Camels on the coffee table. Then he got up. She stood glaring at him. He walked over and put on his hat and coat. "Not a word about this," he said, and laid an index finger against his lips. All Mrs. Barrows could bring out was "Really!" Mr. Martin put his hand on the doorknob. "I'm sitting in the catbird seat," he said. He stuck his tongue out at her and left. Nobody saw him go.

Mr. Martin got to his apartment, walking, well before eleven. No one saw him go in. He had two glasses of milk after brushing his teeth, and he felt elated. It wasn't tipsiness, because he hadn't been tipsy. Anyway, the walk had worn off all effects of the whiskey. He got in bed and read a magazine for a while. He was asleep before midnight.

Mr. Martin got to the office at eight-thirty the next morning, as usual. At a quarter to nine, Ulgine Barrows, who had never before arrived at work before ten, swept into his office. "I'm reporting to Mr. Fitweiler now!" she shouted. "If he turns you over to the police, it's no more than you deserve!" Mr. Martin gave her a look of shocked surprise. "I beg your pardon?" he said. Mrs. Barrows snorted and bounced out of the room, leaving Miss Paird and Joey Hart staring after her. "What's the matter with that old devil now?" asked Miss Paird. "I have no idea," said Mr. Martin, resuming his work. The other two looked at him and then at each other. Miss Paird got up and went out. She walked slowly past the closed door of Mr. Fitweiler's office. Mrs. Barrows was yelling inside, but she was not braying. Miss Paird could not hear what the woman was saying. She went back to her desk.

Forty-five minutes later, Mrs. Barrows left the president's office and went into her own, shutting the door. It wasn't until half an hour later that Mr. Fitweiler sent for Mr. Martin. The head of the filing department, neat, quiet, attentive, stood in front of the old man's desk. Mr. Fitweiler was pale and nervous. He took his glasses off and twiddled them. He made a small, bruffing sound in his throat. "Martin," he said, "you have been with us more than twenty years." "Twenty-two, sir," said Mr. Martin. "In that time," pursued the president, "your work and your — uh — manner have been exemplary." "I trust so, sir," said Mr. Martin. "I have understood, Martin," said Mr. Fitweiler, "that you have never taken a drink or smoked." "That is correct, sir," said Mr. Martin. "Ah, yes." Mr. Fitweiler polished his glasses. "You may describe what you did after leaving the office yesterday, Martin," he said. Mr. Martin allowed less than a second for his bewildered pause. "Certainly, sir," he said. "I walked home. Then I went to Schrafft's for dinner. Afterward I walked home again. I went to bed early, sir, and read a magazine for a while. I was asleep before eleven." "Ah, yes," said Mr. Fitweiler again. He was silent for a moment, searching for the proper words to say to the head of the filing department. "Mrs. Barrows," he said finally, "Mrs. Barrows has worked hard, Martin, very hard. It grieves me to report that she has suffered a severe breakdown. It has taken the form of a persecution complex accompanied by distressing hallucinations." "I am very sorry, sir," said Mr. Martin. "Mrs. Barrows is under the delusion," continued Mr. Fitweiler, "that you visited her last evening and behaved yourself in an — uh — unseemly manner." He raised his hand to silence Mr. Martin's little pained outcry. "It is the nature of these psychological diseases," Mr. Fitweiler said, "to fix upon the least likely and most innocent party as the — uh — source of persecution. These matters are not for the lay mind to grasp, Martin. I've just had my psychiatrist, Doctor Fitch, on the phone. He would not, of course, commit himself, but he made enough generalizations to substantiate my suspicions. I suggested to Mrs. Barrows, when she had completed her — uh — story to me this morning, that she visit Doctor Fitch, for I suspected a condition at once. She flew, I regret to say, into a rage, and demanded — uh — requested that I call you on the carpet. You may not know, Martin, but Mrs. Barrows had planned a reorganization of your department — subject to my approval, of course, subject to my approval. This brought you, rather than anyone else, to her mind — but again that is a phenomenon for Doctor Fitch and not for us. So, Martin, I am afraid Mrs. Barrows' usefulness here is at an end." "I am dreadfully sorry, sir," said Mr. Martin.

It was at this point that the door to the office blew open with the suddenness of a gas-main explosion and Mrs. Barrows catapulted through it. "Is the little rat denying it?" she screamed. "He can't get away with that!" Mr. Martin got up and moved discreetly to a point beside Mr. Fitweiler's chair. "You drank and smoked at my apartment," she bawled at Mr. Martin, "and you know it! You called Mr. Fitweiler an old windbag and said you were going to blow him up when you got coked to the gills on your heroin!" She stopped yelling to catch her breath and a new glint came into her popping eyes. "If you weren't such a drab, ordinary little man," she said, "I'd think you'd planned it all. Sticking your tongue out, saying you were sitting in the catbird seat, because you thought no one would believe me when I told it! My God, it's really too perfect!" She brayed loudly and hysterically, and the fury was on her again. She glared at Mr. Fitweiler. "Can't you see how he has tricked us, you old fool? Can't you see his little game?" But Mr. Fitweiler had been surreptitiously pressing all the buttons under the top of his desk and employees of F & S began pouring into the room. "Stockton," said Mr. Fitweiler, "you and Fishbein will take Mrs. Barrows to her home. Mrs. Powell, you will go with them." Stockton, who had played a little football in high school, blocked Mrs. Barrows as she made for Mr. Martin. It took him and Fishbein together to force her out of the door into the hall, crowded with stenographers and office boys. She was still screaming imprecations at Mr. Martin, tangled and contradictory imprecations. The hubbub finally died out down the corridor.

"I regret that this has happened," said Mr. Fitweiler. "I shall ask you to dismiss it from your mind, Martin. "Yes, sir," said Mr. Martin, anticipating his chief's "That will be all" by moving to the door. "I will dismiss it." He went out and shut the door, and his step was light and quick in the hall. When he entered his department he had slowed down to his customary gait, and he walked quietly across the room to the W20 file, wearing a look of studious concentration.

LIONEL TRILLING

The student in "Of This Time, Of That Place," long a widely discussed story in literary circles, is a strange and haunting figure. He has been so persistently identified as a specific famous poet that the author had to point out that, simply as a matter of dates, such identification is mistaken. Unique as he seems, there has been more than one student like him on a college campus, but it remained for Professor Trilling to do him justice in fiction.

Lionel Trilling was born in 1905 in New York City. He was professor of English at Columbia Universtiy. He was married to Diana Trilling, also a writer, and was eminent both as fiction writer and literary critic.

Of This Time, Of That Place

I

It was a fine September day. By noon it would be summer again, but now it was true autumn with a touch of chill in the air. As Joseph Howe stood on the porch of the house in which he lodged, ready to leave for his first class of the year, he thought with pleasure of the long indoor days that were coming. It was a moment when he could feel glad of his profession.

On the lawn the peach tree was still in fruit and young Hilda Aiken was taking a picture of it. She held the camera tight against her chest. She wanted the sun behind her, but she did not want her own long morning shadow in the foreground. She raised the camera, but that did not help, and she lowered it, but that made things worse. She twisted her body to the left, then to the right. In the end she had to step out of the direct line of the sun. At last she snapped the shutter and wound the film with intense care.

Howe, watching her from the porch, waited for her to finish and called good morning. She turned, startled, and almost sullenly lowered her glance. In the year Howe had lived at the Aikens', Hilda had accepted him as one of her family, but since his absence of the summer she had grown shy. Then suddenly she lifted her head and smiled at him, and the humorous smile confirmed his pleasure in the day. She picked up her bookbag and set off for school.

The handsome houses on the streets to the college were not yet fully awake, but they looked very friendly. Howe went by the Bradby house where he would be a guest this evening at the first dinner party of the year. When he had gone the length of the picket fence, the whitest in town, he turned back. Along the path there was a fine row of asters and he went through the gate and picked one for his buttonhole. The Bradbys would be pleased if they happened to see him invading their lawn and the knowledge of this made him even more comfortable.

He reached the campus as the hour was striking. The students were hurrying to their classes. He himself was in no hurry. He stopped at his dim cubicle of an office and lit a cigarette. The prospect of facing his class had suddenly presented itself to him and his hands were cold; the lawful seizure of power he was about to make seemed momentous. Waiting did not help. He put out his cigarette, picked up a pad of theme paper, and went to his classroom.

As he entered, the rattle of voices ceased, and the twenty-odd freshmen settled themselves and looked at him appraisingly. Their faces seemed gross, his heart sank at their massed impassivity, but he spoke briskly.

"My name is Howe," he said, and turned and wrote it on the blackboard. The carelessness of the scrawl confirmed his authority. He went on, "My office is 412 Slemp Hall, and my office-hours are Monday, Wednesday and Friday from eleven-thirty to twelve-thirty."

He wrote, "M., W., F., 11:30-12:30." He said, "I'll be very glad to see any of you at that time. Or if you can't come then, you can arrange with me for some other time."

He turned again to the blackboard and spoke over his shoulder. "The text for the course is Jarman's *Modern Plays,* revised edition. The Co-op has it in stock." He wrote the name, underlined "revised edition" and waited for it to be taken down in the new notebooks.

When the bent heads were raised again he began his speech of prospectus. "It is hard to explain — " he said, and paused as they composed themselves. "It is hard to explain what a course like this is intended to do. We are going to try to learn something about modern literature and something about prose composition."

As he spoke, his hands warmed and he was able to look directly at the class. Last year on the first day the faces had seemed just as cloddish, but as the term wore on they became gradually alive and quite likeable. It did not seem possible that the same thing could happen again.

"I shall not lecture in this course," he continued. "Our work will be carried on by discussion and we will try to learn by an exchange of opinion. But you will soon recognize that my opinion is worth more than anyone else's here."

He remained grave as he said it, but two boys understood and laughed. The rest took permission from them and laughed too. All Howe's private ironies protested the vulgarity of the joke, but the laughter made him feel benign and powerful.

When the little speech was finished, Howe picked up the pad of paper he had brought. He announced that they would write an extemporaneous theme. Its subject was traditional, "Who I am and why I came to Dwight College." By now the class was more at ease and it gave a ritualistic groan of protest. Then there was a stir as fountain pens were brought out and the writing arms of the chairs were cleared, and the paper was passed about. At last, all the heads bent to work, and the room became still.

Howe sat idly at his desk. The sun shone through the tall clumsy windows. The cool of the morning was already passing. There was a scent of autumn and of varnish and the stillness of the room was deep and oddly touching. Now and then a student's head was raised and scratched in the old, elaborate, students' pantomime that calls the teacher to witness honest intellectual effort.

Suddenly a tall boy stood within the frame of the open door. "Is this," he said, and thrust a large nose into a college catalogue, "is this the meeting place of English 1A? The section instructed by Dr. Joseph Howe?"

He stood on the very sill of the door, as if refusing to enter until he was perfectly sure of all his rights. The class looked up from work, found him absurd and gave a low mocking cheer.

The teacher and the new student, with equal pointedness, ignored the disturbance. Howe nodded to the boy, who pushed his head forward and then jerked it back in a wide elaborate arc to clear his brow of a heavy lock of hair. He advanced into the room and halted before Howe, almost at attention. In a loud, clear voice he announced, "I am Tertan, Ferdinand R., reporting at the direction of Head of Department Vincent."

The heraldic formality of this statement brought forth another cheer.

Howe looked at the class with a sternness he could not really feel, for there was indeed something ridiculous about this boy. Under his displeased regard the rows of heads dropped to work again. Then he touched Tertan's elbow, led him up to the desk and stood so as to shield their conversation from the class.

"We are writing an extemporaneous theme," he said. "The subject is, 'Who I am and why I came to Dwight College.'"

He stripped a few sheets from the pad and offered them to the boy. Tertan hesitated and then took the paper, but he held it only tentatively. As if with the effort of making something clear, he gulped, and a slow smile fixed itself on his face. It was at once knowing and shy.

"Professor," he said, "to be perfectly fair to my classmates" — he made a large gesture over the room — "and to you" — he inclined his head to Howe — "this would not be for me an extemporaneous subject."

Howe tried to understand. "You mean you've already thought about it — you've heard we always give the same subject? That doesn't matter."

Again the boy ducked his head and gulped. It was the gesture of one who wishes to make a difficult explanation with perfect candor. "Sir," he said, and made the distinction with great care, "the topic I did not expect, but I have given much ratiocination to the subject."

Howe smiled and said, "I don't think that's an unfair advantage. Just go ahead and write."

Tertan narrowed his eyes and glanced sidewise at Howe. His strange mouth smiled. Then in quizzical acceptance, he ducked his head, threw back the heavy, dank lock, dropped into a seat with a great loose noise and began to write rapidly.

The room fell silent again and Howe resumed his idleness. When the bell rang, the students who had groaned when the task had been set now groaned again because they had not finished. Howe took up the papers, and held the class while he made the first assignment. When he dismissed it, Tertan bore down on him, his slack mouth held ready for speech.

"Some professors," he said, "are pedants. They are Dryasdusts. However, some professors are free souls and creative spirits. Kant, Hegel and Nietzsche were all professors." With this pronouncement he paused. "It is my opinion," he continued, "that you occupy the second category."

Howe looked at the boy in surprise and said with good-natured irony, "With Kant, Hegel, and Nietzsche?"

Not only Tertan's hand and head but his whole awkward body waved away the stupidity. "It is the kind and not the quantity of the kind," he said sternly.

Rebuked, Howe said as simply and seriously as he could, "It would be nice to think so." He added, "Of course I am not a professor."

This was clearly a disappointment but Tertan met it. "In the French sense," he said with composure. "Generically, a teacher."

Suddenly he bowed. It was such a bow, Howe fancied, as a stage-director might teach an actor playing a medieval student who takes leave of Abelard — stiff, solemn, with elbows close to the body and feet to-gether. Then, quite as suddenly, he turned and left.

A queer fish, and as soon as Howe reached his office, he sifted through the batch of themes and drew out Tertan's. The boy had filled many sheets with his unformed headlong scrawl. "Who am I?" he had begun. "Here, in a mundane, not to say commercialized academe, is asked the question which from time long immemorably out of mind has accreted doubts and thoughts in the psyche of man to pester him as a nuisance. Whether in St. Augustine (or Austin as sometimes called) or Miss Bash-kirtsieff or Frederic Amiel or Empedocles, or in less lights of the intellect than these, this posed question has been ineluctable."

Howe took out his pencil. He circled "academe" and wrote "vocab." in the margin. He underlined "time long immemorably out of mind" and wrote "Diction!" But this seemed inadequate for what was wrong. He put down his pencil and read ahead to discover the principle of error in the theme. "Today as ever, in spite of gloomy prophets of the dismal sci-ence (economics) the question is uninvalidated. Out of the starry depths of heaven hurtles this spear of query demanding to be caught on the shield of the mind ere it pierces the skull and the limbs be unstrung."

Baffled but quite caught, Howe read on. "Materialism, by which is meant the philosophic concept and not the moral idea, provides no aegis against the question which lies beyond the tangible (metaphysics). Exist-ence without alloy is the question presented. Environment and heredity relegated aside, the rags and old clothes of practical life discarded, the name and the instrumentality of livelihood do not, as the prophets of the dismal science insist on in this connection, give solution to the interroga-tion which not from the professor merely but veritably from the cosmos is given. I think, therefore I am (cogito etc.) but who am I? Tertan I am, but what is Tertan? Of this time, of that place, of some parentage, what does it matter?"

Existence without alloy: the phrase established itself. Howe put aside Tertan's paper and at random picked up another. "I am Arthur J. Casebeer, Jr.," he read. "My father is Arthur J. Casebeer and my grandfather was Arthur J. Casebeer before him. My mother is Nina Wimble Casebeer. Both of them are college graduates and my father is in insurance. I was born in St. Louis eighteen years ago and we still make our residence there."

Arthur J. Casebeer, who knew who he was, was less interesting than Tertan, but more coherent. Howe picked up Tertan's paper again. It was clear that none of the routine marginal comments, no "sent. str." or "punct." or "vocab." could cope with this torrential rhetoric. He read ahead, contenting himself with underscoring the errors against the time when he should have the necessary "conference" with Tertan.

It was a busy and official day of cards and sheets, arrangements and small decisions, and it gave Howe pleasure. Even when it was time to attend the first of the weekly Convocations he felt the charm of the beginning of things when intention is still innocent and uncorrupted by effort. He sat among the young instructors on the platform, and joined in their humorous complaints at having to assist at the ceremony, but actually he got a clear satisfaction from the ritual of prayer and prosy speech, and even from wearing his academic gown. And when the Convocation was over the pleasure continued as he crossed the campus, exchanging greetings with men he had not seen since the spring. They were people who did not yet, and perhaps never would, mean much to him, but in a year they had grown amiably to be part of his life. They were his fellow-townsmen.

The day had cooled again at sunset, and there was a bright chill in the September twilight. Howe carried his voluminous gown over his arm, he swung his doctoral hood by its purple neckpiece, and on his head he wore his mortarboard with its heavy gold tassel bobbing just over his eye. These were the weighty and absurd symbols of his new profession and they pleased him. At twenty-six Joseph Howe had discovered that he was neither so well off nor so bohemian as he had once thought. A small income, adequate when supplemented by a sizable cash legacy, was genteel poverty when the cash was all spent. And the literary life — the room at the Lafayette, or the small apartment without a lease, the long summers on the Cape, the long afternoons and the social evenings — began to weary him. His writing filled his mornings and should perhaps have filled his life, yet it did not. To the amusement of his friends, and

with a certain sense that he was betraying his own freedom, he had used
the last of his legacy for a year at Harvard. The small but respectable
reputation of his two volumes of verse had proved useful — he continued
at Harvard on a fellowship and when he emerged as Doctor Howe he
received an excellent appointment, with prospects, at Dwight.

He had his moments of fear when all that had ever been said of the
dangers of the academic life had occurred to him. But after a year in
which he had tested every possibility of corruption and seduction he was
ready to rest easy. His third volume of verse, most of it written in his first
years of teaching, was not only ampler but, he thought, better than its
predecessors.

There was a clear hour before the Bradby dinner party, and Howe
looked forward to it. But he was not to enjoy it, for lying with his mail
on the hall table was a copy of this quarter's issue of *Life and Letters,* to
which his landlord subscribed. Its severe cover announced that its editor,
Frederic Woolley, had this month contributed an essay called "To
Poets," and Howe, picking it up, curious to see who the two poets might
be, felt his own name start out at him with cabalistic power — Joseph
Howe. As he continued to turn the pages his hand trembled.

Standing in the dark hall, holding the neat little magazine, Howe
knew that his literary contempt for Frederic Woolley meant nothing, for
he suddenly understood how he respected Woolley in the way of the
world. He knew this by the trembling of his hand. And of the little
world as well as the great, for although the literary groups of New York
might dismiss Woolley, his name carried high authority in the academic
world. At Dwight it was even a revered name, for it had been here at the
college that Frederic Woolley had made the distinguished scholarly career
from which he had gone on to literary journalism. In middle life he had
been induced to take the editorship of *Life and Letters,* a literary
monthly not widely read but heavily endowed, and in its pages he had
carried on the defense of what he sometimes called the older values. He
was not without wit, he had great knowledge and considerable taste, and
even in the full movement of the "new" literature he had won a certain
respect for his refusal to accept it. In France, even in England, he would
have been connected with a more robust tradition of conservatism, but
America gave him an audience not much better than genteel. It was
known in the college that to the subsidy of *Life and Letters* the Bradbys
contributed a great part.

As Howe read, he saw that he was involved in nothing less than an event. When the Fifth Series of *Studies in Order and Value* came to be collected, this latest of Frederic Woolley's essays would not be merely another step in the old direction. Clearly and unmistakably, it was a turning point. All his literary life Woolley had been concerned with the relation of literature to mortality, religion, and the private and delicate pieties, and he had been unalterably opposed to all that he had called "inhuman humanitarianism." But here, suddenly, dramatically late, he had made an about-face, turning to the public life and to the humanitarian politics he had so long despised. This was the kind of incident the histories of literature make much of. Frederick Woolley was opening for himself a new career and winning a kind of new youth. He contrasted the two poets, Thomas Wormser, who was admirable, Joseph Howe, who was almost dangerous. He spoke of the "precious subjectivism" of Howe's verse. "In times like ours," he wrote, "with millions facing penury and want, one feels that the qualities of the *tour d'ivoire* are well-nigh inhuman, nearly insulting. The *tour d'ivoire* becomes the *tour d'ivresse,* and it is not self-intoxicated poets that our people need." The essay said more: "The problem is one of meaning. I am not ignorant that the creed of the esoteric poets declares that a poem does not and should not *mean* anything, that it *is* something. But poetry is what the poet makes it, and if he is a true poet he makes what his society needs. And what is needed now is the tradition in which Mr. Wormser writes, the true tradition of poetry. The Howes do no harm, but they do no good when positive good is demanded of all responsible men. Or do the Howes indeed do no harm? Perhaps Plato would have said they do, that in some ways theirs is the Phrygian music that turns men's minds from the struggle. Certainly it is true that Thomas Wormser writes in the lucid Dorian mode which sends men into battle with evil."

It was easy to understand why Woolley had chosen to praise Thomas Wormser. The long, lilting lines of *Corn Under Willows* hymned, as Woolley put it, the struggle for wheat in the Iowa fields, and expressed the real lives of real people. But why out of the dozen more notable examples he had chosen Howe's little volume as the example of "precious subjectivism" was hard to guess. In a way it was funny, this multiplication of himself into "the Howes." And yet this becoming the multiform political symbol by whose creation Frederic Woolley gave the sign of a sudden new life, this use of him as a sacrifice whose blood was necessary for the rites of rejuvenation, made him feel oddly unclean.

Nor could Howe get rid of a certain practical resentment. As a poet he had a special and respectable place in the college life. But it might be another thing to be marked as the poet of a willful and selfish obscurity.

As he walked to the Bradbys', Howe was a little tense and defensive. It seemed to him that all the world knew of the "attack" and agreed with it. And, indeed, the Bradbys had read the essay but Professor Bradby, a kind and pretentious man, said, "I see my old friend knocked you about a bit, my boy," and his wife Eugenia looked at Howe with her childlike blue eyes and said, "I shall *scold* Frederic for the untrue things he wrote about you. You aren't the least obscure." They beamed at him. In their genial snobbery they seemed to feel that he had distinguished himself. He was the leader of Howeism. He enjoyed the dinner party as much as he had thought he would.

And in the following days, as he was more preoccupied with his duties, the incident was forgotten. His classes had ceased to be mere groups. Student after student detached himself from the mass and required or claimed a place in Howe's awareness. Of them all it was Tertan who first and most violently signaled his separate existence. A week after classes had begun Howe saw his silhouette on the frosted glass of his office door. It was motionless for a long time, perhaps stopped by the problem of whether or not to knock before entering. Howe called, "Come in!" and Tertan entered with his shambling stride.

He stood beside the desk, silent and at attention. When Howe asked him to sit down, he responded with a gesture of head and hand, as if to say that such amenities were beside the point. Nevertheless, he did take the chair. He put his ragged, crammed briefcase between his legs. His face, which Howe now observed fully for the first time, was confusing, for it was made up of florid curves, the nose arched in the bone and voluted in the nostril, the mouth loose and soft and rather moist. Yet the face was so thin and narrow as to seem the very type of asceticism. Lashes of unusual length veiled the eyes and, indeed, it seemed as if there were a veil over the whole countenance. Before the words actually came, the face screwed itself into an attitude of preparation for them.

"You can confer with me now?" Tertan said.

"Yes, I'd be glad to. There are several things in your two themes I want to talk to you about." Howe reached for the packet of themes on his desk and sought for Tertan's. But the boy was waving them away.

"These are done perforce," he said. "Under the pressure of your requirement. They are not significant; mere duties." Again his great hand flapped vaguely to dismiss his themes. He leaned forward and gazed at his teacher.

"You are," he said, "a man of letters? You are a poet?" It was more declaration than question.

"I should like to think so," Howe said.

At first Tertan accepted the answer with a show of appreciation, as though the understatement made a secret between himself and Howe. Then he chose to misunderstand. With his shrewd and disconcerting control of expression, he presented to Howe a puzzled grimace. "What does that mean?" he said.

Howe retracted the irony. "Yes. I am a poet." It sounded strange to say.

"That," Tertain said, "is a wonder." He corrected himself with his ducking head. "I mean that is wonderful."

Suddenly, he dived at the miserable briefcase between his legs, put it on his knees, and began to fumble with the catch, all intent on the difficulty it presented. Howe noted that his suit was worn thin, his shirt almost unclean. He became aware, even, of a vague and musty odor of garments worn too long in unaired rooms. Tertan conquered the lock and began to concentrate upon a search into the interior. At last he held in his hand what he was after, a torn and crumpled copy of *Life and Letters*.

"I learned it from here," he said, holding it out.

Howe looked at him sharply, his hackles a little up. But the boy's face was not only perfectly innocent, it even shone with a conscious admiration. Apparently nothing of the import of the essay had touched him except the wonderful fact that his teacher was a "man of letters." Yet this seemed too stupid, and Howe, to test it, said, "The man who wrote that doesn't think it's wonderful."

Tertan made a moist hissing sound as he cleared his mouth of saliva. His head, oddly loose on his neck, wove a pattern of contempt in the air. "A critic," he said, "who admits *prima facie* that he does not understand." Then he said grandly, "It is the inevitable fate."

It was absurd, yet Howe was not only aware of the absurdity but of a tension suddenly and wonderfully relaxed. Now that the "attack" was on the table between himself and this strange boy, and subject to the boy's funny and absolutely certain contempt, the hidden force of his feeling was revealed to him in the very moment that it vanished. All unsuspected, there had been a film over the world, a transparent but discoloring haze of danger. But he had no time to stop over the brightened aspect of things. Tertan was going on. "I also am a man of letters. Putative."

"You have written a good deal?" Howe meant to be no more than polite, and he was surprised at the tenderness he heard in his words.

Solemnly the boy nodded, threw back the dank lock, and sucked in a deep, anticipatory breath. "First, a work of homiletics, which is a defense of the principles of religious optimism against the pessimism of Schopen-hauer and the humanism of Nietzsche."

"Humanism? Why do you call it humanism?"

"It is my nomenclature for making a deity of man," Tertan replied negligently. "Then three fictional works, novels. And numerous essays in science, combating materialism. Is it your duty to read these if I bring them to you?"

Howe answered simply, "No, it isn't exactly my duty, but I shall be happy to read them."

Tertan stood up and remained silent. He rested his bag on the chair. With a certain compunction — for it did not seem entirely proper that, of two men of letters, one should have the right to blue-pencil the other, to grade him or to question the quality of his "sentence structure" — Howe reached for Tertan's papers. But before he could take them up, the boy suddenly made his bow-to-Abelard, the stiff inclination of the body with the hands seeming to emerge from the scholar's gown. Then he was gone.

But after his departure something was still left of him. The timbre of his curious sentences, the downright finality of so quaint a phrase as "It is the inevitable fate" still rang in the air. Howe gave the warmth of his feeling to the new visitor who stood at the door announcing himself with a genteel clearing of the throat.

"Doctor Howe, I believe?" the student said. A large hand advanced into the room and grasped Howe's hand. "Blackburn, sir, Theodore Blackburn, vice-president of the Student Council. A great pleasure, sir."

Out of a pair of ruddy cheeks a pair of small eyes twinkled good-naturedly. The large face, the large body were not so much fat as beefy and suggested something "typical" — monk, politician, or innkeeper.

Blackburn took the seat beside Howe's desk. "I may have seemed to introduce myself in my public capacity, sir," he said. "But it is really as an individual that I came to see you. That is to say, as one of your students to be."

He spoke with an English intonation and he went on, "I was once an English major, sir."

For a moment Howe was startled, for the roast-beef look of the boy and the manner of his speech gave a second's credibility to one sense of his statement. Then the collegiate meaning of the phrase asserted itself, but some perversity made Howe say what was not really in good taste even with so forward a student, "Indeed? What regiment?"

Blackburn stared and then gave a little pouf-pouf of laughter. He waved the misapprehesion away. "*Very* good, sir. It certainly is an ambiguous term." He chuckled in appreciation of Howe's joke, then cleared his throat to put it aside. "I look forward to taking your course in the romantic poets, sir," he said earnestly. "To me the romantic poets are the very crown of English literature."

Howe made a dry sound, and the boy, catching some meaning in it, said, "Little as I know them, of course. But even Shakespeare who is so dear to us of the Anglo-Saxon tradition is in a sense but the preparation for Shelley, Keats and Byron. And Wadsworth."

Almost sorry for him, Howe dropped his eyes. With some embarrassment, for the boy was not actually his student, he said softly, "Wordsworth."

"Sir?"

"Wordsworth, not Wadsworth. You said Wadsworth."

"Did I, sir?" Gravely he shook his head to rebuke himself for the error. "Wordsworth, of course — slip of the tongue." Then, quite in command again, he went on. "I have a favor to ask of you, Doctor Howe. You see, I began my college course as an English major," — he smiled — "as I said."

"Yes?"

"But after my first year I shifted. I shifted to the social sciences. Sociology and government — I find them stimulating and very *real*." He paused, out of respect for reality. "But now I find that perhaps I have neglected the other side."

"The other side?" Howe said.

"Imagination, fancy, culture. A well-rounded man." He trailed off as if there were perfect understanding between them. "And so, sir, I have decided to end my senior year with your course in the romantic poets."

His voice was filled with an indulgence which Howe ignored as he said flatly and gravely, "But that course isn't given until the spring term."

"Yes, sir, and that is where the favor comes in. Would you let me take your romantic prose course? I can't take it for credit, sir, my program is full, but just for background it seems to me that I ought to take it. I do hope," he concluded in a manly way, "that you will consent."

"Well, it's no great favor, Mr. Blackburn. You can come if you wish, though there's not much point in it if you don't do the reading."

The bell rang for the hour and Howe got up.

"May I begin with this class, sir?" Blackburn's smile was candid and boyish.

Howe nodded carelessly and together, silently, they walked to the class-room down the hall. When they reached the door Howe stood back to let his student enter, but Blackburn moved adroitly behind him and grasped him by the arm to urge him over the threshold. They entered together with Blackburn's hand firmly on Howe's biceps, the student inducting the teacher into his own room. Howe felt a surge of temper rise in him and almost violently he disengaged his arm and walked to the desk, while Blackburn found a seat in the front row and smiled at him.

II

The question was, At whose door must the tragedy be laid?

All night the snow had fallen heavily and only now was abating in sparse little flurries. The windows were valanced high with white. It was very quiet; something of the quiet of the world had reached the class, and Howe found that everyone was glad to talk or listen. In the room there was a comfortable sense of pleasure in being human.

Casebeer believed that the blame for the tragedy rested with heredity. Picking up the book he read, "The sins of the fathers are visited on their children." This opinion was received with general favor. Nevertheless, Johnson ventured to say that the fault was all Pastor Manders' because the Pastor had made Mrs. Alving go back to her husband and was always hiding the truth. To this Hibbard objected with logic enough, "Well then, it was really all her husband's fault. He *did* all the bad things." De Witt, his face bright with an impatient idea, said that the fault was all society's. "By society I don't mean upper-crust society," he said. He looked around a little defiantly, taking in any members of the class who might be members of upper-crust society. "Not in that sense. I mean the social unit."

Howe nodded and said, "Yes, of course."

"If the society of the time had progressed far enough in science," De

Witt went on, "then there would be no problem for Mr. Ibsen to write about. Captain Alving plays around a little, gives way to perfectly natural biological urges, and he gets a social disease, a venereal disease. If the disease is cured, no problem. Invent salvarsan and the disease is cured. The problem of heredity disappears and li'l Oswald just doesn't get paresis. No paresis, no problem — no problem, no play."

This was carrying the ark into battle, and the class looked at De Witt with respectful curiosity. It was his usual way and on the whole they were sympathetic with his struggle to prove to Howe that science was better than literature. Still, there was something in his reckless manner that alienated them a little.

"Or take birth-control, for instance," De Witt went on. "If Mrs. Alving had some knowledge of contraception, she wouldn't have had to have li'l Oswald at all. No li'l Oswald, no play."

The class was suddenly quieter. In the back row Stettenhover swung his great football shoulders in a righteous sulking gesture, first to the right, then to the left. He puckered his mouth ostentatiously. Intellect was always ending up by talking dirty.

Tertan's hand went up, and Howe said, "Mr. Tertan." The boy shambled to his feet and began his long characteristic gulp. Howe made a motion with his fingers, as small as possible, and Tertan ducked his head and smiled in apology. He sat down. The class laughed. With more than half the term gone, Tertan had not been able to remember that one did not rise to speak. He seemed unable to carry on the life of the intellect without this mark of respect for it. To Howe the boy's habit of rising seemed to accord with the formal shabbiness of his dress. He never wore the casual sweaters and jackets of his classmates. Into the free and comfortable air of the college classroom he brought the stuffy sordid strictness of some crowded, metropolitan high school.

"Speaking from one sense," Tertan began slowly, "there is no blame ascribable. From the sense of determinism, who can say where the blame lies? The preordained is the preordained and it cannot be said without rebellion against the universe, a palpable absurdity."

In the back row Stettenhover slumped suddenly in his seat, his heels held out before him, making a loud, dry, disgusted sound. His body sank until his neck rested on the back of his chair. He folded his hands across his belly and looked significantly out of the window, exasperated not only with Tertan, but with Howe, with the class, with the whole system designed to encourage this kind of thing. There was a certain insolence in the movement and Howe flushed. As Tertan continued to speak, Howe stalked casually toward the window and placed himself in the line of Stettenhover's vision. He stared at the great fellow, who pretended not to see him. There was so much power in the big body, so much contempt in the Greek-athlete face under the crisp Greek-athlete curls, that Howe felt almost physical fear. But at last Stettenhover admitted him to focus and under his disapproving gaze sat up with slow indifference. His eyebrows raised high in resignation, he began to examine his hands. Howe relaxed and turned his attention back to Tertan.

"Flux of existence," Tertan was saying, "produces all things, so that judgment wavers. Beyond the phenomena, what? But phenomena are adumbrated and to them we are limited."

Howe saw it for a moment as perhaps it existed in the boy's mind — the world of shadows which are cast by a great light upon a hidden reality as in the old myth of the Cave. But the little brush with Stettenhover had tired him, and he said irritably, "But come to the point, Mr. Tertan."

He said it so sharply that some of the class looked at him curiously. For three months he had gently carried Tertan through his verbosities, to the vaguely respectful surprise of the other students, who seemed to conceive that there existed between this strange classmate and their teacher some special understanding from which they were content to be excluded. Tertan looked at him mildly, and at once came brilliantly to the point. "This is the summation of the play," he said and took up his book and read, "'Your poor father never found any outlet for the overmastering joy of life that was in him. And I brought no holiday into his home, either. Everything seemed to turn upon duty and I am afraid I made your poor father's home unbearable to him, Oswald.' Spoken by Mrs. Alving."

Yes, that was surely the "summation" of the play and Tertan had hit it, as he hit, deviously and eventually, the literary point of almost everything. But now, as always, he was wrapping it away from sight. "For most mortals," he said, "there are only joys of biological urgings, gross and crass, such as the sensuous Captain Alving. For certain few there are the transmutations beyond these to a contemplation of the utter whole."

Oh, the boy was mad. And suddenly the word, used in hyperbole, intended almost for the expression of exasperated admiration, became literal. Now that the word was used, it became simply apparent to Howe that Tertan was mad.

It was a monstrous word and stood like a bestial thing in the room. Yet it so completely comprehended everything that had puzzled Howe, it so arranged and explained what for three months had been perplexing him that almost at once its horror became domesticated. With this word Howe was able to understand why he had never been able to communicate to Tertan the value of a single criticism or correction of his wild, verbose themes. Their conferences had been frequent and long but had done nothing to reduce to order the splendid confusion of the boy's ideas. Yet, impossible though its expression was, Tertan's incandescent mind could always strike for a moment into some dark corner of thought.

And now it was suddenly apparent that it was not a faulty rhetoric that Howe had to contend with. With his new knowledge he looked at Tertan's face and wondered how he could have so long deceived himself. Tertan was still talking, and the class had lapsed into a kind of patient unconsciousness, a coma of respect for words which, for all that most of them knew, might be profound. Almost with a suffusion of shame, Howe believed that in some dim way the class had long ago had some intimation of Tertan's madness. He reached out as decisively as he could to seize the thread of Tertan's discourse before it should be entangled further.

"Mr. Tertan says that the blame must be put upon whoever kills the joy of living in another. We have been assuming that Captain Alving was a wholly bad man, but what if we assume that he became bad only because Mrs. Alving, when they were first married, acted toward him in the prudish way she says she did?"

It was a ticklish idea to advance to freshmen and perhaps not profitable. Not all of them were following.

"That would put the blame on Mrs. Alving herself, whom most of you admire. And she herself seems to think so." He glanced at his watch. The hour was nearly over. "What do you think, Mr. De Witt?"

De Witt rose to the idea; he wanted to know if society couldn't be blamed for educating Mrs. Alving's temperament in the wrong way. Casebeer was puzzled, Stettenhover continued to look at his hands until the bell rang.

Tertan, his brows louring in thought, was making as always for a private word. Howe gathered his books and papers to leave quickly. At this moment of his discovery and with the knowledge still raw, he could not engage himself with Tertan. Tertan sucked in his breath to prepare for speech and Howe made ready for the pain and confusion. But at that

moment Casebeer detached himself from the group with which he had
been conferring and which he seemed to represent. His constituency
remained at a tactful distance. The mission involved the time of an
assigned essay. Casebeer's presentation of the plea — it was based on the
freshmen's heavy duties at the fraternities during Carnival Week — cut
across Tertan's preparations for speech. "And so some of us fellows
thought," Casebeer concluded with heavy solemnity, "that we could do a
better job, give our minds to it more, if we had more time."

Tertan regarded Casebeer with mingled curiosity and revulsion. Howe
not only said that he would postpone the assignment but went on to talk
about the Carnival, and even drew the waiting constituency into the
conversation. He was conscious of Tertan's stern and astonished stare,
then of his sudden departure.

Now that the fact was clear, Howe knew that he must act on it. His
course was simple enough. He must lay the case before the Dean. Yet he
hesitated. His feeling for Tertan must now, certainly, be in some way
invalidated. Yet could he, because of a word, hurry to assign to official
and reasonable solicitude what had been, until this moment, so various
and warm? He could at least delay and, by moving slowly, lend a poor
grace to the neccessary, ugly act of making his report.

It was with some notion of keeping the matter in his own hands that
he went to the Dean's office to look up Tertan's records. In the outer
office the Dean's secretary greeted him brightly, and at his request
brought him the manila folder with the small identifying photograph
pasted in the corner. She laughed. "He was looking for the birdie in the
wrong place," she said.

Howe leaned over her shoulder to look at the picture. It was as bad as
all the Dean's-office photographs were, but it differed from all that Howe
had ever seen. Tertan, instead of looking into the camera, as no doubt he
had been bidden, had, at the moment of exposure, turned his eyes
upward. His mouth, as though conscious of the trick played on the photographer, had the sly superior look that Howe knew.

The secretary was fascinated by the picture. "What a funny boy," she
said. "He looks like Tartuffe!"

And so he did, with the absurd piety of the eyes and the conscious
slyness of the mouth and the whole face bloated by the bad lens.

"Is he *like* that?" the secretary said.

"Like Tartuffe? No."

From the photograph there was little enough comfort to be had. The records themselves gave no clue to madness, though they suggested sad-ness enough. Howe read of a father, Stanislaus Tertan, born in Budapest and trained in engineering in Berlin, once employed by the Hercules Chemical Corporation — this was one of the factories that dominated the sound end of the town — but now without employment. He read of a mother Erminie (Youngfellow) Tertan, born in Manchester, educated at a Normal School at Leeds, now housewife by profession. The family lived on Greenbriar Street which Howe knew as a row of once elegant homes near what was now the factory district. The old mansion had long ago been divided into small and primitive apartments. Of Ferdinand himself there was little to learn. He lived with his parents, had attended a Detroit high school and had transferred to the local school in his last year. His rating for intelligence, as expressed in numbers, was high, his scholastic record was remarkable, he held a college scholarship for his tuition.

Howe laid the folder on the secretary's desk. "Did you find what you wanted to know?" she asked.

The phrases from Tertan's momentous first theme came back to him. "Tertan I am, but what is Tertan? Of this time, of that place, of some parentage, what does it matter?"

"No, I didn't find it," he said.

Now that he had consulted the sad, half-meaningless record he knew all the more firmly that he must not give the matter out of his own hands. He must not release Tertan to authority. Not that he anticipated from the Dean anything but the greatest kindness for Tertan. The Dean would have the experience and skill which he himself could not have. One way or another the Dean could answer the question, "What is Tertan?" Yet this was precisely what he feared. He alone could keep alive — not forever but for a somehow important time — the question, "What is Tertan?" He alone could keep it still a question. Some sure instinct told him that he must not surrender the question to a clean official desk in a clear official light to be dealt with, settled and closed.

He heard himself saying, "Is the Dean busy at the moment? I'd like to see him."

His request came thus unbidden, even forbidden, and it was one of the surprising and startling incidents of his life. Later when he reviewed the events, so disconnected in themselves, or so merely odd, of the story that unfolded for him that year, it was over this moment, on its face the least notable, that he paused longest. It was frequently to be with fear and never without a certainty of its meaning in his own knowledge of himself that he would recall this simple, routine request, and the feeling of shame and freedom it gave him as he sent everything down the official chute. In the end, of course, no matter what he did to "protect" Tertan, he would have had to make the same request and lay the matter on the Dean's clean desk. But it would always be a landmark of his life that, at the very moment when he was rejecting the official way, he had been, without will or intention, so gladly drawn to it.

After the storm's last delicate flurry, the sun had come out. Reflected by the new snow, it filled the office with a golden light which was almost musical in the way it made all the commonplace objects of efficiency shine with a sudden sad and noble significance. And the light, now that he noticed it, made the utterance of his perverse and unwanted request even more momentous.

The secretary consulted the engagement pad. "He'll be free any minute. Don't you want to wait in the parlor?"

She threw open the door of the large and pleasant room in which the Dean held his Committee meetings, and in which his visitors waited. It was designed with a homely elegance on the masculine side of the eighteenth-century manner. There was a small coal fire in the grate and the handsome mahogany table was strewn with books and magazines. The large windows gave on the snowy lawn, and there was such a fine width of window that the white casements and walls seemed at this moment but a continuation of the snow, the snow but an extension of casement and walls. The outdoors seemed taken in and made safe, the indoors seemed luxuriously freshened and expanded.

Howe sat down by the fire and lighted a cigarette. The room had its intended effect upon him. He felt comfortable and relaxed, yet nicely organized, some young diplomatic agent of the eighteenth century, the newly fledged Swift carrying out Sir William Temple's business. The rawness of Tertan's case quite vanished. He crossed his legs and reached for a magazine.

It was that famous issue of *Life and Letters* that his idle hand had found and his blood raced as he sifted through it, and the shape of his own name, Joseph Howe, sprang out at him, still cabalistic in its power. He tossed the magazine back on the table as the door of the Dean's office opened and the Dean ushered out Theodore Blackburn.

"Ah, Joseph!" the Dean said.

Blackburn said, "Good morning, Doctor." Howe winced at the title and caught the flicker of amusement over the Dean's face. The Dean stood with his hand high on the door-jamb and Blackburn, still in the doorway, remained standing almost under his long arm.

Howe nodded briefly to Blackburn, snubbing his eager deference. "Can you give me a few minutes?" he said to the Dean.

"All the time you want. Come in." Before the two men could enter the office, Blackburn claimed their attention with a long full "Er." As they turned to him, Blackburn said, "Can *you* give *me* a few minutes, Doctor Howe?" His eyes sparkled at the little audacity he had committed, the slightly impudent play with hierarchy. Of the three of them Blackburn kept himself the lowest, but he reminded Howe of his subaltern relation to the Dean.

"I mean, of course," Blackburn went on easily, "when you've finished with the Dean."

"I'll be in my office shortly," Howe said, turned his back on the ready "Thank you, sir," and followed the Dean into the inner room.

"Energetic boy," said the Dean. "A bit beyond himself but very energetic. Sit down."

The Dean lighted a cigarette, leaned back in his chair, sat easy and silent for a moment, giving Howe no signal to go ahead with business. He was a young Dean, not much beyond forty, a tall handsome man with sad, ambitious eyes. He had been a Rhodes scholar. His friends looked for great things from him, and it was generally said that he had notions of education which he was not yet ready to try to put into practice.

His relaxed silence was meant as a compliment to Howe. He smiled and said, "What's the business, Joseph?"

"Do you know Tertan — Ferdinand Tertan, a freshman?"

The Dean's cigarette was in his mouth and his hands were clasped behind his head. He did not seem to search his memory for the name. He said, "What about him?"

Clearly the Dean knew something, and he was waiting for Howe to tell him more. Howe moved only tentatively. Now that he was doing what he had resolved not to do, he felt more guilty at having been so long deceived by Tertan and more need to be loyal to his error.

"He's a strange fellow," he ventured. He said stubbornly, "In a strange way he's very brilliant." He concluded, "But very strange."

The springs of the Dean's swivel chair creaked as he came out of his sprawl and leaned forward to Howe. "Do you mean he's so strange that it's something you could give a name to?"

Howe looked at him stupidly. "What do you mean?" he said.

"What's his trouble?" the Dean said more neutrally.

"He's very brilliant, in a way. I looked him up and he has a top intelligence rating. But somehow, and it's hard to explain just how, what he says is always on the edge of sense and doesn't quite make it."

The Dean looked at him and Howe flushed up. The Dean had surely read Woolley on the subject of "the Howes" and the *tour d'ivresse*. Was that quick glance ironical?

The Dean picked up some papers from his desk, and Howe could see that they were in Tertan's impatient scrawl. Perhaps the little gleam in the Dean's glance had come only from putting facts together.

He sent me this yesterday," the Dean said. "After an interview I had with him. I haven't been able to do more than glance at it. When you said what you did, I realized there was something wrong."

Twisting his mouth, the Dean looked over the letter. "You seem to be involved," he said without looking up. "By the way, what did you give him at mid-term?"

Flushing, setting his shoulders, Howe said firmly, "I gave him A-minus."

The Dean chuckled. "Might be a good idea if some of our nicer boys went crazy — just a little." He said, "Well," to conclude the matter and handed the papers to Howe. "See if this is the same thing you've been finding. Then we can go into the matter again."

Before the fire in the parlor, in the chair that Howe had been occupying, sat Blackburn. He sprang to his feet as Howe entered.

"I said my office, Mr. Blackburn." Howe's voice was sharp. Then he was almost sorry for the rebuke, so clearly and naïvely did Blackburn seem to relish his stay in the parlor, close to authority.

"I'm in a bit of a hurry, sir," he said, "and I did want to be sure to speak to you, sir."

He was really absurd, yet fifteen years from now he would have grown up to himself, to the assurance and mature beefiness. In banks, in consular offices, in brokerage firms, on the bench, more seriously affable, a little sterner, he would make use of his ability to be administered by his job. It was almost reassuring. Now he was exercising his too-great skill on Howe. "I owe you an apology, sir," he said.

Howe knew that he did, but he showed surprise.

"I mean, Doctor, after your having been so kind about letting me attend your class, I stopped coming." He smiled in deprecation. "Extra-curricular activities take up so much of my time. I'm afraid I undertook more than I could perform."

Howe had noticed the absence and had been a little irritated by it after Blackburn's elaborate plea. It was an absence that might be interpreted as a comment on the teacher. But there was only one way for him to answer. "You've no need to apologize," he said. "It's wholly your affair."

Blackburn beamed. "I'm so glad you feel that way about it, sir. I was worried you might think I had stayed away because I was influenced by —— " He stopped and lowered his eyes.

Astonished, Howe said, "Influenced by what?"

"Well, by —— " Blackburn hesitated and for answer pointed to the table on which lay the copy of *Life and Letters*. Without looking at it, he knew where to direct his hand. "By the unfavorable publicity, sir." He hurried on. "And that brings me to another point, sir. I am vice-president of Quill and Scroll, sir, the student literary society, and I wonder if you would address us. You could read your own poetry, sir, and defend your own point of view. It would be very interesting."

It was truly amazing. Howe looked long and cruelly into Blackburn's face, trying to catch the secret of the mind that could have conceived this way of manipulating him, this way so daring and inept — but not en-tirely inept — with its malice so without malignity. The face did not yield its secret. Howe smiled broadly and said, "Of course I don't think you were influenced by the unfavorable publicity."

"I'm still going to take — regularly, for credit — your romantic poets course next term," Blackburn said.

"Don't worry, my dear fellow, don't worry about it."

Howe started to leave and Blackburn stopped him with, "But about Quill, sir?"

"Suppose we wait until next term? I'll be less busy then."

And Blackburn said, "Very good, sir, and thank you."

In his office the little encouter seemed less funny to Howe, was even in some indeterminate way disturbing. He made an effort to put it from his mind by turning to what was sure to disturb him more, the Tertan letter read in the new interpretation. He found what he had always found, the same florid leaps beyond fact and meaning, the same headlong certainty.

But as his eye passed over the familiar scrawl it caught his own name, and for the second time that hour he felt the race of his blood.

"The Paraclete," Tertan had written to the Dean, "from a Greek word meaning to stand in place of, but going beyond the primitive idea to mean traditionally the helper, the one who comforts and assists, cannot without fundamental loss be jettisoned. Even if taken no longer in the supernatural sense, the concept remains deeply in the human consciousness inevitably. Humanitarianism is no reply, for not every man stands in the place of every other man for this other comrade's comfort. But certain are chosen out of the human race to be the consoler of some other. Of these, for example, is Joseph Barker Howe, Ph.D. Of intellects not the first yet of true intellect and lambent instructions, given to that which is intuitive and irrational, not to what is logical in the strict word, what is judged by him is of the heart and not the head. Here is one chosen, in that he chooses himself to stand in the place of another for comfort and consolation. To him more than another I give my gratitude, with all respect to our Dean who reads this, a noble man, but merely dedicated, not consecrated. But not in the aspect of the Paraclete only is Dr. Joseph Barker Howe established, for he must be the Paraclete to another aspect of himself, that which is driven and persecuted by the lack of understanding in the world at large, so that he in himself embodies the full history of man's tribulations and, overflowing upon others, notably the present writer, is the ultimate end."

This was love. There was no escape from it. Try as Howe might to remember that Tertan was mad and all his emotions invalidated, he could not destroy the effect upon him of his student's stern, affectionate regard. He had betrayed not only a power of mind but a power of love. And, however firmly he held before his attention the fact of Tertan's madness, he could do nothing to banish the physical sensation of gratitude he felt. He had never thought of himself as "driven and persecuted" and he did not now. But still he could not make meaningless his sensation of gratitude. The pitiable Tertan sternly pitied him, and comfort came from Tertan's never-to-be-comforted mind.

III

In an academic community, even an efficient one, official matters move slowly. The term drew to a close with no action in the case of Tertan, and Joseph Howe had to confront a curious problem. How should he grade his strange student, Tertan?

Tertan's final examination had been no different from all his other writing, and what did one "give" such a student? De Witt must have his A, that was clear. Johnson would get a B. With Casebeer it was a question of a B-minus or a C-plus, and Stettenhover, who had been crammed by the team tutor to fill half a blue-book with his thin feminine scrawl, would have his C-minus which he would accept with mingled indifference and resentment. But with Tertan it was not so easy.

The boy was still in the college process and his name could not be omitted from the grade sheet. Yet what should a mind under suspicion of madness be graded? Until the medical verdict was given, it was for Howe to continue as Tertan's teacher and to keep his judgment pedagogical. Impossible to give him an F: he had not failed. B was for Johnson's stolid mediocrity. He could not be put on the edge of passing with Stettenhover, for he exactly did not pass. In energy and richness of intellect he was perhaps even De Witt's superior, and Howe toyed grimly with the notion of giving him an A, but that would lower the value of the A De Witt had won with his beautiful and clear, if still arrogant, mind. There was a notation which the Registrar recognized — Inc. for Incomplete, and in the horrible comedy of the situation, Howe considered that. But really only a mark of M for Mad would serve.

In his perplexity, Howe sought the Dean, but the Dean was out of town. In the end, he decided to maintain the A-minus he had given Tertan at mid-term. After all, there had been no falling away from that quality. He entered it on the grade sheet with something like bravado.

Academic time moves quickly. A college year is not really a year, lacking as it does three months. And it is endlessly divided into units which, at their beginning, appear larger than they are — terms, half-terms, months, weeks. And the ultimate unit, the hour, is not really an hour, lacking as it does ten minutes. And so the new term advanced rapidly, and one day the fields about the town were all brown, cleared of even the few thin patches of snow which had lingered so long.

Howe, as he lectured on the romantic poets, became conscious of Blackburn emanating wrath. Blackburn did it well, did it with enormous dignity. He did not stir in his seat, he kept his eyes fixed on Howe in perfect attention, but he abstained from using his notebook, there was no mistaking what he proposed to himself as an attitude. His elbow on the writing-wing of the chair, his chin on the curled fingers of his hand, he was the embodiment of intellectual indignation. He was thinking his own thoughts, would give no public offense, yet would claim his due, was not to be intimidated. Howe knew that he would present himself at the end of the hour.

Blackburn entered the office without invitation. He did not smile; there was no cajolery about him. Without invitation he sat down beside Howe's desk. He did not speak until he had taken the blue-book from his pocket. He said, "What does this mean, sir?"

It was a sound and conservative student tactic. Said in the usual way it meant, "How could you have so misunderstood me?" or "What does this mean for my future in the course?" But there were none of the humbler tones in Blackburn's way of saying it.

Howe made the established reply, "I think that's for you to tell me."

Blackburn continued icy. "I'm sure I can't, sir."

There was a silence between them. Both dropped their eyes to the blue-book on the desk. On its cover Howe had penciled: "F: This is very poor work."

Howe picked up the blue-book. There was always the possibility of injustice. The teacher may be bored by the mass of papers and not wholly attentive. A phrase, even the student's handwriting, may irritate him unreasonably. "Well," said Howe, "let's go through it."

He opened the first page. "Now here: you write, 'In *The Ancient Mariner,* Coleridge lives in and transports us to a honey-sweet world where all is rich and strange, a world of charm to which we can escape from the humdrum existence of our daily lives, the world of romance. Here, in this warm and honey-sweet land of charming dreams we can relax and enjoy ourselves.'"

Howe lowered the paper and waited with a neutral look for Blackburn to speak. Blackburn returned the look boldly, did not speak, sat stolid and lofty. At last Howe said, speaking gently, "Did you mean that, or were you just at a loss for something to say?"

"You imply that I was just 'bluffing'?" The quotation marks hung palpable in the air about the word.

"I'd like to know. I'd prefer believing that you were bluffing to believing that you really thought this."

Blackburn's eyebrows went up. From the height of a great and firm-based idea he looked at his teacher. He clasped the crags for a moment and then pounced, craftily, suavely. "Do you mean, Doctor Howe, that there aren't two opinions possible?"

It was superbly done in its air of putting all of Howe's intellectual life into the balance. Howe remained patient and simple. "Yes, many opinions are possible, but not this one. Whatever anyone believes of *The Ancient Mariner*, no one can in reason believe that it represents a — a honey-sweet world in which we can relax."

"But that is what I *feel*, sir."

This was well-done, too. Howe said, "Look, Mr. Blackburn. Do you really relax with hunger and thirst, the heat and the sea-serpents, the dead men with staring eyes, Life in Death and the skeletons? Come now, Mr. Blackburn."

Blackburn made no answer, and Howe pressed forward. "Now, you say of Wordsworth, 'Of peasant stock himself, he turned from the effete life of the salons and found in the peasant the hope of a flaming revolution which would sweep away all the old ideas. This is the subject of his best poems.' "

Beaming at his teacher with youthful eagerness, Blackburn said, "Yes, sir, a rebel, a bringer of light to suffering mankind. I see him as a kind of Prothemeus."

"A kind of what?"

"Prothemeus, sir."

"Think, Mr. Blackburn. We were talking about him only today and I mentioned his name a dozen times. You don't mean Prothemeus. You mean — " Howe waited, but there was no response.

"You mean Prometheus."

Blackburn gave no assent, and Howe took the reins. "You've done a bad job here, Mr. Blackburn, about as bad as could be done." He saw Blackburn stiffen and his genial face harden again. "It shows either a lack of preparation or a complete lack of understanding." He saw Blackburn's face begin to go to pieces and he stopped.

"Oh, sir," Blackburn burst out, "I've never had a mark like this before, never anything below a B, never. A thing like this has never happened to me before."

It must be true, it was a statement too easily verified. Could it be that other instructors accepted such flaunting nonsense? Howe wanted to end the interview. "I'll set it down to lack of preparation," he said. "I know you're busy. That's not an excuse, but it's an explanation. Now, suppose you really prepare, and then take another quiz in two weeks. We'll forget this one and count the other."

Blackburn squirmed with pleasure and gratitude. "Thank you, sir. You're really very kind, very kind."

Howe rose to conclude the visit. "All right, then — in two weeks."

It was that day that the Dean imparted to Howe the conclusion of the case of Tertan. It was simple and a little anti-climactic. A physician had been called in, and had said the word, given the name.

"A classic case, he called it," the Dean said. "Not a doubt in the world," he said. His eyes were full of miserable pity, and he clutched at a word. "A classic case, a classic case." To his aid and to Howe's there came the Parthenon and the form of the Greek drama, the Aristotelian logic, Racine and the Well-Tempered Clavichord, the blueness of the Aegean and its clear sky. Classic — that is to say, without a doubt, perfect in its way, a veritable model, and, as the Dean had been told, sure to take a perfectly predictable and inevitable course to a foreknown conclusion.

It was not only pity that stood in the Dean's eyes. For a moment there was fear too. "Terrible," he said, "it is simply terrible."

Then he went on briskly. "Naturally, we've told the boy nothing. And, naturally, we won't. His tuition's paid by his scholarship, and we'll continue him on the rolls until the end of the year. That will be kindest. After that the matter will be out of our control. We'll see, of course, that he gets into the proper hands. I'm told there will be no change, he'll go on like this, be as good as this, for four to six months. And so we'll just go along as usual."

So Tertan continued to sit in Section 5 of English 1A, to his classmates still a figure of curiously dignified fun, symbol to most of them of the respectable but absurd intellectual life. But to his teacher he was now very different. He had not changed — he was still the greyhound casting for the scent of ideas, and Howe could see that he was still the same Tertan, but he could not feel it. What he felt as he looked at the boy sitting in his accustomed place was the hard blank of a fact. The fact itself was formidable and depressing. But what Howe was chiefly aware of was that he had permitted the metamorphosis of Tertan from person to fact.

As much as possible he avoided seeing Tertan's upraised hand and eager eye. But the fact did not know of its mere factuality, it continued its existence as if it were Tertan, hand up and eye questioning, and one day it appeared in Howe's office with a document.

"Even the spirit who lives egregiously, above the herd, must have its relations with the fellowman," Tertan declared. He laid the document on Howe's desk. It was headed "Quill and Scroll Society of Dwight College. Application for Membership."

"In most ways these are crass minds," Tertan said, touching the paper. "Yet as a whole, bound together in their common love of letters, they transcend their intellectual lacks since it is not a paradox that the whole is greater than the sum of its parts."

"When are the elections?" Howe asked.

"They take place tomorrow."

"I certainly hope you will be successful."

"Thank you. Would you wish to implement that hope?" A rather dirty finger pointed to the bottom of the sheet. "A faculty recommender is necessary," Tertan said stiffly, and waited.

"And you wish me to recommend you?"

"It would be an honor."

"You may use my name."

Tertan's finger pointed again. "It must be a written sponsorship, signed by the sponsor." There was a large blank space on the form under the heading, "Opinion of Faculty Sponsor."

This was almost another thing and Howe hesitated. Yet there was nothing else to do and he took out his fountain pen. He wrote, "Mr. Ferdinand Tertan is marked by his intense devotion to letters and by his exceptional love of all things of the mind." To this he signed his name, which looked bold and assertive on the white page. It disturbed him, the strange affirming power of a name. With a businesslike air, Tertan whipped up the paper, folded it with decision and put it into his pocket. He bowed and took his departure, leaving Howe with the sense of having done something oddly momentous.

And so much now seemed odd and momentous to Howe that should not have seemed so. It was odd and momentous, he felt, when he sat with Blackburn's second quiz before him, and wrote in an excessively firm hand the grade of C-minus. The paper was a clear, an indisputable failure. He was carefully and consciously committing a cowardice. Blackburn had told the truth when he had pleaded his past record. Howe had consulted it in the Dean's office. It showed no grade lower than a B-minus. A canvass of some of Blackburn's previous instructors had brought vague attestations to the adequate powers of a student imperfectly remembered, and sometimes surprise that his abilities could be questioned at all.

As he wrote the grade, Howe told himself that his cowardice sprang from an unwillingness to have more dealings with a student he disliked. He knew it was simpler than that. He knew he feared Blackburn: that was the absurd truth. And cowardice did not solve the matter after all. Blackburn, flushed with a first success, attacked at once. The minimal passing grade had not assuaged his feelings and he sat at Howe's desk and again the blue-book lay between them. Blackburn said nothing. With an enormous impudence, he was waiting for Howe to speak and explain himself.

At last Howe said sharply and rudely, "Well?" His throat was tense and the blood was hammering in his head. His mouth was tight with anger at himself for his disturbance.

Blackburn's glance was almost baleful. "This is impossible, sir."

"But there it is," Howe answered.

"Sir?" Blackburn had not caught the meaning but his tone was still haughty.

Impatiently Howe said, "There it is, plain as day. Are you here to complain again?"

"Indeed I am, sir." There was surprise in Blackburn's voice that Howe should ask the question.

"I shouldn't complain if I were you. You did a thoroughly bad job on your first quiz. This one is a little, only a very little, better." This was not true. If anything, it was worse.

"That might be a matter of opinion, sir."

"It is a matter of opinion. Of my opinion."

"Another opinion might be different, sir."

"You really believe that?" Howe said.

"Yes." The omission of the "sir" was monumental.

"Whose, for example?"

"The Dean's, for example." Then the fleshy jaw came forward a little. "Or a certain literary critic's, for example."

It was colossal and almost too much for Blackburn himself to handle. The solidity of his face almost crumpled under it. But he withstood his own audacity and went on. "And the Dean's opinion might be guided by the knowledge that the person who gave me this mark is the man whom a famous critic, the most eminent judge of literature in this country, called a drunken man. The Dean might think twice about whether such a man is fit to teach Dwight students."

Howe said in quiet admonition, "Blackburn, you're mad," meaning no more than to check the boy's extravagance.

But Blackburn paid no heed. He had another shot in the locker. "And the Dean might be guided by the information, of which I have evidence, documentary evidence," — he slapped his breast pocket twice — "that this same person personally recommended to the college literary society, the oldest in the country, that he personally recommended a student who is crazy, who threw the meeting into an uproar — a psychiatric case. The Dean might take that into account."

Howe was never to learn the details of that "uproar." He had always to content himself with the dim but passionate picture which at that moment sprang into his mind, of Tertan standing on some abstract height and madly denouncing the multitude of Quill and Scroll who howled him down.

He sat quiet a moment and looked at Blackburn. The ferocity had entirely gone from the student's face. He sat regarding his teacher almost benevolently. He had played a good card and now, scarcely at all unfriendly, he was waiting to see the effect. Howe took up the blue-book and negligently sifted through it. He read a page, closed the book, struck out the C-minus and wrote an F.

"Now you may take the paper to the Dean," he said. "You may tell him that after reconsidering it, I lowered the grade."

The gasp was audible. "Oh, sir!" Blackburn cried. "Please!" His face was agonized. "It means my graduation, my livelihood, my future. Don't do this to me."

"It's done already."

Blackburn stood up. "I spoke rashly, sir, hastily. I had no intention, no real intention, of seeing the Dean. It rests with you — entirely, entirely. I *hope* you will restore the first mark."

"Take the matter to the Dean or not, just as you choose. The grade is what you deserve and it stands."

Blackburn's head dropped. "And will I be failed at mid-term, sir?"

"Of course."

From deep out of Blackburn's great chest rose a cry of anguish. "Oh, sir, if you want me to go down on my knees to you, I will, I will."

Howe looked at him in amazement.

"I will, I will. On my knees, sir. This mustn't, mustn't happen."

He spoke so literally, meaning so very truly that his knees and exactly his knees were involved and seeming to think that he was offering something of tangible value to his teacher, that Howe, whose head had become icy clear in the nonsensical drama, thought, "The boy is mad," and began to speculate fantastically whether something in himself attracted or developed aberration. He could see himself standing absurdly before the

Dean and saying, "I've found another. This time it's the vice-president of the Council, the manager of the debating team and secretary of Quill and Scroll."

One more such discovery, he thought, and he himself would be discovered! And there, suddenly, Blackburn was on his knees with a thump, his huge thighs straining his trousers, his hand outstretched in a great gesture of supplication.

With a cry, Howe shoved back his swivel chair and it rolled away on its casters half across the little room. Blackburn knelt for a moment to nothing at all, then got to his feet.

Howe rose abruptly. He said, "Blackburn, you will stop acting like an idiot. Dust your knees off, take your paper and get out. You've behaved like a fool and a malicious person. You have half a term to do a decent job. Keep your silly mouth shut and try to do it. Now get out."

Blackburn's head was low. He raised it and there was a pious light in his eyes. "Will you shake hands, sir?" he said. He thrust out his hand.

"I will not," Howe said.

Head and hand sank together. Blackburn picked up his blue-book and walked to the door. He turned and said, "Thank you, sir." His back, as he departed, was heavy with tragedy and stateliness.

IV

After years of bad luck with the weather, the College had a perfect day for Commencement. It was wonderfully bright, the air so transparent, the wind so brisk that no one could resist talking about it.

As Howe set out for the campus he heard Hilda calling from the back yard. She called, "Professor, professor," and came running to him.

Howe said, "What's this 'professor' business?"

"Mother told me," Hilda said. "You've been promoted. And I want to take your picture."

"Next year," said Howe. "I won't be a professor until next year. And you know better than to call anybody 'professor.'"

"It was just in fun," Hilda said. She seemed disappointed.

"But you can take my picture if you want. I won't look much different next year." Still, it was frightening. It might mean that he was to stay in this town all his life.

Hilda brightened. "Can I take it in this?" she said, and touched the gown he carried over his arm.

Howe laughed. "Yes, you can take it in this."

"I'll get my things and meet you in front of Otis," Hilda said. "I have the background all picked out."

On the campus the Commencement crowd was already large. It stood about in eager, nervous little family groups. As he crossed, Howe was greeted by a student, capped and gowned, glad of the chance to make an event for his parents by introducing one of his teachers. It was while Howe stood there chatting that he saw Tertan.

He had never seen anyone quite so alone, as though a circle had been woven about him to separate him from the gay crowd on the campus. Not that Tertan was not gay, he was the gayest of all. Three weeks had passed since Howe had last seen him, the weeks of examination, the lazy week before Commencement, and this was now a different Tertan. On his head he wore a panama hat, broad-brimmed and fine, of the shape associated with South American planters. He wore a suit of raw silk, luxurious, but yellowed with age and much too tight, and he sported a whangee cane. He walked sedately, the hat tilted at a devastating angle, the stick coming up and down in time to his measured tread. He had, Howe guessed, outfitted himself to greet the day in the clothes of that ruined father whose existence was on record in the Dean's office. Gravely and arrogantly he surveyed the scene — in it, his whole bearing seemed to say, but not of it. With his haughty step, with his flashing eye, Tertan was coming nearer. Howe did not wish to be seen. He shifted his position slightly. When he looked again, Tertan was not in sight.

The chapel clock struck the quarter hour. Howe detached himself from his chat and hurried to Otis Hall at the far end of the campus. Hilda had not yet come. He went up into the high portico and, using the glass of the door for a mirror, put on his gown, adjusted the hood on his shoulders and set the mortarboard on his head. When he came down the steps, Hilda had arrived.

Nothing could have told him more forcibly that a year had passed than the development of Hilda's photographic possessions from the box camera of the previous fall. By a strap about her neck was hung a leather case, so thick and strong, so carefully stitched and so molded to its contents that it could only hold a costly camera. The appearance was deceptive, Howe knew, for he had been present at the Aikens' pre-Christmas conference about its purchase. It was only a fairly good domestic camera. Still, it looked very impressive. Hilda carried another leather case from which she drew a collapsible tripod. Decisively she extended each of its gleaming legs and set it up on the path. She removed the camera from its case and fixed it to the tripod. In its compact efficiency the camera almost had a life of its own, but Hilda treated it with easy familiarity, looked into its eye, glanced casually at its gauges. Then from a pocket she took still another leather case and drew from it a small instrument through which she looked first at Howe, who began to feel inanimate and lost, and then at the sky. She made some adjustment on the instrument, then some adjustment on the camera. She swept the scene with her eye, found a spot and pointed the camera in its direction. She walked to the spot, stood on it and beckoned to Howe. With each new leather case, with each new instrument, and with each new adjustment she had grown in ease and now she said, "Joe, will you stand here?"

Obediently Howe stood where he was bidden. She had yet another instrument. She took out a tape-measure on a mechanical spool. Kneeling down before Howe, she put the little metal ring of the tape under the tip of his shoe. At her request, Howe pressed it with his toe. When she had measured her distance, she nodded to Howe who released the tape. At a touch, it sprang back into the spool. "You have to be careful if you're going to get what you want," Hilda said. "I don't believe in all this snap-snap-snapping," she remarked loftily. Howe nodded in agreement, although he was beginning to think Hilda's care excessive.

Now at last the moment had come. Hilda squinted into the camera, moved the tripod slightly. She stood to the side, holding the plunger of the shutter-cable. "Ready," she said. "Will you relax, Joseph, please?" Howe realized that he was standing frozen. Hilda stood poised and precise as a setter, one hand holding the little cable, the other extended with curled dainty fingers like a dancer's, as if expressing to her subject the precarious delicacy of the moment. She pressed the plunger and there was the click. At once she stirred to action, got behind the camera, turned a new exposure. "Thank you," she said. "Would you stand under that tree and let me do a character study with light and shade?"

The childish absurdity of the remark restored Howe's ease. He went to the little tree. The pattern the leaves made on his gown was what Hilda was after. He had just taken a satisfactory position when he heard in the unmistakable voice, "Ah, Doctor! Having your picture taken?"

Howe gave up the pose and turned to Blackburn who stood on the walk, his hands behind his back, a little too large for his bachelor's gown. Annoyed that Blackburn should see him posing for a character study in light and shade, Howe said irritably, "Yes, having my picture taken."

Blackburn beamed at Hilda. "And the little photographer?" he said. Hilda fixed her eyes on the ground and stood closer to her brilliant and aggressive camera. Blackburn, teetering on his heels, his hands behind his back, wholly prelatical and benignly patient, was not abashed at the silence. At last Howe said, "If you'll excuse us, Mr. Blackburn, we'll go on with the picture."

"Go right ahead, sir. I'm running along." But he only came closer. "Doctor Howe," he said fervently, "I want to tell you how glad I am that I was able to satisfy your standards at last."

Howe was surprised at the hard, insulting brightness of his own voice, and even Hilda looked up curiously as he said, "Nothing you have ever done has satisfied me, and nothing you could ever do would satisfy me, Blackburn."

With a glance at Hilda, Blackburn made a gesture as if to hush Howe — as though all his former bold malice had taken for granted a kind of understanding between himself and his teacher, a secret which must not be betrayed to a third person. "I only meant, sir," he said, "that I was able to pass your course after all."

Howe said, "You didn't pass my course. I passed you out of my course. I passed you without even reading your paper. I wanted to be sure the college would be rid of you. And when all the grades were in and I did read your paper, I saw I was right not to have read it first."

Blackburn presented a stricken face. "It was very bad, sir?"

But Howe had turned away. The paper had been fantastic. The paper had been, if he wished to see it so, mad. It was at this moment that the Dean came up behind Howe and caught his arm. "Hello, Joseph," he said. "We'd better be getting along, it's almost late."

He was not a familiar man, but when he saw Blackburn, who approached to greet him, he took Blackburn's arm, too. "Hello, Theodore," he said. Leaning forward on Howe's arm and on Blackburn's, he said, "Hello, Hilda dear." Hilda replied quietly, "Hello, Uncle George."

Still clinging to their arms, still linking Howe and Blackburn, the Dean said, "Another year gone, Joe, and we've turned out another crop. After you've been here a few years, you'll find it reasonably upsetting — you wonder how there can be so many graduating classes while you stay the same. But of course you don't stay the same." Then he said, "Well," sharply, to dismiss the thought. He pulled Blackburn's arm and swung him around to Howe. "Have you heard about Teddy Blackburn?" he asked. "He has a job already, before graduation — the first man of his class to be placed." Expectant of congratulations, Blackburn beamed at Howe. Howe remained silent.

"Isn't that good?" the Dean said. Still Howe did not answer and the Dean, puzzled and put out, turned to Hilda. "That's a very fine-looking camera, Hilda." She touched it with affectionate pride.

"Instruments of precision," said a voice. "Instruments of precision." Of the three with joined arms, Howe was the nearest to Tertan, whose gaze took in all the scene except the smile and the nod which Howe gave him. The boy leaned on his cane. The broad-brimmed hat, canting jauntily over his eye, confused the image of his face that Howe had established, suppressed the rigid lines of the ascetic and brought out the baroque curves. It made an effect of perverse majesty.

"Instruments of precision," said Tertan for the last time, addressing no one, making a causal comment to the universe. And it occurred to Howe that Tertan might not be referring to Hilda's equipment. The sense of the thrice-woven circle of the boy's loneliness smote him fiercely. Tertan stood in majestic jauntiness, superior to all the scene, but his isolation made Howe ache with a pity of which Tertan was more the cause than the object, so general and indiscriminate was it.

Whether in his sorrow he made some unintended movement toward Tertan which the Dean checked, or whether the suddenly tightened grip on his arm was the Dean's own sorrow and fear, he did not know. Tertan watched them in the incurious way people watch a photograph being taken, and suddenly the thought that, to the boy, it must seem that the three were posing for a picture together made Howe detach himself almost rudely from the Dean's grasp.

"I promised Hilda another picture," he announced — needlessly, for Tertan was no longer there, he had vanished in the last sudden flux of visitors who, now that the band had struck up, were rushing nervously to find seats.

"You'd better hurry," the Dean said. "I'll go along, it's getting late for me." He departed and Blackburn walked stately by his side.

Howe again took his position under the little tree which cast its shadow over his face and gown. "Just hurry, Hilda, won't you?" he said.

Hilda held the cable at arm's length, her other arm crooked and her fingers crisped. She rose on her toes and said "Ready," and pressed the release. "Thank you," she said gravely and began to dismantle her camera as he hurried off to join the procession.

WALTER VAN TILBURG CLARK

"The Wind and the Snow of Winter" is a story not of a new frontier but of a lost one. Seldom has the Old West been re-evoked so vividly and affectingly as in this tale of an old pioneer. Seldom, too, has the loss of youth to old age been written about more keenly.

Walter Van Tilburg Clark was born in East Orland, Maine, in 1909. He lived in New York State until 1917 when he went to Nevada, where he has lived ever since. Many awards have been bestowed on him for his writing. His short story collection was published under the title of The Watchful Gods. *The best known of his novels are* The Ox-Bow Incident *and* The Track of the Cat.

The Wind and the Snow
of Winter

IT WAS NEAR sunset when Mike Braneen came onto the last pitch of the old wagon road which had led into Gold Rock from the east since the Comstock days. The road was just two ruts in the hard earth, with sagebrush growing between them, and was full of steep pitches and sharp turns. From the summit it descended even more steeply into Gold Rock in a series of short switchbacks down the slope of the canyon. There was a paved highway on the other side of the pass now, but Mike never used that. Cars coming from behind made him uneasy, so that he couldn't follow his own thoughts long, but had to keep turning around every few minutes, to see that his burro, Annie, was staying out on the shoulder of the road, where she would be safe. Mike didn't like cars anyway, and on the old road he could forget about them, and feel more like himself. He could forget about Annie too, except when the light, quick tapping of her hoofs behind him stopped. Even then he didn't really break his thoughts. It was more as if the tapping were another sound from his own inner machinery, and when it stopped, he stopped too, and turned around to see what she was doing. When he began to walk ahead again at the same slow, unvarying pace, his arms scarcely swinging at all, his body bent a little forward from the waist, he would not be aware that there had been any interruption of the memory or the story that was going on in his head. Mike did not like to have his stories interrupted except by an idea of his own, something to do with prospecting, or the arrival of his story at an actual memory which warmed him to closer recollection or led into a new and more attractive story.

An intense, golden light, almost liquid, fanned out from the peaks above him and reached eastward under the gray sky, and the snow which occasionally swarmed across this light was fine and dry. Such little squalls had been going on all day, and still there was nothing like real snow down, but only a fine powder which the wind swept along until it caught under the brush, leaving the ground bare. Yet Mike Braneen was not deceived. This was not just a flurrying day; it was the beginning of winter. If not tonight, then tomorrow, or the next day, the snow would begin which shut off the mountains, so that a man might as well be on a great plain for all he could see, perhaps even the snow which blinded a man at once and blanketed the desert in an hour. Fifty-two years in this country had made Mike Braneen sure about such things, although he didn't give much thought to them, but only to what he had to do because of them. Three nights before, he had been awakened by a change in the wind. It was no longer a wind born in the near mountains, cold with night and altitude, but a wind from far places, full of a damp chill which got through his blankets and into his bones. The stars had still been clear and close above the dark humps of the mountains, and overhead the constellations had moved slowly in full panoply, unbroken by any invisible lower darkness; yet he had lain there half awake for a few minutes, hearing the new wind beat the brush around him, hearing Annie stirring restlessly and thumping in her hobble. He had thought drowsily, Smells like winter this time, and then, It's held off a long time this year, pretty near the end of December. Then he had gone back to sleep, mildly happy because the change meant he would be going back to Gold Rock. Gold Rock was the other half of Mike Braneen's life. When the smell of winter came, he always started back for Gold Rock. From March or April until the smell of winter, he wandered slowly about among the mountains, anywhere between the White Pines and the Virginias, with only his burro for company. Then there would come the change, and they would head back for Gold Rock.

Mike had traveled with a good many burros during that time, eighteen or twenty, he thought, although he was not sure. He could not remember them all, but only those he had had first, when he was a young man and always thought most about seeing women when he got back to Gold Rock, or those with something queer about them, like Baldy, who'd had a great, pale patch, like a bald spot, on one side of his belly, or those who'd had something queer happen to them, like Maria. He could remember just how it had been that night. He could remember it as if it were last night. It had been in Hamilton. He had felt unhappy, because he could remember Hamilton when the whole hollow was full of people and buildings, and everything was new and active. He had gone to sleep in the hollow shell of the Wells Fargo Building, hearing an old iron shutter banging against the wall in the wind. In the morning, Maria had been gone. He had followed the scuffing track she made on account of her loose hobble, and it had led far up the old snow-gullied road to Treasure Hill, and then ended at one of the black shafts that opened like mouths right at the edge of the road. A man remembered a thing like that. There weren't many burros that foolish. But burros with nothing particular about them were hard to remember — especially those he'd had in the last twenty years or so, when he had gradually stopped feeling so personal about them, and had begun to call all the jennies Annie and all the burros Jack.

The clicking of the little hoofs behind him stopped, and Mike stopped too, and turned around. Annie was pulling at a line of yellow grass along the edge of the road.

"Come on, Maria," Mike said patiently. The burro at once stopped pulling at the dead grass and came on up towards him, her small black nose working, the ends of the grass standing out on each side of it like whiskers. Mike began to climb again, ahead of her.

It was a long time since he had been caught by a winter, too. He could not remember how long. All the beginnings ran together in his mind, as if they were all the beginning of one winter so far back that he had almost forgotten it. He could still remember clearly, though, the winter he had stayed out on purpose, clear into January. He had been a young man then, thirty-five or forty or forty-five, somewhere in there. He would have to stop and try to bring back a whole string of memories about what had happened just before, in order to remember just how old he had been, and it wasn't worth the trouble. Besides, sometimes even that system didn't work. It would lead him into an old camp where he had been a number of times, and the dates would get mixed up. It was impossible to remember any other way; because all his comings and goings had been so much alike. He had been young, anyhow, and not much afraid of anything except running out of water in the wrong place; not even afraid of the winter. He had stayed out because he'd thought he had a good thing, and he had wanted to prove it. He could remember how it felt to be out in the clear winter weather on the mountains; the piñon trees and the junipers weighted down with feathery snow, and making sharp, blue shadows on the white slopes. The hills had made blue shadows on one another too, and in the still air his pick had made the beginning of a sound like a bell's. He knew he had been young, because he could remember taking a day off now and then, just to go tramping around those hills, up and down the white and through the blue shadows, on a kind of holiday. He had pretended to his common sense that he was seriously prospecting, and had carried his hammer, and even his drill along, but he had really just been gallivanting, playing colt. Maybe he had been even younger than thirty-five, though he could still be stirred a little, for that matter, by the memory of the kind of weather which had sent him gallivanting. High-blue weather, he called it. There were two kinds of high-blue weather, besides the winter kind, which didn't set him off very often, spring and fall. In the spring it would have a soft, puffy wind and soft, puffy white clouds which made separate shadows that traveled silently across hills that looked soft too. In the fall it would be still, and there would be no clouds at all in the blue, but there would be something in the golden air and the soft, steady sunlight on the mountains that made a man as uneasy as the spring blowing, though in a different way, more sad and not so excited. In the spring high-blue, a man had been likely to think about women he had slept with, or wanted to sleep with, or imaginary women made up with the help of newspaper pictures of actresses or young society matrons, or of the old oil paintings in the Lucky Boy Saloon, which showed pale, almost naked women against dark, sumptuous backgrounds — women with long hair or braided hair, calm, virtuous faces, small hands and feet, and ponderous limbs, breasts, and buttocks. In the fall high-blue, though it had been much longer since he had seen a woman, or heard a woman's voice, he was more likely to think about old friends, men, or places he had heard about, or places he hadn't seen for a long time. He himself thought most often about Goldfield the way he had last seen it in the summer in 1912. That was as far south as Mike had ever been in Nevada. Since then, he had never been south of Tonopah. When the high-blue weather was past, though, and the season worked toward winter, he began to think about Gold Rock. There were only three or four winters out of the fifty-two when he hadn't gone home to Gold Rock, to his old room at Mrs. Wright's, up on Fourth Street, and to his meals in the dining room at the International House, and to the Lucky Boy, where he could talk to Tom Connover and his other friends, and play cards, or have a drink to hold in his hand while he sat and remembered.

This journey had seemed a little different from most, though. It had started the same as usual, but as he had come across the two vast valleys, and through the pass in the low range between them, he hadn't felt quite the same. He'd felt younger and more awake, it seemed to him, and yet, in a way, older too, suddenly older. He had been sure that there was plenty of time, and yet he had been a little afraid of getting caught in the storm. He had kept looking ahead to see if the mountains on the horizon were still clearly outlined, or if they had been cut off by a lowering of the clouds. He had thought more than once, how bad it would be to get caught out there when the real snow began, and he had been disturbed by the first flakes. It had seemed hard to him to have to walk so far, too. He had kept thinking about distance. Also the snowy cold had searched out the regions of his body where old injuries had healed. He had taken off his left mitten a good many times, to blow on the fingers which had been frosted the year he was sixty-three, so that now it didn't take much cold to turn them white and stiffen them. The queer tingling, partly like an itch and partly like a pain, in the patch on his back that had been burned in that old powder blast, was sharper than he could remember its ever having been before. The rheumatism in his joints, which was so old a companion that it usually made him feel no more than tight-knit and stiff, and the place where his leg had been broken and torn when that ladder broke in '97 ached, and had a pulse he could count. All this made him believe that he was walking more slowly than usual, although nothing, probably not even a deliberate attempt, could actually have changed his pace. Sometimes he even thought, with a moment of fear, that he was getting tired.

On the other hand, he felt unusually clear and strong in his mind. He remembered things with a clarity which was like living them again — nearly all of them events from many years back, from the time when he had been really active and fearless and every burro had had its own name. Some of these events, like the night he had spent in Eureka with the little, brown-haired whore, a night in the fall in 1888 or '89, somewhere in there, he had not once thought of for years. Now he could remember even her name. Armandy she had called herself: a funny name. They all picked names for their business, of course, romantic names like Cecily or Rosamunde or Belle or Claire, or hard names like Diamond Gert or Horseshoe Sal, or names that were pinned on them, like Indian Kate or Roman Mary, but Armandy was different.

He could remember Armandy as if he were with her now, not the way she had behaved in bed; he couldn't remember anything particular about that. In fact, he couldn't be sure that he remembered anything particular about that at all. There were others he could remember more clearly for the way they had behaved in bed, women he had been with more often. He had been with Armandy only that one night. He remembered little things about being with her, things that made it seem good to think of being with her again. Armandy had a room upstairs in a hotel. They could hear a piano playing in a club across the street. He could hear the tune, and it was one he knew, although he didn't know its name. It was a gay tune that went on and on the same, but still it sounded sad when you heard it through the hotel window, with the lights from the bars and hotels shining on the street, and the people coming and going through the lights, and then, beyond the lights, the darkness where the mountains were. Armandy wore a white silk dress with a high waist, and a locket on a gold chain. The dress made her look very brown and like a young girl. She used a white powder on her face, that smelled like violets, but this could not hide her brownness. The locket was heart-shaped, and it opened to show a cameo of a man's hand holding a woman's hand very gently, just their fingers laid out long together, and the thumbs holding, the way they were sometimes on tombstones. There were two little gold initials on each hand, but Armandy would never tell what they stood for, or even if the locket was really her own. He stood in the window, looking down at the club from which the piano music was coming, and Armandy stood beside him, with her shoulders against his arm, and a glass of wine in her hand. He could see the toe of her white satin slipper showing from under the edge of her skirt. Her big hat, loaded with black and white plumes, lay on the dresser behind him. His own leather coat, with the sheepskin lining, lay across the foot of the bed. It was a big bed, with a knobby brass foot and head. There was one oil lamp burning in the chandelier in the middle of the room. Armandy was soft-spoken, gentle, and a little fearful, always looking at him to see what he was thinking. He stood with his arms folded. His arms felt big and strong upon his heavily muscled chest. He stood there, pretending to be in no hurry, but really thinking eagerly about what he would do with Armandy, who had something about her which tempted him to be cruel. He stood there, with his chin down into his heavy dark beard, and watched a man come riding down the middle of the street from the west. The horse was a fine black, which lifted its head and feet with pride. The man sat very straight, with a high rein, and something about his clothes and hat made him appear to be in uniform, although it wasn't a uniform he was wearing. The man also saluted friends upon the sidewalks like an officer, bending his head just slightly, and touching his hat instead of lifting it. Mike Braneen asked Armandy who the man was, and then felt angry because she could tell him, and because he was an important man who owned a mine that was in bonanza. He mocked the airs with which the man rode, and his princely greetings. He mocked the man cleverly, and Armandy laughed and repeated what he said, and made him drink a little of her wine as a reward. Mike had been drinking whisky, and he did not like wine anyway, but this was not the moment in which to refuse such an invitation.

Old Mike remembered all this, which had been completely forgotten for years. He could not remember what he and Armandy had said, but he remembered everything else, and he felt very lonesome for Armandy, and for the room with the red, figured carpet and the brass chandelier with oil lamps in it, and the open window with the long tune coming up through it, and the young summer night outside on the mountains. This loneliness was so much more intense than his familiar loneliness that it made him feel very young. Memories like this had come up again and again during these three days. It was like beginning life over again. It had tricked him into thinking, more than once, next summer I'll make the strike, and this time I'll put it into something safe for the rest of my life, and stop this fool wandering around while I've still got some time left — a way of thinking which he had really stopped a long time before.

It was getting darker rapidly in the pass. When a gust of wind brought the snow against Mike's face so hard that he noticed the flakes felt larger, he looked up. The light was still there, although the fire was dying out of it, and the snow swarmed across it more thickly. Mike remembered God. He did not think anything exact. He did not think about his own relationship to God. He merely felt the idea as a comforting presence. He'd always had a feeling about God whenever he looked at a sunset, especially a sunset which came through under a stormy sky. It had been the strongest feeling left in him until these memories like the one about Armandy had begun. Even in this last pass, his strange fear of the storm had come on him again a couple of times, but now that he had looked at the light and thought of God, it was gone. In a few minutes he would come to the summit and look down into his lighted city. He felt happily hurried by this anticipation.

He would take the burro down and stable her in John Hammersmith's shed, where he always kept her. He would spread fresh straw for her, and see that the shed was tight against the wind and snow, and get a measure of grain for her from John. Then he would go up to Mrs. Wright's house at the top of Fourth Street, and leave his things in the same room he always had, the one in front, which looked down over the roofs and chimneys of his city, and across at the east wall of the canyon, from which the sun rose late. He would trim his beard with Mrs. Wright's shears, and shave the upper part of his cheeks. He would bathe out of the blue bowl and pitcher, and wipe himself with the towel with yellow flowers on it, and dress in the good dark suit and the good black shoes with the gleaming box toes, and the good black hat which he had left in the chest in his room. In this way he would perform the ceremony which ended the life of the desert and began the life of Gold Rock. Then he would go down to the International House, and greet Arthur Morris in the gleaming bar, and go into the dining room and eat the best supper they had, with fresh meat and vegetables, and new-made pie, and two cups of hot clear coffee. He would be served by the plump blond waitress who always joked with him, and gave him many little extra things with his first supper, including the drink which Arthur Morris always sent in from the bar.

At this point Mike Braneen stumbled in his mind, and his anticipation wavered. He would not be sure that the plump blond waitress would serve him. For a moment he saw her in a long skirt, and the dining room of the International House, behind her, had potted palms standing in the corners, and was full of the laughter and loud, manly talk of many customers who wore high vests and mustaches and beards. These men leaned back from tables covered with empty dishes. They patted their tight vests and lighted expensive cigars. He knew all their faces. If he were to walk down the aisle between the tables on his side, they would all speak to him. But he also seemed to remember the dining room with only a few tables, with oilcloth on them instead of linen, and with moody young men sitting at them in their work clothes — strangers who worked for the highway department, or were just passing through, or talked mining in terms which he did not understand or which made him angry.

No, it would not be the plump blond waitress. He did not know who it would be. It didn't matter. After supper he would go up Canyon Street under the arcade to the Lucky Boy Saloon, and there it would be the same as ever. There would be the laurel wreaths on the frosted glass panels of the doors, and the old sign upon the window, the sign that was older than Tom Connover, almost as old as Mike Breen himself. He would open the door and see the bottles and the white women in the paintings, and the card table in the back corner and the big stove and the chairs along the wall. Tom would look around from his place behind the bar.

"Well, now," he would roar, "look who's here, boys."

"Now will you believe it's winter?" he would roar at them.

Some of them would be the younger men, of course, and there might even be a few strangers, but this would only add to the dignity of his reception, and there would also be his friends. There would be Henry Bray with the gray walrus mustache and Mark Wilton and Pat Gallagher. They would all welcome him loudly.

"Mike, how are you anyway?" Tom would roar, leaning across the bar to shake hands with his big, heavy, soft hand with the diamond ring on it.

"And what'll it be, Mike? The same?" he'd ask, as if Mike had been in there no longer ago than the night before.

Mike would play that game too. "The same," he would say.

Then he would really be back in Gold Rock: never mind the plump blond waitress.

Mike came to the summit of the old road and stopped and looked down. For a moment he felt lost again, as he had when he'd thought about the plump blond waitress. He had expected Canyon Street to look much brighter. He had expected a lot of orange windows close together on the other side of the canyon. Instead there were only a few scattered lights across the darkness, and they were white. They made no communal glow upon the steep slope, but gave out only single, white needles of light, which pierced the darkness secretly and lonesomely, as if nothing could ever pass from one house to another over there. Canyon Street was very dark, too. There it went, the street he loved, steeply down into the bottom of the canyon, and down its length there were only the few street lights, more than a block apart, swinging in the wind and darting about that cold, small light. The snow whirled and swooped under the nearest street light below.

"You are getting to be an old fool," Mike Braneen said out loud to himself, and felt better. This was the way Gold Rock was now, of course, and he loved it all the better. It was a place that grew old with a man, that was going to die sometime, too. There could be an understanding with it.

He worked his way slowly down into Canyon Street, with Annie slipping and checking behind him. Slowly, with the blown snow behind them, they came to the first built-in block, and passed the first dim light showing through a smudged window under the arcade. They passed the dark places after it, and the second light. Then Mike Braneen stopped in the middle of the street, and Annie stopped beside him, pulling her rump in and turning her head away from the snow. A highway truck, coming down from the head of the canyon, had to get way over into the wrong side of the street to pass them. The driver leaned out as he went by, and yelled, "Pull over, Pop. You're in town now."

Mike Braneen didn't hear him. He was staring at the Lucky Boy. The Lucky Boy was dark, and there were boards nailed across the big window that had shown the sign. At last Mike went over onto the board walk to look more closely. Annie followed him, but stopped at the edge of the walk and scratched her neck against a post of the arcade. There was the other sign, hanging crossways under the arcade, and even in that gloom Mike could see that it said Lucky Boy and had a Jack of Diamonds painted on it. There was no mistake. The Lucky Boy sign, and others like it under the arcade, creaked and rattled in the wind.

There were footsteps coming along the boards. The boards sounded hollow, and sometimes one of them rattled. Mike Braneen looked down slowly from the sign and peered at the approaching figure. It was a man wearing a sheepskin coat with the collar turned up round his head. He was walking quickly, like a man who knew where he was going, and why, and where he had been. Mike almost let him pass. Then he spoke.

"Say, fella — "

He even reached out a hand as if to catch hold of the man's sleeve, though he didn't touch it. The man stopped, and asked impatiently, "Yeah?" and Mike let the hand down again slowly.

"Well, what is it?" the man asked.

"I don't want anything," Mike said. "I got plenty."

"O.K., O.K.," the man said. "What's the matter?"

Mike moved his hand towards the Lucky Boy. "It's closed," he said.

"I see it is, Dad," the man said. He laughed a little. He didn't seem to be in quite so much of a hurry now.

"How long has it been closed?" Mike asked.

"Since about June, I guess," the man said. "Old Tom Connover, the guy that ran it, died last June."

Mike waited for a moment. "Tom died?" he asked.

"Yup. I guess he'd just kept it open out of love of the place anyway. There hasn't been any real business for years. Nobody cared to keep it open after him."

The man started to move on, but then he waited, peering, trying to see Mike better.

"This June?" Mike asked finally.

"Yup. This last June."

"Oh," Mike said. Then he just stood there. He wasn't thinking anything. There didn't seem to be anything to think.

"You knew him?" the man asked.

"Thirty years," Mike said. "No, more'n that," he said, and started to figure out how long he had known Tom Connover, but lost it, and said, as if it would do just as well, "He was a lot younger than I am, though."

"Hey," said the man, coming closer, and peering again. "You're Mike Braneen, aren't you?"

"Yes," Mike said.

"Gee, I didn't recognize you at first. I'm sorry."

"That's all right," Mike said. He didn't know who the man was, or what he was sorry about.

He turned his head slowly, and looked out into the street. The snow was coming down heavily now. The street was all white. He saw Annie with her head and shoulders in under the arcade, but the snow settling on her rump.

"Well, I guess I'd better get Molly under cover," he said. He moved toward the burro a step, but then halted.

"Say, fella — "

The man had started on, but he turned back. He had to wait for Mike to speak.

"I guess this about Tom's mixed me up."

"Sure," the man said. "It's tough, an old friend like that."

"Where do I turn to get to Mrs. Wright's place?"

"Mrs. Wright?"

"Mrs. William Wright," Mike said. "Her husband used to be a foreman in the Aztec. Got killed in the fire."

"Oh," the man said. He didn't say anything more, but just stood there, looking at the shadowy bulk of old Mike.

"She's not dead, too, is she?" Mike asked slowly.

"Yeah, I'm afraid she is, Mr. Braneen," the man said. "Look," he said more cheerfully. "It's Mrs. Branley's house you want right now, isn't it? Place where you stayed last winter?"

Finally Mike said, "Yeah. Yeah, I guess it is."

"I'm going up that way. I'll walk up with you," the man said.

After they had started, Mike thought that he ought to take the burro down to John Hammersmith's first, but he was afraid to ask about it. They walked on down Canyon Street, with Annie walking along beside them in the gutter. At the first side street they turned right and began to climb the steep hill toward another of the little street lights dancing over a crossing. There was no sidewalk here, and Annie followed right at their heels. That one street light was the only light showing up ahead.

When they were halfway up to the light, Mike asked, "She die this summer, too?"

The man turned his body half around, so that he could hear inside his collar.

"What?"

"Did she die this summer, too?"

"Who?"

"Mrs. Wright," Mike said.

The man looked at him, trying to see his face as they came up towards the light. Then he turned back again, and his voice was muffled by the collar.

"No, she died quite a while ago, Mr. Braneen."

"Oh," Mike said finally.

They came up onto the crossing under the light, and the snow-laden wind whirled around them again. They passed under the light, and their three lengthening shadows before them were obscured by the innumerable tiny shadows of the flakes.

JOHN CHEEVER

More like science fiction than any of the author's other work, "The Enormous Radio" also reads like a parable. Cheever's ability to present characters as living, breathing and very human creatures is well to the fore here.

John Cheever was born in Quincy, Massachusetts, in 1912, and was educated at Thayer Academy. Famous primarily for his short stories, of which he published several collections, Cheever also wrote novels.

The Enormous Radio

JIM AND IRENE WESTCOTT were the kind of people who seem to strike that satisfactory average of income, endeavor, and respectability that is reached by the statistical reports in college alumni bulletins. They were the parents of two young children, they had been married nine years, they lived on the twelfth floor of an apartment house in the East Seventies between Fifth and Madison Avenues, they went to the theatre on an average of 10.3 times a year, and they hoped someday to live in Westchester. Irene Westcott was a pleasant, rather plain girl with soft brown hair and a wide, fine forehead upon which nothing at all had been written, and in the cold weather she wore a coat of fitch skins dyed to resemble mink. You could not say that Jim Westcott, at thirty-seven, looked younger than he was, but you could at least say of him that he seemed to feel younger. He wore his graying hair cut very short, he dressed in the kind of clothes his class had worn at Andover, and his manner was earnest, vehement, and intentionally naïve. The Westcotts differed from their friends, their classmates, and their neighbors only in an interest they shared in serious music. They went to a great many concerts — although they seldom mentioned this to anyone — and they spent a good deal of time listening to music on the radio.

Their radio was an old instrument, sensitive, unpredictable, and beyond repair. Neither of them understood the mechanics of radio — or of any of the other appliances that surrounded them — and when the instrument faltered, Jim would strike the side of the cabinet with his hand. This sometimes helped. One Sunday afternoon, in the middle of a Schubert quartet, the music faded away altogether. Jim struck the cabinet repeatedly, but there was no response; the Schubert was lost to them forever. He promised to buy Irene a new radio, and on Monday when he came home from work he told her that he had got one. He refused to describe it, and said it would be a surprise for her when it came.

The radio was delivered at the kitchen door the following afternoon, and with the assistance of her maid and the handy man Irene uncrated it and brought it into the living room. She was struck at once with the physical ugliness of the large gumwood cabinet. Irene was proud of her living room, she had chosen its furnishings and colors as carefully as she chose her clothes, and now it seemed to her that the new radio stood among her intimate possessions like an aggressive intruder. She was confounded by the number of dials and switches on the instrument panel, and she studied them thoroughly before she put the plug into a wall socket and turned the radio on. The dials flooded with a malevolent green light, and in the distance she heard the music of a piano quintet. The quintet was in the distance for only an instant; it bore down upon her with a speed greater than light and filled the apartment with the noise of music amplified so mightily that it knocked a china ornament from a table to the floor. She rushed to the instrument and reduced the volume. The violent forces that were snared in the ugly gumwood cabinet made her uneasy. Her children came home from school then, and she took them to the Park. It was not until later in the afternoon that she was able to return to the radio.

The maid had given the children their suppers and was supervising their baths when Irene turned on the radio, reduced the volume, and sat down to listen to a Mozart quintet that she knew and enjoyed. The music came through clearly. The new instrument had much purer tone, she thought, than the old one. She decided that tone was most important and that she could conceal the cabinet behind a sofa. But as soon as she had made her peace with the radio, the interference began. A crackling sound like the noise of a burning powder fuse began to accompany the singing of the strings. Beyond the music, there was a rustling that reminded Irene unpleasantly of the sea, and as the quintet progressed, these noises were joined by many others. She tried all the dials and switches but nothing dimmed the interference, and she sat down, disappointed and bewildered, and tried to trace the flight of the melody. The elevator shaft in her building ran beside the living-room wall, and it was the noise of the elevator that gave her a clue to the character of the static. The rattling of the elevator cables and the opening and closing of the elevator doors were reproduced in her loudspeaker, and, realizing that the radio was sensitive to electrical currents of all sorts, she began to discern through the Mozart the ringing of telephone bells, the dialing of phones, and the lamentation of a vacuum cleaner. By listening more carefully, she was able to distinguish doorbells, elevator bells, electric razors, and Waring mixers, whose sounds had been picked up from the apartments that surrounded hers and transmitted through her loudspeaker. The powerful and ugly instrument, with its mistaken sensitivity to discord, was more than she could hope to master, so she turned the thing off and went into the nursery to see her children.

When Jim Westcott came home that night, he went to the radio confidently and worked the controls. He had the same sort of experience Irene had had. A man was speaking on the station Jim had chosen, and his voice swung instantly from the distance into a force so powerful that it shook the apartment. Jim turned the volume control and reduced the voice. Then, a minute or two later, the interference began. The ringing of telephones and doorbells set in, joined by the rasp of the elevator doors and the whir of cooking appliances. The character of the noise had changed since Irene had tried the radio earlier; the last of the electric razors was being unplugged, the vacuum cleaners had all been returned to their closets, and the static reflected that change in pace that overtakes the city after the sun goes down. He fiddled with the knobs but couldn't get rid of the noises, so he turned the radio off and told Irene that in the morning he'd call the people who had sold it to him and give them hell.

The following afternoon, when Irene returned to the apartment from a luncheon date, the maid told her that a man had come and fixed the radio. Irene went into the living room before she took off her hat or her furs and tried the instrument. From the loudspeaker came a recording of the "Missouri Waltz." It reminded her of the thin, scratchy music from an old-fashioned phonograph that she sometimes heard across the lake where she spent her summers. She waited until the waltz had finished, expecting an explanation of the recording, but there was none. The music was followed by silence, and then the plaintive and scratchy record was repeated. She turned the dial and got a satisfactory burst of Caucasian music — the thump of bare feet in the dust and the rattle of coin jewelry — but in the background she could hear the ringing of bells and a confusion of voices. Her children came home from school then, and she turned off the radio and went to the nursery.

When Jim came home that night, he was tired, and he took a bath and changed his clothes. Then he joined Irene in the living room. He had just turned on the radio when the maid announced dinner, so he left it on, and he and Irene went to the table.

Jim was too tired to make even a pretense of sociability, and there was nothing about the dinner to hold Irene's interest, so her attention wandered from the food to the deposits of silver polish on the candlesticks and from there to the music in the other room. She listened for a few moments to a Chopin prelude and then was surprised to hear a man's voice break in. "For Christ's sake, Kathy," he said, "do you always have to play the piano when I get home?" The music stopped abruptly. "It's the only chance I have," a woman said. "I'm at the office all day." "So am I," the man said. He added something obscene about an upright piano, and slammed a door. The passionate and melancholy music began again.

"Did you hear that?" Irene asked.

"What?" Jim was eating his dessert.

"The radio. A man said something while the music was still going on — something dirty."

"It's probably a play."

"I don't think it *is* a play," Irene said.

They left the table and took their coffee into the living room. Irene asked Jim to try another station. He turned the knob. "Have you seen my garters?" a man asked. "Button me up," a woman said. "Have you seen my garters?" the man said again. "Just button me up and I'll find your garters," the woman said. Jim shifted to another station. "I wish you wouldn't leave apple cores in the ashtrays," a man said. "I hate the smell."

"This is strange," Jim said.

"Isn't it?" Irene said.

Jim turned the knob again. " 'On the coast of Coromandel where the early pumpkins blow,' " a woman with a pronounced English accent said, " 'in the middle of the woods lived the Yonghy-Bonghy-Bo. Two old chairs, and half a candle, one old jug without a handle . . .' "

"My God!" Irene cried. "That's the Sweeneys' nurse."

" 'These were all his worldly goods,' " the British voice continued.

"Turn that thing off," Irene said. "Maybe they can hear *us*." Jim switched the radio off. "That was Miss Armstrong, the Sweeneys' nurse," Irene said. "She must be reading to the little girl. They live in 17-B. I've talked with Miss Armstrong in the Park. I knew her voice very well. We must be getting other people's apartments."

"That's impossible," Jim said.

"Well, that was the Sweeneys' nurse," Irene said hotly. "I know her voice. I know it very well. I'm wondering if they can hear us."

Jim turned the switch. First from a distance and then nearer, nearer, as if borne on the wind, came the pure accents of the Sweeneys' nurse again: " 'Lady Jingly! Lady Jingly!' " she said, " 'Sitting where the pump-kins blow, will you come and be my wife,' said the Yonghy-Bonghy-Bo . . ."

Jim went over to the radio and said "Hello" loudly into the speaker.

" 'I am tired of living singly,' " the nurse went on, " 'on this coast so wild and shingly, I'm a-weary of my life; if you'll come and by my wife, quite serene would be my life . . .' "

"I guess she can't hear us," Irene said. "Try something else."

Jim turned to another station, and the living room was filled with the uproar of a cocktail party that had overshot its mark. Someone was playing the piano and singing the Whiffenpoof Song, and the voices that surrounded the piano were vehement and happy. "Eat some more sand-wiches," a woman shrieked. There were screams of laughter and a dish of some sort crashed to the floor.

"Those must be the Hutchinsons, in 15-B," Irene said. "I knew they were giving a party this afternoon. I saw her in the liquor store. Isn't this too divine? Try something else. See if you can get those people in 18-C."

The Westcotts overheard that evening a monologue on salmon fishing in Canada, a bridge game, running comments on home movies of what had apparently been a fortnight at Sea Island, and a bitter family quarrel about an overdraft at the bank. They turned off the radio at midnight and went to bed, weak with laughter. Sometime in the night, their son began to call for a glass of water and Irene got one and took it to his room. It was very early. All the lights in the neighborhood were extin-guished, and from the boy's window she could see the empty street. She went into the living room and tried the radio. There was some faint coughing, a moan, and then a man spoke. "Are you all right, darling?" he asked. "Yes," a woman said wearily. "Yes, I'm all right, I guess," and then she added with great feeling, "But, you know, Charlie, I don't feel

like myself any more. Sometimes there are about fifteen or twenty minutes in the week when I feel like myself. I don't like to go to another
doctor, because the doctor's bills are so awful already, but I just don't feel
like myself, Charlie. I just never feel like myself." They were not young,
Irene thought. She guessed from the timbre of their voices that they were
middle-aged. The restrained melancholy of the dialogue and the draft
from the bedroom window made her shiver, and she went back to bed.

The following morning, Irene cooked breakfast for the family — the
maid didn't come up from her room in the basement until ten — braided
her daughter's hair, and waited at the door until her children and her
husband had been carried away in the elevator. Then she went into the
living room and tried the radio. "I don't want to go to school," a child
screamed. "I hate school. I won't go to school. I hate school." "You will
go to school," an enraged woman said. "We paid eight hundred dollars to
get you into that school and you'll go if it kills you." The next number
on the dial produced the worn record of the "Missouri Waltz." Irene
shifted the control and invaded the privacy of several breakfast tables.
She overheard demonstrations of indigestion, carnal love, abysmal vanity,
faith, and despair. Irene's life was nearly as simple and sheltered as it
appeared to be, and the forthright and sometimes brutal language that
came from the loudspeaker that morning astonished and troubled her. She
continued to listen until her maid came in. Then she turned off the radio
quickly, since this insight, she realized, was a furtive one.

Irene had a luncheon date with a friend that day, and she left her
apartment at a little after twelve. There were a number of women in the
elevator when it stopped at her floor. She stared at their handsome and
impassive faces, their furs, and the cloth flowers in their hats. Which one
of them had been to Sea Island, she wondered. Which one had overdrawn
her bank account? The elevator stopped at the tenth floor and a woman
with a pair of Skye terriers joined them. Her hair was rigged high on her
head and she wore a mink cape. She was humming the "Missouri Waltz."

Irene had two Martinis at lunch, and she looked searchingly at her
friend and wondered what her secrets were. They had intended to go
shopping after lunch, but Irene excused herself and went home. She told
the maid that she was not to be disturbed; then she went into the living
room, closed the doors, and switched on the radio. She heard in the
course of the afternoon, the halting conversation of a woman entertain-
ing her aunt, the hysterical conclusion of a luncheon party, and a hostess
briefing her maid about some cocktail guests. "Don't give the best Scotch
to anyone who hasn't white hair," the hostess said. "See if you can get rid

of that liver paste before you pass those hot things, and could you lend me five dollars? I want to tip the elevator man."

As the afternoon waned, the conversations increased in intensity. From where Irene sat, she could see the open sky above Central Park. There were hundreds of clouds in the sky, as though the south wind had broken the winter into pieces and were blowing it north, and on her radio she could hear the arrival of cocktail guests and the return of children and businessmen from their schools and offices. "I found a good-sized diamond on the bathroom floor this morning," a woman said. "It must have fallen out of that bracelet Mrs. Dunston was wearing last night." "We'll sell it," a man said. "Take it down to the jeweller on Madison Avenue and sell it. Mrs. Dunston won't know the difference, and we could use a couple of hundred bucks. . . ." " 'Oranges and lemons, say the bells of St. Clement's,' " the Sweeneys' nurse sang. " 'Half-pence and farthings, say the bells of St. Martin's. When will you pay me? say the bells at old Bailey . . .' " "It's not a hat," a woman cried, and at her back roared a cocktail party. "It's not a hat, it's a love affair. That's what Walter Florell said. He said it's not a hat, it's a love affair," and then, in a lower voice, the same woman added, "Talk to somebody, for Christ's sake, honey, talk to somebody. If she catches you standing here not talking to anybody, she'll take us off her invitation list, and I love these parties."

The Westcotts were going out for dinner that night, and when Jim came home Irene was dressing. She seemed sad and vague, and he brought her a drink. They were dining with friends in the neighborhood, and they walked to where they were going. The sky was broad and filled with light. It was one of those splendid spring evenings that excite memory and desire, and the air that touched their hands and faces felt very soft. A Salvation Army band was on the corner playing "Jesus Is Sweeter." Irene drew on her husband's arm and held him there for a minute, to hear the music. "They're really such nice people, aren't they?" she said. "They have such nice faces. Actually, they're so much nicer than a lot of the people we know." She took a bill from her purse and walked over and dropped it into the tambourine. There was in her face, when she returned to her husband, a look of radiant melancholy that he was not familiar with. And her conduct at the dinner party that night seemed strange to him, too. She interrupted her hostess rudely and stared at the people across the table from her with an intensity for which she would have punished her children.

It was still mild when they walked home from the party, and Irene looked up at the spring stars. "'How far that little candle throws its beams,'" she exclaimed. "'So shines a good deed in a naughty world.'" She waited that night until Jim had fallen asleep, and then went into the living room and turned on the radio.

Jim came home at about six the next night. Emma, the maid, let him in, and he had taken off his hat and was taking off his coat when Irene ran into the hall. Her face was shining with tears and her hair was disordered. "Go up to 16-C, Jim!" she screamed. "Don't take off your coat. Go up to 16-C. Mr. Osborn's beating his wife. They've been quarreling since four o'clock, and now he's hitting her. Go up there and stop him."

From the radio in the living room, Jim heard screams, obscenities, and thuds. "You know you don't have to listen to this sort of thing," he said. He strode into the living room and turned the switch. "It's indecent," he said. "It's like looking in windows. You know you don't have to listen to this sort of thing. You can turn it off."

"Oh, it's so terrible, it's so dreadful," Irene was sobbing. "I've been listening all day, and it's so depressing."

"Well, if it's so depressing, why do you listen to it? I bought this damned radio to give you some pleasure," he said. "I paid a great deal of money for it. I thought it might make you happy. I wanted to make you happy."

"Don't, don't, don't, don't quarrel with me," she moaned, and laid her head on his shoulder. "All the others have been quarreling all day. Everybody's been quarreling. They're all worried about money. Mrs. Hutchinson's mother is dying of cancer in Florida and they don't have enough money to send her to the Mayo Clinic. At least, Mr. Hutchinson says they don't have enough money. And some woman in this building is having an affair with the superintendent — with that hideous superintendent. It's too disgusting. And Mrs. Melville has heart trouble and Mr. Hendricks is going to lose his job in April and Mrs. Hendricks is horrid about the whole thing and that girl who plays the 'Missouri Waltz' is a whore, a common whore, and the elevator man has tuberculosis and Mr. Osborn has been beating Mrs. Osborn." She wailed, she trembled with grief and checked the stream of tears down her face with the heel of her palm.

"Well, why do you have to listen?" Jim asked again. "Why do you have to listen to this stuff if it makes you so miserable?"

"Oh, don't don't don't," she cried. "Life is too terrible, too sordid and awful. But we've never been like that, have we, darling? Have we? I mean we've always been good and decent and loving to one another, haven't we? And we have two children, two beautiful children. Our lives aren't sordid, are they, darling? Are they?" She flung her arms around his neck and drew his face down to hers. "We're happy, aren't we, darling? We are happy, aren't we?"

"Of course we're happy," he said tiredly. He began to surrender his resentment. "Of course we're happy. I'll have that damned radio fixed or taken away tomorrow." He stroked her soft hair. "My poor girl," he said.

"You love me, don't you?" she asked. "And we're not hypercritical or worried about money or dishonest, are we?"

"No, darling," he said.

A man came in the morning and fixed the radio. Irene turned it on cautiously and was happy to hear a California-wine commercial and a recording of Beethoven's Ninth Symphony, including Schiller's "Ode to Joy." She kept the radio on all day and nothing untoward came from the speaker.

A Spanish suite was being played when Jim came home. "Is everything all right?" he asked. His face was pale, she thought. They had some cocktails and went into dinner to the "Anvil Chorus" from *Il Trovatore*. This was followed by Debussy's "La Mer."

"I paid the bill for the radio today," Jim said. "It cost four hundred dollars. I hope you'll get some enjoyment out of it."

"Oh, I'm sure I will," Irene said.

"Four hundred dollars is a good deal more than I can afford," he went on. "I wanted to get something that you'd enjoy. It's the last extravagance we'll be able to indulge in this year. I see that you haven't paid your clothing bills yet. I saw them on your dressing table." He looked directly at her. "Why did you tell me you'd paid them? Why did you lie to me?"

"I just didn't want you to worry, Jim," she said. She drank some water. "I'll be able to pay my bills out of this month's allowance. There were the slipcovers last month, and that party."

"You've got to learn to handle the money I give you a little more intelligently, Irene," he said. "You've got to understand that we won't have as much money this year as we had last. I had a very sobering talk with Mitchell today. No one is buying anything. We're spending all our time promoting new issues, and you know how long that takes. I'm not getting any younger, you know. I'm thirty-seven. My hair will be gray next year. I haven't done as well as I'd hoped to do. And I don't suppose things will get any better."

"Yes, dear," she said.

"We've got to start cutting down," Jim said. "We've got to think of the children. To be perfectly frank with you, I worry about money a great deal. I'm not at all sure of the future. No one is. If anything should happen to me, there's the insurance, but that wouldn't go very far today. I've worked awfully hard to give you and the children a comfortable life," he said bitterly. "I don't like to see all of my energies, all of my youth, wasted in fur coats and radios and slipcovers and — "

"Please, Jim," she said. "Please. They'll hear us."

"*Who'll* hear us? Emma can't hear us."

"The radio."

"Oh, I'm sick!" he shouted. "I'm sick to death of your apprehensiveness. The radio can't hear us. Nobody can hear us. And what if they can hear us? Who cares?"

Irene got up from the table and went into the living room. Jim went to the door and shouted at her from there. "Why are you so Christly all of a sudden? What's turned you overnight into a convent girl? You stole your mother's jewelry before they probated her will. You never gave your sister a cent of that money that was intended for her — not even when she needed it. You made Grace Howland's life miserable, and where was all your piety and your virtue when you went to that abortionist? I'll never forget how cool you were. You packed your bag and went off to have that child murdered as if you were going to Nassau. If you'd had any reasons, if you'd had any good reasons — "

Irene stood for a minute before the hideous cabinet, disgraced and sickened, but she held her hand on the switch before she extinguished the music and the voices, hoping that the instrument might speak to her kindly, that she might hear the Sweeneys' nurse. Jim continued to shout at her from the door. The voice on the radio was suave and noncommittal. "An early-morning railroad disaster in Tokyo," the loudspeaker said, "killed twenty-nine people. A fire in a Catholic hospital near Buffalo for the care of blind children was extinguished early this morning by nuns. The temperature is forty-seven. The humidity is eighty-nine."

JEAN STAFFORD

*It is a cliché to speak of the multitude of lonely lives in a big city. In
"Children Are Bored on Sunday," the loneliness of the characters is
encompassed in a special way, the loneliness of the divorced. Miss Stafford has written of the divorced elsewhere but nowhere so brilliantly as
of these two people in a crowded museum.*

*Jean Stafford was born in Covina, California, in 1915, and was edu-
cated at the University of Colorado and at Heidelberg. She has published
three novels,* Boston Adventure, The Mountain Lion, The Catherine
Wheel; *two collections of short stories; and a children's book.*

Children Are Bored on Sunday

THROUGH the wide doorway between two of the painting galleries, Emma
saw Alfred Eisenburg standing before "The Three Miracles of Zenobius,"
his lean, equine face ashen and sorrowing, his gaunt frame looking under-
nourished, and dressed in a way that showed he was poorer this year than
he had been last. Emma herself had been hunting for the Botticelli all
afternoon, sidetracked first by a Mantegna she had forgotten, and then by
a follower of Hieronymus Bosch, and distracted, in an English room as
she was passing through, by the hot invective of two ladies who were
lodged (so they bitterly reminded one another) in an outrageous and
expensive mare's-nest at a hotel on Madison. Emma liked Alfred, and
once, at a party in some other year, she had flirted with him slightly for
seven or eight minutes. It had been spring, and even into that modern
apartment, wherever it had been, while the cunning guests, on their
guard and highly civilized, learnedly disputed on aesthetic and political
subjects, the feeling of spring had boldly invaded, adding its nameless,
sentimental sensations to all the others of the buffeted heart; one did not

know and never had, even in the devouring raptures of adolescence, whether this was a feeling of tension or of solution — whether one flew or drowned.

In another year, she would have been pleased to run into Alfred here in the Metropolitan on a cold Sunday, when the galleries were thronged with out-of-towners and with people who dutifully did something self-educating on the day of rest. But this year she was hiding from just such people as Alfred Eisenburg, and she turned quickly to go back the way she had come, past the Constables and Raeburns. As she turned, she came face to face with Salvador Dali, whose sudden countenance, with its unlikely mustache and its histrionic eyes, familiar from the photographs in public places, momentarily stopped her dead, for she did not immediately recognize him and, still surprised by seeing Eisenburg, took him also to be someone she knew. She shuddered and then realized that he was merely famous, and she penetrated the heart of a guided tour and proceeded safely through the rooms until she came to the balcony that overlooks the medieval armor, and there she paused, watching two youths of high-school age examine the joints of an equestrian's shell.

She paused because she could not decide what to look at now that she had been denied the Botticelli. She wondered, rather crossly, why Alfred Eisenburg was looking at it and why, indeed, he was here at all. She feared that her afternoon, begun in such a burst of courage, would not be what it might have been; for this second's glimpse of him — who had no bearing on her life — might very well divert her from the pictures, not only because she was reminded of her ignorance of painting by the presence of someone who was (she assumed) versed in it but because her eyesight was now bound to be impaired by memory and conjecture, by the irrelevant mind-portraits of innumerable people who belonged to Eisenburg's milieu. And almost at once, as she had predicted, the air separating her from the schoolboys below was populated with the images of composers, of painters, of writers who pronounced judgments, in their individual argot, on Hindemith, Ernst, Sartre, on Beethoven, Rubens, Baudelaire, on Stalin and Freud and Kierkegaard, on Toynbee, Frazer, Thoreau, Franco, Salazar, Roosevelt, Maimonides, Racine, Wallace, Picasso, Henry Luce, Monsignor Sheen, the Atomic Energy Commission, and the movie industry. And she saw herself moving, shaky with apprehensions and Martinis, and with the belligerence of a child who feels himself laughed at, through the apartments of Alfred Eisenburg's friends, where the shelves were filled with everyone from Aristophanes to Ring

Lardner, where the walls were hung with reproductions of Seurat, Titian, Vermeer, and Klee, and where the record cabinets began with Palestrina and ended with Copland.

These cocktail parties were a *modus vivendi* in themselves for which a new philosophy, a new ethic, and a new etiquette had had to be devised. They were neither work nor play, and yet they were not at all beside the point but were, on the contrary, quite indispensable to the spiritual life of the artists who went to them. It was possible for Emma to see these occasions objectively, after these many months of abstention from them, but it was still not possible to understand them, for they were so special a case, and so unlike any parties she had known at home. The gossip was different, for one thing, because it was stylized, creative (integrating the whole of the garrotted, absent friend), and all its details were precise and all its conceits were Jamesian, and all its practitioners sorrowfully saw themselves in the role of Pontius Pilate, that hero of the untoward circumstance. (It has to be done, though we don't want to do it; 'tis a pity she's a whore, when no one writes more intelligent verse than she.) There was, too, the matter of the drinks, which were much worse than those served by anyone else, and much more plentiful. They dispensed with the fripperies of olives in Martinis and cherries in Manhattans (God forbid! They had no sweet teeth), and half the time there was no ice, and when there was, it was as likely as not to be suspect shavings got from a bed for shad at the corner fish store. Other species, so one heard, went off to dinner after cocktail parties certainly no later than half past eight, but no one ever left a party given by an Olympian until ten, at the earliest, and then groups went out together, stalling and squabbling at the door, angrily unable to come to a decision about where to eat, although they seldom ate once they got there but, with the greatest formality imaginable, ordered several rounds of cocktails, as if they had not had a drink in a month of Sundays. But the most surprising thing of all about these parties was that every now and again, in the middle of the urgent, general conversation, this cream of the enlightened was horribly curdled, and an argument would end, quite literally, in a bloody nose or a black eye. Emma was always astounded when this happened and continued to think that these outbursts did not arise out of hatred or jealousy but out of some quite unaccountable quirk, almost a reflex, almost something physical. She never quite believed her eyes — that is, was never altogether convinced that they were really beating one another up. It seemed, rather, that this was only a deliberate and perfectly honest demonstration of what might have happened often if they had not so diligently dedicated themselves to their intellects. Altogether she had seen them do it, she did not and could not believe that city people clipped each other's jaws, for, to Emma, urban equalled urbane, and ichor ran in these Augustan's veins.

As she looked down now from her balcony at the atrocious iron clothes below, it occurred to her that Alfred Eisenburg had been just such a first-generation metropolitan boy as these two who half knelt in lithe and eager attitudes to study the glittering splints of a knight's skirt. It was a kind of childhood she could not imagine and from the thought of which she turned away in secret, shameful pity. She had been really stunned when she first came to New York to find that almost no one she met had gluttonously read Dickens, as she had, beginning at the age of ten, and because she was only twenty when she arrived in the city and unacquainted with the varieties of cultural experience, she had acquired the idea, which she was never able to shake entirely loose, that these New York natives had been deprived of this and many other innocent pleasures because they had lived in apartments and not in two- or three-story houses. (In the early years in New York, she had known someone who had not heard a cat purr until he was twenty-five and went to a house-party on Fire Island.) They had played hide-and-seek dodging behind ash cans instead of lilac bushes and in and out of the entries of apartment houses instead of up alleys densely lined with hollyhocks. But who was she to patronize and pity them? Her own childhood, rich as it seemed to her on reflection, had not equipped her to read, or to see, or to listen, as theirs had done; she envied them and despised them at the same time, and at the same time she feared and admired them. As their attitude implicitly accused her, before she beat her retreat, she never looked for meanings, she never saw the literary-historical symbolism of the cocktail party but went on, despite all testimony to the contrary, believing it to be an occasion for getting drunk. She never listened, their manner delicately explained, and when she talked she was always lamentably off key; often and often she had been stared at and had been told, "It's not the same thing at all."

Emma shuddered, scrutinizing this nature of hers, which they all had scorned, as if it were some harmless but sickening reptile. Noticing how cold the marble railing was under her hands, she felt that her self-blame was surely justified; she came to the Metropolitan Museum not to attend to the masterpieces but to remember cocktail parties where she had drunk too much and had seen Alfred Eisenburg, and to watch schoolboys, and to make experience out of the accidental contact of the palms of her hands with a cold bit of marble. What was there to do? One thing, anyhow, was clear and that was that today's excursion into the world had been premature; her solitude must continue for a while, and perhaps it would never end. If the sight of someone so peripheral, so uninvolving as Alfred Eisenburg could scare her so badly, what would a cocktail party do? She almost fainted at the thought of it, she almost fell headlong, and the boys, abandoning the coat of mail, dizzied her by their progress toward an emblazoned tabard.

In so many words, she wasn't fit to be seen. Although she was no longer mutilated, she was still unkempt; her pretensions needed brushing; her ambiguities needed to be cleaned; her evasions would have to be completely overhauled before she could face again the terrifying learning of someone like Alfred Eisenburg, a learning whose components cohered into a central personality that was called "intellectual." She imagined that even the boys down there had opinions on everything political and artistic and metaphysical and scientific, and because she remained, in spite of all her opportunities, as green as grass, she was certain they had got their head start because they had grown up in apartments, where there was nothing else to do but educate themselves. This being an intellectual was not the same thing as dilettantism; it was a calling in itself. Emma, for example, did not even know whether Eisenburg was a painter, a writer, a composer, a sculptor, or something entirely different. When, seeing him with the composers, she had thought he was one of them; when, the next time she met him, at a studio party, she decided he must be a painter; and when, on subsequent occasions, everything had pointed toward his being a writer, she had relied altogether on circumstantial evidence and not on anything he had said or done. There was no reason to suppose that he had not looked upon her as the same sort of variable and it made their anonymity to one another complete. Without the testimony of an impartial third person, neither she nor Eisenburg would ever know the other's actual trade. But his specialty did not matter, for his larger designation was that of "the intellectual," just as the man who confines his talents to the nose and throat is still a doctor. It was, in the light of this, all the more extraordinary that they had had that lightning-paced flirtation at a party.

Extraordinary, because Emma could not look upon herself as an intellectual. Her private antonym of this noun was "rube," and to her regret — the regret that had caused her finally to disappear from Alfred's group

— she was not even a bona-fide rube. In her store clothes, so to speak, she was often taken for an intellectual, for she had, poor girl, gone to college, and had never been quite the same since. She would not dare, for instance, go up to Eisenburg now and say that what she most liked in the Botticelli were the human and compassionate eyes of the centurions' horses, which reminded her of the eyes of her own Great-Uncle Graham, whom she had adored as a child. Nor would she admit that she was delighted with a Crivelli Madonna because the peaches in the background looked exactly like marzipan, or that Goya's little red boy inspired in her only the pressing desire to go out immediately in search of a plump cat to stroke. While she knew that feelings like these were not really punishable, she had not perfected the art of tossing them off; she was no flirt. She was a bounty jumper in the war between Great-Uncle Graham's farm and New York City, and liable to court-martial on one side and death on the other. Neither staunchly primitive nor confidently *au courant,* she rarely knew where she was at. And this was her Achilles' heel: her identity was always mistaken, and she was thought to be an intellectual who, however, had not made the grade. It was no use now to cry that she was not, that she was a simon-pure rube; not a soul would believe her. She knew, deeply and with horror, that she was thought merely stupid.

It was possible to be highly successful as a rube among the Olympians, and she had seen it done. Someone calling himself Nahum Mothersill had done it brilliantly, but she often wondered whether his name had not helped him, and, in fact, she had sometimes wondered whether that had been his real name. If she had been called, let us say, Hyacinth Derry-berry, she believed she might have been able, as Mothersill had been, to ask who Ezra Pound was. (This struck her suddenly as a very important point; it was endearing, really, not to know who Pound was, but it was only embarrassing to know who he was but not to have read the "Cantos.") How different it would have been if education had not med-dled with her rustic nature! Her education had never dissuaded her from her convictions, but certainly it had ruined the looks of her mind — painted the poor thing up until it looked like a mean, hypocritical, promiscuous malcontent, a craven and apologetic fancy woman. Thus she continued secretly to believe (but *never* to confess) that the apple Eve had eaten tasted exactly like those she had eaten when she was a child visiting on her Great-Uncle Graham's farm, and that Newton's observation was no news in spite of all the hue and cry. Half the apples she had eaten had fallen out of the tree, whose branches she had shaken for this very purpose, and the Apple Experience included both the descent of the fruit and the consumption of it, and Eve and Newton and Emma understood one another perfectly in this particular of reality.

Emma started. The Metropolitan boys, who, however bright they were, would be boys, now caused some steely article of dress to clank, and she instantly quit the balcony, as if this unseemly noise would attract the crowd's attention and bring everyone including Eisenburg, to see what had happened. She scuttered like a quarry through the sightseers until she found an empty seat in front of Rembrandt's famous frump, "The Noble Slav" — it was this kind of thing, this fundamental apathy to most of Rembrandt, that made life in New York such hell for Emma — and there, upon the plum velours, she realized with surprise that Alfred Eisenburg's had been the last familiar face she had seen before she had closed the door of her tomb.

In September, it had been her custom to spend several hours of each day walking in a straight line, stopping only for traffic lights and outlaw taxicabs, in the hope that she would be tired enough to sleep at night. At five o'clock — and gradually it became more often four o'clock and then half past three — she would go into a bar, where, while she drank, she seemed to be reading the information offered by the *Sun* on "Where to Dine." Actually she had ceased to dine long since; every few days, with effort, she inserted thin wafers of food into her repelled mouth, flushing the frightful stuff down with enormous drafts of magical, purifying, fulfilling applejack diluted with tepid water from the tap. One weighty day, under a sky that grimly withheld the rain, as if to punish the whole city, she had started out from Ninetieth Street and had kept going down Madison and was thinking, as she passed the chancery of St. Patrick's, that it must be nearly time and that she needed only to turn east on Fiftieth Street to the New Weston, where the bar was cool, and dark to an almost absurd degree. And then she was hailed. She turned quickly, looking in all directions until she saw Eisenburg approaching, removing a gray pellet of gum from his mouth as he came. They were both remarkably shy, and, at the time, she had thought they were so because this was the first time they had met since their brief and blameless flirtation. (How curious it was that she could scrape off the accretions of the months that had followed and could remember how she had felt on that spring night — as trembling, as expectant, as altogether young as if they had sat together underneath a blooming apple tree.) But now, knowing that her own embarrassment had come from something else, she thought that perhaps his had, too, and she connected his awkwardness on that September day with a report she had had, embedded in a bulletin on everyone, from her sole communicant, since her retreat, with the Olympian world. This informant had run into Alfred at a party and had said that he was having a very bad time of it with a divorce, with poverty, with a tempest that had carried off his job, and, at last, with a psychoanalyst, whose fees he could not possibly afford. Perhaps the nightmare had been well under way when they had met beside the chancery. Without alcohol and without the company of other people, they had had to be shy or their suffering would have shown in all its humiliating dishabille. Would it be true still if they should inescapably meet this afternoon in an Early Flemish room?

Suddenly, on this common level, in this state of social displacement, Emma wished to hunt for Alfred and urgently tell him that she hoped it had not been as bad for him as it had been for her. But naturally she was not so naïve, and she got up and went purposefully to look at two Holbeins. They pleased her, as Holbeins always did. The damage, though, was done, and she did not really see the pictures; Eisenburg's hypothetical suffering and her own real suffering blurred the clean lines and muddied the lucid colors. Between herself and the canvases swam the months of spreading, cancerous distrust, of anger that made her seasick, of grief that shook her like an influenza chill, of the physical afflictions by which the poor victimized spirit sought vainly to wreck the arrogantly healthy flesh.

Even that one glance at his face, seen from a distance through the lowing crowd, told her, now that she had repeated it to her mind's eye, that his cheeks were drawn and his skin was gray (no soap and water can ever clean away the grimy look of the sick at heart) and his stance was tired. She wanted them to go together to some hopelessly disreputable bar and to console one another in the most maudlin fashion over a lengthy succession of powerful drinks of whiskey, to compare their illnesses, to marry their invalid souls for these few hours of painful communion, and to babble with rapture that they were at last, for a little while, no longer alone. Only thus, as sick people, could they marry. In any other terms, it would be a mésalliance, doomed to divorce from the start, for rubes and intellectuals must stick to their own class. If only it could take place — this honeymoon of the cripples, this nuptial consummation of the abandoned — while drinking the delicious amber whiskey in a joint with a juke box, a stout barkeep, and a handful of tottering derelicts; if it could take place, would it be possible to prevent him from marring it all by talking of secondary matters? That is, of art and neurosis, art and politics, art and science, art and religion? Could he lay off the fashions of the day and leave his learning in his private entrepôt? Could he, that is, see the apple fall and not run madly to break the news to Newton and ask him what on earth it was all about? Could he, for her sake (for the sake of this pathetic rube all but weeping for her own pathos in the Metropolitan Museum), forget the whole dispute and, believing his eyes for a change, admit that the earth was flat?

It was useless for her now to try to see the paintings. She went, full of intentions, to the Van Eyck diptych and looked for a long time at the souls in Hell, kept there by the implacable, impartial, and genderless angel who stood upon its closing mouth. She looked, in renewed astonishment, at Jo Davidson's pink, wrinkled, embalmed head of Jules Bache, which sat, a trinket on a fluted pedestal, before a Flemish tapestry. But she was really conscious of nothing but her desire to leave the museum in the company of Alfred Eisenburg, her cousin-german in the territory of despair.

So she had to give up, two hours before the closing time, although she had meant to stay until the end, and she made her way to the central stairs, which she descended slowly, in disappointment, enviously observing the people who were going up, carrying collapsible canvas stools on which they would sit, losing themselves in their contemplation of the pictures. Salvador Dali passed her, going quickly down. At the telephone booths, she hesitated, so sharply lonely that she almost looked for her address book, and she did take out a nickel, but she put it back and pressed forlornly forward against the incoming tide. Suddenly, at the storm doors, she heard a whistle and she turned sharply, knowing that it would be Eisenburg, as, of course, it was, and he wore an incongruous smile upon his long, El Greco face. He took her hand and gravely asked her where she had been all this year and how she happened to be here, of all places, of all days. Emma replied distractedly, looking at his seedy clothes, his shaggy hair, the green cast of his white skin, his deep black eyes, in which all the feelings were disheveled, tattered, and held together only by the merest faith that change *had* to come. His hand was warm and her own seemed to cling to it and all their mutual necessity seemed centered here in their clasped hands. And there was no doubt about it; he had heard of her collapse and he saw in her face that she had heard of his. Their recognition of each other was instantaneous and absolute, for they cunningly saw that they were children and that, if they wished, they were free for the rest of this winter Sunday to play together, quite naked, quite innocent. "What a day it is! What a place!" said Alfred Eisenburg. "Can I buy you a drink, Emma? Have you time?"

She did not accept at once; she guardedly inquired where they could go from here, for it was an unlikely neighborhood for the sort of place she wanted. But they were *en rapport,* and he, wanting to avoid the grown-ups as much as she, said they would go across to Lexington. He needed a drink after an afternoon like this — didn't she? Oh, Lord, yes, she did, and she did not question what he meant by "an afternoon like this" but said that she would be delighted to go, even though they would have to walk on eggs all the way from the Museum to the place where the bottle was, the peace pipe on Lexington. Actually, there was nothing to fear; even if they had heard catcalls, or if someone had hooted at them, "Intellectual loves Rube!" they would have been impervious, for the heart carved in the bark of the apple tree would contain the names Emma and Alfred, and there were no prerequisites to such a conjugation. To her own heart, which was shaped exactly like a valentine, there came a winglike palpitation, a delicate exigency, and all the fragrance of all the flowery springtime love affairs that ever were seemed waiting for them in the whiskey bottle. To mingle their pain, their handshake had promised them, was to produce a separate entity, like a child that could shift for itself, and they scrambled hastily toward this profound and pastoral experience.

GEORGE P. ELLIOTT

A concentration camp in America? And what kind of people would organize it? And what kind would be its victims? "The NRACP" is more horrible than anything conceived of in 1984. It is a powerful account of something it is to be devoutly hoped will never happen here.

George P. Elliott was born on an Indiana farm in 1918 and from the age of ten he grew up in the southern California desert. He has taught at various colleges and his short stories have been collected in a book, Among the Dangs. *The author of two novels, his most recent book is* A Piece of Lettuce, *a group of essays.*

The NRACP

March 3

DEAR HERB,

Your first letter meant more to me than I can say, but the one I received yesterday has at last aroused me from my depression. I will try to answer both of them at once. You sensed my state of mind; I could tell it from little phrases in your letter — "open your heart, though it be only to a sunset," "try reading *Finnegans Wake*; if you ever get *into* it you won't be able to fight your way out again for months." I cherish your drolleries. They are little oases of half-light and quiet in this rasping, blinding landscape.

How I hate it! Nothing but the salary keeps me here. Nothing. I have been driven into myself in a very unhealthy way. Long hours, communal eating, the choice between a badly lighted reading room full of people and my own cell with one cot and two chairs and a table, a swim in a chlorinated pool, walks in this violent, seasonless, arid land — what is there? There seem to be only two varieties of people here: those who "have culture," and talk about the latest *New Yorker* cartoons, listen to imitation folksongs and subscribe to one of the less popular book clubs; and those who play poker, talk sports and sex, and drink too much. I prefer the latter type as people, but unfortunately I do not enjoy their activities, except drinking; and since I know the language and mores of the former type, and have more inclination toward them, I am thrown with people whom I dislike intensely. In this muddle I find myself wishing, selfishly, that you were here; your companionship would mean so much to me now. But you knew better than I what the CPR would mean — you were most wise to stay in Washington, most wise. You will be missing something by staying there — but I assure you it is something well worth missing.

I must mention the two universal topics of conversation. From the filing clerks to my division chief I know of no one, including myself, who does not talk absorbedly about mystery stories. A few watered-down eclectics say they haven't much preference in mysteries, but the folksongers to a man prefer the tony, phoney Dorothy Sayers-S. S. Van Dine type of pseudo-literary snobbish product, and the horsey folk prefer the Dashiell Hammett romantic cum violent realism; there is one fellow — a big-domed Irishman named O'Doone who wears those heavy-rimmed, owlish glasses that were so popular some years ago — who does nothing but read and reread Sherlock Holmes, and he has won everyone's respect, in some strange way, by this quaint loyalty. He's quite shy, in a talkative, brittle way, but I think I could grow fond of him — Yet everyone finds a strong need to read the damnable things, so strong that we prefer the absolute nausea of reading three in one day — I did it once myself, for three days on end — to not reading any. What is it actually that we prefer not to do? I can only think of Auden's lines, "The situation of our time Surrounds us like a baffling crime." Of our time, and of this job.

What are we doing here? — that is the other subject none of us can let alone. We are paid fantastic salaries — the secretary whom I share with another writer gets $325 a month, tell Mary *that* one — and for one whole month we have done nothing while on the job except to read all the provisions and addenda to the Relocation Act as interpreted by the Authority, or to browse at will in the large library of literature by and about Negroes, from sociological studies to newspaper poetry in dialect. You will know the Act generally of course; but I hope you are never for any reason subjected to this Ph.D.-candidate torture of reading to exhaustion about a subject in which you have only a general interest. But the *why* of this strange and expensive indoctrination, is totally beyond me. I thought that I was going to do much the same sort of PR work here on the spot as we had been doing in the State Department; I thought the salary differential was just a compensation for living in this hell-hole. That's what everyone here had thought too. It appears, however, that there is something more important brewing. In the whole month I have been here — I swear it — I have turned out only a couple of articles describing the physical charms of this desiccated cesspool; they appeared in Negro publications which I hope you have not heard of. And beyond that I have done nothing but bore myself to death by reading Negro novels and poetry.

They are a different tribe altogether; their primeval culture is wonderful enough to merit study — I would be the last to deny it. But not by me. I have enough trouble trying to understand the rudiments of my own culture without having this one pushed off onto me.

— I have been stifled and confused for so long that all my pent-up emotions have found their worthiest outlet in this letter to you, my dear friend. I have been vowing (as we used to vow to quit smoking, remember?) to stop reading mysteries but my vows seldom survive the day. Now I do solemnly swear and proclaim that each time I have the urge to read a mystery, I will instead write a letter to you. If these epistles become dull and repetitious, just throw them away without reading them. I'll put a mark — say an M — on the envelope of these counter-mystery letters, so you needn't even open them if you wish. I'm sure there will be a lot of them.

Does this sound silly? I suppose it does. But I am in a strange state of mind. There's too much sunlight and the countryside frightens me and I don't understand anything.

Bless you,
Andy

March 14

Dear Herb,

It wasn't as bad as I had feared, being without mysteries. We get up at seven and go to work at eight. Between five and six in the afternoon, there's time for a couple of highballs. From seven or so, when dinner is over, till ten or eleven — that's the time to watch out for. After you have seen the movie of the week and read *Time* and *The New Yorker*, then you discover yourself, with that autonomic gesture with which one reaches for a cigarette, wandering toward the mystery shelf and trying to choose between Carter Dickson and John Dickson Carr (two names for the same writer, as I hope you don't know). On Sundays there's tennis in the early morning and bowling in the afternoon. But then those gaping rents in each tightly woven, just tolerable day remain, no matter what you do. At first I thought I should have to tell myself bedtime stories. One evening I got half-drunk in the club-rooms and absolutely potted alone in my own room afterwards. First time in my life. Another time, O'Doone and I sat up till midnight composing an "Epitaph for a Mongoose." I can't tell you how dreary some of our endeavors were; O'Doone still quotes one of mine occasionally. He's a strange fellow, I can't exactly figure him out but I like him in an oblique sort of way. We neither one fit into any of three or four possible schemes of things here and we share a good deal in general outlook. But he can amuse himself with a cerebral horseplay which only makes me uneasy. O'Doone has a French book — God knows where he got it — on Senegalese dialects so he goes around slapping stuffy people on the back and mumbling "Your grandmother on your father's side was a pig-faced gorilla" or else a phrase which in Senegalese has something to do with transplanting date trees but which in English sounds obscene, and then he laughs uproariously. In any event, he's better off than I, who am amused by almost nothing.

Now that you have been spared the threatened dejection of my counter-mystery letters, I must confess to the secret vice which I have taken up in the past week. It grows upon me too, it promises to become a habit which only age and infirmity will break. I had thought it a vice of middle age (and perhaps it is — are we not 38, Herb? When does middle age commence?). I *take walks*. I take long walks alone. If I cannot say that I enjoy them exactly, yet I look forward to them with that eagerness with which an adolescent will sometimes go to bed in order to continue the dream which waking has interrupted.

Not that my walks are in any way dreamlike. They are perfectly real. But they take place in a context so different from any of the social or intellectual contexts of the CPR day, and they afford such a strong emotional relief to it, that I think these walks may be justly compared to a continued dream. My walks, however, have a worth of their own such as dreams can never have, for instead of taking me from an ugly world to a realm of unexplained symbols, they have driven me toward two realities, about which I must confess I have had a certain ignorance:

myself, and the natural world. And standing, as I feel I do, at the starting-point of high adventure, I feel the explorer's excitement and awe, and no self-pity at all.

I have recaptured — and I am not embarrassed to say it — the childhood delight in stars. That's a great thing to happen to a man, Herb — to be able to leave the smoke- and spite-laden atmosphere of bureaucracy, walk a few miles out into the huge, silent desert, and look at the stars with a delight whose purity needs no apology and whose expansiveness need find no words for description. I am astonished by the sight of a Joshua tree against the light blue twilight sky, I am entranced by the vicious innocence of one of the kinds of cactus that abound hereabouts, I enjoy these garish sunsets with a fervor that I once considered indecent. I cannot say I like this desert — certainly not enough to live in it permanently — but it has affected me, very deeply. I think that much of my trouble during my first month here was resisting the force of the desert. Now, I no longer resist it, yet I have not submitted to it; rather I have developed a largeness of spirit, a feeling of calm and magnificence. Which I am sure is in part lightheadedness at having such a weight of nasty care removed all at once, but which is wonderful while it lasts.

But it's not *just* lightheadedness. Some obstruction of spirit, an obstruction of whose existence I was not even aware, has been removed within me, so that now I can and dare observe the complexities of that catalogued, indifferent, unaccountable natural world which I had always shrugged at. One saw it from train windows, one dealt with it on picnics; one admired the nasturtiums and peonies of one's more domesticated friends, one approved of lawns, and shade trees. What then? What did one know of the rigidity of nature's order or of the prodigality with which she wastes and destroys and errs? I came here furnished only with the ordinary generic names of things — snake, lizard, toad, rabbit, bug, cactus, sage-bush, flower, weed — but already I have watched a road-runner kill a rattlesnake, and I am proud that I know how rabbits drink. Do you know how rabbits drink? If you ask what difference it makes to know this, I can happily reply, "None at all, but it gives me pleasure." A pleasure which does not attempt to deny mortality, but accepts it and doesn't care — that is a true pleasure, and one worth cherishing.

II P.M.

I owe it to you, I know, to give a somewhat less personal, less inward account of this place. But a calculated, itemized description of anything, much less of so monstrous a thing as a desert, that is beyond me. Instead I'll try to give you an idea of what effect such physical bigness can have upon one.

Our buildings are situated at the head of a very long valley — the Tehuala River Valley — which is partially arable and which, in both the upper and lower regions, is good for grazing purposes. The highway into the valley, that is, the highway that leads to the East, as well as the railroad, runs not far from our settlement. Being Public Relations, we are located just within the fence (it is a huge, barbarous fence with guards). We have had a rather surprising number of visitors already, and hundreds more are expected during the summer. Our eight buildings are flat-roofed, gray, of a horizontal design, and air-conditioned. But our view of the valley is cut off by a sharp bend about four or five miles below us. The tourists, in other words, can see almost nothing of the valley, and just as little of the Reserve stretching for 800 miles to the southwest, for this is the only public entrance to the Reserve, and no airplanes are permitted over any part of it. Around the turn in the upper valley, is yet another even more barbarous, even better guarded fence, past which no one goes except certain Congressmen, the top officials (four, I believe) in the NRACP, and SSE (Special Service Employees, who, once they have gone past that gate, do not return and do not communicate with the outside world even by letter). All this secrecy — you can fill in details to suit yourself — is probably unnecessary, but it does succeed in arousing an acute sense of mystery and speculation about the Reserve. Well, being no more than human I walked the five miles to the bend, climbed a considerable hill nearby, and looked out over the main sweep of the valley for the first time. I was hot and tired when I reached the foot of the hill, so I sat down — it was around 5:30 — and ate the lunch I had brought. When I reached the top of the hill the sun was about to set; the long shadows of the western hills lay over the floor of the valley and in some places they extended halfway up the hills to the east. Far, far to the west, just to the north of the setting sun, was a snow-capped mountain; and immediately in front of me, that is, a mile and a half or so away, stretched the longest building I have ever seen in my life. It had a shed roof rising away from me; there were no windows on my side of the building; nothing whatsoever broke the line of its continuous gray back; and it was at least a mile long, probably longer. Beyond it, lay dozens of buildings exactly like this one except for their length; some of them ran, as the long one did, east and west, some ran north and south, some aslant. I could not estimate to my satisfaction how large most of them were; they seemed to be roughly about the size of small factories. The effect which their planner had deliberately calculated and achieved was that of a rigidly patterned, unsymmetrical (useless?) articulation of a restricted flat area. Nothing broke the effect, and for a reason which I cannot define, these buildings in the foreground gave a focus and order to the widening scene that lay before me such that I stood for the better part of an hour experiencing a pure joy — a joy only heightened by my grateful knowledge that these Intake buildings were designed to introduce an entire people to the new and better world beyond (and I must confess I felt the better that I myself was, albeit humbly, connected with the project). The fine farms and ranches and industries and communities which would arise from these undeveloped regions took shape in the twilight scene before me, shimmering in the heat waves rising from the earth. But presently it was quite dark — the twilights are very brief here — and I was awakened from my reverie by the lights going on in one of the buildings before me. I returned to the PR settlement, and to my solitary room, in a state of exaltation which has not yet deserted me.

For an hour, the Universe and History co-extended before me; and they did not exclude me; for while I am but a grain on the shore of event, yet only within my consciousness did this co-extending take place and have any meaning. For that long moment, mine was the power.

I will write again soon.

ANDY

March 20

Dear Herb,

You complain that I didn't say anything directly about my voyage of discovery into myself, as I had promised in my last letter. And that the internal high pressures of urban life are blowing me up like a balloon in this rarefied atmosphere.

Maybe so. I'll try to explain what has been going on. But I forgot to take a cartographer on my voyage, so that my account may resemble, in crudeness, that of an Elizabethan freebooter in Caribbean waters. (If I had the energy, I'd try to synthesize these balloon-voyage metaphors; but I haven't.)

It all began when I asked myself, on one of my walks, why I was here, why I had taken this job. $8,000 a year — yes. The social importance of the project — maybe (but not my personal importance to the project).

Excitement at being in on the beginning of a great experiment in planning — yes. The hope of escaping from the pressures of Washington life — yes. These are valid reasons all of them, but in the other balance — why I should want *not* to come here — are better reasons altogether. An utter absence of urban life. No friends. No chance of seeing Betty. The loss of permanent position (this one you pointed out most forcefully) in State for a better paid but temporary job here. Loss of friends. Too inadequate a knowledge of my duties, or of the whole NRACP for that matter, to permit me to have made a decision wisely. And an overpowering hatred of restrictions (never once, Herb, for three years to be allowed to leave this Reserve! I've been sweating here for seven weeks, but that is 156 weeks. Christ!). Now I had known, more or less, all these factors before I came here, all these nice rational, statistical factors. But when I asked myself the other night, in the false clarity of the desert moonlight, why I had chosen to come, why really, I still could not answer myself satisfactorily. For of one thing I was still certain, that none of the logical reasons, none of my recognized impulses, would have brought me here singly or combined.

I also, being in the mood, asked myself why I had continued to live with Clarice for five years after I had known quite consciously that I did not love her but felt a positive contempt for her. Betty accounted for part of it, and the usual fear of casting out again on one's own. But I would not have been on my own in any obvious sense: I am sure you know of my love affairs during those five years; I could have married any of three or four worthy women. And I ask myself why it was that the moment Clarice decided once and for all to divorce me — she did the deciding, not me; I don't think you knew that — from that time on I lost my taste for my current inamorata and have not had a real affair since. These questions I was unable to answer; but at least I was seriously asking them of myself. I was willing and able to face the answers.

The key to the answer came from my long-limbed, mildly pretty, efficient, but (I had originally thought) frivolous and banal secretary — Ruth. She is one of those women who, because they do not have an "intellectual" idea in their noodles, are too frequently dismissed as conveniently decorative but not very valuable. And perhaps Ruth really is that. But she has made two or three remarks recently which seem to me to display an intuitive intelligence of a considerable order. Yet they may be merely aptly chosen, conventional observations. It is hard to tell. — She interests me. She has a maxim which I resent but cannot refute: "There are those who get it and those who dish it out; I intend to be on the side of the dishers." (Is this the post-Christian golden rule? It has its own power, you know.) In any case, the other day I was sitting in my cubicle of an office, in front of which Ruth's desk is placed — she services two of us. I had my feet up on the desk in a rather indecorous fashion, and I had laid the book I was reading on my lap while I smoked a cigarette. I suppose I was daydreaming a little. Suddenly Ruth opened the door and entered. I started, picked up the book and took my feet off the table-top. Ruth cocked an eye at me and said, "You like to feel guilty, don't you? All I wanted to know was whether you could spare time for a cup of coffee." So we went to the café and had coffee, and didn't even mention her statement or its cause.

But it set me thinking; and the longer I thought about it, the better I liked it. I had always discounted wild, Dostoyevskian notions like that as being too perverse to be true. But now I am not at all sure that frivolous, red-nailed Ruth wasn't right. So long as Clarice had been there to reprove me for my infidelities, I had had them. When her censorship was removed, the infidelities, or any love affairs at all, lost their spice — the spice which was the guilt that she made me feel about them. And then, having been divorced from Clarice, I took this job. This job is a sop to my sense of guilt at being white and middle-class, that is to say, one of Ruth's "dishers," a sop because I am participating in an enterprise whose purpose is social justice; at the same time it is a punishment, because of the deprivations I am undergoing; yet the actual luxury of my life and my actual status in the bureaucracy, high but not orthodox, privileged yet not normally restricted, nourishes the guilt which supports it. What it is that causes the sense of guilt in the first place, I suppose Freud could tell me, but I am not going to bother to find out. There are certain indecencies about which one ought not to inquire unless one has to. Social guilt — that is to say, a sense of responsibility toward society — is a good thing to have, and I intend to exploit it in myself. I intend to satisfy it by doing as fine a job as I possibly can; and furthermore I intend to find a worthy European family, say Italian, who are impoverished, and to support them out of my salary. I must confess that the CARE packages we used to send to Europe after the war made me feel better than all the fine sentiments I ever gave words to.

I am grateful that I came here. I have been thrown back upon myself in a way that has only benefited me.

We begin work soon. The first trainload of Negroes arrived today, 500 of them. They are going through Intake (the buildings I described in my last letter) and our work, we are told, will commence within a few days. Exactly what we are to do, we will be told tomorrow. I look forward to it eagerly.

ANDY

I read this letter over before putting it in the envelope. That was a mistake. All the excitement about myself which I had felt so keenly sounds rather flat as I have put it. There must be a great deal for me yet to discover. As you know, I have never spent much of my energy in intimacies, either with myself or with other people. One gets a facsimile of it when talking about the universal stereotypes of love with a woman. But this desert has thrown me back upon myself; and from your letter I take it you would find my explorations of interest. However, you must not expect many more letters in so tiresome a vein. I will seal and mail this one tonight lest I repent in the morning.

April 10

Dear Herb,

I have not known how to write this letter, though I've tried two or three times in the past week to do it. I'm going to put it in the form of a homily, with illustrations, on the text "There are those who get it and those who dish it out; I intend to be on the side of the dishers."

First, in what context did it occur? It is the motto of a charming young woman (any doubts I may have expressed about her are withdrawn as of now; she is all one could ask for) who is not malicious and does not in the least want to impose her beliefs or herself upon other people. She sends $100 a month to her mother, who is dying of cancer in a county hospital in Pennyslvania. When she told me she was sending the money , I asked her why. "Why?" said Ruth. "I'm disappointed in you to ask me such a thing." "All right, be disappointed, but tell me why." She shrugged a little in a humorous way. "She's my mother. And anyway," she added, "we're all dying, aren't we?" The important thing to note about Ruth is — she means it but she doesn't care. Just as she doesn't really care whether you like her clothes or her lovely hair; she does, and you ought to; the loss is yours if you don't. She was reared in a perfectly usual American city, and she has chosen from its unconscious culture the best in custom and attitude.

But she said it here, in the Public Relations division of the Colored

Persons Reserve, here where there is as much getting and dishing out as anywhere in the world, where the most important Negro in the Reserve, the President of it, may be in a very real sense considered inferior to our window-washer. The first time O'Doone heard her say it — he had dropped by to talk awhile, and Ruth had joined us — he made the sign of the cross in the air between himself and Ruth and backed clear out of the room. He didn't return either. I'm sure he's not religious. I don't know why he did that.

Now what does the statement imply. Primarily, it makes no judgment and does not urge to action. It is unmoral. "There is a condition such that some people must inflict pain and others must receive it; since it is impossible to be neutral in this regard and since I like neither to give nor to take injury, I shall choose the path of least resistance — ally myself with the inflictors, not because I like their side and certainly not because I dislike the other side, but only because I myself am least interfered with that way." No regret. No self-deception (*it is impossible to be neutral*). A clear conscience (*I like neither to give nor to take injury*). In other words, true resignation — this circumstance is as it is, and it will not and should not be otherwise. There is a certain intensity of joy possible after resignation of this order, greater than we frustrated hopers know. (Where do I fit into this scheme? I think I have discovered one thing about myself from contemplating Ruth's maxim: that is, I want profoundly to be a disher, but my training has been such, or perhaps I am only so weak, that I am incapable of being one with a clear conscience. Consequently I find myself in a halfway position — dishing it out, yes, but at the behest of people I have never seen, and to people I will never know.) Ruth took a job with the NRACP for the only right reason — not for any of my complicated ones nor for the general greed, but because she saw quite clearly that here was one of the very pure instances of getting it and dishing it out. She left a job as secretary to an executive in General Electric for this. I think she gets a certain pleasure from seeing her philosophy so exquisitely borne out by event. Ruth is 27. I think I am in love with her. I am sure she is not in love with me.

Tell me, Herb, does not this maxim ring a bell in you? Can you not recognize, as I do, the rightness of it? This girl has had the courage to put into deliberate words her sense of the inevitable. Do you not admire her for it? And is she not right? She is right enough. If you doubt it, let me tell you what our job here is.

The authorities consider the situation potentially explosive enough to warrant the most elaborate system of censorship I have ever heard of. To begin with, there is a rule that during his first week in the Reserve every Negro may write three letters to persons on the outside. After that period is over, only one letter a month is permitted. Now all letters leaving here during the first week are sent to PR where they are censored and typed in the correct form (on NRACP letterhead); the typed copies are sent on and the originals are filed. The reason for this elaborate system is interesting enough, and probably sound; every endeavor is to be made to discourage any leaking out of adverse reports on conditions in the CPR. There are some fourteen million Negroes in the nation, not all of whom are entirely pleased with the prospect of being relocated; and there are an indeterminate number of Caucasian sympathizers — civil liberties fanatics for the most part — who could cause trouble if any confirmation of their suspicions about the CPR should leak out. We have put out a staggering amount of data on the climatic, agricultural, power production and mining conditions of the region; and we have propagandized with every device in the book. Yet we know well enough how long it takes for propaganda to counteract prejudice, and sometimes how deceptive an apparent propaganda success can be. We are more than grateful that almost the entire news outlet system of the nation is on our side.

Well then, after the three letters of the first week have been typed and sent, the writer's job begins. Every effort is made to discourage the interned Negroes from writing to the outside. For one thing, we keep in our files all personal letters incoming during the first month. Anyone who continues to write to an internee after this month needs to be answered. The filing clerks keep track of the dates, and forward all personal letters to us. (The clerks think we send the letters on to the internees.) We then write appropriate responses to the letters, in the style of the internee as we estimate it from his three letters. We try to be as impersonal as possible, conveying the idea that everything is all right. Why do we not forward the letters to the internees to answer? First of all we do — if the internees request it. They are told that they will receive letters only from those persons whose letters they request to see, and such a request involves yards of red tape. Very few are expected to use the cumbersome mechanism at all. Then, we write the letters for them simply to save ourselves time and trouble. We would have a lot of rewriting to do anyway; this method assures us of complete control and an efficient *modus operandi*. Any outsider Negro who writes too many insistent letters will be, at our request, relocated within a month; we do not want any unnecessary unhappiness to result from the necessarily painful program. Friends and relatives are to be reunited as fast as possible. Whole communities are to be relocated together, to avoid whatever wrenches in personal relationships we can avoid.

Is not this getting it and dishing it out on a fine scale? All for very good reasons, I know. But then, is it not conceivable that there are always good reasons for the old crapperoo? Sometimes I feel absolutistic enough to say — if it's this bad, for any ultimate reason whatsoever, then to hell with it. After which sentiment, comes the gun at the head. But then reason reinstates my sense of relativity of values, and on I go writing a letter to Hector Jackson of South Carolina explaining that I've been so busy putting up a chickenhouse and plowing that I haven't had a chance to write but I hope to see you soon. (I doubt if I will.)

ANDY

I forgot to mention — I have a special job, which is to censor the letters of all the clerical personnel in PR. One of my duties is to censor any reference to the censorship! A strange state of affairs. None of them know that this job is mine; most think the censor must be some Mail Department employee. I must say you look at some people with new eyes after reading their correspondence.

I need hardly say, but if there is any doubt I will say, that this letter is absolutely confidential. How much of our system will become publicly known, I cannot guess; but naturally I don't want to jump the official gun in this regard.

April 12

Dear Herb,

Let me tell you about the strange adventure I had last evening. I am still not quite sure what to make of it.

Immediately after work I picked up a few sandwiches and a pint of whiskey, and walked out into the desert on one of my hikes. One more meal with the jabber of the café and one more of those good but always good in the same way dinners, and I felt I should come apart at the seams. (Another thing I have learned about myself — I am ill-adapted to prison life.) I had no goal in view. I intended to stroll.

But I found myself heading generally in the direction of the hill from which I had looked over the Tehuala Valley and the city of CPR Intake buildings. I came across nothing particularly interesting in a natural his-

tory way, so that by early dusk I was near to the hill; I decided to climb
it again and see what I could see.

The first thing I saw, in the difficult light of dusk, was a soldier with a
gun standing at the foot of the hill. I came around a large clump of
cactus, and there he was, leaning on his rifle. He immediately pointed it
at me, and told me to go back where I belonged. I objected that I had
climbed this hill before and I could see no reason why I shouldn't do it
again. He replied that he didn't see any reason either, but I couldn't just
the same; they were going to put up another fence to keep people like me
away. I cursed, at the whole situation; if I had dared I would have cursed
him too, for he had been rude as only a guard with a gun can be. Then,
before I left, I pulled out my pint and took a slug of it. The guard was a
changed man.

"Christ," he said, "give me a pull."

"I should give you a pull."

"Come on," he said, "I ain't had a drop since I came to this hole. They
won't even give us beer."

"All right," I replied, "if you'll tell me what the hell's going on around
here."

He made me crouch behind a Joshua tree, and he himself would not
look at me while he talked. I asked him why all the precautions.

"They got a searchlight up top the hill, with machine guns. They
sweep the whole hill all the time. They can see plain as day in the dark.
They keep an eye on us fellows down here. I know. I used to run the
light."

"I haven't seen any light," I said.

He glanced at me with scorn.

"It's black," he said. "They cut down all the bushes all around the top
part of that hill. Anybody comes up in the bare place — pttt! *Any*body.
Even a guard."

"I still don't see any light."

"Man, it's black light. You wear glasses and shine this thing and you
can see better than you can with a regular light searchlight. It's the stuff.
We used to shoot rabbits with it. The little bastards never knew what hit
them!"

I didn't want to appear simple, so I didn't ask any more questions
about the black light. He was an irascible fellow, with a gun and a knife,
and he had drunk most of the bottle already.

"Why do you let me stay at all?" I asked.

"Can't see good in the dusk. Not even them can't."

I couldn't think of anything more to say. I felt overwhelmed.

"I used to be guard on the railroad they got inside. Say, have they got a system. Trains from the outside go through a automatic gate. All the trainmen get on the engine and drive out. Then we come up through another automatic gate and hook on and drag it in. Always in the daytime. Anybody tried to hop train, inside or out, pttt! Air-conditioned box cars made out of steel. Two deep they come. Never come in at night."

"Are you married?" I asked.

"Ain't nobody married up front, huh?" I didn't answer. "There ain't, ain't there?"

"No, but there could be if anybody felt like it."

"Well, there ain't even a woman inside. Not a damn one. They let us have all the nigger women we want. Some ain't so bad. Most of them fight a lot."

He smashed the pint bottle on a rock nearby.

"Why didn't you bring some real liquor, god damn you?" he said in a low voice full of violence. "Get the hell back home where you belong. Get out of here. It's getting dark. I'll shoot the guts out of you too. Bring me something I can use next time, huh? Get going — Stay under cover," he shouted after me. "They're likely to get you if they spot you. They can't miss if it's dark enough."

The last I heard of him he was coughing and spitting and swearing. I was as disgusted as scared, and I must confess I was scared stiff.

I walked homeward bound, slowly recovering my emotional balance, trying to understand what had happened to me with that guard, the meaning of what he had told me. For some absurd reason the tune "In the Gloaming, O, My Darling" kept running through my head in the idiotic way tunes will, so that I was unable to concentrate intelligently upon the situation. (I wonder why that tune business happens.)

I heard a sound at some distance to my left. I stopped, suddenly and inexplicably alarmed to the point of throbbing temples and clenched fists. I saw a slim figure in brown among the cactus; and then, as the figure approached, I could see it was a young woman. She did not see me, but her path brought her directly to where I was standing. I did not know whether to accost her at a distance or to let her come upon me where I stood. By the time I had decided not to accost her, I could see it was Ruth.

"Why, Ruth!" I cried, with all the emotion of relief and gratified surprise in my voice, and perhaps something more. "What are you doing here?"

She started badly, then seeing who it was she hurried up to me and to my intense surprise took my arms and put them around her body.

"Andy," she said, "I am so glad to see you. Some good angel must have put you here for me."

I squeezed her, we kissed, a friendly kiss, then she drew away and shook herself. She had almost always called me Mr. Dixon before; there was a real affection in her "Andy."

"What's the matter?" I asked her. "Where have you been?"

"I didn't know you took walks too."

"Oh, yes. It's one way to keep from going nuts."

She laughed a little, and squeezed my arm. I could not refrain from kissing her again, and this time it was not just a friendly kiss.

"Where did you go?" I asked again.

"To that hill. I went up there a couple of times before. There was a guard there wanted to lay me."

We didn't speak for a few moments.

"I think he almost shot me for giving him the brush-off. I didn't look back when I left, but I heard him click his gun. You don't know how glad I was to see you."

So we kissed again, and this time it was serious.

"Wait a minute," she said, "wait a minute."

She unlocked her arm from mine, and we continued on our way not touching.

"I had some trouble with a guard too," I said. "I wonder why they're so damned careful to keep us away."

"Mine told me they didn't want us to get any funny ideas. He said things aren't what they seem to be in there."

"Didn't you ask him what he meant?"

"Sure. That's when he said I'd better shut up and let him lay me, or else he'd shoot me. So I walked off. I'm not going to call on *him* again."

I put my arm around her — I can't tell you how fond I was of her at that moment, of her trim, poised body, her courage, her good humor, her delightful rich voice and laughter — but she only kissed me gently and withdrew.

"I want to keep my head for a while, darling," she said.

I knew what she meant. We walked on in silence, hand in hand. It was moonlight. This time if I was lightheaded I knew why.

When we were about half a mile from our buildings, we came across O'Doone also returning from a walk.

"Well," he said brightly, "it *is* a nice moon, isn't it?"

It wouldn't do to say that we had met by accident; I was embarrassed, but Ruth's fine laugh cleared the air for me.

"Nicest I ever saw," she said.

"Did you ever walk up that hill," I asked him, "where you can see out over the valley?"

"Once," he said in a surprisingly harsh voice. "I'd rather play chess."

So we went into one of the recreation rooms, and O'Doone beat me at three games of chess. Ruth sat by, knitting — a sweater for a cousin's baby. We talked little, but comfortably. It would have been a domestic scene, if it had not been for the fifty or sixty other people in the room.

Herb, what does it all mean?

ANDY

April 20

Dear Herb,

This is a *Prior* Script. If all goes well you will receive this letter from Ruth's cousin, who will be informed by O'Doone's sister to forward it to you. O'Doone's sister will also send you instructions on how to make the invisible ink visible. When I wrote the letter, I was in a self-destructive frame of mind; I was prepared to take all the certainly drastic consequences that would come from its being read by someone of authority. But O'Doone's invisible ink (what a strange fellow to have brought a quart of it here! He said he had brought it only to play mysterious letter-games with his nephew — I wonder) and Ruth's baby sweater, upon the wrapping of which I write this, combined to save me. If the authorities catch *this,* I don't care what happens. It takes so long to write lightly enough in invisible ink for no pen marks to show on the paper, that I doubt if I will have the patience to use it often. Most of my letters will be innocuous in regular ink. I may add an invisible note or two, between the lines, in the margin, at the end. O'Doone says it's not any of the ordinary kinds and if we're careful the authorities are not likely to catch us. O'Doone is strange. He refused to take this whole ink matter for anything more than a big joke — as though we were digging a tunnel under a house, O'Doone pretending we are just tunneling in a strawstack to hide our marbles, myself trying to protest (but being laughed at for my lapse in taste) that we are really undermining a house in order to blow it up,

Which perhaps we are. In any event, I don't have the energy left to rewrite this letter; I'll merely copy it off, invisibly.

. I cannot tell you how shocked I was to discover the familiar, black, censor's ink over five lines in your last letter. The censor censored! I had not thought of that. In my innocence I had thought that we writers in the higher brackets could be trusted to be discreet. One would think I was still a loyal subscriber to the *Nation,* I was so naïve. But no — I am trusted to censor the letters of inferiors (I suspect my censorship is sample-checked by someone), but my own letters are themselves inspected and their dangerous sentiments excised. And, irony of ironies! your own references to the fact that my letters were censored were themselves blacked out.

Who is it that does this? The head of PR here? That's a strange way to make him waste his time. One of his assistants? Then the head must censor the assistant's letters. And the chief board of the NRACP censors the head's letters? And the President theirs? And God his? And —— ?

Which is the more imprisoned — the jailer who thinks he is free and is not, or the prisoner who knows the precise boundaries of his liberty and accepting them explores and uses all the world he has?

I am a jailer who knows he is not free. I am a prisoner who does not know the limits of his freedom. And all this I voluntarily submitted to in the name of a higher freedom. Ever since my adolescence, when the New Deal was a faith, liberty has been one of the always repeated, never examined articles of my creed. Well, I have been examining liberty recently, and she's a pure fraud.

One thing I have learned — you don't just quietly put yourself on the side of Ruth's dishers, you become one of them yourself; and a disher *has* to dish it out, he cannot help it at all; and he pays for it. Or maybe I am only paying for my guilt-making desire to be a more important disher than I am.

Ruth was surprised at my distress upon receiving your censored letter. She only shrugged. What had I expected, after all? It was inevitable, it was a necessity. That's the key word, Herb — Necessity. Not liberty, Necessity. True liberty is what the prisoner has, because he accepts Necessity. That's the great thing, Herb, to recognize and accept Necessity.

I've slowly been working toward a realization of this. I think my decision to work in the NRACP came from recognizing the social necessity of it. The Negro problem in America was acute and was insoluble by any liberal formula; this solution gives dignity and independence to the

Negroes; it staves off the Depression by the huge demand for manufactured products, for transportation, for the operations of the NRACP itself; but perhaps most important of all, it establishes irrevocably in the American people's mind the wisdom and rightness of the government; for if capitalism must go (as it must) it should be replaced peaceably by a strong and wise planned state. Such a state we are proving ourselves to be. Very well. I accepted this. But what I forgot was that *I*, I the individual, I Andrew Dixon, must personally submit to the stringencies of necessity. The relics of the New Deal faith remained to clutter up my new attitude. This experience, coming when and as it did, particularly coming when Ruth's courageous wisdom was nearby to support me, has liberated me (I hope) into the greater freedom of the Prisoner of Necessity.

Such are my pious prayers at least. I cannot say I am sure I fully understand all the strictures of necessity. I *can* say I do not enjoy those I understand. But pious I will remain.

Remember the days when we thought we could *change* Necessity? Democracy and all that? How much older I feel!

ANDY

May 1

Mary my dear,

Please let me apologize — sincerely too, Mary — for having neglected you so cruelly for the past months. Herb tells me you are quite put out, and well you might be. I can find no excuses for it, but this I will stoutly maintain — it was not a question of hostility or indifference to you, my dear. Actually I have been going through something of a crisis, as Herb may have been telling you. It has something to do with the desert, and something to do with the NRACP, and a lot to do with the charming young woman whose picture I enclose. She is Ruth Cone. We are getting married in a couple of Sundays — Mother's Day. Why Mother's Day, I really don't know. But she wants it, so there's no help. The details of our plighting troth might amuse you.

A couple of evenings ago I was playing chess in the recreation room with a man named O'Doone, my only friend here. Ruth was sitting beside us knitting some rompers for a cousin's baby. From time to time we would chat a little; it was all very comfortable and unromantic. O'Doone, between games, went to the toilet. When he had left, Ruth said to me with a twinkle in her eye, "Andy darling, don't you see what I am

doing?" I replied, "Why yes, my sweet, knitting tiny garments. Is it — ?"
And we both laughed heartily. It was a joke, you see, a mild comfortable
little joke, and no one would have thought of it a second time except that
when we had finished laughing it was no longer a joke. Her face became
very sober, and I am sure mine did too. I said, "Do you want children,
Ruth?" "Yes," she replied. "Do you want to have my children?" "Yes,"
she said again, without looking at me. Then with the most charming
conquest of modesty that you can imagine, she turned her serious little
face to me, and we very lightly kissed. O'Doone had returned by then.
"Well," he said in a bright way, "do I interrupt?" "Not at all," I answered; "we have just decided to get married." He burbled a little, in
caricature of the overwhelmed, congratulating friend, pumped our hands,
and asked us when we were marrying. "I don't know," I said. "Why not
tomorrow?" "Oh no," said Ruth severely, "how can I assemble my trousseau?" At which O'Doone went off into a braying laugh, and we set up
the chess pieces. "Bet you five to one," he said, "I win this game in less
than sixty moves." I wouldn't take his bet. It took him about forty moves
to beat me.

And thus did Dixon and Cone solemnly vow to share their fortunes.

It's the first marriage in PR. Everybody will attend. The chief promised
me Monday off and temporary quarters in one of the guest suites. We are
to get a two-room apartment in the new dormitory that is nearly completed. Such privacy and spaciousness will make us the envy of the whole
community. I'm sure there will be a spate of marriages as soon as the
dormitory is completed. We will not be married by a holy man, partly
because neither of us believes in it and partly because there isn't one of
any kind on the premises. (I wondered why those detailed questions
about religious beliefs on our application forms.) There was a little
trouble at first about who was authorized to marry people here. The PR
chief, as the only person permitted to leave the place, went out and got
himself authorized to do it legally. I think he rather fancies himself in
the capacity of marrier. He runs to paternalism.

Ruth urges me, Mary — she assumes, quite rightly, that I have not
done it already — to tell you some of the homely details of life here. Of
our sleeping rooms, the less said the better. The beds are comfortable
period. We live quite communally, but very well. There's a fine gym-
nasium, with swimming pool and playfields attached — tennis, baseball,
squash, fencing, everything but golf. There's the best library (surely the
best!) in the world on American Negro affairs, and a reasonably good

one of modern literature. We have comfortable working quarters — with long enough hours to be sure. There is a fine desert for us to walk around in, and I have come to need an occasional stroll in the desert for spiritual refreshment. And we eat handsomely, except for vegetables. In fact, the only complaint that I have of the cooking is the monotony of its excellence — roast, steak, chop, stew. Never or seldom, liver and kidneys and omelettes and casseroles. And always frozen vegetables. Well, probably the Negroes will be producing plenty of vegetables within a few weeks. There's lots of liquor of every kind. There is a sort of department store where one can buy everything one needs and most of the luxuries one could want in this restricted life. There's a movie a week — double-feature with news and cartoon — and bridge or poker every day. A micro-cosmic plenitude.

Well, as for the rest of our routine life here, I can think of nothing interesting enough to mention. We work and avoid work, backbite, confide, suspect. It's a bureaucratic existence, no doubt of that.

Will this epistle persuade you to forgive me?

Now you must write to me — soon.

Devotedly yours,

ANDY

(In invisible ink)

O'Doone, who sometimes gives his opinions very obliquely, came to me today with some disturbing figures. He wasn't in the least jaunty about them, and I must confess that I am not either.

According to *Time,* which seems to know more about the CPR than we do, there have been about 50,000 Negroes interned already, and these 50,000 include nearly all the wealthy and politically powerful Negroes in the nation (including an objectionable white-supremacy Senator one of whose great-great-grandmothers turns out to have been black). The leaders were interned first, reasonably enough, to provide the skeleton of government and system in the new State which they are to erect. *But,* O'Doone points out, we have yet to receive from them a request for letters from an outsider; and if any Negroes at all are going to make such requests, it must surely be these, the most important, the least afraid of red tape. (He also pointed out that not one of the entertainers or athletes of prominence has been interned. That, I'm afraid, is all too easily explained.) You see, says O'Doone, you see? But he didn't say Why? to me, and I'm glad he didn't for I can't even guess why.

Another statistic he had concerned the CPR itself. We all know that the figures on natural resources in the CPR are exaggerated. Grossly. Fourteen million people cannot possibly live well in this area, and O'Doone demonstrated that fact to me most convincingly. The Negro problem, economically, in the U.S. has been that they provided a larger cheap labor market than consumer market. Now the false stimulus of capitalizing their beginnings here will keep American industry on an even keel for years and years, but after that what? O'Doone bowed out at that point, but I think I can press the point a little further. They will provide a market for surplus commodities, great enough to keep the pressures of capitalism from blowing us sky-high, meanwhile permitting the transition to a planned State to take place. Very astute, I think, very astute indeed.

June 12

Dear Herb,

Why I have not written, you ought to be able to guess. I will not pretend to any false ardors about Ruth. She is wise and winning as a woman, and everything one could ask for as a wife. I love her dearly. She has not read very widely or profoundly, but I think she is going to do something about that, soon. We are very happy together and I think we shall continue to be happy during the difficult years to come. What more can I say?

Why are happiness and contentment and the sense of fulfillment so hard to write about? I can think of nothing to say, and besides Ruth is just coming in from tennis (it's 9:30 Sunday morning).

10 P.M.

Ruth has gone to bed, so I will continue in another vein.

I have been discovering that the wells of pity, which have lain so long locked and frozen in my eyes, are thawed in me now. I am enclosing a letter which came in from a Negress in Chicago to her lover, in the CPR, and his response. It is the first letter from inside, except for the usual three during the first week, that I have read. Apparently a few have been coming out now and then, but this is my first one. I cannot tell you how I pitied both these unhappy people. When Ruth read them, she said, "My, what a mean man! I hope he has to collect garbage all his life." I cannot agree with her. I think his little note betrays an unhappiness as great as the woman's, and even more pitiable for being unrecognized, unappreciated. Judge for yourself. I can think of nothing to add.

ANDY

Honey dear child, why don't you write to me? Don't you even remember all those things you told me you'd do no matter what? And you're not even in jail, you just in that place where we all going to go to sooner or later. O I sure hope they take me there with you. I can't live without you. But I don't even know who to ask to go there with you. I went to the policeman and they said they didn't know nothing about it. I don't know what to do. You don't know how I ache for you honey. It's just like I got a tooth pulled out but it ain't no tooth it's worse, and there is no dentist for it neither. There's a fellow at the store keeps bothering me now and again, but I assure him I don't want him I got a man. I thought I had a man, you, but I don't hear nothing from you. Maybe you got something there, I don't see how you could do it not after those things you said, but if you have tell me so I can go off in some hole and die. I don't want this Lee Lawson, he's no good, it's you I want, sweetheart, you tell me it's all right. I got to hear from you or I'll just die.

Dear ——— ,
   I've been so busy baby, you wouldn't believe how busy I've been. You'll be coming here pretty soon and then you'll feel better too. It's nice here. We'll get along fine then. You tell that guy to leave you be. You're my gal. Tell him I said so.

Yours truly,
———

(In invisible ink)
   I didn't include these letters because I thought they were in the Héloïse-Abélard class, but because I wanted to say something about them, and also because they gave me more invisible space.
   The man's response came to us already typed. That very much astonished me, and O'Doone, when I told him, let fly a nasty one. "I suppose," he said, "they have a couple of writers in there writing a few letters in place of the Negroes, which we then relay. Complicated, isn't it?" Not complicated, upsetting. Devastating. What if it were true? (And I must say this letter has an air more like the PR rewrite-formula than like a real letter. Then *none* of the Negroes would have even a filtered connection

with the outside world. Why? Why fool even us? Is there no end to the deception and doubt of this place?

O'Doone posed another of his puzzles yesterday. He read in the current PR weekly bulletin that the CPR has been shipping whole trainloads of leather goods and canned meats to China and Europe for relief purposes, under the government's supervision of course. O'Doone came into my office at once, waving the bulletin and chortling. "How do you like it?" he cried. "Before we get a carrot out of them the Chinese get tons of meat." Then a sudden light seemed to dawn on his face. "Where did all the cattle come from?"

A strange thing happened: O'Doone's intelligent, sensitive face collapsed. The great domed forehead remained almost unwrinkled, but his features looked somehow like one of those children's rubber faces which collapse when you squeeze them. No anguish, no anxiety. Only collapse. He left without a word. I wish he had never come here with that news.

Last night I lay awake till three or four o'clock. I could hear trucks and trains rumbling occasionally throughout the night — entering and leaving the Reserve. But that guard I met at the foot of the hill told me that they only bring internees in the daytime. Are those shipments? How can it be? Sometimes I am sick at heart with doubt and uncertainty.

I dreamt last night that I was a Gulliver, lying unbound and unresisting on the ground while a thousand Lilliputians, all of them black, ate at me. I would not write the details of that dream even in invisible ink. Not even in plain water.

July 4

Dear Herb,

Hail Independence Day! Some of the overgrown kids around here are shooting off firecrackers. No one is working. It is all very pleasant. I suppose March 20 will be the Independence Day of the new Negro nation — the day when the first trainload arrived. How long ago that seems already. I do not think I have ever been through so much in so short a time. And now for the real news.

Ruth is pregnant! Amazing woman, she remains outwardly as humorous and self-contained as ever. No one else knows her condition, because she wants to avoid as much as possible of the female chatter that goes with pregnancy. She insists upon playing tennis still. Yet she is not all calmness and coolness; when we are lying in bed together before going to sleep, she croons little nonsense hymns to pregnancy in my ear, and yesterday afternoon at the office she walked into my cubicle, up to where I was sitting very solemnly, and placed my hand over her womb. Then she kissed me with a sort of unviolent passion such as I have never known before in my life. I tell you, she's a wonderful woman.

How miraculous is conception and growth! I no more understand such things than I really understand about the stars and their rushings. One event follows another, but I'm sure I don't know why. You get back to an archaic awe, if you permit yourself to, realizing that you yourself have started off a chain of miracles. I never had a sense of littleness when observing the naked heavens, of man's puniness, of my own nothingness. Perhaps it was a fear of that feeling which for so long prevented me from looking upwards at all. I mentioned my reaction to O'Doone on one of the first occasions of our meeting; he nodded and said, "But is not a man more complex than a star, and in every way but one that we know of, more valuable?" What he said remains with me yet; and when I am presented with the vastness of the stars and the forces which operate within them, I am impressed and excited enough but I am not depressed by the imagined spectacle. Their bigness does not make me little. My own complexity does not make them simple. Man is no longer the center of the universe perhaps, but neither is anything else. That I have learned.

But when I am presented with the proof of the powers that men (and myself) possess, then I still feel a little off balance. When Clarice was pregnant with Betty, I had no such feeling. I felt annoyed chiefly. But now, in this desert, in the CPR, I have been sent back at last to fundamentals, to the sources of things; and I realize fully how unaccountable is birth to life. Ruth, who never departed far from the sources, is less embarrassed in admitting her sense of mystery.

One thing I am going to teach this child, if it can be taught anything: that the humane tradition has been tried and found wanting. It's over, finished, kaput. A new era of civilization commences. Kindness and freedom — once they were good for something, but no more. *Put yourself in his place* — never. Rather, fight to stay where you are. I think we are entering upon an age of reason and mystery. Reason which accepts and understands the uttermost heights and depths of human power, man's depravity and his nobility; and, understanding these, dares use them toward a great and future goal, the goal of that stern order which is indispensable to the fullest development of man. Mystery toward all that is not explainable, which is a very great deal. Rationalism failed, for it asserted that everything was ultimately explainable. We know better. We know that to destroy a man's sense of mystery is to cut him off at one of the sources of life. Awe, acceptance, faith — these are wonderful sources of power and fulfillment. I have discovered them. My child shall never forget them.

ANDY

(*In invisible ink*)

I have put the gun to my temple, Herb, I have pointed the knife at my heart. But my nerve failed me. There were a few days when I was nearly distracted. My division chief told me to stay home till I looked better, but I dared not. I think it was only Ruth's pregnancy that saved me. My newly awakened sense of mystery, plus my powers of reason, have saved me. This is the third letter I have written you in a week, but I knew the others were wild and broken, and I was not sure at all that I was physically able to write in such a manner as to avoid detection.

It came to a head, for me, two weeks ago. O'Doone entered my office, his face looking bright and blasted. He dropped a booklet on my desk and left after a few comments of no importance. The booklet was an anthropologist's preliminary report on certain taboos among American Negroes. The fellow had been interviewing them in Intake. There was nothing of special interest about it that I could see, except that it was written in the past tense.

I expected O'Doone to reclaim the booklet any day. For some reason he had always done the visiting to me, not I to him. He was very restless, and I am slothful. But a week passed, and no O'Doone. I did not meet him in the café nor in the recreation room. I went to his own room, but he did not answer. The next day I went to his office, and his secretary told me he had not shown up for two days. I returned to his room. It was locked. The janitor unlocked it for me. When I entered I saw him lying dead on his bed. "Well, old boy," I said to drive the janitor away, I don't know why, "feeling poorly?" He had drunk something. There was a glass on the table by his bed. There was no note. His face was repulsive. (That is a mystery I have learned to respect, how hideous death is.) He was cold, and somehow a little sticky to the touch. I covered his face with a towel, and sat down. I knew I should call someone, but I did not want to. I knew the janitor would remember letting me in, and my staying too long. Yet I felt that there was something I must do. What it was I could not remember, something important. It took me an eternity to remember

— the invisible ink. I knew where he had kept it. It was not there. I looked throughout his room, and it was simply gone. I left the room.

I still did not notify anyone of his suicide. I was not asking myself why he had done it. Or perhaps I was only shouting Where's the ink? in a loud voice to cover up the little question Why? I went to our rooms and straight to the liquor shelf. I took down the Scotch and poured myself a stiff one, and drank. It was horrible. I spat it out, cursing; then I recognized the odor. O'Doone had come over, poured out the Scotch (I hope he enjoyed it himself) and filled the bottle with the invisible ink. At that, I broke down in the most womanish way, and cried on the bed (never ask Why? Why? Why?).

Ruth found me there some time later. I told her everything that had happened, and she immediately pulled me together. She had the sense to know I had been acting more oddly than was wise. She notified the right people, and O'Doone was disposed of. No one asked me any embarrassing questions, and no official mention of O'Doone's end was made anywhere.

I must continue this on a birthday card.

(In invisible ink, on a large, plain Happy Birthday card to Mary)

I had still not allowed myself to ask why he had done it, but Ruth put the thing in a short sentence. "He was too soft-hearted to stand it here." She was right; he was a Christian relic. He knew more than he could bear. I resolved to go that very evening again to the hill where the black searchlight threatened the night.

Some sandwiches. Four half-pints of whiskey. A hunting-knife (a foolish gesture, I know). Plain drab clothes. The long walk in the still hot, late-afternoon sun. Sunset. The huge, sudden twilight. And I was within sight of a guard (not the same one I had seen before) standing by the new fence at the foot of the hill.

I crept up toward him under cover of brush and cactus, till I was close enough to toss a half-pint of whiskey in his direction. His bored, stupid face immediately became animated by the most savage emotions. He leveled his gun and pointed it in my general direction. He could not see me, however, and rather than look for me he crouched, eyes still searching the underbrush, to reach for the bottle. He drained it in five minutes.

"Throw me some more," he whispered loudly.

"Put the gun down."

I aimed my voice away from him, hoping that he would not spot me. I was lying flat beneath a large clump of sagebrush. There was a Joshua tree nearby, and several cactus plants. He pointed the gun at one of the stalks of cactus, and crept up toward it. Then he suddenly stopped, I don't know why, and walked back to his post.

"What yer want?" he asked.

I tossed out another bottle. He jumped again; then he got it and drank it.

"What's going on in there?" I asked him.

"They're fixing up the niggers," he said. "You know as much about it as I do."

He began to sing "O Susannah" in a sentimental voice. It was beginning to get too dark for my safety. I was desperate.

I tossed out another bottle, only not so far this time. When he leaned for it, I said very clearly, "You look like a butcher."

He deliberately opened the bottle and drank off half of it.

"Butcher, huh? Butcher?" he laid down his gun and took his villainous knife out. "I'm no butcher. I won't have nothing to do with the whole slimy mess. I won't eat them. No, sir, you can do that for me. But I can do a little carving, I think. No butcher, you son of a bitch. You dirty prying nigger-eating son of a bitch. I'll learn you to call me a butcher."

He was stalking the cactus again. He lunged forward at it, and with much monotonous cursing and grunting dealt with it murderously. Meanwhile I crawled out on the other side of the sagebrush and ran for it. He never shot at me. Nothing happened, except that I too ran full tilt into a cactus, and had to walk hours in agony of flesh as well as of spirit. I vomited and retched till I thought I would be unable to walk further.

I must continue this letter some other way.

ANDY

(In invisible ink, on the papers wrapping another sweater for Ruth's cousin's baby)

I told Ruth nothing of what I had learned. Not even *her* great sense of the inevitable could survive such a shock, I think. Yet sometimes it seems to me that she must surely know it all. I do not want to know whether she knows. Could I support it if she did?

It was more painful pulling the cactus needles out than it had been acquiring them. But she removed them all, bathed the little wounds with alcohol and put me to bed. The next morning I awoke at seven and insisted upon going to work. I sat all day in my office, eating crackers and drinking milk. I didn't accomplish a thing. It was that day my chief told me to take it easy for a while. I was in a sort of stupor for a couple of days; yet I insisted, to everyone's consternation, on going to work. I accomplished nothing, and I intended to accomplish nothing. It was just that I could not tolerate being alone. In fact, today was the first day I have been alone for more than five minutes since I returned from the walk. But today I have regained a kind of composure, or seeming of composure, which for a time I despaired of ever possessing again. And I know that by the time I have given shape enough to my thoughts to put them on this paper for you to read, I shall have gained again a peace of mind. To have you to write to, Herb, that is the great thing at this point. Without you there, I do not know what I would have done.

So much for my emotions. My thinking, my personal philosophy, has gone through at least as profound an upheaval as they.

In the chaos of my mind, in which huge invisible chunks of horror hit me unexpectedly from unexpected angles again and again, my first coherent and sensible idea came in the form of a question. "Why did they make it possible for me to find out what has been going on?" For I finally realized that it was no fluke that I had discovered it. Or O'Doone either. Or anyone with the suspicions and the courage for it. When the atom bombs were being produced, the whole vast undertaking was carried off without a single leak to the outside. Therefore, if I had been able in so simple a way to find out what had been going on in the CPR, it was only because they didn't care. They could have stopped me.

Then I thought: invisible ink is scarcely new in the history of things. Perhaps they have been reading my correspondence with you all along and will smile at this letter as they have smiled at others; or perhaps they haven't taken the trouble to read it, because they simply don't care.

Perhaps the authorities not only did not care if we gradually found out, but wanted us to.

Why should they want us to? Why, if that were true, should they have put up so formidable a system of apparent preventatives? Double fences, censorship, lies, etc., etc.?

The only answer that makes sense is this. They want the news gradually and surreptitiously to sift out to the general population — illegally, in the form of hideous rumors to which people can begin to accustom themselves. After all, everyone knew generally that something like the

atom bomb was being manufactured. Hiroshima was not the profound
and absolute shock in 1945 that it would have been in 1935, and a good
deal of the preparation for its general acceptance was rumor. It is in the
people's interest that the CPR function as it does function, and especially
so that they can pretend that they have nothing to do with it. The
experience of the Germans in the Jew-extermination camps demonstrated
that clearly enough. It would do no good for me to go around crying out
the truth about NRACP, because few would believe me in the first place
and my suppression would only give strength to the rumors, which were
required and planned for anyhow.

But I still had to set myself the task of answering Why? What drove
them (whoever they are) to the decision to embark upon a course which
was not only revolutionary but dangerous? I accepted the NRACP as
inevitable, as Necessity; there remained only the task of trying to understand wherein lay the mystery of the Necessity and of adjusting myself to
the situation. The individual, even the leader, has no significant choice to
make in the current of event; that current is part of natural law; it is
unmoral, cruel, wasteful, useless, and mysterious. The leader is he who
sees and points out the course of history, that we may pursue that course
with least pain. It is odd that we Americans have no such leader; what
we have is committees and boards and bureau heads who collectively
possess leadership and who direct our way almost impersonally. There is
nothing whatsoever that I myself would like so much as to be one of
those wise, courageous, anonymous planners. The wisdom I think that I
possess. But in place of courage I have a set of moral scruples dating
from an era when man was supposed to have a soul and when disease
took care of overpopulation. The old vestigial values of Christianity must
be excised in the people as they are being excised in me. The good and
the lucky are assisting at the birth of a new age. The weak and unfit are
perishing in the death of an old. Which shall it be for us?

For my own part, I think I am in a state of transition, from being one
of the unfit to being one of the fit. I feel it. I will it. There are certain
external evidences of it. For example, I was face to face with the truth at
the end of April, but instead of acknowledging what I saw I turned to
my love for Ruth. Yet that refusal to recognize the truth did not long
survive the urgings of my sense of necessity. And I remember, when
being confronted with piecemeal evidences of the truth, that I was unable
to explain a number of them. You know, Herb, how accomplished a

rationalizer I can be; yet this time I did not even *try* to rationalize about many of the facts.

— It is dawn outside. I cannot read this letter over, so I am not entirely sure how incoherent it is. I feel that I have said most of what I wanted to say. I am not very happy. I think I shall sleep the better for having written this. I eat nothing but bread and fruit and milk. A bird is singing outside; he is making the only sound in the world. I can see the hill which separates us from the Intake buildings. It's a pleasant hill, rather like an arm extending out from the valley sides, and I am glad it is there. I am cold now, but in three hours it will be warm and in five hours hot. I am rambling I know. But suddenly all my energy has leaked out. I walk to the door to see Ruth so happily sleeping, mysteriously replenishing life from this nightly portion of death, and I think of that baby she is bearing and will give birth to. If it were not for her and the baby, I am sure I should have gone mad. Is not that a mystery, Herb? Our child shall be fortunate; it is the first conscious generation of each new order in whom the greatest energy is released. There are splendid things ahead for our child.

It is not my fault. I did not know what I was doing. How could I have known? What can I do now?

I stare at the lightening sky, exhausted. I do not know why I do not say farewell, and go to bed. Perhaps it is because I do not want to hear that little lullaby that sings in my ears whenever I stop: I have eaten human flesh, my wife is going to have a baby; I have eaten human flesh, my wife is going to have a baby.

Remember, back in the simple days of the Spanish Civil War, when Guernica was bombed, we speculated all one evening what the worst thing in the world could be? This is the worst thing in the world, Herb. I tell you, the worst. After this, nothing.

Perhaps if I lay my head against Ruth's breast and put her hands over my ears I can go to sleep. Last night I recited Housman's "Loveliest of trees, the cherry now," over and over till I went to sleep, not because I like it particularly but because I could think of nothing else at all to recite.

My wife is going to have a baby, my wife is going to have a baby, my wife is going to have a baby.

Bless you,
ANDY

HORTENSE CALISHER

"In Greenwich There Are Many Gravelled Walks" is a poignant story of another "lost generation," a modern one. The young people in this story are much more lost from childhood on than were even Fitzgerald's people of the twenties. And the older characters who form their background are equally lost.

Hortense Calisher was born in New York and attended the city schools and Barnard College. During the Depression she held various jobs ranging from head of stock in a hat department to caseworker in a family service agency. She is the mother of two children.

In Greenwich
There Are Many Gravelled Walks

ON AN AFTERNOON in early August, Peter Birge, just returned from driving his mother to the Greenwich sanitarium she had to frequent at intervals, sat down heavily on a furbelowed sofa in the small apartment he and she had shared ever since his return from the Army a year ago. He was thinking that his usually competent solitude had become more than he could bear. He was a tall, well-built young man of about twenty-three, with a pleasant face whose even, standardized look was the effect of proper food, a good dentist, the best schools, and a brush haircut. The heat, which bored steadily into the room through a Venetian blind lowered over a half-open window, made his white T shirt cling to his chest and arms, which were still brown from a week's sailing in July at a cousin's place on the Sound. The family of cousins, one cut according to the pattern of a two-car-and-country-club suburbia, had always looked with distaste on his precocious childhood with his mother in the Village and, the few times he had been farmed out to them during those early years, had received his healthy normality with ill-concealed surprise, as if they had clearly expected to have to fatten up what they undoubtedly referred to in private as "poor Anne's boy." He had only gone there at all, this time, when it became certain that the money saved up for a summer abroad, where his Army stint had not sent him, would have to be spent on one of his mother's trips to Greenwich, leaving barely enough, as it was, for his next, and final, year at the School of Journalism. Half out of disheartenment over his collapsed summer, half to provide himself with a credible "out" for the too jovially pressing cousins at Rye, he had registered for some courses at the Columbia summer session. Now these were almost over, too, leaving a gap before the fall semester began. He had cut this morning's classes in order to drive his mother up to the place in Connecticut.

He stepped to the window and looked through the blind at the convertible parked below, on West Tenth Street. He ought to call the garage for the pickup man, or else, until he thought of someplace to go, he ought to hop down and put up the top. Otherwise, baking there in the hot sun, the car would be like a griddle when he went to use it, and the leather seats were cracking badly anyway.

It had been cool when he and his mother started, just after dawn that morning, and the air of the well-ordered countryside had had that almost speaking freshness of early day. With her head bound in a silk scarf and her chubby little chin tucked into the cardigan which he had buttoned on her without forcing her arms into the sleeves, his mother, peering up at him with the near-gaiety born of relief, had had the exhausted charm of a child who has just been promised the thing for which it has nagged. Anyone looking at the shingled hair, the feet in small brogues — anyone not close enough to see how drawn and beakish her nose looked in the middle of her little, round face, which never reddened much with drink but at the worst times took on a sagging, quilted whiteness — might have thought the two of them were a couple, any couple, just off for a day in the country. No one would have thought that only a few hours before, some time after two, he had been awakened, pounded straight up on his feet, by the sharp, familiar cry and then the agonized susurrus of prattling that went on and on and on, that was different from her everyday, artlessly confidential prattle only in that now she could not stop, she could not stop, *she could not stop,* and above the small, working mouth with its eliding, spinning voice, the glazed button eyes opened wider and wider, as if she were trying to breathe through them.

Later, after the triple bromide, the warm bath, and the crooning, practiced soothing he administered so well, she had hiccuped into crying,
then into stillness at last, and had fallen asleep on his breast. Later still,
she had awakened him, for he must have fallen asleep there in the big
chair with her, and with the weak, humiliated goodness which always
followed these times she had even tried to help him with the preparations
for the journey — preparations which, without a word between them,
they had set about at once. There'd been no doubt, of course, that she
would have to go. There never was.

He left the window and sat down again in the big chair and smoked
one cigarette after another. Actually, for a drunkard — or an alcoholic, as
people preferred to say these days — his mother was the least troublesome
of any. He had thought of it while he packed the pairs of daintily kept
shoes, the sweet-smelling blouses and froufrou underwear, the tiny, perfect dresses — of what a comfort it was that she had never grown raddled
or blowzy. Years ago, she had perfected the routine within which she
could feel safe for months at a time. It had gone on for longer than he
could remember: from before the death of his father, a Swedish engineer,
on the income of whose patents they had always been able to live fairly
comfortably; probably even during her life with that other long-dead
man, the painter whose model and mistress she had been in the years
before she married his father. There would be the long, drugged sleep of
the morning, then the unsteady hours when she manicured herself back
into cleanliness and reality. Then, at about four or five in the afternoon,
she and the dog (for there was always a dog) would make their short
pilgrimage to the clubby, cozy little hangout where she would be a
fixture until far into the morning, where she had been a fixture for the
last twenty years.

Once, while he was at boarding school, she had made a supreme effort
to get herself out of the routine — for his sake, no doubt — and he had
returned at Easter to a new apartment, uptown, on Central Park West.
All that this had resulted in was inordinate taxi fares and the repetitious
nightmare evenings when she had gotten lost, and he had found her, a
small, untidy heap, in front of their old place. After a few months, they
had moved back to the Village, to those few important blocks where she
felt safe and known and loved. For they all knew her there, or got to
know her — the aging painters, the newcomer poets, the omniscient news
hacks, the military spinsters who bred dogs, the anomalous, sandalled

young men. And they accepted her, this dainty hanger-on who neither painted nor wrote but hung their paintings on her walls, faithfully read their parti-colored magazines, and knew them all — their shibboleths, their feuds, the whole vocabulary of their disintegration, and, in a mild, occasional manner, their beds.

Even this, he could not remember not knowing. At ten, he had been an expert compounder of remedies for hangover, and of an evening, standing sleepily in his pajamas to be admired by the friends his mother sometimes brought home, he could have predicted accurately whether the party would end in a brawl or in a murmurous coupling in the dark.

It was curious, he supposed now, stubbing out a final cigarette, that he had never judged resentfully either his mother or her world. By the accepted standards, his mother had done her best; he had been well housed, well schooled, even better loved than some of the familied boys he had known. Wisely, too, she had kept out of his other life, so that he had never had to be embarrassed there except once, and this when he was grown, when she had visited his Army camp. Watching her at a post party for visitors, poised there, so chic, so distinctive, he had suddenly seen it begin: the fear, the scare, then the compulsive talking, which always started so innocently that only he would have noticed at first — that warm, excited, buttery flow of harmless little lies and pretensions which gathered its dreadful speed and content and ended then, after he had whipped her away, just as it had ended this morning.

On the way up this morning, he had been too clever to subject her to a restaurant, but at a drive-in place he was able to get her to take some coffee. How grateful they had both been for the coffee, she looking up at him, tremulous, her lips pecking at the cup, he blessing the coffee as it went down her! And afterward, as they flew onward, he could feel her straining like a homing pigeon toward their destination, toward the place where she felt safest of all, where she would gladly have stayed forever if she had just had enough money for it, if they would only let her stay. For there the pretty little woman and her dog — a poodle this time — would be received like the honored guest that she was, so trusted and docile a guest, who asked only to hide there during the season of her discomfort, who was surely the least troublesome of them all.

He had no complaints, then, he assured himself as he sat on the burning front seat of the convertible trying to think of somewhere to go. It was just that while others of his age still shared a communal wonder at what life might hold, he had long since been solitary in his knowledge of what life was.

Up in a sky as honestly blue as a flag, an airplane droned smartly toward Jersey. Out at Rye, the younger crowd at the club would be commandeering the hot blue day, the sand, and the water, as if these were all extensions of themselves. They would use the evening this way, too, disappearing from the veranda after a dance, exploring each other's rhythm-and-whiskey-whetted appetites in the backs of cars. They all thought themselves a pretty sophisticated bunch, the young men who had graduated not into a war but into its hung-over peace, the young girls attending junior colleges so modern that the deans had to spend all their time declaring that their girls were being trained for the family and the community. But when Peter looked close and saw how academic their sophistication was, how their undamaged eyes were still starry with expectancy, their lips still avidly open for what life would surely bring, then he became envious and awkward with them, like a guest at a party to whose members he carried bad news he had no right to know, no right to tell.

He turned on the ignition and let the humming motor prod him into a decision. He would drop in at Robert Vielum's, where he had dropped in quite often until recently, for the same reason that others stopped by at Vielum's — because there was always likely to be somebody there. The door of Robert's old-fashioned apartment, on Claremont Avenue, almost always opened on a heartening jangle of conversation and music, which meant that others had gathered there, too, to help themselves over the pauses so endemic to university life — the life of the mind — and there were usually several members of Robert's large acquaintance among the subliterary, quasi-artistic, who had strayed in, ostensibly en route somewhere, and who lingered on hopefully on the chance that in each other's company they might find out what that somewhere was.

Robert was a perennial taker of courses — one of those non-matriculated students of indefinable age and income, some of whom pursued, with monkish zeal and no apparent regard for time, this or that freakishly peripheral research project of their own conception, and others of whom, like Robert, seemed to derive a Ponce de León sustenance from the young. Robert himself, a large man of between forty and fifty whose small features were somewhat cramped together in a wide face, never seemed bothered by his own lack of direction, implying rather that this was really the catholic approach of the "whole man," alongside of which the serious pursuit of a degree was somehow foolish, possibly vulgar. Rumor connected him with a rich Boston family that had remittanced him at least as far as New York, but he never spoke about himself, although he was extraordinarily alert to gossip. Whatever income he had he supplemented by renting his extra room to a series of young men students. The one opulence among his dun-colored, perhaps consciously Spartan effects was a really fine record-player, which he kept going at all hours with selections from his massive collection. Occasionally he annotated the music, or the advance-copy novel that lay on his table, with foreign-language tags drawn from the wide, if obscure, latitudes of his travels, and it was his magic talent for assuming that his young friends, too, had known, had experienced, that, more than anything, kept them enthralled.

"*Fabelhaft!* Isn't it?" he would say of the Mozart. "Remember how they did it that last time at Salzburg!" and they would all sit there, included, belonging, headily remembering the Salzburg to which they had never been. Or he would pick up the novel and lay it down again. "*La plume de mon oncle,* I'm afraid. *La plume de mon oncle Gide. Eheu,* poor Gide!" — and they would each make note of the fact that one need not read that particular book, that even, possibly, it was no longer necessary to read Gide.

Peter parked the car and walked into the entrance of Robert's apartment house, smiling to himself, lightened by the prospect of company. After all, he had been weaned on the salon talk of such circles; these self-fancying little bohemias at least made him feel at home. And Robert was cleverer than most — it was amusing to watch him. For just as soon as his satellites thought themselves secure on the promontory of some "trend" he had pointed out to them, they would find that he had deserted them, had gone on to another trend, another eminence, from which he beckoned, cocksure and just faintly malicious. He harmed no one permanently. And if he concealed some skeleton of a weakness, some closeted Difference with the Authorities, he kept it decently interred.

As Peter stood in the dark, soiled hallway and rang the bell of Robert's apartment, he found himself as suddenly depressed again, unaccountably reminded of his mother. There were so many of them, and they affected you so, these charmers who, if they could not offer you the large strength, could still atone for the lack with so many small decencies. It was admirable, surely, the way they managed this. And surely, after all, they harmed no one.

Robert opened the door. "Why, hello — Why, hello, Peter!" He seemed surprised, almost relieved. "Greetings!" he added, in a voice whose boom was more in the manner than the substance. "Come in, Pietro, come in!" He wore white linen shorts, a zebra-striped beach shirt, and huaraches, in which he moved easily, leading the way down the dark hall of the apartment, past the two bedrooms, into the living room. All of the apartment was on a court, but on the top floor, so it received a medium, dingy light from above. The living room, long and pleasant, with an old white mantel, a gas log, and many books, always came as a surprise after the rest of the place, and at any time of day Robert kept a few lamps lit, which rouged the room with an evening excitement.

As they entered, Robert reached over in passing and turned on the record-player. Music filled the room, muted but insistent, as if he wanted it to patch up some lull he had left behind. Two young men sat in front of the dead gas log. Between them was a table littered with maps, an open atlas, travel folders, glass beer steins. Vince, the current roomer, had his head on his clenched fists. The other man, a stranger, indolently raised a dark, handsome head as they entered.

"Vince!" Robert spoke sharply. "You know Peter Birge. And this is Mario Osti. Peter Birge."

The dark young man nodded and smiled, lounging in his chair. Vince nodded. His red-rimmed eyes looked beyond Peter into some distance he seemed to prefer.

"God, isn't it but hot!" Robert said. "I'll get you a beer." He bent over Mario with an inquiring look, a caressing hand on the empty glass in front of him.

Mario stretched back on the chair, smiled upward at Robert, and shook his head sleepily. "Only makes me hotter." He yawned, spread his arms languorously, and let them fall. He had the animal self-possession of the very handsome; it was almost a shock to hear him speak.

Robert bustled off to the kitchen.

"Robert!" Vince called, in his light, pouting voice. "Get me a drink. Not a beer. A drink." He scratched at the blond stubble on his cheek with a nervous, pointed nail. On his round head and retroussé face, the stubble produced the illusion of a desiccated baby, until, looking closer, one imagined that he might never have been one, but might have been spawned at the age he was, to mummify perhaps but not to grow. He wore white shorts exactly like Robert's, and his blue-and-white striped shirt was a smaller version of Robert's brown-and-white, so that the two of them made an ensemble, like the twin outfits the children wore on the beach at Rye.

"You know I don't keep whiskey here." Robert held three steins deftly balanced, his heavy hips neatly avoiding the small tables which scattered the room. "You've had enough, wherever you got it." It was true, Peter remembered, that Robert was fonder of drinks with a flutter of ceremony about them — *café brûlé* perhaps, or, in the spring, a *Maibowle,* over which he could chant the triumphant details of his pursuit of the necessary woodruff. But actually one tippled here on the exhilarating effect of wearing one's newest façade, in the fit company of others similarly attired.

Peter picked up his stein. "You and Vince all set for Morocco, I gather."

"Morocco?" Robert took a long pull at his beer. "No. No, that's been changed. I forgot you hadn't been around. Mario's been brushing up my Italian. He and I are off for Rome the day after tomorrow."

The last record on the changer ended in an archaic battery of horns. In the silence while Robert slid on a new batch of records, Peter heard Vince's nail scrape, scrape along his cheek. Still leaning back, Mario shaped smoke with his lips. Large and facilely drawn, they looked, more than anything, accessible — to a stream of smoke, of food, to another mouth, to any plum that might drop.

"You going to study over there?" Peter said to him.

"Paint." Mario shaped and let drift another corolla of smoke.

"No," Robert said, clicking on the record arm. "I'm afraid Africa's démodé." A harpsichord began to play, its dwarf notes hollow and perfect. Robert raised his voice a shade above the music. "Full of fashion photographers. And little come-lately writers." He sucked in his cheeks and made a face. "Trying out their passions under the beeg, bad sun."

"*Eheu,* poor Africa?" said Peter.

Robert laughed. Vince stared at him out of wizened eyes. Not drink, so much, after all, Peter decided, looking professionally at the mottled cherub face before he realized that he was comparing it with another face, but lately left. He looked away.

"Weren't you going over, Peter?" Robert leaned against the machine.

"Not this year." Carefully Peter kept out of his voice the knell the words made in his mind. In Greenwich, there were many gravelled walks, unshrubbed except for the nurses who dotted them, silent and attitudinized as trees. "Isn't that Landowska playing?"

"Hmm. Nice and cooling on a hot day. Or a fevered brow." Robert fiddled with the volume control. The music became louder, then lowered. "Vince wrote a poem about that once. About the Mozart, really, wasn't it, Vince? 'A lovely clock between ourselves and time.'" He enunciated daintily, pushing the words away from him with his tongue.

"Turn it off!" Vince stood up, his small fists clenched, hanging at his sides.

"No, let her finish." Robert turned deliberately and closed the lid of the machine, so that the faint hiss of the needle vanished from the frail, metronomic notes. He smiled. "What a time-obsessed crowd writers are. Now Mario doesn't have to bother with that dimension."

"Not unless I paint portraits," Mario said. His parted lips exposed his teeth, like some white, unexpected flint of intelligence.

"*Dolce far niente,*" Robert said softly. He repeated the phrase dreamily, so that half-known Italian words — "*loggia,*" the "Ponte Vecchio," the "Lungarno" — imprinted themselves one by one on Peter's mind, and he saw the two of them, Mario and Roberto now, already in the frayed-gold light of Florence, in the umber dusk of half-imagined towns.

A word, muffled, came out of Vince's throat. He lunged for the record-player. Robert seized his wrist and held it down on the lid. They were locked that way, staring at each other, when the doorbell rang.

"That must be Susan," Robert said. He released Vince and looked down, watching the blood return to his fingers, flexing his palm.

With a second choked sound, Vince flung out his fist in an awkward attempt at a punch. It grazed Robert's cheek, clawing downward. A thin line of red appeared on Robert's cheek. Fist to mouth, Vince stood a moment; then he rushed from the room. They heard the nearer bedroom door slam and the lock click. The bell rang again, a short, hesitant burr.

Robert clapped his hand to his cheek, shrugged, and left the room.

Mario got up out of his chair for the first time. "Aren't you going to ask who Susan is?"

"Should I?" Peter leaned away from the face bent confidentially near, curly with glee.

"His daughter," Mario whispered. "He said he was expecting his *daughter.* Can you imagine? *Robert?*"

Peter moved farther away from the mobile, pressing face and, standing at the window, studied gritty details of the courtyard. A vertical line of lighted windows, each with a glimpse of stair, marked the hallways on each of the five floors. Most of the other windows were dim and closed, or opened just a few inches above their white ledges, and the yard was quiet. People would be away or out in the sun, or in their brighter front rooms dressing for dinner, all of them avoiding this dark shaft that connected the backs of their lives. Or, here and there, was there someone sitting in the fading light, someone lying on a bed with his face pressed to a pillow? The window a few feet to the right, around the corner of the court, must be the window of the room into which Vince had gone. There was no light in it.

Robert returned, a Kleenex held against his cheek. With him was a pretty, ruffle-headed girl in a navy-blue dress with a red arrow at each shoulder. He switched on another lamp. For the next arrival, Peter thought, surely he will tug back a velvet curtain or break out with a heraldic flourish of drums, recorded by Red Seal. Or perhaps the musty wardrobe was opening at last and was this the skeleton — this girl who had just shaken hands with Mario, and now extended her hand toward Peter, tentatively, timidly, as if she did not habitually shake hands but today would observe every custom she could.

"How do you do?"

"How do you do?" Peter said. The hand he held for a moment was small and childish, the nails unpainted, but the rest of her was very correct for the eye of the beholder, like the young models one sees in magazines, sitting or standing against a column, always in three-quarter view, so that the picture, the ensemble, will not be marred by the human glance. Mario took from her a red dressing case that she held in her free hand, bent to pick up a pair of white gloves that she had dropped, and returned them with an avid interest which overbalanced, like a waiter's gallantry. She sat down, brushing at the gloves.

"The train was awfully dusty — and crowded." She smiled tightly at Robert, looked hastily and obliquely at each of the other two, and bent over the gloves, brushing earnestly, stopping as if someone had said something, and, when no one did, brushing again.

"Well, well, well," Robert said. His manners, always good, were never so to the point of clichés, which would be for him what nervous *gaffes* were for other people. He coughed, rubbed his cheek with the back of his hand, looked at the hand, and stuffed the Kleenex into the pocket of his shorts. "How was camp?"

Mario's eyebrows went up. The girl was twenty, surely, Peter thought.

"All right," she said. She gave Robert the stiff smile again and looked down into her lap. "I like helping children. They can use it." Her hands folded on top of the gloves, then inched under and hid beneath them.

"Susan's been counselling at a camp which broke up early because of a polio scare," Robert said as he sat down. "She's going to use Vince's room while I'm away, until college opens."

"Oh — " She looked up at Peter, "Then you aren't Vince?"

"No. I just dropped in. I'm Peter Birge."

She gave him a neat nod of acknowledgement. "I'm glad, because I certainly wouldn't want to inconvenience —— "

"Did you get hold of your mother in Reno?" Robert asked quickly.

"Not yet. But she couldn't break up her residence term anyway. And Arthur must have closed up the house here. The phone was disconnected."

"Arthur's Susan's stepfather," Robert explained with a little laugh. "Number three, I think. Or is it *four,* Sue?"

Without moving, she seemed to retreat, so that again there was nothing left for the observer except the girl against the column, any one of a dozen with the short, anonymous nose, the capped hair, the foot arched in the trim shoe, and half an iris glossed with an expertly aimed photoflood. "Three," she said. Then one of the hidden hands stole out from under the gloves, and she began to munch evenly on a fingernail.

"Heavens, you haven't still got that *habit?*" Robert said.

"What a heavy papa you make, Roberto," Mario said.

She flushed, and put the hand back in her lap, tucking the fingers under. She looked from Peter to Mario and back again. "Then you're not Vince," she said. "I didn't think you were."

The darkness increased around the lamps. Behind Peter, the court had become brisk with lights, windows sliding up, and the sound of taps running.

"Guess Vince fell asleep. I'd better get him up and send him on his way." Robert shrugged, and rose.

"Oh, don't! I wouldn't want to be an inconvenience," the girl said with a polite terror which suggested she might often have been one.

"On the contrary." Robert spread his palms, with a smile, and walked down the hall. They heard him knocking on a door, then his indistinct voice.

In the triangular silence, Mario stepped past Peter and slid the window up softly. He leaned out to listen, peering sidewise at the window to the right. As he was pulling himself back in, he looked down. His hands stiffened on the ledge. Very slowly he pulled himself all the way in and stood up. Behind him a tin ventilator clattered inward and fell to the floor. In the shadowy lamplight his too classic face was like marble which moved numbly. He swayed a little, as if with vertigo.

"I'd better get out of here!"

They heard his heavy breath as he dashed from the room. The slam of the outer door blended with Robert's battering, louder now, on the door down the hall.

"What's down there?" She was beside Peter, otherwise he could not have heard her. They took hands, like strangers met on a narrow foot-bridge or on one of those steep places where people cling together more for anchorage against their own impulse than for balance. Carefully they leaned out over the sill. Yes — it was down there, the shirt, zebra-striped, just decipherable on the merged shadow of the courtyard below.

Carefully, as if they were made of eggshell, as if by some guarded movement they could still rescue themselves from disaster, they drew back and straightened up. Robert, his face askew with the impossible question, was behind them.

After this, there was the hubbub — the ambulance from St. Luke's, the prowl car, the two detectives from the precinct station house, and finally the "super," a vague man with the grub pallor and shamble of those who live in basements. He pawed over the keys on the thong around his wrist and, after several tries, opened the bedroom door. It was a quiet, unvi-olent room with a tossed bed and an open window, with a stagy significance acquired only momentarily in the minds of those who gath-ered in a group at its door.

Much later, after midnight, Peter and Susan sat in the bald glare of an all-night restaurant. With hysterical eagerness, Robert had gone on to the station house with the two detectives to register the salient facts, to help ferret out the relatives in Ohio, to arrange, in fact, anything that might still be arrangeable about Vince. Almost without noticing, he had ac-quiesced in Peter's proposal to look after Susan. Susan herself, after silently watching the gratuitous burbling of her father, as if it were a phenomenon she could neither believe nor leave, had followed Peter without comment. At his suggestion, they had stopped off at the restau-rant on their way to her stepfather's house, for which she had a key.

"Thanks. I was starved." She leaned back and pushed at the short bang of hair on her forehead.

"Hadn't you eaten at all?"

"Just those pasty sandwiches they sell on the train. There wasn't any diner."

"Smoke?"

"I do, but I'm just too tired. I can get into a hotel all right, don't you think? If I can't get in at Arthur's?"

"I know the manager of a small one near us," Peter said. "But if you don't mind coming to my place, you can use my mother's room for tonight. Or for as long as you need, probably."

"What about your mother?"

"She's away. She'll be away for quite a while."

"Not in Reno, by any chance?" There was a roughness, almost a coarseness, in her tone, like that in the overdone camaraderie of the shy.

"No. My father died when I was eight. Why?"

"Oh, something in the way you spoke. And then you're so competent. Does she work?"

"No. My father left something. Does yours?"

She stood up and picked up her bedraggled gloves. "No," she said, and her voice was suddenly distant and delicate again. "She marries." She turned and walked out ahead of him.

He paid, rushed out of the restaurant, and caught up with her.

"Thought maybe you'd run out on me," he said.

She got in the car without answering.

They drove through the Park, toward the address in the East Seventies that she had given him. A weak smell of grass underlay the gas-blended air, but the Park seemed limp and worn, as if the strain of the day's effluvia had been too much for it. At the Seventy-second Street stop signal, the blank light of a street lamp invaded the car.

"Thought you might be feeling Mrs. Grundyish at my suggesting the apartment," Peter said.

"Mrs. Grundy wasn't around much when I grew up." The signal changed and they moved ahead.

They stopped in a street which had almost no lights along its smartly converted house fronts. This was one of the streets, still sequestered by money, whose houses came alive only under the accelerated, febrile glitter of winter and would dream through the gross summer days, their inte-

riors deadened with muslin or stirred faintly with the subterranean clink-
ings of caretakers. No. 4 was dark.

"I would rather stay over at your place, if I have to," the girl said. Her
voice was offhand and prim. "I hate hotels. We always stopped at them in
between."

"Let's get out and see."

They stepped down into the areaway in front of the entrance, the car
door banging hollowly behind them. She fumbled in her purse and took
out a key, although it was already obvious that it would not be usable. In
his childhood, he had often hung around in the areaways of old brown-
stones such as this had been. In the corners there had always been a soft,
decaying smell, and the ironwork, bent and smeared, always hung loose
and broken-toothed. The areaway of this house had been repaved with
slippery flag; even in the humid night there was no smell. Black-tongued
grillwork, with an oily shine and padlocked, secured the windows and
the smooth door. Fastened on the grillwork in front of the door was the
neat, square proclamation of a protection agency.

"You don't have a key for the padlocks, do you?"

"No." She stood on the curb, looking up at the house. "It was a nice
room I had there. Nicest one I ever did have, really." She crossed to the
car and got in.

He followed her over to the car and got in beside her. She had her head
in her hands.

"Don't worry. We'll get in touch with somebody in the morning."

"I don't. I don't care about any of it, really." She sat up, her face
averted. "My parents, or any of the people they tangle with." She wound
the lever on the door slowly, then reversed it. "Robert, or my mother, or
Arthur," she said, "although he was always pleasant enough. Even Vince
—even if I'd known him."

"He was just a screwed-up kid. It could have been anybody's window."

"No." Suddenly she turned and faced him. "I should think it would be
the best privilege there is, though. To care, I mean."

When he did not immediately reply, she gave him a little pat on the
arm and sat back. "Excuse it, please. I guess I'm groggy." She turned
around and put her head on the crook of her arm. Her words came
faintly through it. "Wake me when we get there."

She was asleep by the time they reached his street. He parked the car as
quietly as possible beneath his own windows. He himself had never felt

more awake in his life. He could have sat there until morning with her sleep-secured beside him. He sat thinking of how different it would be at Rye, or anywhere, with her along, with someone along who was the same age. For they were the same age, whatever that was, whatever the age was of people like them. There was nothing he would be unable to tell her.

To the north, above the rooftops, the electric mauve of midtown blanked out any auguries in the sky, but he wasn't looking for anything like that. Tomorrow he would take her for a drive — whatever the weather. There were a lot of good roads around Greenwich.

RAY BRADBURY

Speaking in St. Paul's Catherdral in London, on his way to accept the Nobel Peace Award, Dr. Martin Luther King said, "The doctrine of black supremacy is as great a danger as the doctrine of white supremacy." "The Other Foot" was written thirteen years before Dr. King's statement and the perceptive Negroes in it are well aware of its truth.

Ray Bradbury may be the most prolific writer on the American literary scene. Born in Waukegan, Illinois, in 1920, he began to write at the age of twelve. He sold his first short story when he was nineteen and since has had more than three hundred stories published in nearly every magazine in the United States. He has published numerous books, including The Martian Chronicles. *In 1954, he received the Benjamin Franklin Award for the best story in a mass magazine, plus a Grant Award from the National Institute of Arts and Sciences for "contributing to American literature."*

The Other Foot

WHEN they heard the news they came out of the restaurants and cafés and hotels and looked at the sky. They lifted their dark hands over their upturned white eyes. Their mouths hung wide. In the hot noon for thousands of miles there were little towns where the dark people stood with their shadows under them, looking up.

In her kitchen, Hattie Johnson covered the boiling soup, wiped her thin fingers on a cloth and walked carefully to the back porch.

"Come on, Ma! Hey, Ma, come on, you'll miss it!"

"Hey, Mom!"

Three little Negro boys danced around in the dusty yard, yelling. Now and then they looked at the house frantically.

"I'm coming," said Hattie, and opened the screen door. "Where you hear this rumor?"

"Up at Jones', Ma. They say a rocket's coming, first one in twenty years, with a white man in it!"

"What's a white man? I never seen one."

"You'll find out," said Hattie. "Yes indeed, you'll find out."

"Tell us about one, Ma. Tell like you did."

Hattie frowned. "Well, it's been a long time. I was a little girl, you see. That was back in 1965."

"Tell us a white man, Mom!"

She came and stood in the yard looking up at the blue clear Martian sky with the thin white Martian clouds, and in the distance the Martian hills broiling in the heat. She said, at last, "Well, first of all, they got white hands."

"White hands!" The boys joked, slapping each other.

"And they got white arms."

"White arms!" hooted the boys.

"And white faces."

"White faces! *Really?*"

"White like *this,* mom?" The smallest threw dust on his face, sneezing. "This way?"

"Whiter than that," she said, gravely, and turned to the sky again. There was a troubled thing in her eyes, as if she was looking for a thunder shower up high, and not seeing it made her worry. "Maybe you better go inside."

"Oh, Mom!" They stared at her in disbelief. "We got to watch, we just got to. Nothing's going to happen, is it?"

"I don't know. I got a feeling, is all."

"We just want to see the ship and maybe run down to the port and see that white man; what's he like, huh, Mom?"

"I don't know, I just don't know," she mused, shaking her head.

"Tell us some more!"

"Well, the white people live on Earth, which is where we all come from, twenty years ago. We just up and walked away and came to Mars and set down and built towns and here we are. Now, we're Martians instead of Earth people. And no white men've come up here in all that time. That's the story."

"Why didn't they come up, Mom?"

"Well, 'cause. Right after we got up here, Earth got in an atom war. They blew each other up terribly. They forgot us. When they finished fighting, after years, they didn't have any rockets. Took them until recently to build more. So here they come now, twenty years later, to visit." She gazed at her children numbly and then began to walk. "You wait here. I'm going down the line to Elizabeth Brown's house. You promise to stay?"

"We don't want to but we will."

"All right, then." And she ran off down the road.

At Brown's she arrived in time to see everybody packed into the family car. "Hey there, Hattie! Come on, along!"

"Where you going?" she said, breathlessly running up.

"To see the white man!"

"That's right," said Mr. Brown, seriously. He waved at his load. "These children never saw one, and I almost forgot."

"What you going to do with that white man?" asked Hattie.

"Do?" said everyone. "Why — just *look* at him is all."

"You sure?"

"What else *can* we do?"

"I don't know," said Hattie. "I just thought there might be trouble."

"What kind of trouble?"

"You *know*," said Hattie, vaguely, embarrassed. "You ain't going to lynch him?"

"Lynch him?" Everyone laughed. Mr. Brown slapped his knee. "Why bless you, child, no! We're going to shake his hand. Ain't we, everyone?"

"Sure, sure!"

Another car drove up from another direction and Hattie gave a cry. "Willie!"

"What you doing way down here, where're the kids?" shouted her husband, angrily. He glared at the others. "You going down like a bunch of fools to see that man come in?"

"That appears to be just right," agreed Mr. Brown, nodding and smiling.

"Well, take your guns along," said Willie. "I'm on my way home for mine right now!"

"Willie!"

"You get in this car, Hattie." He held the door open, firmly, looking at her until she obeyed. Without another word to the others he roared the car off down the dusty road.

"Willie, not so fast!"

"Not so fast, huh? We'll see about that." He watched the road tear under the car. "What right they got coming up here, this late? Why don't they leave us in peace? Why didn't they blow themselves up on that old world and let us be?"

"Willie, that ain't no Christian way to talk."

"I'm not feeling Christian," he said, savagely gripping the wheel. "I'm just feeling mean. After all them years of doing what they did to our folks, my mom and dad, and your mom and dad, you remember? You remember how they hung my father on Knockwood Hill and shot my mother, you remember? Or you got a memory that's short like the others?"

"I remember," she said.

"You remember Doctor Phillips and Mr. Burton and their big houses, and my mother's washing shack, and dad working when he was old, and the thanks he got was being hung by Doctor Phillips and Mr. Burton. Well," said Willie, "the shoe's on the other foot now. We'll see who gets laws passed against him, who gets lynched, who rides the back of streetcars, who gets segregated in shows, we'll just wait and see."

"Oh, Willie, you're talking trouble."

"Everybody's talking. Everybody's thought on this day, thinking it'd never be. Thinking, what kind of day would it be if the white man even came up here to Mars? But here's the day, and we can't run away."

"Ain't you going to let the white people live up here?"

"Sure." He smiled, but it was a wide, mean smile, and his eyes were mad. "They can come up and live and work here, why certainly. All they got to do to deserve it is live in their own small part of town, the slums, and shine our shoes for us, and mop up our trash, and sit in the last row in the balcony. That's all we ask. And once a week we hang one or two of them. Simple."

"You don't sound human, and I don't like it."

"You'll have to get used to it," he said. He braked the car to a stop before the house and jumped out. "Find my guns and some rope. We'll do this right."

"Oh, Willie," she wailed, and just sat there in the car while he ran up the steps and slammed the front door.

She went along. She didn't want to go along, but he rattled around in the attic, cursing like a crazy man until he found four guns. She saw the brutal metal of them glittering in the black attic, and she couldn't see him at all he was so dark, she heard only his swearing, and at last his long legs came climbing down from the attic in a shower of dust and he stacked up bunches of brass shells and blew out the gun chambers and clicked shells into them, his face stern and heavy and folded in upon the gnawing bitterness there. "Leave us alone," he kept muttering, his hands flying away from him suddenly, uncontrolled. "Leave us blame alone, why don't they?"

"Willie, Willie."

"You, too, you, too." And he gave her the same look, and a pressure of his hatred touched her mind.

Outside the window the boys gabbled to each other. "White as milk, she said. White as milk."

"White as this old flower, you *see*?"

"White as a stone, like chalk you write with."

Willie plunged out of the house. "You children come inside, I'm locking you up, you ain't seeing no white man, you ain't talking about them, you ain't doing nothing, come on now."

"But, Daddy —— "

He shoved them through the door and he went and fetched a bucket of paint and a stencil and from the garage a long thick hairy rope-coil into which he fashioned a hangman's knot, very carefully watching the sky while his hands felt their way at their task.

And then they were in the car, leaving bolls of dust behind them down the road. "Slow up, Willie."

"This is no slowing up time," he said. "This is a hurrying time, and I'm hurrying."

All along the road people were looking up in the sky, or climbing in their cars, or riding in cars, and guns were sticking up out of some cars like telescopes sighting all the evils of a world coming to an end.

She looked at the guns. "You been talking," she accused her husband.

"That's what I been doing," he grunted, nodding. He watched the road, fiercely. "I stopped at every house and I told them what to do, to get their guns, to get paint, to bring rope and be ready. And here we all are, the welcoming committee, to give them the key to the city, yes sir!"

She pressed her thin dark hands together, to push away the terror growing in her now, and she felt the car bucket and lurch around other cars, she heard the voices yelling, Hey, Willie, look! and hands holding up ropes and guns as they rushed by! And mouths smiling at them in the swift rushing.

"Here we are," said Willie, and braked the car into dusty halting and silence. He kicked the door open with a big foot and, laden with weapons, stepped out, lugging them across the airport meadow.

"Have you *thought,* Willie?"

"That's all I done for twenty years. I was sixteen when I left Earth and I was glad to leave," he said. "There wasn't anything there for me or you or anybody like us. I've never been sorry I left. We've had peace here, the first time we ever drew a solid breath. Now, come on."

He pushed through the dark crowd which came to meet him.

"Willie, Willie, what we gonna do?" they said.

"Here's a gun," he said. "Here's a gun. Here's another." He passed them out with savage jabs of his arms. "Here's a pistol. Here's a shotgun."

The people were so close together it looked like one dark body with a thousand arms reaching out to take the weapons. "Willie, Willie."

His wife stood tall and silent by him, her fluted lips pressed shut, and her large eyes wet and tragic. "Bring the paint," he said to her. And she lugged a gallon can of yellow paint across the field to where at that moment a trolley car was pulling up, with a fresh-painted sign on its front TO THE WHITE MAN'S LANDING, full of talking people who got off, and ran across the meadow, stumbling, looking up. Women with picnic boxes, men with straw hats, in shirt sleeves. The streetcar stood humming and empty. Willie climbed up, set the paint cans down, opened them, stirred the paint, tested a brush, drew forth a stencil, and climbed up on a seat.

"Hey, there!" The conductor came around behind him, his coin changer jangling. "What you think you're doing, get down off there."

"You see what I'm doing, keep your shirt on."

And Willie began the stenciling in yellow paint. He dabbed on an F and an O and an R with terrible pride in his work. And when he finished it the conductor squinted up and he read the fresh glinting yellow words: FOR WHITES: REAR SECTION. He read it again. FOR WHITES: He blinked. REAR SECTION. The conductor looked at Willie and began to smile.

"Does that suit you?" asked Willie, stepping down.

Said the conductor, "That suits me just fine, sir."

Hattie was looking at the sign from outside, and holding her hands over her breasts.

Willie returned to the crowd, which was growing now, taking size from every auto that groaned to a halt, and every new trolley car which squealed around the bend from the nearby town.

Willie climbed up on a packing box. "Let's have a delegation to paint every streetcar in the next hour. Volunteers?"

Hands leapt up.

"Get going!"

They went.

"Let's have a delegation to fix theatre seats, roped off, the last two rows for whites."

More hands.

"Go on!"

They ran off.

Willie peered around, bubbled with perspiration, panting with exertion, proud of his energy, his hand on his wife's shoulder who stood under him looking at the ground with her downcast eyes. "Let's see now," he declared. "Oh, yes. We got to pass a law this afternoon, no intermarriages!"

"That's right," said a lot of people.

"All shoeshine boys quit their jobs today."

"Quittin' right now!" Some men threw down the rags they had carried, in their excitement, all across town.

"Got to pass a minimum wage law, don't we?"

"Sure!"

"Pay them white folks at least ten cents an hour."

"That's right!"

The Mayor of the town came hurrying up. "Now look here, Willie Johnson, get down off that box!"

"Mayor, I can't be made to do nothing like that."

"You're making a mob, Willie Johnson."

"That's the idea."

"The same thing you always hated when you were a kid. You're no better than some of those white men you yell about!"

"This is the other shoe, Mayor, and the other foot," said Willie, not even looking at the Mayor, looking at the faces beneath him, some of them smiling, some of them doubtful, others bewildered, some of them reluctant and drawing away, fearful.

"You'll be sorry," said the Mayor.

"We'll have an election and get a new Mayor," said Willie. And he glanced off at the town where up and down the streets signs were being hung, fresh-painted: LIMITED CLIENTELE: *Right to serve customer revokable at any time*. He grinned and slapped his hands. Lord! And streetcars were being halted and sections being painted white in back, to suggest their future inhabitants. And theatres were being invaded and roped off by chuckling men, while their wives stood wondering on the curbs and children were spanked into houses to be hid away from this awful time.

"Are we all ready?" called Willie Johnson, the rope in his hands with the noose tied and neat.

"Ready!" shouted half the crowd. The other half murmured and moved like figures in a nightmare in which they wished no participation.

"Here it comes!" called a small boy.

Like marionnette heads on a single string, the heads of the crowd turned upward.

Across the sky, very high and beautiful, a rocket burned on a sweep of orange fire. It circled and came down, causing all to gasp. It landed, setting the meadow afire here and there; the fire burned out, the rocket lay a moment in quiet; and then as the silent crowd watched, a great door in the side of the vessel whispered out a breath of oxygen, the door slid back and an old man stepped out.

"A white man, a white man, a white man——" The words traveled back in the expectant crowd, the children speaking in each other's ears, whispering, butting each other, the words moving in ripples to where the crowd stopped and the streetcars stood in the windy sunlight, the smell of paint coming out their opened windows. The whispering wore itself away and it was gone.

No one moved.

The white man was tall and straight, but a deep weariness was in his face. He had not shaved this day, and his eyes were as old as the eyes of a man can be and still be alive. His eyes were colorless; almost white and sightless with things he had seen in the passing years. He was as thin as a winter bush. His hands trembled and he had to lean against the portway of the ship as he looked out over the crowd.

He put out a hand and half-smiled, but drew his hand back.

No one moved.

He looked down into their faces, and perhaps he saw but did not see the guns and the ropes, and perhaps he smelled the paint. No one ever asked him. He began to talk. He started very quietly and slowly, expecting no interruptions, and receiving none, and his voice was very tired and old and pale.

"It doesn't matter who I am," he said. "I'd be just a name to you, anyhow. I don't know your names, either. That'll come later." He paused, closed his eyes for a moment, and then continued.

"Twenty years ago, you left Earth. That's a long long time. It's more like twenty centuries, so much has happened. After you left, the War came." He nodded slowly. "Yes, the *big* one. The Third One. It went on for a long time. Until last year. We bombed all of the cities of the world. We destroyed New York and London and Moscow and Paris and Shanghai and Bombay and Alexandria. We ruined it all. And when we finished with the big cities we went to the little cities and atom-bombed and burned them."

Now he began to name cities and places, and streets. And as he named them, a murmur rose up in his audience.

"We destroyed Natchez . . ."

A murmur.

"And Columbus, Georgia . . ."

Another murmur.

"We burned New Orleans . . ."

A sigh.

"And Atlanta . . ."

Still another.

"And there was nothing left of Greenwater, Alabama."

Willie Johnson jerked his head and his mouth opened. Hattie saw this gesture, and the recognition coming into his dark eyes.

"Nothing was left," said the old man in the port, speaking slowly. "Cotton fields, burned."

"Oh," said everyone.

"Cotton mills bombed out —— "

"Oh."

"And the factories radio-active, everything radio-active. All the roads and the farms and the foods, radio-active. Everything." He named more names of towns and villages.

"Tampa."

"That's my town," someone whispered.

"Fulton."

"That's mine," someone else said.

"Memphis."

"Memphis, did they burn *Memphis*?" A shocked query.

"Memphis, blown up."

"*Fourth* Street in Memphis?"

"All of it," said the old man.

It was stirring them now. After twenty years it was rushing back. The towns and the places, the trees and the brick buildings, the signs and the churches and the familiar stores, all of it was coming to the surface among the gathered people. Each name touched memory, and there was no one present without a thought of another day, they were all old enough for that, save the children.

"Laredo."

"I remember Laredo."

"New York City."

"I had a store in Harlem."

"Harlem, bombed out."

The ominous words. The familiar, remembered places. The struggle to imagine all of those places in ruins.

Willie Johnson murmured the words, "Greenwater, Alabama. That's where I was born. I remember."

Gone. All of it gone. The man said so.

The man continued. "So we destroyed everything and ruined everything, like the fools that we were and the fools that we are. We killed millions. I don't think there are more than five hundred thousand people left in the world, all kinds and types. And out of all the wreckage we salvaged enough metal to build this one rocket, and we came to Mars in it this month to seek your help."

He hesitated and looked down among the faces to see what could be found there, but he was uncertain.

Hattie Johnson felt her husband's arm tense, saw his fingers grip the rope.

"We've been fools," said the old man, quietly. "We've brought the earth and civilization down about our heads. None of the cities are worth saving, they'll be radio-active for a century. Earth is over and done with. Its age is through. You have rockets here which you haven't tried to use to return to Earth in twenty years. Now I've come to ask you to use them. To come to Earth, to pick up the survivors and bring them back to Mars. To help us go on at this time. We've been stupid. Before God we admit our stupidity and our evilness. All the Chinese and the Indians and the Russians and the British and the Americans. We're asking to be taken in. Your Martian soil has lain fallow for numberless centuries; there's room for everyone; it's good soil, I've seen your fields from above. We'll come and work the soil with you." He paused. "We'll come and work it *for* you. Yes, we'll even do that. We deserve anything you want to do to us, but don't shut us out. We can't force you to act now. If you want I'll get into my ship and go back and that will be all there is to it. We won't bother you again. But we'll come here and we'll work for you, and do the things you did for us, clean your houses, cook your meals, shine your shoes, and humble ourselves in the sight of God for the things we have done over the centuries to ourselves, to others, to you."

He was finished.

There was a silence of silences. A silence you could hold in your hand and a silence that came down like a pressure of a distant storm over the crowd. Their long arms hung like dark pendulums in the sunlight, and their eyes were upon the old man and he did not move now, but waited.

Willie Johnson held the rope in his hands. Those around him watched to see what he might do. His wife Hattie waited, clutching his arm.

She wanted to get at the hate of them all, to pry at it and work at it until she found a little chink, and then pull out a pebble or a stone or a brick and then a part of the wall, and once started, the whole edifice might roar down and be done away with. It was teetering now. But which was the keystone and how to get at it? How to touch them and get a thing started in all of them to make a ruin of their hate?

She looked at Willie there in the strong silence and the only thing she knew about the situation was him and his life and what had happened to him, and suddenly he was the keystone, suddenly she knew that if he could be pried loose, then the thing in all of them might be loosened and torn away.

"Mister —— " She stepped forward. She didn't even know the first words to say. The crowd stared at her back, she felt them staring.

"Mister —— "

The man turned to her with a tired smile.

"Mister," she said. "Do you know Knockwood Hill in Greenwater, Alabama?"

The old man spoke over his shoulder to someone within the ship. A moment later a photographic map was handed out and the man held it, waiting.

"You know the big oak on top of that hill, mister?"

The big oak. The place where Willie's father was shot and.hung and found swinging in the morning wind.

"Yes."

"Is that still there?" asked Hattie.

"It's gone," said the old man. "Blown up. The hill's all gone, and the oak tree, too. You see?" He touched the photograph.

"Let me see that," said Willie, jerking forward and looking at the map. Hattie blinked at the white man, heart pounding.

"Tell me about Greenwater," she said, quickly.

"What do you want to know?"

"About Dr. Phillips, is he still alive?"

A moment, in which the information was found in a clicking machine within the rocket.

"Killed in the war."

"And his son?"

"Dead."

"What about their house?"

"Burned. Like all the other houses."

"What about that other big tree on Knockwood Hill?"

"All the trees went, burned."

"*That* tree went, you're sure?" said Willie.

"Yes."

Willie's body loosened somewhat.

"And what about that Mr. Burton's house and Mr. Burton?"

"No houses at all left, no people."

"You know Mrs. Johnson's washing shack, my mother's place?"

The place where she was shot.

"That's gone, too. Everything's gone. Here are the pictures, you can see for yourself."

The pictures were there to be held and looked at and thought about. The rocket was full of pictures and answers to questions. Any town, any building, any place.

Willie stood with the rope in his hands.

He was remembering Earth, the green Earth and the green town where he was born and raised, and he was thinking now of that town gone to pieces, to ruin, blown up and scattered, all of the landmarks with it, all of the supposed or certain evil scattered with it, all of the hard men gone, the stables, the ironsmiths, the curio shops, the soda founts, the gin mills, the river bridges, the lynching trees, the buckshot-covered hills, the roads, the cows, the mimosas, and his own house as well as those big-pillared houses down near the long river, those white mortuaries where the women as delicate as moths fluttered in the autumn light, distant, far away. Those houses where the cold men rocked with glasses of drink in their hands, guns leaned against the porch newels, sniffing the autumn airs and considering death. Gone, all gone, gone and never coming back. Now, for certain, all of that civilization ripped into confetti and strewn at their feet. Nothing, nothing of it left to hate, not an empty brass gun shell, or a twisted hemp, or a tree or even a hill of it to hate. Nothing but some alien people in a rocket, people who might shine his shoes and ride in the back of trolleys or sit far up in midnight theatres . . .

"You won't have to do that," said Willie Johnson.

His wife glanced at his big hands.

His fingers were opening.

The rope, released, fell and coiled upon itself along the ground.

They ran through the streets of their town and they tore down the new signs so quickly made, and painted out the fresh yellow signs on streetcars, and they cut down the ropes in the theatre balconies, and unloaded their guns and stacked their ropes away.

"A new start for everyone," said Hattie, on the way home in their car.

"Yes," said Willie, at last. "The Lord's let us come through, a few here and a few there. And what happens next is up to all of us. The time for being fools is over. We got to be something else except fools. I knew that when he talked. I knew then that now the white man's as lonely as we've always been. He's got no home now, just like we didn't have one for so long. Now everything's even. We can start all over again, on the same level."

He stopped the car, and sat in it, not moving, while Hattie went to let the children out. They ran down to see their father. "You see the white man, you see him?" they cried.

"Yes, sir," said Willie, sitting behind the wheel, rubbing his face with his slow fingers. "Seems like for the first time today I really seen the white man, I really seen him clear."

TENNESSEE WILLIAMS

*"Three Players of a Summer Game" is among Williams' most impres-
sive short stories. The widow, the alcoholic, the neglected little girl, in
enacting their parts, show the author's dramatic genius. Reading this
story is like watching an absorbing play.*

*Tennessee Williams was born in Columbus, Mississippi, of Tennessee
ancestry. Christened Thomas Lanier Williams he changed his name
because it had "the sound of a writer who turns out sonnet sequences
to Spring." His first play closed during the tryout and he went back to
work as an all-night elevator operator, verse-reciting waiter in Greenwich Village and New Orleans, theater usher and Hollywood writer. He
saved enough money to write* The Glass Menagerie, *a big Broadway
success. Since then he has written many other successful plays as well
as short stories and a novel.*

Three Players of
A Summer Game

CROQUET IS A SUMMER GAME that seems, in a curious way, to be composed
of images, very much as a painter's abstraction of summer or one of its
games would be composed of them. The delicate wire wickets set in a
lawn of smooth emerald that flickers fierily at some points and rests
under violet shadow in others; the wooden poles gaudily painted and like
moments that stand out in a season that was a struggle for something of
unspeakable importance to someone passing through it; the clean and
hard wooden spheres of different colors and the strong, rigid shape of the
mallets that drive the balls through the wickets; the formal design of
those wickets and poles upon the croquet lawn — all this is like a painter's abstraction of a summer and a game played in it. And I cannot
think of croquet without hearing a sound like the faraway booming of a
cannon fired to announce a white ship coming into a harbor. The faraway booming sound is that of a green-and-white striped awning coming

down over a gallery of a white frame house in Meridian, Mississippi. The house is of Victorian design carried to an extreme of improvisation, an almost grotesque pile of galleries and turrets and cupolas and eaves, all freshly painted white — so white and so fresh that it has the blue-white glitter of a block of ice in the sun. The house is like a new resolution not yet tainted by any defection from it. And I associate the summer game with players coming out of this house with the buoyant air of persons just released from a suffocating enclosure. Their clothes are as light in weight and color as the flattering clothes of dancers. There are three players — a woman, a man, and a little girl.

The voice of the woman player is not at all loud, yet it has a pleasantly resonant quality; it carries farther than most voices, and it is interspersed with peals of treble laughter. The woman player, even more than her male opponent in the game, has the grateful quickness of motion of someone let out of a suffocating enclosure; her motion has the quickness of breath released just after a moment of terror, of fingers unclenched when panic is suddenly past, or of a cry that subsides into laughter. She seems unable to speak or move about moderately; she moves convulsively in rushes, whipping her white skirts with long strides that quicken to running. Her skirts make a faint crackling sound as her pumping thighs whip them open — the sound that comes to you, greatly diminished by distance, when fitful fair-weather gusts belly out and slacken the faraway sails of a yawl. This agreeably cool summer sound is accompanied by another, which is even cooler — the ceaseless, tiny chatter of beads hung in long loops from her throat. They are not pearls but they have a milky lustre; they are small, faintly speckled white ovals — polished bird eggs turned solid and strung upon glittery filaments of silver. The woman player is never still for a moment; sometimes she exhausts herself and collapses on the grass in the conscious attitudes of a dancer. She is a thin woman, with long bones and skin of a silky sheen, and her eyes are only a shade or two darker than the blue-tinted bird's-egg beads about her long throat. She is never still — not even when she has fallen in exhaustion on the grass. The neighbors think she's gone mad, but they feel no pity for her, and that, of course, is because of her male opponent in the game. This player is Brick Pollitt, a young Delta planter, a man so tall, with such a fiery thatch of hair, that to see a flagpole on an expanse of green lawn or even a particularly brilliant weather vane or cross on a steeple is sufficient to recall that long-ago summer which his legend belongs to.

This male player of the summer game is a drinker who has not yet fallen beneath the savage axe blows of his liquor. He is not so young any more, but he has not yet lost the slim grace of his youth. He is a head taller than the tall woman player. He is such a tall man that even in those sections of the lawn dimmed under violet shadow his head continues to catch fiery rays of the descending sun, the way the heavenward-pointing index finger of a huge gilded hand atop a Protestant steeple in Meridian goes on drawing the sun's flame for a good while after the lower surfaces of the town have sunk into lingering dusk.

The third player of the summer game is the woman's daughter, a plump twelve-year-old child named Mary Louise. This little girl has made herself distinctly unpopular among the children of the neighborhood by imitating too perfectly the elegant manners and cultivated Eastern voice of her mother. She sits in an electric automobile, on the sort of fat silk pillow that expensive lap dogs sit on, uttering treble peals of ladylike laughter, tossing her copper curls, using grown-up expressions such as "Oh, how delightful!" and "Isn't that just lovely!" She sits in the electric automobile sometimes all afternoon, by herself, as if she were on display in a glass box, only now and then raising a plaintive voice to call her mother and ask if it is all right for her to come in now, or if she can drive the electric around the block, which she is sometimes then permitted to do.

Our house was on the opposite corner, and I was the only child close to her age (I was a boy of fourteen) who could put up with her precocious refinements. For a very short time, she had had another friend, a little girl named Dorothea, and the two of them would get into their mothers' castoff finery and have tea parties on the lawn, but one afternoon Dorothea took umbrage at something, overturned the tea table, and stalked off, chanting a horrid little verse: "Smarty, Smarty, gave a party, Nobody came but a sad old darky!" "Common!" Mary Louise shrieked after her, and they didn't play together any more. Sometimes she called me over to play croquet with her, but that was only when her mother and Brick Pollitt had disappeared into the house too early to play the game. Mary Louise had a passion for croquet. She played it purely for itself; it did not have for her any shadowy connotations.

What the game meant to Brick Pollitt calls for some further account of Brick's life before that summer. He had been a celebrated athlete at Sewanee, and had married a New Orleans débutante who was a Mardi Gras queen and whose father owned a fleet of banana boats. It had seemed a brilliant marriage, with lots of wealth and prestige on both sides, but only two years later Brick started falling in love with his liquor, and Margaret, his wife, began to be praised for her patience and loyalty to him. Brick seemed to be throwing his life away, as if it were something disgusting that he had suddenly found in his hands. This self-disgust came upon him with the abruptness and violence of a crash on a highway. But what had Brick crashed into? Nothing that anybody was able to surmise, for he seemed to have everything that young men like Brick might hope or desire to have. What else is there? There must have been something that he wanted and lacked, or what reason was there for dropping his life and taking hold of a glass that he never let go of for more than one waking hour? His wife, Margaret, took hold of Brick's ten-thousand-acre plantation. She had Brick's power of attorney, and she managed all his business affairs with astuteness. "He'll come out of it," she would say. "Brick is passing through something that he'll come out of." She always said the right thing, took the conventionally right attitude, and expressed it to the world which admired her for it. Everybody admired her as a remarkably fine and brave little woman who had much to put up with. Two sections of an hourglass could not drain and fill more evenly than Brick and Margaret after he took to drink. It was as though she had her lips fastened to some invisible wound in his body through which drained out of him and flowed into her the assurance and vitality that had been his before his marriage. Margaret Pollitt lost her pale, feminine prettiness and assumed in its place something more impressive — a firm and rough-textured sort of handsomeness. Once very pretty but indistinct, a graceful sketch that was done with a very light pencil, she became vivid as Brick disappeared behind the veil of his liquor. She abruptly stopped being quiet and dainty. She was now apt to have dirty fingernails, which she covered with scarlet enamel. When the enamel chipped off, the gray showed underneath. Her hair was now cut short, so that she didn't have to "mess with it." It was wind-blown and full of sparkle; she jerked a comb through it, making it crackle. She had white teeth that were a little too large for her thin lips, and when she threw her head back in laughter, strong cords stood out in her smooth brown throat. She had a booming laugh that she might have stolen from Brick while he was drunk or asleep beside her at night. She had a way of releasing the clutch on a car at the exact instant that her laughter boomed out, and of not calling goodbye but of thrusting one bare, strong arm straight out with the fingers clenched as the car shot off in high gear and disappeared into a cloud of yellow dust. She didn't drive her own little runabout nowadays as much as she did Brick's Pierce-Arrow touring car, for Brick's driver's license had been revoked. She frequently broke the speed limit on the highway. The patrolmen would stop her, but she had such an affability, such a disarming way with her, that they would have a good laugh together and there would be no question of a ticket.

Somebody in her family died in Memphis that spring, and she went there to attend the funeral and collect her inheritance, and while she was away, Brick Pollitt slipped out from under her thumb a bit. Another death occurred during her absence. That nice young doctor who took care of Brick when he had to be carried to the hospital took sick in a shocking way. An awful flower grew in his brain, like a fierce geranium — grew and grew and one day shattered its pot. All of a sudden, the wrong words came out of his mouth; he seemed to be speaking in an unknown tongue; he couldn't find things with his hands; he made troubled signs over his forehead. His wife led him about the house by one hand, yet he stumbled and fell flat; the breath was knocked out of him, and he had to be put to bed by his wife and the Negro yardman; and he lay there laughing weakly, incredulously, trying to find his wife's hand with both of his while she looked at him with eyes that she couldn't keep from blazing with terror. He lived on under drugs for a week, and it was during that time that Brick Pollitt came and sat with Isabel Grey by her dying husband's bed. She couldn't speak; she could only shake her head incessantly, like a metronome, with no lips visible in her white face but two pressed-narrow bands of a dimmer whiteness that shook as if some white liquid flowed beneath them with a rapidity and violence that made them quiver.

"*God*" was the only word she was able to say, but Brick Pollitt somehow understood what she meant by that word, as if it were in a language that she and he, alone of all people, could speak and understand. And when the dying man's eyes opened, as if they were being forced, on something they couldn't bear to look at, it was Brick, his hands suddenly quite sure and steady, who filled the hypodermic needle for her and pumped its contents fiercely into her husband's hard young arm. And it was over.

There was another bed at the back of the house, and he and Isabel lay beside each other on that bed for a couple of hours before they let the town know that her husband's agony was completed, and the only move ment between them was the intermittent, spasmodic digging of their fingernails into each other's clenched palm while their bodies lay stiffly separate, deliberately not touching at any other points, as if they abhorred any other contact with each other.

And so you see what the summer game on the violet-shadowed lawn was—it was a running together out of something unbearably hot and bright into something obscure and cool.

The young widow was left with nothing in the way of material possessions except the house and an electric automobile. By the time Brick's wife, Margaret, had returned from her journey to Memphis, Brick had taken over the various details of the widow's life that a brother or a relative, if she had had one, would have seen to. For a week or two, people thought it was very kind of him, and then all at once they decided that Brick's reason for kindness was by no means noble. It appeared that the widow was now his mistress, and this was true. It was true in the limited way that most such opinions are true. She was his mistress, but that was not Brick's reason. His reason had something to do with that chaste interlocking of hands their first time together, after the hypodermic. It had to do with those hours, now receding and fading behind them, as all such hours must, but neither of them could have said what it was, aside from that. Neither of them was able to think very clearly. But Brick was able to pull himself together for a while and take command of the young widow's affairs.

The daughter, Mary Louise, was a plump child of twelve. She was my friend that summer. Mary Louise and I caught lightning bugs and put them in Mason jars, and we played croquet when her mother and Brick Pollitt were not inclined to play. It was Mary Louise that summer who taught me how to deal with mosquito bites. She was plagued by mosquitoes and so was I. She warned me that scratching the bites would leave scars on my skin, which was as tender as hers. I said that I didn't care. Someday you will, she told me. She carried with her constantly that summer a lump of ice in a handkerchief. Whenever a mosquito bit her, instead of scratching the bite she rubbed it gently with the handkerchief-wrapped lump of ice until the sting was frozen to numbness. Of course, in five minutes it would come back and have to be frozen again, but eventually it would disappear and leave no scar. Mary Louise's skin, where it was not temporarily mutilated by a mosquito bite or a slight rash that sometimes appeared after she ate strawberry ice cream, was ravishingly smooth and tender.

The Greys' house was very run down, but soon after Brick Pollitt started coming over to see the young widow, the house was painted. It was painted so white that it was almost a very pale blue; it had the blue-white glitter of a block of ice in the sun. In spite of his red hair, Brick Pollitt, too, had a cool appearance, because he was still young and thin, as thin as the widow, and he dressed, as she did, in clothes of light weight and color. His white shirts looked faintly pink because of his skin underneath them. Once, I saw him at an upstairs window of the widow's house just a moment before he pulled the shade down. I was in an upstairs room of my house, and I saw that Brick Pollitt was divided into two colors as distinct as two stripes of a flag, the upper part of him, which had been exposed to the sun, almost crimson and the lower part of him white as this piece of paper.

While the widow's house was being repainted, at Brick Pollitt's expense, she and her daughter lived at the Alcazar Hotel, also at Brick's expense. Brick drove in from his plantation every morning to watch the house painters at work. His driving license had been restored to him, and this was an important step forward in his personal renovation — being able to drive his own car again. He drove with elaborate caution and formality, coming to a dead stop at every cross street in the town, sounding the silver trumpet at every corner, with smiles and bows and great circular gestures of his hands inviting pedestrians to precede him. But people did not approve of what Brick Pollitt was doing. They sympathized with Margaret, that brave little woman who had to put up with so much. As for Dr. Grey's widow, she had not been very long in the town; the Doctor had married her while he was an intern at a big hospital in Baltimore. Nobody had formed a definite opinion of her before the Doctor died, so it was no effort now simply to condemn her, without any qualification, as a common strumpet.

Brick Pollitt, when he talked to the house painters, shouted to them as if they were deaf, so that all the neighbors could hear what he had to say. He was explaining things to the world, especially the matter of his drinking.

"It's something that you can't cut out completely right away," he would yell up at them. "That's the big mistake that most drinkers make — they try to cut it out completely, and you can't do that. You can do it for maybe a month or two months, but all at once you go back on it worse than before you went off it, and then the discouragement is awful

— you lose all faith in yourself and just give up. The thing to do, the way to handle the problem is like a bullfighter handles a bull in a ring. Wear it down little by little, get control of it gradually. That's how I'm handling this thing! Yep. Now, let's say that you get up wanting a drink in the morning. Say it's ten o'clock, maybe. Well, you say to yourself, 'Just wait half an hour, old boy, and then you can have one.' . . . Well, at half past ten you still want that drink and you want it a little bit worse than you did at ten, but you say to yourself, 'Boy, you could do without it half an hour ago, so you can do without it now.' You see, that's how you got to argue about it with yourself, because a drinking man is not one person. A man that drinks is two people, one grabbing the bottle, the other one fighting him off it — not one but two people fighting each other to get control of a bottle. Well, sir. If you can talk yourself out of a drink at ten, you can still talk yourself out of a drink at *half past* ten! But at *eleven* o'clock the need for the drink is greater. Now *here's* the important thing to remember about this struggle. You got to watch those scales, and when they tip too far against your power to resist, you got to give in a little. That's not weakness. *That's strategy!* Because don't forget what I told you. A drinking man is not one person but two, and it's a battle of wits going on between them. And so I say at eleven, 'Well, *have* your drink. *Go on* and *have* it! One drink at eleven won't hurt you!"

"What time is it now? . . . Yep! Eleven . . . All right, I'm going to have me that one drink. I could do without it, I don't crave it. But the important thing is . . ."

His voice would trail off as he entered the widow's house. He would stay in there longer than it took to have one drink, and when he came out, there would be a change in his voice as definite as a change of weather or season. The strong and vigorous tone would be a bit filmed over.

Then he would usually begin to talk about his wife. "I don't say my wife Margaret's not an intelligent woman. She is, and both of us know it, but she don't have a good head for property values. Now, you know Dr. Grey, who used to live here before that brain thing killed him. Well, he was my physician, he pulled me through some bad times when I had that liquor problem. I felt I owed him a lot. Now, that was a terrible thing the way he went, but it was terrible for his widow, too; she was left with this house and that electric automobile and that's all, and this house was put up for sale to pay off her debts, and — well, I bought it. I bought it,

and now I'm giving it back to her. Now, my wife Margaret, she. And a
lot of other folks, too. Don't understand about this. . . . What time is it?
Twelve? High noon! . . . This ice is melted . . ."

He'd drift back into the house and stay there half an hour, and when
he'd come back out, it would be rather shyly, with a sad and uncertain
creaking of the screen door pushed by the hand not holding the tall glass.
But after resting a little while on the steps, he would resume his talk to
the house painters.

"Yes," he would say, as if he had paused only a moment before, "it's
the most precious thing that a woman can give to a man — his lost
respect for himself — and the meanest thing one human being can do to
another human being is take his respect for himself away from him. I. I
had it took away from me."

The glass would tilt slowly up and jerkily down, and he'd have to wipe
his chin.

"I had it took away from me! I won't tell you how, but maybe, being
men about my age, you're able to guess it. That was how. Some of them
don't want it. They cut it off. They cut it right off a man, and half the
time he don't even know when they cut it off him. Well, I knew it all
right. I could feel it being cut off me. Do you know what I mean? . . .
That's right.

"But once in a while there's one — and they don't come often — that
wants for a man to keep it, and those are the women that God made and
put on this earth. The other kind come out of Hell, or out of . . . I don't
know what. I'm talking too much. Sure. I know I'm talking too much
about private matters. But that's all right. This property is mine. I'm
talking on my own property and I don't give a hoot who hears me or
what they think! I'm not going to try to fool anybody about it. Whatever
I do is nothing to be ashamed of. I've been through things that I would
rather not mention. But I'm coming out of it now, God damn it, yes, I
am! I can't take all the credit. And yet I'm proud. I'm goddam proud of
myself, because I was in a pitiful condition with that liquor problem of
mine, but now the worst is over. I've got it just about licked. That's my
car out there and I drove it up here myself. It's no short drive, it's almost
a hundred miles, and I drive it each morning and drive it back each
night. I've got back my driver's license, and I fired the man that was
working for my wife, looking after our place. I fired that man and not
only fired him but give him a kick in the britches that made him eat
standing up for the next week or two. It wasn't because I thought he was

fooling around. It wasn't that. But him and her both took about the same attitude toward me, and I didn't like the attitude they took. They would talk about me right in front of me, as if I wasn't there. 'Is it time for his medicine?' Yes, they were giving me dope! So one day I played possum. I was lying out there on the sofa and she said to him, 'I guess he's passed out now.' And he said, 'Jesus, dead drunk at half past one in the afternoon!' Well. I got up slowly. I wasn't drunk at that hour, I wasn't even half drunk. I stood up straight and walked slowly toward him. I walked straight up to them both, and you should of seen the eyes of them both bug out! 'Yes, Jesus,' I said, 'at half past one!' And I grabbed him by his collar and by the seat of his britches and turkey-trotted him right on out of the house and pitched him on his face in a big mud puddle at the foot of the steps to the front veranda. And as far as I know or care, maybe he's still laying there and she's still screaming, 'Stop, Brick!' But I believe I did hit her. Yes, I did. I did hit her. There's times when you got to hit them, and that was one of those times. I ain't been to the house since. I moved in the little place we lived in before the big one was built, on the other side of the bayou, and ain't crossed over there since.

"Well, sir, that's all over with now. I got back my power of attorney which I'd give to that woman and I got back my driver's license and I bought this piece of property in town and signed my own check for it and I'm having it completely done over to make it as handsome a piece of residential property as you can find in this town and I'm having that lawn out there prepared for the game of croquet."

Then he'd look at the glass in his hand as if he had just then noticed that he was holding it. He'd give it a look of slightly pained surprise, as if he had cut his hand and just now noticed that it was cut and bleeding. Then he would sigh like an old-time actor in a tragic role. He would put the tall glass down on the balustrade with great, great care, look back at it to make sure that it wasn't going to fall over, and walk, very straight and steady, to the porch steps and, just as steady but with more concentration, down them. When he arrived at the foot of the steps, he would laugh as if someone had made a comical remark. He would duck his head genially and shout to the house painters something like this: "Well, I'm not making any predictions, because I'm no fortune-teller, but I've got a strong idea that I'm going to lick my liquor problem this summer, ha-ha, I'm going to lick it this summer! I'm not going to take no cure and I'm not going to take no pledge. I'm just going to prove I'm a man again! I'm going to do it step by little step, the way that people play the game of croquet. You know how you play that game. You hit the ball through one wicket and then you drive it through the next one. You hit it through that wicket and then you drive on to another. You go from wicket to wicket, and it's a game of precision — it's a game that takes concentration and precision, and that's what makes it a wonderful game for a drinker. It takes a sober man to play a game of precision. It's better than shooting pool, because a pool hall is always next door to a gin mill, and you never see a pool player that don't have his liquor glass on the edge of the table or somewhere pretty near it, and croquet is also a better game than golf, because in golf you've always got that nineteenth hole waiting for you. Nope, for a man with a liquor problem croquet may seem a little bit sissy, but let me tell you it's a game of precision. You go from wicket to wicket until you arrive at that big final pole, and then, bang, you've hit it, the game is finished, you're there! And then, and not until then, you can go up here to the porch and have you a cool gin drink, a buck or a Collins. Hey! Where did I leave that glass? Aw! Yeah, hand it down to me, will you? Ha-ha. Thanks."

He would take a birdlike sip, make a fiercely wry face, and shake his head violently as if somebody had drenched it with water. *"This God-damned stuff!"*

He would look around to find a safe place to set the glass down again. He would select a bare spot of earth between the hydrangea bushes and deposit the glass there as carefully as if he were planting a memorial tree, and then he would straighten up with a great air of relief and expand his chest and flex his arms. "Ha-ha, yep, croquet is a summer game for widows and drinkers, ha-ha!"

For a few moments, standing there in the sun, he would seem as sure and powerful as the sun itself, but then some little shadow of uncertainty would touch him again, get through the wall of his liquor; some tricky little shadow of a thought, as sly as a mouse, quick, dark, too sly to be caught, and without his moving enough for it to be noticed his still fine body would fall as violently as a giant tree crashes down beneath a final axe stroke, taking with it all the wheeling seasons of sun and stars, whole centuries of them, crashing suddenly into oblivion and rot. He would make this enormous fall without a perceptible movement of his body. At the most, it would show in the faint flicker of something across his face, whose color gave him the name people knew him by. Possibly one knee sagged a little forward. Then slowly, slowly, he would fasten one hand over his belt and raise the other one hesitantly to his head, feel the scalp and the hard round bowl of the skull underneath it, as if he dimly imagined that by feeling that dome he might be able to guess what was hidden inside it — facing now the intricate wickets of the summer to come.

For one reason or another, Mary Louise Grey was locked out of the house a great deal of the time that summer, and since she was a lonely child with little or no imagination, apparently unable to amuse herself with solitary games — except the endless one of copying her mother — the afternoons when she was excluded from the house because her mother had a headache were periods of great affliction. There were several galleries with outside stairs between them, and she would patrol the galleries and wander forlornly about the lawn or go down the front walk and sit in the glass box of the electric. She would vary her steps, sometimes walking sedately, sometimes skipping, sometimes hopping and humming, one plump hand always clutching a handkerchief that contained the lump of ice. This lump of ice to rub her mosquito bites had to be replaced at frequent intervals. "Oh, iceman!" the widow would call sweetly from an upstairs window. "Don't forget to leave some extra pieces for little Mary Louise to rub her mosquito bites with!"

From time to time, Mary Louise would utter a soft cry, and, in a voice that had her mother's trick of carrying a great distance without being loud, call, "Oh, Mother, I'm simply being devoured by mosquitoes!"

"Darling," her mother would answer from the upstairs window, "that's dreadful, but you know that Mother can't help it; she didn't create the mosquitoes and she can't destroy them for you!"

"You could let me come in the house, Mama."

"No, I can't let you come in, precious. Not yet."

"Why not, Mother?"

"Because Mother has a sick headache."

"I will be quiet."

"You say that you will, but you won't. You must learn to amuse yourself, precious; you mustn't depend on Mother to amuse you. Nobody can depend on anyone else forever. I'll tell you what you can do till Mother's headache is better. You can drive the electric out of the garage. You can drive it around the block, but don't go into the business district with it, and then you can stop in the shady part of the drive and sit there perfectly comfortably till Mother feels better and can get dressed and come out. And then I think Mr. Pollitt may come over for a game of croquet. Won't that be lovely?"

"Do you think he will get here in time to play?"

"I hope so, precious. It does him so much good to play croquet."

"Oh, I think it does all of us good to play croquet," Mary Louise would say, in a voice that trembled just at the vision of it.

Before Brick Pollitt arrived — sometimes half an hour before his coming, as though she could hear his automobile on the highway twenty miles from the house — Mary Louise would bound plumply off the gallery and begin setting up the poles and wickets. While she was doing this, her plump little buttocks and her beginning breasts and her shoulder-length copper curls would all bob up and down in unison. I would watch her from our front steps. She worked feverishly against time, for experience had taught her that the sooner she completed the preparations for the game, the greater would be the chance of getting her mother and Mr. Pollitt to play it. Frequently she was not fast enough, or they were too fast for her; by the time she had finished her perspiring job, the veranda would be deserted. Her wailing cries would begin, punctuating the dusk at intervals only a little less frequent than the passing of cars of people going out for evening drives to cool off.

"Mama! Mama! The croquet set is ready!"

Usually there would be a long, long wait for any response to come from the upstairs window toward which the calls were directed. But one time there wasn't. Almost immediately after the wailing voice was lifted, begging for the commencement of the game, Mary Louise's thin, pretty mother showed herself at the window. That was the time when I saw, between the dividing gauze of the bedroom curtains, her naked breasts, small and beautiful, shaken like two angry fists by her violent motion. She leaned between the curtains to answer Mary Louise not in her usual tone of gentle remonstrance but in a shocking cry of rage: "Oh, be still, for God's sake, you fat little monster!"

Mary Louise was shocked into a silence that must have lasted for a quarter of an hour. It was probably the word "fat" that struck her so overwhelmingly, for Mary Louise had once told me, when we were circling the block in the electric, that her mother had told her that she was *not* fat, that she was only plump, and that these cushions of flesh were going to dissolve in two or three more years and then she would be just as thin and pretty as her mother.

Though Mary Louise would call me over to play croquet with her, she was not at all satisfied with my game. I had had so little practice and she so much, and, besides, it was the company of the grown-up people she wanted. She would call me over only when they had disappeared irretrievably into the lightless house or when the game had collapsed owing to Mr. Brick Pollitt's refusal to take it seriously. When he played seriously, he was even better at it than Mary Louise, who practiced sometimes all afternoon in preparation for a game. But there were evenings when he would not leave his drink on the porch but would carry it down onto the lawn with him and play with one hand, more and more capriciously, while in the other hand he carried a tall glass. Then the lawn would become a great stage on which he performed all the immemorial antics of the clown, to the exasperation of Mary Louise and her thin, pretty mother, both of whom would become very severe and dignified on these occasions. They would retire from the croquet lawn and stand off at a little distance, calling softly, like a pair of complaining doves, both in the same ladylike tones of remonstrance. He was not a middle-aged-looking man — that is, he was not at all big around the middle — and he could leap and run like a boy. He could turn cartwheels and walk on his hands, and sometimes he would grunt and lunge like a wrestler or make long, crouching runs like a football player, weaving in and out among the wickets and gaudily painted poles of the croquet lawn. The acrobatics and sports of his youth seemed to haunt him. He would call out hoarsely to invisible teammates and adversaries — muffled shouts of defiance and anger and triumph, to which an incongruous counterpoint was continually provided by the faint, cooing voice of the widow: "Brick! Brick! Stop now, please stop! The child is crying! People will think you've gone crazy!" For Mary Louise's mother knew why the lights had gone out on all the screened porches up and down the street and why the automobiles drove past the house at the speed of a funeral procession while Mr. Brick Pollitt was making a circus ring of the croquet lawn.

Late one evening when he was making one of his crazy dashes across the lawn with an imaginary football hugged against his belly, he tripped over a wicket and sprawled on the lawn, and he pretended to be too gravely injured to get back on his feet. His groans brought Mary Louise and her mother running from behind the vine-screened end of the veranda and out upon the lawn to assist him. They took him by the hands and tried to haul him up, but with a sudden shout of laughter he pulled them both down on top of him and held them there till both of them were sobbing. He got up, finally, to replenish his glass of iced gin, and then returned to the lawn. That evening was a fearfully hot one, and

Brick decided to cool and refresh himself with the sprinkler while he enjoyed his drink. He turned it on and pulled it out to the center of the lawn. There he rolled about on the grass under its leisurely revolving arch of water, and as he rolled about, he began to wriggle out of his clothes. He kicked off his white shoes and one of his pale-green socks, tore off his drenched white shirt and grass-stained linen pants, but he never succeeded in getting off his necktie. Finally, he was sprawled, like some grotesque fountain figure, in underwear and necktie and the one remaining pale-green sock while the revolving arch of water moved with cool whispers about him. The arch of water had a faint crystalline iridescence, a mist of delicate colors, as it wheeled under the moon, for the moon had by that time begun to poke with an air of slow astonishment over the roof of the little building that housed the electric. And still the complaining doves cooed at him from various windows of the house, and you could tell their voices apart only by the fact that the mother murmured "Brick? Brick?" and Mary Louise called him Mr. Pollitt.

"Oh, Mr. Pollitt, Mother is so unhappy! Mother is crying!"

That night, he talked to himself or to invisible figures on the lawn. One of them was his wife, Margaret. He kept saying, "I'm sorry, Margaret, I'm sorry, Margaret, I'm so sorry, so sorry, Margaret. I'm sorry I'm no good, I'm sorry, Margaret, I'm so sorry, so sorry I'm no good, sorry I'm drunk, sorry I'm no good, I'm so sorry it all had to turn out like this . . ."

Later on, much later, after the remarkably slow procession of touring cars had stopped passing the house, a little black sedan that belonged to the police drew up in front of the Greys' and sat there for a while. In it was the chief of police himself. He called "Brick! Brick!" almost as gently and softly as Mary Louise's mother had called from the lightless windows. "Brick! Brick, old boy! Brick, fellow?" he called, till finally the inert fountain figure in underwear and green sock and unremovable necktie staggered out from under the rotating arch of water and stumbled down to the walk and stood there negligently and quietly conversing with the chief of police, under the no longer at all astonished, now quite large and indifferent great yellow stare of the August moon. They began to laugh softly together, Mr. Brick Pollitt and the chief of police, and finally the door of the little black car opened and Mr. Brick Pollitt got in beside the chief of police while the common officer got out to collect the clothes, flabby as drenched towels, on the croquet lawn. Then they drove away, and the summer night's show was over.

It was not quite over for me, for I had been watching it all that time with unabated interest. And about an hour afterward I saw Mary Louise's mother come out onto the lawn; she stood there with an air of desolation for quite a while. Then she went into the garage and backed the electric out. The electric went sedately off into the summer night, with its buzzing no louder than an insect's, and perhaps an hour later it came back again, containing in its glass show box not only the thin, pretty widow but a quiet and chastened Mr. Pollitt. She curved an arm about his immensely tall figure as they went up the front walk, and I heard him say only one word distinctly. It was the name of his wife.

Early that autumn, which was different from summer in nothing except the quicker coming of dusk, the visits of Mr. Brick Pollitt began to take on a spasmodic irregularity. That faraway boom of a cannon at five o'clock was now the announcement that two ladies in white dresses were waiting on a white gallery for someone who was each time a little more likely to disappoint them than the time before. Disappointment was not a thing that Mary Louise was inured to; it was a country that she was passing through not as an old inhabitant but as a bewildered explorer, and each afternoon she lugged the oblong box out of the garage, ceremonially opened it upon the center of the lawn, and began to arrange the wickets in their formal pattern between the two gaudily painted poles that meant beginning, middle, and end. And the widow talked to her from the gallery, under the awning, as if there had been no important alteration in their lives or their prospects. Their almost duplicate voices as they talked back and forth between gallery and lawn rang out as clearly as if the enormous corner lot were enclosed at this hour by a still more enormous and perfectly transparent glass bell that picked up and carried through space whatever was uttered beneath it. This was true not only when they were talking to each other across the lawn but when they were seated side by side in the white wicker chairs on the gallery. Phrases from these conversations became catchwords, repeated and mocked by the neighbors, for whom the widow and her daughter and Mr. Brick Pollitt had been three players in a sensational drama. It had shocked and angered them for two acts, but now as it approached a conclusion it was declining into unintentional farce, which they could laugh at. It was not difficult to find something ludicrous in the talks between the two ladies or the high-pitched elegance of their voices.

Mary Louise would ask, "Will Mr. Pollitt get here in time for croquet?"

"I hope so, precious. It does him so much good."

"He'll have to come soon or it will be too dark to see the wickets."

"That's true, precious."

"Mother, why is it dark so early now?"

"Honey, you know why. The sun goes South."

"But why does it go South?"

"Precious, Mother cannot explain the movements of the heavenly bodies, you know that as well as Mother knows it. Those things are controlled by certain mysterious laws that people on earth don't know or understand."

"Mother, are we going East?"

"When, precious?"

"Before school starts."

"Honey, you know it's impossible for Mother to make any definite plans."

"I hope we do. I don't want to go to school here."

"Why not, precious? Are you afraid of the children?"

"No, Mother, but they don't like me. They make fun of me."

"How do they make fun of you?"

"They mimic the way I talk and they walk in front of me with their stomachs pushed out and giggle."

"That's because they're children and children are cruel."

"Will they stop being cruel when they grow up?"

"Why, I suppose some of them will and some of them won't."

"Well, I hope we go East before school opens."

"Mother can't make any plans or promises honey."

"No, but Mr. Brick Pollitt—"

"Honey, lower your voice! Ladies talk softly.'

"Oh, my goodness!"

"What is it, precious?"

"A mosquito just bit me!"

"That's too bad, but don't scratch it. Scratching can leave a permanent scar on the skin."

"I'm not scratching it. I'm just sucking it, Mother."

"Honey, Mother has told you time and again that the thing to do when you have a mosquito bite is to get a small piece of ice and wrap it up in a handkerchief and rub the bite gently with it until the sting is removed."

"That's what I do, but my lump of ice is melted!"

"Get you another piece, honey. You know where the icebox is!"

"There's not much left. You put so much in the ice bag for your head-ache."

"There must be some left, honey."

"There's just enough left for Mr. Pollitt's drinks."

"Never mind that."

"He needs it for his drinks, Mother."

"Yes, Mother knows what he wants the ice for, precious."

"There's only a little piece left. It's hardly enough to rub a mosquito bite with."

"Well, use it for that purpose, that purpose is better, and anyhow when Mr. Pollitt comes over as late as this, he doesn't deserve to have any ice saved for him."

"Mother?"

"Yes, precious?"

"I love ice and sugar!"

"What did you say, precious?"

"I said I loved ice and sugar!"

"Ice and sugar, precious?"

"Yes, I love the ice and sugar in the bottom of Mr. Pollitt's glass when he's through with it."

"Honey, you mustn't eat the ice in the bottom of Mr. Pollitt's glass!"

"Why not, Mother?"

"Because it's got liquor in it!"

"Oh, no, Mother. It's just ice and sugar when Mr. Pollitt's through with it."

"Honey, there's always a little liquor left in it."

"Oh, no. Not a drop's left when Mr. Pollitt's through with it!"

"But you say there's sugar left in it, and, honey, you know that sugar is very absorbent."

"It's what, Mummy?"

"It absorbs some liquor, and that's a good way to cultivate a taste for it. And, honey, you know what dreadful consequences a taste of liquor can have. It's bad enough for a man, but for a woman it's fatal. So when you want ice and sugar, let Mother know and she'll prepare some for you, but don't ever let me catch you eating what's left in Mr. Pollitt's glass!"

"Mama?"

"Yes, precious?"

"It's almost completely dark now. Everybody is turning on their lights or driving out on the river road to cool off. Can't we go out riding in the electric?"

"No, honey, we can't till we know Mr. Pollitt's not—"

"Do you still think he will come?"

"Precious, how can I say? Is Mother a fortune-teller?"

"Oh, here comes the Pierce, Mummy, here comes the Pierce!"

"Is it? Is it the Pierce?"

"Oh, no. No, it isn't. It's a Hudson Super Six. Mummy, I'm going to pull up the wickets now and water the lawn, because if Mr. Pollitt does come, he'll have people with him or won't be in a condition to play croquet. And when I've finished, I want to drive the electric around the block."

"Drive it around the block, honey, but don't go into the business district with it."

"Are you going with me, Mummy?"

"No, precious, I'm going to sit here."

"It's cooler in the electric."

"I don't think so. The electric goes too slowly to make much breeze."

If Mr. Pollitt did finally arrive those evenings, it was likely to be with a caravan of cars that came from Memphis, and then Mrs. Grey would have to receive a raffish assortment of strangers as if she herself had invited them to a party. The party would not confine itself to the downstairs rooms and galleries but would explode quickly and brilliantly in all directions, filling both floors of the house, spilling out upon the lawn, and sometimes even penetrating the little building that housed the electric automobile and the oblong box that held the packed-away croquet set. On those party nights, the fantastically balustraded and gabled and turreted white building would glitter all over, like one of those huge night-excursion boats that came downriver from Memphis, and it would be full of ragtime music and laughter. But at some point in the evening there would be, almost invariably, a disturbance. Some male guest would start cursing loudly, a woman would scream, you would hear a shattering of glass. Almost immediately afterward, the lights would go out in the house, as if it really were a boat and had run aground. From all the doors and galleries and stairs, people would come rushing forth, and the dispersion would be more rapid than the arrival had been. A little while later, the police car would pull up in front of the house. The thin, pretty widow would come out on the front gallery to receive the chief of police, and you could hear her light voice tinkling like glass chimes. "Why, it was nothing, it was nothing at all, just somebody who drank a little too much and lost his temper. You know how that Memphis crowd is, Mr. Duggan, there's always one gentleman in it who can't hold his liquor. I know it's late, but we have such a huge lawn — it occupies half the block — that I shouldn't think anybody who wasn't overcome with curiosity would have to know that a party had been going on!"

And then something happened that made no sound at all.

It wasn't an actual death, but it had nearly all the external indications of one. When there is a death in a house, the house is unnaturally quiet for a day or two. During that interval, the space that separates a house from those who watch it seems to become a translucent thickness of glass behind which whatever activity is visible goes on with the startling hush of a film when the sound track is broken. So it had been five months ago, when the pleasant young Doctor had died of that fierce flower grown in his skull. There had been an unnatural quiet for several days, and then a peculiar gray car with frosted windows had crashed through the bell of silence and the young Doctor, identifiable by the bronze gleam of hair at one end of the strapped and sheeted figure on the cot, had emerged from the house as if he were giving a public demonstration of how to go to sleep soundly in jolting motion under a glaze of lights.

That was five months ago, and it was now early October.

Mr. Pollitt had not been seen at the Greys' for more than a week when, one day, a truck pulled up before the house and a workman planted a square wooden sign at the front of the lawn. Mrs. Grey came out of the house as if it had caught fire. She ran down the steps, her white skirts making the crackling noise of flame, calling out as she descended, "You, man! What are you doing! What are you putting up there!"

"A 'For Sale' sign," he told her.

"Who told you to put that up? This house isn't for sale!"

"Yes, ma'am, it is!"

"Who said so?"

"Mrs. Pollitt, *she* said so."

He stared at Mrs. Grey and she came no closer. Then he gave the pole of the red-lettered sign a final blow with the back of a shovel and tossed the implement crashing into the truck and drove off. The back of the sign said nothing, so presently Mrs. Grey continued her running advance to the front of the lawn, where the great red letters were visible. She stood in front of it, rapidly shaking her head, finally gasping aloud as if the import of it had just then struck her, and then she turned and went slowly and thoughtfully back to the radiant fantasy of a house just as Mary Louise appeared from behind it with the hose.

"Mother!" she called, "I'm going to water the lawn!"

"*Don't!*" said Mrs. Grey.

The next afternoon, a fat and pleasantly smiling man, whom I had seen times without number loitering around in front of the used-car lot next to the Paramount movie, came up the front walk of the Greys' house with the excessive nonchalance of a man who is about to commit a robbery. He pushed the bell, waited awhile, pushed it again, and then was admitted through an opening that seemed to be hardly wide enough for his figure. He came back out almost immediately with something in his closed fist. It was the key to the little building that contained the croquet set and the electric automobile. He drew its folding doors all the way open, and disclosed the electric sitting there with its usual manner of a lady putting on or taking off her gloves at the entrance to a reception. He stared at it, as if its elegance were momentarily baffling. Then he got in and drove it out of the garage, holding the polished black pilot stick with a look on his round face that was like the look of an adult who is a little embarrassed to find himself being amused by a game that was meant for children. He drove it serenely out into the wide, shady street, and at an upstairs window of the house there was some kind of quick movement, as if a figure looking out had been startled by something and then had retreated in haste.

Later, after the Greys had left town, I saw the elegant square vehicle, which appeared to be made out of glass and patent leather, standing with an air of haughty self-consciousness among a dozen or so other cars for sale in the lot next door to the Paramount movie theatre, and as far as I know, it may be still sitting there, but many degrees less glittering by now.

The Greys had come and gone all in one quick season: the young Doctor, with his understanding eyes and quiet voice, whom everyone had liked in a hesitant, early way and had said would do well in the town; the thin, pretty woman, whom no one had really known except Brick Pollitt; and the plump little girl, who might someday be as pretty and slender as her mother. They had come and gone in one season, yes, like one of these tent shows that suddenly appear in a vacant lot in a Southern town and cross the sky at night with mysteriously wheeling lights and unearthly music, and then are gone, and the summer goes on without them, as if they had never come there.

As for Mr. Brick Pollitt, I can remember seeing him only once after the Greys left town, for my time there was also coming to an end. This last time that I saw him was a brilliant fall morning. It was a Saturday morning in October. Brick's driver's license had been revoked again, and his wife, Margaret, sat in the driver's seat of the Pierce-Arrow touring car. Brick did not sit beside her. He was on the back seat of the car, pitching this way and that way with the car's jolting motion, like a loosely wrapped package being delivered somewhere. Margaret Pollitt handled the car with a wonderful male assurance, her bare arms brown and muscular, and the car's canvas top had been lowered, the better to expose on its back seat the sheepishly grinning and nodding figure of Brick Pollitt. He was immaculately clothed and barbered. The knot of his polka-dot tie was drawn as tight as strong and eager fingers could knot a tie for an important occasion. One of his large red hands protruded, clasping the door to steady his motion, and two bands of gold glittered, a small one about a finger, a large one about the wrist. His cream-colored coat was neatly folded on the seat beside him and he wore a shirt of thin white material. He was a man who had been, and even at that time still was, the handsomest you were likely to remember.

Margaret blew the car's silver trumpet at every intersection. She leaned this way and that way, elevating or thrusting out an arm as she greeted people on porches, merchants beside store entrances, people she barely knew along the walks, calling them all by their familiar names, as if she were running for office in the town, while Brick nodded and grinned with senseless amiability behind her. It was exactly the way that some ancient conqueror, such as Caesar, or Alexander the Great, or Hannibal, might have led in chains through a capital city the prince of a state newly conquered.

JAMES AGEE

James Agee's writing is probably most admired for its deeply moving emotional quality and an equally profound grasp of what André Malraux called "Man's Fate." "A Mother's Tale" is a fable without the traditional moral. For those who have read The Jungle *by Upton Sinclair, which caused such a sensation early in the century, it is interesting to compare Sinclair's direct, sociological treatment with the subtle, more lasting approach of Agee.*

As with so many great artists, James Agee has become far more famous since his death than when he was alive. He was born in Knoxville, Tennessee, in 1909. He went to public schools in his own state and later to Exeter and Harvard. He died in New York City in 1955. He was the author of a book of verse, Permit Me Voyage, *published in 1934, and the Pulitzer Prize-winning* A Death in the Family. *His classic* Let Us Now Praise Famous Men (*with Walker Evans*), *first published in 1941, was reissued by Houghton Mifflin in 1960.*

A Mother's Tale

THE CALF RAN UP THE HILL as fast as he could and stopped sharp. "Mama!" he cried, all out of breath. "What *is* it! What are they *doing!* Where are they *going!*"

Other spring calves came galloping too.

They all were looking up at her and awaiting her explanation, but she looked out over their excited eyes. As she watched the mysterious and majestic thing they had never seen before, her own eyes became even more than ordinarily still, and during the considerable moment before she answered, she scarcely heard their urgent questioning.

Far out along the autumn plain, beneath the sloping light, an immense drove of cattle moved eastward. They went at a walk, not very fast, but faster than they could imaginably enjoy. Those in front were compelled by those behind; those at the rear, with few exceptions, did their best to keep up; those who were locked within the herd could no more help moving than the particles inside a falling rock. Men on horses rode ahead, and alongside, and behind, or spurred their horses intensely back and forth, keeping the pace steady, and the herd in shape; and from man to man a dog sped back and forth incessantly as a shuttle, barking, incessantly, in a hysterical voice. Now and then one of the men shouted fiercely, and this like the shrieking of the dog was tinily audible above a low and awesome sound which seemed to come not from the multitude of hooves but from the center of the world, and above the sporadic bawlings and bellowings of the herd.

From the hillside this tumult was so distant that it only made more delicate the prodigious silence in which the earth and sky were held; and, from the hill, the sight was as modest as its sound. The herd was virtually hidden in the dust it raised, and could be known, in general, only by the horns which pricked this flat sunlit dust like little briars. In one place a twist of the air revealed the trembling fabric of many backs; but it was only along the near edge of the mass that individual animals were discernible, small in a driven frieze, walking fast, stumbling and recovering, tossing their armed heads, or opening their skulls heavenward in one of those cries which reached the hillside long after the jaws were shut.

From where she watched, the mother could not be sure whether there were any she recognized. She knew that among them there must be a son of hers; she had not seen him since some previous spring, and she would not be seeing him again. Then the cries of the young ones impinged on her bemusement: "Where are they going?"

She looked into their ignorant eyes.

"Away," she said.

"Where?" they cried. "Where? Where?" her own son cried again.

She wondered what to say.

"On a long journey."

"But where *to*?" they shouted. "Yes, where *to*?" her son exclaimed, and she could see that he was losing his patience with her, as he always did when he felt she was evasive.

"I'm not sure," she said.

Their silence was so cold that she was unable to avoid their eyes for long.

"Well, not *really* sure. Because, you see," she said in her most reasonable tone, "I've never seen it with my own eyes, and that's the only way to *be* sure; *isn't* it."

They just kept looking at her. She could see no way out.

"But I've *heard* about it," she said with shallow cheerfulness, "from those who *have* seen it, and I don't suppose there's any good reason to doubt them."

She looked away over them again, and for all their interest in what she was about to tell them, her eyes so changed that they turned and looked, too.

The herd, which had been moving broadside to them, was being turned away, so slowly that like the turning of stars it could not quite be seen from one moment to the next; yet soon it was moving directly away from them, and even during the little while she spoke and they all watched after it, it steadily and very noticeably diminished, and the sounds of it as well.

"It happens always about this time of year," she said quietly while they watched. "Nearly all the men and horses leave, and go into the North and the West."

"Out on the range," her son said, and by his voice she knew what enchantment the idea already held for him.

"Yes," she said, "out on the range." And trying, impossibly, to imagine the range, they were touched by the breath of grandeur.

"And then before long," she continued, "everyone has been found, and brought into one place; and then . . . what you see, happens. All of them.

"Sometimes when the wind is right," she said more quietly, "you can hear them coming long before you can see them. It isn't even like a sound, at first. It's more as if something were moving far under the ground. It makes you uneasy. You wonder, why, what in the world can *that* be! Then you remember what it is and then you can really hear it. And then finally, there they all are."

She could see this did not interest them at all.

"But where are they *going?*" one asked, a little impatiently.

"I'm coming to that," she said; and she let them wait. Then she spoke slowly but casually.

"They are on their way to a railroad."

There, she thought; that's for that look you all gave me when I said I wasn't sure. She waited for them to ask; they waited for her to explain.

"A railroad," she told them, "is great hard bars of metal lying side by side, oi so they tell me, and they go on and on over the ground as far as the eye can see. And great wagons run on the metal bars on wheels, like wagon wheels but smaller, and these wheels are made of solid metal too. The wagons are much bigger than any wagon you've ever seen, as big as, big as sheds, they say, and they are pulled along on the iron bars by a terrible huge dark machine, with a loud scream."

"Big as *sheds?*" one of the calves said skeptically.

"Big *enough*, anyway," the mother said. "I told you I've never seen it myself. But those wagons are so big that several of us can get inside at once. And that's exactly what happens."

Suddenly she became very quiet, for she felt that somehow, she could not imagine just how, she had said altogether too much.

"Well, *what* happens," her son wanted to know. "What do you mean, *happens.*"

She always tried hard to be a reasonably modern mother. It was probably better, she felt, to go on, than to leave them all full of imaginings and mystification. Besides, there was really nothing at all awful about what happened . . . if only one could know *why*.

"Well," she said, "it's nothing much, really. They just — why, when they all finally *get* there, why there are all the great cars waiting in a long line, and the big dark machine is up ahead . . . smoke comes out of it, they say . . . and . . . well, then, they just put us into the wagons, just as many as will fit in each wagon, and when everybody is in, why . . ." She hesitated, for again, though she couldn't be sure why, she was uneasy.

"Why then," her son said, "the train takes them away."

Hearing that word, she felt a flinching of the heart. Where had he picked it up, she wondered, and she gave him a shy and curious glance. Oh dear, she thought. I should never have even *begun* to explain. "Yes," she said, "when everybody is safely in, they slide the doors shut."

They were all silent for a little while. Then one of them asked thoughtfully, "Are they taking them somewhere they don't want to go?"

"Oh, I don't think so," the mother said. "I imagine it's very nice."

"*I* want to go," she heard her son say with ardor. "I want to go right now," he cried. "Can I, Mama? *Can* I? *Please?*" And looking into his eyes, she was overwhelmed by sadness.

"Silly thing," she said, "there'll be time enough for that when you're grown up. But what I very much hope," she went on, "is that instead of being chosen to go out on the range and to make the long journey, you will grow up to be very strong and bright so they will decide that you may stay here at home with Mother. And you, too," she added, speaking to the other little males; but she could not honestly wish this for any but her own, least of all for the eldest, strongest and most proud, for she knew how few are chosen.

She could see that what she said was not received with enthusiasm.

"But I want to go," her son said.

"Why?" she asked. "I don't think any of you realize that it's a great *honor* to be chosen to stay. A great privilege. Why, it's just the most ordinary ones are taken out onto the range. But only the very pick are chosen to stay here at home. If you want to go out on the range," she said in hurried and happy inspiration, "all you have to do is be ordinary and careless and silly. If you want to have even a chance to be chosen to stay, you have to try to be stronger and bigger and braver and brighter than anyone else, and that takes *hard work*. *Every day*. Do you see?" And she looked happily and hopefully from one to another. "Besides," she added, aware that they were not won over, "I'm told it's a very rough life out there, and the men are unkind.

"Don't you see," she said again; and she pretended to speak to all of them, but it was only to her son.

But he only looked at her. "Why do you want me to stay home?" he asked flatly; in their silence she knew the others were asking the same question.

"Because it's safe here," she said before she knew better; and realized she had put it in the most unfortunate way possible. "Not safe, not just that," she fumbled. "I mean . . . because here we *know* what happens, and what's going to happen, and there's never any doubt about it, never any reason to wonder, to worry. Don't you see? It's just *Home*," and she put a smile on the word, "where we all know each other and are happy and well."

They were so merely quiet, looking back at her, that she felt they were neither won over nor alienated. Then she knew of her son that he, anyhow, was most certainly not persuaded, for he asked the question she most dreaded: "Where do they go on the train?" And hearing him, she knew that she would stop at nothing to bring that curiosity and eagerness, and that tendency toward skepticism, within safe bounds.

"Nobody knows," she said, and she added, in just the tone she knew would most sharply engage them, "Not for sure, anyway."

"What do you mean, *not for sure*," her son cried. And the oldest, biggest calf repeated the question, his voice cracking.

The mother deliberately kept silence as she gazed out over the plain, and while she was silent they all heard the last they would ever hear of all those who were going away: one last great cry, as faint almost as a breath; the infinitesimal jabbing vituperation of the dog; the solemn muttering of the earth.

"Well," she said, after even this sound was entirely lost, "there was one who came back." Their instant, trustful eyes were too much for her. She added, "Or so they say."

They gathered a little more closely around her, for now she spoke very quietly.

"It was my great-grandmother who told me," she said. "She was told it by *her* great-grandmother, who claimed she saw it with her own eyes, though of course I can't vouch for that. Because of course I wasn't even dreamed of then; and Great-grandmother was so very, very old, you see, that you couldn't always be sure she knew quite *what* she was saying."

Now that she began to remember it more clearly, she was sorry she had committed herself to telling it.

"Yes," she said, "the story is, there was one, *just* one, who ever came back, and he told what happened on the train, and where the train went and what happened after. He told it all in a rush, they say, the last things first and every which way, but as it was finally sorted out and gotten into order by those who heard it and those they told it to, this is more or less what happened:

"He said that after the men had gotten just as many of us as they could into the car he was in, so that their sides pressed tightly together and nobody could lie down, they slid the door shut with a startling rattle and a bang, and then there was a sudden jerk, so strong they might have fallen except that they were packed so closely together, and the car began to move. But after it had moved only a little way, it stopped as suddenly as it had started, so that they all nearly fell down again. You see, they were just moving up the next car that was joined on behind, to put more of us into it. He could see it all between the boards of the car, because the boards were built a little apart from each other, to let in air."

Car, her son said again to himself. Now he would never forget the word.

"He said that then, for the first time in his life, he became very badly frightened, he didn't know why. But he was sure, at that moment, that there was something dreadfully to be afraid of. The others felt this same great fear. They called out loudly to those who were being put into the car behind, and the others called back, but it was no use; those who were getting aboard were between narrow white fences and then were walking up a narrow slope and the men kept jabbing them as they do when they are in an unkind humor, and there was no way to go but on into the car. There was no way to get out of the car, either: he tried, with all his might, and he was the one nearest the door.

"After the next car behind was full, and the door was shut, the train jerked forward again, and stopped again, and they put more of us into still another car, and so on, and on, until all the starting and stopping no longer frightened anybody; it was just something uncomfortable that was never going to stop, and they began instead to realize how hungry and thirsty they were. But there was no food and no water, so they just had to put up with this; and about the time they became resigned to going without their suppers (for now it was almost dark), they heard a sudden and terrible scream which frightened them even more deeply than anything had frightened them before, and the train began to move again, and they braced their legs once more for the jolt when it would stop, but this time, instead of stopping, it began to go fast, and then even faster, so fast that the ground nearby slid past like a flooded creek and the whole country, he claimed, began to move too, turning slowly around a far mountain as if it were all one great wheel. And then there was a strange kind of disturbance inside the car, he said, or even inside his very bones. He felt as if everything in him was *falling*, as if he had been filled full of a heavy liquid that all wanted to flow one way, and all the others were leaning as he was leaning, away from this queer heaviness that was trying to pull them over, and then just as suddenly this leaning heaviness was gone and they nearly fell again before they could stop leaning against it. He could never understand what this was, but it too happened so many times that they all got used to it, just as they got used to seeing the country turn like a slow wheel, and just as they got used to the long cruel screams of the engine, and the steady iron noise beneath them which made the cold darkness so fearsome, and the hunger and the thirst and the continual standing up, and the moving on and on and on as if they would never stop."

"*Didn't* they ever stop?" one asked.

"Once in a great while," she replied. "Each time they did," she said, "he thought, Oh, now *at last! At last* we can get out and stretch our tired legs and lie down! *At last* we'll be given food and water! But they never let them out. And they never gave them food or water. They never even cleaned up under them. They had to stand in their manure and in the water they made."

"Why did the train stop?" her son asked; and with somber gratification she saw that he was taking all this very much to heart.

"He could never understand why," she said. "Sometimes men would walk up and down alongside the cars, and the more nervous and the more trustful of us would call out; but they were only looking around, they never seemed to do anything. Sometimes he could see many houses and bigger buildings together where people lived. Sometimes it was far out in the country and after they had stood still for a long time they would hear a little noise which quickly became louder, and then became suddenly a noise so loud it stopped their breathing, and during this noise something black would go by, very close, and so fast it couldn't be seen. And then it was gone as suddenly as it had appeared, and the noise became small, and then in the silence their train would start up again.

"Once, he tells us, something very strange happened. They were standing still, and cars of a very different kind began to move slowly past. These cars were not red, but black, with many glass windows like those in a house; and he says they were as full of human beings as the car he was in was full of our kind. And one of these people looked into his eyes and smiled, as if he liked him, or as if he knew only too well how hard the journey was.

"So by his account it happens to them, too," she said, with a certain pleased vindictiveness. "Only they were sitting down at their ease, not standing. And the one who smiled was eating."

She was still, trying to think of something; she couldn't quite grasp the thought.

"But didn't they *ever* let them out?" her son asked.

The oldest calf jeered. "Of *course* they did. He came back, didn't he? How would he ever come back if he didn't get out?"

"They didn't let them out," she said, "for a long, long time."

"How long?"

"So long, and he was so tired, he could never quite be sure. But he said that it turned from night to day and from day to night and back again several times over, with the train moving nearly all of this time, and that when it finally stopped, early one morning, they were all so tired and so discouraged that they hardly even noticed any longer, let alone felt any hope that anything would change for them, ever again; and then all of a sudden men came up and put up a wide walk and unbarred the door and slid it open, and it was the most wonderful and happy moment of his life when he saw the door open, and walked into the open air with all his joints trembling, and drank the water and ate the delicious food they had ready for him; it was worth the whole terrible journey."

Now that these scenes came clear before her, there was a faraway shining in her eyes, and her voice, too, had something in it of the faraway.

"When they had eaten and drunk all they could hold they lifted up their heads and looked around, and everything they saw made them happy. Even the trains made them cheerful now, for now they were no longer afraid of them. And though these trains were forever breaking to pieces and joining again with other broken pieces, with shufflings and clashings and rude cries, they hardly paid them attention any more, they were so pleased to be in their new home, and so surprised and delighted to find they were among thousands upon thousands of strangers of their own kind, all lifting up their voices in peacefulness and thanksgiving, and they were so wonderstruck by all they could see, it was so beautiful and so grand.

"For he has told us that now they lived among fences as white as bone, so many, and so spiderishly complicated, and shining so pure, that there's no use trying even to hint at the beauty and the splendor of it to anyone who knows only the pitiful little outfittings of a ranch. Beyond these mazy fences, through the dark and bright smoke which continually turned along the sunlight, dark buildings stood shoulder to shoulder in a wall as huge and proud as mountains. All through the air, all the time, there was an iron humming like the humming of the iron bar after it has been struck to tell the men it is time to eat, and in all the air, all the time, there was that same strange kind of iron strength which makes the silence before lightning so different from all other silence.

"Once for a little while the wind shifted and blew over them straight from the great buildings, and it brought a strange and very powerful smell which confused and disturbed them. He could never quite describe this smell, but he has told us it was unlike anything he had ever known before. It smelled like old fire, he said, and old blood and fear and darkness and sorrow and most terrible and brutal force and something else, something in it that made him want to run away. This sudden uneasiness and this wish to run away swept through every one of them, he tells us, so that they were all moved at once as restlessly as so many leaves in a wind, and there was great worry in their voices. But soon the leaders among them concluded that it was simply the way men must smell when there are a great many of them living together. Those dark buildings must be crowded very full of men, they decided, probably as many thousands of them, indoors, as there were of us, outdoors; so it was no wonder their smell was so strong and, to our kind, so unpleasant. Besides, it was so clear now in every other way that men were not as we had always supposed, but were doing everything they knew how to make us comfortable and happy, that we ought to just put up with their smell, which after all they couldn't help, any more than we could help our own. Very likely men didn't like the way we smelled, any more than we liked theirs. They passed along these ideas to the others, and soon everyone felt more calm, and then the wind changed again, and the fierce smell no longer came to them, and the smell of their own kind was back again, very strong of course, in such a crowd, but ever so homey and comforting, and everyone felt easy again.

"They were fed and watered so generously, and treated so well, and the majesty and the loveliness of this place where they had all come to rest was so far beyond anything they had ever known or dreamed of, that many of the simple and ignorant, whose memories were short, began to wonder whether that whole difficult journey, or even their whole lives up to now, had ever really been. Hadn't it all been just shadows, they murmured, just a bad dream?

"Even the sharp ones, who knew very well it had all really happened, began to figure that everything up to now had been made so full of pain only so that all they had come to now might seem all the sweeter and the more glorious. Some of the oldest and deepest were even of a mind that all the puzzle and tribulation of the journey had been sent us as a kind of harsh trying or proving of our worthiness; and that it was entirely fitting and proper that we could earn our way through to such rewards as these, only through suffering, and through being patient under pain which was beyond our understanding; and that now at the last, to those who had borne all things well, all things were made known: for the mystery of suffering stood revealed in joy. And now as they looked back over all that was past, all their sorrows and bewilderments seemed so little and so fleeting that, from the simplest among them even to the most wise, they could feel only the kind of amused pity we feel toward the very young when, with the first thing that hurts them or they are forbidden, they are sure there is nothing kind or fair in all creation, and carry on accordingly, raving and grieving as if their hearts would break."

She glanced among them with an indulgent smile, hoping the little lesson would sink home. They seemed interested but somewhat dazed. I'm talking way over their heads, she realized. But by now she herself was too deeply absorbed in her story to modify it much. *Let* it be, she thought, a little impatient; it's over *my* head, for that matter.

"They had hardly before this even wondered that they were alive," she went on, "and now all of a sudden they felt they understood *why* they were. This made them very happy, but they were still only beginning to enjoy this new wisdom when quite a new and different kind of restiveness ran among them. Before they quite knew it they were all moving once again, and now they realized that they were being moved, once more, by men, toward still some other place and purpose they could not know. But during these last hours they had been so well that now they felt no uneasiness, but all moved forward calm and sure toward better things still to come; he has told us that he no longer felt as if he were being driven, even as it became clear that they were going toward the shade of those great buildings; but guided.

"He was guided between fences which stood ever more and more narrowly near each other, among companions who were pressed ever more and more closely against one another; and now as he felt their warmth against him it was not uncomfortable, and his pleasure in it was not through any need to be close among others through anxiousness, but was a new kind of strong and gentle delight, at being so very close, so deeply of his own kind, that it seemed as if the very breath and heartbeat of each one were being exchanged through all that multitude, and each was another, and others were each, and each was a multitude, and the multitude was one. And quieted and made mild within this melting, they now entered the cold shadow cast by the buildings, and now with every step the smell of the buildings grew stronger, and in the darkening air the glittering of the fences was ever more queer.

"And now as they were pressed ever more intimately together he could see ahead of him a narrow gate, and he was strongly pressed upon from either side and from behind, and went in eagerly, and now he was between two fences so narrowly set that he brushed either fence with either flank, and walked alone, seeing just one other ahead of him, and knowing of just one other behind him, and for a moment the strange thought came to him, that the one ahead was his ᶜather, and that the one behind was the son he had never begotten.

"And now the light was so changed that he knew he must have come inside one of the gloomy and enormous buildings, and the smell was so much stronger that it seemed almost to burn his nostrils, and the swell and the somber new light blended together and became some other thing again, beyond his describing to us except to say that the whole air beat with it like one immense heart and it was as if the beating of this heart were pure violence infinitely manifolded upon violence: so that the uneasy feeling stirred in him again that it would be wise to turn around and run out of this place just as fast and as far as ever he could go. This he heard, as if he were telling it to himself at the top of his voice, but it came from somewhere so deep and so dark inside him that he could only hear the shouting of it as less than a whisper, as just a hot and chilling breath, and he scarcely heeded it, there was so much else to attend to.

"For as he walked along in this sudden and complete loneliness, he tells us, this wonderful knowledge of being one with all his race meant less and less to him, and in its place came something still more wonderful: he knew what it was to be himself alone, a creature separate and different from any other, who had never been before, and would never be again. He could feel this in his whole weight as he walked, and in each foot as he put it down and gave his weight to it and moved above it, and in every muscle as he moved, and it was a pride which lifted him up and made him feel large, and a pleasure which pierced him through. And as he began with such wondering delight to be aware of his own exact singleness in this world, he also began to understand (or so he thought) just why these fences were set so very narrow, and just why he was walking all by himself. It stole over him, he tells us, like the feeling of a slow cool wind, that he was being guided toward some still more wonderful reward or revealing, up ahead, which he could not of course imagine, but he was sure it was being held in store for him alone.

"Just then the one ahead of him fell down with a great sigh, and was so quickly taken out of the way that he did not even have to shift the order of his hooves as he walked on. The sudden fall and the sound of that sigh dismayed him, though, and something within him told him that it would be wise to look up: and there he saw Him.

"A little bridge ran crosswise above the fences. He stood on this bridge with His feet as wide apart as He could set them. He wore spattered trousers but from the belt up He was naked and as wet as rain. Both arms were raised high above His head and in both hands He held an enormous Hammer. With a grunt which was hardly like the voice of a human being, and with all His strength, He brought this Hammer down into the forehead of our friend: who, in a blinding blazing, heard from his own mouth the beginning of a gasping sigh; then there was only darkness."

Oh, this is *enough!* it's *enough!* she cried out within herself, seeing their terrible young eyes. How *could* she have been so foolish as to tell so much!

"What happened then?" she heard, in the voice of the oldest calf, and she was horrified. This shining in their eyes: was it only excitement? no pity? no fear?

"What happened?" two others asked.

Very well, she said to herself. I've gone so far; now I'll go the rest of the way. She decided not to soften it, either. She'd teach them a lesson they wouldn't forget in a hurry.

"Very well," she was surprised to hear herself say aloud.

"How long he lay in this darkness he couldn't know, but when he began to come out of it, all he knew was the most unspeakably dreadful pain. He was upside down and very slowly swinging and turning, for he was hanging by the tendons of his heels from great frightful hooks, and he has told us that the feeling was as if his hide were being torn from him inch by inch, in one piece. And then as he became more clearly aware he found that this was exactly what was happening. Knives would sliver and slice along both flanks, between the hide and the living flesh; then there was a moment of most precious relief; then red hands seized his hide and there was a jerking of the hide and a tearing of tissue which it was almost as terrible to hear as to feel, turning his whole body and the poor head at the bottom of it; and then the knives again.

"It was so far beyond anything he had ever known unnatural and amazing that he hung there through several more such slicings and jerkings and tearings before he was fully able to take it all in: then, with a scream, and a supreme straining of all his strength, he tore himself from the hooks and collapsed sprawling to the floor and, scrambling right to his feet, charged the men with the knives. For just a moment they were so astonished and so terrified they could not move. Then they moved faster than he had ever known men could — and so did all the other men who chanced to be in his way. He ran down a glowing floor of blood and down endless corridors which were hung with the bleeding carcasses of our kind and with bleeding fragments of carcasses, among blood-clothed men who carried bleeding weapons, and out of that vast room into the open, and over and through one fence after another, shoving aside many an astounded stranger and shouting out warnings as he ran, and away up the railroad toward the West.

"How he ever managed to get away, and how he ever found his way home, we can only try to guess. It's told that he scarcely knew, himself, by the time he came to this part of his story. He was impatient with those who interrupted him to ask about that, he had so much more important things to tell them, and by then he was so exhausted and so far gone that he could say nothing very clear about the little he did know. But we can realize that he must have had really tremendous strength, otherwise he couldn't have outlived the Hammer; and that strength such as his — which we simply don't see these days, it's of the olden time — is capable of things our own strongest and bravest would sicken to dream of. But there was something even stronger than his strength. There was his righteous fury, which nothing could stand up against, which brought him out of that fearful place. And there was his high and burning and heroic purpose, to keep him safe along the way, and to guide him home, and to keep the breath of life in him until he could warn us. He did manage to tell us that he just followed the railroad, but how he chose one among the many which branched out from that place, he couldn't say. He told us, too, that from time to time he recognized shapes of mountains and other landmarks, from his journey by train, all reappearing backward and with a changed look and hard to see, too (for he was shrewd enough to travel mostly at night), but still recognizable. But that isn't enough to account for it. For he has told us, too, that he simply *knew* the way; that he didn't hesitate one moment in choosing the right line of railroad, or even think of it as choosing; and that the landmarks didn't really guide him, but just made him the more sure of what he was already sure of; and that whenever he *did* encounter human beings — and during the later stages of his journey, when he began to doubt he would live to tell us, he traveled day and night — they never so much as moved to make him trouble, but stopped dead in their tracks, and their jaws fell open.

"And surely we can't wonder that their jaws fell open. I'm sure yours would, if you had seen him as he arrived, and I'm very glad I wasn't there to see it, either, even though it is said to be the greatest and most momentous day of all the days that ever were or shall be. For we have the testimony of eyewitnesses, how he looked, and it is only too vivid, even to hear of. He came up out of the East as much staggering as galloping (for by now he was so worn out by pain and exertion and loss of blood that he could hardly stay upright), and his heels were so piteously torn by the hooks that his hooves doubled under more often than not, and in his broken forehead the mark of the Hammer was like the socket for a third eye.

"He came to the meadow where the great trees made shade over the water. 'Bring them all together!' he cried out, as soon as he could find breath. 'All!' Then he drank; and then he began to speak to those who were already there: for as soon as he saw himself in the water it was as clear to him as it was to those who watched him that there was no time left to send for the others. His hide was all gone from his head and his neck and his forelegs and his chest and most of one side and a part of the other side. It was flung backward from his naked muscles by the wind of his running and now it lay around him in the dust like a ragged garment. They say there is no imagining how terrible and in some way how grand the eyeball is when the skin has been taken entirely from around it: his eyes, which were bare in this way, also burned with pain, and with the final energies of his life, and with his desperate concern to warn us while he could; and he rolled his eyes wildly while he talked, or looked piercingly from one to another of the listeners, interrupting himself to cry out, 'Believe me! Oh, believe me!' For it had evidently never occurred to him that he might not be believed, and must make this last great effort, in addition to all he had gone through for us, to make himself believed; so that he groaned with sorrow and with rage and railed at them without tact or mercy for their slowness to believe. He had scarcely what you could call a voice left, but with this relic of a voice he shouted and bellowed and bullied us and insulted us, in the agony of his concern. While he talked he bled from the mouth, and the mingled blood and saliva hung from his chin like the beard of a goat.

"Some say that with his naked face, and his savage eyes, and that beard and the hide lying off his bare shoulders like shabby clothing, he looked almost human. But others feel this is an irreverence even to think; and others, that it is a poor compliment to pay the one who told us, at such cost to himself, the true ultimate purpose of Man. Some did not believe he had ever come from our ranch in the first place, and of course he was so different from us in appearance and even in his voice, and so changed

from what he might ever have looked or sounded like before, that nobody could recognize him for sure, though some were sure they did.
Others suspected that he had been sent among us with his story for some
mischievous and cruel purpose, and the fact that they could not imagine
what this purpose might be, made them, naturally, all the more suspicious.
Some believed he was actually a man, trying — and none too successfully,
they said — to disguise himself as one of us; and again the fact that they
could not imagine why a man would do this, made them all the more
uneasy. There were quite a few who doubted that anyone who could get
into such bad condition as he was in, was fit even to give reliable information, let alone advice, to those in good health. And some whispered,
even while he spoke, that he had turned lunatic; and many came to
believe this. It wasn't only that his story was so fantastic; there was good
reason to wonder, many felt, whether anybody in his right mind would
go to such trouble for others. But even those who did not believe him
listened intently, out of curiosity to hear so wild a tale, and out of the
respect it is only proper to show any creature who is in the last agony.

"What he told, was what I have just told you. But his purpose was
away beyond just the telling. When they asked questions, no matter how
curious or suspicious or idle or foolish, he learned, toward the last, to
answer them with all the patience he could and in all the detail he could
remember. He even invited them to examine his wounded heels and the
pulsing wound in his head as closely as they pleased. He even begged
them to, for he knew that before everything else, he must be believed.
For unless we could believe him, wherever could we find any reason, or
enough courage, to do the hard and dreadful things he told us we must
do!

"It was only these things, he cared about. Only for these, he came back."

Now clearly remembering what these things were, she felt her whole
being quail. She looked at the young ones quickly and as quickly looked
away.

"While he talked," she went on, "and our ancestors listened, men came
quietly among us; one of them shot him. Whether he was shot in kindness or to silence him is an endlessly disputed question which will probably never be settled. Whether, even, he died of the shot, or through his
own great pain and weariness (for his eyes, they say, were glazing for
some time before the men came), we will never be sure. Some suppose
even that he may have died of his sorrow and his concern for us. Others

feel that he had quite enough to die of, without that. All these things are tangled and lost in the disputes of those who love to theorize and to argue. There is no arguing about his dying words, though; they were very clearly remembered:

" 'Tell them! Believe!' "

After a while her son asked, "What did he tell them to do?"

She avoided his eyes. "There's a great deal of disagreement about that, too," she said after a moment. "You see, he was so very tired."

They were silent.

"So tired," she said, "some think that toward the end, he really *must* have been out of his mind."

"Why?" asked her son.

"Because he was so tired out and so badly hurt."

They looked at her mistrustfully.

"And because of what he told us to do."

"What did he tell us to do?" her son asked again.

Her throat felt dry. "Just . . . things you can hardly bear even to think of. That's all."

They waited. "Well, *what?*" her son asked in a cold, accusing voice.

" 'Each one is himself,' " she said shyly. " 'Not of the herd. Himself alone.' That's one."

"What else?"

" 'Obey nobody. Depend on none.' "

"What else?"

She found that she was moved. " 'Break down the fences,' " she said less shyly. " 'Tell everybody, everywhere.' "

"Where?"

"Everywhere. You see, he thought there must be ever so many more of us than we had ever known."

They were silent. "What else?" her son asked.

" 'For if even a few do not hear me, or disbelieve me, we are all betrayed.' "

"Betrayed?"

"He meant, doing as men want us to. Not for ourselves, or the good of each other."

They were puzzled.

"Because, you see, he felt there was no other way." Again her voice altered: " 'All who are put on the range are put onto trains. All who are *put onto trains meet the Man With The Hammer. All who stay home are kept there to breed others to go onto the range, and so betray themselves and their kind and their children forever.*

"*'We are brought into this life only to be victims; and there is no other way for us unless we save ourselves.'*

"Do you understand?"

Still they were puzzled, she saw; and no wonder, poor things. But now the ancient lines rang in her memory, terrible and brave. They made her somehow proud. She began actually to want to say them.

"*'Never be taken,'*" she said. "*'Never be driven. Let those who can, kill Man. Let those who cannot, avoid him.'*"

She looked around at them.

"What else?" her son asked, and in his voice there was a rising valor.

She looked straight into his eyes. "*'Kill the yearlings,'*" she said very gently. "*'Kill the calves.'*"

She saw the valor leave his eyes.

"Kill us?"

She nodded, "*'So long as Man holds dominion over us,'*" she said. And in dread and amazement she heard herself add, "*'Bear no young.'*"

With this they all looked at her at once in such a way that she loved her child, and all these others, as never before; and there dilated within her such a sorrowful and marveling grandeur that for a moment she was nothing except her own inward whisper, "Why, *I* am one alone. And of the herd, too. Both at once. All one."

Her son's voice brought her back: "Did they do what he told them to?"

The oldest one scoffed, "Would we be here, if they had?"

"They say some did," the mother replied. "Some tried. Not all."

"What did the men do to them?" another asked.

"I don't know," she said. "It was such a very long time ago."

"Do you believe it?" asked the oldest calf.

"There are some who believe it," she said.

"Do *you*?"

"I'm told that far back in the wildest corners of the range there are some of us, mostly very, very old ones, who have never been taken. It's said that they meet, every so often, to talk and just to think together about the heroism and the terror of two sublime Beings, The One Who Came Back, and The Man With The Hammer. Even here at home, some of the old ones, and some of us who are just old-fashioned, believe it, or parts of it anyway. I know there are some who say that a hollow at the center of the forehead — a sort of shadow of the Hammer's blow — is a sign of very special ability. And I remember how Great-grandmother used to sing an old, pious song, let's see now, yes, 'Be not like dumb-driven cattle, be a hero in the strife.' But there aren't many. Not any more."

"Do *you* believe it?" the oldest calf insisted; and now she was touched to realize that every one of them, from the oldest to the youngest, needed very badly to be sure about that.

"Of course not, silly," she said; and all at once she was overcome by a most curious shyness, for it occurred to her that in the course of time, this young thing might be bred to her. "It's just an old, old legend." With a tender little laugh she added, lightly, "We use it to frighten children with."

By now the light was long on the plain and the herd was only a fume of gold near the horizon. Behind it, dung steamed, and dust sank gently to the shattered ground. She looked far away for a moment, wondering. Something — it was like a forgotten word on the tip of the tongue. She felt the sudden chill of the late afternoon and she wondered what she had been wondering about. "Come, children," she said briskly, "it's high time for supper." And she turned away; they followed.

The trouble was, her son was thinking, you could never trust her. If she said a thing was so, she was probably just trying to get her way with you. If she said a thing wasn't so, it probably was so. But you never could be sure. Not without seeing for yourself. I'm going to go, he told himself; I don't care *what* she wants. And if it isn't so, why then I'll live on the range and make the great journey and find out what *is* so. And if what she told was true, why then I'll know ahead of time and the one *I* will charge is The Man With The Hammer. I'll put Him and His Hammer out of the way forever, and that will make me an even better hero than The One Who Came Back.

So, when his mother glanced at him in concern, not quite daring to ask her question, he gave her his most docile smile, and snuggled his head against her, and she was comforted.

The littlest and youngest of them was doing double skips in his efforts to keep up with her. Now that he wouldn't be interrupting her, and none of the big ones would hear and make fun of him, he shyly whispered

his question, so warmly moistly ticklish that she felt as if he were licking
her ear.

"What is it, darling?" she asked, bending down.

"What's a train?"

BERNARD MALAMUD

When it was published, "The Magic Barrel" attracted instant attention to its author. The rabbinical student searching for a wife he can love and the over-zealous matchmaker are a wonderful contrast in characterization. There is a beautiful quality of the Old Testament in the ending.

Bernard Malamud was born in Brooklyn and educated at City College and Columbia University. During the forties he taught in evening high schools and then went to Oregon State College where he was assistant professor of English. He has taught at Harvard, and at Bennington College. He is the author of several books of fiction and in 1959 won the National Book Award for fiction.

The Magic Barrel

NOT LONG AGO there lived in uptown New York, in a small, almost meager room, though crowded with books, Leo Finkle, a rabbinical student in the Yeshivah University. Finkle, after six years of study, was to be ordained in June and had been advised by an acquaintance that he might find it easier to win himself a congregation if he were married. Since he had no present prospects of marriage, after two tormented days of turning it over in his mind, he called in Pinye Salzman, a marriage broker, whose two-line advertisement he had read in the *Forward*.

The matchmaker appeared one night out of the dark fourth-floor hallway of the graystone rooming house, grasping a black, strapped portfolio that had been worn thin with use. Salzman, who had been long in the business, was of slight but dignified build, wearing an old hat and an overcoat too short and tight for him. He smelled frankly of fish, which he loved to eat, and although he was missing a few teeth, his presence was not displeasing, because of an amiable manner curiously contrasted by mournful eyes. His voice, his lips, his wisp of beard, his bony fingers were animated, but give him a moment of repose and his mild blue eyes soon revealed a depth of sadness, a characteristic that put Leo a little at ease although the situation, for him, was inherently tense.

He at once informed Salzman why he had asked him to come, explaining that his home was in Cleveland, and that but for his parents, who had married comparatively late in life, he was alone in the world. He had for six years devoted himself entirely to his studies, as a result of which, quite understandably, he had found himself without time for a social life and the company of young women. Therefore he thought it the better part of trial and error — of embarrassing fumbling — to call in an experienced person to advise him in these matters. He remarked in passing that the function of the marriage broker was ancient and honorable, highly approved in the Jewish community, because it made practical the necessary without hindering joy. Moreover, his own parents had been brought together by a matchmaker. They had made, if not a financially profitable marriage — since neither had possessed any worldly goods to speak of — at least a successful one in the sense of their everlasting devotion to one another. Salzman listened in embarrassed surprise, sensing a sort of apology. Later, however, he experienced a glow of pride in his work, an emotion that had left him years ago, and he heartily approved of Finkle.

The two men went to their business. Leo had led Salzman to the only clear place in the room, a table near a window that overlooked the lamp-lit city. He seated himself at the matchmaker's side but facing him, attempting by an act of will to suppress the unpleasant tickle in his throat. Salzman eagerly unstrapped his portfolio and removed a loose rubber band from a thin packet of much handled cards. As he flipped through them, a gesture and sound that physically hurt Leo, the student pretended not to see and gazed steadfastly out the window. Although it was still February, winter was on its last legs, signs of which he had for the first time in years begun to notice. He now observed the round white moon, moving high in the sky through a cloud menagerie, and watched with half-open mouth as it penetrated a huge hen, and dropped out of her like an egg laying itself. Salzman, though pretending through eyeglasses he had just slipped on to be engaged in scanning the writing on the cards, stole occasional glances at the young man's distinguished face, noting with pleasure the long, severe scholar's nose, brown eyes heavy with learning, sensitive yet ascetic lips, and a certain almost hollow quality of the dark cheeks. He gazed around at shelves upon shelves of books and let out a soft but happy sigh

When Leo's eyes fell upon the cards, he counted six spread out in Salzman's hand.

"So few?" he said in disappointment.

"You wouldn't believe me how much cards I got in my office," Salzman replied. "The drawers are already filled to the top, so I keep them now in a barrel, but is every girl good for a new rabbi?"

Leo blushed at this, regretting all he had revealed of himself in a curriculum vitae he had sent to Salzman. He had thought it best to acquaint him with his strict standards and specifications, but in having done so now felt he had told the marriage broker more than was absolutely necessary.

He hesitantly inquired, "Do you keep photographs of your clients on file?"

"First comes family, amount of dowry, also what kind promises," Salzman replied, unbuttoning his tight coat and settling himself in the chair. "After comes pictures, rabbi."

"Call me Mr. Finkle. I'm not a rabbi yet."

Salzman said he would, but instead called him doctor, which he changed to rabbi when Leo was not listening too attentively.

Salzman adjusted his horn-rimmed spectacles, gently cleared his throat and read in an eager voice the contents of the top card:

"Sophie P. Twenty-four years. Widow for one year. No children. Educated high school and two years college. Father promises eight thousand dollars. Has wonderful wholesale business. Also real estate. On the mother's side comes teachers, also one actor. Well known on Second Avenue."

Leo gazed up in surprise. "Did you say a widow?"

"A widow don't mean spoiled, rabbi. She lived with her husband maybe four months. He was a sick boy, she made a mistake to marry him."

"Marrying a widow has never entered my mind."

"This is because you have no experience. A widow, specially if she is young and healthy like this girl, is a wonderful person to marry. She will be thankful to you the rest of her life. Believe me, if I was looking now for a bride, I would marry a widow."

Leo reflected, then shook his head.

Salzman hunched his shoulders in an almost imperceptible gesture of disappointment. He placed the card down on the wooden table and began to read another:

"Lily H. High school teacher. Regular. Not a substitute. Has savings and new Dodge car. Lived in Paris one year. Father is successful dentist thirty-five years. Interested in professional man. Well Americanized family. Wonderful opportunity.

"I know her personally," said Salzman. "I wish you could see this girl. She is a doll. Also very intelligent. All day you could talk to her about books and theyater and what not. She also knows current events."

"I don't believe you mentioned her age?"

"Her age?" Salzman said, raising his brows in surprise. "Her age is thirty-two years."

Leo said after a while, "I'm afraid that seems a little too old."

Salzman let out a laugh. "So how old are you, rabbi?"

"Twenty-seven."

"So what is the difference, tell me, between twenty-seven and thirty-two? My own wife is seven years older than me. So what did I suffer? — Nothing. If Rothschild's a daughter wants to marry you, would you say on account her age, no?"

"Yes," Leo said dryly.

Salzman shook off the no in the yes. "Five years don't mean a thing. I give you my word that when you will live with her for one week you will forget her age. What does it mean five years — that she lived more and knows more than somebody who is younger? On this girl, God bless her, years are not wasted. Each one that it comes makes better the bargain."

"What subject does she teach in high school?"

"Languages. If you heard the way she reads French, you will think it is music. I am in the business twenty-five years, and I recommend her with my whole heart. Believe me, I know what I'm talking, rabbi."

"What's on the next card?" Leo said abruptly.

Salzman reluctantly turned up the third card:

"Ruth K. Nineteen years. Honor student. Father offers thirteen thousand dollars cash to the right bridegroom. He is a medical doctor. Stomach specialist with marvelous practice. Brother-in-law owns own garment business. Particular people."

Salzman looked up as if he had read his trump card.

"Did you say nineteen?" Leo asked with interest.

"On the dot."

"Is she attractive?" He blushed. "Pretty?"

Salzman kissed his fingertips. "A little doll. On this I give you my word. Let me call the father tonight and you will see what means pretty."

But Leo was troubled. "You're sure she's that young?"

"This I am positive. The father will show you the birth certificate."

"Are you positive there isn't something wrong with her?" Leo insisted.

"Who says there is wrong?"

"I don't understand why an American girl her age should go to a marriage broker."

A smile spread over Salzman's face.

"So for the same reason you went, she comes."

Leo flushed. "I am pressed for time."

Salzman, realizing he had been tactless, quickly explained. "The father came, not her. He wants she should have the best, so he looks around himself. When we will locate the right boy he will introduce him and encourage. This makes a better marriage than if a young girl without experience takes for herself. I don't have to tell you this."

"But don't you think this young girl believes in love?" Leo spoke uneasily.

Salzman was about to guffaw but caught himself and said soberly, "Love comes with the right person, not before."

Leo parted dry lips but did not speak. Noticing that Salzman had snatched a quick glance at the next card, he cleverly asked, "How is her health?"

"Perfect," Salzman said, breathing with difficulty. "Of course, she is a little lame on her right foot from an auto accident that it happened to her when she was twelve years, but nobody notices on account she is so brilliant and also beautiful."

Leo got up heavily and went to the window. He felt curiously bitter and upbraided himself for having called in the marriage broker. Finally, he shook his head.

"Why not?" Salzman persisted, the pitch of his voice rising.

"Because I hate stomach specialists."

"So what do you care what is his business? After you marry her, do you need him? Who says he must come every Friday night to your house?"

Ashamed of the way the talk was going, Leo dismissed Salzman, who went home with melancholy eyes.

Though he had felt only relief at the marriage broker's departure, Leo was in low spirits the next day. He explained it as arising from Salzman's failure to produce a suitable bride for him. He did not care for his type of clientele. But when Leo found himself hesitating over whether to seek out another matchmaker, one more polished than Pinye, he wondered if it could be — his protestations to the contrary, and although he honored his father and mother — that he did not, in essence, care for the match-making institution. This thought he quickly put out of mind yet found himself still upset. All day he ran around in a fog — missed an important appointment, forgot to give out his laundry, walked out of a Broadway cafeteria without paying and had to run back with the ticket in his hand; had even not recognized his landlady in the street when she passed with a friend and courteously called out, "A good evening to you, Doctor Finkle." By nightfall, however, he had regained sufficient calm to sink his nose into a book and there found peace from his thoughts.

Almost at once there came a knock on the door. Before Leo couuld say enter, Salzman, commerical cupid, was standing in the room. His face was gray and meager, his expression hungry, and he looked as if he would expire on his feet. Yet the marriage broker managed, by some trick of the muscles, to display a broad smile.

"So good evening. I am invited?"

Leo nodded, disturbed to see him again, yet unwilling to ask him to leave.

Beaming still, Salzman laid his portfolio on the table. "Rabbi, I got for you tonight good news."

"I've asked you not to call me rabbi. I'm still a student."

"Your worries are finished. I have for you a first-class bride."

"Leave me in peace concerning this subject." Leo pretended lack of interest.

"The world will dance at your wedding."

"Please, Mr. Salzman, no more."

"But first must come back my strength," Salzman said weakly. He fumbled with the portfolio straps and took out of the leather case an oily paper bag, from which he extracted a hard seeded roll and a small smoked whitefish. With one motion of his hand he stripped the fish out of its skin and began ravenously to chew. "All day in a rush," he muttered.

Leo watched him eat.

"A sliced tomato you have maybe?" Salzman hesitantly inquired.

"No."

The marriage broker shut his eyes and ate. When he had finished he carefully cleaned up the crumbs and rolled up the remains of the fish in the paper bag. His spectacled eyes roamed the room until he discovered, amid some piles of books, a one-burner gas stove. Lifting his hat he humbly asked, "A glass tea you got, rabbi?"

Conscience-stricken, Leo rose and brewed the tea. He served it with a chunk of lemon and two cubes of lump sugar, delighting Salzman.

After he had drunk his tea, Salzman's strength and good spirits were restored.

"So tell me, rabbi," he said amiably, "you considered any more the three clients I mentioned yesterday?"

"There was no need to consider."

"Why not?"

"None of them suits me."

"What, then, suits you?"

Leo let it pass because he could give only a confused answer.

Without waiting for a reply, Salzman asked, "You remember this girl I talked to you — the high school teacher?"

"Age thirty-two?"

But, surprisingly, Salzman's face lit in a smile. "Age twenty-nine."

Leo shot him a look. "Reduced from thirty-two?"

"A mistake," Salzman avowed. "I talked today with the dentist. He took me to his safety deposit box and showed me the birth certificate. She was twenty-nine years last August. They made her a party in the mountains where she went for her vacation. When her father spoke to me the first time I forgot to write the age and I told you thirty-two, but now I remember this was a different client, a widow."

"The same one you told me about? I thought she was twenty-four?"

"A different. Am I responsible that the world is filled with widows?"

"No, but I'm not interested in them, nor for that matter, in school-teachers."

Salzman passionately pulled his clasped hands to his breast. Looking at the ceiling he exclaimed, "Jewish children, what can I say to somebody that he is not interested in high school teachers? So what then you are interested?"

Leo flushed but controlled himself.

"In who else you will be interested," Salzman went on, "if you not interested in this fine girl that she speaks four languages and has person-ally in the bank ten thousand dollars? Also her father guarantees further twelve thousand. Also she has a new car, wonderful clothes, talks on all subjects, and she will give you a first-class home and children. How near do we come in our life to paradise?"

"If she's so wonderful, why wasn't she married ten years ago?"

"Why?" said Salzman with a heavy laugh "—Why? Because she is *partikler*. This is why. She wants only the *best*."

Leo was silent, amused at how he had trapped himself. But Salzman had aroused his interest in Lily H., and he began seriously to consider calling on her. When the marriage broker observed how intently Leo's mind was at work on the facts he had supplied, he felt positive they would soon come to an agreement.

Late Saturday afternoon, conscious of Salzman, Leo Finkle walked with Lily Hirschorn along Riverside Drive. He walked briskly and erectly, wearing with distinction the black fedora he had that morning taken with trepidation out of the dusty hatbox on his closet shelf, and the heavy black Saturday coat he had thoroughly whisked clean. Leo also owned a walking stick, a present from a distant relative, but had decided not to use it. Lily, petite and not unpretty, had on something signifying the approach of spring. She was *au courant,* animatedly, with all subjects, and he weighed her words and found her surprisingly sound—score another for Salzman, whom he uneasily sensed to be somewhere around, hiding perhaps high in a tree along the street, flashing the lady signals; or perhaps a cloven-hoofed Pan, piping nuptial ditties as he danced his invisible way before them, strewing wild buds on the walk and purple summer grapes in their path, symbolizing fruit of a union, of which there was yet none.

Lily startled Leo by remarking, "I was thinking of Mr. Salzman, a curious figure, wouldn't you say?"

Not certain what to answer, he nodded.

She bravely went on, blushing, "I for one am grateful for his introducing us. Aren't you?"

He courteously replied, "I am."

"I mean," she said with a little laugh—and it was all in good taste, or at least gave the effect of being not in bad—"do you mind that we came together so?"

He was not afraid of her honesty, recognizing that she meant to set the relationship aright, and understanding that it took a certain amount of experience in life, and courage, to want to do it quite that way. One had to have some sort of past to make that kind of beginning.

He said that he did not mind. Salzman's function was traditional and honorable—valuable for what it might achieve, which, he pointed out, was frequently nothing.

Lily agreed with a sigh. They walked on for a while and she said after a long silence, again with a nervous laugh, "Would you mind if I asked you something a little bit personal? Frankly, I find the subject fascinating." Although Leo shrugged, she went on half embarrassedly, "How was it that you came to your calling? I mean was it a sudden passionate inspiration?"

Leo, after a time, slowly replied, "I was always interested in the Law."

"You saw revealed in it the presence of the Highest?"

He nodded and changed the subject. "I understand you spent a little time in Paris, Miss Hirschorn?"

"Oh, did Mr. Salzman tell you, Rabbi Finkle?" Leo winced but she went on, "It was ages and ages ago and almost forgotten. I remember I had to return for my sister's wedding."

But Lily would not be put off. "When," she asked in a trembly voice, "did you become enamored of God?"

He stared at her. Then it came to him that she was talking not about Leo Finkle, but a total stranger, some mystical figure, perhaps even passionate prophet that Salzman had conjured up for her — no relation to the living or dead. Leo trembled with rage and weakness. The trickster had obviously sold her a bill of goods, just as he had him, who'd expected to become acquainted with a young lady of twenty-nine, only to behold, the moment he laid eyes upon her strained and anxious face, a woman past thirty-five and aging very rapidly. Only his self-control, he thought, had kept him this long in her presence.

"I am not," he said gravely, "a talented religious person," and in seeking words to go on, found himself possessed by fear and shame. "I think," he said in a strained manner, "that I came to God not because I loved him, but because I did not."

This confession he spoke harshly because its unexpectedness shook him.

Lily wilted. Leo saw a profusion of loaves of bread sailing like ducks high over his head, not unlike the loaves by which he had counted himself to sleep last night. Mercifully, then, it snowed, which he would not put past Salzman's machinations.

He was infuriated with the marriage broker and swore he would throw him out of the room the moment he reappeared. But Salzman did not come that night, and when Leo's anger had subsided, an unaccountable despair grew in its place. At first he thought this was caused by his disappointment in Lily, but before long it became evident that he had involved himself with Salzman without a true knowledge of his own intent. He gradually realized — with an emptiness that seized him with six hands — that he had called in the broker to find him a bride because he was incapable of doing it himself. This terrifying insight he had derived as a result of his meeting and conversation with Lily Hirschorn. Her probing questions had somehow irritated him into revealing — to himself more than her — the true nature of his relationship with God, and from that it had come upon him, with shocking force, that apart from his parents, he had never loved anyone. Or perhaps it went the other way, that he did not love God so well as he might, because he had not loved man. It seemed to Leo that his whole life stood starkly revealed and he saw himself, for the first time, as he truly was — unloved and loveless. This bitter but somehow not fully unexpected revelation brought him to a point of panic controlled only by extraordinary effort. He covered his face with his hands and wept.

The week that followed was the worst of his life. He did not eat, and lost weight. His beard darkened and grew ragged. He stopped attending lectures and seminars and almost never opened a book. He seriously considered leaving the Yeshivah, although he was deeply troubled at the thought of the loss of all his years of study — saw them like pages from a book strewn over the city — and at the devastating effect of this decision upon his parents. But he had lived without knowledge of himself, and never in the Five Books and all the Commentaries — mea culpa — had the truth been revealed to him. He did not know where to turn, and in all this desolating loneliness there was no *to whom,* although he often thought of Lily but not once could bring himself to go downstairs and make the call. He became touchy and irritable, especially with his land-lady, who asked him all manner of questions; on the other hand, sensing his own disagreeableness, he waylaid her on the stairs and apologized abjectly, until, mortified, she ran from him. Out of this, however, he drew the consolation that he was yet a Jew and that a Jew suffered. But gradually, as the long and terrible week drew to a close, he regained his composure and some idea of purpose in life: to go on as planned. Although he was imperfect, the ideal was not. As for his quest of a bride, the thought of continuing afflicted him with anxiety and heartburn, yet perhaps with this new knowledge of himself he would be more successful than in the past. Perhaps love would now come to him and a bride to that love. And for this sanctified seeking who needed a Salzman?

The marriage broker, a skeleton with haunted eyes, returned that very night. He looked, withal, the picture of frustrated expectancy — as if he had steadfastly waited the week at Miss Lily Hirschorn's side for a telephone call that never came.

Casually coughing, Salzman came immediately to the point: "So how did you like her?"

Leo's anger rose and he could not refrain from chiding the matchmaker: "Why did you lie to me, Salzman?"

Salzman's pale face went dead white, as if the world had snowed on him.

"Did you not state that she was twenty-nine?" Leo insisted.

"I give you my word —"

"She was thirty-five. *At least* thirty-five."

"Of this I would not be too sure. Her father told me —"

"Never mind. The worst of it was that you lied to her."

"How did I lie to her, tell me?"

"You told her things about me that weren't true. You made me out to be more, consequently less than I am. She had in mind a totally different person, a sort of semi-mystical Wonder Rabbi."

"All I said, you was a religious man."

"I can imagine."

Salzman sighed. "This is my weakness that I have," he confessed. "My wife says to me I shouldn't be a salesman, but when I have two fine people that they would be wonderful to be married, I am so happy that I talk too much." He smiled wanly. "This is why Salzman is a poor man."

Leo's anger went. "Well, Salzman, I'm afraid that's all."

The marriage broker fastened hungry eyes on him.

"You don't want any more a bride?"

"I do," said Leo, "but I have decided to seek her in a different way. I am no longer interested in an arranged marriage. To be frank, I now admit the necessity of premarital love. That is, I want to be in love with the one I marry."

"Love?" said Salzman, astounded. After a moment he said, "For us, our love is our life, not for the ladies. In the ghetto they —"

"I know, I know," said Leo. "I've thought of it often. Love, I have said to myself, should be a by-product of living and worship rather than its own end. Yet for myself I find it necessary to establish the level of my need and to fulfill it."

Salzman shrugged but answered, "Listen, rabbi, if you want love, this I can find for you also. I have such beautiful clients that you will love them the minute your eyes will see them."

Leo smiled unhappily. "I'm afraid you don't understand."

But Salzman hastily unstrapped his portfolio and withdrew a manila packet from it.

"Pictures," he said, quickly laying the envelope on the table.

Leo called after him to take the pictures away, but as if on the wings of the wind, Salzman had disappeared.

March came. Leo had returned to his regular routine. Although he felt not quite himself yet — lacked energy — he was making plans for a more active social life. Of course it would cost something, but he was an expert in cutting corners; and when there were no corners left he could make circles rounder. All the while Salzman's pictures had lain on the table, gathering dust. Occasionally as Leo sat studying, or enjoying a cup of tea, his eyes fell on the manila envelope, but he never opened it.

The days went by and no social life to speak of developed with a member of the opposite sex — it was difficult, given the circumstances of his situation. One morning Leo toiled up the stairs to his room and stared out the window at the city. Although the day was bright his view of it was dark. For some time he watched the people in the street below hurrying along and then turned with a heavy heart to his little room. On the table was the packet. With a sudden relentless gesture he tore it open. For a half-hour he stood there, in a state of excitement, examining the photographs of the ladies Salzman had included. Finally, with a deep sigh he put them down. There were six, of varying degrees of attractiveness, but look at them long enough and they all became Lily Hirschorn: all past their prime, all starved behind bright smiles, not a true personality in the lot. Life, despite their anguished struggles and frantic yoohooings, had passed them by; they were photographs in a briefcase that stank of fish. After a while, however, as Leo attempted to return the pictures into the envelope, he found another in it, a small snapshot of the type taken by a machine for a quarter. He gazed at it a moment and let out a cry.

Her face deeply moved him. Why, he could at first not say. It gave him the impression of youth — all spring flowers, yet age — a sense of having been used to the bone, wasted; this all came from the eyes, which were hauntingly familiar, yet absolutely strange. He had a strong impression that he had met her before, but try as he might he could not place her, although he could almost recall her name, as if he had read it written in her own handwriting. No, this couldn't be; he would have remembered her. It was not, he affirmed, that she had an extraordinary beauty — no, although her face was attractive enough; it was that *something* about her moved him. Feature for feature, even some of the ladies of the photographs could do better; but she leaped forth to the heart — had lived, or wanted to — more than just wanted, perhaps regretted it — had somehow deeply suffered: it could be seen in the depths of those reluctant eyes, and from the way the light enclosed and shone from her, and within her, opening whole realms of possibility: this was her own. Her he desired. His head ached and eyes narrowed with the intensity of his gazing, then, as if a black fog had blown up in the mind, he experienced fear of her and was aware that he had received an impression, somehow, of filth. He shuddered, saying softly, it is thus with us all. Leo brewed some tea in a small pot and sat sipping it, without sugar, to calm himself. But before he had finished drinking, again with excitement he examined the face and found it good: good for him. Only such a one could truly understand Leo Finkle and help him to seek whatever he was seeking. How she had come to be among the discards in Salzman's barrel he could never guess, but he knew he must urgently go find her.

Leo rushed downstairs, grabbed up the Bronx telephone book, and searched for Salzman's home address. He was not listed, nor was his office. Neither was he in the Manhattan book. But Leo remembered having written down the address on a slip of paper after he had read Salzman's advertisement in the "personals" column of the *Forward*. He ran up to his room and tore through his papers, without luck. It was exasperating. Just when he needed the matchmaker he was nowhere to be found. Fortunately Leo remembered to look in his wallet. There on a card he found his name written and a Bronx address. No phone number was listed, which, Leo now recalled, was the reason he had originally communicated with Salzman by letter. He got on his coat, put a hat on over his skull cap and hurried to the subway station. All the way to the far end of the Bronx he sat on the edge of the seat. He was more than once tempted to take out the picture and see if the girl's face was as he remembered it, but he refrained, allowing the snapshot to remain in his inside coat pocket, content to have her so close. When the train pulled into the station he was waiting at the door and bolted out. He quickly located the street Salzman had advertised.

The building he sought was less than a block from the subway, but it was not an office building, nor even a loft, nor a store in which one could rent office space. It was an old and grimy tenement. Leo found Salzman's name in pencil on a soiled tag under the bell and climbed three dark flights to his apartment. When he knocked, the door was opened by a thin, asthmatic, gray-haired woman, in felt slippers.

"Yes?" she said, expecting nothing. She listened without listening. He could have sworn he had seen her somewhere before but knew it was illusion.

"Salzman — does he live here? Pinye Salzman," he said, "the match-maker?"

She stared at him a long time. "Of course."

He felt embarrassed. "Is he in?"

"No." Her mouth was open, but she offered nothing more.

"This is urgent. Can you tell me where his office is?"

"In the air." She pointed upward.

"You mean he has no office?" Leo said.

"In his socks."

He peered into the apartment. It was sunless and dingy, one large room divided by a half-open curtain, beyond which he could see a sagging metal bed. The near side of the room was crowded with rickety chairs, old bureaus, a three-legged table, racks of cooking utensils, and all the apparatus of a kitchen. But there was no sign of Salzman or his magic barrel, probably also a figment of his imagination. An odor of frying fish made Leo weak to the knees.

"Where is he?" he insisted. "I've got to see your husband."

At length she answered, "So who knows where he is? Every time he thinks a new thought he runs to a different place. Go home, he will find you."

"Tell him Leo Finkle."

She gave no sign that she had heard.

He went downstairs, deeply depressed.

But Salzman, breathless, stood waiting at his door.

Leo was overjoyed and astounded. "How did you get here before me?"

"I rushed."

"Come inside."

They entered. Leo fixed tea and a sardine sandwich for Salzman.

As they were drinking he reached behind him for the packet of pictures and handed them to the marriage broker.

Salzman put down his glass and said expectantly, "You found maybe somebody you like?"

"Not among these."

The marriage broker turned sad eyes away.

"Here's the one I like." Leo held forth the snapshot.

Salzman slipped on his glasses and took the picture into his trembling hand. He turned ghastly and let out a miserable groan.

"What's the matter?" cried Leo.

"Excuse me. Was an accident this picture. She is not for you."

Salzman frantically shoved the manila packet into his portfolio. He thrust the snapshot into his pocket and fled down the stairs.

Leo, after momentary paralysis, gave chase and cornered the marriage broker in the vestibule. The landlady made hysterical outcries but neither of them listened.

"Give me back the picture, Salzman."

"No." The pain in his eyes was terrible.

"Tell me who she is then."

"This I can't tell you. Excuse me."

He made to depart, but Leo, forgetting himself, seized the matchmaker by his tight coat and shook him frenziedly.

"Please," sighed Salzman. *"Please."*

Leo ashamedly let him go. "Tell me who she is," he begged. "It's very important for me to know."

"She is not for you. She is a wild one — wild, without shame. This is not a bride for a rabbi."

"What do you mean wild?"

"Like an animal. Like a dog. For her to be poor was a sin. This is why she is dead now."

"In God's name, what do you mean?"

"Her I can't introduce to you," Salzman cried.

"Why are you so excited?"

"Why he asks," Salzman said, bursting into tears. "This is my baby, my Stella, she should burn in hell."

Leo hurried up to bed and hid under the covers. Under the covers he thought his whole life through. Although he soon fell asleep he could not sleep her out of his mind. He woke, beating his breast. Though he prayed to be rid of her, his prayers went unanswered. Through days of torment he struggled endlessly not to love her; fearing success, he escaped it. He then concluded to convert her to goodness, himself to God. The idea alternately nauseated and exalted him.

He perhaps did not know that he had come to a final decision until he encountered Salzman in a Broadway cafeteria. He was sitting alone at a rear table, sucking the bony remains of a fish. The marriage broker appeared haggard, and transparent to the point of vanishing.

Salzman looked up at first without recognizing him. Leo had grown a pointed beard and his eyes were weighted with wisdom.

"Salzman," he said, "love has at last come to my heart."

"Who can love from a picture?" mocked the marriage broker.

"It is not impossible."

"If you can love her, then you can love anybody. Let me show you some new clients that they just sent me their photographs. One is a little doll."

"Just her I want," Leo murmured.

"Don't be a fool, doctor. Don't bother with her."

"Put me in touch with her, Salzman," Leo said humbly. "Perhaps I can do her a service."

Salzman had stopped chewing, and Leo understood with emotion that it was now arranged.

Leaving the cafeteria, he was, however, afflicted by a tormenting suspicion that Salzman had planned it all to happen this way.

Leo was informed by letter that she would meet him on a certain corner, and she was there one spring night, waiting under a street lamp. He appeared, carrying a small bouquet of violets and rosebuds. Stella stood by the lamppost, smoking. She wore white with red shoes, which fitted his expectations, although in a troubled moment he had imagined the dress red, and only the shoes white. She waited uneasily and shyly. From afar he saw that her eyes — clearly her father's — were filled with desperate innocence. He pictured, in hers, his own redemption. Violins and lit candles revolved in the sky. Leo ran forward with the flowers outthrust.

Around the corner, Salzman, leaning against a wall, chanted prayers for the dead.

FLANNERY O'CONNOR

There is an eerie, almost fourth-dimensional quality to "A Circle in the
Fire." The author herself said, "My people could come from anywhere but
naturally since I know the South, they speak with a Southern accent."
Long ill, she knew she was dying when she wrote it, and that may be why
it has a peculiar perception.

Although only thirty-eight when she died, Flannery O'Connor had
long been recognized as one of our major short story writers. She was born
in Savannah, Georgia, and graduated from the Georgia State College for
Women. She lived on a farm in Milledgeville, Georgia.

A Circle in the Fire

Sometimes the last line of trees was a solid gray blue wall a little darker
than the sky but this afternoon it was almost black and behind it the sky
was a livid glaring white. "You know that woman that had that baby in
that iron lung?" Mrs. Pritchard said. She and the child's mother were
underneath the window the child was looking down from. Mrs. Pritchard
was leaning against the chimney, her arms folded on a shelf of stomach,
one foot crossed and the toe pointed into the ground. She was a large
woman with a small pointed face and steady ferreting eyes. Mrs. Cope
was the opposite, very small and trim, with a large round face and black
eyes that seemed to be enlarging all the time behind her thick glasses as if
she were continually being astonished. She was squatting down pulling
grass out of the border beds around the house. Both of them had on
sunhats that had once been identical but Mrs. Pritchard's was faded and
out of shape while Mrs. Cope's was still stiff and bright green.

"I read about her," she said.

"She was a Pritchard that married a Brookins and so's kin to me —
about my seventh or eight cousin by marriage."

"Well, well," Mrs. Cope muttered and threw a large clump of nut grass behind her. She worked at the weeds and nut grass as if they were an evil sent directly by the devil to destroy the place.

"Beinst she was kin to us, we gone to see the body," Mrs. Pritchard said. "Seen the little baby too."

Mrs. Cope didn't say anything. She was used to these calamitous stories; she said they wore her to a frazzle. Mrs. Pritchard would go thirty miles for the satisfaction of seeing someone laid away. Mrs. Cope always changed the subject to something cheerful but the child had observed that this only put Mrs. Pritchard in a bad humor.

The child thought the blank sky looked as if it were pushing against the fortress fall, trying to break through. The trees across the near field were a patchwork of gray and yellow greens. Mrs. Cope was always worrying about fires in her woods. When the nights were very windy, she would say to the child, "Oh Lord, do pray there won't be any fires, it's so windy," and the child would grunt from behind her book or not answer at all because she heard it so often. In the evenings in the summer when they sat on the porch, Mrs. Cope would say to the child who was reading fast to catch the last light, "Get up and look at the sunset, it's gorgeous. You ought to get up and look at it," and the child would scowl and not answer or glare up once across the lawn and two front pastures to the gray blue sentinel line of trees and then begin to read again with no change of expression, sometimes muttering for meanness, "It looks like a fire. You better get up and smell around and see if the woods ain't on fire."

"She had her arm around it in the coffin," Mrs. Pritchard went on, but her voice was drowned out by the sound of the tractor that the Negro, Culver, was driving up the road from the barn. The wagon was attached and another Negro was sitting in the back, bouncing, his feet jogging about a foot from the ground. The one on the tractor drove it past the gate that led into the field on the left.

Mrs. Cope turned her head and saw that he had not gone through the gate because he was too lazy to get off and open it. He was going the long way around at her expense. "Tell him to stop and come here!" she shouted.

Mrs. Pritchard heaved herself from the chimney and waved her arm in a fierce circle but he pretended not to hear. She stalked to the edge of the lawn and screamed, "Get off, I toljer! She wants you!"

He got off and started toward the chimney, pushing his head and shoulders forward at each step to give the appearance of hurrying. His head was thrust up to the top in a white cloth hat striated with different shades of sweat. The brim was down and hid all but the lower parts of his reddish eyes.

Mrs. Cope was on her knees, pointing the trowel into the ground, "Why aren't you going through the gate there?" she asked and waited, her eyes shut and her mouth stretched flat as if she were prepared for any ridiculous answer.

"Got to raise the blade on the mower if we do," he said and his gaze bore just to the left of her. Her Negroes were as destructive and impersonal as the nut grass.

Her eyes, as she opened them, looked as if they would keep on enlarging until they turned her wrongsideout. "Raise it," she said and pointed across the road with the trowel.

He moved off.

"It's nothing to them," she said. "They don't have to pay for the gas. It's nothing to anybody but the one with the responsibility. I thank the Lord all these things don't come at once. They'd destroy me."

"Yeah, they would," Mrs. Pritchard shouted against the sound of the tractor. He opened the gate and raised the blade and drove through and down into the field; the noise diminished as the wagon disappeared. "I don't see myself how she had it *in* it," she went on in her normal voice.

Mrs. Cope was bent over, digging fiercely at the nut grass again. "We have a lot to be thankful for," she said. "Everyday you should say a prayer of thanksgiving. Do you do that?"

"Yes'm," Mrs. Pritchard said. "See she was in it four months before she even got thataway. Look like to me if I was in one of them, I would leave off . . . how you reckon they . . ."

"Every day I say a prayer of thanksgiving," Mrs. Cope said. "Think of all we have. Lord," she said and sighed, "we have everything," and she looked around at her rich pastures and hills that were heavy with timber and shook her head as if it all might be a burden she was trying to shake off her back.

Mrs. Pritchard studied the woods. "All I got is four abscess teeth," she remarked.

"Well, be thankful you don't have five," Mrs. Cope snapped and threw back a clump of grass. "We might all be destroyed by a hurricane. I can always find something to be thankful for."

Mrs. Pritchard took up a hoe resting against the side of the house and struck lightly at a weed that had come up between two bricks in the chimney. "Yeah?" she said, her voice a little more nasal than usual with contempt.

"Why, think of all those poor Europeans," Mrs. Cope went on, "that they put in boxcars like cattle and rode them to Siberia. Lord," she said, "we ought to spend half our time on our knees."

"I know if I was in an iron lung there would be some things I wouldn't do," Mrs. Pritchard said, scratching her bare ankle with the end of the hoe.

"Even that poor woman had plenty to be thankful for," Mrs. Cope said.

"She could be thankful she wasn't dead."

"Certainly," Mrs. Cope said, and then she pointed the trowel up at Mrs. Pritchard and said, "I have the best kept place in the county and do you know why? Because I work. I've had to work to save this place and work to keep it." She emphasized each word with the trowel. "I don't let anything get ahead of me and I'm not always looking for trouble. I take it as it comes."

"If it all come at oncet sometime," Mrs. Pritchard began.

"It doesn't all come at once," Mrs. Cope said sharply.

The child could see over to where the dirt road joined the highway. She saw a pick-up truck stop at the gate and let off three boys who started walking up the pink dirt road. They walked single-file, the middle one bent to the side carrying a black pig-shaped valise.

"Well, if it ever did," Mrs. Pritchard said, "it wouldn't be nothing you could do but fling your hands."

Mrs. Cope didn't even answer this. Mrs. Pritchard folded her arms and gazed down the road as if she could easily enough see all these fine hills flattened to nothing. She saw the three boys who had almost reached the front walk by now. "Lookit yonder," she said. "Who you reckon they are?"

Mrs. Cope leaned back and supported herself with one hand behind her and looked. The three came toward them but as if they were going to walk on through the side of the house. The one with the suitcase was in front now. Finally about four feet from her, he stopped and set it down. The three boys looked something alike except that the middle-sized one wore silver-rimmed spectacles and carried the suitcase. One of his eyes had a slight cast to it so that his gaze seemed to be coming from two directions at once as if it had them surrounded. He had on a sweat shirt with a faded destroyer printed on it but his chest was so hollow that the destroyer was broken in the middle and seemed on the point of going under. His hair was stuck to his forehead with sweat. He looked to be about thirteen. All three boys had white penetrating stares. "I don't reckon you remember me, Mrs. Cope," he said.

"Your face is certainly familiar," she said, scrutinizing him, "now let's see. . . ."

"My daddy used to work here," he hinted.

"Boyd?" she said. "Your father was Mr. Boyd and you're J. C.?"

"Nome, I'm Powell, the secont one, only I've growed some since then and my daddy he's daid now. Done died."

"Dead. Well I declare," Mrs. Cope said as if death were always an unusual thing. "What was Mr. Boyd's trouble?"

One of Powell's eyes seemed to be making a circle of the place, examining the house and the white water tower behind it and chicken houses and the pastures that rolled away on either side until they met the first line of woods. The other eye looked at her. "Died in Florda," he said and began kicking the valise.

"Well, I declare," she murmured. After a second she said, "And how is your mother?"

"Mah'd again." He kept watching his foot kick the suitcase. The other two boys stared at her impatiently.

"And where do you all live now?" she asked.

"Atlanta," he said. "You know, out to one of them developments."

"Well, I see," she said, "I see." After a second she said it again. Finally she asked, "And who are these other boys?" and smiled at them.

"Garfield Smith him, and W. T. Harper him," he said nodding his head backward first in the direction of the large boy and then the small one.

"How do you boys do?" Mrs. Cope said. "This is Mrs. Pritchard. Mr. and Mrs. Pritchard work here now."

They ignored Mrs. Pritchard who watched them with steady beady eyes. The three seemed to hang there, waiting, watching Mrs. Cope.

"Well, well," she said, glancing at the suitcase, "it's nice of you to stop and see me. I think that was real sweet of you."

Powell's stare seemed to pinch her like a pair of tongs. "Come back to see how you was doing," he said hoarsely.

"Listen here," the smallest boy said, "all the time we been knowing him he's been telling us about this here place. Said it was everything here.

Said it was horses here. Said he had the best time of his entire life right here on this here place. Talks about it all the time."

"Never shuts his trap about his place," the big boy grunted, drawing his arm across his nose as if to muffle his words.

"Always talking about them horses he rid here," the small one continued, "and said he would let us ride them too. Said it was one name Gene."

Mrs. Cope was always afraid someone would get hurt on her place and sue her for everything she had. "They aren't shod," she said quickly. "There was one named Gene but he's dead now but I'm afraid you boys can't ride the horses because they aren't shod and they're in the pasture and I'm afraid you might get hurt. They're dangerous," she said, speaking very fast.

The large boy sat down on the ground with a noise of disgust and began to finger rocks out of his tennis shoe. The small one darted looks here and there and Powell fixed her with his stare and didn't say anything.

After a minute the little boy said, "Say, lady, you know what he said one time? He said when he died he wanted to come here!"

For a second Mrs. Cope looked blank; then she blushed; then a peculiar look of pain came over her face as she realized that these children were hungry. They were staring because they were hungry! She almost gasped in their faces, and then she asked them quickly if they would have something to eat. They said they would but their expressions, composed and unsatisfied, didn't lighten any. They looked as if they were used to being hungry.

The child upstairs had grown red in the face with excitement. She was kneeling down by the window so that only her eyes and forehead showed over the sill. Mrs. Cope told the boys to come around on the other side of the house where the lawn chairs were and she led the way and Mrs. Pritchard followed. The child moved from the right bedroom across the hall and over into the left bedroom and looked down on the other side of the house where there were three white lawn chairs and a red hammock strung between two hazelnut trees. She was a pale fat girl of twelve with a frowning squint and a large mouth full of silver bands. She knelt down at the window.

The three boys came around the corner of the house and the large one threw himself into the hammock and lit a stub of cigarette. The small boy tumbled down on the grass next to the black suitcase and rested his head on it and Powell sat down on the edge of one of the chairs and looked as if he were trying to enclose the whole place in one encircling stare. The child heard her mother and Mrs. Pritchard in a muted conference in the kitchen. She got up and went out into the hall and leaned over the banisters.

Mrs. Cope's and Mrs. Pritchard's legs were facing each other in the back hall. "Those poor children are hungry," Mrs. Cope said in a dead voice.

"You seen that suitcase?" Mrs. Pritchard asked. "What if they intend to spend the night with you?"

Mrs. Cope gave a slight shriek. "I can't have three boys in here with only me and Sally Virginia," she said. "I'm sure they'll go when I feed them."

"I only know they got a suitcase," Mrs. Pritchard said.

The child hurried back to the window. The large boy was stretched out in the hammock with his wrists crossed under his head and the cigarette stub in the center of his mouth. He spit it out in an arc just as Mrs. Cope came around the corner of the house with a plate of crackers. She stopped instantly as if a snake had been slung in her path. "Ashfield!" she said, "please pick that up. I'm afraid of fires."

"Gawfield!" the little boy shouted indignantly, "Gawfield!"

The large boy raised himself without a word and lumbered for the butt. He picked it up and put it in his pocket and stood with his back to her, examining a tattooed heart on his forearm. Mrs. Pritchard came up holding three Coca-Colas by the necks in one hand and gave one to each of them.

"I remember everything about this place," Powell said, looking down the opening of his bottle.

"Where did you all go when you left here?" Mrs. Cope asked and put the plate of crackers on the arm of his chair.

He looked at it but didn't take one. He said, "I remember it was one name Gene and it was one name George. We gone to Florda and my daddy he, you know, died, and then we gone to my sister's and then my mother she, you know, mah'd, and we been there ever since."

"There are some crackers," Mrs. Cope said and sat down in the chair across from him.

"He don't like it in Atlanta," the little boy said, sitting up and reaching indifferently for a cracker. "He ain't ever satisfied with where he's at except this place here. Lemme tell you what he'll do, lady. We'll be playing ball, see, on this here place in this development we got to play ball on, see, and he'll quit playing and say, 'Goddam, it was a horse down there name Gene and if I had him here I'd bust this concrete to hell riding him!'"

"I'm sure Powell doesn't use words like that, do you Powell?" Mrs. Cope said.

"No, mam," Powell said. His head was turned completely to the side as if he were listening for the horses in the field.

"I don't like them kind of crackers," the little boy said and returned his to the plate and got up.

Mrs. Cope shifted in her chair. "So you boys live in one of those nice new developments," she said.

"The only way you can tell your own is by smell," the small boy volunteered. "They're four stories high and there's ten of them, one behind the other. Let's go see them horses," he said.

Powell turned his pinching stare on Mrs. Cope. "We thought we would just spend the night in your barn," he said. "My uncle brought us this far on his pick-up truck and he's going to stop for us again in the morning."

There was a moment in which she didn't say a thing and the child in the window thought: she's going to fly out of that chair and hit the tree.

"Well, I'm afraid you can't do that," she said, getting up suddenly. "The barn's full of hay and I'm afraid of fire from your cigarettes."

"We won't smoke," he said.

"I'm afraid you can't spend the night there just the same," she repeated as if she were talking politely to a gangster.

"Well we can camp out in the woods then," the little boy said. "We brought our own blankets anyways. That's what we got in thatere suit-case. Come on."

"In the woods!" she said, "Oh no! The woods are very dry now, I can't have people smoking in my woods. You'll have to camp out in the field, in this field here next to the house, where there aren't any trees."

"Where she can keep her eye on you," the child said under her breath.

"Her woods," the large boy muttered and got out of the hammock.

"We'll sleep in the field," Powell said but not particularly as if he were talking to her. "This afternoon I'm going to show them about this place." The other two were already walking away and he got up and bounded after them and the two women sat with the black suitcase between them.

"Not no thank-you, not no nothing," Mrs. Pritchard remarked.

"They only played with what we gave them to eat," Mrs. Cope said in a hurt voice.

"Maybe they don't like soft drinks," Mrs. Pritchard muttered.

"They certainly *looked* hungry," Mrs. Cope said.

About sunset they appeared out of the woods, dirty and sweating, and came to the back porch and asked for water. They did not ask for food but Mrs. Cope could tell that they wanted it. "All I have is some cold guinea," she said. "Would you boys like some guinea and some sand-wiches?"

"I wouldn't eat nothing bald-headed like a guinea," the little boy said. "I would eat a chicken or a turkey but not no guinea."

"Dog wouldn't eat one of them," the large boy said. He had taken off his shirt and stuck it in the back of his trousers like a tail. Mrs. Cope carefully avoided looking at him. The little boy had a cut on his arm.

"You boys haven't been riding the horses when I asked you not to, have you?" she asked suspiciously and they all said, "No mam!" at once in loud enthusiastic voices like the Amens that are said in country churches.

She went into the house and made them sandwiches and, while she did it, she held a conversation with them from inside the kitchen, asking where they went to school and what their fathers did and how many brothers and sisters they had. They answered in short explosive sentences, pushing each other's shoulders and doubling up with laughter as if the questions had meanings that she didn't know about. "And does your mother work, Powell?" she called.

"She ast you does your mother work!" the little boy yelled. "His mind's affected by them horses he only looked at," he said. "His mother she works at a factory and leaves him home to mind the rest of them only he don't mind them much. Lemme tell you, lady, one time he locked his little brother in a box and set it on fire."

"I'm sure Powell wouldn't do a thing like that," she said, coming out with the plate of sandwiches and setting it down on the step. They emptied the plate at once and she picked it up and stood holding it, looking at the sun which was going down in front of them, almost on top of the tree line. It was swollen and flame-colored and hung in a net of

ragged cloud as if it might burn through any second and fall into the
woods. From the upstairs window the child saw her shiver and catch
both arms to her sides. "We have so much to be thankful for," she said
suddenly in a mournful marveling tone. "Do you boys thank God every
night for all He's done for you? Do you thank Him for everything?"

This put an instant hush over them. They bit into the sandwiches as if
they had lost all taste for food.

"Do you?" she persisted.

They were as silent as thieves hiding. They chewed without a sound.

"Well, I know I do," she said at length and turned and went back in
the house and the child watched their shoulders drop. The large one
stretched his legs out as if he were releasing himself from a trap. The sun
burned so fast that it seemed to be trying to set everything in sight on
fire. The white water tower was glazed pink and the grass was an
unnatural green as if it were turning to glass. The child suddenly stuck
her head far out the window and said, "Uggggrhhh," in a loud voice,
crossing her eyes and hanging her tongue out as far as possible as if she
were going to vomit.

The large boy looked up and stared at her. "Jesus," he growled, "another woman."

She dropped back from the window and stood with her back against
the wall, squinting fiercely as if she had been slapped in the face and
couldn't see who had done it. As soon as they left the steps, she came
down into the kitchen where Mrs. Cope was washing the dishes. "If I had
that big boy down I'd beat the daylight out of him," she said.

"You keep away from those boys," Mrs. Cope said, turning sharply.
"Ladies don't beat the daylight out of people. You keep out of their way.
They'll be gone in the morning."

But in the morning they were not gone.

When she went out on the porch after breakfast, they were standing
around the back door, kicking the steps. They were smelling the bacon
she had had for her breakfast. "Why, boys!" she said, "I thought you
were going to meet your uncle." They had the same look of hardened
hunger that had pained her yesterday but today she felt faintly provoked.

The big boy turned his back at once and the small one squatted down
and began to scratch in the sand. "We ain't, though," Powell said.

The big boy turned his head just enough to take in a small section of
her and said, "We ain't bothering nothing of yours."

He couldn't see the way her eyes enlarged but he could take note of the significant silence. After a minute she said in an altered voice, "Would you boys care for some breakfast?"

"We got plenty of our own food," the big boy said. "We don't want nothing of yours."

She kept her eyes on Powell. His thin white face seemed to confront but not actually to see her. "You boys know that I'm glad to have you," she said, "but I expect you to behave. I expect you to act like gentlemen."

They stood there, each looking in a different direction, as if they were waiting for her to leave. "After all," she said in a suddenly high voice, "this is my place."

The big boy made some ambiguous noise and they turned and walked off toward the barn, leaving her there with a shocked look as if she had had a searchlight thrown on her in the middle of the night.

In a little while Mrs. Pritchard came over and stood in the kitchen door with her cheek against the edge of it. "I reckon you know they rode them horses all yesterday afternoon," she said. "Stole a bridle out of the saddle room and rode bareback, because Hollis seen them. He runnum out the barn at nine o'clock last night and then he runnum out at ten and they was smoking both times and then he runnum out the milk room this morning and there was milk all over their mouths like they had been drinking out the cans."

"I cannot have this," Mrs. Cope said and stood at the sink with both fists knotted at her sides. "I cannot have this," and her expression was the same as when she tore at the nut grass.

"There ain't a thing you can do about it," Mrs. Pritchard said. "What I expect is you'll have them for a week or so until school begins. They just figure to have themselves a vacation in the country and there ain't nothing you can do but fold your hands."

"I do not fold my hands," Mrs. Cope said. "Tell Mr. Pritchard to put the horses up in the stalls."

"He's already did that. You take a boy thirteen year old is equal in meanness to a man twicet his age. It's no telling what he'll think up to do. You never know where he'll strike next. This morning Hollis seen them behind the bull pen and that big one ast if it wasn't some place they could wash at and Hollis said no it wasn't and that you didn't want no boys dropping cigarette butts in your woods and he said, 'She don't own them woods,' and Hollis said, 'She does too,' and that there little one he said, 'Man, Gawd owns them woods and her too,' and that there one with the glasses said, 'I reckon she owns the sky over this place too,' and that there littlest one says, 'Owns the sky and can't no airplane go over here without she says so,' and then the big one says, 'I never seen a place with so many damn women on it, how do you stand it here?' and Hollis said he had done had enough of their big talk by then and he turned and walked off without giving no reply one way or the other."

"I'm going out there and tell those boys they can get a ride away from here on the milk truck," Mrs. Cope said and she went out the back door, leaving Mrs. Pritchard and the child together in the kitchen.

"Listen," the child said. "I could handle them quicker than that."

"Yeah?" Mrs. Pritchard murmured, giving her a long leering look, "how'd you handle them?"

The child gripped both hands together and made a contorted face as if she were strangling someone.

"They'd handle you," Mrs. Pritchard said with satisfaction.

The child retired to the upstairs window to get out of her way and looked down where her mother was walking off from the three boys who were squatting under the water tower, eating something out of a cracker box. She heard her come in the kitchen door and say, "They say they'll go on the milk truck, and no wonder they aren't hungry — they have that suitcase half full of food."

"Likely stole every bit of it too," Mrs. Pritchard said.

When the milk truck came, the three boys were nowhere in sight, but as soon as it left without them their three faces appeared, looking out of the opening in the top of the calf barn. "Can you beat this?" Mrs. Cope said, standing at one of the upstairs windows with her hands at her hips. "It's not that I wouldn't be glad to have them — it's their attitude."

"You never like nobody's attitude," the child said. "I'll go tell them they got five minutes to leave here in."

"You are not to go anywhere near those boys, do you hear me?" Mrs. Cope said.

"Why?" the child asked.

"I'm going out there and give them a piece of my mind," Mrs. Cope said.

The child took over the position in the window and in a few minutes she saw the stiff green hat catching the glint of the sun as her mother crossed the road toward the calf barn. The three faces immediately disappeared from the opening, and in a second the large boy dashed across the lot, followed an instant later by the other two. Mrs. Pritchard came out and the two women started for the grove of trees the boys had vanished into. Presently the two sunhats disappeared in the woods and the three boys came out at the left side of it and ambled across the field and into another patch of woods. By the time Mrs. Cope and Mrs. Pritchard reached the field, it was empty and there was nothing for them to go but come home again.

Mrs. Cope had not been inside long before Mrs. Pritchard came running toward the house, shouting something. "They've let out the bull!" she hollered, "let out the bull!" And in a second she was followed by the bull himself, ambling, black and leisurely, with four geese hissing at his heels. He was not mean until hurried and it took Mr. Pritchard and the two Negroes a half hour to ease him back to his pen. While the men were engaged in this, the boys let the oil out of the three tractors and then disappeared again into the woods.

Two blue veins had come out on either side of Mrs. Cope's forehead and Mrs. Pritchard observed them with satisfaction. "Like I toljer," she said, "there ain't a thing you can do about it."

Mrs. Cope ate her dinner hastily, not conscious that she had her sunhat on. Every time she heard a noise, she jumped up. Mrs. Pritchard came over immediately after dinner and said, "Well, you want to know where they are now?" and smiled in an omniscient rewarded way.

"I want to know at once," Mrs. Cope said, coming to an almost military attention.

"Down to the road, throwing rocks at your mailbox," Mrs. Pritchard said, leaning comfortably in the door. "Done already about knocked it off its stand."

"Get in the car," Mrs. Cope said.

The child got in too and the three of them drove down the road to the gate. The boys were sitting on the embankment on the other side of the highway, aiming rocks across the road at the mailbox. Mrs. Cope stopped the car almost directly beneath them and looked up out of her window. The three of them stared at her as if they had never seen her before, the large boy with a sullen glare, the small one glint-eyed and unsmiling, and Powell with his two-sided glassed gaze hanging vacantly over the crippled destroyer on his shirt.

"Powell," she said, "I'm sure your mother would be ashamed of you," and she stopped and waited for this to make its effect. His face seemed to twist slightly but he continued to look through her at nothing in particular.

"Now I've put up with this as long as I can," she said. "I've tried to be nice to you boys. Haven't I been nice to you boys?"

They might have been three statues except that the big one, barely opening his mouth, said, "We're not even on your side the road, lady."

"There ain't a thing you can do about it," Mrs. Pritchard hissed loudly. The child was sitting on the back seat close to the side. She had a furious outraged look on her face but she kept her head drawn back from the window so that they couldn't see her.

Mrs. Cope spoke slowly, emphasizing every word. "I think I have been very nice to you boys. I've fed you twice. Now I'm going into town and if you're still here when I come back, I'll call the sheriff," and with this, she drove off. The child, turning quickly so that she could see out the back window, observed that they had not moved; they had not even turned their heads.

"You done angered them now," Mrs. Pritchard said, "and it ain't any telling what they'll do."

"They'll be gone when we get back," Mrs. Cope said.

Mrs. Pritchard could not stand an anticlimax. She required the taste of blood from time to time to keep her equilibrium. When they returned from town, the boys were not on the embankment and she said, "I would rather to see them than not to see them. When you see them you know what they're doing."

"Ridiculous," Mrs. Cope muttered. "I've scared them and they've gone and now we can forget them."

"I ain't forgetting them," Mrs. Pritchard said. "I wouldn't be none surprised if they didn't have a gun in that there suitcase."

Mrs. Cope prided herself on the way she handled the type of mind that Mrs. Pritchard had. When Mrs. Pritchard saw signs and omens, she exposed them calmly for the figments of imagination that they were, but this afternoon her nerves were taut and she said, "Now I've had about enough of this. Those boys are gone and that's that."

"Well, we'll wait and see," Mrs. Pritchard said.

Everything was quiet for the rest of the afternoon but at supper time, Mrs. Pritchard came over to say that she had heard a high vicious laugh pierce out of the bushes near the hog pen. It was an evil laugh, full of calculated meanness, and she had heard it come three times, herself, distinctly.

"I haven't heard a thing," Mrs. Cope said.

"I look for them to strike just after dark," Mrs. Pritchard said.

That night Mrs. Cope and the child sat on the porch until nearly ten o'clock and nothing happened. The only sounds came from tree frogs and from one whippoorwill who called faster and faster from the same spot of darkness as if he had forgotten what the danger was but remembered the warning. "They've gone," Mrs. Cope said, "poor things," and she began to tell the child how much they had to be thankful for, for she said they might have had to live in a development themselves or they might have been Negroes or they might have been in iron lungs or they might have been Europeans ridden in boxcars like cattle, and she began a litany of her blessings, in a stricken voice, that the child, straining her attention for a sudden shriek in the dark, didn't listen to.

There was no sign of them the next morning either. The fortress line of trees was a hard granite blue, the wind had risen overnight and the sun had come up a pale gold. The season was changing. Even a small change in the weather made Mrs. Cope thankful, but when the seasons changed she seemed almost frightened at her good fortune in escaping whatever it was that pursued her. As she sometimes did when one thing was finished and another about to begin, she turned her attention to the child, who had put on a pair of overalls over her dress and had pulled a man's old felt hat down as far as it would go on her head and was arming herself with two pistols in a decorated holster that she had fastened around her waist. The hat was very tight and seemed to be squeezing the redness into her face. It came down almost to the tops of her glasses. Mrs. Cope watched her with a tragic look. "Why do you have to look like an idiot?" she asked. "Suppose company were to come? When are you going to grow up? What's going to become of you? I look at you and I want to cry! Sometimes you look like you might belong to Mrs. Pritchard!"

"Leave me be," the child said in a high irritated voice. "Leave me be. Just leave me be. I ain't you," and she went off to the woods as if she were stalking out an enemy, her head thrust forward and each hand gripped on a gun.

Mrs. Pritchard came over, sour-humored, because she didn't have anything calamitous to report. "I got the misery in my face today," she said, holding on to what she could salvage. "Theseyer teeth. They each one feel like an individual boil."

The child crashed through the woods, making the fallen leaves sound ominous under her feet. The sun had risen a little and was only a white hole like an opening for the wind to escape through in a sky a little darker than itself, and the tops of the trees were black against the glare. "I'm going to get you," she said. "I'm going to get you one by one and beat you black and blue. Line up. LINE UP!" she said and waved one of the pistols at a cluster of long bare-trunked pines, four times her height, as she passed them. She kept moving, muttering and growling to herself and occasionally hitting out with one of the guns at a branch that got in her way. From time to time she stopped to remove the thorn vine that caught at her shirt and she would say, "Leave me be, I told you. Leave me be," and give it a crack with the pistol and then stalk on.

Presently she sat down on a stump to cool off but she planted both feet carefully and firmly on the ground. She lifted them and put them down several times, grinding them fiercely into the dirt as if she were crushing something under her heels. Suddenly she heard a laugh.

She sat up, prickle-skinned. It came again. She heard the sound of splashing and she stood up, uncertain which way to run. She was not far from where this patch of woods ended and the back pasture began. She eased toward the pasture, careful not to make a sound, and coming suddenly to the edge of it, she saw the three boys, not twenty feet away, washing in the cow trough. Their clothes were piled against the black valise out of reach of the water that flowed over the side of the tank. The large boy was standing up and the small one was trying to climb onto his shoulders. Powell was sitting down looking straight ahead through glasses that were splashed with water. He was not paying any attention to the other two. The trees must have looked like green waterfalls through his wet glasses. The child stood partly hidden behind a pine trunk, the side of her face pressed into the bark.

"I wish I lived here!" the little boy shouted, balancing with his knees clutched around the big one's head.

"I'm goddam glad I don't," the big boy panted, and jumped up to dislodge him.

Powell sat without moving, without seeming to know that the other two were behind him, and looked straight ahead like a ghost sprung upright in his coffin. "If this place was not here any more," he said, " you would never have to think of it again."

"Listen," the big boy said, sitting down quietly in the water with the little one still moored to his shoulders, "it don't belong to nobody."

"It's ours," the little boy said.

The child behind the tree did not move.

Powell jumped out of the trough and began to run. He ran all the way around the field as if something were after him and as he passed the tank coming back, the other two jumped out and raced with him, the sun glinting on their long wet bodies. The big one ran the fastest and was the leader. They dashed around the field twice and finally dropped down by their clothes and lay there with their ribs moving up and down. After a while, the big one said hoarsely, "Do you know what I would do with this place if I had the chance?"

"No, what?" the little boy said and sat up to give him his full attention.

"I'd build a big parking lot on it, or something," he muttered.

They began to dress. The sun made two white spots on Powell's glasses and blotted out his eyes. "I know what let's do," he said. He took something small from his pocket and showed it to them. For almost a minute they sat looking at what he had in his hand. Then without any more discussion, Powell picked up the suitcase and they got up and moved past the child and entered the woods not ten feet from where she was standing, slightly away from the tree now, with the imprint of the bark embossed red and white on the side of her face.

She watched with a dazed stare as they stopped and collected all the matches they had between them and began to set the brush on fire. They began to whoop and holler and beat their hands over their mouths and in a few seconds there was a narrow line of fire widening between her and them. While she stared, it reached up from the brush, snatching and biting at the lowest branches of the trees. The wind carried rags of it higher and the boys disappeared shrieking behind it.

She turned and tried to run across the field but her legs were too heavy and she stood there, weighted down with some new unplaced misery that she had never felt before. But finally she began to run.

Mrs. Cope and Mrs. Pritchard were in the field behind the barn when Mrs. Cope saw smoke rising from the woods across the pasture. She shrieked and Mrs. Pritchard pointed up the road to where the child came loping heavily, screaming, "Mama, Mama, they're going to build a parking lot here!"

Mrs. Cope began to scream for the Negroes while Mrs. Pritchard, charged now, ran down the road shouting. Mr. Pritchard came out of the open end of the barn and the two Negores stopped filling the manure spreader in the lot and started toward Mrs. Cope with their shovels. "Hurry, hurry!" she shouted, "start throwing dirt on it!" They passed her almost without looking at her and headed off slowly across the field toward the smoke. She ran after them a little way, charging them like a fierce dog, shrilling, "Hurry, hurry, don't you see it! Don't you see it!"

"It'll be there when we git there," Culver said and they thrust their shoulders forward a little and went on at the same pace.

The child came to a stop beside her mother and stared up at her face as if she had never seen it before. It was the face of the new misery she felt, but on her mother it looked old and it looked as if it might have belonged to anybody, a Negro or a European or to Powell himself. The child turned her head quickly, and past the Negroes' ambling figures she could see the gray column of smoke rising and widening unchecked inside the granite line of trees. She stood taut, listening, and could just catch in the distance a few wild high shrieks of joy as if the prophets were dancing in the fiery furnace, in the circle the angel had cleared for them. "I known a man oncet that his wife was poisoned by a child she had adopted out of pure kindness," she said.

AUGUSTA WALLACE LYONS

"The First Flower" is that rara avis in American literature, an honest young love story with an honest happy ending. If a reader will try to recall such short stories, going back over the years, he may be amazed at their scarcity. There is as well an appealing delicacy and simplicity here.

Augusta Wallace Lyons was born in Prospect, Kentucky, the daughter of Tom Wallace, the famous Louisville Courier-Journal *editor. She studied at Sweet Briar, Vassar and Barnard. She left Barnard for Broadway and was in several plays, including* Tobacco Road, *in which she played Pearl, the blond child bride. Her short stories have appeared in American and Canadian magazines and she has published a novel,* Season of Desire.

The First Flower

EVA WATCHED the uniformed delivery boy swing off his bicycle and bound up the front steps of Margaret Hall School with a square green carton under his arm.

"Flowers for Miss Digby," she said, plucking a violet from the lawn and laying it on her lap.

"I guess so," Josie agreed, "Harvey would naturally send her an orchid for the dance tonight."

Quite naturally. It was impossible to picture Miss Digby not being twenty-three and beautiful and assured and chosen, all the problems and uncertainties of life behind her. If she'd ever had problems.

The heavy front door of the school swung slowly open and they could see Miss Heideman, their Latin teacher, signing for the package.

"I wonder if she ever got a corsage?" Eva asked, looking thoughtfully at the violet, cool and perfect against the dark blue serge of her skirt.

"Miss Heideman?"

"Well she hasn't been sixty all her life."

"If she'd ever been the type to get orchids, she'd have married," Josie said.

"Not necessarily. She may have loved and lost, like Molly McCloud."

"Oh Molly will marry somebody else eventually," Josie said.

"Not if she really and truly loved Rogers. Real love only happens once, and, if it's unrequited, a woman would rather live alone with her memories than try to deny her deepest feelings and marry for convenience. At least that's the way I would be!"

The prospect even offered a melancholy fascination. Who could know which was the more romantic fate — that of the beloved bride, or that of the rejected one who languishes faithful to the faithless, dedicated without hope, masking heartbreak with a smile. Eva could contemplate such a future without a qualm. But even for that you had to be —

"Josie — there's something I want to ask you. Only you mustn't ever, on your word of honor, even hint to anybody else that the question so much as entered my mind. Because it's something we're too young to have to even think about really, and it's not going to be important to me even when I'm older, so I'm only bringing it up because I just happened to be wondering about it in a vague sort of way. Like I might wonder if I had a chance to be elected most prompt girl at Margaret Hall or something, though I know I'm not the type that gets elected and wouldn't get any thrill out of being most prompt anyway. See what I mean?"

"Yes. There's something you're wondering about, but it's so unimportant that you don't want anybody to know you even bothered wondering."

"Exactly." Josie was such a satisfactory friend. "Well — do you think, if we tried, we could make ourselves pretty? I mean when we're older, of course. Next year, for instance?"

"I don't know. I guess we'd have to get permanents and spend all our time giggling in front of the mirror the way boy-crazy girls do. It would seem so silly."

"Miss Digby's not silly!" She was more like the violet. Beautiful without effort. Or so it seemed.

"We are never going to look like her," Josie said with authority.

Eva crushed the violet against her knee and threw it away. She wished she hadn't brought the subject up. She wished she could be five years younger again. When she was ten she never worried about how she looked. And she wasn't going to worry now. People still didn't expect it of her after all, since she was so young for her age, and when she got older, she could be a war nurse — a lady with a lamp, tall and beautiful in white, moving softly among —

But she checked the fantasy, embarrassed to be caught, even by her own mind, indulging in such ridiculous hopes. The soldiers would want their Florence Nightingale to look like Miss Digby. Or, as a second choice, Molly McCloud. And suddenly she ached to be Molly. To be Miss Digby was too much to ask, but an unrequited love might be within her reach someday. She tried to think of the kind of man she could love in vain — Lord Byron, Heathcliff, François Villon. Villon — poet and thief. By comparison, Harvey Winston really didn't look like much.

A bell rang, a raucous summons. It was ringing for the meeting — the elections. Eva felt a sudden, unpleasant warmth prickle through her at the mere thought of the hour ahead. Foley would be elected best character, best posture, most truthful, and half-a-dozen other things. Lucy, or maybe Margie, would be the girl with the best personality. Edith most melodious voice and maybe best figure. Dorothy best sense of humor. They would be voted for and applauded and their names would be in the annual, and their parents would be proud, and someday they would show the annual to their children.

But she, Eva Stuart, would just sit at her big-bellied desk and vote for others and keep a rejoicing expression on her face and laugh deprecatingly if anybody even nominated her for anything, even most prompt, because who would vote for her, for Pete's sake? She was always prompt, but so were Jonesy and Foley. And being the youngest of the seniors by two years, nobody could expect her to be best at anything and she certainly didn't care, and wished she didn't have to go to the election.

But she did have to go. Otherwise people would think she minded not being chosen, and anyway Miss Digby would be there! That was some consolation.

Miss Digby would sit, still and lovely, among the older women who made up the rest of the faculty, and she could look at her thinking, "Fair as a star when only one is shining in the sky."

The bell had stopped ringing. "We better go," Josie said.

Eva rose reluctantly, brushing the grass off her skirt and wondering what it would feel like to be Miss Digby. To know you yourself were what poems are written about. The serene unwanting center of a wanting world. Until "young Lochinvar came out of the West" and swept you up into ecstasy. Lochinvar or Ivanhoe or François Villon. Villon would be the most thrilling — the most —

She would keep her mind on Villon during the elections.

Sitting beside Josie and drinking in Miss Digby's beauty, she remained detached during the nominating and voting for best posture, best character, most courteous, most prompt, and most consistent user of correct English. Then came "best figure."

And Miss Heideman, of all people, came up with a simply crazy, ridiculous suggestion that spoiled everything and made Eva feel like an utter, absolute fool in front of everybody. It was her idea of a joke of course, and everybody took it that way naturally but still —

What Miss Heideman said was:

"I nominate Eva Stuart for best figure."

Everybody simply hooted of course. Eva loudest of all, because naturally she realized better than anybody that she was a completely childish tomboy type who didn't even think about wanting to be attractive in any way, much less dream she ever could be.

The one person who didn't hoot was Josie. She loyally seconded the nomination. Upon which the other girls all turned to stare at Eva.

She was sitting with her black-stockinged legs screwed around each other and the toe of her left foot stuck behind the rung of the chair. She slumped forward under the group scrutiny to conceal her full, lifting breasts, and twisted a lock of hair around the forefinger of her right hand. A stranger coming in at that moment and asked to guess her age would have said "around twelve." To heighten this effect, she touched her lower lip with the hair-wrapped finger. Not actually putting it in her mouth, but giving the impression she might. It was comforting to know she looked so childish that nobody could think of her as having a figure, good or bad.

Edith was elected best figure of course. While the ballots were being counted Eva glanced surreptitiously at Miss Heideman's withered face. A face that had suffered, loved, and lost, and suddenly Eva wanted to throw her arms around her, comfort her, tell her — Miss Heideman's eyes met hers and Eva ducked her head, confused, ashamed, hoping her stupid impulse hadn't showed in her expression.

When she was alone in her room, dressing for the dance — the Senior spring dance from which she had tried unsuccessfully to be excused —

she found herself wondering about her figure. Not if it was best, for goodness' sake; but if it — if she —

She stood in a white slip before the not too brightly illumined mirror and studied herself a long time. Trying to see, really see, to look objectively without the bias of fear or hope. First she stood very still, then lifted a comb and ran it slowly through her hair. Not a dark cloud of hair like Miss Digby's. Not golden curls like Molly McCloud's, but soft hair nonetheless, with color. There was a song about her kind of color. "Jeanie with the Light Brown Hair." She hummed a snatch of it happily.

"Eva, you don't by any chance imagine that you're pretty?"

The derision in Foley's voice stung like the slap of a wet towel across the face.

Caught completely off guard, Eva was hardly able to stammer a denial, much less toss off the absurd accusation, with an appropriately incredulous laugh. Far from laughing, she had to tense every muscle to keep back the tears, suck her lower lip tight between her teeth to suppress a betraying quiver.

Foley stood in the doorway staring at her with speculative scorn. Foley — the best character, the best posture, the most prompt — the kind of person before whom it was unbearable to seem ridiculous.

"Don't you look in the mirror when you comb your hair?" Eva managed to ask. Foley was a muscular, square-jawed, no-nonsense type but she was always well groomed.

"Oh sure. It was just the look on your mug that gave me the idea you might have illusions. I'm relieved I was wrong. For a minute I was convinced you needed to have your head examined. Can I borrow a couple of bobby pins?"

Sitting on a collapsible chair at the edge of the gym floor, become for tonight a dance floor, Eva held herself stiffly erect, her features severely composed. If she could just get through the evening without letting her treacherous face reflect her feelings before she could censor them — if she could just keep calm. And she ought to be able to, in spite of the dress. The awful pink net formal her mother had sent her. A dress in which nobody could look a day under fifteen. A dress that would make any girl look as if she might actually expect to be danced with no matter how hard she tried to show she'd be simply amazed if anybody asked her even once.

The three-piece orchestra began playing. The boys started moving across the polished floor. First they came in scattered groups of two or three, trying to beat each other to the really attractive girls — Margie, Lucy, and Edith. Then the others surged forward en masse. A white-coated wave. A wave that would sweep all the girls onto the dance floor, except maybe one or two who would be left with miles of empty chairs on either side of them.

Already there were three chairs empty on her right and one on her left. A boy was looking at her. Coming toward her. Or maybe she only imagined — and he would think — the way Foley had thought —

She stood up suddenly, turning her back on the approaching boy, pushing the chair out of her way, fleeing along the wall, toward the rear door of the gym, and out into the protecting night, down the gravel path, across the lawn to the summer house. Now he couldn't think she'd had any false hopes. He'd realized now she wasn't silly enough to imagine herself a Helen Digby. Or even a Lucy or an Edith.

She sat down on the summer house steps, safe at last and close to tears for no good reason.

And if she did cry, it wouldn't be about her appearance or the dance or what Foley thought. She didn't care about those things at all.

If she didn't manage not to cry it would be because there was nothing she could care about — no chance of meeting François Villon, or being the Maid of Orleans, or having anything special or wonderful happen to her, ever.

The tears were still not quite falling when she heard footsteps coming down the gravel path. Perhaps Josie? It was too dark to see. The sophomores sat some twenty chairs down the line from the seniors, so she hadn't noticed whether Josie was chosen or not. Anyway it wasn't too bad being a wallflower when you were a sophomore. There were always several others, but a senior —

The steps came nearer, and she was able to make out a white-coated figure. Then — a boy was standing before her!

Eva stared up at him in utter confusion.

He shifted his weight uneasily from one foot to the other, thrust his hands in his pockets, took them out again, thrust them back.

"Looking for somebody?" Eva asked, feeling impelled to say something.

"Yes. Uh — you."

"Oh!"

"I hope it's all right. I mean — I was going to ask you to dance, but — you — you came out here."

"Well you see I didn't realize — it never occurred to me — but if you had asked me I'd have accepted."

"My name's Russell McClellan. They call me Rusty."

"I'm Eva Stuart."

"It's nice out here," he said, and sat down beside her. Quite close.

Eva had no idea what to say. She could only look at him and try to keep the surprise and joy and relief from showing too much.

He wasn't saying anything either. She wondered how long they could just sit and not talk. Maybe the girl is supposed to open the conversation. But she didn't know at all how to go about it. Then she remembered an article she'd read, surreptitiously, saying you should make a man talk about his interests. The silence was becoming strained. Somebody had to say something.

"Have you any interests?" she asked eagerly.

At which he laughed. The kind of laugh that makes you like to be laughed at, and suddenly he was easy to talk to. As friendly as Josie. Only there was something between them that wasn't between her and Josie. Something new to her.

Once Miss Heideman, patroling the lawn, beamed a flashlight on them, and Eva was afraid she'd order them inside but she didn't. She just said "Oh — Eva," and went on.

They could hear the music out here almost as well as in the gym and when the orchestra was playing the "Merry Widow Waltz," Russell sang softly, "Though I say not, What I may not — " and reached out to a flowering shrub that grew by the steps. He picked a pale pink blossom, and dropped it into Eva's open hand. His fingers brushed hers, and the touch sent a tremor up her arm. Like electricity. Like a miracle.

"For you," he said.

For you! For her. For Eva. The way he said it made being Eva, Eva chosen to receive a flower from Russell, the most wonderful fate in the world.

She looked up from the lovely thing in her hand and smiled at him, not minding that what she was feeling shone clearly in her eyes.

PHILIP ROTH

"The Contest for Aaron Gold" might be called "Portrait of the Artist As a Small Boy." It has two heroes, little Aaron, with his genius, and a sympathetic teacher who tries to help but finds instead that he has hurt him deeply. It is a sensitive picture of two unusual people caught in the rough-and-tumble of life in an ordinary camp with ordinary people.

Philip Roth was born in Newark, New Jersey, in 1933, and educated at Bucknell University and the University of Chicago. His first book, Goodbye, Columbus, *was awarded the Houghton Mifflin Literary Fellowship. He is the author of a novel,* Letting Go *and other novels.*

The Contest For
Aaron Gold

THE CAMP was hot. Two birds jabbered and in the distance Werner could hear a droning sound. As he trudged up the path the drone became louder until ahead of him he saw a half-dozen men milling around a squat, shivering, black machine. The men were at work on the road. For the first time Werner noticed that he was walking not on dirt or grass but asphalt. He set his bag down.

"What the hell do you think I'm running here, Angelo?" one of the men was shouting. He wore a plaid, peaked cap, a white polo shirt that had CAMP LAKESIDE scrawled across the front, and rust trousers. "There's going to be — Angelo! Do you hear me!"

A dark, dumpy man in work clothes answered him. "Yea, Lionel, I hear you, I hear you."

"There's going to be parents bringing their kids. In five days, Angelo, five goddam days!"

"I hear you, Lionel, I hear you."

"I want them to drive their cars all the way to the cabins, Angelo. And

Copyright © 1955 by Philip Roth. Originally published in *Epoch.*

if you can't finish the job, I'll get somebody else. You understand me, Angelo?"

"I understand you, Lionel. I hear you, I understand you."

"Five goddam days, or I get somebody else!"

Angelo shuffled off to the other side of the machine.

"Yea, five goddam days, Lionel. O.K. All right. Five goddam days. . . ."

"Mr. Steinberg," Werner called.

"Werner, Werner Samuelson!" The man in the peaked cap jogged over and swung a sweaty arm around him. In his sporty outfit he did not seem the gray-suited businessman who had stepped unexpectedly into Werner's Philadelphia ceramic shop back in March and offered him a job. "How are you, Werner?"

"A little hot."

"Get out of those clothes and get down to the lake for a dip. For christ sake, you're in the country — " Mr. Steinberg suddenly pulled his arm from Werner's shoulder. "Angelo!" He started racing after the dumpy man. "Werner," he yelled back, "I'll talk to you later . . . Angelo, for christ sake!"

With some difficulty, Werner found the new ceramics shop that was to be both home and classroom. After he had showered and unpacked, he sat down at the potter's wheel that was on the porch of the brown log building and began to toy with a lump of clay, turning it from a vase to a dish to a teacup and back again to a vase by way of a saucer. From the wide porch of the shop he could see the lake, big and blue, and beyond the lake the hills and the smooth green Berkshire mountains. Not since 1940, he remembered, when the Germans had chased him from his studio in southern Austria had he spent a summer in the country; for the past fourteen years the money from his Philadelphia shop had just been enough to scrape ungracefully along on, let alone to allow for vacations. In fact, had not Steinberg offered six hundred dollars plus room and board to be ceramics instructor at his summer camp, Werner suspected that once again, during the hot, customerless, summer months, he would have been on a one-meal-a-day diet. Finally, he might well have had to toss in the one thing he still had left, his shop. Now, however, when September came, with six hundred dollars and a little luck, he could give the shop one last try. It might mean nine weeks with a hundred scream-ing boys, but nevertheless, Steinberg's offer was a godsend.

Across the lake on a high white, wooden tower Werner saw a figure in a white bathing suit waving an arm at him. The figure looked as though it had been held by its hair and dipped in bronze. Mr. Steinberg had mentioned that Werner's salary was to be second only to that of a Mr. Lefty Shulberg, the swimming instructor — that must be him. Lefty Shulberg had been a professional basketball player, Steinberg said, and once, in a Tarzan movie had an underwater battle with Johnny Weissmuller. Werner watched the figure stop waving, push up on its toes, and then from the tower plunge headlong into the lake, more an airplane, Werner thought, than a gull.

The ceramics shop was at the far end of the camp, more than a half mile from the entrance. As the days flicked by Werner could hear the asphalt machine moving noisily from the entrance road into the camp itself. Mr. Steinberg had granted five days, but in four Angelo had the road flattened and finished. The noise, however, did not stop. So many parents had praised the idea that Mr. Steinberg sped to asphalting the other major arteries of the camp: immediately, Angelo's boys were to begin on the road that twisted down to Lefty Shulberg's lake. Werner was pleased that it wasn't to be the dirt path that led to the door of his ceramics shop.

The drone was still comfortably distant the first day a group of twelve boys invaded Werner's shop. The previous evening Werner had learned that the schedule was such that every boy in camp visited the ceramics shop three hours a week, no more than one hour a day. He had finally decided (and he knew he was hedging) that this first day he would let them browse around. Halfway through the hour, however, when it seemed that the boys were restless with browsing — one had just cracked a companion on the skull with a bony elbow — Werner herded them around the wheel and began showing them how to work with clay. As he worked, their twelve blank faces stared rigidly up at him. It was a little upsetting.

"This," Werner told them, "is called a potter's wheel." Nomenclature taken care of, he slipped uncertainly into history. "Men have used it for many hundreds of years to make beautiful and useful things." Unimpressed, the twelve stared on. He cleared a throat that didn't need clearing. "With the potter's wheel and their own hands, people have made vases and pitchers, cups and saucers, pots and pans, vessels and — and gourds. They've made vessels big enough to put two of you boys in." A fat boy in the second row looked disturbed. "But they put grain into them, sometimes water," Werner said quickly; "never boys, I don't think." There was relief.

"The men" — whoever *they* were — "always tried to make these vessels more beautiful and shapely" — somebody giggled. "They painted them red and gold, and blue and green, and they painted their sides with stories and legends. It took hundreds of years until men saw how much happier they could be if they surrounded themselves with beautiful — beautiful objects of art."

"Hey," shouted a boy in glasses and a too big baseball cap, "hey, can I work that wheel, Mr. Werner?" The giggler triggered off again.

"Yes," Werner said. "That is, no. Not right now." The giggles subsided into rhythmic thirty-second hiccups. "It takes time to learn what to do."

The boy in the baseball cap answered with a disgusted ducklike sound, moderately obscene, and Werner, cornered, quickly suggested that instead of working the wheel, each boy could grab a handful of clay and sit at one of the benches scattered around the porch and shape whatever he liked. The clay grabbed, Werner stole around to the opposite side of the porch for a smoke — he needed one; somehow twelve boys seemed like more than twelve boys.

He lit a cigarette, flicked a match out into the dirt path, and then to calm himself, he began counting the yellow buggy sunflowers that slopped across the path. As he counted he inhaled long and deep on the cigarette; with the smoke, ever so faintly, he thought he could taste asphalt.

He was halfway through his second cigarette, when he heard three urgent blasts from a whistle, then three more. Suddenly, on the other side of the shop there was bench-banging and feet scuffling, and by the time Werner raced around to see what had happened, half of the boys had already scrambled off, and the rest were leaping from their benches and high-tailing it away.

Werner managed to grab one boy by the seat of his blue short pants. "Where are you going?"

"What? We got swim now, Mr. Werner. Uncle Lefty just now blew his whistle. We got swim."

"Oh."

"Hey, lemme go, will you?" The boy jerked his head toward where Werner was still clutching at his pants.

"I beg your pardon."

The boy zoomed off, taking the five wooden steps in one leap. Werner looked out toward the lake. Astride the tower Lefty Shulberg raised his megaphone to his mouth and aimed at the ceramics shop.

"You guys in the clay factory, let's go. Swim! On the double!" The megaphone followed the boys. "Last one here gets a swat across the behind!" A yelp went up from the boys, and Lefty laughed into his megaphone.

Werner turned and looked at the benches: there were four of the twelve lumps of clay as lumpy as when they had been grabbed; five others scattered alongside had been expertly rolled into spheres — baseballs, obviously. Two of the original twelve were pancaked against the bench. One was supposed to be a pancake, the other had initials carved into it. Either it was an ashtray without a tray, or, possibly, an initialed pancake. Unable to find the twelfth lump Werner gathered all the pieces together and started to the supply room. In the farthest corner of the porch, however, there was something standing upon the floor, and so he walked to it. It was a small clay figure, a knight apparently, whose chest was covered with armor and whose spindly legs wouldn't have done him much service against a good, fast dragon. Werner mashed all the baseballs and pancakes into a wad, and mounting the wobbly knight in his right hand, he carried everything back to the supply room.

A few sunny days later, when the same twelve boys swarmed into the shop, Werner did not ask who had made the knight. He just gave out the clay and then strolled casually about. Sure enough, in five minutes there was a boy in the corner squatted Indian-style on the floor, the back of his frayed polo shirt to the others. When the whistle blasted six times, and everybody broke for the lake, Werner went to the boy and asked to speak with him a moment. He asked the boy's name.

"It's Aaron," the boy said.

"Aaron what?"

"Aaron Gold, Mr. Werner," the boy admitted. "I'll play with everybody else from now on, promise."

"You'll what?"

"You gonna report me?" Aaron said.

Werner told him that he merely liked his knight and wondered if he might not want some help.

"Can I play alone?" Aaron asked. "Uncle Irv says we gotta learn to play together."

"Who's Uncle Irv?"

"He's the head — the head counselor, I mean. He says we gotta not play alone. Uncle Lefty says so too. It's no good for you."

Werner looked the boy up and down. He was about eight years old, bony, underfed, a little tired-looking. He had thin yellow hair like tinsel, large brown eyes, and the most curious yellow peach fuzz growing down his cheeks that Werner had ever seen.

"You better go to swim."

The boy didn't move, except for a swoop of the head enabling him to scratch the hollow in his chest with his chin.

"Go ahead, go to swim."

The boy remained still.

"Oh," Werner said, "I won't report you — I promise."

That night it was hot and the air was gluey and so Werner strolled along his dirt path. He was figuring out how to push some of the boys beyond the baseball-pancake stage, when he came upon Mr. Steinberg and Angelo. Mr. Steinberg was pointing and thrashing his arms as though he might have been a little angry with the moon, and Angelo had his hands deep in his pockets.

". . . if parents want to drive, then I want them to drive, for christ sake. If you can't understand me, Angelo, maybe somebody else can. What the hell you think I'm running here?"

"A camp, Lionel, a camp. I'll get it done, Lionel." Angelo shuffled away. "Let me go home, will you?"

From the shadows Werner called hello to Mr. Steinberg. "Werner," Steinberg said. He hastened over to him. "Taking a walk, Werner?"

Werner said yes, that was what he was doing.

"Good, Werner, good," Steinberg said. "I've just finished speaking to Angelo. He's going to start asphalting your road so it'll be finished for visiting day. Would you do me a favor, Werner; when he starts, would you detour the kids through the grass?"

Werner nodded.

"Good," Steinberg smiled. "By the way," Steinberg said in an un-by-the-way-tone, "Lefty Shulberg was a little annoyed this morning. Seems the Gold kid came down to swim fifteen minutes late. Would you see if you could do something about that, Werner?"

"What?"

"I don't mean to say you held him up, Werner. I know kids — they dawdle, play around. Just remind him to get down on time." He dropped his voice to a confidential octave. "Lefty tells me that the kid is kind of peculiar. Having a helluva time teaching him to swim."

"Peculiar?"

"Yea. You know, if there's one thing parents want to see visiting day it's their kid swimming around like a goddam fish."

Werner said that was probably true.

"But you know, Werner," Steinberg started away, "even old Lefty can't teach them if they're not there."

"Mr. Steinberg —"

"Damn near forgot," Steinberg called back. "Every kid's going to have something finished by visiting day, Werner. Parents want something for their money."

Werner thought of baseballs and pancakes. "I suppose so, Mr. Steinberg."

A week passed and the machine began blackening its way up the path to the ceramics shop. Inside the shop Werner had laid down his first law. He considered the wisdom of dispensing laws, but near his wit's end, he finally had to dispense: no more baseballs, no more pancakes. By now most of the boys had individual modeling projects under way. Snakes were the favorite, turtles a close second. Aaron was the only one who tried a human figure. He puttered with several knights for a while, then embarked upon a large one, a warrior knight standing and aiming his sword at something. For a while he couldn't decide what that something was. Werner said that since the something wasn't to be shown it didn't matter, but Aaron insisted that it did. Werner suggested a purple dragon with six heads and two tails. Aaron shook his head no. They discussed it. Finally they decided on a purple dragon with six heads and three tails. That seemed satisfactory.

It was on Thursday of the following week, about twenty minutes after the boys had dashed for the lake, that Werner stumbled over Aaron crouching under a bench, at work on his warrior knight.

"Aaron, didn't you hear the whistle?"

"Yes."

"Then why didn't you go to swim?"

"I was working."

"Uncle Lefty will be waiting. Suppose you go now. Quickly."

"But I can't, Uncle Werner. Look." He stuck the clay figure under

Werner's nose. The legs, wobbly and undeserving of knighthood until then, were now solid and finely shaped.

"How in the world did you do that?" Werner said.

"Last night in bed, Uncle Werner, I just started to feel my own legs. They weren't nothing like the ones I was making, so I changed these. Can I stay and finish my legs, Uncle Werner?"

Werner didn't answer.

"Can I finish them, Uncle Werner?"

"Of course," Werner finally said, "of course — what do you think, I'm on the dragon's side?"

Werner feared that he would have a visitor that night, and he did.

"Werner," Steinberg stood framed in the doorway of the shop, "you're lucky it's me who's calling on you and not Lefty."

"Come in, Mr. Steinberg," Werner said, "you're letting in the bugs."

Steinberg slammed the screen door. He had to start again. "I tell you, you're lucky it's not Lefty. He's raging mad about that Gold kid not coming to swim today. He bawled the living hell out of the kid and now he wanted to get at you. I told him I'd take care of it."

Werner said nothing: could taking care of *it* mean firing *him*?

"Look, Werner, let's get squared around. It's good you're taking your job seriously, looking after the kids and all. But if there's one thing we don't want here it's one-sided kids. That's what I tell the parents and that's what they want, an all-around camp, you understand? But if you're going to let one kid play potsy with clay all day, Werner, what the hell are his parents going to say to me? For christ sake, let's be practical — they're not going to be satisfied with nothing but a clay pot."

"The boys aren't making clay pots." From a shelf Werner took down Aaron's knight, what was finished of it.

"That's fine, Werner, fine. But don't tell me that should take a forty-hour week to produce." Mr. Steinberg smirked.

Werner didn't know whether to answer. "Why not?" he said finally.

"For christ sake, we asphalted the whole entrance road, the whole thing, and the parking lot besides in seven days. Seven days, and you stand there and ask me why a kid shouldn't take forty hours to make a pair of goddam legs. Don't kid me, Werner."

It was said before he knew it. "I'm not trying to!"

"Goddamit, what do you think I'm running here! Just let's not hold this kid back any more — I won't stand for it. Lefty tells me he sees how

you hold the kid back." Mr. Steinberg paused a second. "I'd hate like hell
to tell you what he said about you and that kid." At the door he turned
around. "Look, as long as every kid has something by visiting day, we all
finish out the summer together. If Gold has a what-do-you-call-it with
real pretty legs, that's all the better!" He slammed the screen door and
the light bulb over Werner's head trembled.

It began to rain that night, a cold, miserable rain, and it rained for four
days until the lake was a murky brown. The first rainy morning Werner
watched from his porch as a single-file column of raincoated, rainhatted
boys marched to the recreation hall for "rainy-day activities." Lefty
Shulberg, bareheaded, his trousers tucked neatly into brown combat
boots, marched at the front; so close beside him that he might have been
chained, was a boy in a bulky, yellow slicker and a black rainhat. In both
arms, like a wet infant, the boy cradled a basketball. He was out of step.

"Sound off," Lefty bellowed.

A gleeful chant went up. "One . . . Two . . . Three . . . Four . . .
One — two . . . Three — four." And then a barrage of giggles from the
marching boys.

"Suck that gut in, Gold!" The other boys howled. Aaron almost
dropped the big basketball.

When he awoke the morning of the fourth day, Werner knew it had
stopped raining: the asphalt machine was droning up the road. Not
wanting to run into Mr. Steinberg, Werner did not go to breakfast until
late. Steinberg and his speed-up instructions had been on his mind these
past four days, and he had finally reached a decision: after all, Steinberg
was his employer, paying the check, and he was the employee. This was
just no summer to get fired.

At the close of the hour that morning Werner told the boys that he was
going to ask them a favor. "It's not a big favor," he said. "I just wonder
if some of you who have been working slowly, couldn't work a little
faster. Just a little." He put his back to Aaron. "We all want something
finished when our parents come up on Sunday . . ." He felt foolish for
using the plural. "Don't you?" he added. Nobody seemed appalled by the
news.

Before he could say more there came the three blasts, then three more,
then the bellowing voice: "Swim! You guys, let's go. On the double!"
The boys started dropping things and running. "Swim! That means
*every*body. You too, Sir Lancelot!"

Werner looked quickly up and across the lake. From the high tower, Lefty Shulberg waved an arm at him. Then he raised his megaphone. "Get that lead out of your pants! On the double!"

Werner watched as the boys screamed and ran away. He watched as the two fat-ringed legs of the last boy vanished around the bend of the lake.

"Uncle Werner?"

Werner turned. "Aaron. Aaron, you're supposed to be at swim. Now get out."

"Uncle Werner," the boy said sharply, "I can't work *no* quicker."

"Look, Aaron, no time for explanations. Lefty's waiting."

"I can't finish by Sunday, Uncle Werner. I just can't!"

"You have to. Now go, Aaron!" Werner pushed him in the direction of the lake. The boy spun around.

"Hey, whose side you on, Uncle Werner?"

"What?" Werner snapped.

"Whose *side* — me or the dragon?" The boy's eyes looked like two brown egg yolks.

Werner smacked him on the behind. "O.K. O.K. *Don't* work no quicker. Now get down to Lefty. And on the double!" Werner turned, mumbling to himself, "For crying out loud . . ."

"Thank you kindly, Mr. Werner," came a bellow from across the lake. Werner swung around — from the corner of his eye he saw Aaron running away — and there was Lefty on the tower. With one arm across his middle, Lefty Shulberg bowed deeply, gratuitously, toward Werner's ceramics shop.

Sunday was visiting day, but by Friday the asphalt machine buzzed in Werner's ear like a horsefly. After lunch he looked out to see how far along Angelo's workers were. A short man with a scythe was down the road a few feet whisking away the sunflowers with wide, slow strokes. It was Angelo himself.

"How soon you think you'll be done?" Werner said to him. Angelo peeked over his shoulder like a nervous squirrel.

"Yea, sure, I'll tell you — if Steinberg gets his way" — he peeked over his shoulder — "we'll have the goddam thing done in ten goddam minutes."

"I see."

Angelo peeked again. "Yea, sure, then we can start paving the goddam lake." Mr. Steinberg suddenly appeared up the road. Angelo spat in his palms and went back to guillotining sunflowers.

Werner didn't make it inside in time.

"Werner, Werner," Mr. Steinberg shouted, "Angelo's going to have this road finished up for you by the end of the day."

Werner looked at him and said that was fine.

Two steps at a time, Mr. Steinberg hopped onto the porch. "I want to thank you — Lefty says all the kids been on time lately." Mr. Steinberg chuckled. "Kids are funny — got to stay on them, else they'll dawdle."

Werner turned to go inside. Mr. Steinberg followed him. Werner had been praying that Steinberg would keep away until after visiting day; Werner wanted to make sure they finished the summer together.

"Stuff looks all right, Werner, all right." He was at the shelves handling the boys' finished projects. This was no accidental visit.

"Damn nice ashtray," Mr. Steinberg said. Werner made believe he was doing some work of his own.

"Damn nice snake," Werner, damn nice."

There was silence while Mr. Steinberg checked over the rest of the shelves.

"What's this? What's this thing?"

Werner looked up. "That's unfinished."

"Unfinished? Whose is it?"

Werner waited. "Aaron Gold's," he said.

"When's he going to finish?" Steinberg turned the headless-armless knight roughly in his hand. "Tomorrow?"

"He doesn't come tomorrow."

"Well what in hell is he going to show his parents?" Mr. Steinberg jutted his head forward. "Well, what?"

"That."

"That! For christ sake, Werner, what the hell kind of game are you playing, anyhow! Look, I'm a busy man. I pay good money to see the work gets done." He clutched the unfinished knight in his fist. "Angelo gets his roads built on time. Lefty gets those kids in their swimming on time: I don't have to tell them what to do, for christ sake." He slammed the knight down on the table. "Wait'll Lefty hears about this goddam thing. Look at this goddam thing!" He stared right at Werner. "Werner, I'm just about fed up . . . What kind of game are you and that little queer trying to play anyhow!" Suddenly, he walked out of the screen door, bouncing it after him; he yelled a word back through it.

"Forchristsake!"

It was over. Werner lit a cigarette. Mr. Steinberg was fed up, but he hadn't fired him — he hadn't even mentioned it. Werner twisted the unfinished knight in one hand, trying to figure out Mr. Steinberg. He pondered for several minutes — and then it dawned: it was too close to visiting day. The camp wouldn't be all-around if there was a new ceramics shop without a new ceramics instructor. So. Mr. Steinberg had nearly for-christ-saked him into the floor, but he hadn't fired him. And after visiting day, the incident cold and no deadlines to be met, he certainly wouldn't fire him. At least Werner's six hundred dollars seemed safe.

Werner stared at the knight. What *would* Lefty say when he heard about the goddam thing? What he might think was that as far as the contest for Aaron Gold was concerned — for, apparently, that was what it had become to Lefty — he had lost. Lefty probably didn't like to lose, but Werner had had his way, and if that wasn't a loss, at best it was a tie. Ties probably wouldn't do for Lefty either. Maybe he would come over and punch him in the mouth. No, Lefty wouldn't settle up that way. It was too simple. No, but he would think of something. What? That didn't take too much pondering: probably Lefty would make Aaron Gold the most miserable kid in the world. He seemed capable.

Werner rolled the knight from one hand to the other. He heeled out his cigarette, and then he got up and went over to the clay cabinet and grabbed off a big lump of clay. He walked back to the table and picked up the knight. He began to work on it. In ten minutes he had grafted a neck and head on the figure. Then he started on the arms; he stopped first to ask himself at which one of the invisible dragon's invisible heads he should aim the sword. There was room for choice. "O.K.," he said aloud, "don't get cute. Just aim at his goddam stomach."

By nine o'clock Sunday morning it was a steamy eighty-five degrees. Werner perspired as he arranged the boys' projects on the shelves for exhibition. When he turned to get a drink, there was Aaron Gold standing in the doorway of the shop; Werner hadn't seen the boy since the day before Steinberg's visit.

"Hello," Aaron said. He had on a laundry-stiffened camp polo shirt and shorts, and his yellow hair was matted to his head with water. He looked starched.

"Aaron, you're supposed to be at breakfast."

"I snuck out."

"Why?"

"I felt like it."

Werner went to the sink. "Want some water?"

"No."

Werner took a long drink. "If they miss you, you'll get into trouble," Werner said. Aaron widened his eyes and stared on a line toward Werner's navel. He jiggled his head first yes, then, ferociously, no. He was feeling skittish. Werner went to the shelves, a skinny line of perspiration oozing up along his spine. Finally, he turned his head to Aaron.

"Come here a second."

Aaron made believe he skated over to him, on ice skates.

"What?" Aaron said. The boy smelled from toothpaste.

Werner pointed a finger at the shelf. "Look."

In the center of the top shelf there was a lined index card, and on it,

A KNIGHT FIGHTING A DRAGON
By Aaron Gold.

Next to the card stood a knight, whole. Aaron looked at the knight, then he looked up at Werner, then he looked at the knight. Werner's polo shirt felt like wet flannel.

"He got arms, Uncle Werner."

"Uh-huh."

"He got arms."

Werner nodded.

"Who put them arms on?"

"I did," Werner said.

"He got arms," Aaron said.

"Well," Werner said, watching him, "you didn't expect him to fight without arms, did you?"

Aaron didn't move an inch. Werner reached a hand toward his shoulder and, instantaneously, Aaron leaped back, as though it were a game of tag and if Werner touched him that would make him "it."

"Aaron —"

"You ruined him," the boy suddenly shouted, pulling at his yellow hair. "You ruined him." He ran to the screen door and began kicking at it. "You ruined him, you did, you did . . ." And then he ran out the door and off along the edge of the lake, like a small wild animal who gets out of a blazing forest just as fast as he can.

Werner flopped down in a chair. He smelled his own perspiration. He was gripping the knight in his hand — and he didn't even remember picking it up. He set it upon the table before him, contemplating it as one might contemplate a rare piece of sculpture. He stared a full minute, and then, like a mace, he pummeled his right fist down upon it. It shattered, but he pounded and pounded at it with his fist. He pounded until it was a mess, and even then he didn't stop. It was a better job than the dragon himself might have done.

Within an hour Werner had thrown all his things into his suitcase and put on a clean shirt and his old cord suit. He had already kicked open the screen door and started out, when he saw that his right hand was grimy with clay. He went back in and scrubbed it clean and then, once again, he picked up his suitcase and left the shop.

The camp was hot. Above the new, black, sticky road the air squirmed from the heat. Car noises rumbled from around the lake, and as he walked, suitcase in hand, Werner squinted that way. Black cars, red cars, tan cars were twisting slowly down toward the lake and parking near the boathouse; and beyond, astride the high tower, there was Lefty Shulberg in his white bathing suit, talking through his megaphone. Lefty, it seemed, was about to give a special diving exhibition for any parents and kids who might be interested. Loudly, through the megaphone, he was welcoming his audience.

"How you doing, Mike. Sit your parents down right there. That a boy . . . Jeff-boy, what do you say, kid." The names snapped out like sparks, and then, a moment after Werner heard them, they were muffled in a wooly heat. "Artie, that a boy . . . Hey, Joe, how's my — Hey, what do you know! Goldy! How are you doing, Goldy — buddy! That your parents? Good, sit them right down front. What do you know!" Lefty waved his megaphone at Aaron Gold's parents. Mr. Gold, in white shirt and gray Bermuda shorts, waved back; Mrs. Gold nodded. Lefty was treating their boy all right.

Werner just kept walking along the hot, squirming road and out of the camp.

SHIRLEY JACKSON

If the reader of "One Ordinary Day, with Peanuts" suspects from the beginning that Mr. Johnson is too good to be true, he will be right. But how very much so makes a delightful fantasy of a husband and wife playing Dr. Jekyll and Mr. Hyde. This interplay of good and evil is almost a trademark of Miss Jackson's writing.

Shirley Jackson was born in California and grew up there and in Rochester, New York. She attended Syracuse University where she edited the college literary magazine. Shortly after graduation, she married Stanley Edgar Hyman, the well-known critic. Her first novel was The Road Through the Wall. *Her best-known short story collection is* The Lottery.

One Ordinary Day,
with Peanuts

MR. JOHN PHILIP JOHNSON shut his front door behind him and came down his front steps into the bright morning with a feeling that all was well with the world on this best of all days, and wasn't the sun warm and good, and didn't his shoes feel comfortable after the resoling, and he knew that he had undoubtedly chosen the precise very tie which belonged with the day and the sun and his comfortable feet, and, after all, wasn't the world just a wonderful place? In spite of the fact that he was a small man, and the tie was perhaps a shade vivid, Mr. Johnson irradiated this feeling of well-being as he came down the steps and onto the dirty sidewalk, and he smiled at people who passed him, and some of them even smiled back. He stopped at the newsstand on the corner and bought his paper, saying "*Good* morning" with real conviction to the man who sold him the paper and the two or three other people who were lucky enough to be buying papers when Mr. Johnson skipped up. He remembered to fill his pockets with candy and peanuts, and then he set out to get himself uptown. He stopped in a flower shop and bought a carnation for his buttonhole, and stopped almost immediately afterward to give the carnation to a small child in a carriage, who looked at him dumbly, and then smiled, and Mr. Johnson smiled, and the child's mother looked at Mr. Johnson for a minute and then smiled too.

When he had gone several blocks uptown, Mr. Johnson cut across the avenue and went along a side street, chosen at random; he did not follow the same route every morning, but preferred to pursue his eventful way in wide detours, more like a puppy than a man intent upon business. It happened this morning that halfway down the block a moving van was parked, and the furniture from an upstairs apartment stood half on the sidewalk, half on the steps, while an amused group of people loitered, examining the scratches on the tables and the worn spots on the chairs, and a harassed woman, trying to watch a young child and the movers and the furniture all at the same time, gave the clear impression of endeavoring to shelter her private life from the people staring at her belongings. Mr. Johnson stopped, and for a moment joined the crowd, and then he came forward and, touching his hat civilly, said, "Perhaps I can keep an eye on your little boy for you?"

The woman turned and glared at him distrustfully, and Mr. Johnson added hastily, "We'll sit right here on the steps." He beckoned to the little boy, who hesitated and then responded agreeably to Mr. Johnson's genial smile. Mr. Johnson brought out a handful of peanuts from his pocket and sat on the steps with the boy, who at first refused the peanuts on the grounds that his mother did not allow him to accept food from strangers; Mr. Johnson said that probably his mother had not intended peanuts to be included, since elephants at the circus ate them, and the boy considered, and then agreed solemnly. They sat on the steps cracking peanuts in a comradely fashion, and Mr. Johnson said, "So you're moving?"

"Yep," said the boy.

"Where you going?"

"Vermont."

"Nice place. Plenty of snow there. Maple sugar, too; you like maple sugar?"

"Sure."

"Plenty of maple sugar in Vermont. You going to live on a farm?"

"Going to live with Grandpa."

"Grandpa like peanuts?"

"Sure."

"Ought to take him some," said Mr. Johnson, reaching into his pocket. "Just you and Mommy going?"

"Yep."

"Tell you what," Mr. Johnson said. "You take some peanuts to eat on the train."

The boy's mother, after glancing at them frequently, had seemingly decided that Mr. Johnson was trustworthy, because she had devoted herself wholeheartedly to seeing that the movers did not — what movers rarely do, but every housewife believes they will — crack a leg from her good table, or set a kitchen chair down on a lamp. Most of the furniture was loaded by now, and she was deep in that nervous stage when she knew there was something she had forgotten to pack — hidden away in the back of a closet somewhere, or left at a neighbor's and forgotten, or on the clothesline — and was trying to remember under stress what it was.

"This all, lady?" the chief mover said, completing her dismay.

Uncertainly, she nodded.

"Want to go on the truck with the furniture, sonny?" the mover asked the boy, and laughed. The boy laughed too and said to Mr. Johnson, "I guess I'll have a good time at Vermont."

"Fine time," said Mr. Johnson, and stood up. "Have one more peanut before you go," he said to the boy.

The boy's mother said to Mr. Johnson, "Thank you so much; it was a great help to me."

"Nothing at all," said Mr. Johnson gallantly. "Where in Vermont are you going?"

The mother looked at the little boy accusingly, as though he had given away a secret of some importance, and said unwillingly, "Geeenwich."

"Lovely town," said Mr. Johnson. He took out a card, and wrote a name on the back. "Very good friend of mine lives in Greenwich," he said. "Call on him for anything you need. His wife makes the best doughnuts in town," he added soberly to the little boy.

"Swell," said the little boy.

"Goodbye," said Mr. Johnson.

He went on, stepping happily with his new-shod feet, feeling the warm sun on his back and on the top of his head. Halfway down the block he met a stray dog and fed him a peanut.

At the corner, where another wide avenue faced him, Mr. Johnson decided to go on uptown again. Moving with comparative laziness, he was passed on either side by people hurrying and frowning, and people brushed past him going the other way, clattering along to get somewhere quickly. Mr. Johnson stopped on every corner and waited patiently for the light to change, and he stepped out of the way of anyone who seemed to be in any particular hurry, but one young lady came too fast for him, and crashed wildly into him when he stooped to pat a kitten which had run out onto the sidewalk from an apartment house and was now unable to get back through the rushing feet.

"Excuse me," said the young lady, trying frantically to pick up Mr. Johnson and hurry on at the same time, "terribly sorry."

The kitten, regardless now of danger, raced back to its home. "Perfectly all right," said Mr. Johnson, adjusting himself carefully. "You seem to be in a hurry."

"Of course I'm in a hurry," said the young lady. "I'm late."

She was extremely cross and the frown between her eyes seemed well on its way to becoming permanent. She had obviously awakened late, because she had not spent any extra time in making herself look pretty, and her dress was plain and unadorned with collar or brooch, and her lipstick was noticeably crooked. She tried to brush past Mr. Johnson, but, risking her suspicious displeasure, he took her arm and said, "Please wait."

"Look," she said ominously, "I ran into you and your lawyer can see my lawyer and I will gladly pay all damages and all inconveniences suffered therefrom but please this minute let me go because *I am late*."

"Late for what?" said Mr. Johnson; he tried his winning smile on her but it did no more than keep her, he suspected, from knocking him down again.

"Late for work," she said between her teeth. "Late for my employment. I have a job and if I am late I lose exactly so much an hour and I cannot really afford what your pleasant conversation is costing me, be it *ever* so pleasant."

"I'll pay for it," said Mr. Johnson. Now these were magic words, not necessarily because they were true, or because she seriously expected Mr. Johnson to pay for anything, but because Mr. Johnson's flat statement, obviously innocent of irony, could not be, coming from Mr. Johnson, anything but the statement of a responsible and truthful and respectable man.

"What *do* you mean?" she asked.

"I said that since I am obviously responsible for your being late I shall certainly pay for it."

"Don't be silly," she said, and for the first time the frown disappeared. "*I* wouldn't expect you to pay for anything — a few minutes ago I was offering to pay *you*. Anyway," she added, almost smiling, "it *was* my fault."

"What happens if you don't go to work?"

She stared. "I don't get paid."

"Precisely," said Mr. Johnson.

"What do you mean, precisely? If I don't show up at the office exactly twenty minutes ago I lose a dollar and twenty cents an hour, or two cents a minute or . . ." She thought. ". . . Almost a dime for the time I've spent talking to you."

Mr. Johnson laughed, and finally she laughed, too. "You're late already," he pointed out. "Will you give me another four cents worth?"

"I don't understand why."

"You'll see," Mr. Johnson promised. He led her over to the side of the walk, next to the buildings, and said, "Stand here," and went out into the rush of people going both ways. Selecting and considering, as one who must make a choice involving perhaps whole years of lives, he estimated the people going by. Once he almost moved, and then at the last minute thought better of it and drew back. Finally, from half a block away, he saw what he wanted, and moved out into the center of the traffic to intercept a young man, who was hurrying, and dressed as though he had awakened late, and frowning.

"Oof," said the young man, because Mr. Johnson had thought of no better way to intercept anyone than the one the young woman had unwittingly used upon him. "Where do you think you're going?" the young man demanded from the sidewalk.

"I want to speak to you," said Mr. Johnson ominously.

The young man got up nervously, dusting himself and eyeing Mr. Johnson. "What for?" he said. "What'd *I* do?"

"That's what bothers me most about people nowadays," Mr. Johnson complained broadly to the people passing. "No matter whether they've done anything or not, they always figure someone's after them. About what you're going to do," he told the young man.

"Listen," said the young man, trying to brush past him, "I'm late, and don't have any time to listen. Here's a dime, now get going."

"Thank you," said Mr. Johnson, pocketing the dime. "Look," he said, "what happens if you stop running?"

"I'm late," said the young man, still trying to get past Mr. Johnson, who was unexpectedly clinging.

"How much you make an hour?" Mr. Johnson demanded.

"A communist, are you?" said the young man. "Now will you please let me —"

"No," said Mr. Johnson insistently, "*how* much?"

"Dollar fifty," said the young man. "And *now* will you —"

"You like adventure?"

The young man stared, and, staring, found himself caught and held by Mr. Johnson's genial smile; he almost smiled back and then repressed it and made an effort to tear away. "I got to *hurry*," he said.

"Mystery? Like surprises? Unusual and exciting events?"

"You selling something?"

"Sure," said Mr. Johnson. "You want to take a chance?"

The young man hesitated, looked longingly up the avenue toward what might have been his destination and then, when Mr. Johnson said "I'll pay for it" with his own peculiar convincing emphasis, turned and said, "Well, okay. But I got to *see* it first, what I'm buying."

Mr. Johnson, breathing hard, led the young man over to the side where the girl was standing; she had been watching with interest Mr. Johnson's capture of the young man and now, smiling timidly, she looked at Mr. Johnson as though prepared to be surprised at nothing.

Mr. Johnson reached into his pocket and took out his wallet. "Here," he said, and handed a bill to the girl. "This about equals your day's pay."

"But no," she said, surprised in spite of herself. "I mean, I *couldn't*."

"Please do not interrupt," Mr. Johnson told her. "And *here*," he said to the young man, "this will take care of *you*." The young man accepted the bill dazedly, but said, "Probably counterfeit" to the young woman out of the side of his mouth. "Now," Mr. Johnson went on, disregarding the young man, "what is your name, miss?"

"Kent," she said helplessly. "Mildred Kent."

"Fine," said Mr. Johnson. "And you, sir?"

"Arthur Adams," said the young man stiffly.

"Splendid," said Mr. Johnson. "Now, Miss Kent, I would like you to meet Mr. Adams. Mr. Adams, Miss Kent."

Miss Kent stared, wet her lips nervously, made a gesture as though she might run, and said, "How do you do?"

Mr. Adams straightened his shoulders, scowled at Mr. Johnson, made a gesture as though he might run, and said, "How do you do?"

"Now *this*," said Mr. Johnson, taking several bills from his wallet, "should be enough for the day for both of you. I would suggest, perhaps, Coney Island — although I personally am not fond of the place — or perhaps a nice lunch somewhere, and dancing, or a matinee, or even a movie, although take care to choose a really *good* one; there are *so* many bad movies these days. You might," he said, struck with an inspiration, "visit the Bronx Zoo, or the Planetarium. Anywhere, as a matter of fact," he concluded, "that you would like to go. Have a nice time."

As he started to move away Arthur Adams, breaking from his dumbfounded stare, said, "But see here, mister, you *can't* do this. Why — how do you know — I mean, *we* don't even know — I mean, how do you know we won't just take the money and not do what you said?"

"You've taken the money," Mr. Johnson said. "You don't have to follow any of my suggestions. You may know something you prefer to do — perhaps a museum, or something."

"But suppose I just run away with it and leave her here?"

"I know you won't," said Mr. Johnson gently, "because you remembered to ask *me* that. Goodbye," he added, and went on.

As he stepped up the street, conscious of the sun on his head and his good shoes, he heard from somewhere behind him the young man saying, "Look, you know you don't *have* to if you don't want to," and the girl saying, "But unless *you* don't want to . . ." Mr. Johnson smiled to himself and then thought that he had better hurry along; when he wanted to he could move very quickly, and before the young woman had gotten around to saying, "Well, *I* will if *you* will," Mr. Johnson was several blocks away and had already stopped twice, once to help a lady lift several large packages into a taxi and once to hand a peanut to a seagull. By this time he was in an area of large stores and many more people and he was buffeted constantly from either side by people hurrying and cross and late and sullen. Once he offered a peanut to a man who asked him for a dime, and once he offered a peanut to a bus driver who had stopped his bus at an intersection and had opened the window next to his seat and put out his head as though longing for fresh air and the comparative quiet of the traffic. The man wanting a dime took the peanut because Mr. Johnson had wrapped a dollar bill around it, but the bus driver took the peanut and asked ironically, "You want a transfer, Jack?"

On a busy corner Mr. Johnson encountered two young people — for

one minute he thought they might be Mildred Kent and Arthur Adams
— who were eagerly scanning a newspaper, their backs pressed against a
storefront to avoid the people passing, their heads bent together. Mr.
Johnson, whose curiosity was insatiable, leaned onto the storefront next
to them and peeked over the man's shoulder; they were scanning the
"Apartments Vacant" columns.

Mr. Johnson remembered the street where the woman and her little
boy were going to Vermont and he tapped the man on the shoulder and
said amiably, "Try down on West Seventeen. About the middle of the
block, people moved out this morning."

"Say, what do you —" said the man, and then, seeing Mr. Johnson
clearly, "Well, thanks. Where did you say?"

"West Seventeen," said Mr. Johnson. "About the middle of the block."
He smiled again and said, "Good luck."

"Thanks," said the man.

"Thanks," said the girl, as they moved off.

"Goodbye," said Mr. Johnson.

He lunched alone in a pleasant restaurant, where the food was rich,
and only Mr. Johnson's excellent digestion could encompass two of their
whipped-cream-and-chocolate-and-rum-cake pastries for dessert. He had
three cups of coffee, tipped the waiter largely, and went out into the
street again into the wonderful sunlight, his shoes still comfortable and
fresh on his feet. Outside he found a beggar staring into the windows of
the restaurant he had left and, carefully looking through the money in
his pocket, Mr. Johnson approached the beggar and pressed some coins
and a couple of bills into his hand. "It's the price of the veal cutlet lunch
plus tip," said Mr. Johnson. "Goodbye."

After his lunch he rested; he walked into the nearest park and fed
peanuts to the pigeons. It was late afternoon by the time he was ready to
start back downtown, and he had refereed two checker games and
watched a small boy and girl whose mother had fallen asleep and awakened with surprise and fear which turned to amusement when she saw
Mr. Johnson. He had given away almost all of his candy, and had fed all
the rest of his peanuts to the pigeons, and it was time to go home.
Although the late afternoon sun was pleasant, and his shoes were still
entirely comfortable, he decided to take a taxi downtown.

He had a difficult time catching a taxi, because he gave up the first
three or four empty ones to people who seemed to need them more;
finally, however, he stood alone on the corner and — almost like netting a

frisky fish — he hailed desperately until he succeeded in catching a cab which had been proceeding with haste uptown and seemed to draw in toward Mr. Johnson against its own will.

"Mister," the cab driver said as Mr. Johnson climbed in, "I figured you was an omen, like. I wasn't going to pick you up at all."

"Kind of you," said Mr. Johnson ambiguously.

"If I'd of let you go it would of cost me ten bucks," said the driver.

"Really?" said Mr. Johnson.

"Yeah," said the driver. "Guy just got out of the cab, he turned around and give me ten bucks, said take this and bet it in a hurry on a horse named Vulcan, right away."

"Vulcan?" said Mr. Johnson, horrified. "A fire sign on a Wednesday?"

"What?" said the driver. "Anyway, I said to myself if I got no fare between here and there I'd bet the ten, but if anyone looked like they needed the cab I'd take it as a omen and I'd take the ten home to the wife."

"You were very right," said Mr. Johnson heartily. "This is Wednesday, you would have lost your money. Monday, yes, or even Saturday. But never never never a fire sign on a Wednesday. Sunday would have been good, now."

"Vulcan don't run on Sunday," said the driver.

"You wait till another day," said Mr. Johnson. "Down this street, please, driver. I'll get off on the next corner."

"He *told* me Vulcan, though," said the driver.

"I'll tell you," said Mr. Johnson, hesitating with the door of the cab half open. "You take that ten dollars and I'll give you another ten dollars to go with it, and you go right ahead and bet that money on any Thursday on any horse that has a name indicating . . . let me see, Thursday . . . well, grain. Or any growing food."

"Grain?" said the driver. "You mean a horse named, like, Wheat or something?"

"Certainly," said Mr. Johnson. "Or, as a matter of fact, to make it even easier, any horse whose name includes the letters C, R, L. Perfectly simple."

"Tall corn?" said the driver, a light in his eye. "You mean a horse named, like, Tall Corn?"

"Absolutely," said Mr. Johnson. "Here's your money."

"Tall Corn," said the driver. "Thank *you,* mister."

"Goodbye," said Mr. Johnson.

He was on his own corner and went straight up to his apartment. He let himself in and called "Hello?" and Mrs. Johnson answered from the kitchen, "Hello, dear, aren't you early?"

"Took a taxi home," Mr. Johnson said. "I remembered the cheesecake, too. What's for dinner?"

Mrs. Johnson came out of the kitchen and kissed him; she was a comfortable woman, and smiling as Mr. Johnson smiled. "Hard day?" she asked.

"Not very," said Mr. Johnson, hanging his coat in the closet. "How about you?"

"So-so," she said. She stood in the kitchen doorway while he settled into his easy chair and took off his good shoes and took out the paper he had bought that morning. "Here and there," she said.

"I didn't do so badly," Mr. Johnson said. "Couple young people."

"Fine," she said. "I had a little nap this afternoon, took it easy most of the day. Went into a department store this morning and accused the woman next to me of shoplifting, and had the store detective pick her up. Sent three dogs to the pound — *you* know, the usual thing. Oh, and listen," she added, remembering.

"What?" asked Mr. Johnson.

"Well," she said, "I got onto a bus and asked the driver for a transfer, and when he helped someone else first I said that he was impertinent, and quarreled with him. And then I said why wasn't he in the army, and I said it loud enough for everyone to hear, and I took his number and I turned in a complaint. Probably got him fired."

"Fine," said Mr. Johnson. "But you do look tired. Want to change over tomorrow?"

"I *would* like to," she said. "I could do with a change."

"Right," said Mr. Johnson. "What's for dinner?"

"Veal cutlet."

"Had it for lunch," said Mr. Johnson.

FRANK BUTLER

It is no accident that the verses which haunt the woman in the "To the
Wilderness I Wander" were written in 1616. Many would call the story a
fantasy, but it would be more accurate to call it metaphysical, resembling
as it does the metaphysical literature of the seventeenth century. John
Donne is today the most celebrated of its practitioners. Metaphysical
writing, if it is to be differentiated from fantasy, can be said to involve in a
more philosophical way the knowledge of being and reality. This is an
excellent example.

Frank Butler was born in Nashville, Tennessee, in 1929. He did
newspaper work and studied at Columbia University. He asks that
mention be made of "the spiritual debt I owe the MacDowell Colony
which gave me four months' freedom to work when I needed them
desperately."

To the Wilderness I Wander

— To Clare

LET ME SAY this story began one warm May morning in the smart, stale,
and ordinarily preoccupied mind of a sullenly attractive young woman
named Marianne Smith while she was riding uptown on the Seventh
Avenue subway. Let me say it began there only because we do not know
nearly enough to tell where it actually did or could begin, or even
whether the word could apply to what I know happened to her that day.

Something had been disturbing Marianne for several stops, robbing her
of the vaguely pleasurable resentment she occasionally felt toward her
husband Phillip. Today it was for calling her up to Times Square
abruptly and without explanation on the day before the last important
review lecture she would give before finals. But something was usually
disturbing Marianne, so she did not give it the immediate attention that
this time was due. Later she was sorry when she learned that it had been
in her power at the beginning to prevent all the subsequent events.

Reprinted from *The Hudson Review*, Vol. IX, No. 1, Spring 1956. Copyright 1956 by
The Hudson Review, Inc.

But by the time the doors hissed shut at 14th Street and the train roared away again, down into its tunneling dark, the intuition that had sought to warn Marianne had also tunneled a way down into her own trackless consciousness and signaled to her there a distinct worry, and then a growing fear.

She coughed and scratched her right palm where it always itched when she was nervous. It was the one gesture she had not controlled into her system of attractiveness because by now it was her only unconscious one.

Perhaps it was the hiss of the brakes and doors. They seemed slower and more ominous than usual, and to Marianne they had always been ominous. Perhaps the train gathered its speed a bit too quickly, or the slope down seemed too steep for subway tracks, or the tunnel too dark in some odd intangible way. Perhaps she even knew, or almost knew, there was something more. The threads of ordered circumstance are what form our fabric of sanity and the real stuff of madness is when one, then several together begin suddenly and inexplicably to unravel, and the familiar pattern becomes confused and unrecognizable, and finally falls away in a tangle of lunacy. But it was not lunacy, but her old instant fear and fascination of it that breathed on Marianne's skin the chill, sudden breath of the impossible that came then. For decay is a delicate process, as slow in the mind as elsewhere in nature. What happened to Marianne may have seemed insane to her, but it happened far too quickly to be anything but a perverse new reality that jerked across those other subtler ravelings of the world she knew with the speed that only a tangible fact can have, pulling tight and taut in her the whole recent tangle of contradictions into a Gordian knot of indisputable, paradoxical truth: the subway was cold, cold as winter, and this was, as I said, an exceptionally warm morning in May.

All this is what beginning there is, though not the story itself. Yet these first reactions of an intelligent, unhappy and typically befuddled mind under the impact of an unknown and usually terrifying *difference* is possibly a greater part of what ultimately became of Marianne (who was not at all terrified) than we may like to suppose. An instant before the cold had come a warning bell had rung somewhere in her, but too softly and too late for her to escape the living fantasy into which she instinctively felt and even hoped she was traveling. Now with the cold she was sure.

She had begun to grow afraid, but whether from madness or fantasy the larger part of her all the while fully enjoyed the sensation. Since she was responsible and, in a way, even the cause of all that happened to her, I think these details have more than casual importance. But the subway is an incidental instrument. Marianne was not carried down into an infernal region and she would not have accepted it if she had been. I believe she would have indignantly demanded something more original. As usual, she was prepared for the worst, but only the most exciting and diverting worst would do. Marianne did have unique desires for fantasy, but she had more imagination than invention, more brains than real intelligence, and these desires had never been very clear. The truth was that she was too lazy to put them to work for her, even destructively, in any way that could satisfy her dark and usually revengeful yearnings. Marianne would very much have liked to destroy something if she knew how, preferably something plodding and everyday, and she would have loved to destroy it with some unknown, satanic weapon torn from the scarlet supernatural she hoped was always slyly lurking about, waiting to be evoked, waiting to pounce. But as yet the subway had done no more than chill her with an uncomfortable draft, and now she felt the first of many subsequent fears slipping regretfully away.

There were few others in the car and Marianne glanced at them very briefly. With her practiced eye she saw only varying versions of the New York subway riders' mask, ugly, complacent, Daily News faces. The pinkish bald man with the sunset tie and two-toned shoes absorbed in the red headlines of his newspaper would doubtlessly consider any question from her a flattery to his pudgy virility. A brown old lady nearer her was bent in sleep over an immense shopping bag and Marianne was sure the two Puerto Rican boys laughing near the door would pretend they did not speak English. Her attention drifted and for a while she forgot the cold as she looked them over, one by one.

There was a young girl sitting across at an angle from her with a slim leg crossed bobbing over her knee, very aware of the occasional rodent glance of a studious boy with glasses and books a few seats down. She was chewing gum and humming a jukebox tune; pretty in the vulgar and transitory way of the metropolitan peasant. They were like the students her Ph.D. fellowship forced her to teach at Municipal University, and she had never had one she liked. Marianne quickly despised the two and with a cynical sniff convinced herself that she would die before questioning either of them.

That was when a sudden realization snapped her back into her fear: *they* were not cold, nor was anyone else on the car, nor did any of them seem aware of the other less obvious sources of fear she felt all around them. Whatever was happening had chosen her alone.

The train came into a station and suddenly dim light was outside the windows and the fury under the vibrating floor was stilled. For a moment her panic again receded, but soon she clutched it back to her like a defending shield from the newer and nameless terrors outside the car.

Twenty-sixth Street was painted on the pillars. They were squat and arched and of an evil rotting brick that sucked the shadows from the catacomb light. Marianne knew with a memory as exact as it was chill that there was no 26th Street station, not anywhere in New York, but she tried in the one poised second before the doors opened to doubt it, to rise and leave quickly, knowing her sense of direction and knowledge of subway routes to be abominable and her imagination dangerously vivid. But her pride was stubborner than her fear and she would not look out again to see if it could be a 23rd or 28th Street station. It was not cowardice. She knew very well what she had seen and that even if she had read it wrong no subway station had ever looked like the one beyond her window. She had failed to convince herself of any doubt that she was brave enough to test, and she accepted the fact.

The horn-rimmed boy glanced up with a nervous start, gathered his books, looked furtively once more at the girl, and left; an old man stacked with dirty packages came in, seated himself with a weary sigh, and stared his anonymous hopelessness at the floor; and before Marianne could have moved, the doors slid shut, this time, she noticed, with a fast and angry hiss, and the train was on its way.

Marianne knew she should feel trapped now, but she was still more excited and curious than afraid, and she could not project into a complete and genuine fear her knowledge that now there was much of which to be afraid. For Marianne it was an old story: her intellect was only barely acquainted with her emotion and one of them had always been far ahead of the other.

Then down at the far corner of the car a distinguishedly shabby old gentleman she had not noticed before looked up startled, his expression wrinkling with anxious perplexity behind his ribboned glasses and the umbrella between his knees clasped so tightly that it seemed an alert and watching thing, as poised with life as the tail of a pointing dog. For a moment Marianne hoped that he was aware of all that she was, that he alone knew and felt and saw all that she did, but his tenseness loosened and quickly passed and the muscles of his face sagged back into a look of sleepy reflection, the indifferent resignation of the aged.

Marianne debated approaching him. She was sure he had forgot whatever alerted him and she had always very much disliked first approaching people she did not know, even tradesmen. But now, she told herself with appropriate grimness, she was desperate. A wish that Phillip were here to do this for her flashed across her mind as she rose with an irritated sigh and started toward his corner, grasping the straps as she went.

The colored map near the center door caught her eye. That would do as well, if she could figure it out. Maps had always confused Marianne, but then I think she would have been much more confused if the old gentleman she had not noticed at first had consented to speak to her.

She stood and stared at it closely, feigning annoyance and pouting with her large sensual lips, one hand on her hip and the other holding to the strap. She was a voluptuous woman, but tall enough and with a narrow enough waist to seem slimmer than she was, and this pose usually got her aid. But there were no likely prospects in the car; even the bald man had become oblivious to her as he pondered the wise prophecies of his sports pages. So she gave up and tried to puzzle it out herself.

She had thought at first she might be in an old tunnel that some emergency had forced into use. But this was a map of an entirely different system. As she studied its strangely webbed crisscrosses, she realized that she was on a train that did not go to Times Square or to 42nd Street at all, but stopped only at 37th Street and then at 54th before curving west under the Hudson River and into New Jersey, off the map.

Marianne smiled with pride at her skill. There it was on the map; everything was all right. Once more she instantly forgot all that had frightened her. This was some subway line she knew nothing about, probably some private suburban company's she had boarded by mistake. She had vaguely heard of one at a party once as the guests were leaving and this must be it. She would get off at 37th Street and walk up. Let Phillip wait for her for a change.

She sat down. She was relieved but a part of her was troubled. A part of her hoped against the rest of her that no station would appear and that when it did not appear the terrible and beautiful and impossible reality that had been promised would burst suddenly over her and transport her into another sphere, into another world and land. Till now Marianne's fears had been charged with thrills of violent anticipation, so that when the train pulled into another station as frightening as the first but clearly labeled as the 37th Street stop on all the pillars and walls, the sweet deliciousness of her fear passed from her lips as a sour taste. She rose to go, as flat and empty as the animation on a deflated balloon. That same part of her which caused all the trouble was again a disappointment.

It saw her life as a dulled and cheated slave to her rationality and struggled for her against the monotony it hinted too much thought might bring. A perverse imp, she had fed it until it grew fat and sleek, treasuring in the depths of her longing its coiled and winking image of the twisted and macabre. Long after she married Phillip it had crept under her desperate control, beaten but unashamed, waiting. A sly nostalgia would always remind her of how for a few years that image had stirred all the turmoiled waters of her secret self within, never once rippling the slick, silked surface that flowed as smoothly through her neatly channeled marriage and career as that of any other Red Cliff graduate.

It had first grasped her one bored summer in college when she had found herself helplessly plunged into reading all the mystery, fantasy and science fiction stories she could find with the sickly passion of the opium eater. Day after day, for weeks and months, she had lost herself in them until her eyes were red and reality had ceased to exist outside their bright and beckoning covers. The quality of the writing itself gradually meant less and less until the critical judgment of the future English instructor in her had been silenced and ignored by the irrational craving of the fanatic, and her laughing dismissal of it to her friends as "my one little morbid fascination, you know," had eventually been given up. She drifted into a study of the Tarot Cards, into Cabalism and astrology and down finally into occult journals and the supernaturalism of the Sunday supplements before the hot hunger was starved out of her. For it was never sated. Marianne just missed being enough of a fool to trap herself in some Brother- or Sisterhood, but she did miss that. When nothing came through with the strange goods her dissatisfied imagination demanded, and though she continued to read the best fantasy and science fiction, the little imp grew increasingly slender on the more refined diet, lately coming out of hiding only long enough to tease, then frustrate her. That was what it had done today.

When she stepped out the door no one followed and no one was waiting for another train. Now she really was alone. There were no brassière ads, no *Times* posters, no candy machines or transit maps on the leprous, scaling walls; and looking farther she could see no turnstiles or change booth and no stairway that might lead up to them. It was tempting, but she knew the subway waiting behind her to be substantial and at least on its way somewhere. She hesitated, shivering in the dank air, then reason reached to get the best of imagination and she turned awkwardly back to the door.

It shut casually in her face. It shut with the same slow and ominous hiss that had first awakened fear in her. The lights merged into a blurring streak, the roar into a straining whine, and the train was gone. A fading memory of the excited, then patient face of the old man trailed after it into the darkness.

This time it took Marianne several moments to match the quick and primal fear that grasped her with the slower exhilaration at her knowledge that the fear actually did exist. But she did. Her hesitation lessened and for a moment she even crossed to the other extreme, looking all about her with the shallow and giddy curiosity of the tourist who stands, guidebook in hand, wondering where to begin her exploration.

The station, if I may still call it that, was mammoth. The low and heavy archways stretched from the tracks as far as she could see, disappearing in the dim haze of the half-lit distance. Except for the gigantic scale it reminded her of an etching of some moldering German (or was it Dutch?) cathedral crypt she once glimpsed in the Fine Arts course she had taken at Red Cliff. But beneath the aging filth of these columns was a strangeness and a sleek sensuality of design and proportion, and even through the thick, twilight haze which seemed a very part of them gleamed a clean directness which had never known the Gothic mind or felt the soaring sturdiness of its spirit.

It awakened the squelched and dreaming imp in her and loosened its craving for the fantastic adventure which the architects of the place seemed to have dreamed into their design. Freed suddenly by it from her first disappointment, Marianne imagined she heard a hint of bigger things to come, and knew that she would follow wherever it led her, wherever it drove its unreined horse of air, into whatever world and through whatever time.

But nothing happened. The cold settled through her light spring dress and the bleak silence of loneliness began to throb a dull ache deep into her ears. But there were no fireworks; the imp had failed her. Marianne was learning.

She began walking to exercise the damp silence out of her. At first she

walked without aim, a sad and pathetic figure, pausing cautiously ever so
often to peer this way or that, furiously scratching her palm for a few
seconds and then impulsively heading off in a new direction. But gradually a desire for purpose led her where she thought the light might be a
very little stronger. She was not sure, and indeed, it was an illusion, but
now that the imp was proved and dismissed for good as an impostor it
gave her a goal until some more subtle symbol could come to guide her.

Focusing upon it, her thoughts darted back from meandering curiosity
to an intense but largely intellectual awareness of her danger. For Marianne accepted her situation as evident truth much more readily than she
had many of the phenomena of her everyday experience. She was concerned with her own awareness of the situation now, not with the situation itself. It was there she knew her real danger lay, and with each step
ringing its echoes all about her, she stepped a separate way within herself,
balancing on a taut line of rationality that divided her buried hysterical
fear from her bubbling, passionate recklessness. She knew the former
could cripple and the latter instantly destroy her if once she slipped and
fell.

Marianne tried to change the subject in her mind. "Poor Phillip, what
must he be thinking by now?" she managed to murmur aloud, hoping
the volume would strike though the silence and stifle her fear.

She had not really given Phillip much consideration. She wondered
whether she ever had. One advantage to marriage was in being able to
forget that entire department of life which had to do with the serious
importance of men. She did love Phillip, but they did not know each
other very well; each had his own work and interests, and they had only
been married a little over three years. Phillip was educated, liberal, attractive and successful, and that was what she had wanted. Once he had been
more, but she had soon stamped out of him the fresh and eager directness
with which she had originally fallen in love, all the while watching
herself kill his love for her, indifferent and unable to do a thing about it.
He was from Maine and she never let him forget it in her mockery of
what she liked to call his naïveté. He had hoped that her interests would
be her teaching career, her marriage, and the family she refused to have.
He had openly come to dislike her facile friends, saying he "damned well
wasn't one of *her* liberals," and the many educational and political committees which had filled her life since college that he had once merely
called useless, shallow and insincere, he had lately begun quietly to

ıgnore. Still, he was in all other ways as considerate as in their first year
of marriage. If anything, under all her impetuous sarcasm and elaborate
suspicions, Phillip had grown more patient and understanding, sweeter
and kinder to her than he had ever been before. The spark was dead, she
knew, but Marianne had no complaints; they got along.

But anyway — poor Phillip; he would be terribly worried by now.
Marianne wished *she* could worry about something. She had walked
more than half a mile and the chill was seeping back into her again.
Perhaps she could become worried about catching a cold. It did seem
colder now and she had seen nothing but the archways stretching away
in all directions, and no change in the dim light that filtered down from
everywhere with maddeningly equal intensity.

Again she wondered whether she were mad. This time it was an idle
thought, but still not without appeal. It would explain a good many
things about her and about what seemed to be going on, but now she
doubted whether she could ever convince herself of it. Besides, she
smiled, remembering one of the questions she had prepared the night
before for the final, Tom O'Bedlam had described all of it long ago so
accurately that she knew she was blocked from that escape, or at least
blocked from the kind of madness and escape Tom had known:

> *That of your five sounde senses*
> *You never be forsaken,*
> *Nor wander from your selves with Tom*
> *Abroad to begg your bacon.*

"Wander from your selves with Tom" . . . poor Tom, he should
know. Poor Marianne, she smiled, but with a little yearning, *she* could
never know what it was to wander from her five sound senses. She was
too sane to do anything more than toy with them, as was the fashion
among the elite bohemians she knew, and beneath all her muddled moder-
nity Marianne was just smart enough to know it. Poor Phillip, poor
Marianne — she played with the word — never to know the visioned madness that had consumed the mind and soul of poor Elizabethan Tom.

To Marianne, "Tom O'Bedlam's Song" distilled all the terror and fury
of lunacy the world had ever known together with a buried but very
important something more. That last and finest stanza was to her an
embodiment of the whole immense romance of the adventurous spirit,

ever seeking to conquer some new and fantastic unknown:

> With an host of furious fancies,
> Whereof I am commander,
> With a burning speare, and a horse of aire,
> To the wildernesse I wander.
> By a Knight of ghostes and shadowes
> I summon'd am to Tourney
> Ten leagues beyond the wide world's end.
> Me thinke it is noe journey.

And with that song, some anonymous sixteenth-century lunatic had struck the chord that lured the first eccentric cave man on a paddled log across an unknown water, and that one day would drive his ultimate grandchildren to their smug seduction of the stars.

Marianne sighed at the thought, knowing it could not apply to her. Something was lacking. Perhaps if she had been a man. . . . She looked about her at the faintly revolting but ominously beautiful architectural desolation, stretching, it seemed, for miles in all directions. Only to stand and look at it was like sipping the delicacy of a fine and evil wine from a cup crusted by alien ages and distant outer worlds. It made her want to feel that emotion of the poem, that wild, clean passion — that burning spear of adventure gone crazy. But for her there was nothing to kindle it, and even a secondhand emotion — an "understanding" of it — would make no real difference to her now, she was beginning to realize, because she was in the very situation the poem described. What difference could it possibly make how she reacted? This was no story to her; she was a pulsing, breathing participant of a *fantasy*.

But if she were not beyond the wide world's end, and were mad, what were the furious fancies whereof she was commander? The arches? They were stone. The light? It came from nowhere and everywhere but it cast shadow. The cold on the warm spring day? She was still shivering and her nails where the polish was chipped were gray with the damp chill. Tom, poor Tom; he *knew* they were real, where she had the choice to doubt either nothing, or everything. This was not at all the way it was supposed to be. In fact, under the brilliant glaze of her fear, it was drab and uncomfortable.

By the time Marianne turned a corner and saw a staircase spiraling above her into the roof about ten yards to her right she was not in the mood to be impressed. There was no other in sight and no wall or door near it. It stood alone, unmarked by distinction in any way.

She would climb it, there was no question about that. Even if there had been another choice, this was too neatly convenient for Marianne to resist.

She was winded, and leaned back against the stairway's central pillar. She lit a cigarette. There was no end to the arched colonnades and she hoped that whenever she went back there would be some other way out. As she looked around at them for what she hoped was the last time, she again felt attraction mixed with repulsion, and both much too strongly for her ordinarily mild and vague tastes toward any form of sculptured mass. They were too coolly slick under their anciently spotted surfaces; an eloquent architecture sickened and cancered by a clambering organic decay.

Marianne wondered for the hundredth time as she looked at them, groaning under a heavier weight than she knew was anywhere in the world, what the greater structure above her could be or have once been, and how deeply underground she was beneath it. There were only the arches as far as she could see and they gave no clue. Only her one lone staircase could answer her questions and it could well curve spiraling upon itself for thousands of dizzy feet above her before it came to the surface. Or back onto itself, she thought, if that was the trick of the plot, for Marianne still thought she knew them all.

Through habit and a not quite subconscious anticipation, Marianne adjusted her hair, smoothed on lipstick and pulled her bodice down more flatteringly over the generous swell of her bosom. Then she mashed out her cigarette against the wall as cruelly as she could, as was also her habit, and began to climb the stairs, wandering, she was thinking, to whatever wilderness there was above.

But the stairway coiled about itself for only a few yards, about as far as the average climb to a subway exit, and opened suddenly into the shadowed back of a long rubbish-filled room. At the front, it looked out through a dirt-smeared window into an empty and silent street.

Marianne shrugged away her mistake indifferently and snapped on a light switch near the stair. There was no evidence here of the building that was implied by the arches below that she had walked through for more than an hour; no evidence that the room was anything but a part of an ordinary building in a very bad state of repair. Then, unexpectedly, its very ordinariness began to excite her. She had scratched at the worming itch in her palm too often and too hard but now under its surface muscular ache an angry nervousness squirmed again for her attention. She went to the door.

It creaked protestingly but opened easily. It was made of raw unplaned wood and had a wooden lever handle. Marianne could not tell how it was fastened together; the joints were very close but neither nailed nor bolted.

The first thing she noticed was the stillness and silence of the street and the city as far as she could see. Next, and in an instant she realized she was not in any New York City she had ever seen, nor very probably even in the twentieth century.

The streets and sidewalks were cobbled with huge, sea-tinted stones, and fine long grass grew high between them. The sky was bright gray, like sooty buttermilk, and the air was moist and thin and chill. Trickles of clear water curled in worn ruts between and across the cobbles to a great rusty grating at the far curbing. The houses were high-gabled and tall, and had slim, lead-paned and arch-pointed windows and colonnaded verandas that overhung the street. Cool vines hung down from them and coiled about the windows. They were dark and there was no noise of life anywhere behind them, and outside in the streets there was not even the sound of birds.

It was a disappointing landscape for time travel, but Marianne was glad she had not been completely cheated. For a minute she wanted very much to believe she was in seventeenth-century New York and that these buildings were Dutch, but they looked just as much Venetian as Dutch and not really very much like either. If it were the past she was in, she wondered what language would be spoken and whether she would be able to teach the twentieth century to somebody. But — and here she had a moment's uneasiness — everything was a little wrong for any historical identification she could ever hope to make.

The streets twisted through a dead city. But a dead city where the ruin had been held in suspension and the rot drawn back from them by a hand that had touched and arranged everything in a pattern that had no reflection in event or time. No huge, unwieldy incredible world had struck at her eyes as she stepped into the street, but one all too much like the one she knew. It was the similarities, not the differences, that chilled her spirit as numb as that dank city below had chilled her bone and muscle. Yet it would have made no difference how much she knew — no difference how many Fine Arts courses she had taken instead of that short easy one her sophomore year — no one could have positioned this city into a time and place that Marianne could know.

This air was comfortable, but as thin as on a mountain top, and it had a faint innocuous odor she knew she would never place. The colors were dull and heavy; colors drawn from earth and sand and ocean, thick, bulging, and a little tired; even the red berries and blossoms on the vines and shrubs were as dark and secret as their leaves. The pitted stone of the buildings had been cut large for homes, if that is what they were, and their joints were fitted in a mortarless hairline only faintly discernible a few feet way. The glass in the lead panes of the windows was tinged with a green that reflected light with the pale sheen of still, tropical seas. They were deeply set in great rows of darkly patterned tile blocks that bordered each window along the street. Small bells hung over the street above the doors, a thong dangling down from each of them, beaded handles at their tips. The decay eating away at the colonnades below had been here arrested, the force of its hunger imprisoned in a frozen sleep, marred neither by touch nor time.

Marianne was quiet. She no longer heeded the discomforting cold or damp. For Tom, she remembered enviously, it had been much easier. But for her the rules were being broken too frequently, and a dull confusion had replaced the old indifference that had earlier masked her fear. Through that confusion she suspected she could never be excited or thrilled by all that was happening to her, because now her fear had grown far too deep within to permit any shallower level of reaction.

She crossed the street to a diagonally opposite corner. The incongruous sewer grating she had noticed yawned underneath and the bright clean water of the street gurgled softly down into it.

As she stepped to the corner's curbing she saw the street sign for the first time. Marianne started, relieved and yet somehow disappointed at its near-familiarity. It was squat, only waist high, and was brick up to metal arms much like those she had always seen in New York. The sign was in English and told her she was at 37th Street and Ninth Avenue. But this 37th Street was not perpendicular to this Ninth Avenue, as she knew all streets in New York above 14th were to all avenues, but ran crookedly back and forth at a sharp northeast angle up across the city. It was one more incongruous detail, out of place for either world.

But nothing is incongruous if viewed from the correct vantage point, however difficult it sometimes may be to attain it. A surrealist landscape of objects foreign to each other and arranged upon a plane foreign to them all appear commonplace enough once one is within it; after a few minutes of looking about, Marianne understood this. She was not so much bothered by an entire world incongruous to her own as she was by those details that seemed even incongruous to it. This street sign, the sewer grating, the electric light at the stairhead, and the vague likeness of the entire street to seventeenth-century Venice or Holland were bits of the ordinary world she knew which jarred against the total effect of the extraordinary one she was in. They were like the fine, hairlike grass shooting up damp and long between the cobbles at her feet, too pale for the seemingly perpetual water trickling among its roots, and yet too thick and lush ever to be so pale. The grass particularly disgusted her, its sharp and alien beauty more revolting than any familiar ugliness.

Marianne stared at the street sign a moment, considering as quickly as possible. She could find some other, some stranger way to follow, or even go back down into the arches to seek the subway again. But for once her decision was rapid. Since it was a choice of following inconsistencies, she compromised, choosing neither to dare too much nor to cringe back just yet. Instead, she chose the way most nearly like New York, heading up the street toward the traditional location of Times Square. Perhaps the same thing had happened to Phillip; perhaps he would even be there waiting for her. A nervous pang slashed through her so quickly she could not recognize it as guilt, and she instinctively glanced back over her shoulder as she entered the gloom of the narrow twisting street: she did not want to think about Phillip now.

The buildings hung far over her, black and formless in the sudden, too heavy shadow, and Marianne was not surprised when after a hundred yards or so the street turned sharply, became serpentine, and slithered down a long steep hill. She stood still a moment, peering into its narrow spaces. Through the thick gloom cast darkly down upon the cobbles from the hulking structures above her, she could see a gradual widening of the street into a small and desolate square, and in its center could barely discern the dim shape of a dead fountain with a thin tree bending over it.

She smoothed her hand over her hair once, took a deep breath, and headed down the hill, fearing it would fade and vanish as she approached it — that it was all an illusion like the brightening light she had followed through the arches somewhere beneath her. But by now I think that Marianne knew it did not matter, that she realized she had no sure method for distinguishing illusion from reality, and that she must be prepared to accept everything with equal credulity.

The fountain square was dark, but the sky was still a vast bright gray. Its light shone irrelevantly, a huge, remote, and disassociated blank, and cast no shadow on the dark earth spread beneath it. The fountain was nondescript, and, Marianne thought, probably vulgar; and the tree (though a common poplar) was unfamiliar to her. She went on.

"If you hurry, you can make it back."

Marianne turned on her heel, her mouth opened and eyes startled. "What — ?" she gasped, not thinking, not seeing.

"If you hurry, you can make it back."

He was a tall ugly man, ragged, but proud perhaps, and of no particular age. He was standing on the corner of one of the square's side streets. She realized with an irrelevant shame that he had been there all along, watching her.

"I — I don't understand."

"If you hurry *now*, you can make it back."

"But who are you? Where am I? What — ?" She stopped, her lip trembling uncontrollably.

He smiled and bowed his head slightly. "You may call me Benjamin." He stated it directly, a simple and convenient fact for her to know. "Don't worry," he added. "You are no place that matters. But hurry."

"Is it — *time* — I'm caught in? Is this the past? Or the future? I'm from nineteen-fifty — "

"All right." His voice was tired and patient. "Stay."

"But I *do* want to go back. Please, I do! I just wanted — Oh what's the use? Nothing makes sense."

There was no answer. Benjamin was motionless at his corner on the opposite side of the little square. The fountain and tree were between them. He was half turned back into the street behind him, waiting One by one the seconds strained away from each other. Marianne's palm was aching and tingling viciously.

"Tell me!" she screamed, the tension shattering off from her like glass upon the cobbles as she ran down their slope toward Benjamin. "Tell me how to get back to New York. You must tell me!"

Benjamin looked down at her, serene and undisturbed. "It was New York?" he said, with faint interest, almost to himself. "You go back any way — the way you came — it does not matter. But it is late."

He gazed upward, closely reading the flat and featureless sky. "Yes. It is too late," he emphasized slowly. "You come with me." There was weary resignation in his voice. He turned and began climbing the street in back of him. "It is not far," he added.

"Come with you? But — " Again she cut herself short as she realized Benjamin was moving away from her up the hill.

"What do you mean, 'too late'?" she called frenziedly after him.

Benjamin ignored her.

Marianne stood shaking with fury and frustration for a moment of terrible silence. Benjamin would soon be far beyond her. This was the wilderness, Tom's wilderness, and she could not be left alone in it. She could not be left alone to find her own way back out of it, not now.

"Wait," she called, breaking and running suddenly after him, her blouse loose and her thick long hair tumbling wildly about her face. "Please wait for me!"

Benjamin turned, and stood at the top of the hill waiting for her, as lifeless-seeming as the inanimate world in which he moved.

"There was no need to run," he said, when she caught up with him and they began to walk together. "Now there is no hurry."

Marianne decided it was her turn not to answer, her not very penetrating or coordinated mind (which worked well and sometimes even excellently on any one level but which had never once managed to broaden or deepen her grasp of a problem by considering questions that were not immediately related to the situation) considering nothing further than the first vague and obvious plan that had occurred to it: to ingratiate herself and pretend acceptance of all the little which Benjamin would say until she had somehow won his confidence and found out from him a way to get back.

She said nothing for a moment and they walked in silence to the top of the hill. The houses began to thin apart as they began a descent into a wide valley below.

"Well," Marianne began again, tossing her head with inappropriate cuteness, "my name is Marianne Smith."

"Was it Mary once?"

"Why, how did you know?"

"Mary would be too plain for you when you married a man named Smith."

Marianne was stunned, then angry, but I am afraid all she could manage was "That's insulting!" and "How dare you?" and a spluttering "And how did you know I was married, anyway?" before she choked silent.

Benjamin's long ugly face turned heavily toward her. His eyes were large, impenetrable, and very mild. "I meant no harm," he said. As he said that Marianne knew it was true, and she was instantly angered because she did know it and because she could say nothing that could either disguise her shame or her resentment for feeling the shame. She scowled, pouting her lips.

"I am sorry," Benjamin went on, answering her real question with a quick glance at the proud expensiveness of her wedding finger's glittering, modern, ostentatious rings, "but numerous women from your New York dislike plainness. I did not know it would offend you."

Marianne could say nothing. What part of the offense had not been false had been slight and both were now destroyed. But it had been another sidetrack, Benjamin was making a fool out of her and though she disliked it, she could find no handy way to defend herself. She *had* changed her name, and being sophisticated (a quality Benjamin obviously neither recognized nor understood) abhorred plainness, abhorred any simplicity of dress or manner that was not calculated to attract covetous men or impress envious women. She fumed because Benjamin had spotted it, mocked it, and, she thought, used it to keep her from asking too many questions.

But it was not so much Benjamin's polite accusation of pride that silenced her (for which he had reasons designed only to lessen her eventual hurt and despair) as it was the sheer number of unrelated questions that bred together like anxious insects in her throat, finding no escape by tongue into words. Now that she was at last confronted by the most startling questions a mind could ask, she was unable to grasp even one of them with her voice and break the irritation she always felt when she had nothing to say.

For Benjamin frightened her. If she could get at him, Marianne was certain he would answer all that confused or disturbed her. It was a simple, neat answer she wanted and she saw no reason why Benjamin should not have it. Marianne distrusted subtleties. Only on a printed page or in the classroom were they real to her. She best liked the thick, liberal, all-inclusive statements about life, and since she had never found enough respectably intellectual ones to make much sense out of things, she held hard and tightly to the few she did possess.

Benjamin had said nothing since his apology.

"It seems to me you could be a little more honest with me, Benjamin," Marianne remarked with throaty sincerity.

"Not yet," he answered. He nodded. "This is our valley. When near, the details have their own beauty, as in the city. But I am the only one who ever bothers to leave it."

The valley was a deep broad field. It stretched rolling and gross, like a fat woman sleeping under a dull green bedspread, and was dotted by tufts of gaunt, occasional houses like the ones in the city, empty and lifeless, but neat, sealed, and like everything else, waiting.

"It's — it's horrible," Marianne whispered over her shudder. "I don't see how you ever live here."

Benjamin ignored the disgust in her voice. "If you are hungry, someone will find food for you." There was no humorous play on her comment in his remark. He was merely changing the subject again.

"Fine!" Her teeth edged the word with sarcasm, but its thrust was wasted.

"Food is not easy here."

"Why?" she asked. It was another word she could always coat with cold contempt.

Benjamin was silent a moment, wondering whether Marianne was ready for his answer. He decided and spoke. "We must forage," he said, and his own despair caved imperceptibly under the words, like a coffin under the smooth green of its grave.

Marianne turned to him, an echo of his desolation ringing in her voice. "I don't understand. There's a whole city there — fields — land everywhere."

"It is not a city; not in any time. You saw that. And little good grows in the ground. To live is to forage."

To live is to forage: the words were bitter and awful. Out of the chill that fell like a shadow upon her from his flat calm voice a visioned face flashed terror across her mind — a lunatic: the leather cap and straw hair, pale laughing eyes, the nonsense dance of the singsong tenor:

> "... Nor wander from your selves with Tom
> Abroad to begg your bacon."

She clutched at his arm impulsively, violent dizziness flooding through and out of her. "Oh, Phillip — " she cried weakly.

"Your husband?"

"He called me — "

"Yes. I know how it usually happens."

Marianne began to cry as she had never cried before, softly, deeply. "Oh, Phillip, Phillip," she repeated over and over again between her sobs, guilt and regret crowding into her small memory.

Benjamin held her gently and firmly until she ceased. He smelled of damp leaves.

"Marianne," he said softly, "Marianne, there is no way back. There is no way back because there is no way here. It happens."

It was impossible for Marianne to accept his words as truth quite yet. The trouble lay in that sharp division in her of emotion and intellect, the weak double core that simplified onto a single uncoordinated level all that came her way. The jealous two had never worked together and either could allow her moods and ideas to be quickly changed at will, and without the other, either could also let her believe anything she wished. She was instantly afraid and actually incapable of doing anything but ignoring the complex reactions that were demanded by those certain realizations now forced upon her. For the last desperate time she could only try to change the face of her mood — a final coin flipped impulsively into the air to be caught and held for the gamble of a future idle guess.

She flung her head back proudly and the old stimulus was immediate. Against this strange earth she felt the countless human centuries, her brilliant parents, her four years at Red Cliff and three as the youngest member in the English department of Municipal University swell and surge through her. "I'll find a way," she said. It was a simple and satisfying answer and she delivered her favorite smile with bright confidence.

Benjamin's face was expressionless. "No. All would have vanished if you had ever denied it. Others have succeeded. But now — it is too late."

His words knifed through her thin, synthetic courage; she instantly and vividly remembered the old man with the umbrella, and those other crucial seconds after she had met Benjamin. But she soothed the wound of the offending memory. "Don't worry, I'll get back. I have to give a test on Elizabethan lyric poetry to a class of grocers' children." Her voice was gay, a cousin to her cocktail voice.

Benjamin gazed slowly over her face and looked down into her eyes as he patted her gently on the arm. "Please don't try," he said.

She bit her lip as she turned away, but tasted a bitter pleasure in the tension of frustrated suspense she sensed in Benjamin's remarks and answers. She would not pump him for information yet. She could enjoy the huge little mystery, show indifference to him, and pretend to have her own secrets and plans.

Benjamin waited a moment for her to speak and when she did not, turned away from her purposefully and pointed down the hill to a cluster of huts ringed around a flat and shallow hollow in which chairs and tables were scattered haphazardly. No life was visible.

"I will take you there. We are few and it is peaceful. You will find no trouble."

This was the knight of ghosts and shadows who was summoning her to Tourney. It looked a very dull one. She shrugged and fluffed her hair behind her ear. Her anger now was that she could not get ahead of him, that he alone of all men ignored her best tricks, one after the other. Marianne found it attractive and wondered what the secret was; it never occurred to her that Benjamin did not even notice them.

She grasped the advantage of his introspection with a superior tone. "I should think you would live in the houses or in the city. Why don't you want to rebuild things and start over?"

He smiled a quick but patient smile back over his shoulder at her question and began walking down the hill. "Come," he called back.

Marianne knew better than not to follow him this time, but a renewed rage burst hotly over her as she caught up with him.

"Why don't you answer me, you — " She grabbed at his arm as she had before.

He flung it easily from him. "Nothing was built for us and nothing can be used, nothing is over and nothing, nothing at all, can ever be begun. Things here are the way they are and are the same everywhere." He turned to her, small new fires at the centers of his eyes. "Don't you see that?"

Marianne flushed. "Well," she said determinedly, "you said the ground's no good either. Why don't you go somewhere else? You know you could do *something,* Benjamin," she added, a trifle condescendingly.

"We can do nothing. Nor can you."

"But why?" In her earnestness, Marianne had forgotten her anger; now she wanted only to get to the point. "If you didn't build everything here, what happened to the others, the ones who did? And where are *you* from then?"

"Questions and answers have no point. We are from our various places, like you. No 'others' were ever here, Marianne. Please understand that!" He looked at her for a moment and a deep, perhaps a personal pain dimmed his eyes. "Pieces of time, pieces of places, slipped here and almost made another place and time, one as real as the one you knew."

"That's why everything looks so — so *almost* familiar?" Benjamin's tone had quieted her again. "Those streets back there — something like places and times I know about. . . ." Her voice trailed off.

"This is a place of the things that did not quite happen, Marianne,"

Benjamin interrupted her groping thoughts, "a place of man's unchosen alternates. Perhaps there are others; I do not know. But in one way this is failure itself. If it had succeeded, this would have been a world of slightly different wars and histories and slightly different tastes, a world, it seems, whose empire would never have gone far from the sea, a world of people a little different in every way. But, their world and their time were stillborn with them. So you see, they never really existed at all."

A shallow and defensive suspicion flared one last time in Marianne's voice. "How do you know so much about it?" she asked. "I'm not so sure you —"

"I know little; I said that once. It was long before memory here, not long ago, remember, but before memory. So no one can tell what happened, and be certain." Scorn lapped a quick thin wave over his words. "Go, do, and think what you will, Marianne!"

"Benjamin, please — " Marianne stammered. She turned away and looked around her. "It's so confusing — even the air and sky are different here and nothing moves. Everything is — everything — "

"Everything is *stuck,*" he finished for her. "It failed, grew tired and stopped, but 'stuck' is the better word. Now it is outside time, Marianne, outside all space that can be named." His voice fell. "I wish I did know all. But no man knows time and we can see no more of its relativity here, outside, than say, your Phillip, back within it, even though we are victims of that relativity itself. This world is time's refuse heap, or one of them, stuck where it could be conveniently found by those odd few who always wanted it from their own beginnings."

Marianne thought hard a moment. "Oh, Benjamin," she cried then, desperation and humility, despair and sincerity welling up together in her voice. "But this 'time' that is wrong; why — what did it do to me? *When* are we?"

"It did nothing to you, Marianne. Time is not wrong. It is you. You must understand one thing: this is not past or future, not behind or ahead of the world you knew, or slightly knew. It is — *elsewhere.*"

"But it *is* the earth. I mean, in a way. . . ." She tried to begin again. "You said — "

"It is a cousin earth. Look," he nodded down to the ominous valley that stretched westward to a flat and greasy Hudson and eastward to jungled swamps that would be the East River, "only the form, not the features, are here. It is an elsewhere earth, similar, but nothing that ours could have ever been or become within its own directions of time."

Marianne's face was empty, blank from the comfortable mask that had been ripped away from its original, long forgotten foundation. Under it her elaborate inner systems were crumbling fast away, and she was losing the smoothness which had at first allowed her to ignore many things that had displeased her. Her confusion was more and more honest and direct: "But, Benjamin, that's what I was trying to say! Isn't it time that went wrong with me, however it happened? How could I have done — "

"Time does not go wrong. Time," he paused, searching until the possibly telepathic illustration sprang to him, "time is a wilderness we wander in."

The old, newly deepened image startled Marianne, but she did not show it. She was excited and came back quietly, "Then this is like — something like another trail through it?"

"No. There can be only one. That is why everything here is stopped. That is why everything is stuck, leading to no past or future. The random route through time is beaten by any humanity into the only trail it can know. There can be only one. This world is of the unchosen choices that slipped off. But you did not slip, nor did I, Marianne. We sought."

"It's no use. I don't understand." Her voice flattened. "I thought I did but I don't. Can't you — where are we, then?"

"Nowhere — I don't know. I understand little more than you." He sighed. "If I did I could talk and explain and demonstrate and it would be only an adventure story for both of us. But I have no map. This is not Africa, Marianne, and I have found no romance to tell you and no weapons for us to use."

He looked into her puzzled, frightened face. "Think this way," he went on sympathetically, and yet with a certain sense of climax. "If a trail, there are no parallels to it. There are no easy ways, perhaps no ways at all, to the past or future of your own path of time." He paused. "These are the unexplored woods along the wilderness way, Marianne. This is somewhere far beyond the border."

"Wait a moment." Marianne could go no further. She needed time to overtake the racing meanings in Benjamin's deceptively slow speech. She sat down upon a stone, weakly, her arm and hand stretched out stiffly behind her to ease her weight down. The village was very near now and Benjamin stood beside her, facing it. Smoke wisped from a roof-hole in one far hut.

"Wilderness — trails — it's all so confusing! Phillip called me to come — "

"But instead, you see, you had to come here."

"Ten leagues beyond the wide world's end," she added in a leaden monotone.

"Yes." Benjamin's voice was also heavy. "That says it."

They were silent.

"Oh, Benjamin, how was I trapped?" Marianne said wearily, not look-ing up.

He looked at her with a calm and direct dare. "By yourself."

She thought. She was trying, but it seemed very difficult to understand him. "But perhaps — even now, if I went back the way I — " She turned an earnest face up to him. "You see, I only got on the subway — "

"I know; I know how it happens. The subway is an incidental instru-ment. But it is no matter. There is no more a way to talk about it now than there is a way to escape it."

"But I must, I simply must escape it. Surely you understand that? What have I done to — "

Benjamin sharpened his voice. "It is your own fault you are here."

Hers was still calm, because the truth had not even yet effectively struck her. "My fault?" she repeated wearily. "But all I — "

"I know." He was gentle again. Benjamin played his difficult and unhappy part with a perfection of patience. "You are here because you are a fool. You are here because you always wanted to come here. You are — "

The sting was finally sharp and deep. She jumped to her feet. "Me? A fool?" The blood was in her face. She had forgotten herself and was unusually pretty. "You don't know much about me, I see!"

He laid his hand on her arm. "I know you, Marianne. You are not difficult."

She jerked it away and laughed with an assurance revived by her momentary scorn. "Well, anyway, Mr. Benjamin, you're here too, aren't you?"

"When you hear truth, do not act a play against it. Not any more. You are here for good; there is no one left to impress."

His voice beneath the harsh words seemed absurdly compassionate. Marianne knew it would be impossible to be angry or even to contradict it, and that drove her hurt and anger into another bitter and cheated silence.

Benjamin looked over her head, away into the distance. "I am from a time when it was not the fools who slipped and fell into this stagnancy. You are. If you were not a fool you would not be here. If you had ever found anything to do you would never have wandered your life away to search out this wilderness. If you were not a fool you would never have believed in it when you sensed it rising up before you." He looked down into her eyes, piercing, holding them to his. "From your world only the fools get as far as meeting me and many of them manage to get back in time."

Marianne sat dumbly, staring at the unsympathetic ground.

"Let us go, Marianne. You will see we have much to share. Once I thought I desired this, too. Like you I went too far," his voice fell, "though for other reasons. But come."

The truth was staring at her, there in the reiterated word "fool," and she knew it. But Marianne better knew that she could not allow herself to be convinced of it quite yet. She had still to get that other truth settled, the truth that said she could never get back to New York and to Phillip. She had first recognized it when Benjamin had said, "All right. Stay," but she had hurled it from her mind, then and again and again, only to have to seek and reapproach it later. There had to be a final statement before she could contain it as fact.

"No. I do appreciate your analysis of me and your eagerness to guide me farther," she said firmly and coolly and with false irony. "But I'm going back. I'm going back to those arches and somehow find that train."

She rose and adjusted her clothing to approximate neatness, smiled and extended her hand. The act, even if Benjamin knew it was one, was as good as she could make it.

"I have known no eagerness, not for a long time," Benjamin said, rejecting the offered hand. "Please do not try to find the train, Marianne. No one ever has. But if you did find the arches, and if you finally found a train, there still is no return track. Not now. You would only be carried farther out into the wilderness—" his hand waved over the landscape, "somewhere much farther."

He looked down at her. "And if you did not find a train you would never find me again. You would never find our village. You would not only be lost but alone."

Marianne's face contorted in desperation. "But before, you said I could get back—Benjamin, I just can't help it. I must—"

"Be wise, now."

The three words turned the key over the fast click of the lock. She collapsed upon the ground and wept, wrenching terrible sobs like purged devils from out of her breast and grinding her face and fist viciously into the dirt. "Oh, Phillip! I was so unfair, so self —" She bit her lip savagely until she tasted the warm sweet salt of blood. She would at least try to be no more of a fool than she had already been (and instantly she knew that now she had accepted that truth, too). She would keep the bitter grievance that had been her marriage a prisoner of her own self-reproach. She would at last know emotion in enjoying the torture of this one. She gave herself over to her demanding tears, and as she did Benjamin waited beside her, his hand touching her shoulder lightly, until finally they stifled themselves into muffled silence and she looked up to him.

"Benjamin, let me stay with you," she said, still choked with tears, her face glistening wet and anxious. "I want to stay with you. You said we had a lot to share, and I'll change —"

"We change some here, though nothing else does." He brought her gently to her feet. "And we stay together. But there is no pairing, Marianne. Except for duties."

This was what would have to be changed. Experience had taught her how, and fear was teaching her why. She could not face her own guilt alone, and within she had already heard it insisting to know her intimately for the first time. She had been regretting, but with a thin and indifferent blamelessness, the disease she had injected into her marriage, her slow deceptions of her friends and the betrayals of her own promise and dreams long ago. But Benjamin was summoning an unwelcome pang from somewhere beyond the memory of her earliest years that was transforming that vague regret into a keen remorse. Now before the mirror of a lonely inferno — her Inferno — her true features sharpening in the clearing fog that had steamed the glass, she watched the clear pale image of her own self-drowned love fade beyond her remembering reach, her Phillip's eyes accusing her of all she had been and never been, the patient lines of hurt and disappointment that had deepened their corners instantly recalling that other look she knew so well: the cold, young distrust that had always hardened in mockery upon the faces of her students. She would be dead to him and to them soon, a digit in the Missing Persons statistics and a curious, vanishing mystery in the minds of a few. But Phillip would never consent to die in her mind, unless she could focus her feelings upon someone else. She wanted to earn a partial redemption for herself in making up some of her wasted life here, to

Benjamin. But much more, she wanted the safety he offered her from her own memories. Whoever he was and wherever he was from, Marianne had known from the beginning under her fool's automatic defenses that he was a good man, and now that she was learning the nightmare truths about her own life she wanted at least to give that devotion and respect she had never had for anyone to him, in Phillip's name, as not only a sort of penance for a life that had been largely a drab, confused insult to itself and to others, but mainly as certain insurance against the horror of having to live with an increasing realization of her guilt, alone, here in her own hell.

She began with a mild flirtation. "We *could* pair, as you call it, Benjamin, if you think you could ever like me after the way I've been." She groped, then reached deep for the right argument. "You are right about me, you know, but I've been looking in at myself, and found, to my surprise," she smiled prettily, "that it isn't *all* bad in there. I know I could change if you think I'm worth the trouble."

Benjamin could say nothing. Marianne watched his eyes flicker pity, then die to resignation. This was her last chance, or there was nothing. A grenade of anonymous fear burst within her, but she stifled it, and only a slivered fragment quivered in her voice. "Well," she laughed, "Do you think I am?"

"You do not understand. Of course you are worth anything that's possible — "

"Well, then?" Her interruption was pitched high in anxiety.

"There is no love and little emotion here. There are no men and no women. There are only lost *people*. I am so very sorry. For I do believe much of what you say, and I think I understand the rest."

This was the climax of Marianne's life: this one exploding moment of absolute desperation was her summit and summation. In its electric flash over the city of her mind she saw that intricate maze in quick, stark clarity; how happiness had been lost by her almost from the beginning, and how here at this too early end, a bit of it could be regained and even be created out of old regrets and wrongs. That salvation could not be lost to her in some courtyard of chance, and down the alleyways another desperation streaked to catch control of it, loosing the hound of her fear upon her tiring intellect.

Her smile was tragic, horrible. "I'll bet I could change your mind, Benjamin. Why don't you come over here and give me an opportunity to see what I can do?" The garish words grated in her ear, distant and unreal, like the startled outburst of a deep-dreaming sleeper.

Benjamin did not answer and a soft, agonized shame fell in silence between them. It was very long before he spoke. "You will be indifferent to life soon." His voice was quiet. "For think, Marianne, there can be no hope or heart here." He paused again. "In an hour or two, you will be one more of us, and that will be all; that will be all. Most go quicker, but you —" Benjamin faltered that one time, "you are a girl" — he turned away — "of great vitality. I wish you had not had to come here."

He turned quickly back to her and placed both hands upon her shoulders. "Do not worry about what you said to me. I know what was in control of you." His fingers clenched her tightly. "Hold to your memories. They are not emotions, they are not feelings, but they are what you have now, Marianne. Hold to them."

Marianne wanted to cry, but her tears were gone. "How can I hold only to guilt?" she cried in despair. "I must do something — oh, you don't know what it is, what it's like to know all that I know about myself!" She moved to scratch her palm, then noticed that it no longer itched, and knew that it never would again. It bled slightly at the center where she had finally dug away the skin and it was very sore.

"Look what happened to me a moment ago!" she shouted up to his immobile face, and her voice fell. "I am sorry for all that —" she dismissed it, "but I know I'll die if there isn't something left for — for *us*," she blurted down her last barrier, "— besides memory. I shall die; I know I shall! Please don't tell me it's all — that it's all there is here!"

"Yes, memories are all we have left. But you have time for many of them and I am sure they all will not be so bad as that." He tried to be casual. Benjamin had come to like Marianne. "There will be much time for their mellowing. There is no death, you know, where there are no days and nights."

Her eyes glazed wide in sudden, horrified realization and she turned sharply away out of his hold to stare down the hill at the squalid village. She had heard the words of the great curse, and here even that was not to be enough. Now she finally grasped with her own hands the terrible throat of the world that lay in coma around her; the sick, chill fantasy in which she had plunged herself through a trick — a warp, they called it, she remembered from far, dimming memories — in time. And that throat was her own. By merely always desiring it, like the swift dark river of a cave under all the passages of her surface life, she had found this cancered appendage of space and time, and had burrowed her way like a worm down into it where she could live forever, three quarters dead and one quarter ill with her guilt of life. This was a patch of perpetual potentiality, incomplete, overgrown, timeless — a wild jumble of improbability, and it was what she had chosen. She was to be torn sexless by it and strung there head downward, in an eternal suspension of life and death.

Marianne remembered, as a lifetime ago, the colors that had first met her on the street, the old thin air, the filtered light and unbelievable sky, the dead, faceless intelligence watching dumbly from the arches and buildings, and the sensed difference in the subtle mosaic of detail that is the background of familiar experience and that here had been all wrong, distessellated, broken. She understood now why love, why almost all emotion, had spent itself out and died here: they were *extensions* of experience; there could be no room for them in a world without time, for here experience could only be known as a series of unconnected dots. It was not only decay, but all action and life that had become timeless in this terrible land, restrained and self-contained, as if a falling leaf could spin once in the air and shatter it all back into an ordered world of event and place. But because of that it bore a terrible beauty, for one knew the leaf would never fall or spin to break the bubble, and that the long, long moment of its world would always keep an agonized charm as it waited and watched, poised against a space it could never name.

Benjamin was breathing behind her. Like all else here, he was waiting for her to acknowledge the final truth. Now that the time had come, she knew there was no reason to avoid its pain. It was less than she had feared.

She noticed she had been mumbling. "It was an easy trip for me here, Benjamin," she said softly, when she had caught herself.

"Yes, it would seem so." He was silent a moment. "What was that you were repeating?"

"Oh, it doesn't matter. A part of a poem."

"Perhaps you would say it for me, before we — "

"All right." She looked past the village and into the wide, white, unblinking sky.

> *"With an host of furious fancies,*
> *Whereof I am commander,*
> *With a burning speare, and a horse of aire,*

To the wildernesse I wander.
By a Knight of ghostes and shadowes
I summon'd am to Tourney
Ten leagues beyond the wide world's end,
Me thinke it is noe journey."

"Thank you. I think I understand it, Marianne."

She looked at his face and into his eyes and saw what she had not looked for before. She saw the remains of a dreamer, and of the thinker who had driven the dreamer too far. "You understand it better than I do, Benjamin. For me it was only irony."

"It was only that for all of us." Benjamin smiled at her. "We must go now." He took her by the arm as he had done before. "You are tired. I will help you, if you wish."

"No," Marianne said, gently shaking off his hand and moving ahead of him as they began walking the last long slope down to the village. "If I must start sometime, I believe I can make it alone now, Benjamin."

They went through the gate and into the village, and as they did, Marianne passes totally from my interest as the chronicler of her story, for there and ever afterwards it was all as Benjamin had said.

LAWRENCE SARGENT HALL

*"The Ledge" is New England to the core in the hardihood of its
fishermen and the torture of their waiting wives. As the operator of "an
old-fashioned boatyard" on the coast of Maine, the author knows his
characters and has written one of the most forceful sea stories to appear
in recent years.*

*Lawrence Sargent Hall, a native of Haverhill, Massachusetts, was
graduated from Bowdoin College in 1936 and received his Ph.D. from
Yale in 1941. He lives on Orr's Island, Maine, and is chairman of the
English department at Bowdoin. His novel,* Stowaway, *published in
1961, won the Faulkner Foundation Award.*

The Ledge

ON CHRISTMAS MORNING before sunup the fisherman embraced his warm
wife and left his close bed. She did not want him to go. It was Christmas
morning. He was a big, raw man, with too much strength, whose delight
in winter was to hunt the sea ducks that flew in to feed by the outer
ledges, bare at low tide.

As his bare feet touched the cold floor and the frosty air struck his
nude flesh, he might have changed his mind in the dark of this special
day. It was a home day, which made it seem natural to think of the
outer ledges merely as some place he had shot ducks in the past. But he
had promised his son, thirteen, and his nephew, fifteen, who came from
inland. That was why he had given them his present of an automatic
shotgun each the night before, on Christmas Eve. Rough man though he
was known to be, and no spoiler of boys, he kept his promises when he
understood what they meant. And to the boys, as to him, home meant
where you came for rest after you had had your Christmas fill of action
and excitement.

His legs astride, his arms raised, the fisherman stretched as high as he
could in the dim privacy of his bedroom. Above the snug murmur of his

wife's protest he heard the wind in the pines and knew it was easterly as the boys had hoped and he had surmised the night before. Conditions would be ideal, and when they were, anybody ought to take advantage of them. The birds would be flying. The boys would get a man's sport their first time outside on the ledges.

His son at thirteen, small but steady and experienced, was fierce to grow up in hunting, to graduate from sheltered waters and the blinds along the shores of the inner bay. His nephew at fifteen, an overgrown farm boy, had a farm boy's love of the sea, though he could not swim a stroke and was often sick in choppy weather. That was the reason his father, the fisherman's brother, was a farmer and chose to sleep in on the holiday morning at his brother's house. Many of the ones the farmers had grown up with were regularly seasick and could not swim, but they were unafraid of the water. They could not have dreamed of being anything but fishermen. The fisherman himself could swim like a seal and was never sick, and he would sooner die than be anything else.

He dressed in the cold and dark, and woke the boys gruffly. They tumbled out of bed, their instincts instantly awake while their thoughts still fumbled slumbrously. The fisherman's wife in the adjacent bedroom heard them apparently trying to find their clothes, mumbling sleepily and happily to each other, while her husband went down to the hot kitchen to fry eggs — sunny-side up, she knew, because that was how they all liked them.

Always in winter she hated to have them go outside, the weather was so treacherous and there were so few others out in case of trouble. To the fisherman these were no more than woman's fears, to be taken for granted and laughed off. When they were first married they fought miserably every fall because she was after him constantly to put his boat up until spring. The fishing was all outside in winter, and though prices were high the storms made the rate of attrition high on gear. Nevertheless he did well. So she could do nothing with him.

People thought him a hard man, and gave him the reputation of being all out for himself because he was inclined to brag and be disdainful. If it was true, and his own brother was one of those who strongly felt it was, they lived better than others, and his brother had small right to criticize. There had been times when in her loneliness she had yearned to leave him for another man. But it would have been dangerous. So over the years she had learned to shut her mind to his hard-driving, and take what comfort she might from his unsympathetic competence. Only once or twice, perhaps, had she gone so far as to dwell guiltily on what it would be like to be a widow.

The thought that her boy, possibly because he was small, would not be insensitive like his father, and the rattle of dishes and smell of frying bacon downstairs in the kitchen shut off from the rest of the chilly house, restored the cozy feeling she had had before she was alone in bed. She heard them after a while go out and shut the back door.

Under her window she heard the snow grind dryly beneath their boots, and her husband's sharp, exasperated commands to the boys. She shivered slightly in the envelope of her own warmth. She listened to the noise of her son and nephew talking elatedly. Twice she caught the glimmer of their lights on the white ceiling above the window as they went down the path to the shore. There would be frost on the skiff and freezing suds at the water's edge. She herself used to go gunning when she was younger; now, it seemed to her, anyone going out like that on Christmas morning had to be incurably male. They would none of them think about her until they returned and piled the birds they had shot on top of the sink for her to dress.

Ripping into the quiet predawn cold she heard the hot snarl of the outboard taking them out to the boat. It died as abruptly as it had burst into life. Two or three or four or five minutes later the big engine broke into a warm reassuring roar. He had the best of equipment, and he kept it in the best of condition. She closed her eyes. It would not be too long before the others would be up for Christmas. The summer drone of the exhaust deepened. Then gradually it faded in the wind until it was lost at sea, or she slept.

The engine had started immediately in spite of the temperature. This put the fisherman in a good mood. He was proud of his boat. Together he and the two boys heaved the skiff and outboard onto the stern and secured it athwartships. His son went forward along the deck, iridescent in the ray of the light the nephew shone through the windshield, and cast the mooring pennant loose into darkness. The fisherman swung to starboard, glanced at his compass, and headed seaward down the obscure bay.

There would be just enough visibility by the time they reached the headland to navigate the crooked channel between the islands. It was the only nasty stretch of water. The fisherman had done it often in fog or at night — he always swore he could go anywhere in the bay blindfolded — but there was no sense in taking chances if you didn't have to. From the mouth of the channel he could lay a straight course for Brown Cow

Island, anchor the boat out of sight behind it, and from the skiff set their tollers off Devil's Hump three hundred yards to seaward. By then the tide would be clearing the ledge and they could land and be ready to shoot around half-tide.

It was early, it was Christmas, and it was farther out than most hunters cared to go in this season of the closing year, so that he felt sure no one would be taking possession ahead of them. He had shot thousands of ducks there in his day. The Hump was by far the best hunting. Only thing was you had to plan for the right conditions because you didn't have too much time. About four hours was all, and you had to get it before three in the afternoon when the birds left and went out to sea ahead of nightfall.

They had it figured exactly right for today. The ledge would not be going under until after the gunning was over, and they would be home for supper in good season. With a little luck the boys would have a skiff-load of birds to show for their first time outside. Well beyond the legal limit, which was no matter. You took what you could get in this life, or the next man made out and you didn't.

The fisherman had never failed to make out gunning from Devil's Hump. And this trip, he had a hunch, would be above ordinary. The easterly wind would come up just stiff enough, the tide was right, and it was going to storm by tomorrow morning so the birds would be moving. Things were perfect.

The old fierceness was in his bones. Keeping a weather eye to the murk out front and a hand on the wheel, he reached over and cuffed both boys playfully as they stood together close to the heat of the exhaust pipe running up through the center of the house. They poked back at him and shouted above the drumming engine, making bets as they always did on who would shoot the most birds. This trip they had the thrill of new guns, the best money could buy, and a man's hunting ground. The black retriever wagged at them and barked. He was too old and arthritic to be allowed in December water, but he was jaunty anyway at being brought along.

Groping in his pocket for his pipe the fisherman suddenly had his high spirits rocked by the discovery that he had left his tobacco at home. He swore. Anticipation of a day out with nothing to smoke made him incredulous. He searched his clothes, and then he searched them again, unable to believe the tobacco was not somewhere. When the boys inquired what was wrong he spoke angrily to them, blaming them for being in some devious way at fault. They were instantly crestfallen and willing to put back after the tobacco, though they could appreciate what it meant only through his irritation. But he bitterly refused. That would throw everything out of phase. He was a man who did things the way he set out to do.

He clamped his pipe between his teeth, and twice more during the next few minutes he ransacked his clothes in disbelief. He was no stoic. For one relaxed moment he considered putting about and gunning somewhere nearer home. Instead he held his course and sucked the empty pipe, consoling himself with the reflection that at least he had whiskey enough if it got too uncomfortable on the ledge. Peremptorily he made the boys check to make certain the bottle was really in the knapsack with the lunches where he thought he had taken care to put it. When they reassured him he despised his fate a little less.

The fisherman's judgment was as usual accurate. By the time they were abreast of the headland there was sufficient light so that he could wind his way among the reefs without slackening speed. At last he turned his bows toward open ocean, and as the winter dawn filtered upward through long layers of smoky cloud on the eastern rim his spirits rose again with it.

He opened the throttle, steadied on his course, and settled down to the two-hour run. The wind was stronger but seemed less cold coming from the sea. The boys had withdawn from the fisherman and were talking together while they watched the sky through the windows. The boat churned solidly through a light chop, flinging spray off her flaring bows. Astern the headland thinned rapidly till it lay like a blackened sill on the gray water. No other boats were abroad.

The boys fondled their new guns, sighted along the barrels, worked the mechanisms, compared notes, boasted, and gave each other contradictory advice. The fisherman got their attention once and pointed at the horizon. They peered through the windows and saw what looked like a black scum floating on top of gently agitated water. It wheeled and tilted, rippled, curled, then rose, strung itself out and became a huge raft of ducks escaping over the sea. A good sign.

The boys rushed out and leaned over the washboards in the wind and spray to see the flock curl below the horizon. Then they went and hovered around the hot engine, bewailing their lot. If only they had been already set out and waiting. Maybe these ducks would be crazy enough to return later and be slaughtered. Ducks were known to be foolish.

In due course and right on schedule they anchored at mid-morning in the lee of Brown Cow Island. They put the skiff overboard and loaded it with guns, knapsacks, and tollers. The boys showed their eagerness by being clumsy. The fisherman showed his in bad temper and abuse which they silently accepted in the absorbed tolerance of being boys. No doubt they laid it to lack of tobacco.

By outboard they rounded the island and pointed due east in the direction of a ridge of foam which could be seen whitening the surface three hundred yards away. They set the decoys in a broad, straddling vee opening wide into the ocean. The fisherman warned them not to get their hands wet, and when they did he made them carry on with red and painful fingers, in order to teach them. Once the last toller was bobbing among his fellows, brisk and alluring, they got their numbed fingers inside their oilskins and hugged their warm crotches. In the meantime the fisherman had turned the skiff toward the patch of foam where as if by magic, like a black glossy rib of earth, the ledge had broken through the belly of the sea.

Carefully they inhabited their slippery nub of the North American continent, while the unresting Atlantic swelled and swirled as it had for eons round the indomitable edges. They hauled the skiff after them, established themselves as comfortably as they could in a shallow sump on top, lay on their sides a foot or so above the water, and waited, guns in hand.

In time the fisherman took a thermos bottle from the knapsack and they drank steaming coffee, and waited for the nodding decoys to lure in the first flight to the rock. Eventually the boys got hungry and restless. The fisherman let them open the picnic lunch and eat one sandwich apiece, which they both shared with the dog. Having no tobacco the fisherman himself would not eat.

Actually the day was relatively mild, and they were warm enough at present in their woolen clothes and socks underneath oilskins and hip boots. After a while, however, the boys began to feel cramped. Their nerves were agonized by inactivity. The nephew complained and was severely told by the fisherman — who pointed to the dog, crouched unmoving except for his white-rimmed eyes — that part of doing a man's hunting was learning how to wait. But he was beginning to have misgivings of his own. This could be one of those days where all the right conditions masked an incalculable flaw.

If the fisherman had been alone, as he often was, stopping off when the

necessary coincidence of tide and time occurred on his way home from
hauling trawls, and had plenty of tobacco, he would not have fidgeted.
The boys' being nervous made him nervous. He growled at them again.
When it came it was likely to come all at once, and then in a few
moments be over. He warned them not to slack off, never to slack off, to
be always ready. Under his rebuke they kept their tortured peace, though
they could not help shifting and twisting until he lost what patience he
had left and bullied them into lying still. A duck could see an eyelid
twitch. If the dog could go without moving so could they.

"Here it comes!" the fisherman said tersely at last.

The boys quivered with quick relief. The flock came in downwind,
quartering slightly, myriad, black, and swift.

"Beautiful — " breathed the fisherman's son.

"All right," said the fisherman, intense and precise. "Aim at singles in
the thickest part of the flock. Wait for me to fire and then don't stop
shooting till your gun's empty." He rolled up onto his left elbow and
spread his legs to brace himself. The flock bore down, arrowy and
vibrant, then a hundred yards beyond the decoys it veered off.

"They're going away!" the boys cried, sighting in.

"Not yet!" snapped the fisherman. "They're coming round."

The flock changed shape, folded over itself, and drove into the wind in
a tight arc. "Thousands — " the boys hissed through their teeth. All at
once a whistling storm of black and white broke over the decoys.

"Now!" the fisherman shouted. "Perfect!" And he opened fire at the
flock just as it hung suspended in momentary chaos above the tollers.
The three pulled at their triggers and the birds splashed into the water,
until the last report went off unheard, the last smoking shell flew unheeded over their shoulders, and the last of the routed flock scattered
diminishing, diminishing, diminishing in every direction.

Exultantly the boys dropped their guns, jumped up and scrambled for
the skiff.

"I'll handle that skiff!" the fisherman shouted at them. They stopped.
Gripping the painter and balancing himself he eased the skiff into the
water stern first and held the bow hard against the side of the rock shelf
the skiff had rested on. "You stay here," he said to his nephew. "No
sense in all three of us going in the boat."

The boy on the reef gazed at the gray water rising and falling hypnoti-
cally along the glistening edge. It had dropped about a foot since their

arrival. "I want to go with you," he said in a sullen tone, his eyes on the streaming eddies.

"You want to do what I tell you if you want to gun with me," answered the fisherman harshly. The boy couldn't swim, and he wasn't going to have him climbing in and out of the skiff any more than necessary. Besides he was too big.

The fisherman took his son in the skiff and cruised round and round among the decoys picking up dead birds. Meanwhile the other boy stared unmoving after them from the highest part of the ledge. Before they had quite finished gathering the dead birds, the fisherman cut the outboard and dropped to his knees in the skiff. "Down!" he yelled. "Get down!" About a dozen birds came tolling in. "Shoot — shoot!" his son hollered from the bottom of the boat to the boy on the ledge.

The dog, who had been running back and forth whining, sank to his belly, his muzzle on his forepaws. But the boy on the ledge never stirred. The ducks took late alarm at the skiff, swerved aside and into the air, passing with a whirr no more than fifty feet over the head of the boy, who remained on the ledge like a statue, without his gun, watching the two crouching in the boat.

The fisherman's son climbed onto the ledge and held the painter. The bottom of the skiff was covered with feathery black and white bodies with feet upturned and necks lolling. He was jubilant. "We got twenty-seven!" he told his cousin. "How's that? Nine apiece. Boy — " he added, "what a cool Christmas!"

The fisherman pulled the skiff onto its shelf and all three went and lay down again in anticipation of the next flight. The son, reloading, patted his shotgun affectionately. "I'm going to get me ten next time," he said. Then he asked his cousin, "Whatsamatter — didn't you see the strays?"

"Yeah," the boy said.

"How come you didn't shoot at 'em?"

"Didn't feel like it," replied the boy, still with a trace of sullenness.

"You stupid or something?" The fisherman's son was astounded. "What a highlander!" But the fisherman, though he said nothing, knew that the older boy had had an attack of ledge fever.

"Cripes!" his son kept at it. "I'd at least of tried."

"Shut up," the fisherman finally told him, "and leave him be."

At slack water three more flocks came in, one right after the other, and when it was over, the skiff was half full of clean, dead birds. During the subsequent lull they broke out the lunch and ate it all and finished the hot coffee. For a while the fisherman sucked away on his cold pipe. Then he had himself a swig of whiskey.

The boys passed the time contentedly jabbering about who shot the most — there were ninety-two all told — which of their friends they would show the biggest ones to, how many each could eat at a meal provided they didn't have to eat any vegetables. Now and then they heard sporadic distant gunfire on the mainland, at its nearest point about two miles to the north. Once far off they saw a fishing boat making in the direction of home.

At length the fisherman got a hand inside his oilskins and produced his watch.

"Do we have to go now?" asked his son.

"Not just yet," he replied. "Pretty soon." Everything had been perfect. As good as he had ever had it. Because he was getting tired of the boys' chatter he got up, heavily in his hip boots, and stretched. The tide had turned and was coming in, the sky was more ashen, and the wind had freshened enough so that whitecaps were beginning to blossom. It would be a good hour before they had to leave the ledge and pick up the tollers. However, he guessed they would leave a little early. On account of the rising wind he doubted there would be much more shooting. He stepped carefully along the back of the ledge, to work his kinks out. It was also getting a little colder.

The whiskey had begun to warm him, but he was unprepared for the sudden blaze that flashed upward inside him from belly to head. He was standing looking at the shelf where the skiff was. Only the foolish skiff was not there!

For the second time that day the fisherman felt the deep vacuity of disbelief. He gaped, seeing nothing but the flat shelf of rock. He whirled, started toward the boys, slipped, recovered himself, fetched a complete circle, and stared at the unimaginably empty shelf. Its emptiness made him feel as if everything he had done that day so far, his life so far, he had dreamed. What could have happened? The tide was still nearly a foot below. There had been no sea to speak of. The skiff could hardly have slid off by itself. For the life of him, consciously careful as he inveterately was, he could not now remember hauling it up the last time. Perhaps in the heat of hunting he had left it to the boy. Perhaps he could not remember which was the last time.

"Christ —" he exclaimed loudly, without realizing it because he was so entranced by the invisible event.

"What's wrong, Dad?" asked his son, getting to his feet.

The fisherman went blind with uncontainable rage. "Get back down there where you belong!" he screamed. He scarcely noticed the boy sink back in amazement. In a frenzy he ran along the ledge thinking the skiff might have been drawn up at another place, though he knew better. There was no other place.

He stumbled, half falling, back to the boys who were gawking at him in consternation, as though he had gone insane. "God damn it!" he yelled savagely, grabbing both of them and yanking them to their knees. "Get on your feet!"

"What's wrong?" his son repeated in a stifled voice.

"Never mind what's wrong," he snarled. "Look for the skiff — it's adrift!" When they peered around he gripped their shoulders, brutally facing them about. "Down-wind —" He slammed his fist against his thigh. "Jesus!" he cried, struck to madness at their stupidity.

At last he sighted the skiff himself, magically bobbing along the grim sea like a toller, a quarter of a mile to leeward on a direct course for home. The impulse to strip himself naked was succeeded instantly by a queer calm. He simply sat down on the ledge and forgot everything except the marvelous mystery.

As his awareness partially returned he glanced toward the boys. They were still observing the skiff speechlessly. Then he was gazing into the clear young eyes of his son.

"Dad," asked the boy steadily, "what do we do now?"

That brought the fisherman upright. "The first thing we have to do," he heard himself saying with infinite tenderness as if he were making love, "is think."

"Could you swim it?" asked his son.

He shook his head and smiled at them. They smiled quickly back, too quickly. "A hundred yards, maybe, in this water. I wish I could," he added. It was the most intimate and pitiful thing he had ever said. He walked in circles round them, trying to break the stall his mind was left in.

He gauged the level of the water. To the eye it was quite stationary, six inches from the shelf at this second. The fisherman did not have to mark it on the side of the rock against the passing of time to prove to his reason that it was rising, always rising. Already it was over the brink of reason, beyond the margins of thought — a senseless measurement. No sense to it.

All his life the fisherman had tried to lick the element of time, by getting up earlier and going to bed later, owning a faster boat, planning more than the day would hold, and tackling just one other job before the deadline fell. If, as on rare occasions he had the grand illusion, he ever really had beaten the game, he would need to call on all his reserves of practice and cunning now.

He sized up the scant but unforgivable three hundred yards to Brown Cow Island. Another hundred yards behind it his boat rode at anchor, where, had he been aboard, he could have cut in a fathometer to plumb the profound and occult seas, or a ship-to-shore radio on which in an interminably short time he would have heard his wife's voice talking to him over the air about homecoming.

"Couldn't we wave something so somebody would see us?" his nephew suggested.

The fisherman spun round. "Load your guns!" he ordered. They loaded as if the air had suddenly gone frantic with birds. "I'll fire once and count to five. Then you fire. Count to five. That way they won't just think it's only somebody gunning ducks. We'll keep doing that."

"We've only got just two and a half boxes left," said his son.

The fisherman nodded, understanding that from beginning to end their situation was purely mathematical, like the ticking of the alarm clock in his silent bedroom. Then he fired. The dog, who had been keeping watch over the decoys, leaped forward and yelped in confusion. They all counted off, fired the first five rounds by threes, and reloaded. The fisherman scanned first the horizon, then the contracting borders of the ledge, which was the sole place the water appeared to be climbing. Soon it would be over the shelf.

They counted off and fired the second five rounds. "We'll hold off a while on the last one," the fisherman told the boys. He sat down and pondered what a trivial thing was a skiff. This one he and the boy had knocked together in a day. Was a gun, manufactured for killing.

His son tallied up the remaining shells, grouping them symmetrically in threes on the rock when the wet box fell apart. "Two short," he announced. They reloaded and laid the guns on their knees.

Behind thickening clouds they could not see the sun going down. The water, coming up, was growing blacker. The fisherman thought he might have told his wife they would be home before dark since it was Christmas day. He realized he had forgotten about its being any particular day. The tide would not be high until two hours after sunset. When they did not get in by nightfall, and could not be raised by radio, she might send somebody to hunt for them right away. He rejected this arithmetic immediately, with a sickening shock, recollecting it was a two-and-a-half-hour run at best. Then it occurred to him that she might send somebody on the mainland who was nearer. She would think he had engine trouble.

He rose and searched the shoreline, barely visible. Then his glance dropped to the toy shoreline at the edges of the reef. The shrinking ledge, so sinister from a boat, grew dearer minute by minute as though the whole wide world he gazed on from horizon to horizon balanced on its contracting rim. He checked the water level and found the shelf awash.

Some of what went through his mind the fisherman told to the boys. They accepted it without comment. If he caught their eyes they looked away to spare him or because they were not yet old enough to face what they saw. Mostly they watched the rising water. The fisherman was unable to initiate a word of encouragement. He wanted one of them to ask him whether somebody would reach them ahead of the tide. He would have found it possible to say yes. But they did not inquire.

The fisherman was not sure how much, at their age, they were able to imagine. Both of them had seen from the docks drowned bodies put ashore out of boats. Sometimes they grasped things, and sometimes not. He supposed they might be longing for the comfort of their mothers, and was astonished, as much as he was capable of any astonishment except the supreme one, to discover himself wishing he had not left his wife's dark, close, naked bed that morning.

"Is it time to shoot now?" asked his nephew.

"Pretty soon," he said, as if he were putting off making good on a promise. "Not yet."

His own boy cried softly for a brief moment, like a man, his face averted in an effort neither to give or show pain.

"Before school starts," the fisherman said, wonderfully detached, "we'll go to town and I'll buy you boys anything you want."

With great difficulty, in a dull tone as though he did not in the least desire it, his son said after a pause, "I'd like one of those new thirty-horse outboards."

"All right," said the fisherman. And to his nephew, "How about you?"

The nephew shook his head desolately. "I don't want anything," he said.

After another pause the fisherman's son said, "Yes he does, Dad. He wants one too."

"All right —" the fisherman said again, and said no more.

The dog whined in uncertainty and licked the boys' faces where they sat together. Each threw an arm over his back and hugged him. Three strays flew in and sat companionably down among the stiff-necked decoys. The dog crouched, obedient to his training. The boys observed them listlessly. Presently, sensing something untoward, the ducks took off, splashing the wave tops with feet and wingtips, into the dusky waste.

The sea began to make up in the mounting wind, and the wind bore a new and deathly chill. The fisherman, scouring the somber, dwindling shadow of the mainland for a sign, hoped it would not snow. But it did. First a few flakes, then a flurry, then storming past horizontally. The fisherman took one long, bewildered look at Brown Cow Island three hundred yards dead to leeward, and got to his feet.

Then it shut in, as if what was happening on the ledge was too private even for the last wan light of the expiring day.

"Last round," the fisherman said austerely.

The boys rose and shouldered their tacit guns. The fisherman fired into the flying snow. He counted methodically to five. His son fired and counted. His nephew. All three fired and counted. Four rounds.

"You've got one left, Dad," his son said.

The fisherman hesitated another second, then he fired the final shell. Its pathetic report, like the spat of a popgun, whipped away on the wind and was instantly blanketed in falling snow.

Night fell all in a moment to meet the ascending sea. They were now barely able to make one another out through driving snowflakes, dim as ghosts in their yellow oilskins. The fisherman heard a sea break and glanced down where his feet were. They seemed to be wound in a snowy sheet. Gently he took the boys by the shoulders and pushed them in front of him, feeling with his feet along the shallow sump to the place where it triangulated into a sharp crevice at the highest point of the ledge. "Face ahead," he told them. "Put the guns down."

"I'd like to hold mine, Dad," begged his son.

"Put it down," said the fisherman. "The tide won't hurt it. Now brace your feet against both sides and stay there."

They felt the dog, who was pitch black, running up and down in perplexity between their straddled legs. "Dad," said his son, "what about the pooch?"

If he had called the dog by name it would have been too personal. The fisherman would have wept. As it was he had all he could do to keep from laughing. He bent his knees, and when he touched the dog hoisted him under one arm. The dog's belly was soaking wet.

So they waited, marooned in their consciousness, surrounded by a monstrous tidal space which was slowly, slowly closing them out. In this space the periwinkle beneath the fisherman's boots was king. While hovering airborne in his mind he had an inward glimpse of his house as curiously separate, like a June mirage.

Snow, rocks, seas, wind the fisherman had lived by all his life. Now he thought he had never comprehended what they were, and he hated them. Though they had not changed. He was deadly chilled. He set out to ask the boys if they were cold. There was no sense. He thought of the whiskey, and sidled backward, still holding the awkward dog, till he located the bottle under water with his toe. He picked it up squeamishly as though afraid of getting his sleeve wet, worked his way forward and bent over his son. "Drink it," he said, holding the bottle against the boy's ribs. The boy tipped his head back, drank, coughed hotly, then vomited.

"I can't," he told his father wretchedly.

"Try — try —" the fisherman pleaded, as if it meant the difference between life and death.

The boy obediently drank, and again he vomited hotly. He shook his head against his father's chest and passed the bottle forward to his cousin, who drank and vomited also. Passing the bottle back, the boys dropped it in the frigid water between them.

When the waves reached his knees the fisherman set the warm dog loose and said to his son. "Turn around and get up on my shoulders." The boy obeyed. The fisherman opened his oilskin jacket and twisted his hands behind him through his suspenders, clamping the boy's booted ankles with his elbows.

"What about the dog?" the boy asked.

"He'll make his own way all right," the fisherman said. "He can take the cold water." His knees were trembling. Every instinct shrieked for gymnastics. He ground his teeth and braced like a colossus against the sides of the submerged crevice.

The dog, having lived faithfully as though one of them for eleven years, swam a few minutes in and out around the fisherman's legs, not knowing what was happening, and left them without a whimper. He would swim and swim at random by himself, round and round in the blinding night, and when he had swum routinely through the paralyzing water all he could, he would simply, in one incomprehensible moment, drown. Almost the fisherman, waiting out infinity, envied him his pattern.

Freezing seas swept by, flooding inexorably up and up as the earth sank away imperceptibly beneath them. The boy called out once to his cousin, there was no answer. The fisherman, marveling on a terror without voice, was dumbly glad when the boy did not call again. His own boots were long full of water. With no sensation left in his straddling legs he dared not move them. So long as the seas came sidewise against his hips, and then sidewise against his shoulders, he might balance — no telling how long. The upper half of him was what felt frozen. His legs, disengaged from his nerves and his will, he came to regard quite scientifically. They were the absurd, precarious axis around which reeled and surged universal tumult. The waves would come on and on; he could not visualize how many tossing reinforcements lurked in the night beyond — inexhaustible numbers, and he wept in supernatural fury at each because it was higher, till he transcended hate and took them, swaying like a convert, one by one as they lunged against him and away aimlessly into their own undisputed, wild realm.

From his hips upward the fisherman stretched to his utmost as a man does whose spirit reaches out of dead sleep. The boy's head, none too high, must be at least seven feet above the ledge. Though growing larger every minute, it was a small light life. The fisherman meant to hold it there, if need be, through a thousand tides.

By and by the boy, slumped on the head of his father, asked, "Is it over your boots, Dad?"

"Not yet," the fisherman said. Then through his teeth he added, "If I fall — kick your boots off — swim for it — downwind — to the island. . . ."

"You . . . ?" the boy finally asked.

The fisherman nodded against the boy's belly. " — Won't see each other," he said.

The boy did for the fisherman the greatest thing that can be done. He may have been too young for perfect terror, but he was old enough to know there were things beyond the power of any man. All he could do he did, by trusting his father to do all he could, and asking nothing more.

The fisherman, locked to his soul by a sea, held his eyes shut upon the interminable night.

"Is it time now?" the boy said.

The fisherman could hardly speak. "Not yet," he said. "Not just yet. . . ."

As the land mass pivoted toward sunlight the day after Christmas, a tiny fleet of small craft converged off shore like iron filings to a magnet. At daybreak they found the skiff floating unscathed off the headland, half full of ducks and snow. The shooting *had* been good, as someone hearing on the nearby mainland the previous afternoon had supposed. Two hours afterward they found the unharmed boat adrift five miles at sea. At high noon they found the fisherman at ebb tide, his right foot jammed cruelly into a glacial crevice of the ledge beside three shotguns, his hands tangled behind him in his suspenders, and under his right elbow a rubber boot with a sock and a live starfish in it. After dragging unlit depths all day for the boys, they towed the fisherman home in his own boat at sundown, and in the frost of evening, mute with discovering purgatory, laid him on his wharf for his wife to see.

She, somehow, standing on the dock as in her frequent dream, gazing at the fisherman pure as crystal on the icy boards, a small rubber boot still frozen under one clenched arm, saw him exaggerated beyond remorse or grief, absolved of his mortality.

JAMES BALDWIN

"This Morning, This Evening, So Soon" shows what it feels like to be a Negro who has escaped from prejudice and returns to taste its bitterness all over again. With the past humiliations of his father in mind, and the future of his own son, he resents being called "boy!" in a way that most people would not call a dog. This story proves why its author is regarded as a great contemporary writer.

James Baldwin, born in 1924, was educated in New York public schools and worked as a laborer. He was first published by David Burnett in New Story *in Paris and later contributed to many other magazines. He is the author of three novels—*Go Tell It on the Mountain, Giovanni's Room, *and* Another Country—*and two collections of essays. His long essay,* The Fire Next Time, *caused a sensation.*

This Morning, This Evening, So Soon

"You ARE full of nightmares," Harriet tells me. She is in her dressing gown and has cream all over her face. She and my older sister, Louisa, are going out to be girls together. I suppose they have many things to talk about — they have *me* to talk about, certainly — and they do not want my presence. I have been given a bachelor's evening. The director of the film which has brought us such incredible and troubling riches will be along later to take me out to dinner.

I watch her face. I know that it is quite impossible for her to be as untroubled as she seems. Her self-control is mainly for my benefit — my benefit, and Paul's. Harriet comes from orderly and progressive Sweden and has reacted against all the advanced doctrines to which she has been exposed by becoming steadily and beautifully old-fashioned. We never fought in front of Paul, not even when he was a baby. Harriet does not so much believe in protecting children as she does in helping them to build a foundation on which they can build and build again, each time life's high-flying steel ball knocks down everything they have built.

Whenever I become upset, Harriet becomes very cheerful and composed. I think she began to learn how to do this over eight years ago, when I returned from my only visit to America. Now, perhaps, it has become something she could not control if she wished to. This morning, at breakfast, when I yelled at Paul, she averted Paul's tears and my own guilt by looking up and saying, "My God, your father is cranky this morning, isn't he?"

Paul's attention was immediately distracted from his wounds, and the unjust inflicter of those wounds, to his mother's laughter. He watched her.

"It is because he is afraid they will not like his songs in New York. Your father is an *artiste, mon chou,* and they are very mysterious people, *les artistes.* Millions of people are waiting for him in New York, they are begging him to come, and they will give him a *lot* of money, but he is afraid they will not like him.Tell him he is wrong."

She succeeded in rekindling Paul's excitement about places he has never seen. I was also, at once, reinvested with all my glamor. I think it is sometimes extremely difficult for Paul to realize that the face he sees on record sleeves and in the newspapers and on the screen is nothing more or less than the face of his father — who sometimes yells at him. Of course, since he is only seven — going on eight, he will be eight years old this winter — he cannot know that I am baffled, too.

"Of course, you are wrong, you are silly," he said with passion — and caused me to smile. His English is strongly accented and is not, in fact, as good as his French, for he speaks French all day at school. French is really his first language, the first he ever heard. "You are the greatest singer in France" — sounding exactly as he must sound when he makes this pronouncement to his schoolmates — "the greatest *American* singer" — this concession was so gracefully made that it was not a concession at all, it added inches to my stature, America being only a glamorous word for Paul. It is the place from which his father came, and to which he now is going, a place which very few people have ever seen. But his aunt is one of them and he looked over at her. "Mme. Dumont says so, and she says he is a *great actor, too.*" Louisa nodded, smiling. "And she has seen *Les Fauves Nous Attendent* — five times!" This clinched it, of course. Mme. Dumont is our concierge and she has known Paul all his life. I suppose he will not begin to doubt anything she says until he begins to doubt everything.

He looked over at me again. "So you are wrong to be afraid."

"I was wrong to yell at you, too. I won't yell at you any more today."

"All right." He was very grave.

Louisa poured more coffee. "He's going to knock them dead in New York. You'll see."

"Mais bien sûr," said Paul, doubtfully. He does not quite know what "knock them dead" means, though he was sure, from her tone, that she must have been agreeing with him. He does not quite understand this aunt, whom he met for the first time two months ago, when she arrived to spend the summer with us. Her accent is entirely different from anything he has ever heard. He does not really understand why, since she is my sister and his aunt, she should be unable to speak French.

Harriet, Louisa, and I looked at each other and smiled. "Knock them dead," said Harriet, "means *d'avoir un succès fou.* But you will soon pick up all the American expressions." She looked at me and laughed. "So will I."

"That's what he's afraid of." Louisa grinned. "We have *got* some expressions, believe me. Don't let anybody ever tell you America hasn't got a culture. Our culture is as thick as clabber milk."

"Ah," Harriet answered, "I know. I know."

"I'm going to be practicing later," I told Paul.

His face lit up. *"Bon."* This meant that, later, he would come into my study and lie on the floor with his papers and crayons while I worked out with the piano and the tape recorder. He knew that I was offering this as an olive branch. All things considered, we got on pretty well, my son and I.

He looked over at Louisa again. She held a coffee cup in one hand and a cigarette in the other; and something about her baffled him. It was early, so she had not yet put on her face. Her short, thick, graying hair was rougher than usual, almost as rough as my own — later, she would be going to the hairdresser's; she is fairer than I, and better-looking; Louisa, in fact, caught all the looks in the family. Paul knows that she is my older sister and that she helped to raise me, though he does not, of course, know what this means. He knows that she is a schoolteacher in the *American* South, which is not, for some reason, the same place as South America. I could see him trying to fit all these exotic details together into a pattern which would explain her strangeness — strangeness of accent, strangeness of manner. In comparison with the people he has always known, Louisa must seem, for all her generosity and laughter and affection, peculiarly uncertain of herself, peculiarly hostile and embattled.

I wondered what he would think of his Uncle Norman, older and much blacker than I, who lives near the Alabama town in which we were born. Norman will meet us at the boat.

Now Harriet repeats, "Nightmares, nightmares. Nothing ever turns out as badly as you think it will — in fact," she adds laughing, "I am happy to say that that would scarcely be possible."

Her eyes seek mine in the mirror — dark blue eyes, pale skin, black hair. I had always thought of Sweden as being populated entirely by blonds, and I thought that Harriet was abnormally dark for a Swedish girl. But when we visited Sweden, I found out differently. "It is all a great racial salad, Europe, that is why I am sure that I will never understand your country," Harriet said. That was in the days when we never imagined that we would be going to it.

I wonder what she is really thinking. Still, she is right, in two days we will be on a boat, and there is simply no point in carrying around my load of apprehension. I sit down on the bed, watching her fix her face. I realize that I am going to miss this old-fashioned bedroom. For years, we've talked about throwing out the old junk which came with the apartment and replacing it with less massive, modern furniture. But we never have.

"Oh, everything will probably work out," I say. "I've been in a bad mood all day long. I just can't sing any more." We both laugh. She reaches for a wad of tissues and begins wiping off the cream. "I wonder how Paul will like it, if he'll make friends — that's all."

"Paul will like any place where you are, where we are. Don't worry about Paul."

Paul has never been called any names, so far. Only, once he asked us what the word *métis* meant and Harriet explained to him that it meant mixed blood, adding that the blood of just about everybody in the world was mixed by now. Mme. Dumont contributed bawdy and detailed corroboration from her own family tree, the roots of which were somewhere in Corsica; the moral of the story, as she told it, was that women were weak, men incorrigible, and *le bon Dieu* appallingly clever. Mme. Dumont's version is the version I prefer, but it may not be, for Paul, the most utilitarian.

Harriet rises from the dressing table and comes over to sit in my lap. I fall back with her on the bed, and she smiles down into my face.

"Now, don't worry," she tells me, "please try not to worry. Whatever is coming, we will manage it all very well, you will see. We have each other and we have our son and we know what we want. So, we are luckier than most people."

I kiss her on the chin. "I'm luckier than most men."

"I'm a very lucky woman, too."

And for a moment we are silent, alone in our room, which we have shared so long. The slight rise and fall of Harriet's breathing creates an intermittent pressure against my chest, and I think how, if I had never left America, I would never have met her and would never have established a life of my own, would never have entered my own life. For everyone's life begins on a level where races, armies, and churches stop. And yet everyone's life is always shaped by races, churches, and armies; races, churches, armies menace, and have taken, many lives. If Harriet had been born in America, it would have taken her a long time, perhaps forever, to look on me as a man like other men; if I had met her in America, I would never have been able to look on her as a woman like all other women. The habits of public rage and power would also have been our private compulsions, and would have blinded our eyes. We would never have been able to love each other. And Paul would never have been born.

Perhaps, if I had stayed in America, I would have found another woman and had another son. But that other woman, that other son are in the limbo of vanished possibilities. I might also have become something else, instead of an actor-singer, perhaps a lawyer, like my brother, or a teacher, like my sister. But no, I am what I have become and this woman beside me is my wife, and I love her. All the sons I might have had mean nothing, since I *have* a son, I named him, Paul, for my father, and I love him.

I think of all the things I have seen destroyed in America, all the things that I have lost there, all the threats it holds for me and mine.

I grin up at Harriet. "Do you love me?"

"Of course not. I simply have been madly plotting to get to America all these years."

"What a patient wench you are."

"The Swedes are very patient."

She kisses me again and stands up. Louisa comes in, also in a dressing gown.

"I hope you two aren't sitting in here yakking about the *subject*." She looks at me. "My, you are the sorriest-looking celebrity I've ever seen. I've always wondered why people like you hired press agents. Now I know." She goes to Harriet's dressing table. "Honey, do you mind if I borrow some of that *mad* nail polish?"

Harriet goes over to the dressing table. "I'm not sure I know *which* mad nail polish you mean."

Harriet and Louisa, somewhat to my surprise, get on very well. Each seems to find the other full of the weirdest and most delightful surprises. Harriet has been teaching Louisa French and Swedish expressions, and Louisa has been teaching Harriet some of the saltier expressions of the black South. Whenever one of them is not playing straight man to the other's accent, they become involved in long speculations as to how a language reveals the history and the attitudes of a people. They discovered that all the European languages contain a phrase equivalent to "to work like a nigger." ("Of course," says Louisa, "they've had black men working for them for a long time.") "Language is experience and language is power," says Louisa, after regretting that she does not know any of the African dialects. "That's what I keep trying to tell those dicty bastards down South. They get their own experience into the language, we'll have a great language. But, no, they all want to talk like white folks." Then she leans forward, grasping Harriet by the knee. "I tell them, honey, white folks ain't saying *nothing*. Not a thing are they saying—and *some* of them know it, they *need* what you got, the whole world needs it." Then she leans back, in disgust. "You think they listen to me? Indeed they do not. They just go right on, trying to talk like white folks." She leans forward again, in tremendous indignation. "You know some of them folks are *ashamed* of Mahalia Jackson? *Ashamed* of her, one of the greatest singers alive! They think she's common." Then she looks about the room as though she held a bottle in her hand and were looking for a skull to crack.

I think it is because Louisa has never been able to talk like this to any white person before. All the white people she has ever met needed, in one way or another, to be reassured, consoled, to have their consciences pricked but not blasted, could not, could not afford to hear a truth which would shatter, irrevocably, their image of themselves. It is astonishing the lengths to which a person, or a people, will go in order to avoid a truthful mirror. But Harriet's necessity is precisely the opposite: it is of the utmost importance that she learn everything that Louisa can tell her, and then learn more, much more. Harriet is really trying to learn from Louisa how best to protect her husband and her son. This is why they are going out alone tonight. They will have, tonight, as it were, a final council of war. I may be moody, but they, thank God, are practical.

Now Louisa turns to me while Harriet rummages about on the dressing table. "What time is Vidal coming for you?"

"Oh, around seven-thirty, eight o'clock. He says he's reserved tables for us in some very chic place, but he won't say where." Louisa wriggles her shoulders, raises her eyebrows, and does a tiny bump and grind. I laugh. "That's right. And then I guess we'll go out and get drunk."

"I hope to God you do. You've been about as cheerful as a cemetery these last few days. And, that way, your hangover will keep you from bugging us tomorrow."

"What about *your* hangovers? I know the way you girls drink."

"Well, we'll be paying for our own drinks," says Harriet, "so I don't think we'll have that problem. But *you're* going to be fêted, like an international movie star."

"You sure you don't want to change your mind and come out with Vidal and me?"

"We're sure," Louisa says. She looks down at me and gives a small, amused grunt. "An international movie star. And I used to change your diapers. I'll be damned." She is grave for a moment. "Mama'd be proud of you, you know that?" We look at each other and the air between us is charged with secrets which not even Harriet will ever know. "Now, get the hell out of here, so we can get dressed."

"I'll take Paul on down to Mme. Dumont's."

Paul is to have supper with her children and spend the night there.

"For the last time," says Mme. Dumont and she rubs her hand over Paul's violently curly black hair. *"Tu vas nous manquer, tu sais?"* Then she looks up at me and laughs. "He doesn't care. He is only interested in seeing the big ship and all the wonders of New York. Children are never sad to make journeys."

"I would be very sad to go," says Paul, politely, "but my father must go to New York to work and he wants me to come with him."

Over his head, Mme. Dumont and I smile at each other. *"Il est malin, ton gosse!"* She looks down at him again. "And do you think, my little diplomat, that you will like New York?"

"We aren't only going to New York," Paul answers, "we are going to California, too."

"Well, do you think you will like California?"

Paul looks at me. "I don't know. If we don't like it, we'll come back."

"So simple. Just like that," says Mme. Dumont. She looks at me. "It is the best way to look at life. Do come back. You know, we feel that you belong to us, too, here in France."

"I hope you do," I say. "I hope you do. I have always felt — always felt at home here." I bend down and Paul and I kiss each other on the cheek. We have always done so — but will we be able to do so in America? American fathers never kiss American sons. I straighten, my hand on Paul's shoulder. "You be good. I'll pick you up for breakfast, or, if you get up first you come and pick me up and we can hang out together tomorrow, while your *maman* and your Aunt Louisa finish packing. They won't want two men hanging around the house."

"D'accord. Where shall we hang out?" On the last two words he stumbles a little and imitates me.

"Maybe we can go to the zoo, I don't know. And I'll take you to lunch at the Eiffel Tower, would you like that?"

"Oh, yes," he says, "I'd love that." When he is pleased, he seems to glow. All the energy of his small, tough, concentrated being charges an unseen battery and adds an incredible luster to his eyes, which are large and dark brown — like mine — and to his skin, which always reminds me of the colors of honey and the fires of the sun.

"Okay, then." I shake hands with Mme. Dumont. *"Bonsoir, madame."* I ring for the elevator, staring at Paul. *"Ciao, Pauli."*

"Bonsoir, Papa."

And Mme. Dumont takes him inside.

Upstairs, Harriet and Louisa are finally powdered, perfumed, and jeweled, and ready to go: dry martinis at the Ritz, supper, "in some *very* expensive little place," says Harriet, and perhaps the Folies Bergère afterwards. "A real cornball, tourist evening," says Louisa. "I'm working on the theory that if I can get Harriet to act like an American now, she won't have so much trouble later."

"I very much doubt," Harriet says, "that I will be able to endure the Folies Bergère for three solid hours."

"Oh, then we'll duck across town to Harry's New York bar and drink mint juleps," says Louisa.

I realize that, quite apart from everything else, Louisa is having as much fun as she has ever had in her life before. Perhaps she, too, will be sad to leave Paris, even though she has only known it for such a short time.

"Do people drink those in New York?" Harriet asks. I think she is making a list of the things people do or do not do in New York.

"*Some* people do." Louisa winks at me. "Do you realize that this Swedish chick's picked up an Alabama drawl?"

We laugh together. The elevator chugs to a landing.

"We'll stop and say good night to Paul," Harriet says. She kisses me. "Give our best to Vidal."

"Right. Have a good time. Don't let any Frenchman run off with Louisa."

"I did not come to Paris to be protected, and if I had, this wild chick *you* married couldn't do it. I just *might* upset everybody and come home with a French count." She presses the elevator button and the cage goes down.

I walk back into our dismantled apartment. It stinks of departure. There are bags and crates in the hall, which will be taken away tomorrow, there are no books in the bookcases, the kitchen looks as though we never cooked a meal there, never dawdled there, in the early morning or late at night, over coffee. Presently, I must shower and shave but now I pour myself a drink and light a cigarette and step out on our balcony. It is dusk, the brilliant light of Paris is beginning to fade, and the green of the trees is darkening.

I have lived in this city for twelve years. This apartment is on the top floor of a corner building. We look out over the trees and the rooftops to the Champ de Mars, where the Eiffel Tower stands. Beyond this field is the river, which I have crossed so often, in so many states of mind. I have crossed every bridge in Paris, I have walked along every *quai*. I know the river as one finally knows a friend, know it when it is black, guarding all the lights of Paris in its depths, and seeming, in its vast silence, to be communing with the dead who lie beneath it; when it is yellow, evil, and roaring, giving a rough time to tugboats and barges, and causing people to remember that it has been known to rise, it has been known to kill; when it is peaceful, a slick, dark, dirty green, playing host to rowboats and *les bateaux mouches* and throwing up from time to time an extremely unhealthy fish. The men who stand along the *quais* all summer with their fishing lines gratefully accept the slimy object and throw it in a rusty can. I have always wondered who eats those fish.

And I walk up and down, up and down, glad to be alone.

It is August, the month when all Parisians desert Paris and one has to walk miles to find a barbershop or a laundry open in some tree-shadowed, silent side street. There is a single person on the avenue, a paratrooper walking toward École Militaire. He is also walking, almost certainly, and rather sooner than later, toward Algeria. I have a friend, a good-natured boy who was always hanging around the clubs in which I worked in the old days, who has just returned from Algeria, with a recurring, debilitating fever, and minus one eye. The government has set his pension at the sum, arbitrary if not occult, of fifty-three thousand francs every three months. Of course, it is quite impossible to live on this amount of money without working—but who will hire a half-blind invalid? This boy has been spoiled forever, long before his thirtieth birthday, and there are thousands like him all over France.

And there are fewer Algerians to be found on the streets of Paris now. The rug sellers, the peanut vendors, the postcard peddlers and money-changers have vanished. The boys I used to know during my first years in Paris are scattered — or corralled — the Lord knows where.

Most of them had no money. They lived three and four together in rooms with a single skylight, a single hard cot, or in buildings that seemed abandoned, with cardboard in the windows, with erratic plumbing in a wet, cobblestoned yard, in dark, dead-end alleys, or on the outer, chilling heights of Paris.

The Arab cafés are closed — those dark, acrid cafés in which I used to meet with them to drink tea, to get high on hashish, to listen to the obsessive, stringed music which has no relation to any beat, any time, that I have ever known. I once thought of the North Africans as my brothers and that is why I went to their cafés. They were very friendly to me, perhaps one or two of them remained really fond of me even after I could no longer afford to smoke Lucky Strikes and after my collection of American sport shirts had vanished — mostly into their wardrobes. They seemed to feel that they had every right to them, since I could only have wrested these things from the world by cunning — it meant nothing to say that I had had no choice in the matter; perhaps I had wrested these things from the world by treason, by refusing to be identified with the misery of my people. Perhaps, indeed, I identified myself with those who were responsible for this misery.

And this was true. Their rage, the only note in all their music which I could not fail to recognize, to which I responded, yet had the effect of setting us more than ever at a division. They were perfectly prepared to drive all Frenchmen into the sea, and to level the city of Paris. But I could not hate the French, because they left me alone. And I love Paris, I will always love it, it is the city which saved my life. It saved my life by allowing me to find out who I am.

It was on a bridge, one tremendous April morning, that I knew I had fallen in love. Harriet and I were walking hand in hand. The bridge was the Pont Royal, just before us was the great *horloge,* high and lifted up, saying ten to ten; beyond this, the golden statue of Joan of Arc, with her sword uplifted. Harriet and I were silent, for we had been quarreling about something. Now, when I look back, I think we had reached that state when an affair must either end or become something more than an affair.

I looked sideways at Harriet's face, which was still. Her dark blue eyes were narrowed against the sun, and her full, pink lips were still slightly sulky, like a child's. In those days, she hardly ever wore make-up. I was in my shirt sleeves. Her face made me want to laugh and run my hand over her short dark hair. I wanted to pull her to me and say, *Baby, don't be mad at me,* and at that moment something tugged at my heart and made me catch my breath. There were millions of people all around us, but I was alone with Harriet. She was alone with me. Never, in all my life, until that moment, had I been alone with anyone. The world had always been with us, between us, defeating the quarrel we could not achieve, and making love impossible. During all the years of my life, until that moment, I had carried the menacing, the hostile, killing world with me everywhere. No matter what I was doing or saying or feeling, one eye had always been on the world — that world which I had learned to distrust almost as soon as I learned my name, that world on which I knew one could never turn one's back, the white man's world. And for the first time in my life I was free of it; it had not existed for me; I had been quarreling with my girl. It was our quarrel, it was entirely between us, it had nothing to do with anyone else in the world. For the first time in my life I had not been afraid of the patriotism of the mindless, in uniform or out, who would beat me up and treat the woman who was with me as though she were the lowest of untouchables. For the first time in my life I felt that no force jeopardized my right, my power, to possess and to protect a woman; for the first time, the first time, felt that the woman was not, in her own eyes or in the eyes of the world, degraded by my presence.

The sun fell over everything, like a blessing, people were moving all about us, I will never forget the feeling of Harriet's small hand in mine, dry and trusting, and I turned to her, slowing our pace. She looked up at me with her enormous blue eyes, and she seemed to wait. I said, "*Harriet. Harriet. Tu sais, il y a quelque chose de très grave qui m'est arrivé. Je t'aime. Je t'aime. Tu me comprends,* or shall I say it in English?"

This was eight years ago, shortly before my first and only visit home.

That was when my mother died. I stayed in America for three months. When I came back, Harriet thought that the change in me was due to my grief — I was very silent, very thin. But it had not been my mother's death which accounted for the change. I had known that my mother was going to die. I had not known what America would be like for me after nearly four years away.

I remember standing at the rail and watching the distance between myself and Le Havre increase. Hands fell, ceasing to wave, handkerchiefs ceased to flutter, people turned away, they mounted their bicycles or got into their cars and rode off. Soon, Le Havre was nothing but a blur. I thought of Harriet, already miles from me in Paris, and I pressed my lips tightly together in order not to cry.

Then, as Europe dropped below the water, as the days passed and passed, as we left behind us the skies of Europe and the eyes of everyone on the ship began, so to speak, to refocus, waiting for the first glimpse of America, my apprehension began to give way to a secret joy, a checked anticipation. I thought of such details as showers, which are rare in Paris, and I thought of such things as rich, cold, American milk and heavy, chocolate cake. I wondered about my friends, wondered if I had any left, and wondered if they would be glad to see me.

The Americans on the boat did not seem to be so bad, but I was fascinated, after such a long absence from it, by the nature of their friendliness. It was a friendliness which did not suggest, and was not intended to suggest, any possibility of friendship. Unlike Europeans, they dropped titles and used first names almost at once, leaving themselves, unlike the Europeans, with nowhere thereafter to go. Once one had become "Pete" or "Jane" or "Bill" all that could decently be known was

known and any suggestion that there might be further depths, a person,
so to speak, behind the name, was taken as a violation of that privacy
which did not, paradoxically, since they trusted it so little, seem to exist
among Americans. They apparently equated privacy with the unspeakable things they did in the bathroom or the bedroom, which they related
only to the analyst, and then read about in the pages of best sellers. There
was an eerie and unnerving irreality about everything they said and did,
as though they were all members of the same team and were acting on
orders from some invincibly cheerful and tirelessly inventive coach. I was
fascinated by it. I found it oddly moving, but I cannot say that I was
displeased. It had not occurred to me before that Americans, who had
never treated me with any respect, had no respect for each other.

On the last night but one, there was a gala in the big ballroom and I
sang. It had been a long time since I had sung before so many Americans.
My audience had mainly been penniless French students, in the weird
Left Bank bistros I worked in those days. Still, I was a great hit with
them and by this time I had become enough of a drawing card, in the
Latin Quarter and in St.-Germain-des-Prés, to have attracted a couple of
critics, to have had my picture in *France-soir*, and to have acquired a
legal work permit which allowed me to make a little more money. Just
the same, no matter how industrious and brilliant some of the musicians
had been, or how devoted my audience, they did not know, they could
not know, what my songs came out of. They did not know what was
funny about it. It was impossible to translate: It damn well better be
funny, or Laughing to keep from crying, or What did *I* do to be so black
and blue?

The moment I stepped out on the floor, they began to smile, something
opened in them, they were ready to be pleased. I found in their faces, as
they watched me, smiling, waiting, an artless relief, a profound reassurance. Nothing was more familiar to them than the sight of a dark boy,
singing, and there were few things on earth more necessary. It was under
cover of darkness, my own darkness, that I could sing for them of the
joys, passions, and terrors they smuggled about with them like steadily
depreciating contraband. Under cover of the midnight fiction that I was
unlike them because I was black, they could stealthily gaze at those
treasures which they had been mysteriously forbidden to possess and were
never permitted to declare.

I sang "I'm Coming, Virginia," and "Take This Hammer," and "Precious Lord." They wouldn't let me go and I came back and sang a couple

of the oldest blues I knew. Then someone asked me to sing "Swanee River," and I did, astonished that I could, astonished that this song, which I had put down long ago, should have the power to move me. Then, if only, perhaps, to make the record complete, I wanted to sing "Strange Fruit," but, on this number, no one can surpass the great, tormented Billie Holiday. So I finished with "Great Getting-Up Morning" and I guess I can say that if I didn't stop the show I certainly ended it. I got a big hand and I drank at a few tables and I danced with a few girls.

After one more day and one more night, the boat landed in New York. I woke up, I was bright awake at once, and I thought, *We're here*. I turned on all the lights in my small cabin and I stared into the mirror as though I were committing my face to memory. I took a shower and I took a long time shaving and I dressed myself very carefully. I walked the long ship corridors to the dining room, looking at the luggage piled high before the elevators and beside the steps. The dining room was nearly half empty and full of a quick and joyous excitement which depressed me even more. People ate quickly, chattering to each other, anxious to get upstairs and go on deck. Was it my imagination or was it true that they seemed to avoid my eyes? A few people waved and smiled, but let me pass; perhaps it would have made them uncomfortable, this morning, to try to share their excitement with me; perhaps they did not want to know whether or not it was possible for me to share it. I walked to my table and sat down. I munched toast as dry as paper and drank a pot of coffee. Then I tipped my waiter, who bowed and smiled and called me "sir" and said that he hoped to see me on the boat again. "I hope so, too," I said.

And was it true, or was it my imagination, that a flash of wondering comprehension, a flicker of wry sympathy, then appeared in the waiter's eyes? I walked upstairs to the deck.

There was a breeze from the water but the sun was hot and made me remember how ugly New York summers could be. All of the deck chairs had been taken away and people milled about in the space where the deck chairs had been, moved from one side of the ship to the other, clambered up and down the steps, crowded the rails, and they were busy taking photographs — of the harbor, of each other, of the sea, of the gulls. I walked slowly along the deck, and an impulse stronger than myself drove me to the rail. There it was, the great, unfinished city, with all its towers blazing in the sun. It came toward us slowly and patiently, like some enormous, cunning, and murderous beast, ready to devour, impossible to escape. I watched it come closer and I listened to the people around me, to their excitement and their pleasure. There was no doubt that it was real. I watched their shining faces and wondered if I were mad. For a moment I longed, with all my heart, to be able to feel whatever they were feeling, if only to know what such a feeling was like. As the boat moved slowly into the harbor, they were being moved into safety. It was only I who was being floated into danger. I turned my head, looking for Europe, but all that stretched behind me was the sky, thick with gulls. I moved away from the rail. A big, sandy-haired man held his daughter on his shoulders, showing her the Statue of Liberty. I would never know what this statue meant to others, she had always been an ugly joke for me. And the American flag was flying from the top of the ship, above my head. I had seen the French flag drive the French into the most unspeakable frenzies, I had seen the flag which was nominally mine used to dignify the vilest purposes: now I would never, as long as I lived, know what others saw when they saw a flag. "There's no place like home," said a voice close by, and I thought, *There damn sure isn't.* I decided to go back to my cabin and have a drink.

There was a cablegram from Harriet in my cabin. It said: Be good. Be quick. I'm waiting. I folded it carefully and put it in my breast pocket. Then I wondered if I would ever get back to her. How long would it take me to earn the money to get out of this land? Sweat broke out on my forehead and I poured myself some whisky from my nearly empty bottle. I paced the tiny cabin. It was silent. There was no one down in the cabins now.

I was not sober when I faced the uniforms in the first-class lounge. There were two of them; they were not unfriendly. They looked at my passport, they looked at me. "You've been away a long time," said one of them.

"Yes," I said, "it's been a while."

"What did you do over there all that time?" — with a grin meant to hide more than it revealed, which hideously revealed more than it could hide.

I said, "I'm a singer," and the room seemed to rock around me. I held on to what I hoped was a calm, open smile. I had not had to deal with these faces in so long that I had forgotten how to do it. I had once known how to pitch my voice precisely between curtness and servility, and known what razor's edge of a pickaninny's smile would turn away wrath. But I had forgotten all the tricks on which my life had once depended. Once I had been an expert at baffling these people, at setting their teeth on edge, and dancing just outside the trap laid for me. But I was not an expert now. These faces were no longer merely the faces of two white men, who were my enemies. They were the faces of two white people whom I did not understand, and I could no longer plan my moves in accordance with what I knew of their cowardice and their needs and their strategy. That moment on the bridge had undone me forever.

"That's right," said one of them, "that's what it says, right here on the passport. Never heard of you, though." They looked up at me. "Did you do a lot of singing over there?"

"Some."

"What kind — concerts?"

"No." I wondered what I looked like, sounded like. I could tell nothing from their eyes. "I worked a few night clubs."

"Night clubs, eh? I guess they liked you over there."

"Yes," I said, "they seemed to like me all right."

"Well" — and my passport was stamped and handed back to me — "let's hope they like you over here."

"Thanks." They laughed — was it at me, or was it my imagination? — and I picked up the one bag I was carrying and threw my trench coat over one shoulder and walked out of the first-class lounge. I stood in the slow-moving, murmuring line which led to the gangplank. I looked straight ahead and watched heads, smiling faces, step up to the shadow of the gangplank awning and then swiftly descend out of sight. I put my passport back in my breast pocket — *Be quick. I'm waiting* — and I held my landing card in my hand. Then, suddenly, there I was, standing on the edge of the boat, staring down the long ramp to the ground. At the end of the plank, on the ground, stood a heavy man in a uniform. His cap was pushed back from his gray hair and his face was red and wet. He looked up at me. This was the face I remembered, the face of my nightmares; perhaps hatred had caused me to know this face better than I would ever know the face of any lover. "Come on, boy," he cried, "come on, come on!"

And I almost smiled. I was home. I touched my breast pocket. I

thought of a song I sometimes sang, "When will I ever get to be a man?"
I came down the gangplank, stumbling a little, and gave the man my
landing card.

Much later in the day, a customs inspector checked my baggage and
waved me away. I picked up my bags and started walking down the long
stretch which led to the gate, to the city.

And I heard someone call my name.

I looked up and saw Louisa running toward me. I dropped my bags
and grabbed her in my arms and tears came to my eyes and rolled down
my face. I did not know whether the tears were for joy at seeing her, or
from rage, or both.

"How are you? How are you? You look wonderful, but, oh, haven't
you lost weight? It's wonderful to see you again."

I wiped my eyes. "It's wonderful to see you, too, I bet you thought I
was never coming back."

Louisa laughed. "I wouldn't have blamed you if you hadn't. These
people are just as corny as ever, I swear I don't believe there's any hope
for them. How's your French? Lord, when I think that it was I who
studied French and now I can't speak a word. And you never went near
it and you probably speak it like a native."

I grinned. *"Pas mal. Je me défends pas mal."* We started down the wide
steps into the street. "My God," I said. "New York." I was not aware of
its towers now. We were in the shadow of the elevated highway but the
thing which most struck me was neither light nor shade, but noise. It
came from a million things at once, from trucks and tires and clutches
and brakes and doors; from machines shuttling and stamping and rolling
and cutting and pressing; from the building of tunnels, the checking of
gas mains, the laying of wires, the digging of foundations; from the
chattering of rivets, the scream of the pile driver, the clanging of great
shovels; from the battering down and the raising up of walls; from
millions of radios and television sets and jukeboxes. The human voices
distinguished themselves from the roar only by their note of strain and
hostility. Another fleshy man, uniformed and red-faced, hailed a cab for
us and touched his cap politely but could only manage a peremptory
growl: "Right this way, miss. Step up, sir." He slammed the cab door
behind us. Louisa directed the driver to the New Yorker Hotel.

"Do they take us there?"

She looked at me. "They got laws in New York, honey, it'd be the
easiest thing in the world to spend all your time in court. But over at the

New Yorker, I believe they've already got the message." She took my arm. "You see? In spite of all this chopping and booming, this place hasn't really changed very much. You still can't hear yourself talk."

And I thought to myself, Maybe that's the point.

Early the next morning we checked out of the hotel and took the plane for Alabama.

I am just stepping out of the shower when I hear the bell ring. I dry myself hurriedly and put on a bathrobe. It is Vidal, of course, and very elegant he is, too, with his bushy gray hair quite lustrous, his swarthy, cynical, gypsylike face shaved and lotioned. Usually he looks just any old way. But tonight his brief bulk is contained in a dark blue suit and he has an ironical pearl stickpin in his blue tie.

"Come in, make yourself a drink. I'll be with you in a second."

"I am, *hélas!* on time. I trust you will forgive me for my thoughtlessness."

But I am already back in the bathroom. Vidal puts on a record: Mahalia Jackson, singing "I'm Going to Live the Life I Sing About in My Song."

When I am dressed, I find him sitting in a chair before the open window. The daylight is gone, but it is not exactly dark. The trees are black now against the darkening sky. The lights in windows and the lights of motorcars are yellow and ringed. The street lights have not yet been turned on. It is as though, out of deference to the departed day, Paris waited a decent interval before assigning her role to a more theatrical but inferior performer.

Vidal is drinking a whisky and soda. I pour myself a drink. He watches me.

"Well. How are you, my friend? You are nearly gone. Are you happy to be leaving us?"

"No." I say this with more force than I had intended. Vidal raises his eyebrows, looking amused and distant. "I never really intended to go back there. I certainly never intended to raise my kid there —"

"Mais, mon cher," Vidal says, calmly, "you are an intelligent man, you must have known that you would probably be returning one day." He pauses. "And, as for Pauli — did it never occur to you that he might wish one day to see the country in which his father and his father's fathers were born?"

"To do that, really, he'd have to go to Africa."

"America will always mean more to him than Africa, you know that."

"I don't know." I throw my drink down and pour myself another. "Why should he want to cross all that water just to be called a nigger? America never gave him anything."

"It gave him his father."

I look at him. "You mean, his father escaped."

Vidal throws back his head and laughs. If Vidal likes you, he is certain to laugh at you and his laughter can be very unnerving. But the look, the silence which follow this laughter can be very unnerving, too. And, now, in the silence, he asks me, "Do you really think that you have escaped anything? Come. I know you for a better man than that." He walks to the table which holds the liquor. "In that movie of ours which has made you so famous, and, as I now see, so troubled, what are you playing, after all? What is the tragedy of this half-breed troubadour if not, precisely, that he has taken all the possible roads to escape and that all these roads have failed him?" He pauses, with the bottle in one hand, and looks at me. "Do you remember the trouble I had to get a performance out of you? How you hated me, you sometimes looked as though you wanted to shoot me! And do you remember when the role of Chico began to come alive?" He pours his drink. "Think back, remember. I am a very great director, *mais pardon!* I could not have got such a performance out of anyone but you. And what were you thinking of, what was in your mind, what nightmare were you living with when you began, at last, to play the role — truthfully?" He walks back to his seat.

Chico, in the film, is the son of a Martinique woman and a French *colon* who hates both his mother and his father. He flees from the island to the capital, carrying his hatred with him. This hatred has now grown, naturally, to include all dark women and all white men, in a word, everyone. He descends into the underworld of Paris, where he dies. *Les fauves* — the wild beasts — refers to the life he has fled and to the life which engulfs him. When I agreed to do the role, I felt that I could probably achieve it by bearing in mind the North Africans I had watched in Paris for so long. But this did not please Vidal. The blowup came while we were rehearsing a fairly simple, straightforward scene. Chico goes into a sleazy Pigalle dance hall to beg the French owner for a particularly humiliating job. And this Frenchman reminds him of his father.

"You are playing this boy as though you thought of him as the noble savage," Vidal said, icily. *"Ça vient d'où* — all these ghastly mannerisms you are using all the time?"

Everyone fell silent, for Vidal rarely spoke this way. This silence told me that everyone, the actor with whom I was playing the scene and all the people in the "dance hall," shared Vidal's opinion of my performance and were relieved that he was going to do something about it. I was humiliated and too angry to speak; but perhaps I also felt, at the very bottom of my heart, a certain relief, an unwilling respect.

"You are doing it all wrong," he said, more gently. Then, "Come, let us have a drink together."

We walked into his office. He took a bottle and two glasses out of his desk. "Forgive me, but you put me in mind of some of those English *lady* actresses who love to play *putain* as long as it is always absolutely clear to the audience that they are really ladies. So perhaps they read a book, not usually, *hélas! Fanny Hill,* and they have their chauffeurs drive them through Soho once or twice — and they come to the stage with a performance so absolutely loaded with detail, every bit of it meaningless, that there can be no doubt that they are acting. It is what the British call a triumph." He poured two cognacs. "That is what you are doing. Why? Who do you think this boy is, what do you think he is feeling, when he asks for this job?" He watched me carefully and I bitterly resented his look. "You come from America. The situation is not so pretty there for boys like you. I know you may not have been as poor as — as some — but is it really impossible for you to understand what a boy like Chico feels? Have you never, yourself, been in a similar position?"

I hated him for asking the question because I knew he knew the answer to it. "I would have had to be a very lucky black man not to have been in such a position."

"You would have had to be a very lucky *man*."

"Oh, God," I said, "please don't give me any of this equality-in-anguish business."

"It is perfectly possible," he said, sharply, "that there is not another kind."

Then he was silent. He sat down behind his desk. He cut a cigar and lit it, puffing up clouds of smoke, as though to prevent us from seeing each other too clearly. "Consider this," he said. "I am a French director who has never seen your country. I have never done you any harm, except, perhaps, historically — I mean, because I am white — but I cannot be blamed for that — "

"But *I* can be," I said, "and I am! I've never understood why, if *I* have to pay for the history written in the color of my skin, *you* should get off scot-free!" But I was surprised at my vehemence, I had not known I was going to say these things, and by the fact that I was trembling and from the way he looked at me I knew that, from a professional point of view anyway, I was playing into his hands.

"What makes you think I *do?*" His face looked weary and stern. "I am a Frenchman. Look at France. You think that I — we — are not paying for our history?" He walked to the window, staring out at the rather grim little town in which the studio was located. "If it is revenge that you want, well, then, let me tell you, you will have it. You will probably have it, whether you want it or not, our stupidity will make it inevitable." He turned back into the room. "But I beg you not to confuse me with the happy people of your country, who scarcely know that there is such a thing as history and so, naturally, imagine that they can escape, as you put it, scot-free. That is what you are doing, that is what I was about to say. I was about to say that I am a French director and I have never been in your country and I have never done you any harm — but you are not talking to that man, in this room, now. You are not talking to Jean Luc Vidal, but to some other white man, whom you remember, who has nothing to do with me." He paused and went back to his desk. "Oh, most of the time you are not like this, I know. But it is there all the time, it must be, because when you are upset, this is what comes out. So you are not playing Chico truthfully, you are lying about him, and I will not let you do it. When you go back, now, and play this scene again, I want you to remember what has just happened in this room. You brought your past into this room. That is what Chico does when he walks into the dance hall. The Frenchman whom he begs for a job is not merely a Frenchman — he is the father who disowned and betrayed him and all the Frenchmen whom he hates." He smiled and poured me another cognac. "Ah! If it were not for *my* history, I would not have so much trouble to get the truth out of you." He looked into my face, half smiling. "And you, you are angry — are you not? — that I *ask* you for the truth. You think I have no right to ask." Then he said something which he knew would enrage me. "Who are you then, and what good has it done you to come to France, and how will you raise your son? Will you teach him never to tell the truth to anyone?" And he moved behind his desk and looked at me, as though from behind a barricade.

"You have no right to talk to me this way."

"Oh, yes, I do," he said. "I have a film to make and a reputation to maintain and I am going to get a performance out of you." He looked at his watch. "Let us go back to work."

I watch him now, sitting quietly in my living room, tough, cynical, crafty old Frenchman, and I wonder if he knows that the nightmare at the bottom of my mind, as I played the role of Chico, was all the possible fates of Paul. This is but another way of saying that I relived the disasters which had nearly undone me; but, because I was thinking of Paul, I discovered that I did not want my son ever to feel toward me as I had felt toward my own father. He had died when I was eleven, but I had watched the humiliations he had to bear, and I had pitied him. But was there not, in that pity, however painfully and unwillingly, also some contempt? For how could I *know* what he had borne? I knew only that I was his son. However he had loved me, whatever he had borne, I, his son, was despised. Even had he lived, he could have done nothing to prevent it, nothing to protect me. The best that he could hope to do was to prepare me for it; and even at that he had failed. How can one be prepared for the spittle in the face, all the tireless ingenuity which goes into the spite and fear of small, unutterably miserable people whose greatest terror is the singular identity, whose joy, whose safety, is entirely dependent on the humiliation and anguish of others?

But for Paul, I swore it, such a day would never come. I would throw my life and my work between Paul and the nightmare of the world. I would make it impossible for the world to treat Paul as it had treated my father and me.

Mahalia's record ends. Vidal rises to turn it over. "Well?" He looks at me very affectionately. "Your nightmares, please!"

"Oh, I was thinking of that summer I spent in Alabama, when my mother died." I stop. "You know, but when we finally filmed that bar scene, I was thinking of New York. I was scared in Alabama, but I almost went crazy in New York. I was sure I'd never make it back here — back here to Harriet. And I knew if I didn't, it was going to be the end of me." Now Mahalia is singing "When the Saints Go Marching In." "I got a job in the town as an elevator boy, in the town's big department store. It was a special favor, one of my father's white friends got it for me. For a long time, in the South, we all — depended — on the — *kindness* — of white friends." I take out a handkerchief and wipe my face.

"But this man didn't like me. I guess I didn't seem grateful enough, wasn't enough like my father, what he thought my father was. And I couldn't get used to the town again, I'd been away too long, I hated it. It's a terrible town, anyway, the whole thing looks as though it's been built around a jailhouse. There's a room in the courthouse, a room where they beat you up. Maybe you're walking along the street one night, it's usually at night, but it happens in the daytime, too. And the police car comes up behind you and the cop says, Hey, boy. Come on over here. So you go on over. He says, Boy, I believe you drunk. And, you see, if you say, No, no sir, he'll beat you because you're calling him a liar. And if you say anything else, unless it's something to make him laugh, he'll take you in and beat you, just for fun. The trick is to think of some way for them to have their fun without beating you up."

The street lights of Paris click on and turn all the green leaves silver. "Or to go along with the ways *they* dream up. And they'll do anything, anything at all, to prove that you're no better than a dog and to make you feel like one. And they hated me because I'd been North and I'd been to Europe. People kept saying, I hope you didn't bring no foreign notions back here with you, boy. And I'd say, No sir, or No ma'am, but I never said it right. And there was a time, all of them remembered it, when I *had* said it right. But now they could tell that I despised them — I guess, no matter what, I wanted them to know that I despised them. But I didn't despise them any more than everyone else did, only the others never let it show. They knew how to keep the white folks happy, and it was easy — you just had to keep them feeling like they were God's favor to the universe. They'd walk around with great big foolish grins on their faces and the colored folks loved to see this, because they hated them so much. "Just look at So-and-So," somebody'd say. "His white is *on* him today." And when we didn't hate them, we pitied them. In America, that's usually what it means to have a white friend. You pity the poor bastard because he was born believing the world's a great place to be, and you know it's not, and you can see that he's going to have a terrible time getting used to this idea, if he *ever* gets used to it."

Then I think of Paul again, those eyes which still imagine that I can do anything, that skin, the color of honey and fire, his jet-black, curly hair. I look out at Paris again, and I listen to Mahalia. "Maybe it's better to have the terrible times first. I don't know. Maybe, then, you can have, *if* you live, a better life, a real life, because you had to fight so hard to get it away — you know? — from the mad dog who held it in his teeth. But then your life has all those tooth marks, too, all those tatters, and all that blood." I walk to the bottle and raise it. "One for the road?"

"Thank you," says Vidal.

I pour us a drink, and he watches me. I have never talked so much before, not about those things anyway. I know that Vidal has nightmares, because he knows so much about them, but he has never told me what his are. I think that he probably does not talk about his nightmares any more. I know that the war cost him his wife and his son, and that he was in prison in Germany. He very rarely refers to it. He has a married daughter who lives in England, and he rarely speaks of her. He is like a man who has learned to live on what is left of an enormous fortune.

We are silent for a moment.

"Please go on," he says, with a smile. "I am curious about the reality behind the reality of your performance."

"My sister, Louisa, never married," I say, abruptly, "because, once, years ago, she and the boy she was going with and two friends of theirs were out driving in a car and the police stopped them. The girl who was with them was very fair and the police pretended not to believe her when she said she was colored. They made her get out and stand in front of the headlights of the car and pull down her pants and raise her dress — they said that was the only way they could be sure. And you can imagine what they said, and what they did — and they were lucky, at that, that it didn't go any further. But none of the men could do anything about it. Louisa couldn't face that boy again, and I guess he couldn't face her." Now it is really growing dark in the room and I cross to the light switch. "You know, I know what that boy felt, I've felt it. They want you to feel that you're not a man, maybe that's the only way they can feel like men, I don't know. I walked around New York with Harriet's cablegram in my pocket as though it were some atomic secret, in *code,* and they'd kill me if they ever found out what it meant. You know, there's something wrong with people like that. And thank God Harriet was here, she *proved* that the world was bigger than the world they wanted me to live in, I *had* to get back here, get to a place where people were too busy with their own lives, *their private lives,* to make fantasies about mine, to set up walls around mine." I look at him. The light in the room has made the night outside blue-black and golden and the great searchlight of the Eiffel Tower is turning in the sky. "That's what it's like in America, for me, anyway. I always feel that I don't exist there, except in someone else's — usually dirty — mind. I don't know if you know what that means, but I do, and I don't want to put Harriet through that and I don't want to raise Paul there."

"Well," he says at last, "you are not required to remain in America forever, are you? You will sing in that elegant club which apparently feels that it cannot, much longer, so much as open its doors without you, and you will probably accept the movie offer, you would be very foolish not to. You will make a lot of money. Then, one day, you will remember that airlines and steamship companies are still in business and that France still exists. *That* will certainly be cause for astonishment."

Vidal was a Gaullist before De Gaulle came to power. But he regrets the manner of De Gaulle's rise and he is worried about De Gaulle's regime. "It is not the fault of *mon général,*" he sometimes says, sadly. "Perhaps it is history's fault. I *suppose* it must be history which always arranges to bill a civilization at the very instant it is least prepared to pay."

Now he rises and walks out on the balcony, as though to reassure himself of the reality of Paris. Mahalia is singing "Didn't It Rain?" I walk out and stand beside him.

"You are a good boy — Chico," he says. I laugh. "You believe in love. You do not know all the things love cannot do, but" — he smiles — "love will teach you that."

We go, after dinner, to a Left Bank *discothèque* which can charge outrageous prices because Marlon Brando wandered in there one night. By accident, according to Vidal. "Do you know how many people in Paris are becoming rich — to say nothing of those, *hélas!* who are going broke — on the off chance that Marlon Brando will lose his way again?"

He has not, presumably, lost his way tonight, but the *discothèque* is crowded with those strangely faceless people who are part of the night life of all great cities, and who always arrive, moments, hours, or decades late, on the spot made notorious by an event or a movement or a handful of personalities. So here are American boys, anything but beardless, scratching around for Hemingway; American girls titillating themselves with Frenchmen and existentialism while waiting for the American boys to shave off their beards; French painters busily pursuing the revolution which ended thirty years ago; and the young, bored, perverted American *arrivistes* who are buying their way into the art world via flattery and liquor, and the production of canvases as arid as their greedy little faces.

Here are boys, of all nations, one step above the pimp, who are occasionally walked across a stage or trotted before a camera. And the girls, their enemies, whose faces are sometimes seen in ads, one of whom will surely have a tantrum before the evening is out.

In a corner, as usual, surrounded, as usual, by smiling young men, sits the drunken blond woman who was once the mistress of a famous, dead painter. She is a figure of some importance in the art world, and so rarely has to pay for either her drinks or her lovers. An older Frenchman, who was once a famous director, is playing *quatre cent vingt-et-un* with the woman behind the cash register. He nods pleasantly to Vidal and me as we enter, but makes no move to join us, and I respect him for this. Vidal and I are obviously cast tonight in the role vacated by Brando: our entrance justifies the prices and sends a kind of shiver through the room. It is marvelous to watch the face of the waiter as he approaches, all smiles and deference and grace, not so much honored by our presence as achieving his reality from it; excellence, he seems to be saying, gravitates naturally toward excellence. We order two whisky and sodas. I know why Vidal sometimes comes here. He is lonely. I do not think that he expects ever to love one woman again, and so he distracts himself with many.

Since this is a *discothèque,* jazz is blaring from the walls and record sleeves are scattered about with a devastating carelessness. Two of them are mine and no doubt, presently, someone will play the recording of the songs I sang in the film.

"I thought," says Vidal, with a malicious little smile, "that your farewell to Paris would not be complete without a brief exposure to the perils of fame. Perhaps it will help prepare you for America, where, I am told, the populace is yet more carnivorous than it is here."

I can see that one of the vacant models is preparing herself to come to our table and ask for an autograph, hoping, since she is pretty — she has, that is, the usual female equipment, dramatized in the usual, modern way — to be invited for a drink. Should the maneuver succeed, one of her boy friends or girl friends will contrive to come by the table, asking for a light or a pencil or a lipstick, and it will be extremely difficult not to invite this person to join us, too. Before the evening ends, we will be surrounded. I don't, now, know what I expected of fame, but I suppose it never occurred to me that the light could be just as dangerous, just as killing, as the dark.

"Well, let's make it brief," I tell him. "Sometimes I wish that you weren't quite so fond of me."

He laughs. "There are some very interesting people here tonight. Look."

Across the room from us, and now staring at our table, are a group of American Negro students, who are probably visiting Paris for the first time. There are four of them, two boys and two girls, and I suppose that they must be in their late teens or early twenties. One of the boys, a gleaming, curly-haired, golden-brown type — the color of his mother's fried chicken — is carrying a guitar. When they realize we have noticed them, they smile and wave — wave as though I were one of their possessions, as, indeed, I am. Golden-brown is a mime. He raises his guitar, drops his shoulders, and his face falls into the lugubrious lines of Chico's face as he approaches death. He strums a little of the film's theme music, and I laugh and the table laughs. It is as though we were all back home and had met for a moment, on a Sunday morning, say, before a church or a poolroom or a barber shop.

And they have created a sensation in the *discothèque,* naturally, having managed, with no effort whatever, to outwit all the gleaming boys and girls. Their table, which had been of no interest only a moment before, has now become the focus of a rather pathetic attention; their smiles have made it possible for the others to smile, and to nod in our direction.

"Oh," says Vidal, "he does that far better than you ever did, perhaps I will make him a star."

"Feel free, *m'sieu, le bon Dieu,* I got mine." But I can see that his attention has really been caught by one of the girls, slim, tense, and dark, who seems, though it is hard to know how one senses such things, to be treated by the others with a special respect. And, in fact, the table now seems to be having a council of war, to be demanding her opinion or her cooperation. She listens, frowning, laughing; the quality, the force of her intelligence causes her face to keep changing all the time, as though a light played on it. And, presently, with a gesture she might once have used to scatter feed to chickens, she scoops up from the floor one of those dangling ragbags women love to carry. She holds it loosely by the drawstrings, so that it is banging somewhere around her ankle, and walks over to our table. She has an honest, forthright walk, entirely unlike the calculated, pelvic workout by means of which most women get about. She is small, but sturdily, economically, put together.

As she reaches our table, Vidal and I rise, and this throws her for a second. (It has been a long time since I have seen such an attractive girl.)

Also, everyone, of course, is watching us. It is really a quite curious moment. They have put on the record of Chico singing a sad, angry Martinique ballad; my own voice is coming at us from the walls as the girl looks from Vidal to me, and smiles.

"I guess you know," she says, "we weren't *about* to let you get out of here without bugging you just a little bit. We've only been in Paris just a couple of days and we thought for sure that we wouldn't have a chance of running into you anywhere, because it's in all the papers that you're coming home."

"Yes," I say, "yes. I'm leaving the day after tomorrow."

"Oh!" She grins. "Then we really *are* lucky." I find that I have almost forgotten the urchinlike grin of a colored girl. "I guess, before I keep babbling on, I'd better introduce myself. My name is Ada Holmes."

We shake hands. "This is Monsieur Vidal, the director of the film."

"I'm very honored to meet you, sir."

"Will you join us for a moment? Won't you sit down?" And Vidal pulls a chair out for her.

But she frowns contritely. "I really ought to get back to my friends." She looks at me. "I really just came over to say, for myself and all the kids, that we've got your records and we've seen your movie, and it means so much to us" — and she laughs, breathlessly, nervously, it is somehow more moving than tears — "more than I can say. Much more. And we wanted to know if you and your friend" — she looks at Vidal — "your *director*, Monsieur Vidal, would allow us to buy you a drink? We'd be very honored if you would."

"It is we who are honored," says Vidal, promptly, "*and* grateful. We were getting terribly bored with one another, thank God you came along."

The three of us laugh, and we cross the room.

The three at the table rise, and Ada makes the introductions. The other girl, taller and paler than Ada, is named Ruth. One of the boys is named Talley — "short for Talliafero" — and Golden-brown's name is Pete. "Man," he tells me, "I dig you the most. You tore me up, baby, tore me *up*."

"You tore up a lot of people," Talley says cryptically, and he and Ruth laugh. Vidal does not know, but I do, that Talley is probably referring to white people.

They are from New Orleans and Tallahassee and North Carolina; are college students, and met on the boat. They have been in Europe all summer, in Italy and Spain, but are only just getting to Paris.

"We meant to come sooner," says Ada, "but we could never make up our minds to leave a place. I thought we'd never pry Ruth loose from Venice."

"I resigned myself," says Pete, "and just sat in the Piazza San Marco, drinking gin fizz and being photographed with the pigeons, while Ruth had herself driven *all* up and down the Grand Canal." He looks at Ruth. "Finally, thank heaven, it rained."

"She was working off her hostilities," says Ada, with a grin. "We thought we might as well let her do it in Venice, the opportunities in North Carolina are really terribly limited."

"There are some very upset people walking around down there," Ruth says, "and a couple of tours around the Grand Canal might do them a world of good."

Pete laughs. "Can't you just see Ruth escorting them to the edge of the water?"

"I haven't lifted my hand in anger yet," Ruth says, "but, oh, Lord," and she laughs, clenching and unclenching her fists.

"You haven't been back for a long time, have you?" Talley asks me.

"Eight years. I haven't really lived there for twelve years."

Pete whistles. "I fear you are in for some surprises, my friend. There have been some changes made." Then, "Are you afraid?"

"A little."

"We all are," says Ada, "that's why I was so glad to get away for a little while."

"Then you haven't been back since Black Monday," Talley says. He laughs. "That's how it's gone down in Confederate history." He turns to Vidal. "What do people think about it here?"

Vidal smiles, delighted. "It seems extraordinarily infantile behavior, even for Americans, from whom, I must say, I have never expected very much in the way of maturity." Everyone at the table laughs. Vidal goes on. "But I cannot really talk about it, I do not understand it. I have never really understood Americans; I am an old man now, and I suppose I never will. There is something very nice about them, something very winning, but they seem so ignorant — so ignorant of life. Perhaps it is strange, but the only people from your country with whom I have ever made contact are black people — like my good friend, my discovery, here," and he slaps me on the shoulder. "Perhaps it is because we, in Europe, whatever else we do not know, or have forgotten, know about suffering. We have suffered here. You have suffered, too. But most Americans do not yet know what anguish is. It is too bad, because the life of the West is in their hands." He turns to Ada. "I cannot help saying that I think it is a scandal — and we may all pay very dearly for it — that a civilized nation should elect to represent it a man who is so simple that he thinks the world is simple." And silence falls at the table and the four young faces stare at him.

"Well," says Pete, at last, turning to me, "you won't be bored, man, when you get back there."

"It's much too nice a night," I say, "to stay cooped up in this place, where all I can hear is my own records." We laugh. "Why don't we get out of here and find a sidewalk café?" I tap Pete's guitar. "Maybe we can find out if you've got any talent."

"Oh, talent I've got," says Pete, "but character, man, I'm lacking."

So, after some confusion about the bill, for which Vidal has already made himself responsible, we walk out into the Paris night. It is very strange to feel that, very soon now, these boulevards will not exist for me. People will be walking up and down, as they are tonight, and lovers will be murmuring in the black shadows of the plane trees, and there will be these same still figures on the benches or in the parks — but they will not exist for me, I will not be here. For a long while Paris will no longer exist for me, except in my mind; and only in the minds of some people will I exist any longer for Paris. After departure, only invisible things are left, perhaps the life of the world is held together by invisible chains of memory and loss and love. So many things, so many people, depart! and we can only repossess them in our minds. Perhaps this is what the old folks meant, what my mother and my father meant, when they counseled us to keep the faith.

We have taken a table at the Deux Magots and Pete strums on his guitar and begins to play this song:

> *Preach the word, preach the word, preach the word!*
> *If I never, never see you any more.*
> *Preach the word, preach the word.*
> *And I'll meet you on Canaan's shore.*

He has a strong, clear, boyish voice, like a young preacher's, and he is smiling as he sings his song. Ada and I look at each other and grin, and Vidal is smiling. The waiter looks a little worried, for we are already beginning to attract a crowd, but it is a summer night, the gendarmes on the corner do not seem to mind, and there will be time, anyway, to stop us.

Pete was not there, none of us were, the first time this song was needed; and no one now alive can imagine what that time was like. But the song has come down the bloodstained ages. I suppose this to mean that the song is still needed, still has its work to do.

The others are all, visibly, very proud of Pete; and we all join him, and people stop to listen:

> *Testify! Testify!*
> *If I never, never see you any more!*
> *Testify! Testify!*
> *I'll meet you on Canaan's shore!*

In the crowd that has gathered to listen to us, I see a face I know, the face of a North African prizefighter, who is no longer in the ring. I used to know him well in the old days, but have not seen him for a long time. He looks quite well, his face is shining, he is quite decently dressed. And something about the way he holds himself, not quite looking at our table, tells me that he has seen me, but does not want to risk a rebuff. So I call him. "Boona!"

And he turns, smiling, and comes loping over to our table, his hands in his pockets. Pete is still singing and Ada and Vidal have taken off on a conversation of their own. Ruth and Talley look curiously, expectantly, at Boona. Now that I have called him over, I feel somewhat uneasy. I realize that I do not know what he is doing now, or how he will get along with any of these people, and I can see in his eyes that he is delighted to be in the pesence of two young girls. There are virtually no North African women in Paris, and not even the dirty, rat-faced girls who live, apparently, in cafés are willing to go with an Arab. So Boona is always looking for a girl, and because he is so deprived and because he is not Western, his techniques can be very unsettling. I know he is relieved that the girls are not French and not white. He looks briefly at Vidal and Ada. Vidal, also, though for different reasons, is always looking for a girl.

But Boona has always been very nice to me. Perhaps I am sorry that I called him over, but I did not want to snub him.

He claps one hand to the side of my head, as is his habit. "*Comment vas-tu, mon frère?* I have not see you, oh, for long time." And he asks me, as in the old days, "You all right? Nobody bother you?" And he laughs. "Ah! *Tu as fait le chemin, toi!* Now you are *vedette,* big star — wonderful!" He looks around the table, made a little uncomfortable by the silence that has fallen, now that Pete has stopped singing. "I have seen you in the movies — you know? — and I tell everybody, I know *him!*" He points to me, and laughs, and Ruth and Talley laugh with him. "That's right, man, you make me real proud, you make me cry!"

"Boona, I want you to meet some friends of mine." And I go round the table: "Ruth, Talley, Ada, Pete" — and he bows and shakes hands, his dark eyes gleaming with pleasure — *"et Monsieur Vidal, le metteur en scène du film quit'a arraché des larmes."*

"Enchanté." But his attitude toward Vidal is colder, more distrustful. "Of course I have heard of Monsieur Vidal. He is the director of many films, many of them made me cry." This last statement is utterly, even insolently, insincere.

But Vidal, I think, is relieved that I will now be forced to speak to Boona and will leave him alone with Ada.

"Sit down," I say, "have a drink with us, let me have your news. What's been happening with you, what are you doing with yourself these days?"

"Ah," he sits down, "nothing very brilliant, my brother." He looks at me quickly, with a little smile. "You know, we have been having hard times here."

"Where are you from?" Ada asks him.

His brilliant eyes take her in entirely, but she does not flinch. "I am from Tunis." He says it proudly, with a little smile.

"From Tunis. I have never been to Africa, I would love to go one day."

He laughs. "Africa is a big place. Very big. There are many countries in Africa, many" — he looks briefly at Vidal — "different kinds of people, many colonies."

"But Tunis," she continues, in her innocence, "is free? Freedom is happening all over Africa. That's why I would like to go there."

"I have not been back for a long time," says Boona, "but all the news I get from Tunis, from my people, is not good."

"Wouldn't you like to go back?" Ruth asks.

Again he looks at Vidal. "That is not so easy."

Vidal smiles. "You know what I would like to do? There's a wonderful Spanish place not far from here, where we can listen to live music and dance a little." He turns to Ada. "Would you like that?"

He is leaving it up to me to get rid of Boona, and it is, of course, precisely for this reason that I cannot do it. Besides, it is no longer so simple.

"Oh, I'd love that," says Ada, and she turns to Boona. "Won't you come, too?"

"Thank you, mam'selle," he says, softly, and his tongue flicks briefly over his lower lip, and he smiles. He is very moved, people are not often nice to him.

In the Spanish place there are indeed a couple of Spanish guitars, drums, castanets, and a piano, but the uses to which these are being put carry one back, as Pete puts it, to the levee. "These are the wailingest Spanish cats I ever heard," says Ruth. "They didn't learn how to do this in Spain, no, they didn't, they been rambling. You ever hear anything like this going on in Spain?" Talley takes her out on the dance floor, which is already crowded. A very handsome Frenchwoman is dancing with an enormous, handsome black man, who seems to be her lover, who seems to have taught her how to dance. Apparently, they are known to the musicians, who egg them on with small cries of *"Olé!"* It is a very good-natured crowd, mostly foreigners, Spaniards, Swedes, Greeks. Boona takes Ada out on the dance floor while Vidal is answering some questions put to him by Pete on the entertainment situation in France. Vidal looks a little put out, and I am amused.

We are there for perhaps an hour, dancing, talking, and I am, at last, a little drunk. In spite of Boona, who is a very good and tireless dancer, Vidal continues his pursuit of Ada, and I begin to wonder if he will make it and I begin to wonder if I want him to.

I am still puzzling out my reaction when Pete, who has disappeared, comes in through the front door, catches my eye, and signals to me. I leave the table and follow him into the streets.

He looks very upset. "I don't want to bug you, man," he says, "but I fear your boy has goofed."

I know he is not joking. I think he is probably angry at Vidal because of Ada, and I wonder what I can do about it and why he should be telling me.

I stare at him, gravely, and he says, "It looks like he stole some money."

"Stole *money?* Who, Vidal?"

And then, of course, I get it, in the split second before he says, impatiently, "No, are you kidding? Your friend, the Tunisian."

I do not know what to say or what to do, and so I temporize with questions. All the time I am wondering if this can be true and what I can do about it if it is. The trouble is, I know that Boona steals, he would probably not be alive if he didn't, but I cannot say so to these children, who probably still imagine that everyone who steals is a thief. But he has never, to my knowledge, stolen from a friend. It seems unlike him. I have always thought of him as being better than that, and smarter than that. And so I cannot believe it, but neither can I doubt it. I do not know anything about Boona's life, these days. This causes me to realize that I do not really know much about Boona.

"Who did he steal it from?"

"From Ada. Out of her bag."

"How much?"

"Ten dollars. It's not an awful lot of money, but" — he grimaces — "none of us *have* an awful lot of money."

"I know." The dark side street on which we stand is nearly empty. The only sound on the street is the muffled music of the Spanish club. "How do you know it was Boona?"

He anticipates my own unspoken rejoinder. "Who else could it be? Besides — somebody *saw* him do it."

"Somebody saw him?"

"Yes."

I do not ask him who this person is, for fear that he will say it is Vidal.

"Well," I say, "I'll try to get it back." I think that I will take Boona aside and then replace the money myself. "Was it in dollars or in francs?"

"In francs."

I have no dollars and this makes it easier. I do not know how I can possibly face Boona and accuse him of stealing money from my friends. I would rather give him the benefit of even the faintest doubt. But, "Who saw him?" I ask.

"Talley. But we didn't want to make a thing about it — "

"Does Ada know it's gone?"

"Yes." He looks at me helplessly. "I know this makes you feel pretty bad, but we thought we'd better tell you, rather than" — lamely — "anybody else."

Now, Ada comes out of the club, carrying her ridiculous handbag, and with her face all knotted and sad. "Oh," she says, "I hate to cause all this trouble, it's not worth it, not for ten lousy dollars." I am astonished to see that she has been weeping, and tears come to her eyes now.

I put my arm around her shoulder. "Come on, now. You're not causing anybody any trouble and, anyway, it's nothing to cry about."

"It isn't your fault, Ada," Pete says, miserably.

"Oh, I ought to get a sensible handbag," she says, "like you're always
telling me to do," and she laughs a little, then looks at me. "Please don't
try to do anything about it. Let's just forget it."

"What's happening inside?" I ask her.

"Nothing. They're just talking. I think Mr. Vidal is dancing with
Ruth. He's a great dancer, that little Frenchman."

"He's a great talker, too," Pete says.

"Oh, he doesn't mean anything," says Ada, "he's just having fun. He
probably doesn't get a chance to talk to many American girls."

"He certainly made up for lost time tonight."

"Look," I say, "if Talley and Boona are alone, maybe you better go
back in. We'll be in in a minute. Let's try to keep this as quiet as we can."

"Yeah," he says, "okay. We're going soon anyway, okay?"

"Yes," she tells him, "right away."

But as he turns away, Boona and Talley step out into the street, and it
is clear that Talley feels that he has Boona under arrest. I almost laugh,
the whole thing is beginning to resemble one of those mad French farces
with people flying in and out of doors; but Boona comes straight to me.

"They say I stole money, my friend. You know me, you are the only
one here who knows me, you know I would not do such a thing."

I look at him and I do not know what to say. Ada looks at him with
her eyes full of tears and looks away. I take Boona's arm.

"We'll be back in a minute," I say. We walk a few paces up the dark,
silent street.

"She say I take her money," he says. He, too, looks as though he is
about to weep — but I do not know for which reason. "You know me,
you know me almost twelve years, you think I do such a thing?"

Talley saw you, I want to say, but I cannot say it. Perhaps Talley only
thought he saw him. Perhaps it is easy to see a boy who looks like Boona
with his hand in an American girl's purse.

"If you not believe me," he says, "search me. Search me!" And he
opens his arms wide, theatrically, and now there are tears standing in his
eyes.

I do not know what his tears mean, but I certainly cannot search him. I
want to say, I know you steal, I know you have to steal. Perhaps you
took the money out of the girl's purse in order to eat tomorrow, in order

not to be thrown into the streets tonight, in order to stay out of jail. This girl means nothing to you, after all, she is only an American, an American like me. Perhaps, I suddenly think, no girl means anything to you, or ever will again, they have beaten you too hard and kept you in the gutter too long. And I also think, If you would steal from her, then of course you would lie to me, neither of us means anything to you; perhaps, in your eyes, we are simply luckier gangsters in a world which is run by gangsters. But I cannot say any of these things to Boona. I cannot say, Tell me the truth, nobody cares about the money any more.

So I say, "Of course I will not search you." And I realize that he knew that I would not.

"I think it is that Frenchman who say I am a thief. They think we all are thieves." His eyes are bright and bitter. He looks over my shoulder. "They have all come out of the club now."

I look around and they are all there, in a little dark knot on the sidewalk.

"Don't worry," I say. "It doesn't matter."

"You believe me? My brother?" And his eyes look into mine with a terrible intensity.

"Yes," I force myself to say, "yes, of course, I believe you. Someone made a mistake, that's all."

"You know, the way American girls run around, they have their sack open all the time, she could lose the money anywhere. Why she blame me? Because I come from Africa?" Tears are glittering on his face. "Here she come now."

And Ada comes up the street with her straight, determined walk. She walks straight to Boona and takes his hand. "I am sorry," she says, "for everything that happened. Please believe me. It isn't worth all this fuss. I'm sure you're a very nice person, and" — she falters — "I must have lost the money, I'm sure I lost it." She looks at him. "It isn't worth hurting your feelings, and I'm terribly sorry about it."

"I no take your money," he says. "Really, truly, I no take it. Ask him" — pointing to me, grabbing me by the arm, shaking me — "he know me for years, he will tell you that I never, never steal!"

"I'm sure," she says. "I'm sure."

I take Boona by the arm again. "Let's forget it. Let's forget it all. We're all going home now, and one of these days we'll have a drink again and we'll forget all about it, all right?"

"Yes," says Ada, "let us forget it." And she holds out her hand.

Boona takes it, wonderingly. His eyes take her in again. "You are a very nice girl. Really. A very nice girl."

"I'm sure you're a nice person, too." She pauses. "Good night."

"Good night," he says, after a long silence.

Then he kisses me on both cheeks. *"Au revoir, mon frère."*

"Au revoir, Boona."

After a moment we turn and walk away, leaving him standing there.

"Did he take it?" asks Vidal.

"I tell you, I *saw* him," says Talley.

"Well," I say, "it doesn't matter now." I look back and see Boona's stocky figure disappearing down the street.

"No," says Ada, "it doesn't matter." She looks up. "It's almost morning."

"I would gladly," says Vidal, stammering, "gladly — "

But she is herself again. "I wouldn't think of it. We had a wonderful time tonight, a wonderful time, and I wouldn't think of it." She turns to me with that urchinlike grin. "It was wonderful meeting you. I hope you won't have too much trouble getting used to the States again."

"Oh, I don't think I will," I say. And then, "I hope you won't."

"No," she says, "I don't think anything they can do will surprise me any more."

"Which way are we all going?" asks Vidal. "I hope someone will share my taxi with me."

But he lives in the sixteenth arrondissement, which is not in anyone's direction. We walk him to the line of cabs standing under the clock at Odéon.

And we look each other in the face, in the growing morning light. His face looks weary and lined and lonely. He puts both hands on my shoulders and then puts one hand on the nape of my neck. "Do not forget me, Chico," he says. "You must come back and see us, one of these days. Many of us depend on you for many things."

"I'll be back," I say. "I'll never forget you."

He raises his eyebrows and smiles. *"Alors, adieu."*

"Adieu, Vidal."

"I was happy to meet all of you," he says. He looks at Ada. "Perhaps we will meet again before you leave."

"Perhaps," she says. "Good-by, Monsieur Vidal."

"Good-by."

Vidal's cab drives away. "I also leave you now," I say. "I must go home and wake up my son and prepare for our journey."

I leave them standing on the corner, under the clock, which points to six. They look very strange and lost and determined, the four of them. Just before my cab turns off the boulevard, I wave to them and they wave back.

Mme. Dumont is in the hall, mopping the floor.

"Did all my family get home?" I ask. I feel very cheerful, I do not know why.

"Yes," she says, "they are all here. Paul is still sleeping."

"May I go in and get him?"

She looks at me in surprise. "Of course."

So I walk into her apartment and walk into the room where Paul lies sleeping. I stand over his bed for a long time.

Perhaps my thoughts travel — travel through to him. He opens his eyes and smiles up at me. He puts a fist to his eyes and raises his arms. *"Bonjour, Papa."*

I lift him up. *"Bonjour.* How do you feel today?"

"Oh, I don't know yet," he says.

I laugh. I put him on my shoulder and walk out into the hall. Mme. Dumont looks up at him with her radiant, aging face.

"Ah," she says, "you are going on a journey! How does it feel?"

"He doesn't know yet," I tell her. I walk to the elevator door and open it, dropping Paul down to the crook of my arm.

She laughs again. "He will know later. What a journey! *Jusqu'au nouveau monde!"*

I open the cage and we step inside. "Yes," I say, "all the way to the new world." I press the button and the cage, holding my son and me, goes up.

TILLIE OLSEN

The most splendid writing has both laughter and tears. That is why
Don Quixote *has lived all these centuries. And that is why "Tell Me a
Riddle" is such a memorable story. It is a rare quality in all literature
and to be treasured when found.*

    *Tillie Olsen grew up in Nebraska where her formal education stopped
"almost through high school." She has worked most of the time in recent years as a typist and transcriber. A San Franciscan since 1933, she
is the mother of four daughters. A collection of her work appeared in
book form in 1962.*

Tell Me a Riddle

I

FOR FORTY-SEVEN YEARS: they had been married. How deep back the stubborn, gnarled roots of the quarrel reached, no one could say — but only now, when tending to the needs of others no longer shackled them together, the roots swelled up visible, split the earth between them, and the tearing shook even to the children, long since grown.

Why now, why now? wailed Hannah.

As if when we grew up weren't enough, said Paul.

Poor Ma. Poor Dad. It hurt so for both of them, said Vivi. They never had very much; at least in old age they should be happy.

Knock their heads together, insisted Sammy; tell 'em: you're too old for this kind of thing; no reason not to get along now.

Lennie wrote to Clara: They've lived over so much together; what could possibly tear them apart?

Something tangible enough.

Arthritic hands, and such work as he got, occasional. Poverty all his

life, and there was little breath left for running. He could not, could not
turn away from this desire: to have the troubling of responsibility, the
fretting with money, over and done with; to be free, to be *care*free where
success was not measured by accumulation, and there was use for the
vitality still in him.

There was a way. They could sell the house, and with the money join
his lodge's Haven, co-operative for the aged. Happy communal life, and
was he not already an official; had he not helped organize it, raise funds,
served as a trustee?

But she — would not consider it.

"What do we need all this for?" he would ask loudly, for her hearing
aid was turned down and the vacuum was shrilling. "Five rooms" (pushing the sofa so she could get into the corner) "furniture" (smoothing
down the rug) "floors and surfaces to make work. Tell me, why do we
need it?" And he was glad he could ask in a scream.

"Because I'm use't."

"Because you're use't. This is a reason, Mrs. Word Miser? Used to can
get unused!"

"Enough unused I have to get used to already. . . . Not enough
words?" turning off the vacuum a moment to hear herself answer. "Because soon enough we'll need only a little closet, no windows, no furniture, nothing to make work for but worms. Because now I want room.
. . . Screech and blow like you're doing, you'll need that closet even
sooner. . . . Ha, again!" for the vacuum bag wailed, puffed half up,
hung stubbornly limp. "This time fix it so it stays; quick before the
phone rings and you get too importantbusy."

But while he struggled with the motor, it seethed in him. Why fix it?
Why have to bother? And if it can't be fixed, have to wring the mind
with how to pay the repair? At the Haven they come in with their own
machines to clean your room or your cottage; you fish, or play cards, or
make jokes in the sun, not with knotty fingers fight to mend vacuums.

Over the dishes, coaxingly: "For once in your life, to be free, to have
everything done for you, like a queen."

"I never liked queens."

"No dishes, no garbage, no towel to sop, no worry what to buy, what
to eat."

"And what else would I do with my empty hands? Better to eat at my
own table when I want, and to cook and eat how I want."

"In the cottages they buy what you ask, and cook it how you like. *You* are the one who always used to say: better mankind born without mouths and stomachs than always to worry for money to buy, to shop, to fix, to cook, to wash, to clean."

"How cleverly you hid that you heard. I said it then because eighteen hours a day I ran. And you never scraped a carrot or knew a dish towel sops. Now — for you and me — who cares? A herring out of a jar is enough. But when *I* want, and nobody to bother." And she turned off her ear button, so she would not have to hear.

But as *he* had no peace, juggling and rejuggling the money to figure: how will I pay for this now?; prying out the storm windows (there they take care of this); jolting in the streetcar on errands (there I would not have to ride to take care of this or that); fending the patronizing relatives just back from Florida (there it matters what one is, not what one can afford), he gave *her* no peace.

"Look! In their bulletin. A reading circle. Twice a week it meets."

"Haumm," her answer of not listening.

"A reading circle. Chekhov they read that you like, and Peretz. Cultured people at the Haven that you would enjoy."

"Enjoy!" She tasted the word. "Now, when it pleases you, you find a reading circle for me. And forty years ago when the children were morsels and there was a Circle, did you stay home with them once so I could go? Even once? You trained me well. I do not need others to enjoy. Others!" Her voice trembled. "Because *you* want to be there with others. Already it makes me sick to think of you always around others. Clown, grimacer, floormat, yesman, entertainer, whatever they want of you."

And now it was he who turned on the television loud so he need not hear.

Old scar tissue ruptured and the wounds festered anew. Chekhov indeed. She thought without softness of that young wife, who in the deep night hours while she nursed the current baby, and perhaps held another in her lap, would try to stay awake for the only time there was to read. She would feel again the weather of the outside on his cheek when, coming late from a meeting, he would find her so, and stimulated and ardent, sniffing her skin, coax: "I'll put the baby to bed, and you — put the book away, don't read, don't read."

That had been the most beguiling of all the "don't read, put your book away" her life had been. Chekhov indeed!

"Money?" She shrugged him off. "Could we get poorer than once we were? And in America, who starves?"

But as still he pressed:

"Let me alone about money. Was there ever enough? Seven little ones — for every penny I had to ask — and sometimes, remember, there was nothing. But always *I* had to manage. Now *you* manage. Rub your nose in it good."

But from those years she had had to manage, old humiliations and terrors rose up, lived again, and forced her to relive them. The children's needings; that grocer's face or this merchant's wife she had had to beg credit from when credit was a disgrace, the scenery of the long blocks walked around when she could not pay; school coming, and the desperate going over the old to see what could yet be remade; the soups of meat bones begged "for-the-dog" one winter. . . .

Enough. Now they had no children. Let *him* wrack his head for how they would live. She would not exchange her solitude for anything. *Never again to be forced to move to the rhythms of others.*

For in this solitude she had won to a reconciled peace.

Tranquillity from having the empty house no longer an enemy, for it stayed clean — not as in the days when it was her famly, the life in it, that had seemed the enemy: tracking, smudging, littering, dirtying, engaging her in endless defeating battle — and on whom her endless defeat had been spewed.

The few old books, memorized from rereading; the pictures to ponder (the magnifying glass superimposed on her heavy eyeglasses). Or if she wishes, when he is gone, the phonograph, that if she turns up very loud and strains, she can hear: the ordered sounds and the struggling.

Out in the garden, growing things to nurture. Birds to be kept out of the pear tree, and when the pears are heavy and ripe, the old fury of work, for all must be canned, nothing wasted.

And her one social duty (for she will not go to luncheons or meetings) the boxes of old clothes left with her, as with a life-practiced eye for finding what is still wearable within the worn (again the magnifying glass superimposed on the heavy glasses) she scans and sorts — this for rag or rummage, that for mending and cleaning, and this for sending abroad.

Being able at last to live within, and not move to the rhythms of others, as life had helped her to: denying; removing; isolating; taking the children one by one; then deafening, half-blinding — and at last, presenting her solitude.

And in it she had won to a reconciled peace.

Now he was violating it with his constant campaigning: *Sell the house and move to the Haven*. (You sit, you sit — there too you could sit like a stone.) He was making of her a battleground where old grievances tore. (Turn on your ear button — I am talking.) And stubbornly she resisted — so that from wheedling, reasoning, manipulation, it was bitterness he now started with.

And it came to where every happening lashed up a quarrel.

"I will sell the house anyway," he flung at her one night. "I am putting it up for sale. There will be a way to make you sign."

The television blared, as always it did on the evenings he stayed home, and as always it reached her only as noise. She did not know if the tumult was in her or outside. Snap! she turned the sound off. "Shadows," she whispered to him, pointing to the screen, "look, it is only shadows." And in a scream: "Did you say that you will sell the house? Look at me, not at that. I am no shadow. You cannot sell without me."

"Leave on the television. I am watching."

"Like Paulie, like Jenny, a four-year-old. Staring at shadows. *You cannot sell the house.*"

"I will. We are going to the Haven. There you would not hear the television when you do not want it. I could sit in the social room and watch. You could lock yourself up to smell your unpleasantness in a room by yourself — for who would want to come near you?"

"No, no selling." A whisper now.

"The television is shadows. Mrs. Enlightened! Mrs. Cultured! A world comes into your house — and it is shadows. People you would never meet in a thousand lifetimes. Wonders. When you were four years old, yes, like Paulie, like Jenny, did you know of Indian dances, alligators, how they use bamboo in Malaya? No, you scratched in your dirt with the chickens and thought Olshana was the world. Yes, Mrs. Unpleasant, I will sell the house, for there better can we be rid of each other than here."

She did not know if the tumult was outside, or in her. Always a ravening inside, a pull to the bed, to lie down, to succumb.

"Have you thought maybe Ma should let a doctor have a look at her?" asked their son Paul after Sunday dinner, regarding his mother crumpled on the couch, instead of, as was her custom, busying herself in Nancy's kitchen.

"Why not the President too?"

"Seriously, Dad. This is the third Sunday she's lain down like that after dinner. Is she that way at home?"

"A regular love affair with the bed. Every time I start to talk to her."

Good protective reaction, observed Nancy to herself. The workings of hos-til-ity.

"Nancy could take her. I just don't like how she looks. Let's have Nancy arrange an appointment."

"You think she'll go?" regarding his wife gloomily. "All right, we have to have doctor bills, we have to have doctor bills." Loudly: "Something hurts you?"

She startled, looked to his lips. He repeated: "Mrs. Take It Easy, something hurts?"

"Nothing. . . . Only you."

"A woman of honey. That's why you're lying down?"

"Soon I'll get up to do the dishes, Nancy."

"Leave them, Mother, I like it better this way."

"Mrs. Take It Easy, Paul says you should start ballet. You should go to see a doctor and ask: how soon can you start ballet?"

"A doctor?" she begged. "Ballet?"

"We were talking, Ma," explained Paul, "you don't seem any too well. It would be a good idea for you to see a doctor for a checkup."

"I get up now to do the kitchen. Doctors are bills and foolishness, my son. I need no doctors."

"At the Haven," he could not resist pointing out, "a doctor is *not* bills. He lives beside you. You start to sneeze, he is there before you open up a Kleenex. You can be sick there for free, all you want."

"Diarrhoea of the mouth, is there a doctor to make you dumb?"

"Ma. Promise me you'll go. Nancy will arrange it."

"It's all of a piece when you think of it," said Nancy, "the way she attacks my kitchen, scrubbing under every cup hook, doing the inside of the oven so I can't enjoy Sunday dinner, knowing that half-blind or not, she's going to find every speck of dirt. . . ."

"Don't, Nancy, I've told you — it's the only way she knows to be useful. What did the *doctor* say?"

"A real fatherly lecture. Sixty-nine is young these days. Go out, enjoy life, find interests. Get a new hearing aid, this one is antiquated. Old age is sickness only if one makes it so. Geriatrics, Inc."

"So there was nothing physical."

"Of course there was. How can you live to yourself like she does without there being? Evidence of a kidney disorder, and her blood count is low. He gave her a diet, and she's to come back for follow-up and lab work. . . . But he was clear enough: Number One prescription — start living like a human being. When I think of your dad, who could really play the invalid with that arthritis of his, as active as a teenager, and twice as much fun. . . ."

"You didn't tell me the doctor says your sickness is in you, how you live." He pushed his advantage. "Life and enjoyments you need better than medicine. And this diet, how can you keep it? To weigh each morsel and scrape away the bits of fat to make this soup, that pudding. There, at the Haven, they have a dietician, they would do it for you."

She is silent.

"You would feel better there, I know it," he says gently. "There there is life and enjoyment all around."

"What is the matter, Mr. Importantbusy, you have no card game or meeting you can go to?" — turning her face to the pillow.

For a while he cut his meetings and going out, fussed over her diet, tried to wheedle her into leaving the house, brought in visitors:

I should come to a fashion tea. I should sit and look at pretty babies in clothes I cannot buy. This is pleasure?

Always you are better than everyone else. The doctor said you should go out. Mrs. Brem comes to you with goodness and you turn her away.

Because *you* asked her to, she asked me.

They won't come back. People you need, the doctor said. Your own cousins I asked; they were willing to come and make peace as if nothing had happened. . . .

No more crushers of people, pushers, hypocrites, around me. No more in *my* house. You go to them if you like.

Kind he is to visit. And you, like ice.

A babbler. All my life around babblers. Enough!

"She's even worse, Dad? Then let her stew a while," advised Nancy. "You can't let it destroy you; it's a psychological thing, maybe too far gone for any of us to help."

So he let her stew. More and more she lay silent in bed, and sometimes did not even get up to make the meals. No longer was the tongue-lashing inevitable if he left the coffee cup where it did not belong, or forgot to take out the garbage or mislaid the broom. The birds grew bold that summer and for once pocked the pears, undisturbed.

A bellyful of bitterness and every day the same quarrel in a new way and a different old grievance the quarrel forced her to enter and relive. And the new torment: I am not really sick, the doctor said it, then why do I feel so sick?

One night she asked him: "You have a meeting tonight? Do not go. Stay . . . with me."

He had planned to watch "This Is Your Life" anyway, but half sick himself from the heavy heat, and sickening therefore the more after the brooks and woods of the Haven, with satisfaction he grated:

"Hah, Mrs. Live Alone And Like It wants company all of a sudden. It doesn't seem so good the time of solitary when she was a girl exile in Siberia. 'Do not go. Stay with me.' A new song for Mrs. Free As A Bird. Yes, I am going out, and while I am gone chew this aloneness good. Think how you keep us both from where if you want people you do not need to be alone."

"Go, go. All your life you have gone without me."

After him she sobbed curses he had not heard in years, old-country curses from their childhood: Grow, oh shall you grow like an onion, with your head in the ground. Like the hide of a drum shall you be, beaten in life, beaten in death. Oh shall you be like a chandelier, to hang, and to burn. . . .

She was not in their bed when he came back. She lay on the cot on the sun-porch. All week she did not speak or come near him; nor did he try to make peace or care for her.

He slept badly, so used to her next to him. After all the years, old harmonies and dependencies deep in their bodies; she curled to him, or he coiled to her each warmed, warming, turning as the other turned, the nights a long embrace.

It was not the empty bed or the storm that woke him, but a faint singing. *She* was singing. Shaking off the drops of rain, the lightning riving her lifted face, he saw her so; the cot covers on the floor.

"This is a private concert?" he asked. "Come in, you are wet."

"I can breathe now," she answered; "my lungs are rich." Though indeed the sound was hardly a breath.

"Come in, come in." Loosing the bamboo shades. "Look how wet you are." Half helping, half carrying her, still faint-breathing her song.

A Russian love song of fifty years ago.

He had found a buyer, but before he told her, he called together those children who were close enough to come. Paul, of course, Sammy from New Jersey, Hannah from Connecticut, Vivi from Ohio.

With a kindling of energy for her beloved visitors, she arrayed the house, cooked and baked. She was not prepared for the solemn after-dinner conclave, they too probing in and tearing. Her frightened eyes watched from mouth to mouth as each spoke.

His stories were eloquent and funny of her refusal to go back to the doctor; of the scorned invitations; of her stubborn silences or the bile "like a Niagara"; of her contrariness: "If I clean it's no good how I cleaned; if I don't clean, I'm still a master who thinks he has a slave."

("Vinegar he poured on me all his life; I am well marinated; how can I be honey now?")

Deftly he marched in the rightness for moving to the Haven; their money from social security free for visiting the children, not sucked into daily needs and into the house; the activities in the Haven for him; but mostly the Haven for *her:* her health, her need of care, distraction, amusement, friends who shared her interests.

"This does offer an outlet for Dad," said Paul; "he's always been an active person. And economic peace of mind isn't to be sneezed at, either. I could use a little of that myself."

But when they asked: "And you, Ma, how do you feel about it?" could only whisper:

"For him it is good. It is not for me. I can no longer live between people."

"You lived all your life *for* people," Vivi cried.

"Not with." Suffering doubly for the unhappiness on her children's faces.

"You have to find some compromise," Sammy insisted. "Maybe sell the house and buy a trailer. After forty-seven years there's surely some way you can find to live in peace."

"There is no help, my children. Different things we need."

"Then live alone!" He could control himself no longer. "I have a buyer for the house. Half the money for you, half for me. Either alone or with me to the Haven. You think I can live any longer as we are doing now?"

"Ma doesn't have to make a decision this minute, however you feel, Dad," Paul said quickly, "and you wouldn't want her to. Let's let it lay a few months, and then talk some more."

"I think I can work it out to take Mother home with me for a while," Hannah said. "You both look terrrible, but especially you, Mother. I'm going to ask Phil to have a look at you."

"Sure," cracked Sammy. "What's the use of a doctor husband if you can't get free service out of him once in a while for the family? And absence might make the heart . . . you know."

"There was something after all," Paul told Nancy in a colorless voice. "That was Hannah's Phil calling. Her gall bladder. . . . Surgery."

"Her *gall* bladder. If that isn't classic. 'Bitter as gall' — talk of psychosom —— "

He stepped closer, put his hand over her mouth and said in the same colorless, plodding voice. "We have to get Dad. They operated at once. The cancer was everywhere, surrounding the liver, everywhere. They did what they could . . . at best she has a year. Dad . . . we have to tell him."

II

Honest in his weakness when they told him, and that she was not to know. "I'm not an actor. She'll know right away by how I am. Oh that poor woman. I am old too, it will break me into pieces. Oh that poor woman. She will spit on me: 'So my sickness was how I live.' Oh Paulie, how she will be, that poor woman. Only she should not suffer. . . . I can't stand sickness, Paulie, I can't go with you."

But went. And play-acted.

"A grand opening and you did not even wait for me. . . . A good thing Hannah took you with her."

"Fashion teas I needed. They cut out what tore in me; just in my throat something hurts yet. . . . Look! so many flowers, like a funeral. Vivi called, did Hannah tell you? And Lennie from San Francisco, and Clara; and Sammy is coming." Her gnome's face pressed happily into the flowers.

*

It is impossible to predict in these cases, but once over the immediate effects of the operation, she should have several months of comparative well-being.

The money, where will come the money?

Travel with her, Dad. Don't take her home to the old associations. The other children will want to see her.

The money, where will I wring the money?

Whatever happens, she is not to know. No, you can't ask her to sign papers to sell the house; nothing to upset her. Borrow instead, then after. . . .

I had wanted to leave you each a few dollars to make life easier, as other fathers do. There will be nothing left now. (Failure! you and your "business is exploitation." Why didn't you make it when it could be made? — Is that what you're thinking, Sammy?)

Sure she's unreasonable, Dad — but you have to stay with her; if there's to be any happiness in what's left of her life, it depends on you.

Prop me up, children, think of me, too. Shuffled, chained with her, bitter woman. No Haven, and the little money going. . . . How happy she looks, poor creature.

The look of excitement. The straining to hear everything (the new hearing aid turned full). Why are you so happy, dying woman?

How the petals are, fold on fold, and the gladioli color. The autumn air.

Stranger grandsons, tall above the little gnome grandmother, the little spry grandfather. Paul in a frenzy of picture-taking before going.

She, wandering the great house. Feeling the books; laughing at the maple shoemaker's bench of a hundred years ago used as a table. The ear turned to music.

"Let us go home. See how good I walk now." "One step from the hospital," he answers, "and she wants to fly. Wait till Doctor Phil says."

"Look — the birds too are flying home. Very good Phil is and will not show it, but he is sick of sickness by the time he comes home."

"Mrs. Telepathy, to read minds," he answers; "read mine what it says: when the trunks of medicines become a suitcase, then we will go."

The grandboys, they do not know what to say to us. . . . Hannah, she runs around here, there, when is there time for herself?

Let us go home. Let us go home.

Musing; gentleness — *but for the incidents of the rabbi in the hospital and of the candles of benediction.*

Of the rabbi in the hospital:
Now tell me what happened, Mother.
From the sleep I awoke, Hannah's Phil, and he stands there like a devil in a dream and calls me by name. I cannot hear. I think he prays. Go away, please, I tell him, I am not a believer. Still he stands, while my heart knocks with fright.
You scared *him,* Mother. He thought you were delirious.
Who sent him? Why did he come to me?
It is a custom. The men of God come to visit those of their religion they might help. The hospital makes up the list for them — race, religion — and you are on the Jewish list.
Not for rabbis. At once go and make them change. Tell them to write: Race, human; Religion, none.

And of the candles of benediction:
Look how you have upset yourself, Mrs. Excited Over Nothing. Pleasant memories you should leave.
Go in, go back to Hannah and the lights. Two weeks I saw candles and said nothing. But she asked me.
So what was so terrible? She forgets you never did, she asks you to light the Friday candles and say the benediction like Phil's mother when she visits. If the candles give her pleasure, why shouldn't she have the pleasure?
Not for pleasure she does it. For emptiness. Because his family does. Because all around her do.
That is not a good reason too? But you did not hear her. For heritage, she told you. For the boys, from the past they should have tradition.
Superstition! From the savages, afraid of the dark, of themselves: mumbo words and magic lights to scare away ghosts.
She told you: how it started does not take away the goodness. For centuries, peace in the house it means.
Swindler! does she look back on the dark centuries? Candles bought instead of bread and stuck into a potato for there is no other candlestick? Religion that stifled and said: in Paradise, woman, you will be

the footstool of your husband, and in life — poor chosen Jew — ground under, despised, trembling in cellars. And cremated. And cremated.

This is religion's fault? You think you are still an orator of the 1905 revolution? Where are the pills for quieting? Which are they?

Heritage. How have we come from the savages, how no longer to be savages — this to teach. To look back and learn what ennobles man — this to teach. To smash all ghettos that divide man — not to go back, not to go back — this to teach. Learned books in the house, will man live or die, and she gives to her boys — superstition.

Hannah that is so good to you. Take your pill, Mrs. Excited For Nothing, swallow.

Heritage! But when did I have time to teach? Of Hannah I asked only hands to help.

Swallow!

Otherwise — musing; gentleness.

Not to travel. To go home.

The children want to see you. We have to show them you are as thorny a flower as ever.

Not to travel.

Vivi wants you should see her new baby. She sent the tickets — airplane tickets — a Mrs. Roosevelt she wants to make of you. To Vivi's we have to go.

A new baby. How many warm, seductive babies. She holds him stiffly, *away* from her, so that he wails. And a long shudder begins, and the sweat beads on her forehead.

"Hush, shush," croons the grandfather, lifting him back. "You should forgive your grandmamma, little prince, she has never held a baby before, only seen them in glass cases. Hush, shush."

"You're tired, Ma," says Vivi. "The travel and the noisy dinner. I'll take you to lie down."

(*A long travel from, to, what the feel of a baby evokes.*)

In the airplane, cunningly designed to encase from motion (no wind, no feel of flight), she had sat severely and still, her face turned to the sky through which they cleaved and left no scar.

So this was how it looked, the determining, the crucial sky, and this was how man moved through it; remote above the dwindled earth, the concealed human life. Vulnerable life, that could scar.

There was a steerage ship of memory that shook across a great, circular sea: clustered, ill human beings; and through the thick-stained air, tiny fretting waters in a window round like the airplane's — sun round, moon round. (The round thatched roofs of Olshana.) Eye round — like the smaller window that framed distance the solitary year of exile when only her eyes could travel, and no voice spoke. And the polar winds hurled themselves across snow trackless and endless and white — like the clouds which had closed together below and hidden the earth.

Now they put a baby in her lap. Do not ask me, she would have liked to beg. Enough the worn face of Vivi, the remembered grandchildren. I cannot, cannot. . . .

Cannot what? Unnatural grandmother, not able to make herself embrace a baby.

She lay there in the bed of the two little girls, her new hearing aid turned full, listening to the sound of the children going to sleep, the baby's fretful crying and hushing, the clatter of dishes being washed and put away. They thought she slept. Still she rode on.

It was not that she had not loved her babies, her children. The love — the passion of tending — had risen with the need like a torrent; and like a torrent drowned and immolated all else. But when the need was done — oh the power that was lost in the painful damming back and drying up of what still surged, but had nowhere to go. Only the thin pulsing left that could not quiet, suffering over lives one felt, but could no longer hold nor help.

On that torrent she had borne them to their own lives, and the river-bed was desert long years now. Not there would she dwell, a memoried wraith. Surely that was not all, surely there was more. Still the springs, the springs were in her seeking. Somewhere an older power that beat for life. Somewhere coherence, transport, meaning. If they would but leave her in the air now stilled of clamor, in the reconciled solitude, to journey to her self.

And they put a baby in her lap. Immediacy to embrace, and the breath of *that* past: warm flesh like this that had claims and nuzzled away all else and with lovely mouths devoured; hot-living like an animal — intensely and now; the turning maze; the long drunkenness; the drowning into needing and being needed. Severely she looked back — and the shudder seized her again, and the sweat. Not that way. Not there, not now could she, not yet. . . .

And all that visit, she could not touch the baby.

"Daddy, is it the . . . sickness she's like that?" asked Vivi. "I was so glad to be having the baby — for her. I told Tim, it'll give her more happiness than anything, being around a baby again. And she hasn't played with him once."

He was not listening, "Aahh little seed of life, little charmer," he crooned, "Hollywood should see you. A heart of ice you would melt. Kick, kick. The future you'll have for a ball. In 2050 still kick. Kick for your grandaddy then."

Attentive with the older children; sat through their performances (command performance; we command you to be the audience); helped Ann sort autumn leaves to find the best for a school program; listened gravely to Richard tell about his rock collection, while her lips mutely formed the words to remember: *igneous, sedimentary, metamorphic;* looked for missing socks, books and bus tickets; watched the children whoop after their grandfather who knew how to tickle, chuck, lift, toss, do tricks, tell secrets, make jokes, match riddle for riddle. (Tell me a riddle, Grammy. I know no riddles, child.) Scrubbed sills and woodwork and furniture in every room; folded the laundry; straightened drawers; emptied the heaped baskets waiting for ironing (while he or Vivi or Tim nagged: You're supposed to rest here, you've been sick) but to none tended or gave food — and could not touch the baby.

After a week she said: "Let us go home. Today call about the tickets."

"You have important business, Mrs. Inahurry? The President waits to consult with you?" He shouted, for the fear of the future raced in him. "The clothes are still warm from the suitcase, your children cannot show enough how glad they are to see you, and you want home. There is plenty of time for home. We cannot be with the children at home."

"Blind to around you as always: the little ones sleep four in a room because we take their bed. We are two more people in a house with a new baby, and no help."

"Vivi is happy so. The children should have their grandparents a while, she told to me. I should have my mommy and daddy. . . ."

"Babbler and blind. Do you look at her so tired? How she starts to

talk and she cries? I am not strong enough yet to help. Let us go home."
(To reconciled solitude.)

For it seemed to her the crowded noisy house was listening to her, listening for her. She could feel it like a great ear pressed under her heart. And everything knocked: quick constant raps: let me in, let me in.

How was it that soft reaching tendrils also became blows that knocked?

C'mon, Grandma, I want to show you. . . .

Tell me a riddle, Grandma. (*I know no riddles*)

Look, Grammy, he's so dumb he can't even find his hands. (Dody and the baby on a blanket over the fermenting autumn mound)

I made them — for you. (Flat paper dolls with aprons that lifted on scalloped skirts that lifted on flowered pants; hair of yarn and great ringed questioning eyes) (Ann)

Watch me, Grandma. (Richard snaking up the tree, hanging exultant, free, with one hand at the top. Below Dody hunching over in pretend-cooking.) (Climb too, Dody, climb and look)

Be my nap bed, Grammy. (The "No!" too late.) Morty's abandoned heaviness, while his fingers ladder up and down her hearing-aid cord to his drowsy chant: eentsiebeentsiespider. (*Children trust.*)

It's to start off your own rock collection, Grandma. That's a trilobite fossil, 200 million years old (millions of years on a boy's mouth) and that one's obsidian, black glass.

Knocked and knocked.

Mother, I *told* you the teacher said we had to bring it back all filled out this morning. Didn't you even ask Daddy? Then tell *me* which plan and I'll check it: evacuate or stay in the city or wait for you to come and take me away. (Seeing the look of straining to hear.) It's for Disaster, Grandma. (*Children trust*)

Vivi in the maze of the long, the lovely drunkenness. The old old noises: baby sounds; screaming of a mother flayed to exasperation; children quarrelling; children playing; singing; laughter.

And Vivi's tears and memories, spilling so fast, half the words not understood.

She had started remembering out loud deliberately, so her mother would know the past was cherished, still lived in her.

Nursing the baby: My friends marvel, and I tell them, oh it's easy to be such a cow. I remember how beautiful my mother seemed nursing my brother, and the milk just flows. . . . Was that Davy? It must have been Davy. . . .

Lowering a hem: How did you ever . . . when I think how you made everything we wore . . . Tim, just think, seven kids and Mommy sewed everything . . . do I remember you sang while you sewed? That white dress with the red apples on the skirt you fixed over for me, was it Hannah's or Clara's before it was mine?

Washing sweaters: Ma, I'll never forget, one of those days so nice you washed clothes outside; one of the first spring days it must have been. The bubbles just danced up and down while you scrubbed, and we chased after, and you stopped to show us how to blow our own bubbles with green onion stalks . . . you always. . . .

"Strong onion, to still make you cry after so many years," her father said, to turn the tears into laughter.

While Richard bent over his homework: Where is it now, do we still have it, the Book of the Martyrs? It always seemed so, well — exalted, when you'd put it on the round table and we'd all look at it together; there was even a halo from the lamp. The lamp with the beaded fringe you could move up and down; they're in style again, pulley lamps like that, but without the fringe. You know the book I'm talking about, Daddy, the Book of the Martyrs, the first picture was a bust of Socrates? I wish there was something like that for the children, Mommy, to give them what you. . . . (And the tears splashed again)

(What I intended and did not? Stop it, daughter, stop it, leave that time. And he, the hypocrite, sitting there with tears in his eyes — it was nothing to you then, nothing.)

. . . The time you came to school and I almost died of shame because of your accent and because I knew you knew I was ashamed; how could I? . . . Sammy's harmonica and you danced to it once, yes you did, you and Davy squealing in your arms. . . . That time you bundled us up and walked us down to the railway station to stay the night 'cause it was heated and we didn't have any coal, that winter of the strike, you didn't think I remembered that, did you, Mommy? . . . How you'd call us out to see the sunsets. . . .

Day after day, the spilling memories. Worse now, questions, too. Even the grandchildren: Grandma, in the olden days, when you were little. . . .

*

It was the afternoons that saved.

While they thought she napped, she would leave the mosaic on the wall (of children's drawings, maps, calendars, pictures, Ann's cardboard dolls with their great ringed questioning eyes) and hunch in the girls' closet, on the low shelf where the shoes stood, and the girls' dresses covered.

For that while she would painfully sheathe against the listening house, the tendrils and noises that knocked, and Vivi's spilling memories. Sometimes it helped to braid and unbraid the sashes that dangled, or to trace the pattern on the hoop slips.

Today she had jacks and children under jet trails to forget. Last night, Ann and Dody silhouetted in the window against a sunset of flaming man-made clouds of jet trail, their jacks ball accenting the peaceful noise of dinner being made. Had she told them, yes she had told them of how they played jacks in her village though there was no ball, no jacks. Six stones, round and flat, toss them out, the seventh on the back of the hand, toss, catch and swoop up as many as possible, toss again. . . .

Of stones (repeating Richard) there are three kinds: earth's fire jetting; rock of layered centuries; crucibled new out of the old (*igneous, sedimentary, metamorphic*). But there was that other — frozen to black glass, never to transform or hold the fossil memory . . . (let not my seed fall on stone). There was an ancient man who fought to heights a great rock that crashed back down eternally — eternal labor, freedom, labor . . . (stone will perish, but the word remain). And you, David, who with a stone slew, screaming: Lord, take my heart of stone and give me flesh.

Who was screaming? Why was she back in the common room of the prison, the sun motes dancing in the shafts of light, and the informer being brought in, a prisoner now, like themselves. And Lisa leaping, yes, Lisa, the gentle and tender, biting at the betrayer's jugular. Screaming and screaming.

No, it is the children screaming. Another of Paul and Sammy's terrible fights?

In Vivi's house. Severely: you are in Vivi's house.

Blows, screams, a call: "Grandma!" For her? Oh please not for her. Hide, hunch behind the dresses deeper. But a trembling little body hurls itself beside her — surprised, smothered laughter, arms surround her neck, tears rub dry on her cheek, and words too soft to understand whisper into her ear (Is this where you hide too, Grammy? It's my secret place, we have a secret now).

And the sweat beads, and the long shudder seizes.

*

It seemed the great ear pressed inside now, and the knocking. "We have to go home," she told him, "I grow ill here."

"It is your own fault, Mrs. Bodybusy, you do not rest, you do too much." He raged, but the fear was in his eyes. "It was a serious operation, they told you to take care. . . . All right, we will go to where you can rest."

But where? Not home to death, not yet. He had thought to Lennie's, to Clara's; beautiful visits with each of the children. She would have to rest first, be stronger. If they could but go to Florida — it glittered before him, the never-realized promise of Florida. California: of course. (The money, the money, dwindling!) Los Angeles first for sun and rest, then to Lennie's in San Francisco.

He told her the next day. "You saw what Nancy wrote: snow and wind back home, a terrible winter. And look at you — all bones and a swollen belly. I called Phil: he said: 'A prescription, Los Angeles sun and rest.'"

She watched the words on his lips. "You have sold the house. That is why we do not go home. That is why you talk no more of the Haven. Why there is money for travel. After the children you will drag me to the Haven."

"The Haven! Who thinks of the Haven any more? Tell her, Vivi, tell Mrs. Suspicious: a prescription, sun and rest, to make you healthy. . . . And how could I sell the house without *you*?"

At the place of farewells and greetings, of winds of coming and winds of going, they say their good-byes.

They look back at her with the eyes of others before them: Richard with her own blue blaze; Ann with the Nordic eyes of Tim; Morty's dreaming brown of a great-grandmother he will never know; Dody with the laughing eyes of him who had been her springtide love (who stands beside her now); Vivi's, all tears.

The baby's eyes are closed in sleep.

Good-bye, my children.

III

It is to the back of the great city he brought her, to the dwelling places of the cast-off old. Bounded by two lines of amusement piers to the north and to the south, and between a long straight paving rimmed with black benches facing the sand — sands so wide the ocean is only a far fluting.

In the brief vacation season, some of the boarded stores fronting the sands open, and families, young people and children, may be seen. A little tasseled tram shuttles between the piers, and the lights of roller coasters prink and tweak over those who come to have sensation made in them.

The rest of the year it is abandoned to the old, all else boarded up and still; seemingly empty, except the occasional days and hours when the sun, like a tide, sucks them out of the low rooming houses, casts them onto the benches and sandy rim of the walk — and sweeps them into decaying enclosures back again.

A few newer apartments glint among the low bleached squares. It is in one of these Lennie's Jeannie has arranged their rooms. "Only a few miles north and south people pay hundreds of dollars a month for just this gorgeous air, Grandaddy, just this ocean closeness."

She had been ill on the plane, lay ill for days in the unfamiliar room. Several times the doctor came by — left medicine she would not take. Several times Jeannie drove in the twenty miles from work, still in her Visiting Nurse uniform, the lightness and brightness of her like a healing.

"Who can believe it is winter?" he asked one morning. "Beautiful it is outside like an ad. Come, Mrs. Invalid, come to taste it. You are well enough to sit in here, you are well enough to sit outside. The doctor said it too."

But the benches were encrusted with people, and the sands at the sidewalk's edge. Besides, she had seen the far ruffle of the sea: "there take me," and though she leaned against him, it was she who led.

Plodding and plodding, sitting often to rest, he grumbling. Patting the sand so warm. Once she scooped up a handful, cradling it close to her better eye; peered, and flung it back. And as they came almost to the brink and she could see the glistening wet, she sat down, pulled off her shoes and stockings, left him and began to run. "You'll catch cold," he screamed, but the sand in his shoes weighed him down — he who had always been the agile one — and already the white spray creamed her feet.

He pulled her back, took a handkerchief to wipe off the wet and the sand. "Oh no," she said, "the sun will dry," seized the square and smoothed it flat, dropped on it a mound of sand, knotted the kerchief corners and tied it to a bag — "to look at with the strong glass" (for the first time in years explaining an action of hers) — and lay down with the little bag against her cheek, looking toward the shore that nurtured life as it first crawled toward consciousness the millions of years ago.

He took her one Sunday in the evil-smelling bus, past flat miles of
blister houses, to the home of relatives. Oh what is this? she cried as the
light began to smoke and the houses to dim and recede. Smog, he said,
everyone knows but you. . . . Outside he kept his arms about her, but
she walked with hands pushing the heavy air as if to open it, whispered:
who has done this? sat down suddenly to vomit at the curb and for a
long while refused to rise.

One's age as seen on the altered face of those known in youth. Is this
they he has come to visit? This Max and Rose, smooth and pleasant,
introducing them to polite children, disinterested grandchildren, "the
whole family, once a month on Sundays. And why not? We have the
room, the help, the food."

Talk of cars, of houses, of success: this son that, that daughter this.
And *your* children? Hastily skimped over, the intermarriages, the obscure work — "my doctor son-in-law, Phil" — all he has to offer. She
silent in a corner. (Car-sick like a baby, he explains.) Years since he has
taken her to visit anyone but the children, and old apprehensions prickle:
"no incidents," he silently begs, "no incidents," He itched to tell them.
"A very sick woman," significantly, indicating her with his eyes, "a very
sick woman." Their restricted faces did not react. "Have you thought
maybe she'd do better at Palm Springs?" Rose asked. "Or at least a nicer
section of the beach, nicer people, a pool." Not to have to say "money" he
said instead: "would she have sand to look at through a magnifying
glass?" and went on, detail after detail, the old habit betraying of parad-
ing the queerness of her for laughter.

After dinner — the others into the living-room in men- or women-
clusters, or into the den to watch TV — the four of them alone. She sat
close to him, and did not speak. Jokes, stories, people they had known,
beginning of reminiscence, Russia fifty-sixty years ago. Strange words
across the Duncan Phyfe table: *hunger; secret meetings; human rights;
spies; betrayals; prison; escape* — interrupted by one of the grandchildren: "Commercial's on; any Coke left? Gee, you're missing a
real hair-raiser." And then a granddaughter (Max proudly: "look at her,
an American queen") drove them home on her way back to U.C.L.A. No
incident — except that there had been no incidents.

The first few mornings she had taken with her the magnifying glass,
but he would sit only on the benches, so she rested at the foot, where

slatted bench shadows fell, and unless she turned her hearing aid down, other voices invaded.

Now on the days when the sun shone and she felt well enough, he took her on the tram to where the benches ranged in oblongs, some with tables for checkers or cards. Again the blanket on the sand in the striped shadows, but she no longer brought the magnifying glass. He played cards, and she lay in the sun and looked towards the waters; or they walked — two blocks down to the scaling hotel, two blocks back — past chili-hamburger stands, open-doored bars. Next-to-New and Perpetual Rummage Sale stores.

Once, out of the aimless walkers, slow and shuffling like themselves, someone ran unevenly towards them, embraced, kissed, wept: "dear friends, old friends." A friend of *hers,* not his: Mrs. Mays who had lived next door to them in Denver when the children were small.

Thirty years are compressed into a dozen sentences; and the present, not even in three. All is told: the children scattered; the husband dead; she lives in a room two blocks up from the sing hall — and points to the domed auditorium jutting before the pier. The leg? phlebitis; the heavy breathing? that, one does not ask. She, too, comes to the benches each day to sit. And tomorrow, tomorrow, are they going to the community sing? Of course he would have heard of it, everybody goes — the big doings they wait for all week. They have never been? She will come for them to dinner tomorrow and they will all go together.

So it is that she sits in the wind of the singing, among the thousand various faces of age.

She had turned off her hearing aid at once they came into the auditorium — as she would have wished to turn off sight.

One by one they streamed by and imprinted on her — and though the savage zest of their singing came voicelessly soft and distant, the faces roared — the faces densened the air — chorded into

children-chants, mother-croons, singing of the chained;
love serenades, Beethoven storms, mad Lucia's scream;
drunken joy-songs, keens for the dead, work-singing

while from floor to balcony to dome a bare-footed sore-covered little girl threaded the sound-thronged tumult, danced her ecstasy of grimace to flutes that scratched at a cross-roads village wedding

Yes, faces became sound, and the sound became faces; and faces and sound became weight — pushed, pressed

"Air" — her hand claws his.

"Whenever I enjoy myself. . . ." Then he saw the gray sweat on her face. "Here. Up. Help me, Mrs. Mays," and they support her out to where she can gulp the air in sob after sob.

"A doctor, we should bring for her a doctor."

"Tch, it's nothing," says Ellen Mays, "I get it all the time. You've missed the tram. Fix your hearing aid, honey . . . Come to my place . . . close . . . tea. My view.

"See, she *wants* to come. Steady now, that's how."

Adding mysteriously: "Remember your advice, easy to keep your head above water, empty things float. Float."

The singing a fading march for them, tall woman with a swollen leg, weaving little man, and the swollen thinness they help between.

The stench in the hall: mildew? decay? "We sit and rest then climb. My gorgeous view. We help each other and here   we   are."

The stench along into the slab of room. A washstand for a sink, a box with oilcloth tacked around for a cupboard, a three-burner gas plate. Artificial flowers, colorless with dust. Everywhere pictures foaming: wedding, baby, party, vacation, graduation, family pictures. From the narrow couch under a slit of window, sure enough the view: lurching rooftops and a scallop of ocean heaving, preening, twitching under the moon.

"While the water heats. Excuse me . . . down the hall." Ellen Mays has gone.

"You'll live?" he asks mechanically, sat down to feel his fright; tried to pull her alongside.

She pushed him away. "For air," she said; stood clinging to the dresser. Then, in a terrible voice:

After a lifetime of room. Of many rooms.

Shhh.

You remember how she lived. Eight children. And now one room   like a coffin.

She pays rent!

Shrinking the life of her into one room like a coffin Rooms and rooms like this. I lie on the quilt and hear them talk Once you went for coffee I walked I saw

Please, Mrs. Orator Without Breath.

A Balzac a Chekhov to write it Rummage Alone On scraps Better here old than in the old country!

On scraps And they sang like . . . like Wondrous. *Man, one has to believe.* So strong. For what? To rot not grow?

Your poor lungs beg you. They sob between each word.

Singing. Unused the life in them. She in this poor room with her pictures. Max You The children everywhere unused the life. And who has meaning? Century after century still all in man not to grow?

Coffins, rummage, plants: sick woman. Oh lay down. We will get for you the doctor.

"And when will it end. Oh, *the end.*" *That* nightmare thought, and this time she writhed, crumpled beside him, seized his hand (for a moment again the weight, the soft distant roaring of humanity) and on the strangled-for breath, begged: "Man . . . will destroy ourselves?"

And looking for answer — in the helpless pity and fear for her (for *her*) that distorted his face — she understood the last months, and knew that she was dying.

IV

"Let us go home," she said after several days.

"You are in training for a cross-country trip? That is why you do not even walk across the room? Here, like a prescription Phil said, till you are stronger from the operation. You want to break doctor's orders?"

She saw the fiction was necessary to him, was silent; then: "At home I will get better. If the doctor here says?"

"And winter? And the visits to Lennie and to Clara? All right," for he saw the tears in her eyes, "I will write Phil, and talk to the doctor."

Days passed. He reported nothing. Jeannie came and took her out for air, past the boarded concessions, the hooded and tented amusement rides, to the end of the pier. They watched the spent waves feeding the new, the gulls in the clouded sky; even up where they sat, the wind-blown sand stung.

She did not ask to go down the crooked steps to the sea.

Back in her bed, while he was gone to the store, she said: "Jeannie, this doctor, he is not one I can ask questions. Ask him for me, can I go home?"

Jeannie looked at her, said quickly: "Of course, poor Granny. You want your own things around you, don't you? I'll call him tonight. . . . Look, I've something to show you," and from her purse unwrapped a large cookie, intricately shaped like a little girl. "Look at the curls — can you hear me well, Granny? — and the darling eyelashes. I just came from a house where they were baking them."

"The dimples," she marveled, "there in the knees," holding it to the better light, turning, studying, "like art. Each singly they cut, or a mold?"

"Singly," said Jeannie, "and if it is a child only the mother can make them. Oh Granny, it's the likeness of a real little girl who died yesterday — Rosita. She was three years old. *Pan del Muerto,* the Bread of the Dead. It was the custom in the part of Mexico they came from."

Still she turned and inspected. "Look, the hollow in the throat, the little cross necklace. . . . I think for the mother it is a good thing to be busy with such bread. You know the family?"

Jeannie nodded. "On my rounds. I nursed. . . . Oh Granny, it is like a party; they play songs she liked to dance to. The coffin is lined with pink velvet and she wears a white dress. There are candles. . . ."

"In the house?" Surprised, "They keep her in the house?"

"Yes," said Jeannie, "and it is against the health law. I think she is . . . prepared there. The father said it will be sad to bury her in this country; in Oaxaca they have a feast night with candles each year; everyone picnics on the graves of those they loved until dawn."

"Yes, Jeannie, the living must comfort themselves." And closed her eyes.

"You want to sleep, Granny?"

"Yes, tired from the pleasure of you. I may keep the Rosita? There stand it, on the dresser, where I can see; something of my own around me."

In the kitchenette, helping her grandfather unpack the groceries, Jeannie said in her light voice:

"I'm resigning my job, Grandaddy."

"Ah, the lucky young man. Which one is he?"

"Too late. You're spoken for." She made a pyramid of cans, unstacked, and built again.

"Something is wrong with the job?"

"With me. I can't be"—she searched for the word—"what they call professional enough. I let myself feel things. And tomorrow I have to report a family. . . ." The cans clicked again. "It's not that, either. I just don't know what I want to do, maybe go back to school, maybe go to art school. I thought if you went to San Francisco I'd come along and talk it over with Mommy and Daddy. But I don't see how you can go. She wants to go home. She asked me to ask the doctor."

The doctor told her himself. "Next week you may travel, when you are a little stronger." But next week there was the fever of an infection, and by the time that was over, she could not leave the bed—a rented hospital bed that stood beside the double bed he slept in alone now.

Outwardly the days repeated themselves. Every other afternoon and evening he went out to his new-found cronies, to talk and play cards. Twice a week, Mrs. Mays came. And the rest of the time, Jeannie was there.

By the sickbed stood Jeannie's FM radio. Often into the room the shapes of music came. She would lie curled on her side, her knees drawn up, intense in listening (Jeannie sketched her so, coiled, convoluted like an ear), then thresh her hand out and abruptly snap the radio mute— still to lie in her attitude of listening, concealing tears.

Once Jeannie brought in a young Marine to visit, a friend from high-school days she had found wandering near the empty pier. Because Jeannie asked him to, gravely, without self-consciousness, he sat himself cross-legged on the floor and performed for them a dance of his native Samoa.

Long after they left, a tiny thrumming sound could be heard where, in her bed, she strove to repeat the beckon, flight, surrender of his hands, the fluttering footbeats, and his low plaintive calls.

Hannah and Phil sent flowers. To deepen her pleasure, he placed one in her hair. "Like a girl," he said, and brought the hand mirror so she could see. She looked at the pulsing red flower, the yellow skull face; a desolate, excited laugh shuddered from her, and she pushed the mirror away—but let the flower burn.

The week Lennie and Helen came, the fever returned. With it the excited laugh, and incessant words. She, who in her life had spoken but seldom and then only when necessary (never having learned the easy, social uses of words), now in dying, spoke incessantly.

In a half-whisper: "Like Lisa she is, your Jeannie. Have I told you of

Lisa, who taught me to read? Of the highborn she was, but noble in herself. I was sixteen; they beat me; my father beat me so I would not go to her. It was forbidden, she was a Tolstoyan. At night, past dogs that howled, terrible dogs, my son, in the snows of winter to the road, I to ride in her carriage like a lady, to books. To her, life was holy, knowledge was holy, and she taught me to read. They hung her. Everything that happens one must try to understand why. She killed one who betrayed many. Because of betrayal, betrayed all she lived and believed. In one minute she killed, before my eyes (there is so much blood in a human being, my son), in prison with me. All that happens, one must try to understand.

"The name?" Her lips would work. "The name that was their pole star; the doors of the death houses fixed to open on it; I read of it my year of penal servitude. Thuban!" very excited, "Thuban, in ancient Egypt the pole star. Can you see, look out to see it, Jeannie, if it swings around *our* pole star that seems to *us* not to move.

"Yes, Jeannie, at your age my mother and grandmother had already buried children . . . yes, Jeannie, it is more than oceans between Olshana and you . . . yes, Jeannie, they danced, and for all the bodies they had they might as well be chickens, and indeed, they scratched and flapped their arms and hopped.

"And Andrei Yefimitch, who for twenty years had never known of it and never wanted to know, said as if he wanted to cry: but why my dear friend this malicious laughter?" Telling to herself half-memorized phrases from her few books. "Pain I answer with tears and cries, baseness with indignation, meanness with repulsion . . . for life may be hated or wearied of, but never despised."

Delirious: "Tell me, my neighbor, Mrs. Mays, the pictures never lived, but what of the flowers? Tell them who ask: no rabbis, no ministers, no priests, no speeches, no ceremonies: ah, false — let the living comfort themselves. Tell Sammy's boy, he who flies, tell him to go to Stuttgart and see where Davy has no grave. And what?" A conspirator's laugh. "And what? where millions have no graves — save air."

In delirium or not, wanting the radio on; not seeming to listen, the words still jetting, wanting the music on. Once, silencing it abruptly as of old, she began to cry, unconcealed tears this time. "You have pain, Granny?" Jeannie asked.

"The music," she said, "still it is there yet we do not hear; knocks, and our poor human ears too weak. What else, what else we do not hear?"

Once she knocked his hand aside as he gave her a pill, swept the bottles from her bedside table: "no pills, let me feel what I feel," and laughed as on his hands and knees he groped to pick them up.

Night-times her hand reached across the bed to hold his.

A constant retching began. Her breath was too faint for sustained speech now, but still the lips moved:

When no longer necessary to injure others
Pick pick pick Blind chicken
The bell Summon what ennobles
As a human being responsibility for

"David!" imperious, "Basin!" and she would vomit, rinse her mouth, the wasted throat working to swallow, and begin the chant again.

She will be better off in the hospital now, the doctor said.

He sent the telegrams to the children, was packing her suitcase, when her hoarse voice startled. She had roused, was pulling herself to sitting.

"Where now?" she asked. "Where now do you drag me?"

"You do not even have to have a baby to go this time," he soothed, looking for the brush to pack. "Remember, after Davy you told me — worthy to have a baby for the pleasure of the hospital?"

"Where now? Not home yet?" Her voice mourned. "Where *is* my home?"

He rose to ease her back. "The doctor, the hospital," he started to explain, but deftly, like a snake, she had slithered out of bed and stood swaying, propped behind the night table.

"Coward," she hissed, "runner."

"You stand," he said senselessly.

"To take me there and run. Afraid of a little vomit."

He reached her as she fell. She struggled against him, half slipped from his arms, pulled herself up again.

"Weakling," she taunted, "to leave me there and run. Betrayer. All your life you have run."

He sobbed, telling Jeannie. "A Marilyn Monroe to run for her virtue. Fifty-nine pounds she weighs, the doctor said, and she beats at me like a Dempsey. Betrayer, she cries, and I running like a dog when she calls; day and night, running to her, her vomit, the bedpan. . . ."

"She wants you, Grandaddy," said Jeannie. "Isn't that what they call love? I'll see if she sleeps, and if she does, poor worn-out darling, we'll have a party, you and I; I brought us rum babas."

*

They did not move her. By her bed now stood the tall hooked pillar that held the solutions — blood and dextrose — to feed her veins. Jeannie moved down the hall to take over the sickroom, her face so radiant, her grandfather asked her once: "you are in love?" (Shameful the joy, the pure overwhelming joy from being with her grandmother; the peace, the serenity that breathed.) "My darling escape," she answered incoherently, "my darling Granny" — as if that explained.

Now one by one the children came, those that were able. Hannah, Paul, Sammy. Too late to ask: and what did you learn with your living, Mother, and what do we need to know?

Clara, the eldest, clenched:

Pay me back, Mother, pay me back for all you took from me. Those others you crowded into your heart. The hands I needed to be for you, the heaviness, the responsibility.

Is this she? Noises the dying make, the crablike hands crawling over over the covers. The ethereal singing.

She hears that music, that singing from childhood; forgotten sound — not heard since, since. . . . And the hardness breaks like a cry: Where did we lose each other, first mother, singing mother?

Annulled: the quarrels, the gibing, the harshness between; the fall into silence and the withdrawal.

I do not know you, Mother. Mother, I never knew you.

Lennie, suffering not alone for her who was dying, but for that in her which never lived (for that which in him might never live). From him too, unspoken words: *good-bye Mother who taught me to mother myself.*

Not Vivi, who must stay with her children; not Davy, but he is already here, having to die again with *her* this time, for the living take their dead with them when they die.

Light she grew, like a bird, and, like a bird, sound bubbled in her throat while the body fluttered in agony. Night and day, asleep or awake (though indeed there was no difference now) the songs and the phrases leaping.

And he, who had once dreaded a long dying (from fear of himself, from horror of the dwindling money) now desired her quick death profoundly, for *her* sake. He no longer went out, except when Jeannie forced him; no longer laughed, except when in the bright kitchenette, Jeannie coaxed his laughter (and she, who seemed to hear nothing else, would laugh too, conspiratorial wisps of laughter).

Light, like a bird, the fluttering body, the little claw hands, the beaked shadow on her face; and the throat, bubbling, straining.

He tried not to listen, as he tried not to look on the face in which only the forehead remained familiar, but trapped with her the long nights in that little room, the sounds worked themselves into his consciousness, with their punctuation of death swallows, whimpers, gurglings.

Even in reality (swallow) *life's lack of it*
Dungeons slaveships deathtrains hunger Pits whips clubs mur der eeeeeeee (spasm) *eenough end*
78,000 in one minute   78,000 human beings (whisper of a scream) *Man will destroy ourselves?*

"Aah, Mrs. Miserable," he said, as if she could hear, "all your life working, and now in bed you lie, servants to tend, you do not even need to call to be tended, and still you work. Such hard work it is to die? Such hard work?"

The body threshed, her hand clung in his. A melody, ghost-thin, hovered on her lips, and like a guilty ghost, the vision of her bent in listening to it, silencing the record instantly he was near. Now, heedless of his presence, she floated the melody on and on.

"Hid it from me," he complained, "how many times you listened to remember it so?" And tried to think when she had first played it, or first begun to silence her few records when he came near — but could reconstruct nothing. There was only this room with its tall hooked pillar and its swarm of sounds.

An unexamined life not worth
No man one except through others
Strong with the not yet in the now
Dogma dead war dead one country

"It helps, Mrs. Philosopher, words from books? It helps?" And it seemed to him that for seventy years she had hidden a tape recorder, infinitely microscopic, within her, that it had coiled infinite mile on mile, trapping every song, every melody, every word read, heard and spoken — and that maliciously she was playing back only what said nothing of him, of the children, of their intimate life together.

"Left us indeed, Mrs. Babbler," he reproached, "you who called others babbler and cunningly saved your words. A lifetime you tended and loved, and now not a word of us, for us. Left us indeed? Left me."

And he took out his solitaire deck, shuffled the cards loudly, slapped them down.

Lift high   banner of reason   (tatter of an orator's voice)   *justice freedom   light*

Mankind   life worthy   capacities

Seeks (blur of shudder) *belong   human being*

"Words, words," he accused, "and what human beings did *you* seek around you, Mrs. Live Alone, and what mankind think worthy?"

Though even as he spoke, he remembered she had not always been isolated, had not always wanted to be alone (as he knew there had been a voice before this gossamer one; before the hoarse voice that broke from silence to lash, make incidents, shame him — a girl's voice of eloquence that spoke their holiest dreams). But again he could reconstruct, image, nothing of what had been before, or when, or how, it had changed.

Ace, queen, jack. The pillar shadow fell, so, in two tracks; in the mirror depths glistened a moonlike blob, the empty solution bottle. And it worked in him: *of reason and justice and freedom. Dogma dead:* he remembered the full quotation, laughed bitterly. "Hah, good you do not know what you say; good Victor Hugo died and did not see it, his twentieth century."

Deuce, ten, five. Dauntlessly she began a song of their youth of belief:

> *These things shall be, a loftier race*
> *than e'er the world hath known shall rise*
> *with flame of freedom in their souls*
> *and light of knowledge in their eyes*

King, four, jack. "In the twentieth century, hah!"

> *They shall be gentle, brave and strong*
> *to spill no drop of blood, but dare*
> *all that may plant man's lordship firm*
> *on earth and fire and sea and air*

"To spill no drop of blood, hah! So, cadaver, and you too, cadaver Hugo, 'in the twentieth century ignorance will be dead, dogma will be

dead, war will be dead, and for all mankind one country — of fulfilment.'
Hah!"

> *And every life* (long strangling cough) *shall*
> *be a song*

The cards fell from his fingers. Without warning, the bereavement and
betrayal he had sheltered — compounded through the years — hidden
even from himself — revealed itself,

> uncoiled,

> released,

> *sprung*

and with it the monstrous shapes of what had actually happened in the
century.

A ravening hunger or thirst seized him. He groped into the
kitchenette, switched on all three lights, piled a tray — "you have finished
your night snack, Mrs. Cadaver, now I will have mine." And he was
shocked at the tears that splashed on the tray.

"Salt tears. For free. I forgot to shake on salt?"

Whispered: "Lost, how much I lost."

Escaped to the grandchildren whose childhoods were childish, who had
never hungered, who lived unravaged by disease in warm houses of many
rooms, had all the school for which they cared, could walk on any street,
stood a head taller than their grandparents, towered above — beautiful
skins, straight backs, clear straightforward eyes. "Yes, you in Olshana,"
he said to the town of sixty years ago, "they would be nobility to you."

And was this not the dream then, come true in ways undreamed? he
asked.

And are there no other children in the world? he answered, as if in her
harsh voice.

> *And the flame of freedom, the light of knowledge?*
> *And the drop, to spill no drop of blood?*

And he thought that at six Jeannie would get up and it would be his
turn to go to her room and sleep, that he could press the buzzer and she
would come now; that in the afternoon Ellen Mays was coming, and this
time they would play cards and he could marvel at how rouge can stand
half an inch on the cheek; that in the evening the doctor would come,
and he could beg him to be merciful, to stop the feeding solutions, to let
her die.

To let her die, and with her their youth of belief out of which her bright, betrayed words foamed; stained words, that on her working lips came stainless.

Hours yet before Jeannie's turn. He could press the buzzer and wake her to come now; he could take a pill, and with it sleep; he could pour more brandy into his milk glass, though what he had poured was not yet touched.

Instead he went back, checked her pulse, gently tended with his knotty fingers as Jeannie had taught.

She was whimpering; her hand crawled across the covers for his. Compassionately he enfolded it, and with his free hand gathered up the cards again. Still was there thirst or hunger ravening in him.

That world of their youth — dark, ignorant, terrible with hate and disease — how was it that living in it, in the midst of corruption, filth, treachery, degradation, they had not mistrusted man nor themselves; had believed so beautifully, so . . . falsely?

"Aaah, children," he said out loud, "how we believed, how we belonged." And he yearned to package for each of the children, the grandchildren, for everyone, *that joyous certainty, that sense of mattering, of moving and being moved, of being one and indivisible with the great of the past, with all that freed, ennobled man.* Package it, stand on corners, in front of stadiums and on crowded beaches, knock on doors, give it as a fabled gift.

"And why not in cereal boxes, in soap packages?" he mocked himself. "Aah. You have taken my senses, cadaver."

Words foamed, died unsounded. Her body writhed; she made kissing motions with her mouth. (Her lips moving as she read, poring over the Book of the Martyrs, the magnifying glass superimposed over the heavy eyeglasses.) *Still she believed?* "Eva!" he whispered. "Still you believed? You lived by it? These Things Shall Be?"

"One pound soup meat," she answered distinctly, "one soup bone."

"My ears heard you. Ellen Mays was witness: 'Man . . . one has to believe.'" Imploringly: "Eva!"

"Bread, day-old." She was mumbling. "Please, in a wooden box . . . for kindling. The thread, hah, the thread breaks. Cheap thread" — and a gurgling, enormously loud, began in her throat.

"I ask for stone; she gives me bread — day-old." He pulled his hand away, shouted: "Who wanted questions? Everything you have to wake?"

Then dully, "Ah, let me help you turn, poor creature."

Words jumbled, cleared. In a voice of crowded terror:

"Paul, Sammy, don't fight.

"Hannah, have I ten hands?"

"How can I give it, Clara, how can I give it if I don't have?"

"You lie," he said sturdily, "there was joy too." Bitterly: "Ah how cheap you speak of us at the last."

As if to rebuke him, as if her voice had no relationship with her flailing body, she sang clearly, beautifully, a school song the children had taught her when they were little; begged:

"Not look my hair where they cut. . . ."

(The crown of braids shorn.) And instantly he left the mute old woman poring over the Book of the Martyrs; went past the mother treadling at the sewing machine, singing with the children; past the girl in her wrinkled prison dress, hiding her hair with scarred hands, lifting to him her awkward, shamed, imploring eyes of love; and took her in his arms, dear, personal, fleshed, in all the heavy passion he had loved to rouse from her.

"Eva!"

Her little claw hand beat the covers. How much, how much can a man stand? He took up the cards, put them down, circled the beds, walked to the dresser, opened, shut drawers, brushed his hair, moved his hand bit by bit over the mirror to see what of the reflection he could blot out with each move, and felt that at any moment he would die of what was unendurable. Went to press the buzzer to wake Jeannie, looked down, saw on Jeannie's sketch pad the hospital bed, with *her;* the double bed alongside, with him; the tall pillar feeding into her veins, their hands, his and hers, clasped, feeding each other. And as if he had been instructed he went to his bed, lay down, holding the sketch — as if it could shield against the monstrous shapes of loss, of betrayal, of death — and with his free hand took hers back into his.

So Jeannie found them in the morning.

That last day the agony was perpetual. Time after time it lifted her almost off the bed, so they had to fight to hold her down. He could not endure and left the room; wept as if there never would be tears enough.

Jeannie came to comfort him. In her light voice she said: Grandaddy, Grandaddy don't cry. She is not there, she promised me. On the last day, she said she would go back to when she first heard music, a little girl on the road of the village where she was born. She promised me. It is a wedding and they dance, while the flutes so joyous and vibrant tremble in the air. Leave here there, Grandaddy, it is all right. She promised me. Come back, come back and help her poor body to die.

For two of that generation
Seevya and Genya

Death deepens the wonder

GEORGE GARRETT

*Probably every newly recruited soldier has dreamed, à la Walter Mitty, of
having his hard-boiled sergeant at his mercy. It might be considered an
almost universal male dream. In "The old Army Game," vividly written,
the dream does come true. But what happens? One does not have to have
been in the army to enjoy it.*

*George Garrett was born in Orlando, Florida, in 1929. He attended
Princeton University. After serving as a Field Artillery sergeant in the
Second World War, like "most American writers," he says, he held a variety
of jobs, most of them menial and none of them for long. He has been an
associate professor of English at the University of Virginia and Resident
Fellow in Creative Writing at Princeton. He is the author of many books,
including novels, short stories and poems.*

The Old Army Game

EVERYBODY has got a story about the Bad Sergeant in Basic. Sit down
some evening with your buddies, and you'll find that's one subject everybody can deal out like a hand of cards. And that's not a bad image for it,
because those stories, told or written or even finally mounted in memory,
acquire a bright, conventional, two-dimensional character. All the people
in them are face cards. Which seems to me as good a way as any to
introduce Sergeant First Class Elwood Quince.

Lean and hard-faced, a face all angles like a one-eyed jack. Perfectly
turned out, everything tailored skintight, glossy, spit-shined and glowing. Field cap, white from wear and care, two fingers over the nose.
Casts a flat gray semicircular shadow that way. Calls attention to the
mouth. The thin tight lips. Open you'd expect to see even rows of fine
white teeth; instead you'd see them yellow and no good and all awry and
gaping like a worn-out picket fence. And when he did smile, it was all
phony, "like a jackass chewing briars." Back to the field cap. Calls attention to the mouth and hides the eyes in shadow like a mask. The eyes —

with the cap off and resting on a desk and his large restless hands patting his straw-blond hair, long and rich on top, but sidewalled so that with a cap or a helmet on he looks as shaved clean as a chicken ready for the oven — the eyes are peculiarly light and cloudy at the same time, like a clear spring that somebody has spit in or stirred the mud in the bottom of with a stick. Can you see him yet? But he's still. Let's breathe on him and let him walk because Quince's walk is important. He has two of them: (a) the official walk when he's marching troops, in formation, etc. and (b) when he's relaxed and just walking about the area. The former is conventional, ramrod, but natural. Well-trained soldier. The latter is quite special. Light-footed, easy, insinuative, cat- and woman-like. Creepy. He seemed like a ghost to us. You always look over your shoulder before you speak because the chances are he's right there behind you and everywhere at once.

Talk? Oh my, yes, he can talk: Arkansas mountain accent. Part Southern and part Western and a little bit nasal and whiny and hard on the r's. Picturesque. Rural similes abound. Some extended to the epic proportion. For example, to Sachs, our fat boy from New York: "Sachs when I see you draggin' your lardass around the battery area, you put me in mind of a old woreout sow in a hogpen with a measly little scrawny litter of piglets sniffin' and chasin' around behind her and that old sow is just so tired and fat and goddamn lazy she can't even roll over and let 'em suck." Also frequently scatalogical. Here is a dialogue. Sergeant Quince and Me. In open ranks. Inspection. He right in front of Me. I'm looking straight into the shadow his cap casts.

Quince: Do you know how low you are?

Me (learning to play by ear): Pretty low, Sergeant.

Quince: Pretty low? No, I mean just *how* low?

Me: I don't know, Sergeant.

Quince: Well then, since you're so ignorant, I'll tell you. You're lower than whale shit. And you know where that is, don't you?

Me: Yes, Sergeant.

Quince: On the bottom of the ocean.

(Quince passes on to the next victim.)

The tone of voice? Always soft. Never raises his voice except in giving commands. Otherwise speaks just above a whisper. You have to strain to hear him.

When we arrived at Camp Chaffee, Arkansas, the Army's mansion pitched in the seat of excrement now that Camp Polk, La., and Camp

Blanding, Fla., are closed up tight as a drum, left to hobos, rats, bugs, weeds, etc., we were assigned to take Basic Training in Sergeant Quince's outfit. I call it *his* outfit because the Battery Commander had a harelip and was as shy as a unicorn, stayed in his office all day. The First Sergeant had V-shaped wound stripes from the First World War, I swear, and didn't care about anything but getting out a morning report without erasures and also the little flower garden he had all around the Orderly Room shack, that he tended and watered with a cute watering can just like Little Bo Peep's. Nevertheless Sergeant Cobb started out as a *presence*. Austere and lonely and unapproachable, but thought of as an ultimate tribunal where possibly wrongs might be righted, a kind of tired old god we might turn to one day in despair of salvation from Quince, come to him as broken children, and he'd sigh and forgive us. Until there came a test one day. Sergeant Quince marched the whole battery, one hundred and sixty-odd men in four heavy-booted platoons, right across one side of Cobb's garden. By the time the First Platoon had passed by, Cobb was out of the office, hatless, necktie askew and loose like a long tongue, eyes burning. (Ah ha! thought we of Sergeant Quince, the original "young man so spic and span," something unpleasant will hit the fan now.) But it didn't. Cobb stood there looking and wilted. Tears brimmed in his eyes and spilled down his cheeks. He watched his tended stalks and blossoms go down under the irresistible marching feet of Progress, of Mutability, of Change and Decay. And he never said a word. He slumped and shook his fist, a helpless old man. Meanwhile Quince ignored him, counted a crisp cadence for the marching troops and grinned *just* like a jackass chewing briars. And our hearts sank like stones to see the mighty fallen.

So, though he was merely the Field First, it was Quince's outfit to make or break. His little brotherhood of lesser cadre revolved like eager breathless planets around his indubitable magnificence. From our first formation, we in rumpled new ill-fitting fatigues and rough new boots, he sartorial with, glinting in the sun, the polished brass of the whistle he loved so well.

"Gentlemens," he said. "You all are about to begin the life of a soldier. My name is Sergeant Quince. Your name is Shit."

War going on in Korea, etc. We would learn how to soldier and not get our private parts shot off by the gooks whether we liked it or not. We would "rue the day" (his word) we ever saw his face or this godforsaken battery area. We would learn to hate him. We wouldn't have dreamed we were *able* to hate anybody as much as we were going to hate him. Etc., etc., etc.

"Let's be clear about one thing," he said, looking down from the barracks steps into our upraised, motley, melting-pot faces, "I hate niggers. They're black bastards to me, but I'll just call them niggers for short around here, during duty hours." (A Negro standing next to me winced as if he'd been kicked in the stomach.) "If anybody don't like it, let him go and see the I.G. I also hate Jews, wops, spics, micks, cotton pickers, Georgia crackers, Catholics and Protestants. I hate all of you, damn your eyes."

I really believe he meant it.

At this point, according to the conventions of the Tale of the Bad Sergeant, written or told, the story usually takes a turn, a *peripeteia* of a modest sort. You're supposed to be given a hint of *his* problems before moving on. Let's do it. I have no objection. But I reserve the right to call it giving the devil his due.

We were a crazy mixed-up bunch. Farm boys, black and white, from the Deep South. Street boys from the jungle of fists in the big cities. College boys. Accidents: a thirty-five-year-old lawyer who got drafted by mistake, a cripple who was used for some weeks to fire up the boilers and keep the boiler rooms clean before his medical discharge finally came through. Two fat sullen American Indians . . . Mexican wetbacks. I remember one of these had a fine handlebar mustache. Quince walked up to him and plucked it. "Only two kinds of people can wear a mustache and get away with it," he said, "movie stars and queers." (He used another more vividly descriptive term, but I've never seen that particular one in print except in the Henry Miller books that you have to smuggle in, and since I'm not standing on Innovation, I'll let it pass.) "I don't recall seeing your ugly face in the picture show. Shave it off!" So there we were. I'll give Quince this much credit. He wasn't the least bit interested in "molding us into a fighting team." He wasn't crazy that way. His reach didn't exceed his grasp *that much*. He was merely involved in getting us through a cycle of Basic Training. We hated each other, fought each other singly and in groups in the barracks and the privacy of the boiler rooms (with that poor cripple who was responsible for the care and maintenance thereof cowering in a corner behind the boiler, but armed with a poker lest he too became involved). We stole from each other, ratted on each other, goofed off on each other ("soldiering on the job" this is sometimes called in Real Life with good reason) and thus made every bit of work about twice as hard and twice as long as it had to be. And, if anything, this situation pleased Quince. He perched on his mobile (on roller skates) Olympus and chewed briars while we played roothog and grabass in the dust and mud below.

Strict? My Lord yes. I would say so. No passes at all during the whole cycle. G.I. Parties every night until our fatigues fell to shreds from splashed Clorox and the rough wood floors were as smooth and white as a stone by the shore. Polished the nailheads nightly too with matchsticks wrapped in cotton, dipped in Brasso. Long night hikes with full field pack. G.I. haircuts (marched to the so-called barber) once a week. Bald as convicts we were. Police Call was always an agony of duck-waddling "assholes and elbows" on our hands and knees like penitents. How he loved Police Call! How he loved Mail Call! Gave out all the letters himself. That is, threw them into the packed hopeful faces and let them fight and scramble for them in the dark. Opened mail and packages when he pleased. Withheld mail for days at a time as a whim. Didn't make soldiers out of us, but tractable brutes. Brutalized, cowed, we marched to and fro like the zombies in mental hospitals that they haven't got time to bother with, so they pump them full of great jolts of tranquilizers. And when we passed by, eyes front, in step, he was complimented by any high-ranking officers that witnessed.

Let me say this for Quince. I know another sergeant who tried exactly the same thing and failed. He was of the same mold as Quince, but somehow subtly defective. In the end he had to fall his troops out of the barracks with a drawn forty-five. Not Quince. His lips touched to the brass whistle, even before he breathed into it, was quite enough to make us shiver.

A sadist too. Individually. Poor white, soft, round, hairy, Jewish Sachs suffered indignities he couldn't have dreamed of in his worst nightmares. Once or twice was nearly drowned in a dirty toilet bowl. Sachs with the other fat and soft boys, Quince's "Fat Man's Squad," had regularly to participate in "weenie races." What's a weenie race? I think Quince invented it. The fat boys kneel down at the starting line, pants and drawers down. Quince produces a package of frankfurters, wrapped in cellophane. One each frankfurter is firmly inserted into each rectum. All in place? Everybody ready? Quince blows the whistle and away they crawl, sometimes a hundred yards going and coming. Last man back has to eat all the frankfurters on the spot. Tears and pleading move Quince not a whit. Nor puking nor anything else.

One time Quince lost his head about one barracks which had someway failed to live up to his expectations. He and his attendant cadre went raging through that barracks, tearing up beds, knocking over wall lockers, and destroying everything "personal" they could get their hands on: cameras, portable radios, fountain pens, books, letters, photographs, etc.

How did these various things happen? You're bound to ask. Didn't anybody go to the Inspector General, the Chaplain, write a Congressman or Mother? Not to my knowledge. Anyone could have, it's true, but all were very young and in mortal fear of the man. Who would be the first to go? No one went. And — *mirabilis!* — nobody cracked up. If anything we got tougher and tougher every day. Gave our souls to God.

Or maybe — entirely justified in your contempt, "Don't give me no sad tales of woe" — you'll just say: "So what: what do you want me to do, punch your TS Card?" That would be to misunderstand. Agreed that in a century like ours these things are small doings, negligible discomforts. It would be sheer sentimentality to claim otherwise. And I'm not cock-eyed enough to think that such events could arouse your Pity and Terror. Nothing of Great Men Falling from High Place in our time. A battle in the anthill maybe. No, the simple facts, arranged and related, my hand of cards, will never do that. But they are nevertheless not insignificant. "Why?" you say. "Why bother?" Excuse me, but Maxim Gorky said it once and better than I can, so I quote:

Why do I relate these abominations? So that you may know, kind sirs, that all is not past and done with! You have a liking for grim fantasies; you are delighted by horrible stories well told; the gro-tesquely terrible excites you pleasantly. But I know of genuine horrors, everyday terrors, and I have the undeniable right to excite you unpleas-antly by telling you about them, in order that you may remember how we live, and under what circumstances. A low and unclean life it is, ours, and that is the truth.

I am a lover of humanity and I have no desire to make anyone miserable, but one must not be sentimental, nor hide the grim truth with the motley words of beautiful lies. Let us face life as it is! All that is good and human in our hearts needs renewing.

Thus we survived, endured, lived through it, and the cycle came to an end, a screeching halt. Last day on the Range (rocket launchers) we fired

$25,000 worth of ammunition into the side of a hill as fast as we could, so that the Range Officer could get back to camp early. If he didn't use the ammo all up, he'd be issued proportionately less for the following day. We were glad to assist him in his dilemma. We fired it away with joy and abandon. What explosions! What flashes of flame and clouds of smoke! It's a wonder we didn't kill each other.

That night we sat in the barracks packing our duffel bags. A fine cold rain was falling outside. And we were quiet inside, lonesome survivors, because somehow you never quite imagined something like that coming to an end. It was a calm, respectable, barracks-room scene. You could have photographed it and mailed the picture home.

Up the steps, weary-footed, his cap soaking wet and his raincoat beaded with raindrops and dripping, came the old First Sergeant, Cobb. He asked us to gather around, and he talked to us quietly. There had been a personal tragedy in the family of Sergeant Quince. (That bastard had a family?) His wife had been in a terrible automobile accident and was dying. (A *wife* yet?) He wanted to go home before she died. He had to arrange for somebody to look after the children. (*Children?*) The trouble was that this time of the month Sergeant Quince didn't have the money, even for train fare one way. He was broke.

"Why don't he go to the Red Cross?" somebody said.

Sergeant Cobb shrugged. "He ain't got time, I guess," he said. "I know he ain't a kindhearted man, boys. And you don't *have* to do this. It's strictly voluntary. But give a little something. He's human and he needs your help. Give from your heart."

He took a helmet liner off of the top of somebody's wall locker and held it in his hand like a collection plate in church. Somebody hawked and spat on the floor. I didn't think anybody would give anything. We just stood there and stared at Sergeant Cobb until Sachs pushed through to the front.

"Here's my contribution," he said. And he dropped a dime into the helmet liner.

Everybody started to laugh, and even the thick-headed ones caught on. Each of us put a dime in the pot. Ten cents for Sergeant Quince in his hour of need. Sergeant Cobb emptied the liner, put the dimes in his raincoat pocket, placed the liner back on top of the wall locker and started to leave. At the front door he turned around, shook his head and giggled.

"Don't that beat all?" he said. "They done exactly the same thing in all the other barracks too."

Half an hour later we had the exquisite pleasure of looking out of the windows and seeing Sergeant Quince in his Class-A uniform with his double row of World War II ribbons stand in the rain in the middle of the battery area and get soaking wet. He cussed and cussed us and threw those dimes high, wide and handsome and away. He wished us all damnation, death and hell.

This is where it ought to end. It would be a swell place to end, with the picture of Quince *furioso* throwing fountains of dimes in the air. Enraged and possessed and frustrated, like that man wildly digging for nonexistent gold at the end of William Faulkner's *The Hamlet*. Yes, Quince in insane rage, hurling our proffered dimes in the air, wild and black-faced with frustration and tribulation, would be a fine fade-out in the modern manner. But not so. Not so soon did he fade out of my life. Nor, I guess, did I expect him to.

Sachs and I went to Leadership School. What happened to the rest of them I wouldn't know and couldn't care less. But Sachs and myself took our duffel bags and waited in front of the orderly room. The harelipped Captain came out and painfully wished us well. We climbed over the tailgate of a deuce and a half and rode to the other side of camp where they try and make you into an NCO in three months flat or turn you into jelly.

"Why are you going?" Sachs asked me. As if I understood at the outset why *he* was doing it. I had hardly spoken to Sachs before that.

"Because that sonofabitch Quince is trash," I said. "I don't like to be pushed around by trash."

Sachs grinned. "You Southerners," he said. "You Southerners and your pride and your squabbles!"

I won't bore you with the sordid details of that place except to say that they made us and we made it. It worked. Sachs shed thirty pounds, went at every bit of it with fury and determination and emerged the top man in the class. Believe it or not. Many a husky specimen fell among the thorns and withered out of school, but Sachs thrived, grew, bloomed. I was in the top ten myself, and both of us made Sergeant out of it. We soldiered night and day like madmen. We learned all the tricks of the trade. When we were finished we were sharp. Bandbox soldiers. The metamorphosis was complete. Still, it's only fair to point out that we kept laughing about it. Sachs called it "being in disguise" and referred to his uniform as a costume. He called us both "the masqueraders." I called myself "the invisible white man."

One anecdote only of that time I'll insert. The Anecdote of the Word. It helps to explain the game we were playing. One week early in the course I was doing badly and it looked like I would wash out. I'd get good marks and only a few gigs one day, poor marks and many the next. The TAC/NCO wrote on my weekly report that he thought I was "a good man," but that I had been "vacillating." He was a college boy himself and used that word. Well, shortly thereafter the Company Commander called us both into his inner sanctum. We got shaped up in a big hurry and reported. His office was a room as bare as a monk's cell except for one huge sign on the wall that read "THIS TOO SHALL PASS." He, the Captain, was a huge hulk of a man, a former All-American tackle from some place or other, a bull neck, a bulging chest behind the desk, and all jaw, lantern and /or granite with the Mussolini thrust to it. He was dead serious. We were quivering arrows at attention in front of him.

"I have this here report before me," he said. "You say here that this soldier has been *vacillating*. What do you mean?"

The TAC gulped and patiently tried to explain what he had meant by means of the image of the pendulum of a grandfather's clock swinging back and forth. The Captain heard him out, nodded.

"Clerk!" he roared.

The Company Clerk came tearing into the room like somebody trying to steal second. Saluted. Quivered too!

"Get me a dictionary."

We waited in breathless anticipation. The clerk soon returned with the dictionary. Captain opened it to the *v*'s and followed his index finger, thick and blunt-ended as a chisel, down the line of words. Looked at the word a while and the definition. It was a pocket dictionary and defined as follows:

VAC-IL-LATE, V.I.,-LATED,-LATING. I. Waver; stagger 2. fluctuate 3. be irresolute or hesitant.

"Nothing about pendulums," he noted. "Damn good word, though. Good word."

He wrote it down on a pad in capitals and underlined it several times. That was that. We were dismissed.

Now from that Orderly Room issued forth each week reams of mimeographed material for the benefit of all students. Ever after that incident the Captain cautioned that those who wished to complete the course successfully *must not vacillate!* This got to be a standing joke in that mirthless place.

"If I catch any of you guys *vacillating* in the company area," the TAC used to tell us, "you've had it."

Sachs and I made it, were transformed from anarchists to impeccable sergeanthood. We didn't end up going to Korea to be shot at, but instead were sent to Europe to join a very sharp outfit where we would be able to maintain the high standards we had so recently acquired. Which we did for the rest of our service time. Sachs was so good he even made Sergeant First Class without time in grade.

More than a year later we were in Germany for maneuvers. It was the middle of summer and we were living in tents. In the evenings we used to go to a huge circus tent of a beer hall and get drunk. It was there one hot night that we met Quince again. He was sitting all alone at a table with a big crowd of empty 3.2 beer cans around him. He was a corporal now, two stripes down, and by the patch on his shoulder we knew he was in a mucked-up oufit, a whole division of stumblebums with a well-known cretin commanding. He looked it, too. His uniform was dirty. His shirt was open all the way down the front, revealing a filthy, sweat-soaked T-shirt. Of course it's hard to look sharp if you're living in the field in the middle of the summer. But Sachs and I took pride in our ability to look as sharp in the field as in garrison. It took some doing, but we could do it.

"Let's buy the bastard a beer," Sachs said.

He seemed glad to see us as if we were dear, old, long-lost friends. Once we had introduced ourselves, that is. He didn't recognize us at first. He marveled at our transformation and good luck. We couldn't help marveling at *his* transformation too. ("This is the worst outfit I was ever with," he admitted. "The Battery Commander has got it in for me.") He bought us a round and we bought more.

Late, just before they shut the place down and threw everybody out, Quince went maudlin. A crying drunk.

"I can't explain it, but it makes me feel bad to see you guys like this," he said. "I hated you guys, I'll admit that. Long before the dimes. But I didn't know you hated me so much."

"What do you mean by that?"

"To hunt me down after all this time and shame me. Soldiering is my life. It's just a couple of years for you guys. And here you are with all this rank looking like old soldiers. Sergeants! Goddamn, it isn't fair."

"Do you know what the Army is, Quince?"

"What? What's that?"

"I'll tell you what the Army is to me," Sachs said. "It's just a game, a stupid, brutal, pointless, simple-minded game. And you know what, Corporal Quince? I beat that game. I won. I'm a better soldier now than you ever were or ever will be and it doesn't mean a thing to me."

Quince turned his head away from us so we wouldn't see him crying.

"You hadn't ought to have said that," he said. "You can't take everything away from a guy. You got to leave a guy something."

We left him to cry in his beer until they tossed him out, and walked back under the stars to our tents, singing the whole way. We sat in our sleeping bags and had a smoke before we flaked out.

"You were great," I told Sachs. "That was worth waiting for."

But Sachs was a moody kind of a guy. He didn't see it that way. He was angry, in fact.

"You can't beat them down," he said. "No matter what you do. They always win out in the end. Sure I got in my licks. But he won anyway. *He made me do it.* That was the Quince in me kicking him while he's down. So in the end he still beat me."

"You worry about yourself too much."

"That's just the way I am," he said bitterly.

"You don't feel *sorry* for him, do you?"

That was a dumb question. Sachs was no Herman Wouk.

"Hell no," he said. "You don't get it. The trouble is I still hate him. I hate him worse than ever."

And he stubbed out his cigarette and turned over and went to sleep without another word, leaving me to ponder on that for a while.

JOHN UPDIKE

"Pigeon Feathers" is about a boy with a problem that has bewildered not only the young but people of all ages—what is death? "Purification or purgation of the emotions by art" is one dictionary definition of catharsis. Thanks to the art of the author, the reader shares such a catharsis with the boy.

John Updike was born in Shillington, Pennsylvania, in 1932. He attended Harvard College and the Ruskin School of Drawing and Fine Art in Oxford, England, and he has worked for The New Yorker. *He is the author of* The Carpentered Hen, *a book of poems; many novels, including* The Poorhouse Fair, Rabbit, Run, The Centaur; *and several volumes of short stories, among them* The Same Door *and* Pigeon Feathers and Other Stories. *In 1964 he received the National Book Award for fiction.*

Pigeon Feathers

WHEN they moved to Firetown, things were upset, displaced, rearranged. A red cane-back sofa that had been the chief piece in the living room at Olinger was here banished, too big for the narrow country parlor, to the barn, and shrouded under a tarpaulin. Never again would David lie on its length all afternoon eating raisins and reading mystery novels and science fiction and P. G. Wodehouse. The blue wing chair that had stood for years in the ghostly, immaculate guest bedroom in town, gazing through windows curtained with dotted swiss at the telephone wires and horse-chestnut trees and opposite houses, was here established importantly in front of the smutty little fireplace that supplied, in those first cold April days, their only heat. As a child, David had always been afraid of the guest bedroom — it was there that he, lying sick with the measles, had seen a black rod the size of a yardstick jog along at a slight slant beside the edge of the bed, and vanish when he screamed — and it was disquieting to have one of the elements of its haunted atmosphere basking by the fire, in the center of the family, growing sooty with use. The books that at home had gathered dust in the case beside the piano were here hastily stacked, all out of order, in the shelves that the carpenters had built low along one wall. David, at fourteen, had been more moved than a mover; like the furniture, he had to find a new place, and on the Saturday of the second week tried to work off some of his disorientation by arranging the books.

It was a collection obscurely depressing to him, mostly books his mother had acquired when she was young: college anthologies of Greek plays and Romantic poetry; Will Durant's *Story of Philosophy*; a soft-leather set of Shakespeare with string bookmarks sewed to the bindings; *Green Mansions,* boxed and illustrated with woodcuts; *I, the Tiger,* by Manuel Komroff; novels by names like Galsworthy and Ellen Glasgow and Irvin S. Cobb and Sinclair Lewis and "Elizabeth." The odor of faded taste made him feel the ominous gap between himself and his parents, the insulting gulf of time that existed before he was born. Suddenly he was tempted to dip into this time. From the heaps of books around him on the broad old floorboards, he picked up Volume II of a four-volume set of *An Outline of History,* by H. G. Wells. The book's red binding had faded to orange-pink in the spine. When he lifted the cover, there was a sweetish, atticlike smell, and his mother's maiden name written in unfamiliar handwriting on the flyleaf — an upright, bold, yet careful signature, bearing a faint relation to the quick scrunched backslant that flowed with marvelous consistency across her shopping lists and budget accounts and notes on Christmas cards to college friends from this same, vaguely menacing long ago.

He leafed through, pausing at drawings, done in an old-fashioned stippled style, of bas-reliefs, masks, Romans without pupils in their eyes, articles of ancient costume, fragments of pottery found in unearthed homes. The print was determinedly legible, and smug, like a lesson book. As he bent over the pages, yellow at the edges, they were like rectangles of dusty glass through which he looked down into unreal and irrelevant worlds. He could see things sluggishly move, and an unpleasant fullness came into his throat. His mother and grandmother fussed in the kitchen; the puppy, which they had just acquired, "for protection in the country," was cowering, with a sporadic panicked scrabble of claws, under the dining table that in their old home had been reserved for special days but that here was used for every meal.

Then, before he could halt his eyes, David slipped into Wells's account of Jesus. He had been an obscure political agitator, a kind of hobo, in a minor colony of the Roman Empire. By an accident impossible to reconstruct, he (the small *h* horrified David) survived his own crucifixion and presumably died a few weeks later. A religion was founded on the freakish incident. The credulous imagination of the times retrospectively assigned miracles and supernatural pretensions to Jesus; a myth grew, and then a church, whose theology at most points was in direct contradiction of the simple, rather communistic teachings of the Galilean.

It was as if a stone that for weeks and even years had been gathering weight in the web of David's nerves snapped them, plunged through the page, and a hundred layers of paper underneath. These fantastic falsehoods (plainly untrue; churches stood everywhere, the entire nation was founded "under God") did not at first frighten him; it was the fact that they had been permitted to exist in an actual human brain. This was the initial impact — that at a definite spot in time and space a brain black with the denial of Christ's divinity had been suffered to exist; that the universe had not spit out this ball of tar but allowed it to continue in its blasphemy, to grow old, win honors, wear a hat, write books that, if true, collapsed everything into a jumble of horror. The world outside the deep-silled windows — a rutted lawn, a whitewashed barn, a walnut tree frothy with fresh green — seemed a haven from which he was forever sealed off. Hot washrags seemed pressed against his cheeks.

He read the account again. He tried to supply out of his ignorance objections that would defeat the complacent march of these black words, and found none. Survivals and misunderstandings more farfetched were reported daily in the papers. But none of them caused churches to be built in every town. He tried to work backward through the churches, from their brave high fronts through their shabby, ill-attended interiors back into the events at Jerusalem, and felt himself surrounded by shifting gray shadows, centuries of history, where he knew nothing. The thread dissolved in his hands. Had Christ ever come to him, David Kern, and said, "Here. Feel the wound in My side"? No; but prayers had been answered. What prayers? He had prayed that Rudy Mohn, whom he had purposely tripped so he cracked his head on their radiator, not die, and he had not died. But for all the blood, it was just a cut; Rudy came back the same day, wearing a bandage and repeating the same teasing words. He could never have died. Again, David had prayed for two separate photographs of movie stars he had sent away for to arrive tomorrow, and though they did not, they did arrive, some days later, together, popping through the clacking letter slot like a rebuke from God's mouth: *I answer your prayers in My way, in My time.* After that, he had made his prayers less definite, less susceptible of being twisted into a scolding. But what a tiny, ridiculous coincidence this was, after all, to throw into battle against H. G. Wells's engines of knowledge! Indeed, it proved the enemy's point: Hope bases vast premises on foolish accidents, and reads a word where in fact only a scribble exists.

His father came home. They had supper. It got dark. He had to go to the bathroom, and took a flashlight down through the wet grass to the outhouse. For once, his fear of spiders there felt trivial. He set the flashlight, burning, beside him, and an insect alighted on its lens, a tiny insect, a mosquito or flea, so fragile and fine that the weak light projected its X-ray onto the wall boards: the faint rim of its wings, the blurred strokes, magnified, of its long hinged legs, the dark cone at the heart of its anatomy. The tremor must be its heart beating. Without warning, David was visited by an exact vision of death: a long hole in the ground, no wider than your body, down which you are drawn while the white faces above recede. You try to reach them but your arms are pinned. Shovels pour dirt into your face. There you will be forever, in an upright position, blind and silent, and in time no one will remember you, and you will never be called. As strata of rock shift, your fingers elongate, and your teeth are distended sidewise in a great underground grimace indistinguishable from a strip of chalk. And the earth tumbles on, and the sun expires, and unaltering darkness reigns where once there were stars.

Sweat broke out on his back. His mind seemed to rebound off of a solidness. Such extinction was not another threat, a graver sort of danger, a kind of pain; it was qualitatively different. It was not even a conception that could be voluntarily pictured; it entered you from outside. His protesting nerves swarmed on its surface like lichen on a meteor. The skin of his chest was soaked with the effort of rejection. At the same time that the fear was dense and internal, it was dense and all around him; a tide of clay had swept up to the stars; space was crushed into a mass. When he stood up, automatically hunching his shoulders to keep his head away from the spider webs, it was with a numb sense of being cramped between two huge volumes of rigidity. That he had even this small freedom to move surprised him. In the narrow shelter of that rank shack, adjusting his pants, he felt — his first spark of comfort — too small to be crushed.

But in the open, as the beam of the flashlight skidded with frightened quickness across the remote surfaces of the barn wall and the grape arbor and the giant pine that stood by the path to the woods, the terror descended. He raced up through the clinging grass pursued not by one of the wild animals the woods might hold, or one of the goblins his superstitious grandmother had communicated to his childhood, but by specters out of science fiction, where gigantic cinder moons fill half the turquoise sky. As David ran, a gray planet rolled inches behind his neck. If he looked back, he would be buried. And in the momentum of his terror, hideous possibilities — the dilation of the sun, the triumph of the insects — wheeled out of the vacuum of make-believe and added their weight to his impending oblivion.

He wrenched the door open; the lamps within the house flared. The wicks burning here and there seemed to mirror one another. His mother was washing the dishes in a little pan of heated pump water; Granmom fluttered near her elbow apprehensively. In the living room — the downstairs of the little square house was two long rooms — his father sat in front of the black fireplace restlessly folding and unfolding a newspaper.

David took from the shelf, where he had placed it this afternoon, the great unabridged Webster's Dictionary that his grandfather had owned. He turned the big thin pages, floppy as cloth, to the entry he wanted, and read:

soul . . . **1.** An entity conceived as the essence, substance, animating principle, or actuating cause of life, or of the individual life, esp. of life manifested in physical activities; the vehicle of individual existence, separate in nature from the body and usually held to be separable in existence.

The definition went on, into Greek and Egyptian conceptions, but David stopped short on the treacherous edge of antiquity. He needed to read no farther. The careful overlapping words shingled a temporary shelter for him. "Usually held to be separable in existence" — what could be fairer, more judicious, surer?

Upstairs, he seemed to be lifted above his fears. The sheets on his bed were clean. Granmom had ironed them with a pair of flatirons saved from the Olinger attic; she plucked them hot off the stove alternately, with a wooden handle called a goose. It was a wonder, to see how she managed. In the next room, his parents made comforting scratching noises as they carried a little lamp back and forth. Their door was open a

crack, so he saw the light shift and swing. Surely there would be, in the
last five minutes, in the last second, a crack of light, showing the door
from the dark room to another, full of light. Thinking of it this vividly
frightened him. His own dying, in a specific bed in a specific room,
specific walls mottled with wallpaper, the dry whistle of his breathing,
the murmuring doctors, the nervous relatives going in and out, but for
him no way out but down into the funnel. Never touch a doorknob
again. A whisper, and his parents' light was blown out. David prayed to
be reassured. Though the experiment frightened him, he lifted his hands
high into the darkness above his face and begged Christ to touch them.
Not hard or long; the faintest, quickest grip would be final for a lifetime.
His hands waited in the air, itself a substance, which seemed to move
through his fingers; or was it the pressure of his pulse? He returned his
hands to beneath the covers uncertain if they had been touched or not.
For would not Christ's touch *be* infinitely gentle?

Through all the eddies of its aftermath, David clung to this thought
about his revelation of extinction: that there, in the outhouse, he had
struck a solidness *qualitatively different,* a rock of horror firm enough to
support any height of construction. All he needed was a little help; a
word, a gesture, a nod of certainty and he would be sealed in, safe. The
assurance from the dictionary had melted in the night. Today was Sunday, a hot fair day. Across a mile of clear air the church bells called,
Celebrate, celebrate. Only Daddy went. He put on a coat over his rolled-
up shirtsleeves and got into the little old black Plymouth parked by the
barn and went off, with the same pained, hurried grimness of all his
actions. His churning wheels, as he shifted too hastily into second, raised
plumes of red dust on the dirt road. Mother walked to the far field, to see
what bushes needed cutting. David, though he usually preferred to stay
in the house, went with her. The puppy followed at a distance, whining
as it picked its way through the stubble but floundering off timidly if one
of them went back to pick it up and carry it. When they reached the crest
of the far field, his mother asked, "David, what's troubling you?"

"Nothing. Why?"

She looked at him sharply. The greening woods cross-hatched the space
beyond her half-gray hair. Then she turned her profile, and gestured
toward the house, which they had left a half mile behind them. "See how
it sits in the land? They don't know how to build with the land any

more. Pop always said the foundations were set with the compass. We must try to get a compass and see. It's supposed to face due south; but south feels a little more *that* way to me." From the side, as she said these things, she seemed handsome and young. The smooth sweep of her hair over her ear seemed white with a purity and calm that made her feel foreign to him. He had never regarded his parents as consolers of his troubles; from the beginning they had seemed to have more troubles than he. Their confusion had flattered him into an illusion of strength; so now on this high clear ridge he jealously guarded the menace all around them, blowing like a breeze on his fingertips, the possibility of all this wide scenery sinking into darkness. The strange fact that though she came to look at the brush she carried no clippers, for she had a fixed prejudice against working on Sundays, was the only consolation he allowed her to offer.

As they walked back, the puppy whimpering after them, the rising dust behind a distant line of trees announced that Daddy was speeding home from church. When they reached the house he was there. He had brought back the Sunday paper and the vehement remark "Dobson's too intelligent for these farmers. They just sit there with their mouths open and don't hear a thing he's saying."

David hid in the funny papers and sports section until one-thirty. At two, the catechetical class met at the Firetown church. He had transferred from the catechetical class of the Lutheran church in Olinger, a humiliating comedown. In Olinger they met on Wednesday nights, spiffy and spruce, in the atmosphere of a dance. Afterward, blessed by the brick-faced minister from whose lips the word "Christ" fell like a burning stone, the more daring of them went with their Bibles to a luncheonette and smoked. Here in Firetown, the girls were dull white cows and the boys narrow-faced brown goats in old men's suits, herded on Sunday afternoons into a threadbare church basement that smelled of stale hay. Because his father had taken the car on one of his countless errands to Olinger, David walked, grateful for the open air and the silence. The catechetical class embarrassed him, but today he placed hope in it, as the source of the nod, the gesture, that was all he needed.

Reverend Dobson was a delicate young man with great dark eyes and small white shapely hands that flickered like protesting doves when he preached; he seemed a bit misplaced in the Lutheran ministry. This was his first call. It was a split parish; he served another rural church twelve miles away. His iridescent green Ford, new six months ago, was spattered to the windows with red mud and rattled from bouncing on the rude back roads, where he frequently got lost, to the malicious satisfaction of many. But David's mother liked him, and, more pertinent to his success, the Haiers, the sleek family of feed merchants and innkeepers and tractor salesmen who dominated the Firetown church liked him. David liked him, and felt liked in turn; sometimes in class, after some special stupidity, Dobson directed toward him out of those wide black eyes a mild look of disbelief, a look that, though flattering, was also delicately disquieting.

Catechetical instruction consisted of reading aloud from a work booklet answers to problems prepared during the week, problems like "I am the ——, the ——, and the ——, saith the Lord." Then there was a question period in which no one ever asked any questions. Today's theme was the last third of the Apostles' Creed. When the time came for questions, David blushed and asked, "About the Resurrection of the Body — are we conscious between the time when we die and the Day of Judgment?"

Dobson blinked, and his fine little mouth pursed, suggesting that David was making difficult things more difficult. The faces of the other students went blank, as if an indiscretion had been committed.

"No, I suppose not," Reverend Dobson said.

"Well, where is our soul, then, in this gap?"

The sense grew, in the class, of a naughtiness occurring. Dobson's shy eyes watered, as if he were straining to keep up the formality of attention, and one of the girls, the fattest, simpered toward her twin, who was a little less fat. Their chairs were arranged in a rough circle. The current running around the circle panicked David. Did everybody know something he didn't know?

"I suppose you could say our souls are asleep," Dobson said.

"And then they wake up, and there is the earth like it always is, and all the people who have ever lived? Where will Heaven be?"

Anita Haier giggled. Dobson gazed at David intently, but with an awkward, puzzled flicker of forgiveness, as if there existed a secret between them that David was violating. But David knew of no secret. All he wanted was to hear Dobson repeat the words he said every Sunday morning. This he would not do. As if these words were unworthy of the conversational voice.

"David, you might think of Heaven this way: as the way the goodness Abraham Lincoln did lives after him."

"But is Lincoln conscious of it living on?" He blushed no longer with embarrassment but in anger; he had walked here in good faith and was being made a fool.

"Is he conscious now? I would have to say no; but I don't think it matters." Dobson's voice had a coward's firmness; he was hostile now.

"You don't?"

"Not in the eyes of God, no." The unction, the stunning impudence, of this reply sprang tears of outrage in David's eyes. He bowed them to his book, where short words like Duty, Love, Obey, Honor were stacked in the form of a cross.

"Were there any other questions, David?" Dobson asked with renewed gentleness. The others were rustling, collecting their books.

"No." He made his voice firm, though he could not bring up his eyes.

"Did I answer your question fully enough?"

"Yes."

In the minister's silence the shame that should have been his crept over David; the burden and fever of being a fraud were placed upon *him,* who was innocent, and it seemed, he knew, a confession of this guilt that on the way out he was unable to face Dobson's stirred gaze, though he felt it probing the side of his head.

Anita Haier's father gave him a ride down the highway as far as the dirt road. David said he wanted to walk the rest, and figured that his offer was accepted because Mr. Haier did not want to dirty his bright blue Buick with dust. This was all right; everything was all right, as long as it was clear. His indignation at being betrayed, at seeing Christianity betrayed, had hardened him. The straight dirt road reflected his hardness. Pink stones thrust up through its packed surface. The April sun beat down from the center of the afternoon half of the sky; already it had some of summer's heat. Already the fringes of weeds at the edges of the road were bedraggled with dust. From the reviving grass and scruff of the fields he walked between, insects were sending up a monotonous, automatic chant. In the distance a tiny figure in his father's coat was walking along the edge of the woods. His mother. He wondered what joy she found in such walks; to him the brown stretches of slowly rising and falling land expressed only a huge exhaustion.

Flushed with fresh air and happiness, she returned from her walk earlier than he had expected, and surprised him at his grandfather's Bible. It was a stumpy black book, the boards worn thin where the old man's fingers had held them; the spine hung by one weak hinge of fabric.

David had been looking for the passage where Jesus says to the one thief on the cross "Today shalt thou be with me in paradise." He had never tried reading the Bible for himself before. What was so embarrassing about being caught at it was that he detested the apparatus of piety. Fusty churches, creaking hymns, ugly Sunday-school teachers and their stupid leaflets — he hated everything about them but the promise they held out, a promise that in the most perverse way, as if the homeliest crone in the kingdom were given the prince's hand, made every good and real thing, ball games and jokes and big-breasted girls, possible. He couldn't explain this to his mother. Her solicitude was upon him.

"David, what are you doing at Granpop's Bible?"

"Trying to read it. This is supposed to be a Christian country, isn't it?"

She sat down on the green sofa that used to be in the sun parlor at Olinger, under the fancy mirror. A little smile still lingered on her face from the walk. "David, I wish you'd talk to me."

"What about?"

"About whatever it is that's troubling you. Your father and I have both noticed it."

"I asked Reverend Dobson about Heaven and he said it was like Abraham Lincoln's goodness living after him."

He waited for the shock to strike her. "Yes?" she said, expecting more.

"That's all."

"And why didn't you like it?"

"Well; don't you see? It amounts to saying there isn't any Heaven at all."

"I don't see that it amounts to that. What do you want Heaven to be?"

"Well, I don't know. I want it to be *some*thing. I thought *he'd* tell me what it was. I thought that was his job." He was becoming angry, sensing her surprise at him. She had assumed that Heaven had faded from his head years ago. She had imagined that he had already entered, in the secrecy of silence, the conspiracy that he now knew to be all around him.

"David," she asked gently, "don't you ever want to rest?"

"No. Not forever."

"David, you're so young. When you get older, you'll feel differently."

"Grandpa didn't. Look how tattered this book is."

"I never understood your grandfather."

"Well, I don't understand ministers who say it's like Lincoln's memory going on and on. Suppose you're not Lincoln?"

"I think Reverend Dobson made a mistake. You must try to forgive him."

"It's not a *question* of his making a mistake! It's a question of dying and never moving or seeing or hearing anything ever again."

"But" — in exasperation — "darling, it's so *greedy* of you to want more. When God has given us this wonderful April day, and given us this farm, and you have your whole life ahead of you — "

"You think, then, that there is God?"

"Of course I do" — with deep relief that smoothed her features into a reposeful oval. He was standing, and above her, too near for his comfort. He was afraid she would reach out and touch him.

"He made everthing? You feel that?"

"Yes."

"Then who made Him?"

"Why, Man. Man." The happiness of this answer lit up her face radiantly, until she saw his gesture of disgust.

"Well that amounts to saying there is none."

Her hand reached for his wrist but he backed away. "David, it's a mystery. A miracle. It's a miracle more beautiful than any Reverend Dobson could have told you about. You don't say houses don't exist because Man made them."

"No. God has to be different."

"But, David, you have the *evidence*. Look out the window at the sun; at the fields."

"Mother, good grief. Don't you see" — he gasped away the roughness in his throat — "if when we die there's nothing, all your sun and fields and what not are all, ah *horror?* It's just an ocean of horror."

"But David, it's not. It's so clearly not that." And she made an urgent opening gesture with her hands that expressed, with its suggestion of a willingness to receive his helplessness, all her grace, her gentleness, her love of beauty gathered into a passive intensity that made him intensely hate her. He would not be wooed away from the truth. *I am the Way, the Truth —*

"No," he told her. "Just let me alone."

He found his tennis ball behind the piano and went outside to throw it against the side of the house. There was a patch high up where the brown stucco that had been laid over the sandstone masonry was crumbling away; he kept trying with the tennis ball to chip more pieces off. Superimposed upon his deep ache was a smaller but more immediate worry that he had hurt his mother. He heard his father's car rattling on the straightaway, and went into the house, to make peace before he arrived. To his relief, she was not giving off the stifling damp heat of her anger but instead was cool, decisive, maternal. she handed him an old green book, her college text of Plato.

"I want you to read the Parable of the Cave," she said.

"All right," he said, though he knew it would do no good. Some story by a dead Greek just vague enough to please her. "Don't worry about it, Mother."

"I *am* worried. Honestly, David, I'm sure there will be something for us. As you get older, these things seem to matter a great deal less."

"That may be. It's a dismal thought, though."

His father bumped at the door. The locks and jambs stuck here. But before Granmom could totter to the catch and let him in, he had knocked it open. Although Mother usually kept her talks with David a confidence, a treasure between them, she called instantly, "George, David is worried about death!"

He came to the doorway of the living room, his shirt pocket bristling with pencils, holding in one hand a pint box of melting ice cream and in the other the knife with which he was about to divide it into four sections, their Sunday treat. "Is the kid worried about death? Don't give it a thought, David. I'll be lucky if I live till tomorrow, and I'm not worried. If they'd taken a buckshot gun and shot me in the cradle I'd be better off. The *world'd* be better off. Hell, I think death is a wonderful thing. I look forward to it. Get the garbage out of the way. If I had the man here who invented death, I'd pin a medal on him."

"Hush, George. You'll frighten the child worse than he is."

This was not true; he never frightened David. There was no harm in his father, no harm at all. Indeed, in the man's steep self-disgust the boy felt a kind of ally. A distant ally. He saw his position with a certain strategic coldness. Nowhere in the world of other people would he find the hint, the nod, he needed to begin to build his fortress against death. They none of them believed. He was alone. In a deep hole.

In the months that followed, his position changed little. School was some comfort. All those sexy, perfumed people, wisecracking, chewing gum, all of them doomed to die, and none of them noticing. In their company David felt that they would carry him along into the bright, cheap paradise reserved for them. In any crowd, the fear ebbed a little; he

had reasoned that somewhere in the world there must exist a few people
who believed what was necessary, and the larger the crowd, the greater
the chance that he was near such a soul, within calling distance, if only
he was not too ignorant, too ill-equipped, to spot him. The sight of
clergymen cheered him; whatever they themselves thought, their collars
were still a sign that somewhere, at some time, someone had recognized
that we cannot, *cannot,* submit to death. The sermon topics posted outside churches, the flip hurried pieties of disc jockeys, the cartoons in
magazines showing angels or devils — on such scraps he kept alive the
possibility of hope.

For the rest, he tried to drown his hopelessness in clatter and jostle.
The pinball machine at the luncheonette was a merciful distraction; as he
bent over its buzzing, flashing board of flippers and cushions, the weight
and constriction in his chest lightened and loosened. He was grateful for
all the time his father wasted in Olinger. Every delay postponed the
moment when they must ride together down the dirt road into the heart
of the dark farmland, where the only light was the kerosene lamp waiting on the dining room table, a light that made their food shadowy,
scrabbled, sinister.

He lost his appetite for reading. He was afraid of being ambushed
again. In mystery novels people died like dolls being discarded; in science
fiction enormities of space and time conspired to crush the humans; and
even in P. G. Wodehouse he felt a hollowness, a turning away from
reality that was implicitly bitter and became explicit in the comic figures
of futile clergymen. All gaiety seemed minced out on the skin of a void.
All quiet hours seemed invitations to dread.

School stopped. His father took the car in the opposite direction, to a
construction job where he had been hired for the summer as a
timekeeper, and David was stranded in the middle of acres of heat and
greenery and blowing pollen and the strange, mechanical humming that
lay invisibly in the weeds and alfalfa and dry orchard grass.

For his fifteenth birthday his parents gave him, with jokes about his
being a hillbilly now, a Remington .22. It was somewhat like a pinball
machine to take it out to the old kiln in the woods, where they dumped
their trash, and set up tin cans on the kiln's sandstone shoulder and shoot
them off one by one. He'd take the puppy, who had grown long legs and
a rich coat of reddish fur — he was part chow. Copper hated the gun but
loved David enough to accompany him. When the flat acrid crack rang

out, he would race in terrified circles that would tighten and tighten until they brought him, shivering, against David's legs. Depending upon his mood, David would shoot again or drop to his knees and comfort the dog. Giving this comfort to a degree returned comfort to him. The dog's ears, laid flat against his skull in fear, were folded so intricately, so — he groped for the concept — *surely*. Where the dull-studded collar made his fur stand up, each hair showed a root of soft white under the length, black-tipped, of the metal color that had given the dog its name. In his agitation Copper panted through nostrils that were elegant slits, like two healed cuts, or like the keyholes of a dainty lock of black, grained wood. His whole whorling, knotted, jointed body was a wealth of such embellishments. And in the smell of the dog's hair David seemed to descend through many finely differentiated layers of earth: mulch, soil, sand, clay, and the glittering mineral base.

But when he returned to the house, and saw the books arranged on the low shelves, fear returned. The four adamant volumes of Wells like four thin bricks, the green Plato that had puzzled him with its queer softness and tangled purity, the dead Galsworthy and "Elizabeth," Grandpa's mammoth dictionary, Grandpa's Bible, the Bible that he himself had received on becoming a member of the Firetown Lutheran Church — at the sight of these, the memory of his fear reawakened and came around him. He had grown stiff and stupid in its embrace. His parents tried to think of ways to entertain him.

"David, I have a job for you to do," his mother said one evening at the table.

"What?"

"If you're going to take that tone perhaps we'd better not talk."

"What tone? I didn't take any tone."

"Your grandmother thinks there are too many pigeons in the barn."

"Why?" David turned to look at his grandmother, but she sat there staring at the orange flame of the burning lamp with her usual expression of bewilderment.

Mother shouted, "Mom, he wants to know why?"

Granmom made a jerky, irritable motion with her bad hand, as if generating the force for utterance, and said, "They foul the furniture."

"That's right," Mother said. "She's afraid for that old Olinger furniture that we'll never use. David, she's been after me for a month about those poor pigeons. She wants you to shoot them."

"I don't want to kill anything especially," David said.

Daddy said, "The kid's like you are, Elsie. He's too good for this world. Kill or be killed, that's my motto."

His mother said loudly, "Mother, he doesn't want to do it."

"Not?" The old lady's eyes distended as if in horror, and her claw descended slowly to her lap.

"Oh, I'll do it, I'll do it tomorrow," David snapped, and a pleasant crisp taste entered his mouth with the decision.

"And I had thought, when Boyer's men made the hay, it would be better if the barn doesn't look like a rookery," his mother added needlessly.

A barn, in day, is a small night. The splinters of light between the dry shingles pierce the high roof like stars, and the rafters and crossbeams and built-in ladders seem, until your eyes adjust, as mysterious as the branches of a haunted forest. David entered silently, the gun in one hand. Copper whined desperately at the door, too frightened to come in with the gun yet unwilling to leave the boy. David stealthily turned, said, "Go away," shut the door on the dog, and slipped the bolt across. It was a door within a door; the double door for wagons and tractors was as high and wide as the face of a house.

The smell of old straw scratched his sinuses. The red sofa, half hidden under its white-splotched tarpaulin, seemed assimilated into this smell, sunk in it, buried. The mouths of empty bins gaped like caves. Rusty oddments of farming — coils of baling wire, some spare tines for a harrow, a handleless shovel — hung on nails driven here and there in the thick wood. He stood stock-still a minute; it took a while to separate the cooing of the pigeons from the rustling in his ears. When he had focused on the cooing, it flooded the vast interior with its throaty, bubbling outpour: there seemed no other sound. They were up behind the beams. What light there was leaked through the shingles and the dirty glass windows at the far end and the small round holes, about as big as basketballs, high on the opposite stone side walls, under the ridge of the roof.

A pigeon appeared in one of these holes, on the side toward the house. It flew in, with a battering of wings, from the outside, and waited there, silhouetted against its pinched bit of sky, preening and cooing in a throbbing, thrilled, tentative way. David tiptoed four steps to the side, rested his gun against the lowest rung of a ladder pegged between two upright beams, and lowered the gunsight into the bird's tiny, jauntily cocked head. The slap of the report seemed to come off the stone wall behind him, and the pigeon did not fall. Neither did it fly. Instead it stuck in the round hole, pirouetting rapidly and nodding its head as if in frantic agreement. David shot the bolt back and forth and had aimed again before the spent cartridge stopped jingling on the boards by his feet. He eased the tip of the sight a little lower, into the bird's breast, and took care to squeeze the trigger with perfect evenness. The slow contraction of his hand, abruptly sprang the bullet; for a half second there was doubt, and then the pigeon fell like a handful of rags, skimming down the barn wall into the layer of straw that coated the floor of the mow on this side.

Now others shook loose from the rafters, and whirled in the dim air with a great blurred hurtle of feathers and noise. They would go for the hole; he fixed his sights on the little moon of blue, and when a pigeon came to it, shot him as he was walking the ten inches or so of stone that would carry him into the open air. This pigeon lay down in that tunnel of stone, unable to fall either one way or the other, although he was alive enough to lift one wing and cloud the light. It would sink back, and he would suddenly lift it again, the feathers flaring. His body blocked that exit. David raced to the other side of the barn's main aisle, where a similar ladder was symmetrically placed, and rested his gun on the same rung. Three birds came together to this hole; he got one, and two got through. The rest resettled in the rafters.

There was a shallow triangular space behind the crossbeams supporting the roof. It was here they roosted and hid. But either the space was too small, or they were curious, for now that his eyes were at home in the dusty gloom David could see little dabs of gray popping in and out. The cooing was shriller now; it apprehensive tremolo made the whole volume of air seem liquid. He noticed one little smudge of a head that was especially persistent in peeking out; he marked the place, and fixed his gun on it, and when the head appeared again, had his finger tightened in advance on the trigger. A parcel of fluff slipped off the beam and fell the barn's height onto a canvas covering some Olinger furniture, and where its head had peeked out there was a fresh prick of light in the shingles.

Standing in the center of the floor, fully master now, disdaining to steady the barrel with anything but his arm, he killed two more that way. He felt like a beautiful avenger. Out of the shadowy ragged infinity of the vast barn roof these impudent things dared to thrust their heads, presumed to dirty its starred silence with their filthy timorous life, and he cut them off, tucked them back neatly into the silence. He had the sensations of a creator; these little smudges and flickers that he was clever to see and even cleverer to hit in the dim recesses of the rafters — out of each of them he was making a full bird. A tiny peek, probe, dab of life, when he hit it, blossomed into a dead enemy, falling with good, final weight.

The imperfection of the second pigeon he had shot, who was still lifting his wing now and then up in the round hole, nagged him. He put a new clip into the stock. Hugging the gun against his body, he climbed the ladder. The barrel sight scratched his ear; he had a sharp, bright vision, like a color slide, of shooting himself and being found tumbled on the barn floor among his prey. He locked his arm around the top rung — a fragile, gnawed rod braced between uprights — and shot into the bird's body from a flat angle. The wing folded, but the impact did not, as he had hoped, push the bird out of the hole. He fired again, and again, and still the little body, lighter than air when alive, was too heavy to budge from its high grave. From up here he could see green trees and a brown corner of the house through the hole. Clammy with the cobwebs that gathered between the rungs, he pumped a full clip of eight bullets into the stubborn shadow, with no success. He climbed down, and was struck by the silence in the barn. The remaining pigeons must have escaped out the other hole. That was all right; he was tired of it.

He stepped with his rifle into the light. His mother was coming to meet him, and it amused him to see her shy away from the carelessly held gun. "You took a chip out of the house," she said. "What were those last shots about?"

"One of them died up in that little round window and I was trying to shoot it down."

"Copper's hiding behind the piano and won't come out. I had to leave him."

"Well, don't blame me. *I* didn't want to shoot the poor devils."

"Don't smirk. You look like your father. How many did you get?"

"Six."

She went into the barn, and he followed. She listened to the silence. Her hair was scraggly, perhaps from tussling with the dog. "I don't suppose the others will be back," she said wearily. "Indeed, I don't know why I let Mother talk me into it. Their cooing was such a comforting noise." She began to gather up the dead birds. Though he didn't want to touch them, David went into the mow and picked up by its tepid, horny, coral-colored feet the first bird he had killed. Its wings unfolded disconcertingly, as if the creature had been held together by threads that now were slit. It did not weigh much. He retrieved the one on the other side of the barn; his mother got the three in the middle, and led the way across the road to the little southern slope of land that went down toward the foundations of the vanished tobacco shed. The ground was too steep to plant or mow; wild strawberries grew in the tangled grass. She put her burden down and said, "We'll have to bury them. The dog will go wild."

He put his two down on her three; the slick feathers let the bodies slide liquidly on one another. He asked, "Shall I get you the shovel?"

"Get it for yourself; *you* bury them. They're your kill," she said. "And be sure to make the hole deep enough so he won't dig them up."

While he went to the tool shed for the shovel, she went into the house. Unlike her, she did not look up, either at the orchard to the right of her or at the meadow on her left, but instead held her head rigidly, tilted a little, as if listening to the ground.

He dug the hole, in a spot where there were no strawberry plants, before he studied the pigeons. He had never seen a bird this close before. The feathers were more wonderful than dog's hair; for each filament was shaped within the shape of the feather, and the feathers in turn were trimmed to fit a pattern that flowed without error across the bird's body. He lost himself in the geometrical tides as the feathers now broadened and stiffened to make an edge for flight, now softened and constricted to cup warmth around the mute flesh. And across the surface of the infinitely adjusted yet somehow effortless mechanics of the feathers played idle designs of color, no two alike, designs executed, it seemed, in a controlled rapture, with a joy that hung level in the air above and behind him. Yet these birds bred in the millions and were exterminated as pests. Into the fragrant, open earth he dropped one broadly banded in shades of slate blue, and on top of it another, mottled all over with rhythmic patches of lilac and gray. The next was almost wholly white, yet with a salmon glaze at the throat. As he fitted the last two, still pliant, on the top, and stood up, crusty coverings were lifted from him, and with a feminine, slipping sensation along his nerves that seemed to give the air hands, he was robed in this certainty: that the God who had lavished such craft upon these worthless birds would not destroy His whole Creation by refusing to let David live forever.

H. W. BLATTNER

As with the traditional clown, there are tears behind the laughter of the whore in "Sound of a Drunken Drummer," which takes its title from Omar Khayyam. She finds lust but no love. The skill with which the flippancies of her frank conversations are related is remarkable.

H. W. Blattner was born of Swiss parents in Buenos Aires. As a child she lived in New York, in Havana, Cuba, and in Switzerland. As a result, she speaks, reads and writes German and Spanish, is competent in French and knows the German-Swiss dialect. Married to an American, she and her husband have lived since 1941 in California where she works as a secretary.

Sound of a Drunken Drummer

DOING FIFTY UP MISSION she said to Rob, sober and upright beside her, "Don't worry, boy, no cop's going to catch us if I have to do ninety. They'd have to shoot me in the tires," but there weren't any around, probably all in their station houses counting poker chips, and when he gave her a glance she said, "That's right, I don't like cops. Instinctively I don't like them, verstehst Du?"

He seemed to. He always did. It was one of the beautiful things about him. He had so many: sweet disposition, handsome intelligent presence, a strong uninhibited capacity for love. Plus good manners. A sterling type.

"Oh love me love me love me true," she sang low with the radio, "cause there's no one in the world but yew-hoo-hoo," and gave out there arbitrarily recollecting the woman back in the drugstore where she'd gone to get the prescription filled that she'd put the arm on the nice young doctor for: the naïve swimming look that surprisingly often got to them, the young sweet — helpless — not too much, careful there, that's right, got it now just the right pitch — "You see doctor I'm a stranger here, I'll be going back East soon but I'm under rather a severe strain — "

Reprinted from *The Hudson Review*, Vol. XV, No. 3, Autumn, 1962. Copyright 1962 by The Hudson Review, Inc.

Here something quick about the death of a beloved relative . — "And I can't sleep so if you could let me have something a bit strong perhaps so I'll be sure to get some rest, I do need it badly."

Hadn't failed her yet any of these young ones that at times jockeyed for the moment with expectation, unlike most of the older trouts rendered wily and callous by suffering, other people's of course — for whom it was all déjà vu like the movie operator who dozes on the job. You could practically read the diagnosis forming up behind the scientific foreheads: "Neurotic. Drinks —" But she was always dead sober at these times and anyway she didn't drink so much most of the time that it was anything like a matter of leaping to the eye, when you considered people like Toni and her clique who went in for it seriously in order not to be, as what's-his-name had said, or had he — I think not, therefore I am not — Men, types. Autumn leaves. Oh, sheets.

But where, what had she started to — no matter, possibly some little thing she was going to say to Rob here who understood one well enough anyway so it wasn't actually necessary to say anything, and slowing for the turn into Ocean Avenue she looked at him and coarsely taken with his companionable air of capable interest flung an arm about his shoulders and said cheek to cheek, "I like you, you know? Men are foul. Dogs are noble." He cut a wet swipe at her chin as she let him go raking way roughly tender, and his profile level with hers faced forward.

Tooling along in the ghost-gray night inside the snug tent of the convertible they wound their way to Junipero Serra and idled on through Portola to where the fine houses slept aristocratic, one couldn't picture people snoring inside. "Richard does, though," she said. "Quite obscenely. I don't know, it simply sounds that way. Look," she pointed, "there's where he is this instant, back in his bedroom there, snoring. Perhaps why Mrs. Wrighthill sleeps separate. *And* à cause de moi, it goes without saying. Marriage one long bore, did someone say. Of *course* she knows, silly. You don't imagine this is the first time, do you? But being a lady she naturally resents not being first fiddle. I suppose she kept her eyes on all that gold paving her way up the aisle, and who am I to scorn her for a natural feminine instinct. No, let's be broad about the thing. He must have been young once, oilily tender. Oi Lily — bei mir bist Du a sister under your skin. No, in truth a formidable woman. A lady. Aren't many of them left, it's said. Stepping all in white with hymen intact and cool authority lo these many years to where attended the gentleman who these days pays for our keep, your horsemeat and my scotch and minks. Not that I asked for any of that barbarity of dead skins but he insisted, Richard's that generous. I'm sure he'd offer to put me through college if I didn't already have my sheepskin. Which I got through the skin of my ass being nice to Professor O'Rourke — you're quite right, it does sound like a fart in a bathtub. Old but still serviceable, like an international playboy. The genius of the people comes out in these things. Like dirty jokes. And him poor devil, the professor I mean, scared stiff he'd be found out. Those intellectuals, they don't overdo that sort of thing although who knows, with the student body constantly changing. If those ivied walls had tongues, mercy. Richard's house too, such a coincidence. Boy, am I in the Ivy League. However that Elise Lynch, she always did turn a hand or an ass to anything. Way back I was told I'd come to a bad end, and that I have testifies to my powers of application because if you think it's anything but a rocky road to hell you're off the beam, boy." She reached over and rubbed the back of his ear. "Did you know, in a happy home even the animals are happy — the dogs, cats, lions, snakes? When I was a kid we had dogs by the half dozen and not one but was a snarler and biter. Pavlov would have been enchanted — you never saw such conditioning. Still it wasn't that so much made me take to other people's beds. I had my smattering of virtue. More of a built-in inclination, I should say. Got it from Daddy, no question. Who couldn't climb off one playmate than he was casting about for another. Kept poor Mother in a constant state of two-mindedness, like having two heads. And the kids getting the psychic fallout, naturally." She rubbed his ear again. He liked it, leaning to get the full satisfaction. "Well, all I can say is I bet you'd be every bit as generous as Richard if you were a man, which thank heaven you're not. This way it's a much more satisfactory relationship. Men and women can't help being dishonest with each other, it's one of the unwritten laws. Listen, if they ever went crazy and told each other the truth there'd be a massacre in the streets."

They were wandering around easy like that, just riding around as they did most nights — Richard left around nine or half-past, not alone because of Mrs. Wrighthill. A man of fifty-three had his sedate routines — she going on talking to him who was such a good listener, as she had got into the habit of doing because if you stayed too long in saloons you got stinking and it was more comfortable as well as seemly to do it inside your own subsidized walls or next door with Toni and her crowd who all they had was money and carrying their cargo of hooch or H according to preference had jettisoned their souls long ago, when of all things there was a pair of dogs exuberantly copulating on the sidewalk, the right time if the wrong place but how naturalistic compared to humans: in the darkened rooms, the walleyed fumbling. Rob spied them too and whimpered, looking back through the rear window. "Don't take it so to heart," she said, "or wherever. You've had yours, if you'll remember the charming bit you ran across in Sutro Heights last week. In broad daylight too." One walked on pretending not to notice and after a suitable interval turned and whistled, on his return slipping the leash on with a mild scold to make it appear as if he'd done no worse than lift a leg on the nasturtiums. So proud and set-up he looked, similar to Richard when he'd put over one of his big deals.

"We'll celebrate," he would say, beaming some — he had the smooth round pink-tinted kind of face to which it came natural, at such times he definitely did have the bland chic, a combination of smoothness and éclat, of a minister in charge of a large and wealthy congregation. By the same token there was his voice to play around one in clerical compass, warm, resonant yet urbane, undoubtedly the instrument that had increased him his fortune, for he came of one of those elite Western clans whose heads started out grubbily as prospectors and wound up sleeping on gold-knobbed beds. When they didn't sail off to chivvy simpleminded natives on tropic isles, trading beads and Mother Hubbards for the real estate. Or on that order — how could she be expected properly to know, an effete New Yorker ignorant of their large Western ways.

"All right," she would say. "Let's." So then he'd have a champagne supper sent in, and top off the whole with some love play. Not too much. Richard had his age and health in addition to his dignity to think of.

But she saw she had come around to his house again, and on a whim stopped the car in front of the tall red-brick white-trim house back of the fine meandering date-palmed street and observing it imagined how he'd disapprove, silently of course, if he knew she was sitting there at her midnight loafing. For being a wellbred man, in the — what, eight, ten months they'd been in association — so hard to say, they came and they went and when they came you wished they'd went — in all this time he had never once said a word about her drinking which naturally he abominated, except to refer in a roundabout manner to the evils of liquor. Himself, a wine man and maybe one two martinis a month. Tout à fait comme il faut. A man of breeding and substance. Gentleman, gentleman friend: mousing around sedate, broad-bottomed, always the cheese and never a nip of the trap.

A patrol car pulled in to the curb. The door slammed and a cop walked back toward her on flat, let's see what we've got here feet.

"Having any trouble, miss?" He peered in as into a cave.

"Since you mention it officer, yes, some," she said. "Nothing you could fix, though, thanks all the same."

He measured her out of his ruddy bull-terrier face and said with something of a hard, accustomed sigh, "Well now, let's have a look at your license."

"Sure, if you must."

He held a flashlight on it, peering, and handed it back. "Like to know what you're parked here for, if you don't mind."

"Well, taking one thing with another I should say I do but that's neither here nor there, is it."

"It sure isn't," he said heavily, leaning the elbow of a thigh-sized arm in on her. Rob growled but she casually laid a hand on him and he didn't follow up.

She relaxed, hands idle on the wheel and congratulated herself on having drunk vodka and then not enough to cause a hassle. "It's this way, officer," she said. "I like to ride around dreaming nights. Kind of a therapy, you see, when you can't sleep. Therapy, that means —"

"I know what it means," he said, his dewlaps contracting a bit.

"Well, good. They're doing an excellent job of training, aren't they. So I drove in here and stopped because it's so peaceful I can hear my motor purr."

"Sounds all right to me," he said.

"Oh, it's a superb motor," she said. "None better."

They gazed at each other, eyes glistening in the witching light of the dashboard.

"All right now," he said. "That'll be all. Better run along before I change my mind, however."

"Yes *sir,* officer. That's just what I'll do. But may I say it's good to see the law right in there, protecting property and what's the other — yes, life." She turned on her nicest debutante smile. "Arrivederci," she said, backed up and swept off around him.

Well, it had got to him of course. Her smile really could have been her fortune, if she'd bothered to lift her little finger instead of her skirt, so much too soon and too often. But then she got to thinking of Wimberley, for no ready reason except the usual: dead now poor devil, done in despite the specialists, all the crazy care. Hadn't belonged to him long, and him on his last lung then, being eaten by the cancer. A bachelor, it had been all right for her to live in and he gave it out that she was his secretary — clever, that. All the same rather a decent solid type, Wim. A shame, wrenched off at thirty-nine and from out of all that wealth, too. One time money didn't talk loud enough. And so thoughtful of him, seeing to it virtually in extremis that she found a fresh bed-down. Befitting a man who inheriting his fortune was above the vulgarity of treating money lightly, and so left every last penny to a foundation bearing his name.

"I'll never forget the day," she said to Rob. He yawned and slid down, paws drooping over the seat edge and snuggling his chin down on them. " 'I've been thinking of your future,' he says in that awful weak staggered voice, and the shadow of death on the wall, 'and I think I've got the answer — ' "

A slant of sun lay on the bed, that if it had fallen on him would have shown him up transparent, rendered down to nothing as he was. Out the window to one side the Golden Gate bridge draped its harp hang in the clear silver air — a wind drove with fury across the sky, blanching it — Tamalpais rising farther on its remote majestic drag, dark blue and the contours fuzzed in silver. Straight ahead and below the ruins of the Palace of Fine Arts foamed up out of the hags'-hair trees, the Yacht Harbor spread out a rich show of boats and over across the blue-iron white-starched water squatted the serene hump of Belvedere like some huge furry animal taking a foot bath. Another eye-jump and there was Alcatraz, a pedantic impregnable reminder, while a further shift brought in the Contra Costa hills beginning to be smogged in, faintly sulphurous, safely far off. Altogether a glorious view, fit to die in sight of.

The man engaged in it — hardly, gamely fighting every inch of the way — courage for the sheer sake of it, a noble thing — laid his egg-size haunted eyes on her and said, "Never got to — know each other right — did we," the words pulled out of him like nails.

"No," she said.

"But no time — go into that." Then it was he said that about her future. "Richard Wrighthill — you know him — "

"I should," she said. "He's been around often enough." And as it didn't sound quite right, "Seems to think a lot of you, Wim."

"Always been — good friend. Wants to — wants you to — come to him."

She thought it over, her dark blue eyes made lighter, more intense by the breezed light so that the effect was of a cool burning, and held in a fixed observance suggesting some jewel-hard inner amusement totally disconnected from the world contemplated. His stare on them was like that of a man walking to the scaffold taking his last fill of the sky.

"Married, isn't he?" she said.

"Not — very. Never — got along. Take good care of you. Told me he's — very much — in love."

"Well, at least sounds as if I wouldn't want for a good home," she said. "And I do appreciate your thinking of me, Wim. Up to now though I've always landed on my feet."

He shook his head, it rolled slowly back and forth on the pillow like a marble in the hand. As if mustering his strength he stared at her with a gaunt longing, a far light deep in his eyes like the twist at the core of a whirlpool — or maybe it was merely his condition accounted for that spectered air. Then he began to talk, weak, halting from the effort of delicacy as well, reminding her of the time she had taken an overdose of sleeping pills, he didn't want to feel she'd ever do anything so terrible and cruel again, and if she had someone like Richard, a steady kind man to take care of her, he felt sure she never would.

He paused, for breath. And said then suddenly, "I'm — dying," without any theatrics, but it cost him a slight gasp. "Elise, you're so — lovely, young — for God's sake live, if you knew — if you knew what it's like — "

As though some merciless outside force were attacking his face it twisted, wrung by a rising agonized ecstasy that dissolving in sudden improbability reshaped with a kind of gradual successive integration and sank like a spear profound, strengthless into the evacuating eyes.

She was on her feet to run for the nurse but weakly, like a tendril his hand caught hers and she saw he wasn't being worked over any more, just infinitely exhausted, and when feebly imperious he shook his head she said at once, "Okay, I won't. Isn't there anything I can — here, let me fix your pillow," and driven to action, with a subtly frowning face smoothed and settled the pillow, fussed around with the covers, all the while trying to keep her face out of his sight because he hated pity. Even her own crude kind, that could extend only a short lawless way.

He lay with his eyes shut and the look of a ghost on him for a considerable time, while sitting on the edge of the bed she held his hand feeling that that at least fit into the picture. And when at length his eyes came open with an ancient, blurred look she said, "All right, Wim, I'll go with this, what's his name, Wrighthill. So don't worry about it. Goodness, I'm not worth it. You lie there and rest, concentrate on that."

A little knife of a smile twisted in on the pale sensitized lips, the smile of a wounded knight. It faded and he said, "You — promise — promise you'll never try — "

"Wim, it was just an accident. Or supposing it wasn't, all I must have been after was some attention. If we have to get Freudish about it. Do you think if I'd really want to — no, it's too silly to waste any more talk on."

A feeble frown drew his brows together Christlike. After a little he said, a whisper, "Whole life — before you." Took a minute for breath, and: "Go to Richard — right away. I'll tell him. No good for you — here. Life — you want life."

So what could she do but agree, especially as the door opened and the nurse glanced in anxious at this long visiting.

A buxom elderly type, she said out in the hall with a brisk matron authority, "You shouldn't, dear. It's hard on people that aren't accustomed to it, and you can't do any good anyway."

Elise shrugged her shoulders. "He asked for me. Still stands, does it? No dice?"

The woman shook her head. "Honestly, dear, you shouldn't go in there any more. You come out looking shaky and after all there's nothing you or anyone can do. It's only a matter of time now."

"Looks like I won't be around much longer, anyhow."

"Good, I'm glad. You're too young — "

"Nuts. At twenty-seven who should be so young."

"You're kidding," the woman said, her face ungainly with amazement. "I would have sworn twenty-one, at the most twenty-two."

"It's true, to look at me you wouldn't take me for a lush, would you? It's my peachy complexion. Holding up real good, nothing seems to touch it. So if I look shaky it's more from hangover than poor Wim. By the way, got anything on you? I'm out of Veronal again."

The nurse starched up at once. "No I haven't," she said with a quick severity. "Excuse me." Brushing past she went in to her patient, and Elise ambled on down to her quarters.

That night the Chinese houseboy came to say there was a gentleman to see her, so she went down and there was Wrighthill in the study, nervous as a tomcat on the scent.

He stammered a greeting, they sat down opposite each other and after a short somewhat soggy silence he pitched in, his gaze filmed-over, heroic, the grim dedication of him conferring the seal of acceptance.

"Miss Lynch — or may I call you Elise, I — I guess I'll come right to the point." He cleared his throat, to eliminate the gravel which whether due to guilt or the nervousness of desire or both choked out the resonance: one got vaguely the impression of a man unjustly suffering an indignity, and in the rear of his mind an eventual revenge forming.

"Wim tells me he's spoken to you about a — a certain, *hrrum,* matter," he said, switching around to something like an intransigent distraction.

"Right. You want to shack up with me, that it?"

His eyelids quivered, rose up to expose his stare — cooling, cooler, stopping just short of cold. But at any rate he was jolted out of most of the jitters. "Isn't that rather an unnecessary way of putting it — "

"I prefer straightforward. Look, we don't have to play footsie, being as we're both with it. Make your pitch, I'll listen and if the terms are right it's a deal."

She slid down a little, relaxed in her chair and lit a cigarette. Silence, a groping. She smoked her cigarette, relaxed, looking as if she didn't have a thing on her mind. Which being exactly the way it was, after a couple more minutes she glanced over at him and grinned. He must have read something of his own into it, because all at once getting up with a sort of twitched nonchalance, and a short rather sad-sounding laugh he came and lowered himself into a chair beside her, taking her hand in his warm pincushion one.

And said richly warm, quite returned to his old harmony, "You're acting this way because you're scared, poor darling. But dearest, you must believe me, there's nothing to be afraid of. I — the fact is I care for you a great deal, a very great deal. I have from the first time I saw you. You were standing at the top of the stairs, and I had never seen a more beautiful girl. Your lovely golden hair, there was a halo — yes, angelic is the word." He paused a moment. "I'm not the kind of man who loses his head easily, but at that instant something happened to me, something I had never expected to feel again. And each time we spoke a few words you — you attracted me more and more. But I don't have to go on, you can see well enough what you've done to me," he said tying it up with a hint of jovial brusqueness — leaving the door open for a dignified exit, just in case.

She was looking at him with an unswerving bright interest not quite amusement but near it, as if for the moment she found him novel in his brash advocate's substance.

Rousing she said, "I suppose Wim's filled you in on the background."

He nodded. "Born in New York City. Married at sixteen, the marriage annulled. College."

"Right, broadly speaking. But you'll want the gaps filled. Where did you leave off — college, yes. Well, it was there I started to go to the bad, really I mean, not just playing around at it like before I got married. And the less said about that the better. Not because there's any pain in it but because it was plain adolescent and birdbrained. But to go on, about the only thing stuck with me from college was a few tricks of copulation. Oh, and I mustn't omit the interval in Switzerland. Shipped me off in a last desperate attempt at regeneration. Came back reeking of the continental polish: rectitude, and when it won't work discretion. So it's good stock you're getting, if the family did kick me out owing to a little scandal involving gin and gigolo. Never touch the stuff now. The gin that is. In any case I don't come at any bargain rates, it's only fair to tell you."

"I'm prepared to go, um, as high as necessary." And he looked, perhaps because the commercialism distressed him, a shade unnerved. Then she thought it might be That Word that had titillated him, warmed his guilt and thus made him doubly determined to get her: since he was suffering already, why not go whole hog. And later simply through the osmosis of association she found out that was about how it shaped up, his puritanism uneasing him despite the out of his wife's spurning though you could say this for him, it never caused him enough discomfort to rumble any foundations.

"Just thought I'd get the lay of the land," she said. "Because it's always best to get clear on the essentials, then everybody knows where he stands. It worked out pretty good with my former comrades."

His eyes that had begun assiduously to stroke her like a collector with a new choice item backed off infiltrated by alarm, suspicion and a gaining uncertainty.

"Sorry," she said. "Forgot that's a verboten word. Now if I had said comrades in arms, but the obviousness of it. Because lovers is pretentious and old-novelish, like soul. That leaves what, intimates, which rings coy, and lays, too defensive. Well, do we come down to the deal or go on with the preambles?"

But he remained mute regarding her with a hung lovesickness, caught with his lust down, and for a moment she had almost a compunction. But what, not such a cinch for her either being at constant beck and call and never calling your body your own except when you sneaked some guy pour le sport, which wasn't cricket. But then who after all was perfect and what was so special about her she should do the noble.

So she allowed him some more time but when he just lumped there with that rather dreamy melancholy as though trying to summon up some approvable manner or expression out of her, and his hand now and again contracting hers in slight nervous spasms she suddenly got bored and vulgarly crossing her arms over her chest said breezy, hoydenish, "Well open the safe door, Richard, and let's see the shine of your gelt."

However, it happened to amuse him, after a hesitant low-keyed manner. "You write your own ticket, little girl," he said, his smile moving by fits. "I guess I could say I'll live to regret those words, but I don't think I will." And with an assurance as smooth, confident and full-bodied as it was peremptory, "I'm a pretty fair judge of character. And I believe in you, in your basic sweetness, the good stuff you're made of."

Watching his principles pop out all over him she grinned. "All I can say to that is we'll hope for the best. As for me, I'm totally inconnu to myself. French. Had to show off some."

"Your accent is perfect," he said. "I never can get that 'u.' "

"Easy. Purse, the lips. U. U. No extra charge for coaching. Little, you said? Five seven and lithe as a panther. And there's two of everything — eyes, arms, breasts, legs. One mouth, one — you'll find everything in satisfactory working order."

He took her hand back in his, which was moist, and twitched it.

"I'm sure it is," he said, his pink richening. Then in a minute with the care of a superficially restored composure, "There's an apartment four blocks from here. Everything's furnished, all you have to bring is your suitcase."

"Plural. There's three. Plus a trunk. Wim's not stingy. I was on my uppers when he took me in and now look at the wardrobe."

"Nothing to what I'll give you, darling," he said, and began stroking her arm.

"Keep talking." Just testing, for the hell of it.

"A car will be waiting for you the day you move in."

"Make it a Cad convertible. No mistress should be without one."

He had the good manners to let it flow on past. "When can you make it, tomorrow?"

"No reason why not. I know Wim wants me out the sooner the better."

He darkened somewhat, right off. "It's such a horrible thing," he said. "At his age, with all he's got to live for."

A pause, his lover's clasp settling with a sort of restraint. "It just came to me," she said. "Some say this here, now is Hell. What if it's Heaven, after all?"

The darkening become a frown, then cleared. "You mustn't trouble your lovely head with such things," he said. His hand put loving pressure on hers. "I'll see you then around five at the Rochester Arms. It's at the corner of — "

"I know where it is."

"The eighth floor. Gorgeous view. I happened to hear of a vacancy, a friend of mine moved out so I went right around and took it, I was sure you'd like it."

"I can see you're a man not given to doubts." Her smile was charming, slanted, with a tangle of lashes and her eyes glinting like water through ferns. A certain perverse quirk at the corners of the lips went ignored — he stared with a sudden jowled barrenness before with a uniform snap-to coming out of it he said, "I had talked to Wim and both of us felt, that is we thought since you'd be at loose ends — "

"Now there, that's what I call an apt turn of phrase. Not everyone could have come out with it so neatly. I must say, I *am* a lucky type. It's not every girl can transfer from bed to bed without having to go out and hustle. I'm *so* grateful, Mr. Wrighthill."

"You called me Richard a while back," he said.

"So I did. I like Richard. I won't call you Dick or Rich."

"Nobody ever has."

"Not even your wife?"

"No." A silence came down, and the fallen-curtain sense didn't lift when he said, "Elise, dear, there's one condition — my wife is never to be mentioned between us."

"Of course. Sorry."

He brought his bulk a little closer and she drew away a fraction before noticing it wasn't a threatening but an amorous move. "You're so lovely," he said in a pressured voice and she could hear his breath coming through the hairs in his nose — a rather large one, the kind described as commanding on the face of a successful man and bazoo on a Skid Row character.

"So lovely," he said, breathing, and his arm going around her he drew her to her feet.

Now this is where I clinch it, she said in herself as with a bull dignity his head loomed. Then the large solid pressure of his body was against hers with the large meaty arms wrapping and the warm-breathed mouth coming down quivering, a rabid diffidence.

When in time their bodies parted it wasn't unlike a stopper leaving a bottle. Dark oxblood suffused his face and his eyes were stunned, dimly questing. They watered as the red sank down leaving a fevered pink and his breath strongly sweeping from his nostrils.

"My darling," he said, "my dearest," with the repressed grunted pain of pleasure, a muted tone of agonized worry. His arms enclosed her with the manipulating lightness of a relentless grasp, and when his eyes lurched over to the couch she said, "Okay, but it'll have to be quick. The houseboy could come in."

He smiled hazed, staggered round in a dream. "That's how it mustn't ever be," he said, mumbled. "There's tomorrow, and all the other tomorrows — oh, I'll wait for my darling." He drew her up close, and into her mind came the time she had wrestled a mattress over. "We're going to be happy, so happy," his breath chuffed in her ear. "Aren't we? My sweetheart, my lovely girl."

"Sure," she said.

"Darling, sweetest," he nuzzled her ear. "I know you're going to make me the happiest man in the world, in all the world." And with a sort of trespassing helplessness his hand began making free of her breast.

"I don't anticipate any complaints," she said. "It's all those amateurs screw it up for us pros."

His hand came regretful away, he gazed at her gently chiding, with the hazed smile. 'You mustn't be hard, dearest," he said. "Love is a beautiful thing; the love of a man and a woman . . . a beautiful thing."

She took his hand and put it back on her breast. "I'm not hard," she said. "Feel." And when his eyes started to glaze she said leaning back on the log of his arm with a roll of warm young passion, audacious and free, "I'm yours. Go ahead. Have some."

So then of course it happened, over on the couch. With him first jamming a chair under the doorknob, from a stealthy presence of mind. Although no one disturbed them he was impelled to hurry and fumble, but she accommodated herself and bringing all her resources into play caused him to cry out once, a sharp hoarse reaching that was the sincerest form of homage.

And afterwards, sitting on the edge of the couch following his set-faced, absorbed zippering and resettling and her casual straightening he gathered her in his arms and told her, in a tone mixing a shining wonder with the dash of gallantry that foresees a dazzling future, how wonderful she was, with a profusion of darlings, belovedests and sweetests which after a while she interrupted by saying she didn't like to bring it up at a time like this, but shouldn't she be going up to take some measures.

He rose immediately, a bulked fluster in the movement. "Yes, I — I wasn't thinking — but how could I have thought of anything but you, my most wonderful dearest — "

"My goodness, that was only a coming attraction," she said. "Save the rave notices for the main feature. Well, I've got to get cracking. Not that it's really too urgent, I've never got pregnant, can't probably, but why take chances?"

He nodded flushing a bit and then quickly said he'd see her the next day. "I'll try to make it before five — Oh wait, wait, you wouldn't go without a kiss, sweetheart — "

She grinned before she could think not to, at his bugeyed entreaty like a schoolboy demanding a promised lollipop, a tuft of hair standing up in front, horn of a dilemma. "Sure," she said. "We'll lip it up a little." But too taken up with the terse acknowledgment of his need to care, or even listen he gathered her up.

Upon her leaving finally she looked back from the door: the manner of his standing there was remindful of a tree just before it starts to fall.

In the morning she said goodbye to Wim, who said it took a big load off his mind and wished her all the best. "I do want you — to be — happy, darling," he said, in his great eyes the involuntary longing and disassociation of the terminally ill. She bent to kiss him quick, with almost an intolerance, and got out of the room. In the hall she was obscurely astonished to find herself undergoing a sinking spell, or something of the kind, but it went away quietly.

Over at the Rochester Arms true to the man's word a Cad awaited, and in the evening there was a sumptuous meal with champagne, which she didn't much go for and afterwards his heavy middle-aged embrace, ditto, but it kept her in scotch and silks and Rob in his two pounds of horsemeat a day, so there was no cause to grumble.

"Be there soon, boy," she said to him, watching the minuscule bayonet tips of the fog fall before the headlights. He pricked up his ears but didn't lift his head, sleepy from his long walk on the beach that afternoon. "I should be too but I never felt more wide awake," she said. Only one o'clock, too. Suddenly all those hours to be lived through before daylight heaved up like the horizon from a pitching ship. Something, a slime like a psychic excretion was released, she sat up, stumbling after memory — hadn't Toni mentioned a party or was it the next night — what difference, always one long party recessed by a day or two. Peculiar how it all balled up so one day ran into the next, and harder and harder to remember things. Right in there, working away drilling all those holes and when the job was finished, that would be the day.

She hummed to "Some Enchanted Evening," coming through the radio. Cheesecloth. Wrap that Dutch one in, with the glowing red skin — Edam. Tiny greasy holes, can't tell one from another. From a hole in the ground. No, the other much more sanitary. How the hair sizzles in the fierce blue flame. Yes, dear, that's Auntie Elise doing a slow burn. Anne, safe and sound with husband and child. Junior League. Suckering the poor. Deeply ashamed of the kid sister and trying not to show it, poor dear. Go in peace, Annie girl. She shall never darken your heart again. Well, one in every barrel.

Motion, a shift, oblique — the woman in the drugstore on Mission, prototype of the embattled respectable poor: virulence like a fling of acid in the look. "Stands to reason," she said. "Us representing the beautiful and damned — nobody ever counts the ugly and damned. And them, the plain and saved, backs to the wall and showing a coyote tooth."

But he just gave a tiny yelp well into his sleep and they rode on carried in the womb of the car past the dark houses and apartments and their own less than two minutes away when in the crashed-monument way of it the entire unit started to give coming deadly alive to the swift scurry of the brittle iced brilliance lashing out the trail of iced fire and then fast, windrush the quaked gathering, stream-up for the giant bursting and up, up — straining to the higher — highest —

No. No. — The shuddered-braking.

Under the dead hand the car swerved to the curb.

The break, as into a death. Long, strong temblor drag. Penultimate: erratic, capersome almost the spasms of decline, down waft by sighed levels. And the arrival, touched bottom: organization of drummed calm, gears meshing in cotton wool.

As in a return to consciousness, new-grotesque the street emerged to perception, the gray gauze-bandage fog over a recognizable front of building.

And now the cold. Oh, the cold. Teeth chattering she shook so it woke up Rob who pulled himself up and in calm wakefulness sat by, a mute staff.

She said rattling, tattered, with a lamenting dribble of laughter, "Not this time, not yet," and shaking with the laughter dribbling grabbed hold putting her face to him and he braced strong, grave, planted firm by her side.

Took a spell but then it was over, the worst of it. From time to time she would be hauled tacking on her side but the worst was done: twister receding to distance. Digging with a hand cold and rigid as a spade for cigarettes, "Boy, that one really whirled me," she said. Voice with a timbre like nickelodeon piano. The match kept hitting up beyond the cigarette tip but eventually she got it going, and smoked it down to the tar.

"All right, boy, end of the line." She got out and held the door for him in a prickled dizzy glitter that passed off in a couple of shakes, waited while he took a leak on a small snobbish maple planted in the concrete, then they went through a tall glass door backed by scrolled iron.

Jay the elevator boy said hello with his usual soft look disordering on a devious concern for her stormed whiteness with the bluish corpse tinge she had glimpsed in the lobby mirror: poor kid, kind of a job never went anywhere and his head turned by all the plush living, a wonder more of them didn't fetch up in Alcatraz. Giving him a dollar bill she said, "Put it to bed for me, will you, Jay?"

"Sure will, Miss Lynch. Thanks."

In the corridor she followed the low sounds of revelry to Toni's door and pushing it open the voices and music blew up warm, broken up. A burn of light, active mouths party-loud and suddenly Toni's elegant parrot screech: "Where *have* you been, baby? We've been brawling here for hours." She laid a predatory hand on her, her sleek mouth writhing with her talk under the harassed eyes, a party was a desperate thing to Toni because if they didn't have a good time they wouldn't come back and she'd drown in the silence. "And I want you to come and meet an Indian, honey — a real one, not one of our scrofulous kind. A superb fawn of a boy, you wouldn't believe the lashes. He's been at the blondes already but wait till he sees *you*."

Elise obligingly said she'd have at him and asked Rob to lie down. His forelegs slid out sticklike, he laid his chin on his paws and narrowly, with a well-mannered skepticism, eyed a woman who leaned over to shriek baby talk at him.

"This way, sweetheart," Toni took her hand. Following the working machinery of the sleek parceled hips she felt her own slapped and said hi to one of the hard core, a specimen who for some time had been trying to get close, whose dank Hitler look and the mouth with the spittled corners made her feel objectively sick so when in a warning voice he called, "Elise, I want you," she kept going, deaf. Then her hand was caught and a face young still but with an old-boy rakishness looked down braced, a tipped desperateness barging in and out of the eyes. "Hello, what's this?"

"Not now, Og," Toni pulled on Elise's other hand. "I'm taking her to meet Sri. Later, baby."

He reared, an ineffectual rage and said withering, "Just because he's dark-skinned. And I'll bet only one diaper to his name."

"*Shhh.* If he should hear think what it'll do to Asian-American relations."

He stared with a pointer desperateness at Elise. "Hell with 'em, I say. I've got my rights, a full-blooded American boy. Honey, I'm telling you, they itch under those diapers and when they die their wives go up in smoke. Gee, baby, you and me could have a ball. Ah, come *on* . . ."

"Later I said," and Toni yanked her off.

To set her before a milk-chocolate young man with large ogling mahogany eyes in a beautiful face alive with a gay and sportive charm, the overall look of him, passionate and dashing, outlandish as an antelope among cattle.

"Sri Rhamapandra, darling — he's here to study our primitive migrant workers aren't you sweetheart," Toni said and in a streak was off in pursuit of a couple at the door, leaving. Her screech cut through: "My God you're not *going*."

Their eyes on a level Elise and the beautiful young man confronted each other. A sparkle and effervescence swiftly came over him, as if he was being shaken up and all his manhood rising to the surface.

"This is a pleasure, well, I must say," he said in a half gabble with a British accent and a joyful shoulder play, his ravished eyes all over her like a frisking. "My word, yes. *Indeed.*"

"How's the name again," Elise said.

"Sri Rhamapandra."

"I had a panda once. Lost it in a blizzard outside a saloon in Nebraska."

"Pandra," he said. "And yours, please? It is all so noisy."

She told him.

"Charming, charming. You are French?"

"My mother was."

"Elise," he said with a small sportive wrench of delight. "I love the sound. It fits you to perfection. My word, you are a beautiful girl."

She glanced casually around. "I'm dry, where's she got the booze this time?"

For a second mystified, then overcome by delight he charmingly laughed, pointing. "There."

"Think she'd keep it in the same place so a person could find it blind," she said. "Well, what're we waiting for?"

He started forward with her. "I shall accompany you with pleasure but I drink only fruit juices and what is that, soft drinks."

"Stomach trouble, religion?"

"Religion." And laughing, with a giddy happiness he suddenly performed a little dancing quickstep, screwing up his face at her with an enticing charm. "Forgive me, but I am quite bowled over."

She briefly regarded him with the absence of a jailer watching the futile escape antics of a prisoner and at the bottles helped herself to scotch with a splash of water while he chose a Seven-Up.

Moving off to a side, away from the worst of it she gulped a large swallow and said past a light belch, "Toni says you're studying our peons."

He gazed at her as if just to look excitedly, supremely enchanted him. "Not quite," he said gabbling on a joyous tilt. "I am studying sociology at Stanford University. My word, what a beautiful girl you are. A real smasher."

"The things one learns in those seats of higher whatchamacallit," she said, closed her eyes and leaned back stiff on the wall. Tacking her to windward somewhat, not too rough. Through her closed eyes she could feel him fizzing in front of her.

"An excellent university, yes," he disposed of it. And with a stab of maddened bliss, "But you are without *question* the most beautiful girl I have seen. Please, please may I see your eyes."

They opened, on a stagger. "Precisely," he said confirming with almost a fanged triumph. "In a novel I read it was stated that the heroine's eyes

were an angel's blue. I scoffed since rationally they could as well have
been brown or green, but now I unreservedly accept the fact of it . . .
Oh, but there is an angel's shining about you."

"Then there's my hair," she said. "Spun gold."

"Yes yes — precisely. And your features, in the classic mold — really I
do not know why in America the truly beautiful women with one or two
exceptions are not to be found in the films. Those are merely pretty.
Shallow tinklers. But you . . . you . . . Oh, I am at a confounded loss of
words." And standing on one foot he lifted the other behind him wob-
bling a little as with a delirious drinking expression his face lowered
towards her, on the point of losing his balance bringing his leg back
down and making her a deep arm-swinging bow in the nature of a
passionate wallow. Yet curiously it wasn't altogether freakish: like a
shaft of sun falling on a jungle an appreciable area of feeling was lit
up.

"Beauty is as beauty does," Elise said and took another large dose of
the scotch. She leaned back on the streaming wall. "So what's your
opinion of our culture, if it's not too strong a word?"

He raised on tiptoe as if to lift himself above the rising swell and
boister, cackle of the party. "Good Lord, it is an intelligent angel in the
bargain," he said loud, accusing with appreciation. And coming down
slowly on his heels marveled, "You are the first person to refer in that
fashion — it is singular, is it not, that they should resent admitting to
flaws when all cultures, being human inventions, are of necessity flawed.
Thus *your* flaw is excessive materialism, ours excessive mysticism." Winding up with a lively shrug of the shoulders, "Well then, in brief I should
say I am appreciative of American culture while not an enthusiast, primarily I think because in this country the word 'intellectual' has acquired
an aura of indecency, do you not find?"

"I find for the accused," she said as it seemed involuntary, with a kind
of numbness, and with a lankiness blinked around. But then delivering
him a remote-control glance, "After all there's something crummy, not
the first-class ones but those others, with their domed earnestness.
Cheeeese."

He made a grab for her hands, laughing with a startled admiration.
"Splendid, I instantly recognize the genus. The attitudinizers, yes. All the
same, my angel, there are those who make forays into the outside to
drink whiskies and pinch the world's bottom — no, I *like* intellectuals,
truly."

"Just thought I'd bring in the niggling human element," she said and leaned back, yanked for the prick of an instant. "Maybe it's different chez vous, but here we're all sick to death of each other, you know? Life and death and all that jazz, like a mental heave." Then with a sluttish, naïve sway, "But who am I. The hell, poor crapped-up bastards, keeping going on nothing."

He laughed on a tortured burst of love, lust, perplexity. "If you knew how inexpressibly lovely you are, angel of blue and gold, you who are laying waste my poor bloody heart. Oh my heavens . . ." He stilled like the victim of a holdup, sluggish, his head quivered. With a sleeper's fumbled motion he raised her hand, kissed it, laid it by the side of his. "So gloriously white," he said, quivering. "How good that you did not spoil it by sunbathing."

She stood remarking with a careless depression their two skins, until laying on her waist his trembling hands he softly turned her around so they were reflected in the mirror above the fireplace. "See," he said. "The twain who have met." Joyous tears came brightening, distorting into his eyes. "Oh, I — oh — "

"Ohio, yes, I should say," she said, a diffident nearing little smile forming.

Then her elbow dug him in the ribs. She was grinning. "Pull yourself together, man," she said. "The cavalry are on the way."

He tried for a smile to disguise the wretchedness of a forsaken dog. "You do not believe me because I am sincere. No one here believes me when I am sincere." His hand dashed the tears away. "Ah, you are too much, too much for me. I adored you from the first moment," he said with a deep stitched sigh, resigned.

She cast a draggled look around. "Getting gamey in here — better beat it before the management comes pounding. By an odd coincidence I live right next door."

A startled, then adoring gratitude overran his face but she had started off and single file they tracked through the rout, the voices got whooping out of hand, the smash of a glass, on a fringe a pair of drunks trading punches, butting solemn as goats. Sprawled in a chair a woman sobbed with drunken persistence while a man stood over her making pacific gestures with a glass in each hand. Luckily Toni wasn't in evidence. Elise dodged the lunge the sodden Og made at her and Rob becoming visible through the shifting latticework of bodies she said, "He's mine. We'll collect him and run for it."

"A fine breed, German shepherd. Gentle, trustworthy," said Sri, like a manual.

They found a man with a precariously tilted glass leaning over Rob saying with a phlegmed roll, "Deutschland über alles." Rob lying at full stretch had his head lazily raised eyeing the man incurious and was about to drop it back when spying Elise he got to his feet and the three of them slipped out.

Closing the door of her apartment Elise turned the key in the lock and led the way into the living room. "Made it. If Toni should bang don't pay any attention. She's people-hungry. Other-directed, in the current coinage. Christ, labels. All of 'em phony, like where it says sugar and it's arsenic inside."

Sri threw himself full length on the sofa, stretching in luxury. "Peculiarly, rather a child-dominated society," he said. "Really most puzzling for so industrious and efficient a people. Or is it unreasonable to expect maturity from the majority of adults. Then also, pragmatism may tend to retard the growth of intellectual maturity . . ."

"Baby, you don't know," said Elise behind the bar fixing herself a screwdriver and a ginger ale for him. "Take the man pays for this layout. Couldn't ask for a more mature specimen. Dotes on responsibility. A rescuer of waifs and strays. Why, I'd be in the gutter. More daddy than sugar, actually."

She carried the glasses to the sofa. Swinging his legs down he took his and set in frankly, avidly to study her. "A girl so beautiful, and clever also," he said wondering, with a sadness but predominantly fascinated.

"Instead she makes do with the other end," she kicked off her pumps and slid down putting her head back. "That's life for you. And death. What's your thought on death, toi?"

"A release, a commencement." His hand clasped hers in a soft desirous grasp. "My dearest Elise, you are terribly lovely," he said, both fantasy and passion muted: around his eyes lurked a faint barbaric rarefaction like an inchoate suffering. "Do you know, my angel, I believe I perceive in you a potential mysticism . . ."

Elise took a long swallow, the shadowy lamplight fuzzing her profile to a lineament of abstraction. "Is there a Suicides Anonymous," she said with a sauntered wag of the head. "I suppose so — not a one of our whims is left unsatisfied. Rushing in to fill one void with another. You need it? We got it."

His head slowly approaching hers hesitated a moment, then continued until the nose of his hazed face came to rest on her cheek. "My eyes are gluttonous of your beauty. Elise, Elise . . . you cannot possibly know your bewitchment." His breath warm and clean was like a child's, but with a man's strained shortness.

"So they could get together and discuss ways and means, easiest roads to the great beyond," she said taking another swallow. "But then of course there's always the chance they'd talk it all out and decide not to. Words are tricky bastards."

"Quite so. Your skin of alabaster, your hands like flowers," and he nibbled on a finger. "What an exquisite ring."

"Sapphire. Compliments of my current owner."

"And does he truly love you, is he kind to you?" he worked his lips across the palm of her hand.

"He's never hit me. Not like one of my types who came in one day and gave me a drubbing, saying it'd teach me but not what."

He held her arm out like opening a folding rule, getting the perspective, and sensuously ran a finger up to the elbow. "Never have I seen a skin to approximate this — it is absolutely an idealization of a skin."

"Evidence of things unseen. That part's even better."

The meaning sifting in immobilized him, then suddenly with the ferocious ardor of a man groveling before a deity: "Do not torment me . . . You could not be cruel, not you. Other girls yes but not you, beloved, never you—"

Raising her head she looked at him down her nose with the fragile scintillance and mystery of a movie queen. "Good gracious, we both knew what was up when we ran out on Toni," she said and kicked him intimately in the ankle. "But I'll just have another drink first. Priming the pump, what it's called."

Feeble he smiled and his eyes hung on her like a train as she went to the bar.

She came back and in a flash he was cozily loving, drawing her close, hugging, patting her all over like a cushion, crooning and gabbling a speech of love as passionate as it was disjointed.

She drank her drink allowing him his play as she would have a puppy, but of a sudden he said in a fainting voice, "Ohh, I love you. Oh my heavens how I love you," and his rounded mouth fell on her neck like a hot petal. But she had lost him somewhere along for some time so she just moved off a little as one does from too importunate a puppy, while like a puppy he clung on.

"Because it's certain to get lousier as it goes along, no getting away from it," she said. "No use fooling around. Either-or, and the devil in between." With a scarcely registering annoyance she found that he had uncovered her shoulder and was working on it pet-tiger fashion. "So in the long run it makes sense. The only sense there is, when you analyze it. It's all very well to say, but what do they know. If ignorance is bliss, knowledge is death. Wonder if this guy. Hey there, you with my gland in your hand."

"Oh heavens," he said, and was all over her.

"All right then," she said. "Your need's greater than mine."

Getting up she walked him off stiff-legged, Rob following. "You don't mind him, do you?" she said. "Because of course they don't know. I suppose. If they do they approve. All for the natural life."

"An utter love," he muttered holding on, sliding his hand up and down her front, not offensive, only to the navel. "Utter precious bewitching love."

In the bedroom she stripped, with a run leaped on the bed and rolled herself up in a ball. "Come along, baby," she said. "Don't be so slow on the drawer." But when he came up a bit diffident in his slender brown nudity his eye met hers peering up at him, a bright blue bloodshot marble, and he paused. "This is how it was in the womb," she said and snuggled her face into her drawn-up knees. "Some ancient races buried like this too. Try it. Feels good."

Crawling in a trifle self-conscious he looked on as if undecided whether or not to smile, becoming then unknowing an observer of a darkened meditating tenderness.

"Feels good, honest," she said muffled, the golden hair shining in the light over the bed with a rioted childish frailness.

"My dearest," he said gently making no move to touch her, and presently she peered up at him with a gleam of cock-eyed insight, unwound and brought her upper body down on his. Staring with a kind of jaded curiosity into his love-warm, lazy eyes as into a mirror she said, "Who knows, it might even be a success. If the cycles are right."

With a soft unsteady passion his hand stroked her back. "My most beloved angel. Words cannot express — "

"They never do. Deeds, baby. Incidentally, would you be ambisextrous?"

"Eh?" His hand stopped.

"Take on male or female. A new fad, starting to catch on."

"Good Lord no. How could one, when it is so good like this. *Oh* so very good." He groaned with ecstasy, squirming.

"Just checking. Okay, ready?"

"Yes, oh *yes* . . ."

Her mouth lowered in a sweet rough grinding. From the outer dark sounded the thump of Rob's scratching leg followed after a space by the low wrung-off yowl of his yawn, his licking settling chops.

And silence, of a sort.

"Oh my darling," said Sri, on his back and his eyes sliding away and closing in ecstasy. "Oh, oh, oh. . . ."

Propped on an elbow with her cheek in her hand she watched him, smoking. "You're a nice kid," she said. "But you sure go all out. Whyn't you save some for the next round?"

His eyes opened and darkly barbaric rolled round to her. "Beloved," he said on a moan, like a sick man. "Beloved beloved beloved," and crawled dragging the weight of his love over to her.

He left towards dawn protesting his love and rapture — he acted like a man hounded by happiness — ("Don't call me," she said. "I'll call you — ") and she slept on and off till nearly nine which was better than average and lay waiting for Nettie to show. Who blew in at a quarter past on a rush of excuses: the bus again, they didn't no way know how to run a transportation route, that was for sure, her brown face wearing its usual hectic anxiousness. She dashed off to put on the coffee water and draw the bath while Elise had a quick one to start off on, which even with the first hot shudder was one of the nicer things of the day. Then breakfast, three cups of coffee, nothing solid with her peckish stomach, at the window with the View to the gaze and after that Toni bursting in indignant because her showpiece had been snatched. "Honey, how lousy — I said *entertain* him not kidnap," and in the next breath said come downtown, want to buy one of those new bucket hats and we'll have lunch and rustle around see who else we can scare up.

Getting back around three she put the leash on Rob and drove out to Sutro Heights. One of those terrific days when the whole city under a free-swinging wind had the translucence of things seen through clear ice, everywhere a flap and toss and glitter, a gloss to the buildings as if they had sprung new-made out of the ground. And currents of energy in the air like a vast electric network — the kind of day that made some people swear because their hats blew off and others want to leap in the streets. A bad day for the incitement of alcoholics and potential suicides, and people in love. Hardly anybody out on the Heights where the wind ripped and screamed, shook and flung the trees like a furious spirit released for one day of magnificent destruction. Barking his elation Rob raced up the path now and then turning to see if she was coming, rushing on with a bound of dizzied joy and freedom.

She let him run himself out before going on out to the point where in one great sweeping disclosure ocean and sky came rising up, the sheet-metal water striking away the eyes. Away off to the left boiled the spray-misted beach on which crept a few solitary figures, with nearer at hand the powered heave, curl-over of green glass and foam-toothed onslaught petering out on the sand in overlapping caracoles that sloped up to a bubbled nibble mild and poignant, the exhausted end. Out on their rocks the seals took the sun, about the Cliff House people congregated, fell away, formed fresh groupings like insects carrying out an intricate project. Up the street the Victorian dome of Sutro Baths stood out quaint and somehow dismal, like a building where a crime has been committed. Farther along on the other side Playland wasn't doing much playing: onion-sizzle, spin and lurch and dazzle, riffle-plink and lopsided revolving blare was for the shoddy glamour of the night, neonstain smudged by the mist, lone seawind tumbling candy wrappers — sailors and teenagers, older folk come to gamble, couples snaking off into a hot-oil metal black and coming out shift-faced, having gone the crooked circle. And over it all light or dark the sword of the wind, and the sense of paucity, the starved grasping for what didn't have a name — full stop, and the beginning of nowhere.

Her gaze went back to the scaled sea, the sky whose clear strong blue deepened in the west to a silken burning. The wind punched at her, blew the hair wanton about her face. Her eyes stung with cold, her ears ached, but she stood on braced before the parapet with Rob leaning his shoulder on her knee.

Unannounced as always it came on, then — the thrown darkening, growing tumor of nightmare. Very gently, almost caressingly the ground swelled and dipped, she lost her footing an instant, clumsily regained it. A knotted interval, and like a blow from behind, the silence. Slicing of the cord. Shut in, closed off. Bone in the earth. Shell at the bottom of the sea.

Bludgeoned Christ-dangle —

Now. Now. Scalpel, prying: collapsed loosening like bowels — a hemorrhage of light poured.

Far down in the core of the earth, thunder.

Slow, mammoth the intermeshed movement. Crust, grind down. Gray slime of brain, meat pulped glistening the warm blood, gut twined loving in the shard of bone. Wormed mass, grave-drip — take, stuff in the sodden flesh bottle-green, gorge on the purple-toed meat of the obscene Christ and jazzed cathedral lights flying in crossed trajectory —

"You all right, miss?"

Raw cut of danger: retreating in confusion, the accelerated beginning descent. "What — "

"You seem faint, may I help you to a bench?"

"No." She made speech from marble lips. "It's all right. Thanks."

The cataract, terraced strip-off. Bearing her derelict self gone over irreversible to the crumbling, a vague driveled solace in the knowledge her eyes bungled at a sweep-back of silver hair under a crush hat, black lair-thick eyes and brows, pink and white skin fed by the cream of self-esteem. Black overcoat with velvet collar, cane. Large gestures around a gleaming dinner table — old-time impresario, and/or molester of shop-girls.

"Are you sure you wouldn't like to sit down?"

"No, I'm all right. Dizzy spell. Nothing to speak of."

He smiled, the carved wrinkles jumping to attention. "Surely. We all have, at some time or other — that's a nice dog you've got there. Here sir, here. I'm very much of a dog fancier myself."

"I'm afraid he doesn't take to strangers," she said, and began to saunter off. "Well. Time to go." She put a bit of an effort into making a pleasant face.

He tipped his hat. "Good afternoon," turning of course to watch the careful stagger. Drunk. Such a lovely girl. Great pity.

In a small sunny hollow she dropped down on the sand with her back against a bank and gradually the feeling of walking on balloons passed away. Her eyes closed, taking the good warm sun, ignoring the rear-guard skirmish. A moisture seeped out rolling cool and erratic down her cheeks. The wind. Stimulus on the duct — ductless — anyway it was good, the impersonal undertaker handling of it. "You like it too boy don't you," she said not bothering to wipe off the moisture, sun take care of it. Panting already a little from the sun and then he yawned, ran his tongue around his mouth and looked at her: what next?

She laughed and pulled him to her. "Rob," she said, "Rob," and found that she was shaking, shaking him too along with her. His tongue flipped out to her cheek. She hugged him hard. "We'll go in a little while," she said and suddenly there was a stony swell of excitement like heartburn — she grew still, her arm around him jogging to his panting. Then abruptly she rose and they walked off, but glancing at her watch she broke into a run and Rob into a lope alongside.

At a bend under the trees she ran square into a young man, rocking him, almost knocking him down. Steadying his hands grasped her shoulders, and swiftly his stare of annoyance gave way to a softening, a mellowing, and then the mold to a deep-lighted smile. In a moment with a twist she was free and running on up the path.

Panting, a pain in her side, she rested a minute in the car before turning the key, dizzy, but it soon quit and they were off on a jackrabbit start.

At three minutes to five she opened the door, listened — beat him to it, and sprinted in to the bar. Putting the empty shot glass down she heard him at the door. She just had time to fling off her jacket, light a cigarette and sit down with a magazine.

"Hi there," she said and rose to get him the sherry he had lately taken to having on arrival. And that he made last a long while, taking small sips and toying with the stem. You could see he really didn't go for the stuff but it went with the stance and served to loosen him up some besides — he hadn't got over a certain stiffness at first and usually it wasn't till after dinner that he unlimbered. And naturally nothing so obvious as a kiss on entering, after all he was no Frenchman or even anything like the man to flaunt an emotion. For it looked as if that night in Wim's study had proved to be the impetus from which he was still revolving but on a narrower orbit, adjusted to the proper discretion and reserve. Which moreover if you cared to look at it that way tended to put *her* in the proper perspective of things. And why not, part of the job.

"Well, dear," he said as she came up bearing the sherry. "Have a nice day?"

With her bending to set down the glass a frown, a very small one, made its appearance. There, see. Should have stuck to the vodka. However it smoothed off and he regarded her calmly, a wide calm solid man — the benignity still there but not nearly so detectable any more — attendant upon a problem he had lived with for some time and had no doubt he could solve. When he judged the time to be ripe. Which from the look of it could be any time now, and she couldn't say it was unexpected.

"Pretty good," she said. "I had lunch with Toni and furnished moral support while she bought a hat. Then I took Rob over to Sutro. You should have seen the wind. Like to tear you apart."

"We usually get it around this time," he said, and dipped into the sherry.

"Run out of cigars? I can send for some." By this time he'd usually lighted one.

"I've decided to give up smoking. All this lung cancer, and other diseases. It's foolish to take chances."

"Thought cigarettes were supposed to be the culprit," she said, conversational.

His glance lowered to hers. "The evidence certainly seems conclusive that they're very dangerous. It would be wise to cut down, if you can't or won't quit. Two packs a day is suici — is entirely too much."

"You can say it, Richard. I don't mind a bit. My one silly little gesture, goodness. I thought it was long buried and forgotten."

A complimentary urbanity spread over his face. "I like to see you taking that sensible attitude, dear. I will say this way you have of not brooding is just about your most attractive trait," he said with the fine gloss of a man who perfectly trusts his intuitions.

"Well thank you, Richard. But you're an optimist yourself. It's our great American heritage, think where our pioneers would have been without it. Pessimism simply isn't in us."

"For which we should be everlastingly grateful," he said going rather into the mature overseer, or flock-addressing bit. "Defeatism will always be alien to us. This existentialist rottenness, for instance." Of all things to get around to, gee. "I feel kind of sorry for a man like that French fellow, Sartre — I started to read one of his things and had to quit — who's degenerated that far. It takes a warped brain to go against the grain of its own great tradition and culture."

"Doesn't it. Not so long ago though they were shooting down Arab women and children, which does seem kind of a funny end result of a culture. But now if you don't mind, Richard, I think I'll have a drink to celebrate our being so well in accord," she said rising and going to the bar. "Which we are practically all the time, when you think. What I mean, pretty unheard of in this quarreling world, wouldn't you say?"

Abruptly, in almost a harsh tone he said, "That's the Communist line," but in a moment moderating his expression to a kind of upper-class reticence.

Going back to her chair she swallowed a good third of her highball and smacked her lips. "Mm, good. What kind things it does." And looked over at him sociably, disposed to pass the time in a civilized manner. "Is it? No, actually any resemblance is purely coincidental. Just that it does look like a whimsical way to bring civilization to the untutored masses."

He gazed back congealing in composure, every inch the informed man of affairs dealing with a fowl-brained female. Of distinction you couldn't quite say, first because of the too too solid flesh. If he shed about forty pounds. But no, since thick or thin the parvenu quality would remain, legacy no doubt of the grubbing ancestor on whom nonetheless his own brand of plucky vulgarity must have looked rather good, aside from being an indispensable in that bearded milieu: a bona fide rawness packed its own picturesque punch. While Richard here, with his sad little crust of nice-nellyism. But hold on there, gal. Come now, be nice to the man, the stranger in our midst.

She said, "So here we are, the two of us with our drinks and the sun setting beyond the Golden Gate just like in the ads," and looked out the window. "Sure is a hell of a view. Whenever I look at this time of day I get that wanton Frisco feeling — worldly, but with verve. Sort of rich-meaty. As if something in the air said get going and do all the good things fast — *live*," she made a devil-may-care squandering gesture, "in a word."

Didn't fetch a thing. Maybe he didn't fancy the Frisco, they were so touchy about it. Or more likely the honeymoon was over. Time was when he'd at least have sent out a mild beam, if only from good manners, but now nothing, except his sausage finger kept sliding sedate up and down the stem of his glass. Then in the dusking light she took note of the subtle frown, of a sort of sublime concentration, way off somewhere: wrong, in effect quite close to home, for just then with a level air he said, "Elise — I feel there's something I should talk to you about."

"Really," she said, interested. "I'm listening."

For a second his level gaze dug in on her like a brand, then it paled back to normal. "It concerns this woman, this — Toni. I have no inten-tion of regulating your choice of friends. But this woman and her crowd aren't the kind of people I'd care to have you associate with. A divor-cee — "

"Three times, and a fabulous settlement from each."

"A divorcee," he said plowing on past the irrelevance, "can of course also be a decent person, but from my impression of this woman I don't think she can do you any good. Frankly I consider her a bad moral influence. The manager's received complaints about those parties of hers, and he told me not long ago he'd be glad to get her out of the building. As a matter of fact and strictly between us he's going to try to break her lease. In view of all this don't you think it would be wise to taper off, when she asks you to go out with her you could say you have other plans. And I must ask you not to go to any more of her parties. I understand there was one last night."

"Oh, I didn't stay long. An hour, maybe less."

"I'm sorry you went at all. A bad crowd, very bad. Ever since that woman moved in the place hasn't been the same. I'm surprised they allowed her in in the first place, and if they don't get her out soon I guess I'll have to move my girl to better quarters," he said giving a hitch to his trouser leg, and on his face a look close to a kind of arid archness.

"Well, I'm only a woman," she said. "Do with me what you will."

But he wasn't amused, where back in the beginning her every quip had brought his smile. Definitely a case of the honeymoon being over. "I hardly think that was called for," he said.

She traced the hair-fine sneer of sensitivity, lost almost among the solidity. Funny too how he rarely came out with his sweetests and belovedests anymore. Always dear nowadays. Well, maybe she did cost him more than he'd expected. "By way of a gag, all it was," she said. "To jazz it up some. Been turning all-fired serious lately, hasn't it?"

A stolidly enduring look moved in on him: most of his expressions took time rising, like yeast. "I've always been a serious person," he said. "It should have been obvious from the start."

"Can't say it wasn't. But a mistress' touch, you know. Supposed to bring out the frolic in a man. Or so goes the tradition."

She stood up well, never batting an eye under the long unmoving stare that ten to one caused junior executives to freeze in their flannel suits and women secretaries to run for a bit of quiet hysteria in the washroom. Blowing their nose on the toilet paper and flushing it down the bowl, wishing peevishly murderous *he* were along —

Then she noticed another thing: underlying the stare she caught like a furtive movement in the dark, an attenuated equivalent of what had blazed out of the face of the woman in the drugstore. Universality of hate and contempt. Rich, poor, everybody knew how to hate. While it was the rare ones who knew how to love. So much easier, more instinctive to hate. *Wanting* to love didn't do it, on that you could rely. Had to be learned, step by painful twisted step. Herself, high on the roster of accomplished, or intuitive haters. Or as the poet had it, *trau, schau, wem?* Eh? *Ach, du lieber.*

"Elise." Could as well have said Miss Lynch.

"Yessir."

And as he said no more but continued to look, with a hardening of the eyes: "Sorry, no flippancy intended. I seem to be in an unhandleable mood today, like my psyche took the bit in its teeth — ever feel anything of the sort?"

Silence, the lump of it. No steering around this Scylla. And as for Charybdis, yonder — get to you in due course.

"Well, you're lucky," she said. "Possibly due to my bad genes. Put the blame on heredity, so much easier. But enough of these puerile interruptions. You were saying."

The square bulk of his shoulders rose a fraction, moved back in place like a bull quietly rebelling against a weight. "Elise," he said, in tone and manner on the grim side but restrained of course, gentleman's disagreement, "Elise, you force me to have a serious talk with you. I had hoped it wouldn't be necessary, thinking that if you were given enough rope you'd straighten yourself out. But I'm sorry to say it's been just the opposite."

"Richard, you're quite right. People like me should never be given any rope, they think it's to hang themselves with."

With no change in his voice and looking the same, only more so he said, "I'd appreciate it one hell of a lot if you'd consent to be serious for ten minutes. What I've got to say is for your own good, and if you'll use the sense you've got you'll listen to me. Your refusal to face facts stopped being amusing some time ago, and I think I'm justified in saying that any other man would have lost patience long before this. I've had a lot more experience of life than you have — "

"Of a somewhat dissimilar kind, Richard. But do go on. Merely wanted to keep things straight."

"Which is exactly what you should concentrate on doing from now on. You're — it's not pleasant to say it, but it's got to be said — you're not the same girl you were, the girl I saw standing on those stairs. In a relatively short time there's been a change in you, a very great change. You're young, basically healthy I'm certain, it shouldn't be hard to put yourself back on the right track."

"I know," she said in a tone of polite discovery. "What you're trying to say is I'm rather too fond of the drink."

"You understate it. What I'm trying to say is that you're well on the road to alcoholism."

"Richard, it's nice of you to try and spare my feelings. Truth is I'm there. Why, if you knew," she said. "I can't face the day without a stiff shot, half a glass full. Water glass. When you've come to that, well."

"I thought you had agreed to be serious."

"I am. Dead serious. You don't see any smile, do you? Course it's getting dark, but — "

"And I can assure you I'm not smiling either. In plain talk, and I don't know how I can say it any more clearly, you haven't got much more time to pull yourself together. It's — getting more than objectionable, I'll go so far as to say I'm seriously disappointed in you. Yet if you'll show me you're really in earnest about pulling out I'll do what I can to help. There are treatments, all kinds of aids. Others have been helped, have gone on to become better men and women. If they did it so can you. Now listen, Elise. You can't doubt that I'm — that I think a great deal of you. You've given me quite a lot of pleasu — happiness. I'll go further and say that I've come in a way to depend on you. But this degrading drinking business has simply got to stop. Now. Before you completely wreck your beauty and health." He paused, and when he spoke again a note of quiet anger nullified the intent of persuasiveness. "I just can't understand why you insist on throwing everything away when with some plain ordinary will power you could overcome this weakness. Once you've taken the first step the rest will be easy. If you really want to, I know you can do it."

Here the tone became more stabilized as he went along on his faith kick for a spell, but it all flowed on by pretty well after the pleasu-happiness bit. Because translated it meant she was a damn good lay, best one he'd had in all probability, otherwise he'd have shown her the exit long ago. Stinking of drink the way she did when he went to fold her in those mattress arms even though she rinsed her mouth out beforehand. And showered in perfume. My Sin. *And* his, for the record. But he could close his eyes in that sublime-torture look while she had to peg away at the job, keep the rear end mobile and play it from all angles so as to keep him happy and well evacuated — damn near died from the ecstasy of it and then lay gasping and heaving like a beached whale. Christ she *deserved* a drink. All right, so he didn't care for her boozy breath. Well neither did she, particularly. But as long as she was able to deliver that was all that really counted. Stink or no, once it got to working and the delicious agony shivers flashing around his belly who gave a crumpet. Assuredly not lover-boy. "So how if we can the sentiment, Richard," she said. "And keep our eye on the balls and the hind end in proper oiled operating condition. Which is my fuckuppation, to get coarse for a moment, and yours is to keep me in Black Label. And one or two other necessaries. Thing is, you're worried if I go on belting the mash I'll lay down on the job. But trust me, man. I been trained by experts. You never heard of a firehorse not rearing at the bell."

She noticed his voice had stopped. "Well, Richard, thanks for the pep talk," she said. "And if you're as fond of me as you say you won't object to my having another before we feed, I'm sure. Small short one, or rather medium would be better. You wouldn't want to stop cold this minute, too drastic. D.t.'s likely to result."

In the gloom he could be felt more or less grimly coping, so to take it out of his hands she went to the bar. Silence, of the more bitter kind. Then he said, "I can't very well stop you, can I. But you've got to promise you'll put yourself under treatment."

She grinned, slopping some token water into the glass. "Well now, you know, I'm pretty strong. Good for some time yet. Really you shouldn't let it fidget you. Man like you, all those investments to worry about, fussing about little old me, goodness." Glass in hand she went and sat on the arm of his chair. "The thing with you is you're getting kind of restless," she said. "In the midst of trust funds we are in death. You ought to get yourself a hobby. Like another girl. Then you'd have two of us to fuss with. Take up the slack, like."

A pause. Could be he'd revolved it and decided against. Question of expense, not improbably. Reason the rich were. Moreover, required a certain amount of daring.

Then he was shaking his head, his arm going loglike about her waist. "You don't know me very well, if you can talk like that. My happiness is with you, dear . . . So you won't promise."

"Oh, catch 'em young and they'll train your way. Can I get you another sherry?"

But of course he said one was enough. She tossed off her scotch. "Say, I know what. We'll eat out. Here we are in this city of gourmandism and how often have we joined the public trough — twice is it. New place opened on Hyde very Frenchy is the word where it's doubtful anyone'd catch us. Anyway you can always say I'm your niece. Crude I know, but one's got to think of these things."

His silence while consenting also had a constraint, main reason being a worry that if he flaunted her about the missus might take it into her head to raise a stink: scandal, divorce, depleted coffers. Gloomy inbitten sort of woman, from picture in the society section. Type could take a notion to do anything. Wrote verses, only thing he'd ever said about her. With a touch of complaisance grafted on to the armistice kind of enmity. An artistic wife what with temperament and all excusing many a man's pecadilloes.

"I'll go gussy up, won't take but ten minutes," she said.

"But first," and his finger put nervous-roguish pressure on her waist. She swung her legs over and slid down on his lap: not the kind of gambit meant business, he didn't care to exert himself this early. Sort of an imprimatur rather, mouth warm and rubbery-moist as a hot dog. When with a certain complacence he released her she said, "Ask the man who owns one," and went off whistling Shake That Thing.

On her return exquisite in the mink he rose and gazed with the blur of infatuation at the core of which was something of a checked resistance: moments lately when he positively set himself against her for her beauty and above all, her youth. Christ, she said. This beatup bag a million years old. And to him: "Will I do? Nobody'd take me for a strumpet, would they?"

"You look very nice," he said, and went with dignity to get his hat. They went down and got in the Continental.

At the restaurant she let it be known she wouldn't refuse a cocktail, however it came as no surprise when he said it would spoil her appetite. "I want you to eat a good hearty dinner, dear," he said. "You're getting so thin and pale. With some flesh on you you'll look and feel so much better."

And that much more energy for the bedwork. However, one didn't argue — his privilege.

"I'll order for us both," he said. "You sit there looking pretty," a kind of affability went with it, "and sharpen that appetite."

So she sat watching the trays loaded with cocktails go by. And when the food came tried to wade into the opulent sauced stuff for which she had no stomach, while at a regular untiring pace he fell to working his way through.

There was no talk, this eating rite commanding all his attention. All about the elegant room others were likewise engaged, bent obeisant to the plate or chewing with a misted gaze as though the food's inner steaming clouded their vision. And soon the air rich with food-incense in the templed light, the waiters gliding with their offertory trays, the headwaiter presiding with a sharp sacerdotal eye began to have a somnolent, shrinking effect — suddenly she could hardly push the fork up to her mouth.

She started to feel dizzy, queasy, and then a sudden plunged drop into a fatigue pocket caused the food on the plate to loom like a mountain on which the fork couldn't get so much as a toehold. She raised her eyes and the sickeningly ornate room was set in motion as though it had been placed on a merry-go-round, the diners rising and falling in stately distortion. Closer, across the shining white cloth upon which the lamp pooled a rosy light like diluted blood, the silver gleaming like expectant weapons, the faintly levitating man continued to eat ponderous, systematic as a boa gorging its prey.

"Eat," he said, "eat," he murmured flushed, copious, a seedpearl sweat standing out on his forehead and even around his eyes. Tranced, congested they went to her plate. "Good for you. Eat."

In her hand the fork lay inert at the base of the mountain. Segment by segment the mass of food disappeared into the erratically floating rapacious mouth, with a neat tail-flip at the end and the lips closing down smooth grease-glistening over the crushing jaws.

Nausea rushed together, fumed up. Stumbling to her feet she mumbled an excuse and was off, reaching the bowl without a second to spare.

Drained, shaky she found her way back. "Anything wrong?" he said. He had finished his dessert and lighted a cigar. "To go with the coffee," he said a shade curt. "After such a wonderful meal." His eyes sharpened. "There is something wrong."

"I heaved," she said. "If you'll pardon the expression. Guess I'll have to stay away from this rich stuff."

He sized her up through a snarl of smoke, the cigar sticking out of his mouth like a small club: his hand stroked up and removed it.

"I've been expecting it to happen any time. You're going to get sick, seriously sick, if you go on. I wish you could see yourself. You look half dead." Master's voice dry, dry and hardened, baked on slow anger. Dragged contempt in the eyes, in the slant of the cigar in the power-fleshed hand.

Considerable outlay. Done everything for her. And all because of stubbornness, stupidity — bad blood after all. Maverick, never take a brand.

"All that and more," she said. "No, really, Richard, I see your point. The right is on your side, no question."

"You won't make the slightest effort to stop. You never will."

Bulked, strapped taut and firm in his integrity he expanded, grown larger with the authority of rank. A big man. Leader in the community. Good works. At death, obituaries this long. Of such is the kingdom.

"Poor Wim," she said. "He may not have made it. Too much the shepherd at heart, when organizers is what's wanted."

"You're still drunk. You went to have a drink, didn't you . . . *Didn't* you?"

At any rate he still had his good cigar to enjoy. There was a large crap-colored gravy spot by the side of his coffee cup. "Well," she said. "It's like this."

"Answer me straight for once. *Didn't* you?"

"I went straight and had a big slug in the bar. It's around the turn there, convenient to the can. Then I went and heaved it up and went back for a refill."

His eyelids came down, blanking his face in a sort of vicious pondering. Then he turned and signaled the waiter, a motion peremptory and harsh as an obscene gesture.

All the way in the car, not a word. Upstairs along the hall like warden and condemned prisoner. Rob came forward wagging and, it could have been accident, the man's knee bumped him hard in the side. She dropped back as he went on into the living room and squatting took the rough-smooth dogface in her hands. "Don't mind it, boy," she said. "Happened to me too lots of times. Sit tight. We'll go out later."

He gave heed with his customary solid rapport. Dropping a kiss on his ear she proceeded to the living room, where slipping out of the mink she said to the held-up newspaper, "What'll it be, scrabble, gin?"

"I thought your taste ran to scotch," the voice issued dry from behind the print.

"Well, vodka's nice too," she said, and went to the bar.

"By all means, help yourself. Take all you want. When it's gone call up for more. They deliver day and night."

"Like me," she said. And laughed, sound of gay abandon. "Gay abandon," she said pouring the vodka. "Name for a bra. More fun at night though isn't it. In the morning too much like champagne for breakfast."

He was looking at her where she stood drinking, over his paper, and she said, "Richard, it'll all come out in the leak. Believe me." It got through. Throwing off a laugh vulgar with revulsion he said, in a new voice, a level run with no inflection, "Come here. Come on here to daddy."

She went, remembering first to down the vodka. He took hold and pulled her down. "Sweetheart," he said, in the voice. "Baby girl."

There was only one light on, from the side. It fell on her breast and left both their faces in a pink overcast in which his with a commencing faint pullback, as though exposed to a savage wind, a dim peaked frown stared at the pale-gold flesh offering twin hummocks perversely virgin, shatterable. Then the hair-knuckled hand entered the light and lay weighted, twitching, blotting — pressed down, lifted, pressed down.

A quiver, as through a great steamer. "Baby girl. Sweetheart. Come to daddy. Come — Give. Come. Come."

Cigar-rancid, widening cave of vellicating snake tongue. The forcep hand dug, ripped the fabric, shook, spilled. "Baby girl. Baby."

She held fast, rigid against the rising constriction of pain.

"Hurry. *Hurry.*"

The laying on of massive flamed hands.

She screamed.

"Baby. Baby girl." Mutter grinding, grunted. "Baby — Baby — Mine — "

She screamed.

In a white silk dressing gown she sat on the bed with a glass and a cigarette facing the other way from the circumspect large-animal movement going on methodical — comb drop, clink of silver, thud-pattern of the controlled sedate feet.

Coming around, halting. Her eyes hitched up the length of the mannerly bulk, from the polished black shoes orderly on the carpet to the perfect exactitude of the tie.

"Sweet. You look about ten in that thing."

The white face stared up, directed, the blue eyes full of light.

A laugh. "Come, I'll tuck you in before I go."

The golden head moved, negative. "Not yet. I'll go soon."

"You won't stay up late, will you. Got to get that beauty sleep."

They kept on looking at each other.

"Sweet. My sweet. Mine."

Deep sag of the bed alongside, and inside the silk the warm bloated hand stroked. "Say it. Say you belong to me."

"I belong to you."

In spasms, brutal-soft the hand pressed and molded the flesh. "You're mine. Say it."

She said it.

The hand slowly came away, was joined by the other to draw and belt the silk over the inflamed and bleeding flesh. Pause, a concentrate of powerful tranquil repletion.

"I want you to go to bed now. Sleep. Sleep deep and good."

"Yes," she said.

The bed slowly rose, snapped in place frivolous.

"Go to sleep now."

The feet in black distinguished shoes, kindly august side by side. And then empty space, and the crushed twin imprint.

She stood in the shadowed hallway. Blood trickled down her somewhere and the darkness billowed. Then Rob was there. She fell down on her knees and said something, the rough coat under her hand. His tongue flicked out and a wet coolness touched her cheek.

Then she was in the bedroom throwing on some clothes and she said, "Be right there," but shaking so much it was hard to go fast, then she remembered and ran to get it out of the closet, holding the heavy coil of it in her hand. Cigarettes — yes there and the lighter for Christ's sake get going get —

"Come on boy run —"

"Sailing along, on moonlight bay," sang the radio. And it was, smooth and easy on the maternal purr in the crouch of the late late night. In time for the late late show.

"What's the thing happens at the same time to many people at different times?"

No answer.

"TV show, darling. Live. You live but a show's live. English is a ridiculous language."

The radio sang low in the glow of the dashboard. "I love you," she said. "For being so strong and silent. Keeps right on, drop by drop. Drip, warm, drip. Trickle, tickle. So I *do* know how to love. Where love is due. In lieu of. Mauve. Lovely color. Muller. Boy wrote me mash notes. Engemmed with acne. Took off the umlaut and there he was, virtually British."

The car just drove itself, rolling up the carpet miles. Oil and rubber.

Rubbers. Evil flowers of the night growing by the wayside. Among the empty beer cans and whiskey fifths. J'accuse Mother Nature.

Nobody, nobody in all the. "Save the two of us. Sunken bloody world drowning in its own semen. Poetry. A word for everything. Where science, cosmic — the cosmic, the comic probe. Proboscis. Ora pro nobis. Novice. No, not that one. Expert, and that large Italian knows-what's-what nose to prove it. Maria, Mariucia. Eh, Mariucia. Putta somewhere else da stiletto, it makea da hole in you stocking. Sorry, lady. I am an admirer of the Gracchi. Sure you do. Gracchi Bros., the pasta makers. *Ecco.*"

A truck roared down the stretch, crashed past.

A yell: "Go." He gave a short joyful bark, the speedometer jumped and climbed seventy, eighty, ninety. Ripping the night in two and the tatters streaming haggard, smashing forward and the world left mangled and bloody behind.

Yelling, so damn much alive it kicked around inside like a thousand devils. He barked, pitchforked by excitement — screaming in the curves, swaying and lurching into the straight and the wheel sliding from side to side and the rock and roll, buck and reel, righting the forward plunge once more and suddenly the screeching skid: recollected swerve onto humped dirt.

"Now's the time," she said, "and this is the place."

Bump and sway, towards a gather of tall grave trees.

Here. Good. The motor sighed off. Instantly crickets, frogs took over. Smelled good, of eucalyptus and night earth.

Out, and he bounded off for a run. Overhead the light clack of leaves turning silver bellies to the moon. A spray of stars in their tiny immensity, and the sweet play of the breeze. Except for the fiddling crickets it was still, good: the night breathed deep and easy like God.

He trotted back and she opened the door for him, shut it and went back to the trunk, dragged out the coil and dumped it on the earth, where it lay like a great snake. Squatting she took hold of one end and went to work but it was a job getting it on, her hand was too impatient: "Goddam," she said through a grunt, "toujours le — " But then it held good and tight, she dragged the length of it around to the front and feeding it in through the window said, "See, you *can* pull the hole in after you."

She turned the key and the engine sprang on with a hitch, settled and murmured even.

Supposed to be a fifth in the glove compartment. After the good long lasting pull she dropped it in her lap and took him up close to her.

"Because I love you it's all right," she said. "Thank God you trust me."

He whimpered a little but she held him and he quieted, leaning on her. Long and gentle she kissed him and faced forward past the tree clot to where the moon lapped light. Holes in the ground here and there, black as eye sockets.

She scrounged down resting her head on the back of the seat, and took a deep relaxed breath. "Okay, lady," she said in a grinned rounded-off voice. "But it's me that wins."

JOHN STEWART CARTER

*Reading "The Keyhole Eye," one remembers the comment that read-
ing Henry James is like watching someone watching someone else
through a keyhole. Sartre, as cited in this story, wrote of a man looking
through a keyhole into an empty room to see the eye of a stranger
looking back. This moving story of an uncle and his adoring nephew,
with its wealth of characters and situations, has Jamesian and Proustian
overtones, but John Stewart Carter is his own man and a good author in
his own right.*

*John Stewart Carter was born in Chicago and still lives next door to
the house in which he was reared. He attended Northwestern and
Harvard Universities and received a Ph.D. from the University of Chicago. Except for a four-year stint in the Navy, he has spent most of his
professional life as a professor of English at Chicago Teachers College.
He is married and has two daughters. His poetry has appeared frequently in literary magazines, and his first book,* Full Fathom Five, *was
awarded the Houghton Mifflin Literary Fellowship and published early
in 1965.*

The Keyhole Eye

MY UNCLE TOM was the last of my grandfather's ten sons and was fourteen years old the year I was born. He left Princeton halfway through his
freshman year to join the A.E.F. and was briefly a flier in France. I
remember, or begin remembering, him best around 1920 when I would
see him at my grandmother's. He looked like Wallace Reid—if you
recall. I don't, but I know I thought so at the time. Later I equated him
with one of Scott Fitzgerald's rich boys, and for years I scarcely thought
of him at all. What has just happened is why I am writing this.

He was always nice to me in an offhand way and called me "kid,"
which was racy of him because we were not supposed to use the word
and were always being told that a kid was a goat, which of course it was
not. I suppose I was a nuisance, but he never acted as if I were, and I

used to hang around his bedroom at my grandmother's, much preferring it to my own. I know he was the first adult male I ever saw walking around naked, and the sight fascinated me mightily — whatever the amateur psychiatrists will make of it. Also he muttered to himself and used very bad words like "bastard" and "bitch," and even worse. He never said these things outside of his own room, and it was wonderful for me at six to hear them. He would let me get into his bed and watch him dress to go out, and I would keep very quiet — all eyes, all ears — until finally he'd snap up his silk hat, fit his silver flask into his pocket, and lean over the bed to punch me in the belly.

"You think I'll get it tonight, kid?" I had no idea what "it" was; I don't think I was even curious; the whole thing was a ritual as set as that in Proust.

My answer was, "Sure thing, Tom," and his, as he closed the door, "Keep your pecker up, kid." This left me limp with delicious, giggly laughter. I knew what a pecker was, but that a grownup should use any other than our nursery word to *me* was almost beyond hope. I never had to ask him or beg or anything; he just always left the light on in his bathroom and the door enough ajar so that I saw it but not so far as to be too light or to catch the bulb in his dresser mirror. I didn't have to ask to stay in his bed either. He just left me there, and, when he got home, he'd carry me in his wonderful dance-stinky shirtsleeve arms across the lounge, down the three steps into the east wing to my own room and my own bed, all shivery cool after so much warmth. Most of the time I wouldn't wake up at all, although I always tried to so I would know about being carried, feeling so bundled and sweaty in his arms and all the whiskey and cigarette smoke deliciously sour on his breathing breath, the enormous dark house around us.

Eleven bedrooms gave off the central upstairs hall at my grandmother's. The hall itself — it was called "Palm Court" on the blueprints — was nearly square and was lighted by a series of skylights. We called it the lounge, and it was furnished as a living room; in fact it was the main living room of the house for the children who were visiting. My grandfather's idea was that each of his ten children should be able to come and stay, and each of the rooms had a name: Tom's room, Fred's room, and so on. All but Tom were married and had families of their own at the time I am writing of, and each of them had a house in town. But in the summer and at Christmas they would come to the big house on the lake where each set of parents occupied the father's old room, and the children, along with nursemaids, the east wing. I don't think all ten were ever there at once, but five or six with their families at a time were not unusual; so the house was run really like a very luxurious men's club. My brother has the household books, and in 1932, when my grandmother died, there were twelve indoor servants. The west wing was more elegant than the east, and that's where houseguests other than the family were put. It had an indoor swimming pool — very Pompeian — in the basement, and there is an entry in the books of $1800.00 for "swimming pool towels," in case any social historian is looking; and, in case anyone wants a *sic transit gloria mundi* note, the last time I saw one of them, a sort of Pompeian brown with black pillars across the border (they must have been specially woven), it was being used by a great-great-grandson to polish his car.

On each side of the doorway, where three steps led down from the lounge to the east wing, was a large console with a big pagoda-shaped mirror over it. If I were just pretending to be asleep when Tom carried me back, I would try to see us in the mirror. The lounge itself was light enough because of the skylights, which in summer were open to the moon and stars. I don't know whether Tom knew about my habit of peeking or whether he always looked himself, but one night he stopped before the mirror, and his eyes came together with mine and we looked full upon ourselves — upon ourselves, wide-eyed, and each other.

After a minute he said, "You're a faker, kid. Why the hell can't you walk to your own goddamned room?" I just kept looking at him and us and he at me. His arms tightened around me and pushed me to his chest where I could no longer see. He put his lips into my hair. I could feel its fineness catch on the scratchiness of his whiskering face.

He put me down then, and we walked, our hands fingered together, down the three steps to my room. We looked at each other once more, no mirror between, after I had climbed into bed. He gave my belly its punch and said, "We're the two loneliest goddamned bastards in the whole beautiful world." Even today, when I see moonlight through an open window in a darkened room, it is partly the moonlight of that night when weak with love and happiness I went to sleep.

I don't think he carried me much after that. I was getting bigger. But he didn't stop right away, and, if I were really asleep, he still carried me for a long time, because in the morning I'd wake up in my own bed. When I wasn't really asleep, he'd know, but he'd walk me by hand, and as we'd pass the mirror he'd say "Hi there, kids" in a conspiratorial whisper and wave, but that's the only reference either of us ever made to the night. When I was twelve, Tom married Jay Henry, who was a girl we had always known; indeed I am married to her cousin now. It was a big society wedding, and all the cousins read every line in the papers for weeks beforehand. We were much less sophisticated then. There were dances and dinners, and people came from all over. Lady Moira Burton, the daughter of an earl, was the bridesmaid the papers gave the most linage to even before she arrived, and we were all amazed when she turned out to be nineteen and brought her own lady's maid. We had expected something at least forty. She always said "Thank you, deeply," and so do I and all my cousins to this day.

Of course the family was very much involved with the wedding, which took place in the church we all went to. We didn't really go, but, if we had gone, that's where we would have gone when we were at my grandmother's. The reception was at the Henrys', a mile or so down the road. The night before the wedding, my grandmother gave a big dinner dance with tables on the terraces, marquees in the garden, and my grandmother herself in a completely beaded dress, long gloves, and her diamond tiara. We have moving pictures of the wedding the next day, and we used to look at them on Christmas after dinner. They were very funny with Jay in a dress that cleared her knees, a court train, and yards of Brussels lace. Tom very young and handsome waving at everybody as he got out of his shiny Packard Twin-Six wedding present, and everyone moving in the jerky way movies had then. My Uncle Harry took the pictures, and I suppose they are still around someplace.

But the night before is what I remember without any moving pictures. It was the first grown-up party I was allowed. I was the youngest of the eight older cousins assigned a table on the terrace, and it was the first time — the last time — I saw my grandmother's really *en fête*. My younger brothers and cousins of course never saw it like that, and some of them cannot remember the house; all of them must, I suppose, have some of the furniture, dishes, silver, or pictures. I didn't dance or anything. I just sat and looked. I didn't even talk much to my cousins, who were trying so hard to be old that I was disgusted. I was too young — in knickerbockers I called plus-fours — even to try to be old, to talk about Lady Moira, the dresses, the cars, the two orchestras, the bootleggers who had delivered the booze — that was the word we used — that afternoon in a hearse. Tom himself came in for a good deal of talk.

"I wonder what poor little Miss Payne is thinking tonight." This was

my oldest cousin, Edith. A great frump of a girl of whom it was said —
in her hearing, I shouldn't wonder, because the family was that way —
that it was to be hoped that she would be married for her money because
no one would marry her for any other reason. She was, however, a
stinker of the first water, and even now I can't feel sorry for her. "Poor-
little-Miss-Payne" — at seventeen; you can see the way we were brought
up.

"HEARTBROKEN. GNASHing PEARLY TEETH. SIMPLY
DEVastated." This was Corinne, who talked like this all the time. John
Held, Jr., was her idol, and she had her own subscription to the old *Life*.

"Who's Miss Payne?" Pete, who had told us earlier that he had cut
himself shaving. He was always saying, "A man has to," too. "A man has
to have at least a dozen bow ties" — that sort of thing.

"Boys never know anything." Slobby Edith again. Tom Charlestoned
by us with Jay looking happy, and waved. "She was the blonde Uncle
Doctor had one summer for their kids" — that was us — "and they had
to get rid of her on account of Tom." I guess we all still looked blank
because Corinne said, all in caps, "TOM'S FATAL CHARM."

"Don't you remember, Pete? All that WEEPING and getting
SHOVED out of ROOMS, and GRANNY utterly FRANTIC? Some
SOPHomore from the University of MassaCHUsetts." Edith began talk-
ing like Corinne, but she'd get the accents all wrong. "And her father
worked at the BANK, which made it so emBARrassing for poor dear
GRANNY and all of us because THAT'S how she got the JOB. A
PIECE of imPERTinence is what GRANNY SAID."

"Aw nuts. I'm sure you were just terribly, terribly embarrassed" — my
cousin Georgie's voice cracked; nobody could ever stand Edith — "like
heck." And then he said the cruelest thing he could have said. I don't
think he knew it was cruel, but somehow he always said the cruelest
thing without knowing it even though I, who was younger, knew it was
cruel and, if it had been anyone but oafy Edith, would have felt sorry.

"Who else ever called Grandmama" — we all used the French accentua-
tion but found our contemporaries' *"grand'mères"* highly affected —
"Granny, for Pete's sake. You make me sick." And he pretended to puke
into his finger bowl.

Corinne, too, must have seen Edith cower, because she said, "There's
no HOPE from THESE SAVAGES, Edie. Let's see what we can find
ELSEwhere," and the two of them left, shaking what we called their
rumps.

I left, too, and walked down to the lake. Up above me on the bluff the party went on, and the waves lapped the shore at my feet. I sailed some stones out into the water, saying Tom's and my dirty words, and looked at the sky where there were more stars than I had ever seen. I made up a phrase, then and there, which is one of the first phrases I ever made up. I've always remembered it, and I must have used it in almost every story I wrote in school and in college: "The sky was vaporous with stars." To a twelve-year-old, it was a marvelous phrase, and there was the wonder under the wonderful sky of having thought it up. It had nothing to do with the ache in my heart at all or with what was happening. There was no one to use it to in my world; I didn't write poetry yet; I just thought it, and it made up somehow for the sorrow that beat under my thin breastbone.

Edie was probably right. There had been a Miss Payne, but we called her Miss Charlotte. She had taken care of us one summer and had disappeared suddenly in August. She was a wonderful reader and very pretty with naturally curly — she told us — blond hair. She let us play with her curls as she read, slipping them out with our fingers and watching them bounce back into place. I remember one such scene. It must have been raining out and late in the afternoon, because Miss Charlotte is reading to us in the lounge and there is lamplight on her head. She is sitting on the floor and the book is on the needlepoint seat — unicorns, flowers, vines, Persian huntsmen with bows and arrows — of the huge couch. I am lying on the couch, my knees over one of its arms, my head at the very edge of the book from which she is reading. There are children — cousins, brothers, neighbors — all over the couch, some on the floor beside her, but I am looking up at her freckly skin, her golden hair and blue eyes, and she reaches over and pats me. Is it "Rapunzel, Rapunzel" she reads? At any rate, when it is over she puts her head down and spreads her hair as a fan over the unicorns, flowers, vines, and me. The children rush to gather it in their hands, to pull it — "It's all right. She lets you. Pull as hard as you can. You can't hurt her" — but I just lie there still, the hair on my face, and reach out with my tongue to pull a few strands to my mouth to taste. I have just tasted it now as I write.

The purpose of all such girls — there was a new one every summer — was to keep us out of the grownups' way. I don't suppose we really knew this or would have minded if we had. It was just the way we were brought up. We slept in the east wing. We were dressed and taken down to the beach. Now that I remembered it, Tom did play with us a lot that summer, and it might have been that summer that I found a hairpin in his bed, but, if he was tolerant of me, I was tolerant of him.

"What would you have a hairpin in your bed for, Tom?" He didn't start that I could remember, but I do remember his answer even though I didn't think it the least bit strange.

"Well, you're not the only caller I have, kid." I suppose the measure of affection I had for him is that he never underrated me. He knew he didn't have to say "Don't tell on me, kid," or make up an elaborate explanation. That was all he said, and, even though I didn't know the answer, I would never have thought of mentioning it to anyone else.

Couples began to drift down from the party then, and I heard one high-pitched, fashionable voice exclaim, "What wonderful, wonderful stars," as if Grandmama had provided them along with the champagne, and I hugged my "vaporous with stars" even closer to my heart. I heard someone else say, "Oh, it's just one of the kids. There are literally millions; you don't dare imagine," so, when I had a chance, I got up the bluff steps, skirted the party, and went up the billiard-room stairs to my room. I got undressed in the dark and it was very pretty. All the lanterns swaying in the garden, the lighted marquees, and the stars in the sky. The orchestra was playing "I'm Forever Blowing Bubbles" real soft with brushes on the drums, and you could hear the feet shuffling as you sometimes can if you only listen.

I didn't have any definite feeling. There was no sense of loss that I was losing Tom or anything like that. If I had to say, I would have said that I was trembly sad because the night was so beautiful and my vaporous stars so far away. But I didn't have to say. I just had to do what I did, and I did it so naturally that there was no thought behind it at all. Although I hadn't done it in at least a couple of years, although I hadn't missed doing it, or thought about it, I just walked up the three steps, across the lounge to Tom's room, and climbed into his bed. Outside, the party went on, and I could hear the orchestra, the laughter, the glasses tinkling.

I may have been asleep a little time or a long time; I don't remember; but I heard the door open and saw the shaft of light in the dresser mirror. Then I heard a girl say, "I thought you said this was Tom's room."

"It is. Shut up."

"But what's he got there?"

"Will you shut up? How do I know what he's got there? Just somebody's there, that's all." Then the door closed, and I could hear the girl's thin, drunken voice remonstrating, but I didn't know what they were saying and just drifted back to sleep.

It was broad daylight — 10:00 or so — when I woke again, still in Tom's bed. Tom was looking at me, clear as the day, in the reflection which shimmered, hung in the air, somewhere between the dresser mirror in which he was tying his tie and me, whose eyes had been drawn from the sprawl of the bed to meet his looking back.

" 'Bout time you got up kid, huh? Today's the wedding day." My gaze went past the reflection into the mirror, and he looked very happy there. I smiled and stretched, drawing my eyes back into myself. "*You* sure look comfortable."

"I am," I said through my yawn.

I shook my head and found him again in the mirror. "You looked so comfortable, so damned asleep when I came in — rough night, kid, rough night — " (I lost his eyes then when he began to fuss with his cuff links) "that I just went to your bed, and that's where I slept."

Inside of me warm, wet, sudden tears began. I can still feel them flood my heart; so I know and knew what they were. But of course I didn't cry them then and I don't now. They just exist in me and always have. I hope I have them in some poems somewhere. I hope I have them here. Anyway, we never looked at each other, ever again.

Another incident in connection with the wedding I suppose is significant enough for me to tell, although I — and I am the one who is writing this — really don't know, nearing fifty, just how it is important. Jay and Tom were married in the afternoon, so I suppose it was 10:00 or so that night when they got ready to leave the Henrys'. All the cousins had been running around like mad at the reception, although the younger ones had been taken off sometime earlier. I was out on the side lawn with the older ones, but they had given up acting older. The girls had kicked off their high heels, and the boys had thrown their blue flannel blazers in a heap on one of the stone benches. All of us had grass stains on our white trousers because we had played real kid games like stoop tag and even statues, trying to whirl up the girls' skirts, trying to bump into what we called their "boobs." At the end we were all stretched out on the side lawn looking at the stars and trying to catch fireflies without moving anything except our arms and hands. Somehow, without anyone mentioning it, we all knew the rules and would have cried "cheat" had anyone sat up. On the other side of the house, the jazz band was still playing, and beneath us we could hear the lake. We had had a good time all week, but now we were exhausted with excitement the way kids get and just lay there. After a while our grandmother appeared on the side porch and called out, "Edith, Edith, round up those children. Your Uncle Tom and Aunt Jay are going to be leaving soon, and you'll want to be there." She peered over the railing to see how many of us were there, still in her gold lamé mother-of-the-groom's dress, her brown velvet hat still firmly on her head. Only her gloves were gone, and I could see the great diamonds on her fingers — blue fire in the August night. Georgie tried to say, "Last one to the porch is a stink-pot," but it didn't work. The girls had to put on their pumps — that was the word — and the boys had to pick up their coats.

Our grandmother just stood there looking out over the lake, related hands gripping the porch railing. I was the last one to struggle up into the light, and I was the one she caught. "What a mess you are!" This wasn't unkindly. "Come, let me fix your tie. And button your belly button." The big diamonds fiddled with my collar button and pulled my tie up.

"You don't have to choke me."

"I'm not going to have you looking like that. And the grass stains. But come on." Then she did something that was strange for her; she took my hand and kept it even when I tried to get away to join the others. "I'm not letting you out of my sight, young man."

Now this is what I don't know even though it is my story and I am writing it. It is what I *can't* know unless I pretend I'm Henry James, which I can't do. Did she realize or sense the state of my unconscious excitement and want to protect me from myself, or did she want me for her own protection? All day long people had been saying, "Oh Barbara, your very last baby," and relating things to her, and she'd been smiling and social, and she was as old as I was young. There is so much that you don't know about people. What aches are at work at any given time, what frustrations rage hectic in the blood to ravage so the moment-open heart. She had married my grandfather at eighteen. He was twenty years older than she, the daughter of an Akron judge, and the son of one of the real robber barons. Her wedding present had been the tiara she had worn last night. I sit here now and try to imagine one of my own daughters — and they certainly have had a more sophisticated upbringing than the belle of Akron at eighteen — transported to such a world, giving birth to ten boys, and then standing, nearly sixty, to watch the last leave.

It will not work at all. So many truths, facts, operate at the same time that it is impossible to know even your own blood, and, unless the intuition intuits the impossible whole, the separating of it, the ordering, must distort forever the part with which it is dealing.

I say again I do not know why she held me by the hand. Anything I can reconstruct, I can at the same time tumble down. I was annoyed then at being restricted and dragged her around to the scrunchy drive where the ushers were handing out rice and all the guests were standing and waiting for Tom and Jay to appear. When they did come and stopped to kiss Grandmama, I got free so that in their dash to the car I was after them like a skinny dervish — arms and legs flying every whichway, frantically tossing rice more on myself than on them and screaming in my high soprano voice, "Keep your pecker up, Tom."

I don't even know that anyone heard me, but my grandmother got me iron by the shoulder with one hand, there was a cruel flash of diamonds, and I was hit hard across the mouth with those great rings. My inner lip was cut against my teeth. I could taste the salt blood. Thirty-five years later I can put my tongue to the very place my mouth was cut and make physical again what I suppose was a psychic scar. The tyranny, the horror of cruelty, plunged to my heart. But was it cruel? Was I indeed hysterical? The woman had brought up ten boys and diamonds grew from the bones of her fingers. I certainly couldn't be allowed to make a spectacle of myself. At all costs I would want to keep my emotion private, and wasn't she helping me to do just that? All this reasoning comes now. At the time, or if I were to tell the story to a psychiatrist, the diamonds would become symbolic, and she was a woman viciously loath to give up her son.

Tom and Jay went to England for two years. Tom to run the London branch, so I didn't see them, and I don't even now know what happened. At any rate Jay went to Reno when they returned, and I saw little of Tom that summer. In the fall he returned to London. When I went away to college, he sent me a check for $2000.00 and one of the three or four notes I have had from him in my life:

Hi Kid,
   They tell me your real bright. I am not real bright and never was. But I will tell you something about the family. You can always have any money you want, but somebodies always going to want to know

what you do with it. Here is a lot of money just put it into some *other* bank and when you need something use it if you don't want to tell anybody.

> Keep your pecker up,
> Tom

Somebody had always even spelled for Tom, and if the letter had been dictated of course it wouldn't have appeared as it did; but he had written it himself and I kept it and am quite unable, typing it out now, to add the necessary *sic*'s. He was thirty when he wrote it, and I was sixteen.

Two years later he came home for a while when my grandmother died, but we all stayed in town, and he stayed at Fred's. I was only back a few days and returned to Cambridge as soon as I could. The brothers were fantastically busy. It was the bottom of the Depression, and they set about salvaging what they could. We were still very rich people, but when it was all over the brothers no longer owned the bank lock, stock, and barrel as they had, and none of them could have afforded to keep up the house even had they wanted to. Actually it stood empty until 1942 when, as a tax deduction, it was rented to the Navy for $1.00 a year. My cousins as they married took a few acres here and there and built houses, and finally five years ago the house was torn down and the whole place subdivided into what the ads called (honestly!) "Junior Estates." A kind of Levittown for the rich was the way Corinne described it.

Tom went back to London afterward and was briefly married to an English movie star, whom he himself divorced in a real English divorce case with "m'luds" and corespondents and full coverage in the international press. At the time of the abdication, he was mentioned once or twice, and Edith had a picture of him in the *Tatler* where he was correctly identified and Mrs. Simpson was "and friend." If that's not fame, I don't know what it is. The *sic transit gloria mundi* boys will be happy to know that my daughters didn't even know who Mrs. Simpson was when I mentioned her the other day.

I saw Tom maybe a dozen times in as many years. I had gone through college and got a check, and got a doctor's degree and got a check, and he bought and gave away 100 copies of my first book — I suppose to people who could have had no idea at all what it was about. He came to my wedding and there was some of the old warmth, but I was too excited to pay much attention. Two months later I was in the Navy, and so was Tom, a retread at forty-two. He was in Washington for most of the war, and I was in and out and saw him often. I was the best man when he married Mrs. Paget Armstrong — Nan.

Mrs. Paget Armstrong was not at all what she sounded. She taught French at the University of Maryland and was a quiet, restful, enormously well read, and deeply sophisticated woman. She was five or six years older than Tom — at least she had a married daughter — and two people more utterly unprepared for, although not at all unsuited to, each other, it is hard to imagine. They moved into her apartment in Bethesda amid the department-store furniture that was all that was left of her marriage to a Spokane dentist and which had not been improved by its move across the continent.

Tom was perfectly happy and she was too. I liked going there very much, although the food was lukewarm and ill-prepared and I had to sleep on what she called a "davenport." Even the bath towels were sleazy. She herself simply radiated sympathy, and it was touching to see how proud Tom was of me when the two of us talked books and poetry. Little by little I noticed the furniture being replaced, and the "davenport" became a "sofa," and I thought to myself, "Aha, the little woman is learning."

They had been married a little more than a year when, late in December, I called her up. She told me that Tom wasn't there, but said she really wanted to see me and would I please come. I had a hard time getting all the way out there, so it was later than she thought it would be when I got there and she had already had a couple of drinks. She was wearing a most beautiful navy wool dress — she had had nothing like it that I had ever seen — with a diamond clip at the neck and my grandmother's big ring on her engagement finger.

"What a wonderful dress!" I said as I kissed her cheek. She looked pleased an instant and said, "Molyneux." As I followed her into the living room, she went on, " 'Molly Ner' is what you people say, you know." Never, never act to the rich as if they were richer than you. It floods them with shame. I guess she felt this go through my mind because right away she said, "I'm sorry. But Tom's overdue a week."

"Hush-hush?" My own heart stopped a minute, too.

"Very. I don't know which way to turn or who to talk to."

"Well, talk to me."

"I've been meaning to for a long time, you know."

"The Molly Ner set doesn't go in for talking?"

"Something like that. But even so I don't suppose you generally say to a nephew —" She stopped and you could see an agony hit her full in the face, and her hand went to her breast as if to ward off a blow. You could tell, too, that it was the sort of thing that recurred, that had been recurring for quite a while. "Why did I marry him? Why did I ever marry him? I could have just slept with him, just slept" — she drew the word out and made it seem simple and beautiful and restful — "with him." She had the trick of repetition even under ordinary circumstances, and now it was exaggerated. "He's an economic primitive. He doesn't read. He can't spell." There were tears in her eyes and you could see that she had just about reached the end of her rope. "He doesn't know anything. Anything at all. Nothing. He's been every goddamned place in the world. He knows every important person in the world. But he's, he's —" she shook her head at the incomprehensibility of it — "innocent." She looked to me for help.

"Is that bad?"

"For me, yes." She twisted the ring in. "When you can't be innocent yourself, yes. I don't even remember when I didn't know. For me there's always a feather of guilt." She looked to see if I understood, and was satisfied, because she went on. "Put me on the witness stand, accuse me of the most monstrous act, and always, always there'd be the moment's hesitation before I could deny it. In that moment I'd remember and I'd think, Yes, I could have done it because I know it has been done by people just as good as me, and I can imagine that I might have done it. I'd feel that it was only accidental — there but for the grace of God go I — that I hadn't done it. The feather of guilt."

"There be much matter in this madness." I tried to laugh her out of it, but you could see that she was hurt at my failure to follow her. I didn't want her to try any harder to make it clear, so I just said, "You mean you could have married him for his money?"

"Oh, you Molly Ners, you Molly Ners. What in Christ's name do you think money is? What's so goddamned special about your money? Of course I could have married him for it and it wouldn't have been any trouble at all. He was married for it twice, wasn't he? That flat-chested Molly Ner bitch. That fantastic bosooooomed Frigidaire. No, no. What haunts me is that I'm really worse than they, I married him for his simple loving kindness." Her eyes drooped closed with a vast weariness, and when she opened them again they were full of love. "You see how that could be worse? Do you know the French word *accueillir?* It means *to receive,* but as a host receives a guest. This is the way Tom loves. He opens himself up completely. He's all there for the taking. But, like a guest, you have to take." Her eyes were so earnest, so pleading, that I took her hand and held it. "You see, he's afraid of embarrassing you by offering you more than you want, more than you are ready for, and yet his own hunger is so deep, his own heart is so transparent, that you can't help wondering — the feather of guilt, and God I love him — if there's enough of you to receive all that he has to give." She took her hand from mine, turned the diamond around and looked at it. "I can't say this sort of thing to him, or at least I haven't yet, so I say it to you. He wouldn't be able to follow. It's not the sort of thing he thinks about; it's not the sort of thing he has to think about. That gorgeous, blooming innocence. But it's sure not a very practical way of loving."

She got up then, smoothed her dress over her hips and said, "I'm glad I said it. To you. To myself. To Bethesda, Maryland. But I don't know if I can stand much more of this kindness, this *gentillesse,* this christawful consideration." I smiled what I suppose was ruefully because she said, "The two with-rue-my-heart-is-laden boys."

"Oh, come off it. It is funny. You're all torn up because you haven't heard from him when you expected, so you complain about his kindness and consideration. Really, now."

She did smile then, but said, "Seriously, you don't know what it is. If he'd just *say*. But no. It's all by the most godawful indirection. How the hell did I know this place was a horror? I didn't know you could pay $350.00 for a wool dress. Yet you come in and your face lights up when you see it in the half dark. As far as I know — really, honestly, truly — it doesn't look any different from $49.95. Why didn't he just buy a house in Georgetown? I — I might feel uncomfortable. Nothing about his being strangled here. D'ya know what he did?" The frantic light came back in her eyes. "I'll tell you. For six months he kept a room at the Shoreham — everybody in Washington is screaming for rooms — to keep his thirty uniforms, his 100 shirts, his forty pairs of shoes in. Because he didn't like to say that there wasn't room for them here. He didn't like to say." She nodded the words out syllable by syllable. "I'm dizzy, just dizzy. I said to him, but they're all alike, aren't they, and he said he supposed so, so he just gave them all away. Just like that. It never occurred to him that I might suppose a room at the Shoreham meant a mistress, you know?"

I was laughing and said, "He isn't acquainted with the subject of French literature."

"It's impossible. Oh, I've seen you in Henry James and Fitzgerald and

Proust and all over the place — and you've seen yourselves, but it doesn't do any good. I'm not prepared for you. You're not prepared for yourselves."

I've often had occasion to remember that "you're not prepared for yourselves," and I've wondered just when she said it to him, for from what happened I am sure she must have. Critics, speaking of Gatsby, always point out his romanticizing the rich; what they don't know is that the rich themselves romanticize the poor. It never occurs to Daisy that she is loved because her "voice is money," and her weeping over Gatsby's shirts — at his thinking that they can make any difference — is as marvelously revealing in its way as Nick's last sight of Daisy eating chicken. Take the ring. Nan wore it as a status symbol — although the phrase had not then been invented. It was the only way she could wear it. Twelve-carat diamonds did not grow from her bones. To Tom, who must have given his movie star an even larger one, it was his mother's ring. To me — well, I've told you about that.

Tom did get back, did survive the war, and it was Nan who died cruelly of cancer toward the end of the '40s. She was in the hospital for nearly a year, and, although he never told her, toward the end Tom had a room on the floor above to be near her. I saw her two weeks before she died, and, in her own phrase, she "received me like a guest." She asked me to be good to Tom, to watch over him as he had watched over her, but then went on, "But how can you? How can anyone? There always will be the moment when, like Sartre's man looking through the keyhole into the empty room, he will see the eye of a stranger looking back. It happened to me a long, long time ago. I don't think it has happened to you yet, but it will, and I guess it will be all right." A spasm of pain came over her then, but she was so intent on finishing that she let it clutch her without closing her eyes. "What will happen to Tom when he plasters his goddamned, clear-blue boy's eye to that goddamned keyhole" — you could see the pain run like a river of fire through her — "I can't even think. Let Sartre think for me. It's his phrase — 'the burning presence' of the 'stare of Another.' Never to have known shame. Jesus, I envy the rich."

I went into the hall to hurry the nurse.

Nan was buried in the family plot. I asked Tom if she had ever seen it and was sorry that she hadn't. It would have amused her greatly because it was dedicated to the proposition that even in death we were different. It was in the oldest city cemetery, one of a half-dozen or so national

Catholic, Protestant, and Jewish strung along what at one time had been the end of the streetcar line. The street widened out, and when I was little, and went there with my grandmother, there was generally a holiday air about the place. Streetcars clanged; huge Polish, German, and Bohemian families would wander around clutching flags, diaper bags, trowels, and watering cans. You'd see widows in black pricing monuments in the empty lots, shawled women looking at grave plants in the enormous greenhouse, and kids eating popcorn, hot dogs from the whistling wagons. In the summer there was an American Legion carnival with a Ferris wheel. None of these delights was for us. The limousine would have to slow almost to a stop, and we on the jump seats often had to take the thumbed noses — "Pay no attention, children. Act as if you didn't see them" — directed toward us by kids our very own age. Inside the cemetery gates there was none of the egalitarian nonsense of today's "Memorial Parks" where all the markers are the same and everyone has to buy "perpetual care." If you were poor, the stone was poor, the grave sunken, and the grasses grew up around you. If you were rich, you crossed over a little river that our father called the Styx on a rattly bridge, and looking back you could see the welter of domino stones where, crowded more closely even than they had been in life, lay the many dead.

On our side of the river, little hills rose, covered with a chaos of tombs, vaults, angels, columns, Greek porticoes, stone catafalques. The merchant princes, the robber barons sometimes had whole hills to themselves, and one of them had been flattened off for us. There is a picture of ours in the book the family had written about itself, and they used to sell a postcard of it at the cemetery gates — a blue sky, white clouds, and geraniums, aromatic with July, in the flower boxes. Corinne bought a pack of them once and used to send them to us from time to time with "Happy Birthday" scrawled across the back, or even, on occasion, "Wish you were here." The robber baron himself lay under an enormous obelisk of polished black marble, his name cut deep in letters as tall as a man. Around him in an ever-widening circle lay the graves of his sons, my grandfather, granduncles, and their sons and sons' sons. Each grave had its heavy slab of matching marble, and, if such a thing can be said to have taste, I suppose the architect's conception can be admired. The obelisk stood as the center of an enormous sundial or clock face, and four flights of three steps each — at 12:00, 3:00, 6:00, and 9:00 — led up to it. The other hours were marked by either black marble benches or flower boxes, and it was because of the filling of these as one set of flowers died that we usually drove out with my grandmother and her gardener.

Well, the streetcar's gone long since; the monument makers have fled; the greenhouses stood empty for a while and were pelted with stones before they were torn down to make room for a shopping plaza, as if the dead could eat, wear shoes, or attend one-cent sales at the drugstore. Very few people are buried there now, mostly people like us who had graves to spare, but even so, when I was there for Fred's funeral, the narrow, winding gravel roads were all marked "One Way." This greatly delighted Corinne, who said, as we rattled over the bridge on our way back, "Remember the Ferris wheel we never could ride?"

Early this year I ran into Tom in the reading room of the public library. I had gone in to look up some things in connection with an article I was trying to do, and there he was, surrounded by encyclopedias, a big blue college notebook in front of him. He was nearly sixty; his older brothers had died, my father among them, and even his grandnieces and nephews were getting married. He only appeared on such occasions, and the members of the family had commented with asperity that, if you wanted to talk to Tom, you had to call him at the bank because he was never home, and half the time your message wasn't delivered. He had even disappeared from the society columns, as indeed had the rest of us, and the only place you were likely to see his name was on the letterheads of charity solicitations.

"Well, look at the elder statesman," was what I said when I saw him, and he really looked caught out.

"I'm sure glad it's you," he laughed, but I felt sorry I had said what I did. A twinge of class consciousness, of course, because we were brought up to act as if there was nothing strange in the behavior, however outrageous, of anyone we knew or were related to. "Come on, I'll buy you lunch." He spoke to the librarian as we left about leaving his stuff out, and she said, "Surely, Mr. Thomas."

He was attending night classes in the downtown branch of the University, and he told me with pride that he was a senior. He hadn't said anything to them about Princeton; indeed, having become committed to education, he was ashamed, much as a Seventh Day Adventist might be ashamed of an Episcopal past. The detail which cost him the greatest effort to confess, however, was his use of the name Richard Thomas, but I quite understood the reservation. He was a trustee of the University; his own name was immediately recognizable. I didn't learn that day, but

I did shortly afterward when I began to see a good deal of him, that Tom was living with a girl he had met in one of his classes, and that she had no idea that he was anything other than an older student rather better off than usual. He had taken an apartment for her and her two children — one Negro, one blond as light — in a high-rise insurance company project, and spent two or three nights a week there. Her name was Mrs. Temple — Jo.

She was very beautiful, with long, brown-red dancer's hair, and she moved like a queen. I often had dinner with them, and she went to no end of trouble with paperback French cookbooks and that sort of thing if she felt like it; otherwise we'd just have something sent in. She was witty, well read in a curious sort of way, and never said anything at all about her former life. One of the neighbors sat with her kids while she was in class, and Jo did the same for the girl during the day. It was all very free, casual, messy, highbrow. Tom was not the least self-conscious about it, and I suppose I would never have seen this kind of life if it hadn't been for him. I was fascinated. The idea of Tom's writing a paper of the effect of the restricted vocabulary in Racine and Hemingway was staggering. Yet the paper was very good, and the three of us talked it over, late into the coffee night, for many weeks. We'd argue and walk up and down as if it were the most important literary discovery since the beginning of time. But, if Jo and I were excited about it, it was Tom's idea, Tom's paper, Tom's passion. He really knew what he was doing, and brought to the job the kind of sensitivity that the late or self-educated seldom have, but which no teacher can ever teach.

One night Jo was going to read Cleopatra in a Shakespeare class they were both taking, and Tom and I picked her up. She was wearing a thin silk dress, cut away to show her magnificent shoulders, and you could tell that she was wearing nothing but a slip underneath — not at all the sort of thing she ordinarily would have worn to class. She must have had quite a reputation around the college, because there wasn't room in the classroom for all the visitors, and the instructor, a Mr. Newberry, laughed and said, "I see that word has got around that Mrs. Temple is to read tonight. I'll have to find us a bigger room." We all moved down the hall then to a chemistry demonstration room.

I suppose those who have never seen one have little notion of what a night course is like at any university, however eminent. On the one hand it is a shabby, heartbroken operation: the university intends to make money out of it; the only big boys who teach are those who want to spend the summer in Europe; the students intend to get credit. Yet if the teacher is any good — and Newberry was good — there is a cohesion, an interest, a completely democratic camaraderie never attainable in day classes where the division into cliques — both intellectual and social — is evident from the very beginning.

I had intended to watch Tom as Jo read, but this was impossible. The students read their parts from behind a long, waist-high sink desk normally used for chemistry demonstrations, the symbols for which still smeared the chalky blackboards. Yet in that bare, dirty room in a reconstructed office building, under fluorescent lights, no one had eyes for anyone or anything but Jo. It was a reading, you understand; they hadn't learned the parts, they didn't act them; there was no business. They would read a scene; Newberry would comment; and they might take up at his cue hundreds of lines later on. Jo didn't even look up very often, and I am perfectly positive that she used only four gestures in the two hours we were there. Her voice was eloquent, varied, and wonderfully colored, but each of the gestures I will remember until the day I die.

When she first stood up — Enobarbus was speaking and she was obviously reading ahead — her hands went to her hair and took out, one at a time, the three or four hairpins that held it loosely up. Each she put to her mouth, never taking her eyes from the text until the hair had spilled, coil by lustrous coil, over her shoulders, clouding her breast. Her hand went to her lips then, and I could feel the tiny slick of her tongue collecting the pins, which she laid between the pages of her book at — oh God — the spine. There was a little shake of her head and the hair streamed back as her breasts rose and the marvelously supple voice began the cadenced lines. If there had been anything conscious about it, had it for a moment seemed calculated, it would have been the most naked striptease. But it was pure, unobserved "Woman Reading" — a woman who knew in her blood that what she was to read had to be read with her hair down.

I wouldn't be so sure about my recollection, I would distrust it as overobserved, over-written, except that in the last scene, just before she got to "Give me my robe, put on my crown," her bare arm arched, gathered the richness of that brown-red hair with its shadows, and the flower fingers pinned it again to her queenly head. Before this, in the scene with the messenger, her voice all whips and scorns, she had put out her hand, instinctively without looking up, toward the huge blond oaf who was doubling the minor parts. As she came to the words, "My bluest veins to kiss," she looked him straight in his goggling eyes, and turned her hand palm upward, baring the underside of her wrist and its bluest veins. At the tenderness of the coquetry, the boy blushed crimson, even as Shakespeare must have intended, and the ceiling lifted with the roar of delight from the class.

The last gesture she used was less overt, but I am just as sure it was noticed because I could hear the comments as we left the classroom. When it came to the asp, Jo — at once Jo and Cleopatra, Jo becoming Cleopatra despite the fluorescent lights, the demonstration sink, Jo with Cleopatra in her bluest veins — put her hand involuntarily to her breast. Her fingers trembled at the silk as if exploring the horror of hurt in

> *With thy sharp teeth this knot intrinsicate*
> *Of life at once untie. Poor venomous fool,*
> *Be angry and dispatch.*

Her voice was utterable tears, but when she spoke

> *Oh, coulds't thou speak,*
> *That I might hear thee call great Caesar ass*
> *Unpolicied,*

it whiplashed into such scorn as I have never heard in the human voice, and her hand pressed flesh to its limit.

The power of her reading was such that the others were swept along with her. Antony was Antony and every man there read the lines with him — not only "I am dying, Egypt, dying" and the great bravura passages, but even single lines and phrases. I know because when Antony said "Eros, ho! The shirt of Nessus is upon me," sixty-year-old Tom's hand became a vise on my suit-coat arm.

After it was all over, a bunch of people including Newberry went up to Jo and thanked her, and I suppose *exalted* is the word to express the look in her eyes. I, of course, was irretrievably and forever in love with her.

Tom and I sat back when the others were making over her. He was deep in thought and said nothing. I did say, "That sure was something," but he just grunted and looked very old. We walked out with the rest of the cast and Newberry — Jo had invited them back to the apartment — and they were all laughing excitedly, Jo very flirtatious, triumphant, and young, swinging her hips joyously, tossing her red-brown head. The halls were empty by that time, and a janitor was standing by the elevator, waiting to turn off the lights. Of course it was Tom who said, "Come on. Let's get going. This poor guy wants to get home," but I don't think anyone heard him above the jabber. While we waited for the elevator, the not-at-all pallid Mr. Newberry made a sort of pass at Jo. I don't think he had an idea in the world that Tom was her lover. (I write *lover* now, but when I phrased it to myself then, it was "Tom was the man who paid the rent," and an admonitory shiver went through me that should have warned me of the horror in store.) Jo avoided Newberry with a little dance step — I suppose he was thirty-two or -three — and came toward me, slipping her hands under my coat — cupped palms, moving fingers — across the small of my back.

"Here's the man who's Antony's age, you Dollabellas, you Eno-barbuses, you Caesars." It was so outrageous that everyone hooted except Tom and me.

In the elevator going down, I was pressed close to her, and I know she knew my excitement because she murmured to me, "Not every soldier's pole has fallen" in the confusion of getting out.

The party at Jo's was very beery, young, and stupid. Lots of gossip about teachers and classes that greatly intrigued Newberry, who would be sorry the next day, and lots of wandering in and out of the bedrooms, the kitchen, and even into the public corridor. All I did was watch my chance, and it seemed to come when Tom went into their bedroom, saying he was going to make a phone call. I knew that Jo had been watching, too, because she was on her feet right away, pulling me into the front hall. The urgency of our kiss was so complete that when I looked at her there was horror in her eyes, and she could only return my gaze for a moment before she pressed my head to her breast and whispered to herself more than to me, "My bluest veins, my very bluest veins."

I don't think we were gone more than a few minutes; at any rate Tom came back after we had reappeared and were already sitting on the floor.

He stood over us, looking down — paternal, avuncular, what you will — and said, "I just talked to Mary" — Mary is my wife — "on the phone and invited myself out for the long weekend."

"Sure, Tom, fine. The girls will love it." I couldn't find his eyes, and I don't think I would have known what to do with them had I caught them, because I was totally unprepared for what followed.

"They're picking me — us — up in twenty minutes. I told them we'd meet downstairs. They don't know the name on the bell."

To say that my heart sank is less than true. Of course there was that awful, bottomless sinking, but I was flooded with a fire of shame as fierce as my desire had been. A stain, like one of those oxblood birthmarks you sometimes see on faces, spread through me as if to devour my bones. I could look nowhere, least of all toward Jo. Tom mercifully walked away, and in a few minutes Jo got up and went into the children's bedroom. I don't know — I still don't know — if I was meant to follow her, but the fact that she had chosen the children's room stopped me — oh shit on Henry James — for long enough to realize that my knees would never have supported me. I just sat there dazed, and I supposed I would be thought drunk. In a little while Jo came back through the door to their room — there was a bath connecting it to the children's. She had our coats in her hand and said, "The Bobbsey Twins are on their way."

Everyone got up — goddamn them — the way the young do for the old, and Jo helped us on with our coats. She pecked us both at the door, but didn't come to the elevator with us. I wondered if it would be Enobarbus or Newberry. On the way down Tom said, "When I said *they* were coming for us, I just meant Taylor. I phoned and told him to bring a car and pack me a bag." His voice was perfectly normal, but mine broke over the "Sure," which was all I could get out. I wanted to say with Jo's scorn, "I'd call great Caesar pretty goddamned policied."

I was on fire with rage at what had been done to me. My tongue had shot between my lip and teeth as if to ward off the diamond blow. I was still, as Nan had said, "unprepared for myself."

Taylor came then with the big bank-president limousine, and it was clear that Tom intended to have him drive us the sixty toll-road miles to my house in the country. Great Caesar was afraid to be alone with me, was he? As if he had read my mind, Tom leaned forward and closed the glass partition, and another wave of humiliation filled me. "In the morning," I thought, "this is what I'll wake up to. And every morning it will be there, uneasy at my heart at first and then known in the blood. The walk to the bathroom, the very shiver as I pee, polluted." My hands trembled with *horror carnis* at the thought of touching myself in the shower, the look in the eyes looking back at me as I shaved. Tom. Tom had done this to me. Tom. As if I were a little boy who had disgraced himself at a birthday party. And I had allowed it. Had been powerless. The Bobbsey Twins. The Bobbsey Twins. Sissy, Sissy. Shitty sissy.

The paroxysm that seized me was completely real. My teeth chattered, my feet would not hold still, and I was in the grip of a wholly unvoluntary memory: the memory of sitting on a black marble bench, cold as the death that surrounded me, my six-year-old thighs, in their thin De Pinna flannel shorts, rigid with ache. It was the day before my mumps began. I had driven out with my grandmother in just such a limousine, glassed-in in April, to see about planting the boxes with hyacinths. It was a weekday, so we had not had to run the gantlet at the gates. The Ferris wheel had stopped. There was a poor little funeral — two cars and the hearse — at one point before we crossed the rattly bridge, but we scrunched past it. The obelisk was very black against the dead gray sky, but the branches of the scarcely greening trees moved, reflected in the elegiac marble. I thought of my grandfather, whom I never knew, dying blind. Of the girl sixteen who had hanged herself. Of the little boy who one hundred years ago had wandered into a Canadian wheat field and died in the August sun, his hair blonder than the wheat which hid him until he was dead. He was a favorite of mine, and the phrases were my grandmother's as she told the story to impress on us how we must never wander away. She moved now with the gardener, as if the two of them were hands on that enormous clock, from box to box, and I climbed on one of the benches. She called out, "You'd better get in the car, honey; you'll get cold," but I just sat there in terrible sadness watching not the trees or the monument but the movement of the trees deep in its blackness.

My grandmother and the gardener had passed to the other side of the obelisk and were out of my sight when suddenly a black cloud of purple martins on their way north hovered above the monument, supposing in its depths a pool. There were literally thousands of them, layered, chirping, their formation abandoned as, purpled black from brown, wheeling, pecking, they swooped down to the marble waters of our graves. I could hear my grandmother's "Oh! Oh!" and the gardener ran out of the shadows, swinging his rake and waving his trowel. The deceived birds rose with a cry but, in the rising and wheeling round the obelisk, swooped over me on the bench. Their wings beat lice-feathered against my face; their claws caught in my hair; their dirt befouled my jacket; they thudded against my hunched breast and back in their wild determination to escape. When they were gone I was frozen with terror that burst within me, and I wet my pants.

My grandmother came running and took me in her arms, but I was far gone in the deep compulsive tremor which had lasted forty years to be relived now with such exactness that I thought it was really urine which trickled through the hairs of my trousered leg and not the memory of a six-year-old shame. I had to put out my hand to know it was not.

After it was over, Tom pressed the button that lowered the window on my side, and I leaned back, limp with quiet exhaustion.

"If it's too cold, say so, kid."

"Kid? I'm forty-six years old."

"Kid." I drank in the real air that blew the graveyard air away and felt calmer. My hand lay on the seat between us, and after a while Tom put his hand over it and pressed it.

"Kid, kid, I had to do it."

"Sure."

He withdrew his hand and for a long time said nothing. The revulsions of my original *horror carnis* set up decreasing echoes as we lapped the night in toll-road miles until finally, as we stopped at one of the gates in the blue-green, unreal light and Taylor flung the coins in the basket, I gave a great sigh, and it was as finished as it was ever going to be.

For a while then I thought Tom was going to say, "Please don't see Jo again," or "If I ask you, will you promise not to go by the flat again," or "I'm warning you, don't go back." My mind phrased and rephrased the possible sentences, made up answers in a dizzy succession — evading, consenting, refusing — until the whole jewel-box cab of the limousine seemed ready to explode. I suppose I was never so far away from him as I was in those moments, for, when he did speak, it was to say, "Did Nan ever tell you that about the man looking into an empty room, a room he knew was empty, through a keyhole?"

"And being amazed that an eye was looking back? Yes. A couple of weeks before she died. I've read it since, of course."

"So have I. You don't know who it is looking back. Whether it is the eye of God or your own eye or Shakespeare's eye." He cleared his throat. "You know that's why I went to night school? I never knew any of the things you and she were talking about. She once even told me that from something you said she was pretty sure you were in love with Charlotte Payne. At six? I just laughed. I sure unlaughed it tonight. I guess that's what comes from knowing things."

The old tenderness flooded me, washing clear like sweet water against a bitter clay bank. Poor Tom's a-cold. Did he still think that learning, even understanding, had anything to do with desire or happiness — Nan's *innocence* again?

"She said she didn't know what would happen when you did look through the keyhole and saw the eye looking back. The burning presence."

"Well, now it's happened," he said. "It was your eye looking back."

WILLIAM EASTLAKE

An Indian and a white man debating their respective cultures and religions while the missing son of the white man is struggling for life in a quicksand create almost too much suspense in "A Long Day's Dying." Their dialogue is tremendously rich in its illuminations of both cultures and the end is fable-like.

William Eastlake was born in New York of Cornish parents but has lived most of his life in the far West. For many years he has been living on a cattle ranch in northern New Mexico. His work has appeared in many magazines. He has published several novels, including Portrait of an Artist with Twenty-Six Horses.

A Long Day's Dying

THE SUMMER SOLSTICE was another implacable, fierce, pure blue New Mexican day, another wide panorama of empty, impossible void without faint sign or distant signal for the very young man dying at the bottom of a vast and lonely canyon called the La Jara Arroyo. Quicksand. The young man tried to remove the word from his thoughts. Quicksand, a viscid, unsubstantial whorl — phantom. Neither is quicksand fluid nor solid; neither can you stand nor swim. Quicksand, the stuff a nightmare and the rest of my life is made of. But try to think of something else, try to think of something pleasant to pass this short time. Think of your Indian friend and the day you said to Rabbit Stockings:

"How many chiefs are there in that summer wickiup?"

"It's not that wickiup, it's my home."

"How many chiefs are there?"

"Plenty. You know, Santo, you've got to stop thinking like a white person."

"That's going to be difficult."

"You've got to try. You know, the whites are going to be extincted."

?"

Isn't that what you're trying to do?"

when you're all gone and then you try to come back again
we Indians are not going to be so nice next time."

"You Indians are not going to let the next Columbus land?"

"That's right, Santo."

The boy Sant thought about this odd, unimportant conversation. He
had a great deal of time to think now so he let his mind wander over all
of his short, rich past, because he had tried everything to keep from
sinking, but nothing worked. The thing that seemed to work best was to
lie backward and try to float on the cool boiling sand. That seemed to
work best, but each long alone hour that passed he was getting in deeper.
It's a grave. That's it. It's as though the earth wanted you, decided to
take you now, could not wait for you to become a man. So Sant did not
whine or complain, he did not cry, because he wanted to behave now like
a man. When you have tried absolutely everything else and there is no
way out, then you try resignation and courage. Quicksand is heavy water
in which swimming is impossible and it's as if the drain below were open
and you were being sucked down into the earth. Sant had been struggling
alone down at the bottom of the lonely arroyo for six hours now.

Six hours before he had begun to cross on his great black horse and the
animal had refused. Sant got off and tried to pull the horse, but Luto
stood rooted on the edge. Sant did not notice that he himself was going
down, he did not realize it was impossible to move until the rein broke
and the horse moved back to firmer ground. "All right," Sant called to
the horse, "when I get out of here — !" But the young man was already
descending like a slow elevator. It was not until the quicksand reached
his chest that he realized the horse might go forever unpunished. What
had the horse done? Behaved sensibly, that's all. But they had crossed at
this point at the bottom of this arroyo many times. "Yes, but I know —."
Sant tried to go more on his back. "I know," he said to the sky, "that
quicksand moves. It needs water to percolate from below the sand like a
spring, and at this exact spot of the percolation it will keep the sand in
suspension and trap anything that enters. But this spot changes." Why
had he entered? To get on the other side. That horse, Luto, continues to
brood there in the shadow of the arroyo, continues to wait for me to
finish whatever I am up to. I wonder if he knows I'm drowning. Maybe

he suspects there's something wrong. Then why doesn't he go back to the corral with his empty saddle so they will know that something happened to me? Because I did not train him. That's the last time I'll neglect a horse. Yet, it's the last time you'll neglect anything. It's the last time you'll even think about it. Sant splashed the water with his arms as it flowed around him on its way to the Rio Grande.

If I was four hundred yards up the arroyo I would be on the other side of the Continental Divide and die into the Pacific. Now I am dying into the Rio Grande and the Atlantic. It's the last time you'll die into anything. It's the first and last time. Wait. They will find me. How? They will miss me and track me here. How are they going to track you over all those hard sand rock formations between here and the house? Well then, Rabbit Stockings will know where I am. How would any Indian know where you are? Particularly one as brainless as Rabbit Stockings. Because Indians have got a lot of intuition. The less brains the more intuition? Something like that.

Sant said abruptly, "Oh God!" aloud up into the sky and then resumed his dialogue with himself. He was swimming gently and softly in fluid earth to keep taking air and he was talking to himself to beat the death that tugged on him from somewhere there below. What about the time you tamed the thunder? It will be the last time for that too. I don't think the thunder will be tamed any more. The time all of the Indians convinced you — Afraid Of His Own Horses, and Rabbit Stockings was in on it too — the time they convinced you that if you could climb a high enough ridge and shoot enough arrows, throw enough rocks into the air and shout horrible shouts, the thunder would go away and never come back. It worked. That's right. As we flew along the high pine-crested ridge hollering and shooting, the thunder paid us back. Remember it sent a bolt of lightning that nearly killed Rabbit Stockings when it shattered a tree that Rabbit Stockings was shouting under. It all proves that there is something in the Indian religion of worshipping things, and it proves that things don't like us very much. I must ask Rabbit Stockings if they worship quicksand. I will never get the chance.

The sun was fire hot on the young man's face but he had to lie back in this position to present as much body surface as he could to the fluid sand. At times he could relieve his burning face with his wet hands but very quickly because he had to use them as flippers, swinging them gently to stay alive.

On the great haunch of the Sangre de Cristo Mountains that rose like another planet above the flat arroyo-cut land there were two riders appearing like centaurs at a distance.

"Rabbit Stockings," Big Sant said, "it's a superstition or something you dreamed up, I don't know which." The man called Big Sant, who didn't know which, was the father of the boy at the bottom of the arroyo. He had a very wide open face and a sharp, red, alive scar on his left jaw.

"I just have this feeling that Santo did not go to the mountains."

"But feeling is not enough, Rabbit Stockings."

"I have this feeling that he went the other way. Something happened to him."

"What happened?"

"He drowned."

"In the small stream from the spring in the arroyo? It would be quite a trick."

"Well, I've got this feeling." The young Indian who had this feeling was a Navajo Indian, about the same age as his partner, at the bottom of the arroyo. He dressed like all the other Indians in this part of New Mexico, that is he dressed like a cowboy except the way his bun of hair was tied in the back. Cowboys didn't do that. It saves on barber's bills, Big Sant thought. But he couldn't take this Indian seriously about his son at the bottom of the arroyo. The Indian religion was part of their way of life that the white man had not been able to make a dent in. The Indians still insisted on getting their inspiration from their guardian spirit. Sometimes it was a bear, an elk, or even a certain pine tree isolated and clinging to a ledge on the mesa which they would watch from below each day. Sometimes it was only a rock, a large yellow concretion about to tumble from a ledge, threatening and high.

"Where did you get your information, Rabbit Stockings?"

"From a snake."

"I thought so. We will continue up the mountain." And he touched his horse to increase their pace to a trot, the Indian keeping up on his matching Appaloosa that had to work hard to maintain the pace. They had been traveling for about an hour now, ever since Big Sant decided that Little Sant must have gotten into some kind of difficulty. Not serious. Probably a lame horse. Indians are alarmists. Little Sant was overdue about six hours on his trip up the mountain to gather the horses, and one hour ago the remuda had come in by themselves without the boy. A strange stallion had gathered up their mares and taken them to the mountain, but it must still be too cold on the Sangre de Cristos at ten thousand feet this time in June so their mares must have turned tail and fled back down to the ranch as soon as the stallion dropped his vigilance. The stallion was not bad, but the warm weather down here must be better. But what happened to the boy? What happened to Little Sant? Probably his horse went lame. Don't ask Rabbit Stockings; Indians are alarmists. "You are, you know, Rabbit Stockings."

"What's that?"

"You want to make a big thing out of nothing. Does the peace pipe go from right to left or from left to right?"

"What's a peace pipe?"

"You see, you have gotten over many of your superstitions. Why don't you get over the rest?"

"If an Indian believes something it's called superstition; when a white man believes something it's called progress."

"How did you figure that, Rabbit Stockings?"

"Why it's everywhere around you," Rabbit Stockings said carefully. "It's everywhere around you. Aren't they going to the moon now? Well, the white man doesn't even know the earth. What do they know about quicksand?"

"Little Sant didn't go that way, Rabbit Stockings." Big Sant was annoyed at this pecking away at the ridiculous. Indians will never let a thing go, particularly if it's a prejudice. This Indian has no evidence for his belief.

"You still didn't tell me what is quicksand," Rabbit Stockings queried.

"It's caused by water rising from below a table of sand. This causes a turbid —"

"What's that mean?"

"Something that is neither water nor sand, Rabbit Stockings. You can't swim in it, neither can you get any purchase on it to get out. You founder and die."

"There's nothing down there pulling you below? Nothing that wants you? Something that says, now is the time?"

"No, Rabbit Stockings. It's like your snake again. There is nothing to it."

"Nothing to it," Rabbit Stockings repeated, bouncing on his smaller horse. "Nothing to it. Another Indian superstition. Well, maybe you're right," Rabbit Stockings announced suddenly. "After all, we didn't chase away the thunder."

"Try to remember that, Rabbit Stockings," Big Sant said.

The young man sinking into eternity at the bottom of the arroyo was looking up at the soft gray-green slopes that led away to the world and thinking small thoughts to fight the insidious and larger thoughts as he lay dying.

Another thing about Indians, Little Sant thought, another thing about Indians is they don't plan for the future. Their future is now. Why plan for something that's happening? You notice this in the Navajo language, the past becomes the future and the present dissolves into their language mist of the day before yesterday. Navajos don't communicate, they confuse. No wonder they don't believe in progress. They couldn't tell you if they did, so it's more comfortable for the Navajos not to believe in the future. I bet they would pass a law against the future if they could — if they believed in laws. I remember Rabbit Stockings touching his head and saying, the future is here. In other words, the future isn't. It's another idea. That true? Yes, I guess it is. So why should we waste time with the future if it doesn't exist? Progress is part of the future, so that's a waste of time too. Right? Words, words, words. Now your snakes. Snakes exist, don't they? Bears, deer, elk, coyotes — they're real, really real. Right?

Really real. Right. Anything you say, Rabbit Stockings. And then the boy with the red hair, in the quicksand at the bottom of the long, deep, lonely arroyo cried suddenly up into the big, empty space. "But get me out! Find me, if your magic works." It was a quiet cry with no attempt to reach anyone, a cry to himself and the quiescent spirit of the rocks and sage, yucca and gray sad tamarisk that wept toward the Rio Grande. But there is no one, the young man thought. There is no spirit, no life, no death — no death outside this one right here. It's only a word until it happens to you. Where is the horse, Luto? I can see him there in the half shadows. Luto seems waiting for me to get it over with so he can carry me away. Was he in on this too? Was this exact time and place absolutely and perfectly arranged to the second? Luto is all black, a pure black horse. I never did like that horse waiting there in the checkered shade of the funeral tamarisk. But there was an understanding, there was always an understanding that he was the best horse in the country, the fastest, the quickest, and the best cow horse in the country. We were never friendly.

We never spoke. I should have sold him, but when I had a customer Luto disappeared as though he knew. And I never bought him; that day he just showed up, unbranded, little more than a colt, but he knew everything, wasn't even green broke but he behaved like a ten year old. I wonder where he came from and where he will go back to now.

Little Sant felt himself sink a little more into the heavy fluid sand. He waved his slim arms, fluttered them like a wounded bird, but he could feel himself being pulled down deeper. No, no, no, he told himself. You are behaving like an Indian, thinking like a Navajo. You've been around them too long, like father, like Big Sant says, you should associate more with white boys. But where did the funeral-black horse come from? Why does Luto wait there in the solemn dappled shadows, and where is he going soon?

Sant ceased all movement and Luto emerged out of the shadow tentatively, the black horse bringing the shade, the darkness with him. Death is a cessation of movement, but more, the young man thought, life is the idea of movement. Death is a coffin-black horse, a shadow interlaced among the shadows in the tamarisk. And it wasn't my idea to cross this arroyo at this point, it was Luto who pushed down and across in that steady, stately stride, refusing only at the last second, and it was again Luto that flew, almost airborne, down Blind Wolf Canyon to bring us around in back of the ranch so that even Rabbit Stockings in his infinite stupidity would not select this arroyo as a place to search.

But it was Luto with terrific, almost deathless delicacy, who had been able to cut out a calf from its mother, a colt from a stallion, and charge from cover, then whip a mule deer to the mesa and in the snow gambol like a hoyden with a jack until the rabbit, wraithlike in the matching frost, would founder in abject capitulation to the dark mountain that moved like a cougar. The sudden darkness of Luto ascending, then descending the pine-feathered slopes of the Sangre de Cristos like a writhing storm, somber and wild. Yes, the young man thought, Luto, yes, Luto is alive. Luto is the best horse, queer, yes, but Luto is the best damn horse.

Now watch. Luto, the shadow, has moved out of the tamarisk shadows, moving catlike, moving over here, the young man thought. Because I have been silent, ceased to struggle for seconds, now Luto is moving in. I will wait and when his tail passes by I will grab it and hold on. I will foil the horse. I will make it out of here. The young man did not believe this, he had been settling in the quicksand for too long now to have grand hope. Little Sant's helplessness had long since turned to hopelessness, but against utter despair he told to himself, I will make it out, I will make it out, as the horse nuzzled forward, fretting its monster nose towards the young man in long sweeping casts, but treading delicately in the beginning soft sand, trailing the broken reins like a shroud. Then Luto jerked up his head in discovery and wheeled to escape as Little Sant's arms rose to catch the flying, gossamer tail. He had it in his hands. It was like threads of ice, new-forming, fragile ice that exploded in his grip and Luto was gone. Now Luto came slowly back, then stopped ten feet away — Luto staring out of the beginning darkness, merging again into the shadows, spectral and huge.

"Luto!" Sant called weakly. "Luto!" Little Sant felt himself settling more into the quicksand. "Luto boy, what's happening?"

The pair of horsemen moving fast up the precipitous slope merged with mountain mahogany, then fled between brakes of aspen, trampling columbine, mariposa lilies, found a trail strewn red with gilias that led straight to the peaks, then entered a lowering and ominous cloud.

"Do you know what day it is, Rabbit Stockings?" Big Sant asked.

"Shrove Tuesday? The day after tomorrow? The day before yesterday? Ash Wednesday? What other days have you invented?"

"Invent one yourself."

"Can I?"

"It's may I, Rabbit Stockings."

"Sure, you can," Rabbit Stockings said. "You whites are always doing it."

"Today is the day, three years to the day, we got Luto. I remember because it's the summer solstice."

"What's that?"

"The twenty-first of June."

"I mean, what's the summer solstice."

"It's the longest day and the shortest night of the year."

Rabbit Stockings thought about this as they cantered through bowers of ponderosa, then debouched into a quiet explosion of orange Cowboy's Delight on the old Circle B, ringed with high wavering Indian Paintbrush midst the gaunt and verdigrised collapse of a homestead, a monument to unhardihood and puerile myth; but some eastern hollyhocks rose in towering, weedlike formidability from out New England ruins in the yellow New Mexican sky. Rabbit Stockings plucked one as he passed and placed the garish Boston flower in his black Indian head knot.

"You see," Rabbit Stockings said, in sham Indian solemnity, "I've been thinking about your summer solstice. It could be the twenty-first but it could be the twenty-second because it seems to my thick Indian head that both days share that shortest night."

"Yes." Big Sant touched his head and blew out a forced breath, annoyed, and the Appaloosa horse started in sympathy. "Yes, but it was the twenty-first we got Luto." Then he said, flat and peremptory, "Rabbit Stockings, you should be a scientist."

"Yes," Rabbit Stockings said.

"They tell me, Rabbit Stockings," Big Sant said, "that an Indian can tell, that is, his religion gives him some secret insight into animals."

"That's not true," Rabbit Stockings said.

"That, for example, a horse like Luto, do you suppose — ? What do you suppose? I've always felt that Luto was too damn co-operative, that it had some ulterior purpose."

"Ulterior?"

"That there is something wrong with Luto, I mean."

"What do you mean?" the Indian asked.

"If Indians believe that each person has a guardian spirit like a rock, a stone, a snake, could it be a horse?"

"I guess it could."

"Would the guardian spirit take care of everything?"

"Except dig the grave," the Indian said. "And sometimes that."

"What do you mean?"

"Well, if it were quicksand," Rabbit Stockings said.

"Why have you got this obsession with quicksand, Rabbit Stockings?"

"Because it's the only way a horse could kill Santo."

"Oh?"

"Yes. Santo is too smart for horses with the usual tricks."

"And why would Luto want to kill Sant?"

"I don't know. I'm only a poor Indian. I only work here."

"Do you have a guardian spirit, Rabbit Stockings?"

"No, I don't," Rabbit Stockings said. "Or maybe I do, but it doesn't count because I don't believe in it, not all the time. It's difficult to believe in anything all the time. You see, if you don't believe in your guardian spirit he can't help you."

"Or hurt you?"

"That's right. In other words, if Santo doesn't believe in the horse it can't hurt him or help him. In other words, if Santo's time had come and he didn't believe the horse was anything but a horse, then the horse would have no power."

"Well, I think there is something wrong with Luto. As I said, he's too perfect for a horse. What can we do?"

"It's probably too late now," Rabbit Stockings said. "All we can do is continue up the mountain. I guess your direction is as good as mine."

"I'm sure it is, Rabbit Stockings. A horse is a horse, no matter how perfect a horse."

"My guardian spirit is a snake."

"When we get back," Big Sant said, "we'll have a drink to the snakes."

"You don't believe it? The trouble with this country is — what is it? The trouble with this country is, we are overdeveloped."

"That's a profound thought, Rabbit Stockings, but we will leave all the profound Indian thoughts for later. Right now — "

"Look! Right now there's a snake!"

The horses plunged back, rising to enormous height on their hinder feet in blurred Appaloosa furious fright and comic dance, in high awkward prance before the dice, the hard clean rattle in the sage ahead.

"I don't see. I hear, but I don't see. Can you see the diamond-back?"

"There!" Rabbitt Stockings hollered and the diamond-back rattler exploded toward the plunging and furious motions of the horses, some grenade, anti-personnel or anti-horse weapon planted in the innocent sage, lashing out with shrapnel speed and sidewind perfect accuracy to the falling mark and missing the falling-away Appaloosa, but recoiling, rearming itself in fluid automation before the rapt and cold stricken-eyed terror of the horse, as Big Sant slid off and seized himself a great, varicolored trunk of petrified wood and hefted it in a vast surging motion above his head to crush the snake.

"Wait!"

"Why?"

"He's trying to tell us something."

"Yes, that's true, Rabbit Stockings. I got the message."

"You don't understand."

"Oh, I do. I understand rattlesnakes perfectly, and they understand me. Get out of the way before the snake kills you."

Rabbit Stockings stepped deftly and quickly in a timed ballet cadence as the snake exploded again and then quickly again and then again, the snake in surly, dusty diamonds, flinging itself at the mad Indian before the Indian gained a high boulder in an unfrantic, graceful leap, resting and looking down from there at the snake, his arms akimbo.

"Well done, Rabbit Stockings. Now can I kill the other half of the act?"

"Why do you, even in your overdeveloped country, why do you have to kill things?"

"Rattlesnakes."

"Still?"

"Rattlesnakes. Oh yes." From his safe distance Big Sant let down his trunk of petrified wood and sat on it. "Or is this one a friend of yours?"

"No."

"Your guardian spirit maybe, telling you to go back?"

"I don't know."

"Some Indian nonsense like that," Big Sant said. "Still, if you want to check the arroyo instead of the mountain we will check the arroyo instead of the mountain. Anything you say. Anything your snake says, any opinion a rattler holds. If you don't kill 'em, join 'em. What do you think?"

"We will check the arroyo," Rabbit Stockings said.

"Not that I hold with snakes," Big Sant said as they quickly mounted the trembling, subdued Appaloosas, "but in an overdeveloped country I'll always go along with a legend, a good Navajo myth. Look, Rabbit Stockings, your snake has called it quits."

They scattered down the mountain, their horses tumbling in mad pursuit of home, wild and uncontrolled, the riders allowing their horses to plunge downward in furious gyrations, careening and bouncing with awful abrupt speed like some kind of huge bright chunks of ore hurtling downward from a blast above on the high, still snow-coifed in June, scintillant, far peaks of the Sangre de Cristos, flashing down, down, down in twisting horse rapture to the sage avenues of the flat earth.

"The La Jara Arroyo," Rabbit Stockings hollered to Big Sant, and beginning now to direct the horse. "That's where Little Sant must be. That's where the quicksand is. The La Jara Arroyo."

"Yes," Big Sant said quietly to himself and the horse. "Yes. Yes, at my age I'm taking orders from a fool Navajo Indian and a snake, a guardian spirit Rabbit Stockings called it, but you and I," he told the still raging horse, "you and I saw a rattler. Wait! This way," and Big Sant went the way of Rabbit Stockings, both fleeing now between yellow plumes of yucca and among a bright festooned desert carpet of the twenty-first of June.

At the bottom of the arroyo nothing moved where the young man had been struggling. The water ran serene now, limpid and innocent. Where they watched from their horses atop the great canyon their searching eyes could see all the way to where the La Jara joined the Puerco but no sign, no clue of Little Sant, only the dusky, burnished copper fire sky above the arroyo heralding the slow end of a long day.

"The summer solstice you called it?"

"Yes, Rabbit Stockings."

"It was a long day all right."

"Rabbit Stockings, we should have continued to the mountain."

"No, I'm afraid we came in the right direction," Rabbit Stockings said. "But I don't understand. I don't understand why we weren't told sooner."

"We should have continued to the mountain," Big Sant insisted. "I don't know why I had to listen to a Navajo Indian and a rattlesnake."

Rabbit Stockings slid off down the sleek sweat of his speckled horse and stared from the ground with incredulous and uncomprehending disbelief at the vast empty cut one hundred feet deep, bottomed with a thin thread of water feeding the Rio Grande and becoming bronze now as it refracted in quick shimmers the maddening and molten sky. Rabbit Stockings crawled forward on the hard earth up to the sage-sprinkled lip of the arroyo, then he thumped the earth with the palm of his small rough red hand. "Yes."

"Yes, what?"

"Yes, they crossed here, Little Sant and Luto. Look, this is Luto's hoofprint. See how it goes like a heart in front?"

"Yes, almost cloven. Yes, that's Luto. But where did they go?"

"Down," Rabbit Stockings said, capping his vision and staring across. "But I don't see where they went up." Rabbit Stockings continued to search all along the arroyo while Big Sant sat frozen. "But there's something moving down there in the tamarisk," Rabbit Stockings said finally.

"Hello!" Big Sant shouted. "Who's there?"

"It's me!"

"It sounds like Little Sant," Rabbit Stockings said. "A little weak but what can you expect. That you, Santo? Okay?"

"Yes," the voice of Little Sant called up. "But don't come down. Please don't come down."

But Big Sant had already started his Appaloosa in a steep dive down the awful slope. Rabbit Stockings tried to arrest him with an upraised hand but Big Sant was already hurtling halfway to the bottom, horse and rider commingled in a vortex of riotous earth spinning down to the sliver of bronzed stream that lazied to the big river, guiltless.

"Me too," Rabbit Stockings shouted as he gained his horse and catapulted it in one great leap out and down, the horse sprawling as it hit and never quite recovering; foundering like a novice skier on busted skis it cavorted crazy to the bottom where it righted on all four scattered legs and stood amazed and triumphant.

"Don't come!" Little Sant shouted toward them both. "Don't come over here!"

"Why not?"

There was a long silence from the tamarisks.

"Because there's a snake here, a dangerous rattler. He killed a horse. The snake killed Luto."

"Where's the snake?" Rabbit Stockings dropped off his horse and moved into the thick interlacing tamarisk. "Where's the snake, Santo?"

"He's gone. The snake was coiled there, where you're standing now. He's gone."

"What snake?" the heavy voice of Big Sant moved into the tamarisk. "What snake? Where's the horse? Where's Luto?"

"Luto's dead. Luto went down in the quicksand." Sant stood up, a small tower of mud. "I was stuck in the quicksand and Luto just stood here and watched. Then Luto was struck by this big snake. I could see the snake strike at Luto, then Luto panicked into the quicksand, got stuck, but I was able to get out using Luto to crawl up, but Luto got stuck worse and began to go under and there was nothing I could do. Luto's dead."

"No," Rabbit Stockings announced, "Luto's not dead."

"I saw Luto die."

"No, you saw Luto sink in the sand, that's all. Luto will be back."

"Oh, you bet I'll never buy a horse that looks like that again."

"Luto won't look like that again," Rabbit Stockings said. "The next time Luto could appear as a beautiful woman, for example."

"Well, I'll never buy a beautiful woman for example."

"Get up in back," Big Sant said down from his horse.

Little Sant squished up and clasped his mudded arms around Big Sant.

"And another thing," Rabbit Stockings advised in his advising tone, "Never do anything on Shrove Tuesday."

"It's not Shrove Tuesday, it's the summer solstice," Big Sant said.

"All right, be careful of that too," Rabbit Stockings advised. "Now that we don't have any medicine bundles—"

"What?"

"So now we've got to be careful all the time," Rabbit Stockings finished.

As they passed the stream in muddy file Little Sant pointed at the spot. "That's where it almost happened."

Rabbit Stockings turned in his saddle. "That's where it did happen."

"I mean to me."

"You're not the center of the world."

"I suppose the Indians are."

"That's nice of you, Santo. I've always supposed they were too."

The horses pounded now in wild scurry up out of the fast darkening arroyo and they gained the long flat country gilded in light, all of them in the gaudy sunset.

"Well, I'll tell you," Little Sant said, "it was terrible, my almost, then Luto's death down there, but outside of that—" He stared from behind his huge father with muddied eyes at the Indian. "Outside of that I don't believe any of it."

The Indian, Rabbit Stockings, trotted forward in a wild rhythm on his dazzling pony and pointed his luminous arm up at the faltering fire going out. "Don't you believe this was the day of the white man's summer solstice?"

"Yes," Little Sant said, grabbing his hard father with stiffening arms and looking towards the darkness back at the arroyo. "Yes, Rabbit Stockings, today was very long, today was the most long, the longest day there ever was." Now Little Sant looked straight ahead into the end of a Midsummer Day. "Yes, we've all got to pray we never have a summer solstice again."

JOYCE CAROL OATES

*Tension is supreme in "Upon the Sweeping Flood." The man in Mrs.
Oates' tale not only has to contend with the raging water but with the
madness that descends upon the other two characters and himself. A good
story to read when one is safe and dry indoors.*

*Joyce Carol Oates was born in Lockport, New York, and received her
B.A. degree from Syracuse University, her M.A. from the University of
Wisconsin. She was the winner of the 1959 Mademoiselle Fiction Contest
and her stories have appeared in many magazines. She has also published
numerous novels.*

Upon the Sweeping Flood

NOT LONG AGO in Eden County, in the remote marsh and swamplands to
the south, a man named Walter Stuart was stopped in the rain by a
sheriff's deputy along a country road. Stuart was in a hurry to get home
to his family — his wife and two daughters — after having endured a
week at his father's old farm, arranging for his father's funeral, surrounded by aging relatives who had sucked at him for the strength of his
youth. He was a stern, quiet man of thirty-nine, beginning to lose some
of the muscular hardness that had always baffled others, masking as it
did Stuart's remoteness, his refinement, his faith in discipline and order
which seemed to have belonged, even in his youth, to a person already
grown safely old. He was a district vice-president for one of the gypsum
mining plants, a man to whom financial success and success in love had
come naturally, without fuss. When only a child he had shifted his faith
with little difficulty from the unreliable God of his family's tradition to
the things and emotions of this world, which he admired in his thoughtful, rather conservative way, and this faith had given him access, as if by
magic, to a communion with persons vastly different from himself —

Reprinted from the *Southwest Review*, Spring, 1963. Copyright © 1963 by Southern
Methodist University Press.

with someone like the sheriff's deputy, for instance, who approached him that day in the hard, cold rain. "Is something wrong?" Stuart said. He rolled down the window and had nearly opened the door when the deputy, an old man with gray eyebrows and a slack, sunburned face, began shouting against the wind, "Just the weather, mister. You going far along here? How far are you going?"

"Two hundred miles," Stuart said. "What about the weather? Is it a hurricane?"

"A hurricane — yes — a hurricane!" the man said, bending to shout at Stuart's face. "You better go back to town and stay put. They're evacuating up there. We're not letting anyone through."

A long line of cars and pickup trucks, tarnished and gloomy in the rain, passed them on the other side of the road. "How bad is it?" said Stuart. "Do you need help?"

"Back at town, maybe, they need help," the man said. "They're putting up folks at the schoolhouse and the churches, and different families — The eye was spost to come by here, but last word we got it's veered further south. Just the same, though — "

"Yes, it's good to evacuate them," Stuart said. At the back window of an automobile passing them two children's faces peered out at the rain, white and blurred. "The last hurricane here — "

"Ah, God, leave off of that!" the old man said, so harshly that Stuart felt, inexplicably, hurt. "You better turn around, now, and get on back to town. You got money they can put you up somewheres good — not with these folks coming along here."

This was said without contempt, but Stuart flinched at its assumptions. "I'm going in to see if anybody needs help," he said. He had the car going again before the deputy could even protest. "I know what I'm doing! I know what I'm doing!" Stuart said.

The car lunged forward into the rain, drowning out the deputy's outraged shouts. The slashing of rain against Stuart's face excited him. Faces staring out of oncoming cars were pale and startled, and Stuart felt rising in him a strange compulsion to grin, to laugh madly at their alarm. . . . He passed cars for some time. Houses looked deserted, yards bare. Things had the look of haste about them, even trees — in haste to rid themselves of their leaves, to be stripped bare. Grass was twisted and wild. A ditch by the road was overflowing and at spots the churning, muddy water stretched across the red clay road. Stuart drove splashing through it. After a while his enthusiasm slowed, his foot eased up on the gas pedal. He had not passed any cars or trucks for some time.

The sky had darkened and the storm had increased. Stuart thought of turning back when he saw, a short distance ahead, someone standing in the road. A car approached from the opposite direction. Stuart slowed, bearing to the right. He came upon a farm — a small, run-down one with just a few barns and a small pasture in which a horse stood drooping in the rain. Behind the roofs of the buildings a shifting edge of foliage from the trees beyond curled in the wind, now dark, now silver. In a neat harsh line against the bottom of the buildings the wind had driven up dust and red clay. Rain streamed off roofs, plunged into fat, tilted rainbarrels, and exploded back out of them. As Stuart watched another figure appeared, running out of the house. Both persons — they looked like children — jumped about in the road, waving their arms. A spray of leaves was driven against them and against the muddy windshield of the car that approached and passed them. They turned: a girl and a boy, waving their fists in rage, their faces white and distorted. As the car sped past Stuart water and mud splashed up in a vicious wave.

When Stuart stopped and opened the door the girl was already there, shouting, "Going the wrong way! Wrong way!" Her face was coarse, pimply about her forehead and chin. The boy pounded up behind her, straining for air. "Where the hell are you going, mister?" the girl cried. "The storm's coming from this way. Did you see that bastard, going right by us? Did you see him? If I see him when I get to town — " A wall of rain struck. The girl lunged forward and tried to push her way into the car; Stuart had to hold her back. "Where are your folks?" he shouted. "Let me in!" cried the girl savagely. "We're getting out of here!" "Your folks," said Stuart. He had to cup his mouth to make her hear. "Your folks in there!" "There ain't anybody there — Gah*dam* you!" she said, twisting about to slap her brother, who had been pushing at her from behind. She whirled upon Stuart again. "You letting us in, mister? You letting us in?" she screamed, raising her hands as if to claw him. But Stuart's size must have calmed her, for she shouted hoarsely and mechanically: "There ain't nobody in there. Our pa's been gone the last two days. LAST TWO DAYS. Gone into town BY HIMSELF. Gone drunk somewhere. He ain't here. He left us here. LEFT US HERE!" Again she rushed at Stuart, and he leaned forward against the steering wheel to let her get in back. The boy was about to follow when something caught his eye back at the farm. "Get in," said Stuart. "Get in. Please. Get in." "My horse there," the boy muttered. "You little bastard! You get in here!" his sister screamed.

But once the boy got in, once the door was closed, Stuart knew that it was too late. Rain struck the car in solid walls and the road, when he could see it, had turned to mud. "Let's go! Let's go!" cried the girl, pounding on the back of the seat. "Turn it around! Go up on our drive and turn it around!" The engine and the wind roared together. "Turn it! Get it going!" cried the girl. There was a scuffle and someone fell against Stuart. "It ain't no good," the boy said. "Let me out." He lunged for the door and Stuart grabbed him. "I'm going back to the house!" the boy cried, appealing to Stuart with his frightened eyes, and his sister, giving up suddenly, pushed him violently forward. "It's no use," Stuart said. "Gahdam fool," the girl screamed, "gahdam fool!"

The water was ankle deep as they ran to the house. The girl splashed ahead of Stuart, running with her head up and her eyes wide open in spite of the flying scud. When Stuart shouted to the boy his voice was slammed back to him as if he were being mocked. "Where are you going? Go to the house! Go to the house!" The boy had turned and was running toward the pasture. His sister took no notice but ran to the house. "Come back, kid!" Stuart cried. Wind tore at him, pushing him back. "What are you — "

The horse was undersized, skinny and brown. It ran to the boy as if it wanted to run him down but the boy, stooping through the fence, avoided the frightened hooves and grabbed the rope that dangled from the horse's halter. "That's it! That's it!" Stuart shouted as if the boy could hear. At the gate the boy stopped and looked around wildly, up to the sky — he might have been looking for someone who had just called him; then he shook the gate madly. Stuart reached the gate and opened it, pushing it back against the boy, who now turned to gape at him. "What? What are you doing here?" he said.

The thought crossed Stuart's mind that the child was insane. "Bring the horse through!" he said. "We don't have much time."

"What are you doing here?" the boy shouted. The horse's eyes rolled, its mane lifted and haloed about its head. Suddenly it lunged through the gate and jerked the boy off the ground. The boy ran in the air, his legs kicking. "Hang on and bring him around!" Stuart shouted. "Let me take hold!" He grabbed the boy instead of the rope. They stumbled together against the horse. It had stopped now and was looking intently at something just to the right of Stuart's head. The boy pulled himself along the rope, hand over hand, and Stuart held onto him by the strap of his overalls. "He's scairt of you!" the boy said. "He's scairt of you!" Stuart reached over and took hold of the rope above the boy's fingers and tugged gently at it. His face was about a foot away from the horse's. "Watch out for him," said the boy. The horse reared and broke free, throwing Stuart back against the boy. "Hey, hey!" screamed the boy, as if mad. The horse turned in midair as if whirled about by the wind, and Stuart looked up through his fingers to see its hooves and a vicious flicking of its tail, and the face of the boy being yanked past him and away with incredible speed. The boy fell heavily on his side in the mud, arms outstretched above him, hands still gripping the rope with wooden fists. But he scrambled to his feet at once and ran alongside the horse. He flung one arm up around its neck as Stuart shouted, "Let him go! Forget about him!" Horse and boy pivoted together back toward the fence, slashing wildly at the earth, feet and hooves together. The ground erupted beneath them. But the boy landed upright, still holding the rope, still with his arm about the horse's neck. "Let me help," Stuart said. "No," said the boy, "he's my horse, he knows me — " "Have you got him good?" Stuart shouted. "We got — we got each other here," the boy cried, his eyes shut tight.

Stuart went to the barn to open the door. While he struggled with it the boy led the horse forward. When the door was open far enough Stuart threw himself against it and slammed it around to the side of the barn. A cloud of hay and scud filled the air. Stuart outstretched his arms, as if pleading with the boy to hurry, and he murmured, "Come on. Please. Come on." The boy did not hear him, or even glance at him: his own lips were moving as he caressed the horse's neck and head. The horse's muddy hoof had just begun to grope about the step before the door when something like an explosion came against the back of Stuart's head, slammed his back, and sent him sprawling out at the horse.

"Damn you! Damn you!" the boy screamed. Stuart saw nothing except rain. Then something struck him, his shoulder and hand, and his fingers were driven down into the mud. Something slammed beside him in the mud and he seized it — the horse's foreleg — and tried to pull himself up, insanely, lurching to his knees. The horse threw him backward. It seemed to emerge out of the air before and above him, coming into sight as though out of a cloud. The boy he did not see at all — only the hooves — and then the boy appeared, inexplicably, under the horse, peering intently at Stuart, his face struck completely blank. "Damn you!" Stuart heard, "He's my horse! My horse! I hope he kills you!" Stuart crawled back in the water, crab fashion, watching the horse form and dissolve, hearing its vicious tattoo against the barn. The door, swinging madly back and forth, parodied the horse's rage, seemed to challenge its frenzy; then the door was all Stuart heard, and he got to his feet, gasping, to see that the horse was out of sight.

The boy ran bent against the wind, out toward nowhere, and Stuart ran after him. "Come in the house, kid! Come on! Forget about it, kid!" He grabbed the boy's arm. The boy struck at him with his elbow. "He was my horse!" he cried.

In the kitchen of the house they pushed furniture against the door. Stuart had to stand between the boy and the girl to keep them from fighting. "Gahdam sniffling fool!" said the girl. "So your gahdam horse run off for the night!" The boy crouched down on the floor, crying steadily. He was about thirteen: small for his age, with bony wrists and face. "We're all going to be blownt to hell, let alone your horse," the girl said. She sat with one big thigh and leg outstretched on the table, watching Stuart. He thought her perhaps eighteen. "Glad you came down to get us?" she said. "Where are you from, mister?" Stuart's revulsion surprised him; he had not supposed there was room in his stunned mind for emotion of this sort. If the girl noticed it she gave no sign, but only grinned at him. "I was — I was on my way home," he said. "My wife and daughters — " It occurred to him that he had forgotten about them entirely. He had not thought of them until now and, even now, no image came to his mind: no woman's face, no little girls' faces. Could he have imagined their lives, their love for him? For an instant he doubted everything. "Wife and daughters," said the girl, as if wondering whether to believe him. "Are they in this storm too?" "No — no," Stuart said. To get away from her he went to the window. He could no longer see the road. Something struck the house and he flinched away. "Them trees!" chortled the girl. "I knew it! Pa always said how he ought to cut them down, so close to the house like they are! I knew it! I knew it! And the old bastard off safe now where they can't get him!"

"Trees?" said Stuart slowly.

"Them trees! Old oak trees!" said the girl.

The boy, struck with fear, stopped crying suddenly. He crawled on the floor to a woodbox beside the big old iron stove and got in, patting the disorderly pile of wood as if he were blind. The girl ran to him and pushed him. "What are you doing?" Stuart cried in anguish. The girl took no notice of him. "What am I doing?" he said aloud. "What the hell am I doing here?" It seemed to him that the end would come in a minute or two, that the howling outside could get no louder, that the howling inside his mind could get no more intense, no more accusing. A goddam fool!A goddam fool! he thought. The deputy's face came to mind, and Stuart pictured himself groveling before the man, clutching at his knees, asking forgiveness and for time to be turned back. . . . Then he saw himself back at the old farm, the farm of his childhood, listening to tales of his father's agonizing sickness, the old peoples' heads craning around, seeing how he took it, their eyes charged with horror and delight. . . . "My wife and daughters," Stuart muttered.

The wind made a hollow, drumlike sound. It seemed to be tolling. The boy, crouching back in the woodbox, shouted: "I ain't scairt! I ain't scairt!" The girl gave a shriek. "Our chicken coop, I'll be gahdammed!" she cried. Try as he could Stuart could see nothing out the window. "Come away from the window," Stuart said, pulling the girl's arm. She whirled upon him. "Watch yourself, mister," she said, "you want to go out to your gahdam bastardly worthless car?" Her body was strong and big in her men's clothing; her shoulders looked muscular beneath the filthy shirt. Cords in her young neck stood out. Her hair had been cut short and was now wet, plastered about her blemished face. She grinned at Stuart as if she were about to poke him in the stomach, for fun. "I ain't scairt of what God can do!" the boy cried behind them.

When the water began to bubble up through the floorboards they decided to climb to the attic. "There's an ax!" Stuart exclaimed, but the boy got on his hands and knees and crawled to the corner where the ax was propped before Stuart could reach it. The boy cradled it in his arms. "What do you want with that?" Stuart said, and for an instant his heart was pierced with fear. "Let me take it. I'll take it." He grabbed it out of the boy's dazed fingers.

The attic was about half as large as the kitchen and the roof jutted down sharply on either side. Tree limbs rubbed and slammed against the roof on all sides. The three of them crouched on the middle beam, Stuart with the ax tight in his embrace, the boy pushing against him as if for warmth, and the girl kneeling with her thighs straining her overalls. She watched the little paneless window at one end of the attic without much emotion or interest, like a large, wet turkey. The house trembled beneath them. "I'm going to the window," Stuart said, and was oddly relieved when the girl did not sneer at him. He crawled forward along the dirty beam, dragging the ax along with him, and lay full length on the floor about a yard from the window. There was not much to see. At times the rain relaxed, and objects beneath in the water took shape: tree stumps, parts of buildings, junk whirling about in the water. The thumping on the roof was so loud at that end that he had to crawl backward to the middle again. "I ain't scairt, nothing God can do!" the boy cried. "Listen to the snivelling baby," said the girl, "he thinks God pays him any mind! Hah!" Stuart crouched beside them, waiting for the boy to press against him again. "As if God gives a good damn about him," the girl said. Stuart looked at her. In the near dark her face did not seem so coarse; the set of her eyes was almost attractive. "You don't think God cares about you?" Stuart said slowly. "No, not specially," the girl said, shrugging her shoulders. "The hell with it. You seen the last one of these?" She tugged at Stuart's arm. "Mister? It was something to see. Me an' Jackie was little then — him just a baby. We drove a far ways north to get out of it. When we come back the roads was so thick with sightseers from the cities! They took all the dead ones floating in the water and put them in one place, part of a swamp they cleared out. The families and things — they were mostly fruit-pickers — had to come by on rafts and rowboats to look and see could they find the ones they knew. That was there for a day. The bodies would turn round and round in the wash from the boats. Then the faces all got alike and they wouldn't let anyone come anymore and put oil on them and set them afire. We stood on top of the car and watched all that day. I wasn't but nine then."

When the house began to shake, some time later, Stuart cried aloud: "This is it!" He stumbled to his feet, waving the ax. He turned around and around as if he were in a daze. "You goin' to chop somethin' with that?" the boy said, pulling at him. "Hey, no, that ain't yours to — it ain't yours to chop — " They struggled for the ax. The boy sobbed, "It ain't yours! It ain't yours!" and Stuart's rage at his own helplessness, at the folly of his being here, for an instant almost made him strike the boy with the ax. But the girl slapped the boy furiously. "Get away from him! I swear I'll kill you!" she screamed.

Something exploded beneath them. "That's the windows," the girl muttered, clinging to Stuart, "and how am I to clean it again! The old bastard will want it clean, and mud over everything!" Stuart pushed her away so that he could swing the ax. Pieces of soft, rotted wood exploded back onto his face. The boy screamed insanely as the boards gave way to a deluge of wind and water, and even Stuart wondered if he had made a mistake. The three of them fell beneath the onslaught and Stuart lost the ax, felt the handle slam against his leg. "You! You!" Stuart cried, pulling at the girl — for an instant, blinded by pain, he could not think who he was, what he was doing, whether he had any life beyond this moment. The big-faced, husky girl made no effort to hide her fear and cried, "Wait, wait!" But he dragged her to the hole and tried to force her out. "My brother — " she gasped. She seized his wrists and tried to get away. "Get out there! There isn't any time!" Stuart muttered. The house seemed about to collapse at any moment. He was pushing her through the hole, against the shattered wood, when she suddenly flinched back against him and he saw that her cheek was cut and she was choking. He snatched her hands away from her mouth as if he wanted to see something secret: blood welled out between her lips. She coughed and spat blood onto him. "You're all right," he said, oddly pleased, "now get out there and I'll get the kid. I'll take care of him." This time she managed to crawl through the hole, with Stuart pushing her from behind; when he turned to seize the boy the boy clung to his neck sobbing something about God. "God loves you!" Stuart yelled. "Loves the least of you! The least of you!" The girl pulled her brother up in her great arms and Stuart was free to climb through himself.

It was actually quite a while — perhaps an hour — before the battering of the trees and the wind pushed the house in. The roof fell slowly, and the section to which they clung was washed free. "We're going somewheres!" shouted the girl. "Look at the house! That gahdam old shanty seen the last storm!"

The boy lay with his legs pushed in under Stuart's and had not spoken for some time. When the girl cried, "Look at that!" he tried to burrow in farther. Stuart wiped his eyes to see the wall of darkness dissolve. The rain took on another look — a smooth, piercing, metallic glint, like nails driving against their faces and bodies. There was no horizon. They could see nothing except the rushing water and a thickening mist that must have been rain, miles and miles of rain, slammed by the wind into one great wall that moved remorselessly upon them. "Hang on," Stuart said, gripping the girl. "Hang on to me."

Waves washed over the roof, pushing objects at them with soft, muted thuds — pieces of fence, boards, branches heavy with foliage. Stuart tried to ward them off with his feet. Water swirled around them, sucking at them, sucking the roof, until they were pushed against one of the farm buildings. Something crashed against the roof — another section of the house — and splintered, flying up against the girl. She was thrown backward, away from Stuart, who lunged after her. They fell into the water while the boy screamed. The girl's arms threshed wildly against Stuart. The water was cold and its aliveness, its sinister energy, surprised him more than the thought that he would drown — that he would never endure the night. Struggling with the girl he forced her back to the roof, pushed her up. Bare, twisted nails raked his hands. "Gahdam you, Jackie, you give a hand!" the girl said as Stuart crawled back up. He lay, exhausted, flat on his stomach and let the water and debris slush over him.

His mind was calm beneath the surface buzzing. He liked to think that his mind was a clear, sane circle of quiet carefully preserved inside the chaos of the storm — that the three of them were safe within the sanctity of this circle; this was how man always conquered nature, how he subdued things greater than himself. But whenever he spoke to the girl it was in short grunts, in her own idiom: "This ain't so bad!" or "It'll let up pretty soon!" Now the girl held him in her arms as if he were a child, and he did not have the strength to pull away. Of his own free will he had given himself to this storm, or to the strange desire to save someone in it — but now he felt grateful for the girl, even for her brother, for they had saved him as much as he had saved them. Stuart thought of his wife at home, walking through the rooms, waiting for him; he thought of his daughters in their twin beds, two glasses of water on their bureau. . . . But these people knew nothing of him: in his experience now he did not belong to them. Perhaps he had misunderstood his role, his life? Perhaps he had blundered out of his way, drawn into the wrong life, surrendered to the wrong role. What had blinded him to the possibility of many lives, many masks, many arms which might so embrace him? A word not heard one day, a gesture misinterpreted, a leveling of someone's eyes in a certain unmistakable manner, which he had mistaken just the same! The consequences of such errors might trail on insanely into the future, across miles of land, across worlds. He only now sensed the incompleteness of his former life. . . . "Look! Look!" the girl cried, jostling him out of his stupor. "Take a look at that, mister!"

He raised himself on one elbow. A streak of light broke out of the dark. Lanterns, he thought, a rescue party already. . . . But the rain dissolved the light; then it reappeared with a beauty that startled him. "What is it?" the boy screamed. "How come it's here?" They watched it filter through the rain, rays knifing through and showing, now, how buildings and trees crouched close about them. "It's the sun, the sun going down," the girl said. "The sun!" said Stuart, who had thought it was night. "The sun!" They stared at it until it disappeared.

The waves calmed sometime before dawn. By then the roof had lost its peak and water ran unchecked over it, in generous waves and then in thin waves, alternately, as the roof bobbed up and down. The three huddled together with their backs to the wind. Water came now in slow drifts. "It's just got to spread itself out far enough so's it will be even," said the girl, "then it'll go down." She spoke without sounding tired, only a little disgusted — as if things weren't working fast enough to suit her. "Soon as it goes down we'll start toward town and see if there ain't somebody coming out to get us, in a boat," she said, chattily and comfortably, into Stuart's ear. Her manner astonished Stuart, who had been thinking all night of the humiliation and pain he had suffered. "Bet the old bastard will be glad to see us," she said, "even if he did go off like that. Well, he never knew a storm was coming. Me and him get along pretty well — he ain't so bad." She wiped her face; it was filthy with dirt and blood. "He'll buy you a drink, mister, for saving us how you did. That was something to have happen — a man just driving up to get us!" And she poked Stuart in the ribs.

The winds warmed as the sun rose. Rain turned to mist and back to rain again, still falling heavily, and now objects were clear about them. The roof had been shoved against the corner of the barn and a mound of dirt, and eddied there without much trouble. Right about them, in a kind of halo, a thick blanket of vegetation and filth bobbed. The fence had disappeared and the house had collapsed and been driven against a ridge of land. The barn itself had fallen in, but the stone support looked untouched, and it was against this they had been shoved. Stuart thought he could see his car — or something over there where the road used to be.

"I bet it ain't deep. Hell," said the girl, sticking her foot into the water. The boy leaned over the edge and scooped up some of the filth in his hands. "Lookit all the spiders," he said. He wiped his face slowly. "Leave them gahdam spiders alone," said the girl. "You want me to shove them down your throat?" She slid to the edge and lowered her legs. "Yah, I touched bottom. It ain't bad." But then she began coughing and drew herself back. Her coughing made Stuart cough: his chest and throat were ravaged, shaken. He lay exhausted when the fit left him and realized, suddenly, that they were all sick — that something had happened to them. They had to get off the roof. Now, with the sun up, things did not look so bad: there was a ridge of trees a short distance away on a long, red clay hill. "We'll go over there," Stuart said. "Do you think you can make it?"

The boy played in the filth, without looking up, but the girl gnawed at her lip to show she was thinking. "I spose so," she said. "But him — I don't know about him."

"Your brother? What's wrong?"

"Turn around. Hey, stupid. Turn around." She prodded the boy, who jerked around, terrified, to stare at Stuart. His thin bony face gave way to a drooping mouth. "Gone loony, it looks like," the girl said with a touch of regret. "Oh, he had times like this before. It might go away."

Stuart was transfixed by the boy's stare. The realization of what had happened struck him like a blow, sickening his stomach. "We'll get him over there," he said, making his words sound good. "We can wait there for someone to come. Someone in a boat. He'll be better there."

"I spose so," said the girl vaguely.

Stuart carried the boy while the girl splashed eagerly ahead. The water was sometimes up to his thighs. "Hold on another minute," he pleaded. The boy stared out at the water as if he thought he were being taken somewhere to be drowned. "Put your arms around my neck. Hold on," Stuart said. He shut his eyes and every time he looked up the girl was still a few yards ahead and the hill looked no closer. The boy breathed hollowly, coughing into Stuart's face. His own face and neck were covered with small red bites. Ahead the girl walked with her shoulders lunged forward as if to hurry her there, her great thighs straining against the water, more than a match for it. As Stuart watched her something was on the side of his face — in his ear — and with a scream he slapped at it, nearly dropping the boy. The girl whirled around. Stuart slapped at his face and must have knocked it off — probably a spider. The boy, upset by Stuart's outcry, began sucking in air faster and faster as if he were dying. "I'm all right, I'm all right," Stuart whispered, "just hold on another minute. . . ."

When he finally got to the hill the girl helped pull him up. He set the boy down with a grunt, trying to put the boy's legs under him so he could stand. But the boy sank to the ground and turned over and vomited into the water; his body shook as if he were having convulsions. Again the thought that the night had poisoned them, their own breaths had sucked germs into their bodies, struck Stuart with an irresistible force. "Let him lay down and rest," the girl said, pulling tentatively at the back of her brother's belt, as if she were thinking of dragging him farther up the slope. "We sure do thank you, mister," she said.

Stuart climbed to the crest of the hill. His heart pounded madly, blood pounded in his ears. What was going to happen? Was anything going to happen? How disappointing it looked, ridges of land showing through the water, and the healthy sunlight pushing back the mist. Who would believe him when he told of the night, of the times when death seemed certain . . . ? Anger welled up in him already, as he imagined the tolerant faces of his friends, his children's faces ready to turn to other amusements, other oddities. His wife would believe him; she would shudder, holding him, burying her small face in his neck. But what could she understand of his experience, having had no part in it? — Stuart cried out; he had nearly stepped on a tangle of snakes. Were they alive? He backed away in terror. The snakes gleamed wetly in the morning light, heads together as if conspiring. Four — five of them — they too had swum for this land, they too had survived the night, they had as much reason to be proud of themselves as Stuart.

He gagged and turned away. Down by the water line the boy lay flat on his stomach and the girl squatted nearby, wringing out her denim jacket. The water behind them caught the sunlight and gleamed mightily, putting them into silhouette. The girl's arms moved slowly, hard with muscle. The boy lay coughing gently. Watching them Stuart was beset by a strange desire: he wanted to run at them, demand their gratitude, their love. Why should they not love him, when he had saved their lives? When he had lost what he was just the day before, turned now into a different person, a stranger even to himself? Stuart stooped and picked up a rock. A broad hot hand seemed to press against his chest. He threw the rock out into the water and said, "Hey!"

The girl glanced around but the boy did not move. Stuart sat down on the soggy ground and waited. After a while the girl looked away; she spread the jacket out to dry. Great banked clouds rose into the sky, reflected in the water — jagged and bent in the waves. Stuart waited as the sun took over the sky. Mist at the horizon glowed, thinned, gave way to solid shapes. Light did not strike cleanly across the land, but was marred by ridges of trees and parts of buildings, and around a corner at any time Stuart expected to see a rescuing party — in a rowboat or something.

"Hey, mister!" He woke; he must have been dozing. The girl had called him. "Hey! Whyn't you come down here? There's all them snakes up there."

Stuart scrambled to his feet. When he stumbled downhill, embarrassed and frightened, the girl said chattily, "The sons of bitches are crawling all over here. He chast some away." The boy was on his feet and looking around with an important air. His coming alive startled Stuart — indeed, the coming alive of the day, of the world, evoked alarm in him. All things came back to what they were. The girl's alert eyes, the firm set of her mouth, had not changed — the sunlight had not changed, or the land, really; only Stuart had been changed. He wondered at it . . . and the girl must have seen something in his face that he himself did not yet know about, for her eyes narrowed, her throat gulped a big swallow, her arms moved slowly up to show her raw elbows. "We'll get rid of them," Stuart said, breaking the silence. "Him and me. We'll do it."

The boy was delighted. "I got a stick," he said, waving a thin whiplike branch. "There's some over here."

"We'll get them," Stuart said. But when he started to walk a rock slipped loose and he fell back into the mud. He laughed aloud. The girl, squatting a few feet away, watched him silently. Stuart got to his feet, still laughing. "You know much about it, kid?" he said, cupping his hand on the boy's head.

"About what?" said the boy.

"Killing snakes," said Stuart.

"I spose — I spose you just kill them."

The boy hurried alongside Stuart. "I need a stick," Stuart said; they got him one from the water, about the size of an ax. "Go by that bush," Stuart said, "there might be some there."

The boy attacked the bush in a frenzy. He nearly fell into it. His enthusiasm somehow pleased Stuart, but there were no snakes in the bush. "Go down that way," Stuart ordered. He glanced back at the girl: she watched them. Stuart and the boy went on with their sticks held in midair. "God put them here to keep us awake," the boy said brightly, "see we don't forget about Him." Mud sucked at their feet. "Last year we couldn't fire the woods on account of it so dry. This year can't either on account of the water. We got to get the snakes like this."

Stuart hurried as if he had somewhere to go. The boy, matching his steps, went faster and faster, panting, waving his stick angrily in the air. The boy complained about snakes and, listening to him, fascinated by him, in that instant Stuart saw everything. He saw the conventional dawn that had mocked the night, had mocked his desire to help people in trouble; he saw, beyond that, his father's home emptied now even of ghosts. He realized that the God of these people had indeed arranged things, had breathed the order of chaos into forms, animated them, had animated even Stuart himself forty years ago. The knowledge of this fact struck him about the same way as the nest of snakes had struck him — an image leaping right to the eye, pouncing upon the mind, joining itself with the perceiver. "Hey, hey!" cried the boy, who had found a snake: the snake crawled noisily and not very quickly up the slope, a brown-speckled snake. The boy ran clumsily after it. Stuart was astonished at the boy's stupidity, at his inability to see, now, that the snake had vanished. Still he ran along the slope, waving his stick, shouting, "I'll get you! I'll get you!" This must have been the sign Stuart was waiting for. When the boy turned Stuart was right behind him. "It got away up there," the boy said. "We got to get it." When Stuart lifted his stick the boy fell back a step but went on in mechanical excitement, "It's up there, gotten hid in the weeds. It ain't me," he said, "it ain't me that — " Stuart's blow struck the boy on the side of the head, and the rotted limb shattered into soft wet pieces. The boy stumbled down toward the water. He was coughing when Stuart took hold of him and began shaking him madly, and he did nothing but cough, violently and with all his concentration, even when Stuart bent to grab a rock and brought it down on his head. Stuart let him fall into the water. He could hear him breathing and he could see, about the boy's lips, tiny flecks or bubbles of blood appearing and disappearing with his breath.

When the boy's eyes opened Stuart fell upon him. They struggled savagely in the water. Again the boy went limp; Stuart stood, panting, and waited. Nothing happened for a minute or so. But then he saw something — the boy's fingers moving up through the water, soaring to the surface! "Will you quit it!" Stuart screamed. He was about to throw himself upon the boy again when the thought of the boy's life, bubbling out between his lips, moving his fingers, filled him with such outraged disgust that he backed away. He threw the rock out into the water and ran back, stumbling, to where the girl stood.

She had nothing to say: her jaw was hard, her mouth a narrow line, her thick nose oddly white against her dirty face. Only her eyes moved, and these were black, lustrous, at once demanding and terrified. She held a board in one hand. Stuart did not have time to think, but, as he lunged toward her, he could already see himself grappling with her in the mud, forcing her down, tearing her ugly clothing from her body — "Lookit!" she cried, the way a person might speak to a horse, cautious and coaxing, and pointed behind him. Stuart turned to see a white boat moving toward them, a half mile or so away. Immediately his hands dropped, his mouth opened in awe. The girl still pointed, breathing carefully, and Stuart, his mind shattered by the broken sunshine upon the water, turned to the boat, raised his hands, cried out, "Save me! Save me!" He had waded out a short distance into the water by the time the men arrived.